THE
PLAYBOY®
INTERVIEWS

OTHER BOOKS IN **THE PLAYBOY INTERVIEWS** SERIES

THEY PLAYED THE GAME | Henry Aaron • Kareem Abdul-Jabbar • Lance Armstrong • Barry Bonds • Jim Brown • Dale Earnhardt Jr. • Brett Favre • Wayne Gretzky • Allen Iverson • Derek Jeter • Michael Jordan • Billie Jean King • Joe Namath • Shaquille O'Neal • Pete Rose • O.J. Simpson • Mike Tyson

THE
PLAYBOY®
INTERVIEWS

THE DIRECTORS

**EDITED BY STEPHEN RANDALL AND
THE EDITORS OF *PLAYBOY* MAGAZINE**

PRESS™
Milwaukie

M Press
10956 SE Main Street
Milwaukie, OR 97222

mpressbooks.com

Portions of this book are reprinted from issues of *Playboy* magazine.
Cover and series design by Tina Alessi & Lia Ribacchi

Library of Congress Cataloging-in-Publication Data

The Playboy interviews : the directors / edited by Stephen Randall and the editors of Playboy magazine. -- 1st M Press ed.
    p. cm.
  Includes index.
  ISBN-13: 978-1-59582-028-0
  ISBN-10: 1-59582-028-0
  1. Motion picture producers and directors--Interviews. 2. Motion pictures--Production and direction. I. Randall, Stephen. II. Playboy (Chicago, Ill.)
  PN1998.2.P63 2006
  791.43023'30922--dc22
  [B]
                        2006018412

ISBN-10: 1-59582-028-0
ISBN-13: 978-1-59582-028-0
First M Press Edition: October 2006

10 9 8 7 6 5 4 3 2 1

Printed in U.S.A.
Distributed by Publishers Group West

CONTENTS

vii INTRODUCTION by Stephen Randall

11 ROBERT ALTMAN | August 1976, interviewed by Bruce Williamson

39 INGMAR BERGMAN | June 1964, interviewed by Cynthia Grenier

51 JOEL AND ETHAN COEN | November 2001, interviewed by Kristine McKenna

73 FRANCIS FORD COPPOLA | July 1975, interviewed by William Murray

103 CLINT EASTWOOD | February 1974, interviewed by Arthur Knight and Gretchen McNeese | March 1997, interviewed by Bernard Weinraub

161 FEDERICO FELLINI | February 1966, interviewed by Curtis Pepper

185 JOHN HUSTON | September 1985, interviewed by Lawrence Grobel

215 STANLEY KUBRICK | September 1968, interviewed by Eric Norden

247 SPIKE LEE | July 1991, interviewed by Elvis Mitchell

275 DAVID MAMET | April 1995, interviewed by Geoffrey Norman and John Rezek

297 ROMAN POLANSKI | December 1971, interviewed by Larry DuBois

343 MARTIN SCORSESE | April 1991, interviewed by David Rensin

373 OLIVER STONE | February 1988, interviewed by Marc Cooper | November 2004, interviewed by David Sheff

417 QUENTIN TARANTINO | November 2003, interviewed by Michael Fleming

433 ORSON WELLES | March 1967, interviewed by Kenneth Tynan

453 BILLY WILDER | June 1963, interviewed by Robert Gehman

465 INDEX

INTRODUCTION

By Stephen Randall
Deputy Editor, Playboy magazine

In the world of film, directors occupy a unique niche. While the actors who star in movies are as famous offscreen as they are onscreen—their personal lives are often more captivating than their acting—directors are known almost exclusively for their work. Their names might go above the title, they might have zealous fans—they might even be the major factor in drawing audiences into theaters, but they exist one or two steps to the side of the celebrity machinery. They're the big names who rarely sit on Jay Leno's couch or show up in the paparazzi shots in Us Weekly.

But their power over what we see and their impact on the culture is undeniable. While their films speak for themselves, the person behind the work is often a mystery. How did directors like Stanley Kubrick, Federico Fellini, Ingmar Bergman, John Huston, Orson Welles and Billy Wilder make movies that have become classics? What motivates the unique visions of Francis Ford Coppola, Martin Scorsese, Spike Lee, the Coen Brothers, Oliver Stone and Quentin Tarantino? Sometimes that answer lies beyond the soundstage, in the lives they lead far away from the set. Sitting in a director's chair, they have a singular role. But off the clock, during an in-depth interview about film, life and the world around us, a different, more revealing portrait emerges.

That's what makes the *Playboy Interview* unusual. It is the only monthly magazine feature that allows important people from various walks of life to engage in a lengthy, intelligent and unpredictable conversation about a variety of subjects. Directors often talk to the media to promote their films, but rarely do they get the opportunity to speak about other aspects of their lives, including the forces and events that have shaped their vision.

Playboy magazine has long been a movie lover's paradise—Hugh Hefner has said that his view of the world was forged in the darkened movies theaters of his youth. Through regular coverage of film and DVDs, to our annual "Sex in Cinema" feature, to conversations with the biggest stars in Hollywood, *Playboy* knows film. And the *Playboy Interview* knows directors. As you'll see when you read these 18 interviews, the story behind the man is as riveting as what he does behind the camera.

THE
PLAYBOY®
INTERVIEWS

August 1976

ROBERT ALTMAN

A candid conversation with the maverick who constantly confounds Hollywood: the director of M*A*S*H

With *Buffalo Bill and the Indians*—his ninth movie since 1970, when M*A*S*H became the most successful antiwar comedy in film history—Robert Altman seems virtually certain to rekindle the controversy that raged after *Nashville*. Sparked by Paul Newman's startling performance in the title role, *Buffalo Bill* is also apt to be hailed as another myth-shattering masterwork when the more vehement Altman addicts take the floor. All the stylistic hallmarks that make an Altman film unique are there in abundance: the spontaneous, seemingly improvised acting; the breezy, ballsy throwaway humor; the indifference toward traditional storytelling structure; and the eight-track overlapping sound, judged either inaudible or boldly innovative, depending on where one stands in that debate.

No director since Sam Peckinpah has provoked such passionate disputes; perhaps no director ever has taken such undisguised delight in watching himself become a cult figure and quasi legend under the very noses of the incumbent Hollywood moguls, who still consider him a freewheeling maverick with an erratic track record.

Actually, M*A*S*H was not only Altman's first but, to date, his only financial blockbuster; his subsequent movies, hits and flops alike, have been less memorable for making money than for making waves. But he has built a formidable reputation as the American director whose vigorous, uncompromisingly personal films have put him in the superstar pantheon with Stanley Kubrick, Ingmar Bergman and Federico Fellini.

Last year's *Nashville* was widely touted in advance as a breakthrough work that would both captivate critics and achieve a huge commercial success. But though it won the Best Film and Best Director awards from the New York Film Critics' Circle and earned five Oscar nominations, *Nashville* failed to break box-office records. No one remained indifferent about Altman's aggressively funny, colorful collage—a kind of grassroots *Grand Hotel* about two dozen oddly assorted characters who while away five days in America's country-music capital before destiny brings them together at the moment of an inexplicable assassination. Music critics, book critics, political commentators, columnists and composers were seemingly compelled to take a position on *Nashville*. As *New York Times* book editor John Leonard noted: "Writing articles about *Nashville* and writing articles about the articles that have been written about *Nashville* is almost a light industry."

Altman, born 51 years ago in Kansas City, Missouri, is a product of America's heartland and a renegade Roman Catholic from the Bible Belt. He sprang from English-Irish-German stock. "The usual mélange," Altman calls it. "When my grandfather opened a jewelry store in K.C., he dropped one *n* from Altman because they told him the sign would be cheaper." His father is still a practicing insurance broker back home. The first and feistiest of three children, Robert used to sneak out of bed to see such seminal epics as *King Kong*. After a stretch in a military academy, he piloted a B-24 bomber through World War II, chalking up 45 missions over the Dutch East Indies before going home to Kansas City and joining an industrial film outfit to learn about making movies. When he decided he knew how, he flew a few sorties into Hollywood armed with radio scripts, short stories and screenplays. In 1957, he coproduced a documentary, *The James Dean Story*, which impressed Alfred Hitchcock. For the next six years, Altman was the whiz kid of TV, directing episodes of *Alfred Hitchcock Presents, Combat, Bonanza, Whirlybirds* and their ilk, earning—and recklessly spending or gambling away—up to $125,000 per annum.

Altman quit TV in 1963 to direct *Countdown*, a melodrama starring newcomer James Caan. He was fired from that job, prophetically, for letting two actors talk at the same time because he thought it would sound more natural. It was 1968 before he got another feature, *That Cold Day in the Park*, a muddled suspense drama starring Sandy Dennis.

Then came M*A*S*H, which 15 directors had rejected before Altman claimed it by default. The rest is history—but hardly one of financial triumph. *Brewster McCloud* (1971), an anarchic comedy about a boy who longs to be a bird and crash-dives into the Houston Astrodome, itself took a header. *McCabe & Mrs. Miller* (1971) co-starred Warren Beatty and Julie Christie as a plucky pair of American free-enterprisers in a frontier town and got the director's bandwagon rolling again. *Images*, made in Ireland, was generally ignored, despite a 1973 Best Actress award at Cannes for Susannah York's performance, and *The Long Goodbye* (1973), with Elliott Gould, brought private-eye Philip Marlowe into the 1970s. *Thieves Like Us* (1974), a warmly vital social drama of the Depression era, was followed by *California Split* (1974), which was a moderate success and teamed Gould and George Segal as a pair of compulsive gamblers.

Through the highs and lows of his prolific output, Altman has remained a loner. His list of sworn enemies, fast friends and those who haven't made up their minds is impressive, even for Hollywood. His friends include a tight floating repertory company: Shelley Duvall, Michael Murphy, Bert Remsen and Keenan Wynn are among those who would rather work for Altman than eat. Nowadays, it's relatively easy to manage both. Lion's Gate Films, his bustling production headquarters, occupies a two-story California-Tudor warren of cubbyholes and cutting rooms on Westwood Boulevard in L.A.

While he makes no secret of his fondness for booze and pot, Altman has been too busy of late to indulge his vices to capacity. But he does little to dispel his reputation as a hard-living, high-rolling roustabout, and once when an inquisitive lady journalist gingerly broached the subject of his three marriages, he twitted her by jovially responding: "I've had many, many mistresses. Keep 'em coming. I just giggle and give in!" Giggles aside, he has been married for 17 years to his third wife, Kathryn—a former Earl Carroll showgirl and a bright, witty, unstoppable redhead who appears more than capable of fighting the battle of the sexes to a draw. Altman has three children by his former wives; he and Kathryn have a son, Bobby, 15, and have adopted a black boy named Matthew, aged nine. When one tries to picture Altman simultaneously as devoted family man, all-American hedonist, savage social realist, veteran Hollywood rebel and major influence on the films we'll be seeing today, tomorrow and three years from now, the images tend to blur, not unlike the voice track in one of his own movies. To find out how the man keeps it all together, *Playboy* movie critic and Contributing Editor Bruce Williamson headed west toward Lion's Gate with a sheaf of questions. Williamson reports:

"During a casual acquaintanceship dating back several years—drinking with Altman in Cannes, getting stoned with him in New York—I believe I have seen the best and worst of him as a private person who is convivial, erratic, difficult, generous, funny, vulnerable and incredibly, sometimes bitingly, perceptive about people. In physical appearance, he has been compared to Santa Claus, Mephistopheles and a benevolent Captain Bligh, and he fits all three descriptions.

"The day I arrived at his Lion's Gate inner office, a homey baronial den with a pinball machine twinkling just outside, Altman spent the first hour or so rapping with Cleavon Little about his role in the film version of Kurt Vonnegut Jr.'s *Breakfast of Champions*, an Altman project they wouldn't be ready to begin shooting for at least a year. What Altman didn't want to do was get on with our interview. It would be better to start talking after I'd seen *Buffalo Bill and the Indians*, Altman decided. If I loathed it, of course, all bets were off. We marked time until Paul Newman arrived, clean-shaven, along with 40 or 50 other people who were visibly itching to see a rough cut of the movie. Later, Altman collared at least half of them to ask point-blank how they had liked it. A mindblower, nearly everyone, myself included, agreed.

"Altman's reluctance to begin our taping lessened the next day, as a series of phone calls reaffirmed the good vibes about the unveiling of *Buffalo Bill*. Finally, Altman settled down to talk. 'At first,' he said, 'I thought, well, I could probably thwart you, but that would be a waste of time.' He would just give straight stuff, no performances, he promised, maybe fill a couple of tapes . . . then we'd have a drink or two and go on with it the next day. That sounded like the best offer I'd be getting."

PLAYBOY: Isn't there a natural link between your two latest pictures, *Buffalo Bill and the Indians* and *Nashville*, in what they say about our passion for celebrities in America? Is it true, as one critic observed, that we're a nation of groupies?

ALTMAN: You people—critics and writers—always pigeonhole these things. Me, I just take a subject and say, Hey, this could be fun; let's make a movie out of it. *Buffalo Bill*, in many ways, is closer to *McCabe & Mrs. Miller* than to *Nashville*, though, like *Nashville*, it is about show business. Buffalo Bill Cody was the first movie star, in one sense, the first totally manufactured American hero. That's why we needed a movie star, Paul Newman, to play the title role. I don't think we could have made it with a nonstar, someone like, say, Gene Hackman.

PLAYBOY: You mean you wouldn't consider Hackman, who is asking $1,000,000 or more a picture, a star?

ALTMAN: Not in the terms that Newman and Robert Redford and Steve McQueen are. In any picture where he can be Steve McQueen, McQueen is worth his $3,000,000, because his pictures can be booked around the world and earn back the tab. Hackman is a fine actor, but I don't believe he's worth paying that kind of money, unless he's in a very good picture. In a bad picture, he just goes down with the whole crew. McQueen can overcome that handicap. The same thing might be true of Redford, who's next in line, then maybe Newman. Jack Nicholson, with an Academy Award now, is probably in their league, and certainly Marlon Brando.

PLAYBOY: What's the real difference in the star quality these actors project?

ALTMAN: It's something that happens, there's no telling why. It happens with politicians, singers . . . they've got to have a certain amount of ability. But primarily they hit on a kind of heroism a mass audience likes to identify with. You can't judge simply by the U.S. and Canada, because it's a worldwide market. For Europe and Japan, you put McQueen in some kind of action picture and they'll flock to see him . . . or Charles Bronson or Alain Delon, or even Terence Hill, whom most people here have never heard of. *The Drowning Pool*, which was just a little Lew Archer detective story that didn't do well at all in the U.S., did terrific business in Europe because it had Paul Newman. European audiences are about 20 years behind us. They're still not judging films as art but as entertainment.

PLAYBOY: Were you required by your backers to cast a major star as Buffalo Bill?

ALTMAN: Yes, because there's $6,000,000 or $7,000,000 tied up in the picture; it's the most expensive picture I've ever made. But we wanted a major star, anyway, as I said, because stardom is part of what we're talking about in *Buffalo Bill*. Before we knew quite which way we intended to go, I talked to Brando on the phone because of his interest in the Indian thing. I talked a long, long time to Nicholson. But Newman was our first choice.

PLAYBOY: Was Newman aware that your approach to *Buffalo Bill* had him spoofing his own golden-boy image to some extent?

ALTMAN: Oh, sure. That's why I wanted him and the reason he wanted to do it. He was very consciously deflating not only Buffalo Bill but Paul Newman, Movie Star. Nobody can live up to that kind of image.

PLAYBOY: In fact, aren't most of your films exercises in debunking, if not of specific historical characters, at least of classic genres? *M*A*S*H* was a spoof of war movies; *McCabe & Mrs. Miller*, of the cliché Western; *The Long Goodbye*, of detective yarns, and so on.

ALTMAN: Apparently, it's something that attracts me. But I see it only after the fact, and then I say to myself, Well, there I go again. I think what happens is that I research these subjects and discover so much bullshit that it just comes out that way. I have a lot of sympathy for these characters, however; they're the victims of their own publicity.

PLAYBOY: You had a lot of fun depicting Buffalo Bill Cody as a frontier dandy with a weakness for opera singers. Is the film historically accurate?

ALTMAN: It's based on fact, though we took off from there. Cody was a very handsome guy, very impressionable, a ladies' man. When he started moving into the social whirl, he got mixed up with a bunch of Italian actresses; we used the idiom of opera as typical of the kind of cultural thing he was reaching for and really couldn't grasp. I feel a great deal of sympathy for Buffalo Bill. He was pure, I think. My intention was just to take a more honest look—satirical or not—at some of our myths, to see what they are. It's no accident that the picture is subtitled *Sitting Bull's History Lesson*. We like to think of Cody as a brave man, a great buffalo hunter, an Indian scout. Well, he shot a lot of buffaloes. But lots of guys who lived in the West at that time got jobs as scouts; that's like saying you worked on the railroad. Cody was a very sad character. I'd equate him with Willy Loman in *Death of a Salesman*.

PLAYBOY: Is *Buffalo Bill and the Indians* intended to be your Bicentennial valentine to America?

ALTMAN: Nope. When I first got the call from David Susskind about doing *Buffalo Bill*, I didn't know there *was* a Bicentennial. We're making a statement about a culture that happens to be American; you can probably make the same statement about France or Italy or England.

I don't know what aboriginal tribes were chased out of Europe by the Europeans, but I'm quite sure they were treated pretty much the same way we treated the Indians we found here. My attitudes and my political statements, however, aren't nearly as harsh as people seem to think. When *Nashville* came out, there was this wild reaction: Oh, what a terrible view of America! It's a view of America, all right, but I don't agree that it's terrible. I'm not condemning America. I'm condemning the corruption of ideas, condemning complacency, the feeling that any way *we* do things must be the right way.

All my films deal with the same thing: striving, socially and culturally, to stay alive. And once any system succeeds, it becomes its own worst enemy. The good things we create soon create bad things. So nothing is ever going to be utopian, and when I make films like *Nashville* and *Buffalo Bill*, it's not to say we're the worst country in the world, or God, what awful people these are. I'm just saying we're *at* this point and it's sad.

PLAYBOY: Do you feel as sad about the country's future as you do about its past and present?

ALTMAN: If I were to make a real judgment about this country, I would say I'm optimistic. I think that parts of the system no longer work, but we're very young; there's a good chance we'll survive all this. It's probably the best place to live that I know. I mean, if you're rich, you can go anywhere. But if you're poor—well, I'd rather be poor here than poor in India. There's always a sense that you can rise above your trappings in this country, whereas even in England, for example, you don't feel the same hope—unless you can become a rock star.

PLAYBOY: Behind the laughs in *Buffalo Bill*, there's an implication that that kind of manufactured hero still walks among us. Can you spot any on the current political scene?

ALTMAN: Yes, all of them. Any person who develops a public and packaged personality is the same as a movie star, unfortunately. They *can't* be real, regular people. You take a Teddy Kennedy or a Jerry Brown: He has to maintain the public's image of him, and he finally *becomes* that image, at which point he's lost a lot of freedom. No way is Teddy Kennedy going to walk around your kitchen with his shoes off and level with you; he's not going to be loose, because he can't afford to be. There's no such thing as a private life anymore. The media are so vast, you're caught up and made an eccentric. It's just like this interview or any interview done with someone like me, to be printed in so many words: The words you guys pick may not give a true picture of an individual, whether it's to sell magazines or political candidates.

PLAYBOY: Is that why you have been so reluctant to do this interview?

ALTMAN: No, I'm just afraid I'll start listening to myself. I wonder how much bullshit an interview will be, because I have nothing to say about anything. I'm not interested in analyzing myself. What I'm doing right now is a very dangerous thing for an artist to do.

PLAYBOY: Why?

ALTMAN: Because when you start trying to explain what you do . . . well, once you find out, you probably won't be able to do it again. Things come out of me only when I relax and let them come as an unconscious, emotional expression rather than an intellectual expression.

I tend to say a lot of arbitrary, contradictory things, and if I don't like a person, I'll get very hostile and say, Aw, fuck it, and purposely try to antagonize him. Yet there's usually some truth in everything anyone says. Again, it's a question of freeing your subconscious.

PLAYBOY: Do you or don't you use booze to free your subconscious? In a *Newsweek* cover story, you were quoted as saying, "I work a lot when I'm drunk and trust that all of it will eventually appear in my films." On other occasions, you have insisted you never drink on the job. What's the truth?

ALTMAN: The fact is, I don't drink while I'm working. But I work a lot while I'm drinking. No matter what you read or hear, I never get drunk on a film set.

PLAYBOY: But when *aren't* you working? You've made nine movies in the past six years, virtually without taking a vacation. Don't you ever have to stop and catch a breath or recharge your creative batteries?

ALTMAN: Perhaps I should stay home on the beach, but all I say is, I can't remember a time when I haven't been working on a project. I come in every day, whether there's anything to do or not. If I don't have something to do, I create it. This is the life, man. I can be here in the office, get drunk, go next door and edit out a piece of film. It's terrific, like owning the world's biggest erector set.

PLAYBOY: Someone has suggested that with Lion's Gate you're founding a mini-MGM. Are you?

ALTMAN: If I am, it's in self-defense. Most of my money goes into the place; it costs about $600,000 a year just to keep the doors open. But I'm trying to keep a group of people together who are very important to me. I'm producing films for them to write or direct, to keep them available to me as need arises. All of them could get better jobs. They could improve their incomes, their status by working somewhere else.

PLAYBOY: Are you referring to their having to buck the anti-Altman sentiment among members of the Hollywood establishment?

ALTMAN: Yes, but that sentiment is understandable. I've never been very nice to the establishment, either. I've always been very outspoken in the press; my tendency is always to be a little loud. I'm a little arrogant and they're a little afraid.

PLAYBOY: Do you believe your maverick status in Hollywood had anything to do with *Nashville's* relatively poor showing in the Oscar awards?

ALTMAN: I was thrilled that we got as far as we did with recognition for the film, which had been turned down by all the major studios; Paramount merely picked it up for distribution. But *One Flew Over the Cuckoo's Nest* wasn't a major Hollywood production, either—the money was put up by a record company—and Milos Forman is not a Hollywood director. Even *Dog Day Afternoon* was a New York picture, so maybe what it really shows is that there's a lack of good product coming from the major studios. The main value of these awards, anyway, other than to rub your ego a little bit, is that they may open the door a crack wider for people with ideas that aren't run of the mill.

PLAYBOY: But with five nominations for *Nashville*, didn't you expect to win more than Keith Carradine's prize for Best Song?

ALTMAN: Well, the Academy is a private club, so its members can do whatever they want with it, I guess. They declared *Nashville* ineligible for an editing award. *Nashville* was more edited than directed, for Christ's sake. They ruled us out on costume design, art direction and camera, and even disqualified our musical score on a technical point. Johnny Green and Jeff Alexander, the old men who run that Academy section, are determined to keep it all to themselves. When Green did a score made up of standard songs of his for *They Shoot Horses, Don't They?* they had to change the rules that year so *he* could qualify and be nominated for an Oscar.

PLAYBOY: In the categories in which *Nashville* was qualified, did you do any active campaigning?

ALTMAN: Paramount did a little, not much. I wouldn't have wanted them to do any more. I don't know what United Artists spent promoting *Cuckoo's Nest*, but I'll guarantee you it was over $80,000. That's the trouble, the whole thing becomes like a national election, with primaries. I won the New York primary, *Cuckoo's Nest* won the foreign primary—six Golden Globe awards—and so on. But nobody knows who votes. I think if a magazine took photographs of each of those Academy members—the ones who actually cast the ballots—and published them all and said who they were, you'd be able to make a pretty good evaluation of what an Academy Award is really worth and how it's arrived at.

PLAYBOY: Louise Fletcher, who took the Best Actress award for *Cuckoo's Nest*, was originally supposed to play the role that got Lily Tomlin a Best Supporting Actress nomination for *Nashville*. Some follow-up stories, commenting on this behind-the-scenes irony, hinted that you had given the role to Lily because she had a bigger name. Is there some misunderstanding?

ALTMAN: Not on my part. That role as the mother of the deaf-mute children was written for Louise, whose parents are deaf. But her husband, Jerry Bick, who was my producer on *Thieves Like Us*, came to me and said he didn't see how Louise would be able to leave her kids and go off on location in Nashville for eight or 10 weeks . . . and what was he supposed to do during that time? I felt very guilty then, because there was no money in the part . . . we felt all the actors in *Nashville* were doing us a great big favor, and it seemed to me we were just asking a little too much of Louise. I'm not sure Jerry went back and *told* her that he had indicated she shouldn't take the part, since they have to live together. But that's when I started considering Lily. In any case, Louise is a deserving actress. I coaxed her out of retirement for *Thieves Like Us* and we showed film on her to Forman and Mike Douglas to help convince them she should get *Cuckoo's Nest*.

PLAYBOY: Is it true that Robert Duvall was supposed to play the Henry Gibson role in *Nashville*?

ALTMAN: The part was written for Duvall. It was one of the last characters added and turned out to be one of the most important. Duvall came down here and said he wanted to be in the picture and could sing country-and-western. So I said, "Fine, you can write your own songs." Then I guess we broke over money.

PLAYBOY: In view of everything you said a moment ago about the Academy, how would you have felt if you *had* won an Oscar?

ALTMAN: Surprised. And I'd be very pleased. Going in as an underdog and winning an uphill battle makes anybody feel good. But, my God, people get crazy; they call you up and say how sorry they are, they were so sure you'd win. It's not a *foot race*; one doesn't set out to make a movie with that goal in mind. Or maybe some do. Recently, I saw an interview in the L.A. *Times* with Billy Friedkin, talking about his new picture, a remake of *Wages of Fear*, apparently meant to top *The Exorcist*. Mr. Friedkin, who has some kind of chronic diarrhea of the mouth, was very humble, as usual; for the $10,000,000 he's been given to spend, he said, "Well, to be frank—I'm going for a classic." But nobody really cares what he intends to do or what I intend to do; it's what we end *up* doing that counts.

PLAYBOY: But a lot of the controversy about *Nashville* centered on exactly that question: What *did* you intend to do? How would you sum up the central metaphor of *Nashville?*

ALTMAN: If you take all those 24 characters in the film, you can break each one down into an archetype. We carefully picked those archetypes to represent a cross section of the whole culture, heightened by the country-music scene and extreme nationalism, or regionalism, of a city like Nashville. When you say Nashville, you immediately focus on an image of great wealth and instant popular success. It's like Hollywood 40 years ago. Kids still get off buses with guitars; two years later they can own a guitar-shaped swimming pool.

Another thing Nashville signifies is that we don't listen to words anymore. The words of a country song are as predictable as the words of a politician's speech. When President Ford announces that the state of the Union is that we're solving problems in the Middle East, we don't listen; we don't read or pay attention to what he says. It becomes rhythm and music rather than meaningful words. No one can quote one thing Ford has said since he's been in office.

Nashville is merely suggesting that you think about these things, allowing you room to think. Many people, I guess, want to know exactly what it is they're supposed to think. They want to know what your message is. Well, my message is that I am not going to do their work for them.

PLAYBOY: *Nashville* never became the commercial blockbuster that you and many pro-Altman critics anticipated. Why?

ALTMAN: Well, I can only think it's because we didn't have King Kong or a shark. I don't mean to take anything away from *Jaws*, but *Nashville* was not a one-focus thing like that. Also, maybe there was too *much* critical response; the word masterpiece frightens people away. It's still been more profitable for me personally than any film I've ever made; it's grossed about $8,000,000 and may go to $10,000,000. I think *Buffalo Bill* is going to be easier for audiences than *Nashville*, because it doesn't pose a threat: The indictment is in history, so we can always put that blame somewhere else. *Nashville*'s indictment made too many people nervous. The whole community of Nashville disowned it; the country-music people said it was no good, it was a lie; and that kept a lot of those fans away.

PLAYBOY: Wasn't the specific charge they leveled against you that the music was phony, wouldn't pass muster at the Grand Ole Opry?

ALTMAN: This crap about a Nashville sound is mainly a matter of opinion. I wasn't making records, goddamn it, I was making a movie. Take any song in there, I can point out a current hit or failure that's better and worse—musically, lyrically and every other way. The main reason for that criticism was that they saw the names of actors, not professional songwriters, on the songs; and Richard Baskin, who did all the arrangements, was not a country-and-western guy. It's my contention that anybody can write a song. The Nashville people have to claim they're more professional; otherwise, how are they going to justify the $1,000,000 a year they make?

PLAYBOY: One last question about *Nashville*. In the assassination scene at the end—

ALTMAN: I know what's coming. When I go around to the universities—where quite a number of kids don't understand my pictures and don't especially like them—they always want to know: Why'd he kill *her*?

PLAYBOY: Well, why did he?

ALTMAN: When you ask why he killed the singer instead of the politician, you've already answered your question—and discovered my motive. The point is that we can accept the assassination of the politician but not that of the girl. Because we *condone* political assassination in our culture. We say that's all right, we understand *that*. Assassination has become acceptable in this society and it's going to spread, the way hijacking did. I think we're in a very dangerous situation. And now, with the Patricia Hearst trial and all its implications, it's becoming almost nightmarish.

PLAYBOY: What implications do you see in the Patty Hearst trial?

ALTMAN: I mean that the Patty Hearst case was not about her at all, and it's the worst thing that's happened in this country since the Julius and Ethel Rosenberg trial. You knew she would be found guilty, she had to be found guilty; there was no way that judge and jury could *not* convict Patty Hearst, because they're afraid, afraid of Hearst power; so now they've stripped that away to prove that money can't protect her. They're afraid of revolution.

PLAYBOY: You suggest that society as a whole demanded her conviction?

ALTMAN: Absolutely. And I think we're going to see that girl's mother, Catherine Hearst, become so radicalized that I would not be surprised at any act she might perform in the next year or so. It turns out that Cinque, or DeFreeze, was a prophet. "If you go back there," he told Patty, "they'll put you in jail." And, by God, that's what happened. We're now in the full swing of the Nixon-Kissinger heritage, with all their philosophy coming down to us. We're even beginning to look at Gerald Ford as if he were a nice guy and pretty smart.

Patty Hearst had to be convicted for not being a well-trained soldier. She shouldn't have gone on trial in the first place. Jesus Christ, she was 19 years old, thrown into the trunk of a car, locked in a closet, absolutely terrorized; and I think from that point on you've got to discount every single thing she has done. I have spoken to several people who are very strong in the ACLU, real liberals, people who suffered through the McCarthy era, the Hollywood Ten and all that. And when they said they thought this kid should be convicted, I couldn't believe it.

The Hearst case deals with exactly the same kind of collective fear the Rosenberg trial did. The fear then was of communism, that Russia might get the bomb. Now there's terrorism and anarchy throughout the world and everyone is panicky. We're afraid of Patty Hearst because she lived with a guy willingly and wrote letters, made statements. What society is actually reacting to is its fear of hippies, and of sexual freedom, and of revolutionaries, people with beards and long hair who don't keep their pants pressed or wear neckties.

PLAYBOY: Would you consider making a film that dealt directly with this kind of volatile social problem?

ALTMAN: Funny you should ask, because I'm just concluding a deal with Ed Doctorow to coproduce a movie based on his novel *The Book of Daniel*; he'll write the script and I'll direct. It's a fictionalized story about the children of the Rosenbergs, about the hysteria of an era when people are frightened and people get sacrificed.

PLAYBOY: You and Doctorow are thick as thieves since he presented your New York Film Critics' Award and introduced himself as "Altman's new best friend." You're also making the movie version of his novel *Ragtime* together. When will that be?

ALTMAN: Not for a while. I've got a first-draft screenplay from Doctorow that is about 340 pages long and brilliant; I'm thrilled with it. The son of a bitch is uncanny, really an artist, and I just like him a lot. I mean, we don't hug or anything, but we talk on the phone almost every day. He came up to Calgary while we were on location and was pressed into service; he makes his screen debut as a presidential assistant in *Buffalo Bill.*

PLAYBOY: Isn't 340 pages pretty long for a screenplay?

ALTMAN: I think we'll make two films out of it, of about two and a half hours each, then expand that into 10 hours of television. This will not be just another movie. It'll be an event.

PLAYBOY: Didn't you once have similar plans for *Nashville?*

ALTMAN: That's already done and re-edited as two two-hour television programs, which will probably air on two Sunday nights to start the 1977 fall television season. Eventually, we're going to do the same thing with *Buffalo Bill;* we've already made the deal.

PLAYBOY: Do these projected films for TV indicate that you feel some dissatisfaction with the shorter original versions?

ALTMAN: No, but there are really good sequences from *Nashville,* for example, that weren't in the movie because you cannot ask people to sit that long in a theater. Some movie buffs will gladly sit for five hours, but people generally won't do it. On television, that's not offensive. You've got breaks. You can eat, stretch, go to the bathroom.

PLAYBOY: You're working with heavyweights now, between Doctorow's *Ragtime* and your plans to film Kurt Vonnegut Jr.'s *Breakfast of Champions.* Is it intimidating for you to tackle movies based on two such famous novels?

ALTMAN: Well, it's no worse than making a movie about something like the Civil War.

PLAYBOY: Have you considered making an epic nonfiction film, as it were? Something like *All the President's Men?*

ALTMAN: To me, doing that movie would be like making an illustrated lecture, because you're not able to deviate from the facts much. I understand the success of it, because everyone knows who the bad guys and good guys are, and you've got that big face of Nixon's looming over all of it. The majority of people in this country—61 percent of them, remember—are exactly like Nixon. They chose him, he betrayed them, and those are the cats who respond to *President's Men* as much as you and I and the liberals who say, "Aw, shit, I told you so." They've got to love it because it's *real,* it's revenge. Nixon was the perfect President for this country, but he dumped on them and they're still feeling hurt.

PLAYBOY: Could you work up greater enthusiasm for making a movie based on Woodward and Bernstein's sequel, *The Final Days?*

ALTMAN: Well, long before Watergate, we thought about a movie of that kind from a book—not a very good book—called *A Night at Camp David*. It's about a president who goes insane. We were flirting with buying it, then I suddenly realized it was all actually happening. The book was almost prophetic, but it was not for me.

PLAYBOY: Are you an activist in politics?

ALTMAN: I get involved. I mean, I give money and support. I supported Gene McCarthy, I supported George McGovern. Right now there's nobody to get passionate about. Intellectually, Morris Udall seemed the best. Jerry Brown is attractive to me; I think he's getting set up for four years from now. But the rest offer nothing fresh.

Actually, I don't think it makes a lot of difference who gets elected in 1976. I doubt that we're going to have a president of any value this term. Probably the next time around will be better. In fact, maybe we shouldn't care who's president. Maybe it should be someone like the chief executive of AT&T, a board chairman whose name we don't even know. Because government today is only a firm that builds highways, maintains a system of courts to keep people from infringing on other people's rights. As for genuine leadership and philosophy . . . well, I think we're past that.

PLAYBOY: Some feminists have tried to make your *films* a political issue. What do you say when your work is attacked for projecting—and we quote—"an adolescent view of women as sex objects"?

ALTMAN: I simply don't understand that. Again, let's look at the films. Women had most of the major roles in *Nashville*. I did *Images* with Susannah York, which was certainly a sympathetic treatment of women. I think Julie Christie as Mrs. Miller is a very accurate portrait of a woman's role in the West if she wanted to survive in that era. Maybe the accusation harks back to Hot Lips in M*A*S*H, but the precise point of that character was that women *were* treated and *are* treated as sex objects. They can't blame me for the condition because I report it. We're dealing with a society in which most of the significant activity until now has been initiated by males. If you make a Western or a sports story or a story about big business or gangsters, it's automatically going to reflect the secondary positions women hold.

PLAYBOY: You retain complete control over your movies, as Francis Ford Coppola, Stanley Kubrick and a few other privileged directors do. Is there never any pressure brought to bear to make you change a film?

ALTMAN: Oh, sure. But nobody has ever cut a film on me. There was a lot of pressure up front from Barry Diller at Paramount, who wanted me to cut one sequence in *Nashville* so we'd get a PG rating rather than an R. The Motion Picture Association's ratings board said it would make a deal with us: It would let us keep the striptease scene with Gwen Welles if we would cut the word fucker somewhere else.

PLAYBOY: Did you give up the "fucker"?

ALTMAN: No, I didn't. We finally took an R. The word itself didn't make much difference to me one way or the other, but I felt I couldn't cut it because that would put the ratings board in a position in which it's not supposed to be. The ratings people are supposed to be advisors, not censors. If they are what they say they are, there shouldn't be any appeal from their rulings. They should just give you an R or a P or an X or a Q or whatever and make it stick.

This whole MPAA thing is so unwieldy, and also corrupt—though by corrupt I don't mean you can buy them off. But they represent a privileged group of industry people, and if you belong to that group, you get slightly different treatment. More money has gone into some pictures, so they're considered more important and handled accordingly; but there's no way anybody can show me the justification for *Papillon*'s getting a PG rating while *Thieves Like Us* got an R. There's no consistency. I took an R for *California Split* because we had 12 fucks and a couple of cocksuckers. But the minute they say they want to trade me a tit for a fucker, that proves to me they're corrupt.

PLAYBOY: If you are so often at odds with the Hollywood establishment, why do you continue to live and work in the enemy camp, so to speak?

ALTMAN: Well, it's a big town, and I've got an awful lot of people I depend on who also depend on me. It doesn't make a bit of difference where you are, anyway. *Nashville* was made in Nashville. *Buffalo Bill* and *McCabe* were made in Canada. *Thieves Like Us* was made in Mississippi. My feeling about Hollywood is that all of that has nothing to do with the pictures I make. I'm the catalyst, I guess, for a kind of East Coast–West Coast cultural separation, the Great Divide, which drives the studio people crazy. Because they want moneymaking pictures, sure, but they also want the snob appeal of critical acceptance and prestige—meaning films that get good reviews.

PLAYBOY: The New York critics love you, but do you get much support from the press here in Los Angeles?

ALTMAN: I always get a kind of left-handed criticism out here, except from a few people. Charles Champlin on the *Times* practically runs ads predicting who will win the Oscars and who he believes *should* win. He never misses. The people who vote read Champlin and think: Oh, Champlin's right, because he's not one of those East Coast people who are always pushing us around.

At the Academy Awards, I ran into Ruth Batchelor, whoever she is; she's a chairman of the Los Angeles critics' group, which was just formed to give out prizes the way the New York critics do. She came up to me and said, "You know, on the first ballot, *Nashville* won everything, but we use a point system and had to keep revoting." And I told her, "You had to keep revoting until you didn't coincide with the New York film critics." She said, "Well, uh . . . yes, that's right." It's all pretty silly.

PLAYBOY: Is it just that they want to be different from their New York colleagues?

ALTMAN: No, I think it reflects the quality of the critics. The same division exists between France and England. They love me at Cannes, while in England they say, "Well, he was just lucky." Generally, I think the Eastern critics are more appreciative of art and exploration in films. I think the California people are more interested in preserving their traditions. I'm not charging that Champlin is a bad critic. But this town responds to him because it feels he represents the industry. It's chauvinistic, like people who live in Chicago rooting for the Cubs or the White Sox. But we shouldn't discuss only New York versus Hollywood. Seattle is a terrific movie town, much closer in taste to the New York anti-Hollywood attitude; and Denver's the same way. I think we're talking about Hollywood versus the rest of the country, not just the East.

PLAYBOY: How closely do you follow what critics write about you?

ALTMAN: The main function of critics, for me, is that they furnish some sort of guidelines. You don't go to a king, you don't go before a jury of 12 citizens picked at random to judge a film. I don't go to the guys at my dad's country club in Kansas City, because they would be bored to death watching one of my movies. I'm trying to reach the several millions of people in the country, or the world, who are film oriented. The critics, who see virtually all films, are in touch with that audience, so I read what they say. There are certain critics I tend to agree with almost straight down the line.

PLAYBOY: Do you want to name them?

ALTMAN: I'd rather not, because it might seem to alienate or discredit anyone who's left out. And if I say Rex Reed is my favorite critic, Rex will get intimidated and start writing bad things about me.

PLAYBOY: We could probably guess that Reed *isn't* your favorite critic, since he is one of those who have called you a lazy artist, a sloppy worker who improvises too much with too little control. How about Jay Cocks of *Time*, who has suggested that you should take your work more seriously than you do?

ALTMAN: Jay Cocks has always made personal comments about me; he can't seem to separate me as an individual from my films. I've never met him and can't answer his assumptions.

I probably am a lazy artist and probably don't control things as much as some people would like—but that's my business. And if my style is too loose or improvised for some people's taste, that's their problem—totally. The fact is, I'm not the greatest Hollywood director and all that bullshit, but I'm not the opposite, either. And I am not careless. I may be irresponsible, I may strive for things and not always succeed, but that's never the result of sloppiness. Maybe it's lack of judgment.

PLAYBOY: Stephen Farber, who recently became *New West*'s film critic, described you as one of the New Has-beens a couple of years ago, just before your reputation started to soar. How did that grab you?

ALTMAN: Well, Farber ought to have his typewriter taken away from him or go get a job working for the oil companies. He is not a critic, he doesn't qualify as a critic. He's a hatchet man and paid assassin, a guy *The New York Times* knows it can go to if it wants an "anti" piece because there's been too much praise of something. I'm sure Clay Felker hired Farber for the same reason he hired John Simon as *New York*'s critic—because he wanted somebody to really get the shiv out and sell magazines. I don't like Simon at all, but at least I give him credit for being a critic. I can't give that much to Rex Reed, who's basically a gossip columnist, but Farber's worse than any of those guys.

PLAYBOY: The loudest member of the pro-Altman critical claque has been *The New Yorker*'s Pauline Kael, who created a stir when she wrote an ecstatic review of *Nashville* based on an unfinished early version. This year, Kael reportedly claimed that she's qualified to review Altman movies in this manner because she knows your work so well she can tell in advance what's going to be left in and taken out. Is that true?

ALTMAN: Did she say that? Well, I suppose she can. Pauline is such a student of film, she probably knows pretty well in which direction a movie is likely to go. In general, I don't mind who sees a film in rough cut. I show them to lots of people without fear of reprisals, though I wouldn't let Rex Reed see one of my films in *finished* form. He'll have to buy his own ticket.

PLAYBOY: Is it true that you threw Barbra Streisand out of your office after one such screening?

ALTMAN: Yes, because she was rude.

PLAYBOY: Do you want to tell us about it?

ALTMAN: She came as a guest of mine with her boyfriend, Jon Peters—to see *Nashville*, at her request, as a matter of fact—because Peters was planning to direct a rock *Star Is Born* or something. So we screened the picture for them and for 20 or 30 other people, including some of the actors in the film. Then we came back here to the office; Barbra sat down and all her conversation was about "Jon and I." "Listen," she said, "Jon and I want to know how you did this, how you did that." Finally, I said, "Don't you think you owe a comment to a few of the people in this room?" She had nothing to say. She was so completely wrapped up in herself, she didn't even know what I was talking about. I just asked them to leave.

PLAYBOY: Aren't there pitfalls in your practice of screening rough cuts of your films for friends, colleagues, sometimes even for critics?

ALTMAN: Well, sure, a little masochism is part of it, you can't delude yourself. But we don't just pull people off the street. I have to be very careful not to load a preview with people I *know* are duck soup, who will just go for the film no matter what. I'm also arrogant enough to invite people who I'm sure will want *not* to like it, who really hope to see it fail. I love to make them commit themselves up front, then turn it around on them later. You see, the way I edit films is to start showing them as I'm pulling them together. I don't actually pay much attention to what people say, but I make decisions while looking at the backs of their heads, seeing the movie through someone else's eyes. If I get embarrassed by a certain sequence, that tells me something.

PLAYBOY: How did you arrive at your free-and-easy approach to film-making?

ALTMAN: Well, I don't like to rehearse a scene before we're actually ready to shoot it. If I do, the freshness is gone for me when we go back to it later; everything seems set and kind of dry.

PLAYBOY: Your unorthodox methods must be a little unnerving for some actors. How did it go with Newman?

ALTMAN: Oh, Paul was sensational. He had no problem at all. Donald

Sutherland in M*A*S*H loved working that way and his improvisation was profound; he's a hell of an actor. Warren Beatty in *McCabe* probably had the toughest time. But Warren was already a star, dealing with an unknown director and properly nervous about it. And Warren doesn't trust anybody very much.

My work is not really as loose and frenetic and unorthodox as everyone seems to think and it's not nearly as improvisational as I get credit for. I suspect that some actors see my films and sense a certain kind of freedom or fantasize about it. But most of the actors who have worked for me don't work for anybody else. Shelley Duvall has given absolutely marvelous performances in four or five of my films; her work in *Thieves Like Us* is as good as any performance I can imagine. I'm always amazed that other directors don't pick up on her, but nobody has; she can't get a job . . . I guess because she doesn't have big tits. Ronee Blakley was looking for an agent, so I had a few of them down here to see film on her while we were cutting *Nashville*. I showed them her hospital scene, her breakdown scene, and they said, "Gee, she's terrific, but . . . you know, she's a country-and-western singer." I said, "No, there's nothing country-and-western about her. If anything, she's a hip West Coast girl." They could not get it through their heads that she was *acting*. They finally said to me, "Well, uh, you've got a way of making real people look like actors." And I told them, "Well, I hope I have a way of making actors look like real people."

PLAYBOY: Have you done any casting for either *Ragtime* or *Breakfast of Champions?*

ALTMAN: We have no cast in mind for *Ragtime*, but *Breakfast* seems pretty well set. Peter Falk will play Dwayne Hoover; Sterling Hayden will play Kilgore Trout; Cleavon Little will play Wayne Hoobler; Alice Cooper will play Bunny Hoover; and Ruth Gordon will play Eliott Rosewater, the richest man in the world.

PLAYBOY: Ruth Gordon will play a male part?

ALTMAN: Sure; she's an actor, why not? All the feminists say we shouldn't discriminate. We're using Alice Cooper as the fag piano player, and Ruth Gordon can certainly look like an old man. Our sexual differences tend to disappear with age, anyway; all she has to do is cut her hair and sit in a wheelchair.

PLAYBOY: You once indicated that *Breakfast* would be a breakthrough movie sexually, in which you'd let it all hang out. Is that still the plan?

ALTMAN: No, that was one of those early ideas that just didn't develop. I was going to deal primarily with the Kilgore Trout section of the story, where his books were being turned into pornographic movies, but we've abandoned that whole concept.

PLAYBOY: Which films will you do next?

ALTMAN: I'll be starting with *Yig Epoxy*, based on a book by Robert Grossbach called *Easy and Hard Ways Out*. It'll be a studio picture for Warner Bros. all shot on a sound stage, with Falk and Hayden again, Henry Gibson and a big, big cast. The whole thing takes place in one of those huge engineering-firm think tanks. It's a flat-out comedy, a cross between *Dr. Strangelove* and M*A*S*H, a really funny situation; and I'm going to see if I can make the audience wet their pants.

PLAYBOY: What does *Yig Epoxy* mean?

ALTMAN: Epoxy, of course, is glue. A YIG is a sort of radar device, and there's a YIG filter, which is used in aircraft for evasive action with ground-air missiles. They can't find the right glue to hold this thing together; consequently, all these planes crash. . . .

PLAYBOY: Sounds like a million laughs. What else is on your calendar?

ALTMAN: I produced a film that's coming in, an original by Robert Benton, called *The Late Show*, with Art Carney and Lily Tomlin. Then there's Alan Rudolph's film *Welcome to L.A.*, which I'm producing, and another thing we're working on for Lily, *The Extra*, which is about the life of a Hollywood extra, an exploration of people who believe the publicity of their own defeat.

PLAYBOY: Haven't you had some difficulties with extras?

ALTMAN: I will not tolerate the Screen Extras Guild. If I rent the shoemaker's shop next door to shoot a scene in front of it, I'm supposed to take out the two guys in there who know how to run all the machines and replace them with two extras who try to *act* like they know what they're doing. There's no way I can get the same effect. So who am I putting out of work—a couple of unskilled people. I haven't used the Extras Guild since M*A*S*H.

PLAYBOY: Do you draw any royalties from the M*A*S*H television series?

ALTMAN: None whatsoever. The TV show is still using the M*A*S*H theme song, *Suicide Is Painless*, for which my son Michael wrote the lyrics when he was 14 years old, and he's made a lot of money out of it. I didn't get a fucking dime out of M*A*S*H, except for my director's fee. Ingo

Preminger, who produced it, personally made at least $5,000,000, and God knows how much Fox collected. Yet I can't even get an audience at Fox. They don't want to talk to me.

I sometimes think that if we were all paid less money and nobody could make a big killing, most of these clever manipulators who are in this business strictly for the money would stay away from the movies and leave them to the artists—to people who really love what they're doing.

PLAYBOY: Let's be realistic. Isn't one of the reasons backers balk at putting money into your pictures the fact that, with more than one person talking at the same time, they find your soundtracks unintelligible?

ALTMAN: I could go back and show you some of Howard Hawks's early pictures and you'd find exactly the same effect. Somebody picked up on it in my films after *McCabe* because it irritated a lot of people; yet I've got a file of reviews and letters saying the sound track was the best thing in the picture.

PLAYBOY: Wasn't Warren Beatty, the star of *McCabe*, one of those who were irritated?

ALTMAN: Warren was infuriated, he is still infuriated and he'll just have to stay infuriated.

Sometimes, though, I'm afraid audiences have a legitimate reason to complain, because we record dialogue under ideal circumstances. In theaters where the speakers aren't working properly, you get a muddled version of the sound track. But that can happen to any director on any film.

PLAYBOY: Are there any directors on the scene now whom you especially admire?

ALTMAN: I admire anybody who can get a film finished. Kurosawa's films impress me. I was very impressed with Fellini's *La Dolce Vita*. I like Bergman, who has always gone his own way and never had a success, really.

PLAYBOY: You've been called an American Fellini, though John Simon recently hinted that Fellini might learn a lot from Lina Wertmuller.

ALTMAN: Well, Simon has finally found someone to fall in love with and I'm glad for him.

When I first saw Bertolucci's *Last Tango in Paris*, I was about ready to quit. He dealt with certain sexual attitudes that are usually kept under wraps and I thought it was a great step. I admire Kubrick, but I can't say I like him. I mean, I don't know him personally. What he does is terrific and the opposite of what I do. He supervises every little detail of his films down to the last inch. But I leave a gap so wide that anything between A and X may be acceptable. With Kubrick, it's between A and A 1.

PLAYBOY: Whom would you single out from the ranks of the younger directors?

ALTMAN: Well, I think Martin Scorsese's going to endure. I think Steven Spielberg will endure, though it's tough when a picture like *Jaws* brings you a lot of success and money overnight that may not strictly be related to the merit of your work. I am not knocking *Jaws*, which was a magnificent accomplishment for a kid that age. But will he now be able to go off and make a small personal film? There's too much coming at you. It's the same with actors. Keith Carradine's suddenly hotter than a pistol since *Nashville*; they keep telling him, "We've got this great part for a street singer." He doesn't want to do those things.

Ivan Passer is a brilliant director; his *Intimate Lighting* I consider one of the best films ever made, though he, again, gets caught up on subjects he's not really familiar with and, consequently, fails. Coppola, of course, is a good producer-director. I get bored, as an audience, with John Cassavetes; though John is terrific, I always have the feeling that if he ever made a movie that was generally accepted and successful, it would really worry him. Paul Mazursky at least makes films that are recognizable as Mazursky films, though I personally don't like them; and I can get by pretty well without Peter Bogdanovich. Like Friedkin, he's constantly talking about his movies; he seems to know too much, and I've never seen a film of his that I thought was even passable.

But my idea of total mediocrity is Richard Brooks's last Gene Hackman thing, *Bite the Bullet*, which is about the worst kind of obvious, commercially inspired movie I can imagine. I guess people like it. I am not acquainted with Brooks, who's done some fine films, but that certainly isn't one of them.

PLAYBOY: You must be buttonholed by many aspiring young filmmakers. What do you say to them?

ALTMAN: I tell them that the only advice I can give is never to take advice from anybody. I've had a lot of experience doing industrial films, documentary films, films I hated doing. I've plugged in the lights, cleaned up, cooked the lunches, learned where to waste time and where to spend it. I also tell them they'd better be lucky. You don't need a lot of money to be a painter or to write a song, but it costs minimally $1,000,000 to make a movie and nobody's going to hand you $1,000,000. There probably should be a system of apprenticeships.

PLAYBOY: Do you hire apprentices?

ALTMAN: Sure, all the time. I don't care whether they come out of schools or off the street. We take a lot of people if they can serve us and we think we can serve them, but many fall by the wayside because they discover it isn't as much fun as they'd thought. They expect they're going to sit around listening in on heavyweight discussions about art; they soon find out that what they're doing is driving 300 miles a day getting film to the airport.

PLAYBOY: One of the least celebrated chapters of your professional life, before you broke into television, was a period you spent tattooing dogs. Where did you do that?

ALTMAN: Inside the groin of the right front leg. We'd tattoo their state and county license numbers.

PLAYBOY: Fascinating—but we meant where *geographically*.

ALTMAN: It started here. After the war, in 1947, I bought a bull terrier from a guy named H. Graham Connar. He had this idea for dog tattooing, which he called Identi-Code. I was writing then with a friend, Jim Rickard; we'd decided to become press agents. Then we got the idea of setting up this whole scam on a national basis. We invented our own tattooing machine, developed a numbering system and moved to New York and Washington. I was the tattooer.

PLAYBOY: How did you make out?

ALTMAN: Pretty well, for a while. I tattooed Truman's dog while he was still in the White House. We were lobbying in Washington and on the verge of being bought out by National Dog Week—which is a corporation owned by four major dog-food companies—when we went broke.

PLAYBOY: A couple of years ago, you claimed you were practically broke again. Isn't your financial picture today on an upswing?

ALTMAN: My percentages are bigger, but I seldom see any of the money. I have no wealth of any kind that would allow me to take three months or a year off. It's nice to be able to borrow from the bank now, because they think I can work, but there's never been a time I wasn't in debt. My personal take from *Nashville* will be a few hundred thousand, which is terrific. But the Government grabs half of it right off the bat and the rest goes to support this Lion's Gate operation.

PLAYBOY: Aren't you a pretty big spender?

ALTMAN: I'm not an extravagant person, no. I have to travel quite a bit. I live reasonably well. I buy a lot of whiskey and a lot of dinners.

PLAYBOY: How's your luck at cards? Do you still have a passion for gambling?

ALTMAN: It's not quite a passion, but it's something I really like. I like to play poker, like going to the races, but I can't allocate any time to it. I love betting on football.

PLAYBOY: Are you a heavy bettor?

ALTMAN: Yeah, within limits. I have good years and bad years. Year before last, I won about $26,000; but I never stop while I'm winning. I may bet $500 or $1,000 on a game, but you always lose in the long run because of the percentages. I never bet on the Dallas Cowboys. There's just something about that team I don't like. I'm not sure what it is, though Texas is not my favorite place.

PLAYBOY: Do you suppose there's a connection between your gambling instincts and your career?

ALTMAN: Only in the sense that if you've experienced life as a gambler, you realize you can get along without great security. Consequently, it doesn't bother me when there's no money in the bank. I have this optimistic attitude that nobody's going to starve.

PLAYBOY: Maybe having grown up during the Depression helps. What was your childhood like?

ALTMAN: I probably had the most normal, uneventful upbringing possible. My parents were stricter with me than with my two younger sisters. As a youngster, I was not a good student, but I just loved movies. I saw them all, went all the time. I got into a lot of trouble once because I sat through Wallace Beery's *Viva Villa!* about four times, until my parents came looking for me. I went to military school for a couple of years and lost my virginity, neither of which made me unhappy. It was generally just a regular childhood.

PLAYBOY: Hasn't your son Michael written a book about your life and your work?

ALTMAN: Oh, yes. It's a slender volume, and he even got some of the facts wrong. He came up to Calgary to talk about it during the filming of *Buffalo Bill*, and I almost threw him off the set, though I sort of admired him for going ahead anyway.

PLAYBOY: What's the title?

ALTMAN: *The World of Robert Altman.* Just a nothing book, with a little synopsis of each picture, quotes, interviews, condensed reviews—oh,

God, it was awful. I read the proofs in about four and a half seconds, and I think now it's going to be shelved. If ever I did a service to my son Michael, it was to keep that tome from being published.

PLAYBOY: You mean you've killed it?

ALTMAN: Well, he had some material in there he didn't have rights to, so we just intimated that we might sue Simon & Schuster, who were supposed to release it. Michael seemed to analyze all my films as being failures in terms that were rather interesting, and they had a whole horoscope in there, with an astrological chart that tried to explain why I am the way I am. There's another unauthorized biography being written by some guy who called and asked if I'd assist him.

PLAYBOY: And did you?

ALTMAN: Jesus, no. Let them wait and write a book about me when I'm dead, if anyone's still interested.

PLAYBOY: You're now on your third marriage, but that has lasted 17 years. What do you think makes it work?

ALTMAN: Well, I suppose it's a matter of growth. And Kathryn is terrific. If I were married to someone who tried to influence me or push her personal feelings into my films, it probably wouldn't last. Yet Kathryn is the one who brought *Breakfast of Champions* to my attention. She'd read it first and just said casually, "You could probably make a movie out of this." She's around, she goes to screenings, she sets up a home with Matthew and Bobby wherever I happen to be shooting, she entertains; but she never intrudes intellectually into what I'm doing. We really live quite separate lives, but we live them together.

PLAYBOY: Before we wind this up, can you tell us which Robert Altman film is your own personal favorite?

ALTMAN: *Brewster McCloud.* I wouldn't say it's my best film; it's flawed, not nearly as finished as some work I've done since, but it's my favorite, because I took more chances then. It was my boldest work, by far my most ambitious. I went way out on a limb to reach for it. After a while, you become more cautious. People keep telling you you've got to be careful, you shouldn't do that. Nevertheless, I don't think there's a question in the world that the films we'll be making and seeing 20 years from now will be films that none of us would understand today. Music's the same way; if you had put a Bob Dylan song on the radio back in 1941, they would have thought you were crazy, closed the station. And I feel it's the obligation of the artist to keep pushing ahead, to stay within range of his audience but to keep pushing and educating them one step at a time.

PLAYBOY: When you look into your own future, what do you want to have accomplished?

ALTMAN: I can't imagine getting up in the morning without the same frustrations, the same fears and the same elation I experience every day. All I want is to do what I'm doing. What else would I do?

PLAYBOY: Then you don't think, as some have claimed, that the ultimate Altman movie has already been made?

ALTMAN: I certainly hope not. I'm just warming up.

June 1964

INGMAR BERGMAN

*A candid conversation with
Sweden's one-man new wave of
cinematic sorcery*

In the months since Ingmar Bergman's *The Silence* world-premiered
in Stockholm, moviegoers in a dozen countries have been lining up
around the block. Some longed to see the final third of the Swedish
filmmaker's celebrated trilogy (following *Through a Glass Darkly* and
Winter Light) on the quest for love as a salvation from emotional
death. Others came to verify the judgment of some critics that this
anatomy of lust is the masterwork of Bergman's 20-year career. But
most, quite unabashedly, have come to ogle the most explicitly erotic
movie scenes on view this side of a stag smoker—even after the snip-
ping of more than a minute's film for the toned down U.S. version.
The film has precipitated a rain of abuse on its 45-year-old creator—as
a pornographer (by members of the Swedish parliament), purveyor of
obscenity (from Lutheran pulpits all over Sweden) and corrupter of
youth and decency (via anonymous calls and letters). Outraged at
the outcry, Bergman was most offended by the accusation that he
filmed the sex scenes merely to shock and titillate his audiences. "I'm
an artist," he told a reporter. "Once I had the idea for *The Silence* in
my mind, I had to make it—that's all." The son of an Evangelical
Lutheran parson who became the chaplain to Sweden's royal family,
Bergman remembers his years at home "with bitterness," as a period
of emotional sterility and rigid moral rectitude from which he with-
drew into the private world of fantasy. It was on his ninth birthday
that he traded a set of tin soldiers for a toy that was to become the
catalyst of his creativity: a battered magic lantern. A year later, he
was building scenery, fashioning marionettes, working all the strings

and speaking all the parts in his own puppet theater productions of Strindberg. Perhaps foreshadowing his directorship of a youth club theater during his years at Stockholm University, where he produced, in 1940, an anti-Nazi version of *Macbeth*, which became a minor cause célèbre—and scandalized his family.

Fired with the zeal of social protest, Bergman quit school the next year, moved into the city's bohemian quarter, began to dress and act accordingly—and to germinate plot lines for satiric and irreverent plays which he never got around to writing. He finally found steady employment as an assistant stage manager, rose swiftly to become a director, and began to earn the reputation for dramatic genius, arrogance and irresistibility to women (he's been married four times) that has become part and parcel of the Bergman legend. Trying his hand at writing a screenplay in 1944, he submitted the manuscript to Svensk Filmindustri, Sweden's largest movie company, which decided to film it. Appropriately entitled *Torment*, it set the tone and theme for a new career, and for the 25 films that followed. In the eight years since his "discovery" abroad with the international release of *The Seventh Seal*, *Smiles of a Summer Night*, *Wild Strawberries*, *The Magician*, *Brink of Life* and *The Virgin Spring*, he has become the acknowledged guru of the art-film avant-garde, and many critics have joined fellow professionals in hailing him as the world's first-ranking filmmaker.

An exacting taskmaster, he does not brook the slightest deviation from the script in the course of shooting, nor countenance the presence of outsiders anywhere in the studio—especially journalists, of whom he has never been fond, on or off the set.

It was with some trepidation, therefore, that we approached the mercurial moviemaker with our request for an exclusive interview. But he replied with a cordial invitation to visit him in Stockholm—which we accepted, arriving late last February, in the middle of the somber Nordic winter, for a week-long stay.

Our conversations took place in his small, sparsely furnished office backstage at the Royal Dramatic Theater in downtown Stockholm, where, as the newly appointed manager of the national theater, he was devoting his directorial energies full time on an extended sabbatical from filmmaking, to staging the works of such theatrical iconoclasts as Brecht, Albee and Ionesco. Meeting with us for an hour or so each morning ("when I'm most alive," he told us), he would arrive promptly at nine, dressed always, indoors and out, in heavy flannel slacks, polo shirt, wool cap and a tan windbreaker with a dry cleaner's tag still stapled to a cuff. Our interview began with a wry smile from our subject—and a disarming greeting in which he reversed roles by asking the first question. [Interview conducted by Cynthia Grenier.]

BERGMAN: Well, are you depressed yet?

PLAYBOY: Should we be?

BERGMAN: Perhaps you haven't been here long enough. But the depression will come. I don't know why anybody lives in Stockholm, so far away from everything. When you fly up here from the south, it's very odd. First there are houses and towns and villages, but farther on there are just woods and forests and more woods and a lake. Perhaps, and then still more woods with, just once in a while, a long way off, a house. And then, suddenly, Stockholm. It's perverse to have a city way up here. And so here we sit, feeling lonely. We're such a huge country, yet we are so few, so thinly scattered across it. The people here spend their lives isolated on their farms—and isolated from one another in their homes. It's terribly difficult for them, even when they come to the cities and live close to other people—it's no help, really. They don't know how to get in touch, to communicate. They stay shut off. And our winters don't help.

PLAYBOY: How do you mean?

BERGMAN: Well, we have light in the winter only from maybe eight-thirty in the morning till two-thirty in the afternoon. Up north, just a few hours from here, they have darkness all day long. No daylight at all. I hate the winter. I hate Stockholm in the winter. When I wake up during the winter—I always get up at six, ever since I was a child—I look at the wall opposite my window. November, December, there is no light at all. Then, in January, comes a tiny thread of light. Every morning I watch that line of light getting a little bigger. This is what sustains me through the black and terrible winter: Seeing that line of light growing as we get closer to spring.

PLAYBOY: If that's how you feel, why not leave Stockholm during the winter and work in the warmer climates of such film capitals as Rome or Hollywood?

BERGMAN: New cities arouse too many sensations in me. They give me too many impressions to experience at the same time. They all crowd in on me. Being in a new city overwhelms me, unsettles me.

PLAYBOY: There've been reports that you feel what you've called "the great fear" whenever you leave Sweden. Is that why you've never made a film outside the country?

BERGMAN: Not really, all that has very little to do with making movies. After all, actors and studios are basically the same all over the world. What worries me about making a film in another country is the loss of artistic control I might run into. When I make a film, I must control it from the beginning until it opens in the movie houses. I grew up in Sweden, I have my roots here, and I'm never frustrated professionally here—at least not by producers. I've been working with virtually the same people for nearly 20 years: They've watched me grow up. The technical demands of moviemaking are enslaving, but here, everything runs smoothly in human terms: the cameraman, the operator, the head electrician. We all know and understand one another. I hardly need to tell them what to do. This is ideal and it makes the creative task—always a difficult one—easier. The idea of making a film for an American company is very tempting, for obvious reasons. But it's not one's first Hollywood film that's so difficult—it's the second. To work in another country with more modern equipment, but with my same crew, with the same relationship to my producers, with the same control over the film as I have here? I don't think that's very likely.

PLAYBOY: You're said to be no less indisposed to come into contact with outsiders even on your own sets in Stockholm, from which all visitors are barred. Why?

BERGMAN: Do you know what moviemaking is? Eight hours of hard work each day to get three minutes of film. And during those eight hours there are maybe only 10 or 12 minutes, if you're lucky, of real creation. And maybe they don't come. Then you have to gear yourself for another eight hours and pray you're going to get your good 10 minutes this time. Everything and everyone on a movie set must be attuned to finding those minutes of real creativity. You've got to keep the actors and yourself in a kind of enchanted circle. An outside presence, even a completely friendly one, is basically alien to the intimate process going on in front of him. Any time there's an outsider on the set, we run the risk that part of the actors' absorption, or the technicians', or mine, is going to be impinged upon. It takes very little to destroy the delicate mood of total immersion in our work. We can't risk losing those vital minutes of real creation. The few times I've made exceptions, I've always regretted it.

PLAYBOY: You've been criticized not only for barring and even ejecting intruders from your sets, but for outbursts of a rage in which, reportedly, you've ripped phones off walls and thrown chairs through glass control booths. Is there any truth to these accounts?

BERGMAN: Yes, there is—or rather, *was*. When I was younger, much younger, like so many young men, I was unsure of myself. But I was very ambitious. And when you're unsure, when you're insecure and need to assert yourself, or think you do, you become aggressive in trying to get your own way. Well, that's what happened to me—in a provincial theater where I was a new director. I couldn't behave that way now and hope to keep the respect of my actors and my technicians. When I know the importance of every minute in a working day, when I realize the supreme necessity of establishing a mood of calm and security on the set, do you think I could, or would have any right to, indulge myself that way? A director on a movie set is a little like the captain of a ship—he must be respected in order to be obeyed. I haven't behaved that way at work since I was maybe 25 or 26.

PLAYBOY: Yet these stories of temper tantrums continue to circulate in print.

BERGMAN: Of course they do. Such stunts as ripping out telephones and hurling chairs around make the sort of copy that journalists love to give their editors and their readers. It's more colorful to read about a violent temper than about someone instilling confidence in his actors by talking quietly to them. It's to be expected that people will go on writing—and reading—this sort of nonsense about a man year after year. Do you begin to understand why I don't like to talk to the press? You know, people also say I don't like to see journalists, that I refuse to talk to them anymore. For once they are right. When I am nice to reporters, when I give them my time and I talk to them sincerely, they go off and print a lot of old gossip, or their editors throw it in, because they think those old stories are more entertaining than the truth. Take that cover story done on me a few years ago by one of those American magazine of yours.

PLAYBOY: *Time* magazine?

BERGMAN: Yes, that's it. My wife read it to me when it came out here. The man they described sounds like someone I'd like to meet—perhaps a little difficult, not such a nice person, yet still an interesting fellow. But I didn't find myself in it. He was nobody I know.

PLAYBOY: It's been reported that you've had no less difficulty recognizing some of your own films when you read what the critics have to say about their merit and meaning. Is this true?

BERGMAN: I've given up reading what's written either about me or about my films. It's pointless to get annoyed. Most film critics know very little about how a film is made, have very little general film knowledge or culture. But we are beginning to get a new generation of film critics who are sincere and knowledgeable about the cinema. Like some of the young French critics—them I read. I don't always agree with what they have to say about my films, but at least they're sincere. Sincerity I like, even when it's unfavorable to me.

PLAYBOY: Well, your films have been unfavorably reviewed for, among other reasons, the private meanings and obscurity of many of their episodes and much of their symbolism. Do you think these accusations may have some validity?

BERGMAN: Possibly, but I hope not—because I think that making a film comprehensible to the audience is the most important duty of any moviemaker. It's also the most difficult. Private films are relatively easy to make, but I don't feel a director should make easy films. He should try to lead his audience a little further in each succeeding film. It's good for the public to work a little. But the director should never forget who it is he's making his film for. In any case, it's not as important that a person who sees one of my films understands it here, in the head, as it is that he understands it here, in the heart. This is what matters.

PLAYBOY: Whatever the nature of their understanding, a great many international critics concur in ranking you foremost among the world's filmmakers. How do you feel about this approbation?

BERGMAN: Success abroad has made my work much easier in Sweden. I don't have to fight so much on matters really external to actual creative work. Thanks to success, I've earned the right to be left to my work. But, of course, success is so transitory. It's such a flimsy thing to be á la mode. Take Paris, a few years ago I was their favorite director. Then came Antonioni. Who's the new one? Who knows? But you know, when these young men of the nouvelle vague first started making films, I was envious of them, envious of their having seen all the films at the cinèmathéque [film library], of their knowing all the techniques of moviemaking. Not anymore. On the technical side, I have become very sound. I have acquired confidence in myself. Now, I can see other directors' work and no longer feel jealous or afraid. I know I don't have to.

PLAYBOY: Have their films influenced or instructed you in the development of your own moviemaking style and skills?

BERGMAN: I've had to learn everything about movies by myself. For the theater, I studied with a wonderful old man in Göteborg, where I spent four years. He was a hard, difficult man, but he knew the theater—and I learned from him. For the movies, however, there was no one. Before the War, I was a schoolboy. Then, during the War, we got to see no foreign films at all. By the time it was over, I was working hard to support a wife and three children. But fortunately, I am by nature an autodidact, one who can teach himself—though it's an uncomfortable thing to be at times. Self-taught people sometimes cling too much to the technical side, the sure side and place technical perfection too high. I think what is important, most important, is having something to say.

PLAYBOY: Do you feel that America's New Wave directors have something to say?

BERGMAN: Yes, I do. I have seen just a few examples of their work—only *The Connection, Shadows* and *Pull My Daisy*. I should like very much to see more. But from what I've seen, I like the American New Wave much more than the French. They are so much more enthusiastic, idealistic, in a way . . . cruder, technically less perfect and less knowing than the French filmmakers. But I think they have something to say, and that is good. That is important. I like them.

PLAYBOY: Have you enjoyed the Russian films you've seen?

BERGMAN: Very much. I think something very good will be coming from them soon. I don't know why, but I feel it. Did you see *Childhood of Ivan*? There are extraordinary things in it. Some of it's very bad, of course, but there is real talent and power.

PLAYBOY: How do you feel about the Italian directors?

BERGMAN: Fellini is wonderful. He is everything I'm not. I should like to be him. He is so baroque. His work is so generous, so warm, so easy, so un-neurotic. I liked *La Dolce Vita* very much, particularly the scene with the father. That was good. And the end, with the giant fish. Visconti, I liked his first film, *La Terra Trema*—his best, I think. I liked Antonioni's *La Notte* a great deal, too.

PLAYBOY: Would you classify these among the best films you've ever seen?

BERGMAN: No, right now I think I have three favorite contemporary films: *The Lady with the Dog, Rashomon* and *Umberto D*. Oh, yes, and a fourth: *Mr. Hulot's Holiday*. I love that one.

PLAYBOY: Let's return to the subject of your own work, if we may.

*Where did you get the idea for your latest and most controversial film,
The Silence?*

BERGMAN: From a very big, fat old man. That's right. Four years ago, when
I was visiting a friend in a hospital here, I noticed from his window a very
old man, enormously fat and paralyzed, sitting in a chair under a tree in
the park. As I watched, four jolly, good-natured nurses came marching
out, lifted him up, chair and all, and carried him back into the hospital.
The image of him being carried away like a dummy stayed in my mind,
although I didn't really know exactly why. It all grew from that seed,
like most of my films have grown—from some small incident, a feeling
I've had about something, an anecdote someone's told me. Perhaps from
a gesture or an expression on an actor's face. It sets off a very special
sort of tension in me, immediately recognizable as such to me. On the
deepest level, of course, the ideas for my films come out of the pressures
of the spirit; and these pressures vary. But most of my films begin with
a specific image or feeling around which my imagination begins slowly
to build an elaborate detail. I file each one away in my mind. Often, I
even write them down in note form. This way I have a whole series of
handy files in my head. Of course, several years may go by before I get
around to transforming these sensations into anything as concrete as a
scenario. But when a project begins to take shape, then I dig into one of
my mental files for a scene, into another for a character. Sometimes the
character I pull out doesn't get on at all with the other ones in my script,
so I have to send him back to his file and look elsewhere. My films grow
like a snowball, very gradually from a single flake of snow. In the end, I
often can't see the original flake that started it all.

PLAYBOY: In the case of *The Silence*, the "original flake"—that paralyzed
old man—is certainly hard to discern in the explicit scenes of inter-
course and masturbation that aroused such heated reactions, pro and
con. What made you decide to depict sex so graphically on the screen?

BERGMAN: For many years, I was timid and conventional in the expression
of sex in my films. But the manifestation of sex is very important, and particularly to me. For, above all, I don't want to make merely intellectual films.
I want audiences to feel, to sense my films. This to me is much more important than their understanding them. There is much in common between
a beautiful summer morning and the sexual act; but I feel I've found the
cinematic means of expressing only the first, and not the other, as yet. What
interests me more, however, is the interior anatomy of love. This strikes me
as far more meaningful than the depiction of sexual gratification.

PLAYBOY: Do you agree with those who say that the American version of *The Silence* has been emasculated by the excision of almost two minutes of film from the erotic scenes?

BERGMAN: I'd rather not comment on that.

PLAYBOY: All right. But is it possible that this encounter with American censorship regulations will induce you to exercise a certain degree of self-censorship in future films?

BERGMAN: No. Never.

PLAYBOY: How did you persuade actresses Thulin and Lindblom to perform the actual acts depicted in the picture's controversial scenes?

BERGMAN: The exact same way I have gotten them, with all my other actors, to perform in any scene in any of my other films. We simply discuss quietly and easily what they must do. Some people claim I hypnotize my actors—that I use magic to bring the performances out of them that I get. What nonsense! All I do is try to give them the one thing everyone wants, the one thing an actor *must* have: confidence in himself. That's all any actor wants, you know. To feel sure enough of himself that he'll be able to give everything he's capable of when the director asks for it. So I surround my actors with an aura of confidence and trust. I talk with them, often not about the scene we're working on at all, but just to make them feel secure and at ease. If that's magic, then I am a sorcerer. Then, too, working with the same people—technicians and actors—in our own private world for so many years together has facilitated my task of creating the necessary mood of trust.

PLAYBOY: How do you reconcile this statement with the following declaration, which you made five or six years ago in discussing your filmmaking methods: "I'd prostitute my talents if it would further my cause, steal if there was no other way out, kill my friends or anyone else if it would help my art"?

BERGMAN: Let's say I was pretty defensive when I said that. When one is unsure of himself, when he's worried about his position, worried about being a creative artist, he feels the need, as I said before, to express himself very strongly, very assertively, in order to withstand any potential criticism. But once you've finally become successful, you feel freed from the imperatives of success. You stop worrying about striving, and can devote yourself to your work. Life becomes so much easier. You like yourself better. I find that I'm beginning to enjoy much that I never did before, to learn that there is much I haven't seen. I feel a little older—not much, but a little—and I like it.

You know, I used to think that compromise in life, as in art, was unthinkable, that the worst thing a man could do was make compromises. But, of course, I did make compromises. We all do. We have to. We couldn't live otherwise. But for a long time I wouldn't admit to myself—although, of course, at the same time I knew it—that I, too, was a man who compromised. I thought I could be above it all. I have learned that I can't. I have learned that what matters, really, is being alive. You're alive. You can't stand dead or half-dead people, can you? To me, what counts is being able to feel. That's what *Winter Light*—the film of mine that people seem to understand the least—is trying to say. Now that you've been in Stockholm in midwinter for a few days, I think you can begin to understand, a little, what this film is about. What do you make of it?

PLAYBOY: We're more interested in learning what *you* make of it.

BERGMAN: Well, it was a difficult film, one of the hardest I've made so far. The audience has to work. It's a progression from *Through a Glass Darkly*, and it in turn is carried forward to *The Silence*. The three stand together. My basic concern in making them was to dramatize the all-importance of communication, of the capacity for feeling. They are not concerned—as many critics have theorized—with God or His absence, but with the saving force of love. Most of the people in these three films are dead, completely dead. They don't know how to love or to feel any emotions. They are lost because they can't reach anyone outside of themselves.

The man in *Winter Light*, the pastor, is nothing. He's nearly dead, you understand. He's almost completely cut off from everyone. The central character is the woman. She doesn't believe in God, but she has strength. It's the women who are strong. She can love. She can save with her love. Her problem is that she doesn't know how to express this love. She's ugly, clumsy. She smothers him, and he hates her for it and for her ugliness. But she finally learns how to love. Only at the end, when they're in the empty church for the three o'clock service that has become perfectly meaningless for him, her prayer in a sense is answered: He responds to her love by going on with the service in that empty country church. It's his own first step toward feeling, toward learning how to love. We're saved not by God, but by love. That's the most we can hope for.

PLAYBOY: How is this theme carried out in the other two films of the trilogy?

BERGMAN: Each film, you see, has its moment of contact, of human communication: The line, "Father spoke to me," at the end of *Through a Glass Darkly*; the pastor conducting the service in the empty church for Marta at the end of *Winter Light*; the little boy reading Ester's letter on the train at the end of *The Silence*. A tiny moment in each film—but the crucial one. What matters most of all in life is being able to make that contact with another human. Otherwise you are dead, like so many people today are dead. But if you can take that first step toward communication, toward understanding, toward love, then no matter how difficult the future may be—and have no illusions, even with all the love in the world, living can be hellishly difficult—then you are saved. This is all that really matters, isn't it?

PLAYBOY: Many reviewers felt that this same message—that of salvation from solitude through love—was also the theme of your best-known and most commercially successful film, *Wild Strawberries*—in which the old physician, as one critic wrote, "After a life of emotional detachment, learns the lesson of compassion, and is redeemed by this change of heart." Are they right?

BERGMAN: But he doesn't change. He can't. That's just it. I don't believe that people *can* change, not really, not fundamentally. Do you? They may have a moment of illumination, they may see themselves, have awareness of what they are, but that is the most they can hope for. In *Winter Light*, the woman, the strong one, she can see. She has her moment of awareness, but it won't change their lives. They will have a terrible life. I wouldn't make a film about what happens to them next for anything in the world. They'll have to get along without me.

PLAYBOY: Speaking of the character of Marta in *Winter Light*, you've been widely praised for your sympathetic depiction of, and insight into, the feminine protagonists in your films. How is it—

BERGMAN: You're going to ask how it is I understand women so well. Women used to interest me as subjects because they were so ridiculously treated and shown in movies. I simply showed them as they actually are—or at least closer to what they are than the silly representations of them in the movies of the 1930s and 1940s. Any reasonably realistic treatment looked great by comparison with what was being done. In the past few years, however, I have begun to realize that women are essentially the same as men, that they both have the same problems. I don't think of there being women's problems or women's stories any more than I do of there being men's problems or men's stories. They are all human problems. It's people who interest me now.

PLAYBOY: Will your next film be in any way a continuation of the theme elaborated in your recent trilogy?

BERGMAN: No, my new film, and my last for a while, is a comedy, an erotic comedy, a ghost story—and my first film in color.

PLAYBOY: What's it called?

BERGMAN: *All the Women.* They may like it in America—the theme song is *Yes, We Have No Bananas.* It amuses *me*, anyway. I've already told one Swedish writer that I'm hoping it will start the Bergman Ballyhoo Era. It's not long since I finished the final cutting. You know, I don't at all mind editing or cutting my films. I don't have any of this love-hate feeling that some directors have toward cutting their own work. David Lean told me once that he can't bear the task of cutting, that it literally makes him sick. I don't feel that way at all. I'm completely un-neurotic in that respect.

PLAYBOY: You said a moment ago that this will be your last film "for a while." How long is a while?

BERGMAN: Two years, probably. I want to immerse myself in my work as director at the Royal Dramatic Theater here. Theater fascinates me for several reasons. For one thing, it's so much less demanding on you than making films. You're less at the mercy of equipment and the demand for so many minutes of footage every day. You aren't nearly so alone. It's between you and the actors, and later on, the audience. It's wonderful—the sudden meeting of the actor's expression and the audience's response. It's all so direct and alive. A film, once completed, is inalterable. In the theater, you can get a different response from every performance. There's constant change, always the chance to improve. I don't think I could live without it.

JOEL & ETHAN COEN

A candid conversation with the maverick filmmakers about blowing up cows and rabbits, avoiding the studio system and working the Hollywood baby pit

A barber pole twirls outside the window and three barber chairs are in a row, facing a wall of mirrors. On a shelf is a collection of razors, clippers, scissors and aftershave lotion. When a man lazily sits in one of the chairs, the barber, who is dressed in white, asks, "What'll it be?" The guy answers, "Just a trim."

It's a scene replayed throughout America every day, but this isn't a real barbershop. This barber isn't really a barber, either. It's Billy Bob Thornton, the actor and director renowned for the 1996 movie *Sling Blade*, whose lack of training as a barber doesn't stop him from cutting hair. There's a line of people—mostly extras who are here with the hope of a quick scene in the movie—waiting for haircuts. "The sad thing is that Billy Bob thinks he's good," says the movie's co-writer Ethan Coen. "He's like one of those guys who trains to be a boxer for a boxing movie, then thinks he can beat people up." Ethan and his brother, Joel Coen, cackle about Thornton's "victims." "We've seen some pretty gruesome haircuts."

Bad haircuts are only one of the offbeat things moviegoers are likely to find in a Coen brothers movie. Joel and Ethan, who jointly write, direct, edit and produce their movies, have been called the Merry Pranksters of filmmaking. Working mostly outside of the traditional studio system, the Coens produce movies that are black, hilarious and violent, with thin or confused plots and twisted, grotesque, if unforgettable, characters. The movie business is known for adhering to formula and its aversion to risk, but many of the Coens' movies seem not only noncommercial but anticommercial. Woody Allen may be the only other director who is consistently able to make whatever movies he wants without regard for box-office potential (which isn't to say that some Coen brothers movies haven't done well at the box office). And while Woody Allen's movies are sweet and somewhat predictable, the Coens' are neither.

Who else would have brutally and messily exploded a cow in *O Brother, Where Art Thou?*, or hand-grenaded a rabbit in *Raising Arizona?* But their most violent moments have been saved for humans, leaving such indelible images as John Goodman charging through an inferno while blasting a shotgun in *Barton Fink*. Or Steve Buscemi being stuffed into a wood chipper (blood spraying everywhere) in *Fargo*. Or Dan Hedaya being buried alive in their first movie, *Blood Simple*. (When he tries to rise up, he's furiously beaten back down with a shovel.) In their latest movie, *The Man Who Wasn't There*, the Coens knock off Tony Soprano. The character in the film played by *Sopranos* star James Gandolfini dies slowly, thick blood gurgling from a tiny hole in his jugular vein.

Shot in black and white and set in the California town of Santa Rosa in 1949, the movie is inspired by Alfred Hitchcock and James M. Cain. Thornton, as barber Ed Crane, starts out as one of the bleakest characters in movie history. His wife, played by Frances McDormand (Joel's wife, who won an Academy Award for her performance in *Fargo*), has an affair with Gandolfini, who winds up on the wrong end of a cigar cutter. The movie does the film noir genre proud not only with a generous amount of infidelity, greed and bad luck but with a sleazy toothpick-chewing detective, an oily defense lawyer and a sexy but sad shaving scene (in which Thornton shaves McDormand's legs). Ethan says the movie is about "ordinary middle-American people who get into a situation that spirals out of control."

There is nothing ordinary about the characters in any Coen brothers film, beginning with 1984's *Blood Simple*, another film noir about infidelity and greed. "It is the most inventive and original thriller in many a moon," wrote David Ansen in *Newsweek*, "a maliciously entertaining murder story."

Next came *Raising Arizona*, a surreal comedy with Holly Hunter and Nicolas Cage that moved at the pace of a Roadrunner cartoon, then *Miller's Crossing*, a meditation on loyalty and betrayal set in America's organized crime community of the 1930s.

In 1991 the Coens released *Barton Fink*, a scathing look at the Hollywood film industry of the early 1940s that quickly became a classic and won the Palme d'Or at the Cannes Film Festival. Throughout their ascent, the Coens worked with a regular crew of unusual actors, including McDormand, Goodman, John Turturro, Hunter and Buscemi, whose careers were propelled by their performances in Coen brothers films. The Coens' successes gave them access to bigger stars, including Tim Robbins and Paul Newman, who appeared in *The Hudsucker Proxy*, a lyrical fable in the tradition of Frank Capra and Preston Sturges. It was McDormand, however, who helped catapult their biggest hit, *Fargo*, to six Independent Spirit Awards and seven Oscar nominations. It won two—McDormand for best actress and Joel and Ethan for best screenplay.

The Big Lebowski (1998) cast Jeff Bridges as a Venice Beach stoner and John Goodman as a slightly unhinged Vietnam vet pitted against avant-garde artists, pornographers and German nihilists. Last year's *O Brother, Where Art Thou?*, a Depression-era tale of a mismatched trio who escape a chain gang and then have a series of adventures rambling around the Old South, features a hilarious performance by George Clooney.

After *The Man Who Wasn't There* opens, the Coens head for Japan to shoot an adaptation of James Dickey's third and final novel, *To the White Sea*. Published in 1993, it's a stark story that chronicles the adventures of a World War II tailgunner shot down on a mission over Tokyo. The movie, starring Brad Pitt, has a budget of $45 million, which makes it their most expensive film to date. A big chunk of the budget will be spent re-creating the 1945 firebombing of Tokyo. The film is almost dialogue free, a modern-day silent film.

The Coens were born in a suburb of Minneapolis called St. Louis Park—Joel in 1954, Ethan in 1957. Their father was an economics professor at the University of Minnesota and their mother an art history professor at St. Cloud State. Smart, sophisticated kids but unexceptional students, they mostly skied and watched movies. They saw Truffaut's *400 Blows* in a high school cinema club but claim to have been more inspired by Dean Jones and Doris Day comedies, cheap horror flicks and Tarzan movies.

In their early teens the Coens mowed lawns and saved money to buy a Vivitar camera. With it, they began shooting Super-8 movies, including such early efforts as a remake of *Naked Prey* called *Zeimers* in *Zambia*; a remake of *Lassie Come Home* called *Ed, a Dog* that featured Ethan as the female lead (costumed in his older sister's tutu) and *The Banana Film*, the story of a man with an uncanny ability to smell bananas.

As teenagers, both Coens attended Simon's Rock College of Bard, a college for high-school-age students in Great Barrington, Massachusetts. Joel spent a lot of his free time in Manhattan and in the mid-1970s he enrolled in the film studies program at New York University. Of his years at NYU, Joel says, "I was a cipher there. I sat at the back of the room with an insane grin on my face." After college, he spent the early 1980s working as an assistant in various capacities on a series of low-budget films. As related in Ronald Bergan's book on the brothers, filmmaker Barry Sonnenfeld hired Joel to be a production assistant on an industrial film. "Without a doubt the worst PA I ever worked with," Sonnenfeld recalls. "He got three parking tickets, came late and set fire to the smoke machine."

Ethan, meanwhile, headed to Princeton, where he studied philosophy and wrote a senior thesis titled "Two Views of Wittgenstein's Later Philosophy." During that time, he temporarily left school and then applied for readmission. When he was late getting the forms in, he wrote that he'd had his arm blown off in a hunting accident. He was readmitted only after a meeting with the college psychiatrist. In 1979, he moved to Manhattan and had a series of temporary jobs. The brothers soon began writing scripts together in their spare time. By 1981, they had written *Blood Simple*. They shot a three-minute trailer for their nonexistent movie and used it to secure funding for the film. In September 1982, the Coens went to Austin, Texas and shot *Blood Simple* in eight weeks. They divided up the credits on the movie the way they've subsequently appeared on all their films: written by Joel and Ethan Coen, produced by Ethan Coen, directed by Joel Coen. In fact, it's an arbitrary listing, because both of them share all the duties on all of their films. They even jointly edit their movies under the pseudonym Roderick Jaynes.

Joel's first marriage fell by the wayside. When Frances McDormand was cast as the female lead in *Blood Simple*, he fell in love with her. They married in 1984 and now live on Manhattan's Upper West Side with their seven-year-old son. Ethan met his wife, editor Tricia Cooke, on the set of *Miller's Crossing*. They live in lower Manhattan and have a five-year-old son and an infant daughter.

The Coen brothers work nonstop and are notoriously reluctant interview subjects, but *Playboy* managed to sit them down while they were completing *The Man Who Wasn't There*. Kristine McKenna, who recently spoke with Tim Burton for the magazine, was tapped for the assignment. Here's her report:

"Besides their strange sensibility and moviemaking talent, the most remarkable thing about the Coen brothers is their relationship. They spend an extraordinary amount of time together, yet they don't interrupt each other, they laugh at each other's jokes, listen to each other's ideas with interest and seem to genuinely like each other. They talk like they make their films—one of them mentions a fragment of an idea, the other takes it further and they bounce it back and forth until it metamorphoses into something interesting, provocative, silly or—often—weird."

PLAYBOY: How important is commercial success to you?

JOEL: We want the movies to be seen. At the same time, we're resigned to the fact that we're not making commercial movies and the appeal will be limited.

ETHAN: On the other hand, if a movie does better than you thought it would, it's gratifying. Conversely, it's disappointing if it doesn't perform up to your expectations.

PLAYBOY: What hasn't?

ETHAN: *The Hudsucker Proxy* was the worst commercially. *Miller's Crossing* didn't do any business, either. From a financial point of view, they were disasters.

PLAYBOY: Do you know why they failed?

JOEL: That's the same as trying to find out why one worked. After the fact, it's bogus. Who knows?

PLAYBOY: Is there no relationship between commercial success and good movies? Can you see reasons why *Fargo* was a hit and *The Hudsucker Proxy* wasn't?

ETHAN: No.

JOEL: No.

ETHAN: Within certain broad parameters you know a movie might appeal to a wider audience than another one, but we're not kidding ourselves.

JOEL: We thought *O Brother, Where Art Thou?* could appeal to a wider audience, and we knew *Barton Fink* never would.

ETHAN: But we had no idea *Fargo* was going to do any business at all.

JOEL: That's true. We thought it was like *Barton Fink*. We thought, We're going to make it really cheaply and nobody will get hurt. We used to try to figure this stuff out. We thought it was important to know why some movies were successful and some weren't if we wanted to survive in the business. We gave up. After the fact, it's easy to come up with reasons. Fran's performance had a lot to do with *Fargo*. People loved it. However, while we were shooting the film we had no idea the public was going to love that character. On the other hand, I thought Jennifer Jason Leigh was really funny in *The Hudsucker Proxy*, but the performance seemed to rub people the wrong way. Why? Who knows?

PLAYBOY: Do the awards feel random, too?

JOEL: You have a better sense of the awards. We knew *The Big Lebowski* wasn't an awards kind of movie.

PLAYBOY: Why not?

JOEL: It's a silly comedy. *Raising Arizona* was another silly comedy.

ETHAN: Comedy in general doesn't get invited on that circuit.

JOEL: On the other hand, we knew that *The Man Who Wasn't There* would be invited to Cannes, where it won a big prize.

ETHAN: It's in black and white.

JOEL: Black and white invites prizes.

ETHAN: Especially from the French.

PLAYBOY: Where does quality come in?

ETHAN: Awards are not about quality.

JOEL: We go to competitions because the movies get more attention. That's the main reason. The press attention is important with our movies. We don't have the advertising budget that, say, *Pearl Harbor* does.

ETHAN: The awards put a movie on people's radar. Festivals are good, even though the idea of putting movies in competitions—this one is the best this, that one is the best that—is ridiculous.

PLAYBOY: Are you able to make virtually any movie you want without interference from movie studios?

JOEL: We're mercifully free of the Hollywood committee development process and the process of making the movie. They understand that if they are going to do a movie with us, they'll let us do it our way.

ETHAN: We've never been messed with.

JOEL: For a couple reasons.

ETHAN: For one, we write the script. We tell the story the way we want and no one tells us what we should be doing. Also, our movies are cheap. It's nothing for them. Most of the movies they're making give them bigger headaches.

JOEL: No one will get fired over one of our movies.

ETHAN: Nobody even had much to say about *O Brother*, which cost more than the others, because the financial health of the movie studio didn't depend on such a small movie.

PLAYBOY: Joel once said, "Ethan has a nightmare of one day finding me on the set of something like *The Incredible Hulk*, wearing a gold chain and saying 'I've got to eat, don't I?'" Could you ever sell out?

JOEL: The whole selling-out thing really isn't an issue because neither of us finds money that interesting.

ETHAN: The movie people let us play in the corner of the sandbox and leave us alone. We're happy here.

PLAYBOY: Do you agree that it's a small and uncrowded corner? Who else besides you and perhaps Woody Allen can make whatever movies they want?

JOEL: Maybe Woody Allen and us. Yeah.

ETHAN: There are some big directors who've made huge hits who can do what they want.

JOEL: But they aren't as marginal as we are. There aren't many who have marginally commercial movies and have our freedom. We're lucky. We know it. It's back to the fact that we work cheap.

ETHAN: That's really the long and the short of it.

JOEL: Our movies are inexpensive because we storyboard our films in the same highly detailed way Hitchcock did. As a result, there's little improvisation. Preproduction is cheap compared with trying to figure things out on a set with an entire crew standing around.

ETHAN: So we're left alone, which is indeed sort of miraculous.

PLAYBOY: Do the distributors have a say at all?

ETHAN: No. They say things, but we don't necessarily listen. They were nervous about the new movie.

JOEL: Principally because it was in black and white.

ETHAN: People were terrified of that. Black and white stigmatizes a movie in the eyes of the exhibitors. It means it's an art film. They are leery of it. They may have good reasons, I don't know. However, it was important to us to make it black and white, though it was harder to get the financing.

PLAYBOY: Did you consider switching to color?

ETHAN: No. We just wouldn't have made it, at least not now. We would have put it in a drawer.

JOEL: We got away with it because, once again, the movie was cheap. It was under $20 million. That said, we know we're lucky. We're in an enviable position. We've made enough of these things—it's not as if we're just starting out. We're a known quantity. When we first started, we were lucky because there was a lot less activity in the independent film world. There weren't 700 movies submitted a year to the Sundance Film Festival. It was easier to get some attention. There was less noise.

PLAYBOY: Would it be tougher to release *Blood Simple* now?

JOEL: I imagine it would be. We're lucky because now people know who we are. We have a track record in the market, for what it's worth.

ETHAN: Our record goes both ways, though.

JOEL: Yes, they know they can lose a little money on us, too [*laughs*].

PLAYBOY: You have been called the "grandfathers of the independent filmmaker movement." Are you proud of your progeny?

ETHAN: God! You're not going to make us responsible for that, are you?

PLAYBOY: Is that a bad thing?

ETHAN: The thing is, people have always been making films outside of the studios.

JOEL: For decades there was marginal, nonnarrative stuff. The current variety of independent films started in the 1960s with people like Roger Corman, Russ Meyer and, later, John Sayles.

ETHAN: We aren't the grandfathers of any movement. In the 1980s, the so-called indie film movement was a media creation. What I found irritating is that "independent" became an encomium. If it was independent, it was supposed to be good, and studio films were bad. Obviously, there are bad independent films and good studio films.

PLAYBOY: *The Hudsucker Proxy* was the first time you worked with a big-name Hollywood producer, Joel Silver. Were you apprehensive about working with him?

JOEL: We were a little, because of his reputation. However, Joel is a smart guy and he knew what we were looking for when we got into business with him. We weren't looking for a partner in terms of the nitty-gritty of the production. We were looking for someone to help us with the studio and help us finance the movie. He offered his services on that basis. When he says he'll do something, he does it.

PLAYBOY: Another thing that has come with your success are big-name actors. Is it different working with people such as George Clooney, Brad Pitt or Paul Newman?

JOEL: The bigger stars we've worked with have been without the movie-star vanities or meshugaas that you read about and dread. Clooney, for example, was the opposite. He has no entourage. He's a big movie star, but he's a nice guy.

ETHAN: Paul Newman, too. It's in part self-selecting. We pay so little. The people who want to have their movie-star things indulged wouldn't work with us.

JOEL: We couldn't give them the stuff they're used to.

ETHAN: Someone who wanted a big salary and a lot of attention would tell us to get lost. If they work with us, they are doing it for other reasons. They wouldn't be doing it if they were coming with some movie-star agenda.

JOEL: Definitely not for the money.

ETHAN: Or more fame. Our movies don't make them recognized on the street, necessarily.

PLAYBOY: Are you recognized on the street?

JOEL: If people recognize me, it's because they're looking at my credit card. Frankly, nobody gives a shit. I get a little more of it when I'm with Fran, because people recognize her. Her fame can occasionally be intrusive, but she's not in the category of people who can't go out.

PLAYBOY: Do you ever take advantage of her celebrity?

JOEL: Sometimes Fran will be in a crowded New York restaurant and the manager will give her a card with a number she can call so she can get a reservation even if there aren't any available. Has she ever used that? Yeah, probably.

PLAYBOY: Do you write movies with actors—Fran or anyone else—in mind?

ETHAN: Half-and-half. We often think about people we know and have worked with before. With Fran, with John Turturro. With some of the other people.

PLAYBOY: Did you discover Turturro?

JOEL: We knew him before we did *Miller's Crossing*. He went to school with Fran. You get to know one actor and you're on a slippery slope.

PLAYBOY: Is it gratifying to set people like him off on successful careers?

JOEL: It's a mutual thing.

PLAYBOY: How about Steve Buscemi?

JOEL: We met him in an audition. When there's a great collaboration like the one with him, you want to work together again.

PLAYBOY: When you first cast John Goodman, he was about to begin work on *Roseanne*.

ETHAN: The TV show hadn't begun and he wasn't well known. He just came in on an audition.

JOEL: We work with someone and—I don't know. It works or not. There's sympathy to a working style and getting along well. There's also the actor's ability, of course. Something just happens.

ETHAN: They understand the material in a full way. In addition, they surprise you by what they bring to the roles.

PLAYBOY: How have you cast people like Billy Bob Thornton, Jeff Bridges or Paul Newman?

JOEL: We write these things and we need actors. Other than the parts for the people we always work with, we don't really have an idea who will play the parts. Sometimes we think about the role and about actors we know from their work.

PLAYBOY: Did you ask Paul Newman?

ETHAN: Yes. We asked and he said yes. We couldn't believe it.

PLAYBOY: Did you feel intimidated working with him?

JOEL: Not at all. Paul is a regular guy in the very best way. He is completely unaffected. The only actor I imagine might make us nervous is Brando. You'd never know whether he was going to show up and want to play the part as a bagel or something. I think he's gone off the deep end.

PLAYBOY: How did you cast *Fargo*?

JOEL: We wrote Fran's part for Fran and Steve Buscemi's part for Steve. But Bill Macy came in during a casting session.

PLAYBOY: *Fargo* was loosely based on a 1987 kidnapping that took place in Minnesota. Are you often inspired by real events?

JOEL: We found the story compelling, but we weren't interested in rendering the details as they were. We're not big on research and we just don't care at a certain point.

PLAYBOY: Did a real person inspire the Dude, Jeff Bridges' character in *The Big Lebowski*?

ETHAN: Yes.

JOEL: Definitely [*they laugh*].

ETHAN: A couple people in L.A. did, especially one guy. We spent time in L.A. and met a few people who were quintessentially L.A. people. One guy in particular—a producer—was like the guy in the movie.

PLAYBOY: Did you do a lot of research about the drug culture, or do you know about it from personal experience?

ETHAN: It's just this guy. The guy is a pothead and stuck in the 1960s. A former SDS guy. There are a lot of those people out there like him.

PLAYBOY: Do you often base your characters on real people?

JOEL: Often the characters are composites. Normally.

ETHAN: And sometimes they're not.

PLAYBOY: Are there actors you've written parts for who have repeatedly turned you down?

JOEL: It took us a long time to get Jeff Bridges to take the part in *The Big Lebowski*. He danced around it for a while. I've heard that he does that on every movie. He's slow to take a part and has a lot of insecurity about it before he commits to it. But once he does, the insecurity evaporates. That was another fun working experience.

PLAYBOY: Which star from the past do you most regret having missed the opportunity to work with?

ETHAN: Richard Burton would have been good.

JOEL: I'd like to have worked with Fred MacMurray.

PLAYBOY: Do you think you're better filmmakers when you're working with actors you like?

ETHAN: We only work with actors we like.

PLAYBOY: After *Miller's Crossing*, Gabriel Byrne said, "It was not a fun set." Why not?

JOEL: Gabriel can be moody, but we had a good time with him. Tex Cobb, who played the biker in *Raising Arizona*, is the only person we've worked with who posed problems. He's not an actor, and he was going through some shit at the time. He was a bit of a pain in the ass.

PLAYBOY: How about Nicolas Cage in that movie?

ETHAN: He was great. We're hoping to do something else with him. We've written a Cold War comedy called *62 Skidoo* that we want him to do. It deals with amnesia, mistaken identity and that very 1960s question, "Who am I?" It's vaguely in the tradition of *Seconds* and *The Manchurian Candidate*, which are incredibly groovy movies that were very much of their time.

PLAYBOY: Did you write *Raising Arizona* with Cage in mind?

JOEL: We actually wrote it for Holly Hunter—with her in mind.

PLAYBOY: Was it challenging to direct all the babies you had in that movie?

JOEL: It was bizarre. Whenever you have an infant, you have to triple or quadruple them. When we had five kids in the movie, we had to have 15 babies on the set.

ETHAN: The picture babies and the standby babies. Cacophonous, nightmarish.

JOEL: We had the baby pit—a big padded pit that they were tossed into when we weren't using them. The mothers all sat around the perimeter knitting.

ETHAN: Whenever we needed a baby, we reached into the pit and grabbed one. It was kind of like a barbecue pit.

JOEL: You can't really direct a baby, which is the problem. You take one out of the pit, put it in front of the camera and see if it behaves. If not, you toss it back into the pit and get another one. It's a lot like working with animals, actually.

ETHAN: Yeah. If an animal doesn't do what you want it to do, you just grab another one. But the rules for working with animals are a lot more stringent than those for working with babies.

JOEL: There is definitely no comparison.

PLAYBOY: What can you do with a baby that you can't do with an animal?

ETHAN: A million things.

JOEL: The pit. We could never do that with animals.

ETHAN: Believe me. It's a remarkable thing to see how animals are monitored. You cannot kill a mosquito on-screen.

JOEL: When you do a Screen Actors Guild movie that uses animals in any way you have to get the American Humane Society to sign off on it. We blew up a cow in *O Brother*, which meant we had to send the Humane Society work tapes while the film was being shot. When they saw the cow scene they didn't believe it was computer generated, but I assure you it was.

ETHAN: There is a rule that you can't get a cow anywhere near a moving car.

JOEL: It might cause the cow stress.

ETHAN: You can't upset the animals.

JOEL: We had to have a lizard crash pad for *Raising Arizona*.

PLAYBOY: What's a lizard crash pad?

ETHAN: A lizard shoots off a rock in the movie, and we had to have a preapproved soft place for it to land.

PLAYBOY: Is there a reason you tend to put animals in peril?

JOEL: No. For fun.

ETHAN: We don't put them in any more peril than we put people.

PLAYBOY: That's true. With the exception of *The Hudsucker Proxy*, all of your films have included a fair amount of violence and killing.

ETHAN: It's called drama.

PLAYBOY: Do some of your movies' dark scenes—burying someone alive in *Blood Simple*, for example—come from your nightmares?

JOEL: Not really. They are the general phobias people experience, I suppose, but it's not personal to us.

ETHAN: It's just stuff that creeps people out. We like that.

JOEL: The reason we killed the cow in *O Brother, Where Art Thou?* is that we think it's funny.

PLAYBOY: How would you respond to someone who is offended?

JOEL: I recognize that some people might not think it's funny, but really [*laughing*], what's not to like? It's interesting to me that people are so upset about the cow scene. We blew up a rabbit in *Raising Arizona* and people were upset about that, too. In a focus group, people were really upset about the rabbit. Shooting people was fine, but they didn't like seeing a rabbit get hurt. Eating cows is fine, but hitting a cow with a car is not.

ETHAN: It's easy to offend people. People get uncomfortable, for instance, when the main character in a movie is not sympathetic in a Hollywood formula way. Our movies are loaded with things that aren't to everyone's taste. On the other hand, there's a scene in *O Brother* where a frog gets squished that everyone seems to like. It's all right to do frog squishing.

JOEL: In our next movie, Brad Pitt plays a character who identifies intensely with animals, yet he kills many animals over the course of the story. Those killings are potentially more alienating to an audience than the scenes in which he kills people.

ETHAN: I don't know exactly why.

PLAYBOY: You murder James Gandolfini in your new movie. Are you fans of *The Sopranos?*

JOEL: Not really.

ETHAN: We don't watch TV. I don't have HBO. We knew him from character parts he had played in other movies.

JOEL: Before *The Sopranos* he played small parts, and we always really liked him. I hear he's great in *The Sopranos*, though.

PLAYBOY: Is it a moral or practical decision not to watch TV?

JOEL: I don't know what it is.

ETHAN: I'm just not interested.

JOEL: I watch the news.

ETHAN: I watch the news, too. But I couldn't tell you about any of the regular shows that are on now.

PLAYBOY: How about movies? Do you try to keep up with them?

ETHAN: I go when I get a chance. I see whatever is nearby and playing at the right time, which means I don't necessarily see the movies I'm particularly interested in seeing.

JOEL: Our moviegoing habits have changed over the past five or six years, mostly because we have kids.

ETHAN: We see a lot of kid movies.

PLAYBOY: Is that good or bad?

ETHAN: It's not good. With some exceptions. *Chicken Run* was good. It might be the last good movie I've seen.

JOEL: I'm curious about *Shrek* because my kid saw it four times. The kids want to see every Disney movie that comes out. Some are hard to sit through.

ETHAN: There were many years when we saw a lot of movies—the cold weather of the Midwest drives you inside to watch movies. Now we don't.

JOEL: Recently I liked *Amores Perros*. I also liked *Sexy Beast*.

PLAYBOY: Do you generally prefer art and foreign movies?

JOEL: Yeah. If I have a chance, I try to see those kinds.

PLAYBOY: We've discussed violence in your movies, but how about sex? British film writer Ronald Bergan wrote, "The Coens avoid the obligatory sex scenes found in most adult films." Why?

ETHAN: What about the orgy scene in *The Big Lebowski*?

JOEL: Yeah, and there's a sex scene in *Barton Fink*, too, although it does end up with the woman being decapitated.

PLAYBOY: What about—

JOEL: And the scene in *Barton Fink* where John Turturro and John Goodman wrestle? We consider that a sex scene. [*Ethan laughs heartily*]. I don't know. We're of the school of panning away to the waterfall or the steaming kettle or the flock of geese flying.

PLAYBOY: Is it that you dislike sex scenes?

JOEL: It's that there aren't many scenes of that sort that are done well. Pedro Almodóvar does them well, but he's the only one. It's not that I don't find that aspect of film interesting, but I'm not interested in doing it.

PLAYBOY: *The Man Who Wasn't There* has been described as a return to your beginnings. Is it?

ETHAN: I suppose so. It's definitely more hard-boiled than *O Brother* is.

JOEL: The movie takes place in Santa Rosa in 1949, the same time and setting as Hitchcock's *Shadow of a Doubt*, which, along with *Psycho*, is probably my favorite Hitchcock film.

PLAYBOY: *O Brother, Where Art Thou?* is said to be loosely based on *The Wizard of Oz*. Is that true?

JOEL: That was definitely an inspiration and a big influence on the movie. In fact, one of my favorite shots in the film is strongly reminiscent of *The Wizard of Oz*. It's a shot of George Clooney, Tim Nelson and John Turturro peering through some bushes while looking down on a Ku Klux Klan meeting.

PLAYBOY: The Klan members perform an elaborately choreographed dance. What inspired that bizarre scene?

JOEL: The dance combines aspects of the witch's castle scene in *The Wizard of Oz*, a number from a Busby Berkeley musical and some interesting old films we saw of the Klan. They marched in formation like that. It really was like a synthesis of Busby Berkeley and Nuremberg.

PLAYBOY: *Barton Fink* features a character named W. P. Mayhew who's played by John Mahoney and is loosely based on William Faulkner, who you've both expressed great admiration for. What's your favorite Faulkner book?

JOEL: *Light in August*, but don't ask me why. The other one I like a lot is *The Wild Palms*. We steal many names from Faulkner, but we haven't attempted to steal a whole book, yet [*laughing*]. *O Brother*, for instance, has a character named Vernon T. Waldrip, and we got that name from *The Wild Palms*.

PLAYBOY: At what point does an homage to a genre become a spoof of a genre?

JOEL: We've always tried to emulate the sources of genre movies rather than the movies themselves. For instance, *Blood Simple* grew out of the fact that we started reading James M. Cain's novels in 1979 and liked the hard-boiled style. We wanted to write a James M. Cain story and put it in a modern context. We've never considered our stuff either homage or spoof. Those are things other people call it, and it's always puzzled me that they do.

PLAYBOY: *The Man Who Wasn't There* was also based on Cain's work. What do you like about his stories?

JOEL: What intrigues us about Cain is that the heroes of his stories are nearly always schlubs—loser guys involved in dreary, banal existences. Cain was interested in people's workaday lives, and he wrote about guys who worked as insurance salesmen or in banks, and we took that as a cue. Even though there's a crime in this story, we were still interested in what this guy, who's a barber, does as a barber. We wanted to examine exactly what the day-to-day was like for a guy who gives haircut after haircut.

PLAYBOY: On the set, Billy Bob Thornton was giving real haircuts to extras and crew members. Did you get one?

ETHAN: Are you kidding?

JOEL: No way. We had to hire someone to fix the haircuts he was giving people.

PLAYBOY: You've said that you're more attracted to film noir as a literary form than as a film genre. Are noir books better than the movies that are based on them?

JOEL: Most of the movies aren't as good as the books, although there are exceptions. John Huston's film noirs like *The Maltese Falcon* and *The Asphalt Jungle* are great, but many film noirs are crummy. Everyone loves *Out of the Past*, for instance, and Kirk Douglas is good in it, but it's a little overcooked.

PLAYBOY: Critics write about your films as if they are challenged to crack some sort of code in order to grasp your real intentions. Are they reading in too much?

JOEL: That's how they've been trained to watch movies. Several critics interpreted *Barton Fink* as a parable for the Holocaust. They said the same thing about *Miller's Crossing*. The critic J. Hoberman cooked up this elaborate theory about the scene where Bernie is taken into the woods to be killed. In *Barton Fink*, we may have encouraged it—like teasing the animals at the zoo. The movie is intentionally ambiguous in ways they may not be used to seeing.

PLAYBOY: Your critics seem to hold you to a higher standard. Do you think about them when you're making movies?

ETHAN: Never.

PLAYBOY: Are you consciously trying to do something different each time out?

JOEL: Not really. We were out filming this scene in *Fargo* where a car is approaching in the distance on an empty stretch of highway as Steve Buscemi is dragging a state trooper's body off the road. As we were shooting that scene, Ethan and I looked at each other and we both said, "It seems like we've been here before." There's an almost identical scene in *Blood Simple*. It's a complete accident.

ETHAN: We don't generally worry about repeating ourselves. Being original and always doing the new thing is incredibly overrated.

PLAYBOY: All of your movies are set in the past. Are you less interested in the present or future?

JOEL: The past has a kind of exoticism. Setting a story in the past is a way of further fictionalizing it. It's not about reminiscence, because our movies are about a past that we have never experienced. It's more about imagination. Right before we made *Barton Fink*, for instance, we read a book called *City of Nets* by Otto Friedrich that was essentially a history of Los Angeles and Hollywood in the 1940s. It was an intensely evocative book and played a role in how we conceived the film.

ETHAN: Books often play a role in our becoming interested in a period or a place. We considered trying to get the rights to *Mildred Pierce*, which wasn't much of a movie but was a great James M. Cain novel set in Glendale in the 1940s. The book *Mildred Pierce* is actually the saga of Glendale, but the movie didn't bother getting into any of that.

PLAYBOY: Several of your films incorporate elements of screwball comedies. What's your favorite of that genre?

JOEL: *The Miracle of Morgan's Creek*, although I'm not sure that it's technically a screwball comedy.

ETHAN: As for contemporary attempts at screwball comedy, *I Wanna Hold Your Hand* was pretty funny, in a screwball kind of way. *Used Cars*, too.

PLAYBOY: Did you watch them when you were kids?

ETHAN: I like all of Preston Sturges' comedies.

PLAYBOY: What's your earliest memory?

ETHAN: I remember moving across the street. We moved from one house into the house across the street.

JOEL: Our parents liked the neighborhood. I remember climbing on top of the stove and setting my pajamas on fire when I was three years old. [*Laughing*] I remember the expression on my parents' faces.

PLAYBOY: What was the first film that made an impression on you?

JOEL: I remember going to see *David Copperfield* when I was four and being completely freaked out by the scene where David's father beats the shit out of him. It upset me so much that I had to leave. Right after that I saw *All Hands on Deck*, which was much more my speed.

ETHAN: I have a vivid memory of seeing a film called *Hatari*. There's an elephant stampede at the end of it.

JOEL: From an early age we were into what we thought were adult movies—things like *Splendor in the Grass* and *A Summer Place*.

ETHAN: They don't make that shit anymore. It's been usurped by significant, disease-of-the-week theme TV movies.

JOEL: Yes, but when we were kids, films like *Tea and Sympathy* served the purpose. *Tea and Sympathy* was a lot better than a TV movie about somebody who gets spina bifida.

PLAYBOY: Were you movie fanatics in those years?

ETHAN: There are movie nuts who are filmmakers—Scorsese and Truffaut, for instance. Not us. We're not collectors of film and we're not as knowledgeable about movies as many of those guys. We're fond of stories; movies are a way of telling stories. We found out that we had some facility for writing them and we got an opportunity to actually make one. It's not as if we have some mystical attachment to film.

PLAYBOY: You've described your childhood as bland. Is that an accurate characterization?

JOEL: I've described it as bland to people who were digging for some explanation of why we do what we do. I remember the blandness fondly. At the same time, I was quite eager to leave when I was in my teens. As soon as I saw New York City, I wanted to be there.

PLAYBOY: How important was religion in your childhood?

ETHAN: Judaism was a central part of the house we grew up in. We had a religious upbringing. I went to Hebrew school every Saturday and had a bar mitzvah, but that just meant I got presents. I never took it seriously. Some part of it probably seeps in, but I think that's more of an ethnic than a religious thing.

JOEL: Yes, I imagine some of it influenced my point of view to a degree. But neither Ethan nor I have maintained a great deal of interest in the traditions.

PLAYBOY: Will your sons be bar mitzvahed?

JOEL: My wife is the daughter of a Disciples of Christ minister, and her sister is a minister in that church. Our son [who's adopted] was born in Paraguay to a Catholic family, so it's complicated. Fran's more into summer solstice. I guess you could say our son's being brought up as a pagan.

PLAYBOY: Do you believe in God?

JOEL: Not in the Jewish sense. I don't believe in the angry God, Yahweh.

PLAYBOY: What do you think happens after death?

JOEL: You rot and decompose.

PLAYBOY: Do you believe in the law of karma—that we reap what we sow? Or do some people get away with murder?

JOEL: Some people do get away with murder.

PLAYBOY: Do you believe in capital punishment?

JOEL: No.

ETHAN: No.

PLAYBOY: How did having your children change you?

JOEL: I certainly see fewer movies.

PLAYBOY: Has it changed your filmmaking at all?

JOEL: Mmm. No.

PLAYBOY: Does filmmaking ever become tedious?

JOEL: Parts of the business are tedious. We had no idea how much promotion you have to do. It wasn't until we were assaulted with all that during the release of *Blood Simple* that it crossed my radar. We say no to a lot and we won't do television, but you have to do a certain amount.

ETHAN: If they give you millions of dollars to make a movie, they expect you to promote it. You make these movies and a year later you have homework.

JOEL: Watching dailies can be tedious, too. Frequently you'll shoot something over and over because you're looking for a small detail. It can be nothing more than an insert, but you'll have to sit through hours of dailies with a room full of people wondering why you shot an hour of a hand holding a coffee cup.

ETHAN: There's another thing, too. You wait around a lot. Mostly you just sit around and bullshit during those long stretches of waiting.

JOEL: It takes time to light the scene—whatever.

PLAYBOY: How do you spend the time?

JOEL: You can gain 20 pounds in six weeks, so I try to stay away from the craft services table. I used to drink a lot of coffee. Ethan still does, but my stomach can't take it. I drink a lot of tea.

PLAYBOY: Have you two ever had a ferocious disagreement?

JOEL: This seems to disappoint people, but no, we haven't.

ETHAN: Occasionally we get a little testy with each other, but that's about the extent of it.

JOEL: We wouldn't be doing this if we had ferocious disagreements. We share the same fundamental point of view toward the material. In fact, the credits on our movies don't reflect the extent of our collaboration. We take separate credits, but we actually do everything together.

PLAYBOY: Why do you edit under a pseudonym?

ETHAN: Because it would be bad taste to have our names on our movies that many times.

PLAYBOY: What's the process? Who sits behind the word processor? Who sits behind the camera?

ETHAN: We both sit behind the camera. We both watch the actors. I tend to be at the word processor more because I type faster.

JOEL: On the set it's completely equal. We talk to the actors and cinematographer and designers. Whenever a decision has to be made, it's made by the one of us who is closer to the problem. The movies really are co-directed.

ETHAN: After they are shot, it's a mirror, in a way. When we're editing, Joel actually makes the physical cuts and splices.

JOEL: Because I have had more practice on the machine from when I was an assistant editor. But we're editing the movies cut by cut together.

PLAYBOY: How about dreaming up your projects?

JOEL: We don't do high-concept movies. It's not that one of us will say, "*Das Boot* in a spaceship." We just talk about ideas.

ETHAN: It's impossible to say after the fact whose idea it was. Ideas just get expanded and developed, and there's an informal discussion until we have the framework to start writing.

JOEL: Sometimes we just start writing to see where it goes. It might start off with, literally, "John Goodman and John Turturro in a hotel room."

PLAYBOY: You have said that your next movie, a film adaptation of James Dickey's *To the White Sea*, is a silent movie. Why a silent movie?

JOEL: I wouldn't call it a silent movie, but after the first 10 or 15 minutes there isn't any dialogue. It's about an American airman who's shot down over Tokyo the night before the city is firebombed. He then walks from Honshu to Hokkaido. Because he's alone, there's no dialogue for 90 percent of the movie.

PLAYBOY: What made Brad Pitt right for the leading role?

JOEL: The lead character is a tailgunner in a B-29, and there's something all-American about Brad that's appropriate. Brad is actually far too old to play the part, so the fact that he has a boyish quality is good. Basically, he's supposed to be a kid who was drafted.

ETHAN: He also kills a lot of people, so the actor can't be somebody you're going to detest. He's killing to survive, but the killings are fairly graphic.

PLAYBOY: More violence?

JOEL: The issue of violence in movies bores me. The discussion about it is endless. We get asked about it frequently. There's all this political stuff around it. It's a bore.

ETHAN: I was just reading one of Philip Roth's novels, and there's a character in it who talks about trees. He says, "Who gives a shit about a tree," and I feel the same way. I find trees boring.

PLAYBOY: If not in your movies, do you ever have qualms about violence in other movies? Where do you draw the line on movie violence?

JOEL: I don't draw a line anywhere. I won't watch a film like *Faces of Death* or depictions of actual violence or newsreels of people killing themselves, because I don't want that stuff in my psyche. But generally I find myself more repulsed by maudlin, overly sentimental films than by violent films.

PLAYBOY: When was the last time you cried in a movie?

JOEL: I hate when people cry in movies. It's particularly disconcerting when you're sitting at a really awful movie and you hear people all around you sobbing and blowing their noses.

PLAYBOY: Do you ever cry?

JOEL: I cried during *Dancer in the Dark* [*laughing*]. Actually, I barely sat through it. I hate to say this, but the best part of the movie was when Björk beat David Morse to death with a metal box.

PLAYBOY: Joel, you once said, "Ethan is unbelievably sentimental and sloppy and he's always trying to sneak that into our movies." Were you kidding?

JOEL: Actually, it's true.

ETHAN: I admit it—there's that exploding cow, for instance.

JOEL: He's trying to sneak a love interest into our new movie. It doesn't make any sense at all because it's not in the novel, but he wants Brad Pitt to meet a girl along the way.

ETHAN: Yeah, I want him to run into a Japanese girl walking through the snow dressed in animal skins and a sable hat. Kind of a *Clan of the Cave Bear* thing. I also wanted to give the lead character a buddy, it being a war picture and all.

JOEL: Then we could kill the buddy.

ETHAN: And Brad Pitt would get to say, "They killed my buddy."

JOEL: That's funny! We should do it. Then everyone can talk more about violence in the movie.

FRANCIS FORD COPPOLA

A candid conversation with the Midas-touch director of The Godfather

Every year or so, the American movie industry comes up with a talented new young director whose current flick is hailed as the greatest piece of goods since *The Birth of a Nation*; he usually finds himself an overnight celebrity, the darling of TV talk shows and magazine profiles. Few deserve such treatment and even fewer manage to survive it. The latest of Hollywood's directorial darlings is a portly, bearded, fast-talking 36-year-old dynamo named Francis Ford Coppola (pronounced Cope-uh-lah), who made headlines this year by being nominated for five Academy Awards—and winning three of them. In the history of the awards, only the venerable Walt Disney received more nominations (six) in a single year. Coppola was also named best motion-picture director of the year by the Directors' Guild of America.

Unlike most of the other boy geniuses, however, Coppola might actually be every bit as talented as the reviewers say he is. His present eminence rests largely on having made *The Godfather Part II* an even bigger artistic success than the original *Godfather*, which, in addition to grossing a staggering $285,000,000, has been acclaimed by most serious movie critics here and abroad as the greatest gangster picture ever made. For the first time in Hollywood history, a sequel to a tremendously successful motion picture has surpassed the original in critical estimation and is likely to do the same at the box office.

Just three years ago, Coppola was broke and so little in demand that he was reportedly only fourth or fifth on Paramount's list of possible candidates to direct what the studio envisaged all along as no more than a big-budget thriller to be carved out of Mario Puzo's sprawling bestseller. Since *The Godfather*, Coppola has become the one person in the movie industry more in demand than Clint Eastwood. "If he took all the offers now coming his way in any one week," a studio executive recently said, "he'd have to work uninterruptedly for the next 50 years and might get to be rich enough to buy up Fort Knox."

The wonder is not that Coppola is so young to be in such a position but that it took Hollywood so long to find out about him. Francis remembers his childhood as an agitated series of crises, with much shouting, passion and tears. His father, Carmine, was a virtuoso flutist who played with several leading orchestras, including Arturo Toscanini's celebrated NBC Symphony. Unable to achieve recognition as a composer, he moved the family back and forth across the country in pursuit of his career, which was finally capped with an Oscar for the score of *Godfather II*. Francis' older brother, August, a writer, was handsome, brilliant and popular with girls; his sister, Talia, an actress (she played Connie, Michael Corleone's sister in both *Godfathers*), was the baby of the family. Francis retreated for a while into a fantasy world in which, for hours on end, he played with puppets, watched TV and read comic books.

He aspired to playwrighting but quickly changed his mind when he saw his first Eisenstein film, *Ten Days That Shook the World*, at the age of 17. "On Monday I was in theater," Coppola has said, "and on Tuesday I wanted to be a filmmaker."

At UCLA's film school, Coppola won the Samuel Goldwyn writing award and at 22 he landed a job as a staff writer with Seven Arts, a major production company, where he directed a low-budget horror picture for producer Roger Corman. Coppola's master's-thesis film, *You're a Big Boy Now*, a knockabout farce with a rock score, brought him to the attention of Warner Bros., which signed him to direct a musical, *Finian's Rainbow*. It flopped. Mostly on his own, Coppola put together *The Rain People*, a film he wrote and directed about a pregnant woman who leaves her husband, despite the fact that she loves him, because she doesn't want to be married anymore. The movie antedated women's lib and is now considered to have been ahead of its period, a polite way of saying that it didn't make much money. But by that time, Coppola had also co-authored the screenplay of *Patton*, for which he won an Oscar. He was barely 28 and the odds were he'd make it big, if he just stuck around long enough.

By 1969, however, Coppola had had enough of Hollywood's cha-otic financing methods, antiquated production techniques and rigidly entrenched craft unions. He talked Warner's into letting him set up his own production company, American Zoetrope, and moved to San Francisco, where he proposed to turn out high-quality, low-budget features. The company's first project, *THX 1138*, a futuristic script directed by his friend George Lucas that has since become a cult clas-sic, all but sank it. Warner's canceled its contract, leaving Coppola stranded under a mountain of debts, from which he quickly extricated himself with *The Godfather*, followed not only by *Godfather II* but by its rival for best-picture honors in the 1974 Oscars competition, *The Conversation*.

Today, Coppola's only worry is deciding what to do next. He has enough money to indulge himself and he has a number of projects that have been sitting on his desk and/or maturing in his head for years. In addition to Lucas, whom he prodded into writing and direct-ing the enormously successful *American Graffiti*—which he produced after the script had been rejected by 11 studios—Coppola has gath-ered around him in San Francisco a small army of young supremely talented individualists. They swarm in and out of the Coppola Com-pany headquarters an old eight-story San Francisco office building that Coppola is restoring. Coppola listens to everyone and overlooks nothing.

Some people feel this may be his undoing as an artist. Coppola willingly delegates authority and listens to advice, but he clearly feels capable of undertaking just about anything interesting that comes his way. He has also set up his own distribution company, has acquired a small legitimate theater, where he plans to produce and direct his own plays as well as those of others, is wheeling and dealing in real estate and publishes a biweekly magazine called *City* that aspires to do for the San Francisco region something of what *New York* does for its area. He enjoys a warm home life with his artist wife, Eleanor, and their three small children, as well as an active social one with a wide circle of friends and cronies whom he calls "the family." To find out more about this artist-mogul, *Playboy* assigned contributor William Murray to track him down on his home grounds and interview him. Murray reports:

"Getting to see Francis Ford Coppola these days is about as dif-ficult as setting up a tête-à-tête with the Godfather himself. It took weeks and dozens of long-distance phone calls, filtered through the usual guard screen of secretaries and superefficient business managers, before a meeting was finally arranged.

"I finally caught up with Coppola at his house, a light-blue, turn-of-the-century, 28-room mansion with a magnificent view of the Golden Gate Bridge. The huge rooms are stocked with gadgets, including an old jukebox, a player grand piano, hi-fi equipment and a fully equipped projection room. It was exactly the sort of palazzo I'd have envisioned for a self-exiled Hollywood tycoon, but I hadn't been in the place more than 20 minutes before I realized that, far from being a self-advertisement for power and success, everything in the house reflected the highly personal, even eccentric tastes of Francis or Eleanor Coppola.

"The first thing Coppola did was to make me a cappuccino on his own espresso machine, imported from Turin. We sat and sipped coffee. Everything was moving at such a leisurely pace that I couldn't imagine at first how I'd ever be able to get a real conversation under way with him.

"I needn't have worried. The minute I switched on my tape recorder, Coppola came to life. This was work. First, he corrected the position of the machine, then he fiddled with the volume and tone controls till he had them set to his satisfaction. Finally, he allowed me to question him. All you have to do with Coppola is get him going. After that, the problem is slowing him down, much less stopping him; I got the feeling he could have been a tremendous politician or an eloquent preacher. We talked for several hours that first day, then continued the next two days at his office.

"Our final session was held at his home. Coppola, wearing an Arab caftan that failed to conceal his bulk, ushered me into one of the Bay Areas' largest backyards, where a Moorish-style pool is heated to body temperature. He leaped into the water and for the next five minutes he moaned—very loudly. 'What if the neighbors complain?' he was asked. 'It's my pool,' he answered, 'and I'll moan if I like.' Sipping a cup of espresso while standing in the water, he added: 'Y' know, I like this. It's my idea of real decadence.'

"Back in the living room, Coppola, his robe billowing about him, pirouetted, gavotted and jigged without a trace of self-consciousness to a record of carnival music that he'd brought back from Rio, where he'd gone to unwind for a couple of weeks. Then, I think, I saw the key to Coppola: He throws himself completely into everything he does, whether it's work or play. The man is a block of pure energy, with the powers of concentration of a leopard stalking prey. If anyone can pull off what he proposes to do to the film business, I'm convinced he can and I came away hoping he'd succeed."

COPPOLA: This is my last interview.

PLAYBOY: Why?

COPPOLA: I decided recently that enough is enough. Basically, there's only one story I can tell and I've told it. I think it's time I kind of go on my way out of respect for the public.

PLAYBOY: All right, let's start with your recent Oscar haul for *Godfather II*. How did it feel to walk away with so many awards?

COPPOLA: Two years ago, I went to the Academy Awards ceremonies feeling blasé, not caring. I thought *Godfather I* would win most of the awards, but how important was the Oscar, anyway? Then it became clear that *Cabaret* was running away with the awards, and I suddenly started wanting to win desperately. When I didn't, I got very depressed. I figured I'd never make another film that would win an Oscar; I was going to go off and make small, personal films, the kind that rarely win awards. I had wanted to leave a winner.

This year, I thought *Chinatown* would clean up. I had two pictures nominated—*Godfather II* and *The Conversation*—and I figured that would split my vote. I was intrigued with the idea of losing twice after coming so close, which might be a record in itself. So when it all happened, I was so elated I didn't know what to do. I never expected Best Picture. I felt *Godfather II* was too demanding, too complex. But when it won, I felt the members were telling me they appreciated the fact that we'd tried to make a film with integrity.

PLAYBOY: What did you think when Bert Schneider, the producer of the antiwar documentary *Hearts and Minds*, read a telegram from a Viet Cong representative?

COPPOLA: Many people voted for *Hearts and Minds* as best documentary, not because it was a great film—it wasn't, particularly—but because of what the film said. And so when Schneider accepted the award, it was certainly appropriate for him to comment on what the film was saying. It wasn't as if they were giving him an award as best tap dancer only to have him turn around and give a political speech. The academy was sanctioning that documentary, was rewarding it for the message it conveyed. So his statement was really a response to that.

PLAYBOY: The incident caused quite an uproar. How did you personally feel about it?

COPPOLA: Imagine, in 1975, getting a telegram from a so-called enemy extending friendship to the American people. I mean, after what we did to the Vietnamese people, you'd think they wouldn't forgive us for 300 years! Getting this positive human, optimistic message was such a beautiful idea to me—it was overwhelming. If the telegram had said, "You Yankee dogs have been killing us for 30 years and now we've got you, so screw you!" I wouldn't have read it. But it didn't say that.

As for the uproar caused by Frank Sinatra's reading the disclaimer expressing his and Bob Hope's reactions, well, men at that point in their lives can't understand what a message like that really means. They're not interested in the truth; they still think all Communists are bad, less than human. When people are against something, they don't even listen.

PLAYBOY: Your career as a director has been made by the two *Godfather* movies, and most of the critics seem to have recognized what you were trying to do with them, but none has had a kind word for the novel nor for its author, Mario Puzo. *The New Yorker's* Pauline Kael, in fact, calls the book trash. Could you have made two fine movies out of trash?

COPPOLA: When I was first offered the project, I started to read the book and I got only about 50 pages into it. I thought it was a popular, sensational novel, pretty cheap stuff. I got to the part about the singer supposedly modeled on Frank Sinatra and the girl Sonny Corleone liked so much because her vagina was enormous—remember that stuff in the book? It never showed up in the movie. Anyway, I said, "My God, what *is* this—*The Carpetbaggers?*" So I stopped reading it and said, "Forget it."

Four or five months later, I was again offered the opportunity to work on it and by that time, I was in dire financial straits with my own company in San Francisco, so I read further. Then I got into what the book is really about—the story of the family, this father and his sons, and questions of power and succession—and I thought it was a terrific story, if you could cut out all the other stuff. I decided it could be not only a successful movie but also a *good* movie. I wanted to concentrate on the central theme, and that's what I tried to do.

So the fact is, it wasn't a piece of trash. Like me, Mario went after the money at first. He's very frank about that. But if the two movies are strong, it's because of what Mario originally put in his book that was strong and valid. Mario himself, by the way, doesn't think *The Godfather* is his best book, but it's the only one of his novels that sold really well. I have great respect for Mario. He created the story, he created the characters, even in *Part II*, which I wrote more of than *Part I*. But all the key elements go back to his book.

PLAYBOY: Did you work together on the screenplays?

COPPOLA: Never. I would do the first draft and send it to him and he would make corrections and rewrite and change anything he wanted to and send it back to me, and then I'd rework it again, and it went back and forth. We work in totally different ways. He's much lazier than I am, which I think he'd admit. What we mainly have in common is that we both like to play baccarat and shoot dice. I like Mario very much.

PLAYBOY: Since you weren't a famous director at the time, why did Paramount approach you about making the film?

COPPOLA: The book hadn't yet made an impression. A lot of directors, including Richard Brooks and Costa-Gavras, had already turned it down. At that time, I had an interesting reputation as a director who could make a film economically. Also, I was a writer and I was Italian, so I seemed like an intelligent shot.

PLAYBOY: Had you heard about *The Godfather* before reading it and hating it?

COPPOLA: Yes, and it's a strange story. One Sunday afternoon, I was sitting around my home in San Francisco, reading *The New York Times*, and I saw an ad for a new book. Couldn't tell what it was about from the book cover—it looked kind of solemn. I thought it might be an intellectual work by some new Italian author named Mario Puzo, so I clipped the ad. I was just going to inquire about it. Right then, Peter Bart, a friend of mine, came by with someone I'd never met before: Al Ruddy, who later became producer of *The Godfather* but at that time had nothing to do with the project. We started talking and Peter mentioned a book he'd just heard about: *The Godfather*, by Mario Puzo. He explained what it was about. I had no interest in filming a bestseller, so I said, "No kidding—I just noticed an ad for it." At that very moment, the phone rang. It was Marlon Brando. I'd contacted him to ask if I might send by the script of *The Conversation*, which I'd written with him in mind. He was just calling to say, "Sure, send the script over."

That all happened in one afternoon. Several months later, Al Ruddy was named producer of *The Godfather*, I received my first offer to direct it and Marlon Brando would shortly have the lead. It still seems bizarre to me that the various elements came together that day in my home.

PLAYBOY: Once you'd decided to direct the film, how did you get Brando for the title role?

COPPOLA: I must have interviewed 2000 people. We videotaped every old Italian actor in existence. But it became apparent that the role called for an actor of such magnetism, such charisma, just walking into a room had to be an event. We concluded that if an Italian actor had gotten to be 70 years old without becoming famous on his own, he wouldn't have the air of authority we needed. Robert Evans, who was in charge of production at Paramount, wanted Carlo Ponti, which was an interesting idea: Get someone already important in life, that sort of thinking. But we finally figured that what we had to do was hire the best *actor* in the world. It was that simple. It boiled down to Laurence Olivier or Marlon Brando, who *are* the greatest actors in the world. We went back and forth on it, and I finally called Mario to ask him. He told me that, ironically enough, he'd been thinking of Brando as the Godfather all along and had, in fact, written him a letter to that effect over two years before. Brando seemed too young, even to me, but sometimes when you go out on a limb and connect with someone—Mario, in this case—you say, "It's God signaling me." So we narrowed it down to Brando. He had turned down the role in *The Conversation* some months earlier, but after he'd had a chance to read *The Godfather*, he called back and said he was interested, that he thought it was a delicious part—he used that word, delicious.

PLAYBOY: Were the studio moguls pleased?

COPPOLA: Hell, no. Ruddy liked Brando, but he said flatly that the studio heads would never buy it. We got in touch with Evans, pitched Brando and listened to him yell at us for being fools. By now, the book was becoming more and more successful, and it was outstripping me in terms of my potency as a director. It was getting bigger than I was. And they were starting to wonder if they hadn't made a big mistake in choosing me as the director.

Time passed, the book got bigger, the budget increased and I refused to send them any new casting ideas. Besides Brando, I already had it in my mind that I wanted Al Pacino, Jimmy Caan, Bobby Duvall, and so on. So a big meeting was scheduled with Evans, Stanley Jaffe, who was then the young president of the studio, and assorted lawyers.

Halfway into the meeting, I made another pitch for Brando. Jaffe replied, and these are his exact words, "As president of Paramount Pictures, I assure you that Marlon Brando will never appear in this motion picture and, furthermore, as president of the company, I will no longer allow you to discuss it." Boom. Final. Maybe from his point of view, at that time, it made sense. Paramount, before *Love Story*, had made a number of flops. And Brando's track record was even worse. But I insisted they hear me out, and Evans persuaded Jaffe to give me five minutes. I stood up as if I were a lawyer pleading for someone's life and went through all the reasons I thought only Brando could play the part. After I'd finished, I pretended to collapse in a heap on the floor.

So Jaffe finally relented, but he gave me certain conditions, the main one being that Brando take a screen test. I'd won. Now all I had to figure was how to get Marlon Brando to take a screen test.

PLAYBOY: How did you?

COPPOLA: Well, you have to realize that despite our telephone conversation, I was still scared shitless of Brando. So I called him and said I wanted to explore the role with him. At which point he jumped in and said he wasn't entirely sure he *could* play the role, and if he couldn't, he shouldn't, so why not get together and try it out? Wonderful, I said, let's videotape it. Fine, he said.

PLAYBOY: So he never really agreed to take the screen test?

COPPOLA: No. But he's a fantastic guy, so I'm sure if I'd been up front with him and told him the spot I was in, he'd have done it.

PLAYBOY: How did the nonscreen test go?

COPPOLA: I got a video recorder from some friends and showed up at Brando's house the next morning with a photographer and an Italian barber I'd already picked for the role of Bonasera, the undertaker in the film. I'd dressed him in a black suit and asked him to memorize the speech at the beginning of the movie, where Bonasera asks the Godfather for a favor. But I kept him outside. Brando met us in his living room, wearing a Japanese kimono, hair tied back in a ponytail. I just started videotaping him. He began to slide into character. He took some shoe polish and put it in his hair. His speech changed: "You t'ink I need a mustache?" I was anxious to make an intelligent comment, so I said, "Oh, yeah, my Uncle Louis has a mustache." He dabbed on a phony mustache and, as I videotaped him, he reached for some Kleenex. "I want to be like a bulldog," he mumbled, and stuffed wads of it into his mouth. He kept talking to himself, mumbling, and finally said, "I just wanna improvise."

I told my guys to keep quiet; I'd heard that noise bothers him. He always wears earplugs when he's working.

Then, without warning, I ushered in my barber friend, who went up to Brando and launched right into his speech. Brando didn't know what was going on for a moment, but he listened and then just started doing the scene. It was my shot. The thing worked, I had it down on tape. I'd watched 47-year-old Marlon Brando turn into this aging Mafia chief. It was fantastic.

Later, when I showed the tape to Evans and Jaffe, their reaction—and this is where I give them credit—was instantaneous. They both said he was great.

PLAYBOY: How was it, working with Brando?

COPPOLA: Well, we all wanted to impress Brando with the fact that each of us was special in some way or other. Jimmy Caan was always trying to make him laugh, Al Pacino would be moody and try to impress him with his intensity, and when Marlon would sit down to talk about Indians or politics, Duvall would sit behind him and do Brando imitations. I got along very well with Marlon. One of the most affectionate, warm men I've ever known. He'd come in late once in a while, but he'd make up for it with his sense of humor.

PLAYBOY: What's an example of his sense of humor?

COPPOLA: Besides "mooning" actors on the set? Well, there's this scene in *Godfather I* where they've brought Brando home from the hospital, and the orderlies are supposed to carry him up the stairs in a stretcher. The actors couldn't manage it, so I asked a couple of muscle-bound guys on the set—real physical-fitness types—to do it. They bragged that it would be no problem for them; so while they were off being costumed and made up, Brando got the other guys to load the stretcher with 1000 pounds of lead weights. So these two guys swagger out, pick up the weighted stretcher with Brando on it—and don't let on that they can hardly lift the thing. Well, about four steps up, they both yell, "Jee-sus, does he weigh a ton!" and they drop the stretcher, which breaks up everybody on the set. That sort of thing went on all the time.

PLAYBOY: Was it *all* as much fun as that?

COPPOLA: No, that's hindsight. If you'd checked with the crew while we were filming, they'd have said *The Godfather* was going to be the biggest disaster of all time. *The French Connection* came out while we were filming, and people who'd seen the film and who saw the *Godfather* rushes implied that our film was boring by comparison. There were rumors that

I was going to be fired every day. I was trying to save money during that time, sacking out on Jimmy Caan's couch. A bad period for me. I couldn't get to sleep at night. When I did, I had nightmares of seeing Elia Kazan walk onto the set, come up to me and say, "Uh, Francis, I've been asked to . . ." But Marlon was a great help. When I mentioned the threatening noises, he told me he wouldn't continue the picture if I got fired.

PLAYBOY: Were you given your head by the studio, were you allowed to improvise, or did you have to stick faithfully to the script?

COPPOLA: I wasn't given my head, by any means. A lot of the energy that went into the film went into simply trying to convince the people who held the power to let me do the film my way. But there was some spontaneity. For instance, Lenny Montana, who plays Luca Brasi, the *mafioso* in the picture who calls on the Godfather to thank him for being invited to the wedding—that's before he gets his hand pinned to a bar with a knife, of course—is not a professional actor, and he was terrified of playing the scene with Brando. We shot the scene a dozen times, but he froze on every take and forgot his lines. We finally gave up. Later, I wrote a new little scene where he was at the party, before his visit to the Godfather, practicing his speech perfectly over and over. We shot that and kept one of the scenes with Brando where Brasi froze, and it made the whole thing work well with the context of the story.

As for Brando himself, what an improviser! I told him at one point that I didn't really know how to shoot his final scene, just before he dies. What could we do to make his playing with his grandson believable? He said, "Here's how *I* play with kids," and took an orange peel, cut it into pieces that looked like fangs and slipped them into his mouth.

PLAYBOY: Orange peel along with the Kleenex?

COPPOLA: Right. And I thought, what a ridiculous idea. Then suddenly I saw it: Of course! The Godfather dies as a monster! And once I'd seen him with the orange-peel fangs, I knew I could never shoot it any other way.

PLAYBOY: How about Pacino, who really had the major role in both movies? How was he cast?

COPPOLA: We were ready to go into production before we found our Michael Corleone. The studio guys wanted Jimmy Caan to play him. I love Jimmy, but I felt he'd be wrong for Michael—and perfect for Sonny. Other people suggested Robert Redford, Warren Beatty, Jack Nicholson, Ryan O'Neal. But all I could see was Al Pacino's face in that camera. I couldn't get him out of my head. Even when I read the book, I kept seeing him as Michael. I nearly got fired over insisting on him, but it worked out in the end.

PLAYBOY: That's an understatement. After *The Godfather* went on to unparalleled success, what got you interested in doing a sequel?

COPPOLA: Initially, the idea of a sequel seemed horrible to me. It sounded like a tacky spin-off, and I used to joke that the only way I'd do it was if they'd let me film *Abbott and Costello Meet the Godfather*—that would have been fun. Then I entertained some Russian film executives who were visiting San Francisco and they asked me if I was going to make *The Godfather Part II*. That was the first time I heard the phrase used; I guess you could say I stole the title from the Russians.

In short, it seemed like such a terrible idea that I began to be intrigued by the thought of pulling it off. Simple as that. Sometimes I sit around thinking I'd like to get a job directing a TV soap opera, just to see if I could make it the most wonderful thing of its kind ever done. Or I imagine devoting myself to directing the plays of a cub-scout troop and having it be the most exciting theater in the country. You know that feeling when something seems so outrageous, you just have to do it? That's what happened to me.

Then after I started thinking about the idea, when I considered that we'd have most of the same actors, the scenes we might be able to develop in depth, I started feeling it really might be something innovative.

PLAYBOY: Do you, like some critics, think *Godfather II* is a better film than *Godfather I*?

COPPOLA: The second film goes much further than the first one. It's much more ambitious and novelistic in its structure. If you get off on the wrong foot with it, I can imagine that it would be like a Chinese water torture to sit through it. But it's a more subtle movie, with its own heartbeat. And it was very tough on some of the actors, especially Al Pacino.

PLAYBOY: Is it true that you had to stop shooting for two or three weeks when you were on location in Santo Domingo because Pacino was exhausted?

COPPOLA: Yes. The role of Michael is a very strange and difficult one and it put a terrific strain on him. It was like being caught in a kind of vise. In the first picture, he went from being a young, slightly insecure, naïve and brilliant young college student to becoming this horrible Mafia killer. In *Godfather II*, he's the same man from beginning to end—working on a much more subtle level, very rarely having a big climactic scene where an actor can unload, like blowing the spittle out of the tube of a trombone. The entire performance had to be kind of vague and so understated that, as an actor, you couldn't really be sure what you were doing. You had the tremendous pressure of not knowing whether your performance would have a true, cumulative effect, whether you were creating a monster or just being terrible. The load on Al was terrific and it really ran him down physically.

PLAYBOY: You obviously had a lot more control over *Godfather II* than *Godfather I*, didn't you?

COPPOLA: Absolutely. I had to fight a lot of wars the first time around. In *Godfather II*, I had no interference. Paramount backed me up in every decision. The film was my baby and they left it in my hands.

PLAYBOY: It would have been stupid of them not to, after all the money the first one made.

COPPOLA: But Paramount was fully aware of some of the chances I was taking and went along. I guess they had to, but they did.

PLAYBOY: One of the most important areas you explore in *Godfather II* is the connection between Mafia operations and some of our legitimate big-business interests. Are you saying that some corporations are no better and no worse than organized crime?

COPPOLA: Right from the very beginning it became clear, as I was doing my research, that though the Mafia was a Sicilian phenomenon, there was no way it could really have flowered except in the soil of America. America was absolutely ripe for the Mafia. Everything the Mafia believed in and was set up to handle—absolute control, the carving out of territories, the rigging of prices and the elimination of competition—everything was here. In fact, the corporate philosophy that built some of our biggest industries and great personal fortunes was a Mafia philosophy. So when those Italians arrived here, they found themselves in the perfect place.

It became clear to me that there was a wonderful parallel to be drawn, that the career of Michael Corleone was the perfect metaphor for the new land. Like America, Michael began as a clean, brilliant young man endowed with incredible resources and believing in a humanistic idealism. Like America, Michael was the child of an older system, a child of Europe. Like America, Michael was an innocent who had tried to correct the ills and injustices of his progenitors. But then he got blood on his hands. He lied to himself and to others about what he was doing and why. And so he became not only the mirror image of what he'd come from but worse. One of the reasons I wanted to make *Godfather II* is that I wanted to take Michael to what I felt was the logical conclusion. He wins every battle; his brilliance and his resources enable him to defeat all his enemies. I didn't want Michael to die. I didn't want Michael to be put into prison. I didn't want him to be assassinated by his rivals. But, in a bigger sense, I also wanted to destroy Michael. There's no doubt that, by the end of this picture, Michael Corleone, having beaten everyone, is sitting there alone, a living corpse.

PLAYBOY: Is that your metaphor for America today?

COPPOLA: Unlike America, Michael Corleone is doomed. There's no way that man is ever going to change. I admit I considered some upbeat touch at the end, like having his son turn against him to indicate he wouldn't follow in that tradition, but honesty—and Pacino—wouldn't let me do it. Michael is doomed. But I don't at all feel that America is doomed. I thought it was healthy to make this horror-story statement—as a warning, if you like—but, as a nation, we don't have to go down that same road, and I don't think we will.

PLAYBOY: A number of critics feel that you and others—including, perhaps, *Playboy*, with its series on organized crime—helped romanticize the Mafia in America. How do you respond to that?

COPPOLA: Well, first of all, the Mafia was romanticized in the book. And I was filming that book. To do a film about my real opinion of the Mafia would be another thing altogether. But it's a mistake to think I was making a film about the Mafia. *Godfather Part I* is a romance about a king with three sons. It is a film about power. It could have been the Kennedys. The whole idea of a family living in a compound—that was all based on Hyannisport. Remember, it wasn't a documentary about Mafia chief Vito Genovese. It was Marlon Brando with Kleenex in his mouth.

PLAYBOY: Where do the films depart most radically from the truth?

COPPOLA: Where you get into the mythic aspects of the Godfather, the great father who is honorable and will not do business in drugs. The character was a synthesis of Genovese and Joseph Profaci, but Genovese ordered his soldiers not to deal in drugs while he himself did just that on the side; Profaci was dishonorable at a lot of levels. The film Godfather would never double-cross anyone, but the real godfathers double-crossed people over and over.

PLAYBOY: Still, you won't deny that, whatever your intentions, *Godfather I* had the effect of romanticizing the Mafia?

COPPOLA: I felt I was making a harsh statement about the Mafia and power at the end of *Godfather I* when Michael murders all those people, then lies to his wife and closes the door. But obviously, many people didn't get the point I was making. And so if the statement I was trying to make was outbalanced by the charismatic aspects of the characters, I felt *Godfather II* was an opportunity to rectify that. The film is pretty rough. The essence of *Godfather I* is all Mario Puzo's creation, not mine. With *Godfather II*, which I had a greater part in writing, I emerged a bit to comment on the first film.

But the fact still may be that people like Marlon and Jimmy and Al too much. If you were taken inside Adolf Hitler's home, went to his parties and heard his stories, you'd probably have liked him. If I made a film of Hitler and got some charismatic actor to play him, people would say I was trying to make him a good human being. He wasn't, of course, but the greatest evil on earth is done by sane human beings who are miserable in themselves. My point is that you can't make a movie about what it's like inside a Mafia family without their seeming to be quite human.

PLAYBOY: What about those who say *not* that the Mafia is romanticized but that it simply doesn't exist?

COPPOLA: When people say the Mafia doesn't exist, in a way they're right. When they say it does exist, they're right, too. You have to look at it with different eyes: It's not a secret Italian organization, as it's portrayed. The most powerful man in the Mafia at one time wasn't Italian—he was a Jew. Meyer Lansky became powerful because he was the best at forging their common interests—that's just good business practice.

PLAYBOY: Except that, as far as we know, AT&T hasn't killed anyone in pursuit of its business.

COPPOLA: Who says? Who says?

PLAYBOY: Have you got something on AT&T?

COPPOLA: AT&T I don't know about, but ITT in Chile? I wouldn't bet my life that it hadn't. And it's not just business. How about the Yablonski murders in that coal miners' union? That was just the union equivalent of a Mafia hit. How about politics? Assassination of a president is the quickest way to bring about lasting and enormous social change. What's the difference between the United States' putting a guy like Trujillo in power so our companies can operate in the Dominican Republic, and the Mafia's handing the Boston territory to one of its *capos*? Then, after 20 years, either guy gets a little uppity and either organization feels free to knock him off.

PLAYBOY: Do you have any stories to tell about how the *real* Mafia reacted to the *Godfather* films?

COPPOLA: No.

PLAYBOY: And you wouldn't tell if you had any?

COPPOLA: No, I *would*. But the fact is I got some terrific advice from Mario Puzo. He told me that, in his experience, Mafia guys loved the glamor of show business and that, if you let them, they'd get involved. So Mario told me that I'd probably be contacted and when I was, I should refuse to open up to them. I shouldn't take their phone number, I shouldn't let them feel they could visit me. Because if there's one thing about them, it's that they respect that attitude. If you turn them off, they won't intrude into your life. Al Ruddy, the producer, was out having dinner with a lot of them, but I wouldn't participate in any way whatsoever with them.

Funny thing is, I've never been very interested in the Mafia—even though some important guys in the Mob have the same name as I do. "Trigger Mike" Coppola was one of Vito Genovese's lieutenants, I think. Terrible man.

PLAYBOY: Any relation?

COPPOLA: You mean Uncle Mike? No, of course not. Coppola is a common Italian name.

PLAYBOY: One Hollywood person who has been mentioned in connection with the Mafia is Frank Sinatra. How are your relations with him, considering that most people believe he was the model for Johnny Fontane, the singer-actor in *The Godfather?*

COPPOLA: I met Sinatra several times before filming started. They were very friendly meetings, since I never liked the idea of exploiting a fictionalization of a man, any man—and I told him so. I let him know that I didn't like that part of the book and that I'd minimize it in the film. Sinatra was very appreciative. Then he turned to me and said, "I'd like to play the Godfather."

PLAYBOY: *What?*

COPPOLA: It's true. He said, "Let's you and me buy this goddamned book and make it ourselves." I said, "Well, it sounds great, but. . . ."

PLAYBOY: Didn't Sinatra yell at Puzo once when they met in a restaurant?

COPPOLA: That incident was caused by some guy trying to make points with Sinatra by introducing the two of them very provocatively. Puzo never meant to embarrass him in person, and he told me he thought Sinatra behaved very understandably, considering the way they were introduced. But the fact remains that Mario, who is a very fine writer, was going broke with several good novels out, so he set out to write the biggest best seller in history. He was going to do anything he had to in order to get off the merry-go-round. So he wrote the perfect commercial book. And exploiting celebrities like Sinatra was something he felt he had to do. In the film, the Sinatra character plays a very small role. I'd have cut it out altogether if I'd had the power.

PLAYBOY: *Godfather II* was supposedly cut down from almost six hours. What did we miss?

COPPOLA: My heart was really in the Little Italy sequences, in the old streets of New York, the music, all that turn-of-the-century atmosphere. I had great scenes in the script that we couldn't include in the movie: There was one where Enrico Caruso showed up in the neighborhood and sang "Over There" to get guys to enlist for World War One; I had scenes of Italians building the subways, of young Vito courting his girl and joining his friends for music and mandolins and wine. . . . But it all got too long and too expensive.

PLAYBOY: Have you ever considered recutting the two movies into one giant film?

COPPOLA: It's an exciting thought, and it's just what I plan to do, believe it or not. In two years, I'm going to take both pictures, look over all the outtakes and recut them any way I want to, into *one* film. You don't often do that, because there's a certain inertia: Once a film is done, it's done, and you tend not to want to open things up again.

I've had an idea for a film I want to make, which I'd call *Remake*. I'd buy a film—any film—decide what I felt about it, then recut it, maybe shoot some things and make it into a whole new work.

PLAYBOY: Some critics have charged that in cutting *Godfather II*, you gave the picture a jerky, disjointed quality.

COPPOLA: Oh, they're full of baloney. They think a movie has to be what the last four movies were. There isn't a critic out there who knows what he's talking about. There may be three. Most are special-interest critics.

PLAYBOY: Meaning?

COPPOLA: Meaning that there's a lot of extortion and blackmail practiced by critics. A lot of them force the filmmaker to participate in certain things that accrue to the critics' advantage under the implied threat of a bad review.

PLAYBOY: Can you be more specific?

COPPOLA: No, because of course I'm not saying they're all that way. But suffice it to say that if this sort of extortion continues, it may blow up in the biggest scandal the field of criticism has known. It's corrupt right down to the bottom. And I'm speaking as one who has enjoyed generally good favor from the critics.

PLAYBOY: Which critics do you admire?

COPPOLA: Pauline Kael of *The New Yorker*. When she writes about a film, she does it in depth. When I make a bad picture, I expect her to blast me higher than a kite and I'll be grateful for that. I like *Time*'s Jay Cocks, who's a friend; Steven Farber and *Playboy*'s Bruce Williamson, who have liked some of my films; and Stanley Kauffmann of the *New Republic*, who often hasn't.

PLAYBOY: Your last three films, *Godfather I* and *II* and *The Conversation*, have been negative. Does that mean you've become more of a pessimist about life?

COPPOLA: Really, I'm not a negative person. Just the opposite. Starting now, I'm going to try to let the other side of me be more evident in my movies. It's funny, but I've noticed that very often filmmakers reflect things in their movies that are the opposite of what they really feel. I know some men whose films are highly sexual but who lead very tame home lives.

PLAYBOY: Why, in both *Godfather* films, are your female characters so submissive and acquiescent?

COPPOLA: That was how the women were represented in the original book and, from what I know, it was the role of women in the Mafia fabric. In *Godfather Part II*, I was interested in developing a more contemporary, political view of women in the person of his wife, Kay, and in her symbolic statement of power when she had her unborn son killed.

PLAYBOY: If Kay was such a liberated and defiant woman, why did it take her so long to leave Michael when she was no longer happy with him?

COPPOLA: It may seem like a long time, but actually they're together only six or seven years. How many people do we know who stay together unhappily for 15 years or more before they finally split? Also, during the 1950s, there were a lot of forces that tended to keep men and women together way beyond the point when they should have parted. Think of how many husbands have kept their wives and held their families together by promising that things would change just as soon as they became vice-presidents or had $100,000 in the bank or closed the big deal. I've strung my own wife along for 13 years by telling her that as soon as I was done with this or that project, I'd stop working so hard and we'd live a more normal life. I mean, that's the classic way husbands lie. Often the lies aren't even intentional. And it's easy to string a woman along for years by doing exactly that. Michael lies to Kay in that way and she believes him at first—because she wants to believe him.

PLAYBOY: Why *do* people tend to get sucked in by their own lies? Do they just sell out to the system?

COPPOLA: Well, people like myself, who decide that it's necessary to work within a system in order to be able either to change it or eventually to go off on their own to subsidize the kind of work they believe in, inevitably become changed by the process, if they go along with it. I know a lot of bright young writers and directors in Hollywood who are very success-ful—some of them I gave jobs to four or five years ago—and they're making a lot of money; but they're no longer talking about the things they used to talk about. Their conversation now is all about deals, about what's going to sell and what isn't. And they rave about their new cars and their new $400,000 houses. They don't even see or hear the changes in themselves. They've become the very people they were criticizing three years ago. Like Michael, they've become their fathers.

PLAYBOY: You don't think the same thing could happen to you?

COPPOLA: Sure, it could happen to me. One of the reasons I live here and not in Los Angeles is that I'm trying to keep my bearings. I have nothing against Los Angeles; it's a terrific center of talent right now, with the finest actors and certainly the best musicians and top people in every area, but there's always been a kind of collective madness that takes place in Hollywood, and it's very attractive and seductive, but you could lose yourself in it.

PLAYBOY: With the power and authority you wield, do you find it hard to keep a grip on your ego?

COPPOLA: Well, I'm 36 now, but I directed my first play in 1956—which is nearly 20 years ago—so I haven't been overwhelmed by power over-night. But sure, everyone has that problem. Let me give you an example: Al Ruddy, who's a nice guy but who's more of a wheeler-dealer than I am, used to walk onto the *Godfather* set now and then to suggest that an actor wear a hat for such and such a scene. I'd say, "No, I already thought this scene out, thanks, anyway." And no sooner would the sen-tence be out of my mouth than I'd think, fuck it, he's right, the actor *should* be wearing a hat. But I wouldn't, or couldn't, change it. If it had been George Lucas or someone like that, I'd have accepted the suggestion. But there are some people you can't take criticism from, perhaps because you feel threatened.

PLAYBOY: How would you feel threatened?

COPPOLA: The artist's worst fear is that he'll be exposed as a sham. I've heard it from actors, directors, everyone. I remember hearing Peter Sellers say, "Someday they're going to uncover me and realize I'm just a fake." Deep down, we're all living with the notion that our success is beyond our ability. In the last couple of years, I've grown more confident that I have ideas, that I can solve problems. That's as much as I'll give myself for now.

PLAYBOY: Do you ever feel uneasy about the power you have to influence other people's minds through film—or in other ways?

COPPOLA: I had a thought about that, a little fantasy that goes like this: I'm getting to be an influential person in San Francisco; what if I and five other powerful guys with cigars got together in a smoke-filled room to decide who would be the next mayor of San Francisco? We do it because we're good guys and we really want the city to be wonderful for everybody. Then I thought, what's the difference between five good guys holding that kind of power and five bad guys? Just good intentions, and intentions can be corrupted. And it's not just, say, in the political field. Let me make a statement about power: From now on, I'm determined to give tremendous thought to the impact any project I undertake will have on the public. It may sound wordy, it may sound obvious, but very few filmmakers ever really do that.

PLAYBOY: Did you think that way about *The Godfather?*

COPPOLA: No. How could I? I've spoken about the circumstances surrounding that project. But if the picture seems to some to be irresponsible because it celebrates violence, that was never my intent. In fact, there's very little actual violence in the film. It occurs very quickly. It's just that the violence happens to characters you like. If I were to roast 50 people alive in *The Towering Inferno*, it would be less horrible than shooting up a guy you've come to know and believe in. I once saw a fistfight in a New York restaurant that was modest by movie standards. But I'd never seen anything so frightening; they were real people.

PLAYBOY: How will this determination to consider public impact affect your next film?

COPPOLA: My next project is going to be delicate in that context. It's going to be a film about Vietnam, although it won't necessarily be political—it will be about war and the human soul. But it's dangerous, because I'll be venturing into an area that is laden with so many implications that if I select some aspects and ignore others, I may be doing something irresponsible. So I'll be thinking hard about it.

People are hungry for film now, susceptible to it because it reaches them on an emotional level. We're living in a time when things are changing quickly: Zip, there went the Catholic Church; zoom, that was the traditional family unit you just saw go by. People aren't sure of what they are feeling or what to believe in, so film can be a very influential medium now. Millions of people watched *The Godfather* around the world, each person spending three hours in a dark theater. Imagine how valuable that time with them is. It's priceless, and yet a filmmaker has it. I think that's an extraordinary thing.

PLAYBOY: Do you feel that Hollywood directors in the past have been irresponsible in propagating stereotypes, in exerting the wrong kind of influence over the public?

COPPOLA: Perhaps to some extent, but American films have *followed* the stereotypes, not set them. I read somewhere recently that the American film was responsible for our view of what an Indian was. But it isn't. The American film merely echoed and amplified the image that already existed in the national consciousness. It reinforced attitudes people already had about Indians when they first came here. The people who write films and the people who direct them have also been programmed. That isn't to say we shouldn't have the courage to try to break the mold, but it takes more courage and more originality than most people have.

PLAYBOY: Isn't Hollywood much more open to new ideas, new ways of doing things than it used to be?

COPPOLA: Yes, but it's chaotic. There's no leadership, maybe because the country itself has no leadership, either. Making movies is a great, complex, writhing crap game. No one is running anything and the only priority is the one that's become uppermost in America today: to make a profit.

PLAYBOY: When you started out in your career, did you have to do work you were ashamed of, just to make a profit?

COPPOLA: Well, I've done some stuff that hasn't worked out too well. But I never took on anything with the attitude that it was going to be terrible. It may have turned out that way, but I thought it was great while I was doing it. I was worried about certain films, though. I was worried while I was making them that things were going wrong and I didn't have the power to change them. During the shooting of *Finian's Rainbow* at Warner's years ago, I was brought in to direct a project that had already been cast and structured. I was also working in a big studio, in a methodology I didn't understand very well and over which I had no control. I'd express some doubts about the way things were going, and the people around me would say, "It's going great." I'll never get myself caught in that kind of situation again, because I now surround myself with people whose taste I respect and who have the right to hit all the sour notes they want. We had no sour notes on *Finian's Rainbow*; everyone kept saying how terrific everything was all the time. They were sincere, their motives were pure. But today I try to work with people who won't hesitate to say, "We're making a mistake." And if after thinking about it I agree with them, we stop and make changes. The one good thing I'd say about the old Hollywood, however autocratic and restrictive it may have been, is that you really got opinions from people who weren't afraid to give them and you always knew where you stood.

PLAYBOY: You mean from men such as Harry Cohn and Louis B. Mayer, the men who used to run the studios?

COPPOLA: Yes, and Darryl Zanuck and David Selznick and all the others. People weren't afraid to back up their opinions. Today everything is very confused and people kind of float around amorphously. Nobody backs up his hunches. There are a handful of directors today who have total authority and deserve it. And then there are a lot of other directors who really ought to be working with strong producers and strong writers, but they all think they're Stanley Kubrick. The *auteur* theory is fine, but to exercise it you have to qualify, and the only way you can qualify is by having *earned* the right to have control, by having turned out a series of really incredibly good films. Some men have it and some men don't. I don't feel that one or two hits or one or two beautiful films entitle anyone to that much control. A lot of very promising directors have been destroyed by it. It's a big dilemma, of course, because, unfortunately, the authority these days is almost always shared with people who have no business being producers and studio executives. With one or two exceptions, there's no one running the studios who's qualified, either, so you have a vacuum, and the director has to fill it.

PLAYBOY: Then Hollywood today isn't as good a place to make movies as it was when it was dominated by the big studios?

COPPOLA: There are maybe 10,000 of the finest actors in the world living in Hollywood, and there are fine writers and all kinds of talented people, but it's a sad, pent-up place. The actors are frustrated; they don't feel they have anyplace to work. When good actors say work, they mean work that uses the best of their talent, that uses them fully and creatively. And the truth of the matter is that there is nowhere to work that way these days. So they become petulant, they become depressed and they hate themselves for it. I feel that the film business today, with its tremendous potential to make profits, with a huge new audience of people all over the world who love to go to the movies, should be providing not only a product, something it can sell, but a hospitable place for creative people to work. Now, at a time when we stand on the eve of incredible profits, to think that no money, no percentage of any money is being used to provide a really stimulating place for actors and writers and directors to work, that all the energy is going into nothing but deal making, well, that's incredible to me. L.A. ought to be the acting and theater and film capital of the world, but nothing is happening.

PLAYBOY: Do you think you can make something happen with your own company?

COPPOLA: What I'm talking about can't be accomplished by a little company like mine. It would take a major company to really grab this thing by the tail.

PLAYBOY: There are rumors that you actually *were* offered control of a major studio.

COPPOLA: Really? Where'd you hear that?

PLAYBOY: From several people. Is it true?

COPPOLA: Let's say that I was approached by certain people and there were discussions, but that's all. Look, I must be honest with you. I've just finished a film and I'm 36. I have a good future in front of me and I'm trying to figure out what's the most exciting, positive way to go on working in films, and taking over a studio might have been a way. But as I see things now, that would take so much energy that I'm not sure it'd be worth it. I mean, if I were running a studio, it might take me 100 BTUs worth of energy to bend something a quarter inch; if I stay independent and use my own resources, those 100 BTUs could bend something a foot. I think events can make the decision for you, though.

If someone were to come up to me and offer me the most incredible film company in history and say, "Do what you want, we're behind you," then I'd interpret that as a cosmic indication that I should do it.

But look: The average executive of a movie studio may make $150,000 a year, and have a corresponding power over his company. As a film artist, I make much, much more than that and, consequently, have that much more power over my company. I've already made a million dollars for directing a film. So what do I do—ask for a million and a half? Perhaps the wisest thing to do is to use all my energies to make a film that grosses some stupendous amount, then go out and buy a major company and change it from the top. But I don't know. As soon as you become that big, you get absorbed.

PLAYBOY: You mean absorbed into a corporate structure?

COPPOLA: Yes, and not just in the movie business. Traditionally, our greatest heroes have been creators and inventors. A hundred years ago, what we paraded before the world was something called Yankee ingenuity. Every one of our great cartels and corporations was started by—that is, the original impulse came from—an Andrew Carnegie or a Thomas Edison or a Henry Ford, guys who used their inventive genius to create something better. And we made the best products in the world! And what those men created evolved into cartels, with their rules of property and profit. By the 1940s, after the United States had demonstrated that the ultimate result of this ingenuity was our emergence as the most powerful nation in the world, we were being run by huge, entrenched institutions completely hostile to that kind of inventiveness. By 1941, Henry Ford couldn't have built his cheap car. We might have *had* a Henry Ford in the 1940s. His name was Preston Tucker.

Tucker designed a car that could be built for a fraction of the kind of money the major companies were spending on their new models. It was a safe car, a revolutionary car in terms of engineering, and it was a beautiful car. In every way, it was a much better machine than the stuff the major companies were offering, the companies created by Ford and the others. But Tucker was called a fraud and he was destroyed. If he were alive today, he'd be hired by one of the major car companies and his inventions would be shelved or filtered out to the public as the company deemed economically prudent. Not to benefit the public but the company, and only the company. I'm going to make a film of Tucker's story someday.

PLAYBOY: Many of the opinions you've expressed to us, including this one, reflect the antiestablishment views of the radical movement. Are you politically active?

COPPOLA: No. Politically, no one knows what I am, including me. I have a lot of very articulate, superradical friends who criticize me for living in a big, expensive house; they apparently believe the world would be a better place if I moved into a shack. I notice, though, that, like me, they send their children to private schools. You see, I believe *everybody* should live in a nice house. I also believe in public education; until last year, I had my own kids in public schools, but I decided I wasn't going to sacrifice my children to an egalitarian ideal. The public schools in this city and all over the country are bad. I refuse to make my children guinea pigs to some social ideal, so I'm not going to send them to our crappy schools anymore. The whole school system has to be changed in this country. Just believing in certain things or giving your own money away isn't going to change anything.

PLAYBOY: What have you done yourself to help bring about change?

COPPOLA: In a self-sacrificing, personal way, probably nothing. Look, if someone announced next year that everyone should put all of his money in escrow and that we'd elect a board of men and women guided by the highest humanistic principles to administer the money to build homes and parks and educational centers for everyone, I'd do it in a minute. A lot of people would. But if half of the people in the world gave up their money and half didn't, the givers would be exploited by the keepers. Wealth is the only protection in a society that works on a system of property, of exploiter and exploitee. So that if I gave up what I earn, it wouldn't really improve anyone else's situation as much as it would deteriorate mine. There's no middle ground. If you have money, you're an exploiter; if you don't, you're exploited. We're in a fish tank in which there are only fish who eat and others who are eaten. If that's the only choice I'm offered, then I hope to be a fish that eats. We have to drain the tank and get into a newer, higher system altogether.

PLAYBOY: You certainly have the money now to afford beautiful things, and you've bought plenty of them. You also seem to have a craving for gadgets and expensive toys, like the $50,000 Mercedes you own. What kind of things do you like to spend money on?

COPPOLA: I've spent money on my house because I need space and because I want to enjoy my family. I've found that there are some things money can buy that truly make life more pleasant and give you more time to do the things that are really important, such as your work. When I was very young, I thought I needed a lot of things, but I've discovered that the more I have, the less I need. I've had terrific sports cars in my day, so now I drive a Honda car—not to be cute or anything like that but because I really like it. An XKE pulls up alongside and the guy looks at me in my little Honda. Nothing happens. I'm not jealous, because I've had that other car, I know I could have one and I don't need it anymore. There's something about possessions, living wealth, that really has to do with trying to prove something to yourself. My lifestyle is going to get simpler and simpler with the coming years.

PLAYBOY: What about that Mercedes?

COPPOLA: I didn't buy it. It was a gift, and I hardly ever use it. I also own a private jet. When I bought it, it was because I had once thought, "Wow, wouldn't it be crazy to have a private jet!" I do a lot of things and live in the same fantasy spirit that I write in. It's all make-believe to me. It's a fairy tale and I get to do all the things I can imagine. But I find that as I actually do them, I don't need them anymore. If I keep the private jet, it will be because I've found it useful. Even when I began buying things, I'd take whatever I'd bought out of the box and often I'd realize immediately that I really didn't need it or want it. I gave a lot of things away to people as presents, things I'd bought for myself the day before.

PLAYBOY: What does make you happy, besides your work?

COPPOLA: What brings me the greatest joy is the company of nice people and to be able to go through all the rituals with them, to eat dinner with them, cook with them, talk with them. I'm very European in that respect.

PLAYBOY: Do you have a lot of people around all the time?

COPPOLA: No. My wife is a very private person, which is probably why I'm still married to her, because I'm a big consumer of things and people, but I know I can't consume her, so I could never get tired of her.

PLAYBOY: Is she a big influence on your life?

COPPOLA: No, I can't say that. Everybody's wife is a big influence, but I don't want to give the mistaken impression that she's the quiet conceptualizer of my life. I discuss things with her and I think she's really bright and I respect her values a lot. She's not interested at all in money or material objects. She's interested in ideas. The best definition I can give you of my wife is that she's an impossible person to buy a present for, because there's nothing she wants. You know what I once gave her for Christmas? The kids were opening their presents and I went into the other room and made her a cappuccino, put it in a box, wrapped it up, brought it out and gave it to her. To this day, she maintains it's the best present she ever got, because she really wanted that cup of coffee. That's the way she is.

PLAYBOY: Generally speaking, what kind of women do you like to have around you?

COPPOLA: I've always enjoyed being around women older than myself. My wife is three years older than I am. I'm very attracted to intelligent women.

PLAYBOY: A lot of men in the movie industry use their power and their status as celebrities to play around sexually. Have you ever been tempted along those lines?

COPPOLA: I'd like to point out that it's not only the men who play around, as you put it. I know a female casting executive who uses her position just as a man might. It's incredible how this woman operates. She uses her position to keep five or six men going at one time and she's just as exploitive of her position as any man might be. I'm convinced that men and women are basically very similar in many more respects than we've been brought up to believe. We've been taught so-called masculine roles, just as women have been programed into so-called feminine ones. But the lines aren't so clearly drawn anymore, partly because of the women's movement. What I'm talking about has nothing to do with what people do in bed, necessarily. I know a great many heterosexual women who are very masculine in many ways, and many heterosexual men who are very feminine. I include myself among the latter and I always have.

PLAYBOY: Pardon us for mentioning it, but you didn't really answer our question about playing around. Would you rather not?

COPPOLA: What can I say? I love women. I can be walking down the street with my wife, and I'll see a beautiful woman and I'll pat my wife on the shoulder and say, "Hey, look at *her!*" But to some extent, the myth about famous movie directors' being pursued by women is not quite accurate. For one thing, there's so little time and so much work to be done. I once asked one of my assistants, who's always with beautiful girls, how he met so many of them. He said, "Easy; I tell them I'm going to introduce them to you." But he never does. And it would seem to me that although the life of a swinging bachelor might have some temporary appeal, it would be something that would run out pretty fast. I'm happy living with my wife and I enjoy the format of the traditional family. And I love kids. If I had my way, I'd have 10 of them. I've always been like that. One of my happiest summers was being a camp counselor. Even as a kid, I liked littler kids.

PLAYBOY: Were you happy as a kid?

COPPOLA: My childhood was very warm, very tempestuous, full of controversy and a lot of passion and shouting. My father, who is an enormously talented man, was the focus of all our lives, the three children and my mother. Our lives centered on what we all felt was the tragedy of his career. He was a very frustrated man, because, though he played first flute for the NBC Symphony under Toscanini, he felt that his own music never really emerged. I worked for Western Union one summer when I was 14 and, for some unknown reason—I still don't know *why*—I wrote up a phony telegram to my father telling him he'd landed a job writing the musical score for such and such a film. I signed it with the name of the guy who was in charge of music at Paramount Pictures. My father was overjoyed and yelled, "It's my break! It's my break!" And I had to tell him it wasn't true. He was heartbroken. Is that a terrible story?

Well, at least you know why I was so delirious when he shared the Oscar for best musical score with Nino Rota. Much of what is called source music—the compositions played by marching bands, performed on stage, and so on—in both *Godfathers* is his, and I used him not because he's my father but because he's an excellent composer.

PLAYBOY: When you were younger, did you dream of success on a scale like this?

COPPOLA: I always dreamed, I always fantasized. While I was in college, I'd tell people I was going to be a famous director, I was going to be rich. People who knew me then tell me they felt it would happen. But I never really believed it would happen, not like this.

PLAYBOY: Would you say the success has come easily to you, or did you have to take risks?

COPPOLA: I've been taking small chances all along. I've always been a good gambler and I've never been afraid to take a chance. I don't think the risks I've taken have been that dramatic, but even so, there have been times when I've stuck my neck out and almost had my head chopped off. But ultimately, I've been rewarded. I've been treated very well by Hollywood. And I've been treated very well by this country. The main reason I've been treated well is that I have taken risks, and people have some respect for that.

Of course, when you gamble, sometimes you lose. It goes in streaks. When the streak goes your way, you build on it as fast as you can, utilizing *their* money, not yours. You try to catch your streak in anything.

PLAYBOY: One last question: You've said you'd never make a *Godfather III*. But is the story of Michael Corleone really over?

COPPOLA: Nine times out of 10, people who say they're never going to do something wind up doing it. Right now, I don't want to make another sequel. But maybe 30 years from now, when I and all the actors have gotten really old, then it might be fun to take another look.

February 1974

CLINT EASTWOOD

A candid conversation with the world's number-one box-office star

About 10 years ago, rumors started drifting back to Hollywood that a new movie, directed by an Italian, shot in Spain and starring an American actor hitherto known only for his labors as the second lead in the moderately popular television series *Rawhide*, was packing moviehouses from Rome to Frankfurt. Studio heads shrugged. Flash in the pan, they said, scornfully dubbing *A Fistful of Dollars* a spaghetti Western. When *Fistful* was followed by the equally profitable *For a Few Dollars More* and *The Good, the Bad and the Ugly*, skeptics were forced to take a more serious look at the lanky, laconic star of these runaway hits: Clint Eastwood.

Eastwood's films have grossed some $150,000,000 worldwide to date, and nothing is more indicative of his rapid upward mobility than the rise in what the studios have been willing to pay for his services. From $75 a week as a contract player to a flat $15,000 for *A Fistful of Dollars*, Eastwood's price went to $400,000 for his first American-based feature, *Hang 'Em High*—and to participate in its production he formed his own company, The Malpaso Company, which promptly made a $1,000,000 deal with Universal Pictures for *Coogan's Bluff*. To help finance Malpaso projects, Eastwood began renting his increasingly costly services to other studios—to Paramount for the musical *Paint Your Wagon* ($750,000 and a piece of the profits, including those made by the record album from the film, in which surprised Eastwood aficionados discovered that the previously semi-inarticulate lone stranger could sing creditably, if not operatically); and to MGM for *Kelly's Heroes* ($1,000,000) and *Where Eagles Dare* ($1,000,000).

All plus percentages, of course. Since then, he and Malpaso have virtually been able to write their own ticket—a ticket that has often specified, of late, that Eastwood tackle directorial as well as acting chores.

Malpaso is a small, highly mobile operation, consisting essentially of Eastwood himself; Robert Daley, who acts as the company's producer; Sonia Chernus, the story editor; and a tall blonde secretary and troubleshooter named Carol Rydall. Eastwood likes to keep things simple. His personal tastes are equally unpretentious. Invariably dressed in jeans, hatless and tieless, he's the antithesis of everything that once stood for Hollywood glamor. He and his wife, the former Margaret Johnson—to whom he's been married for 20 years—live quietly with their two children, Kyle, five, and Alison, one, in Carmel, not far from Eastwood's native San Francisco and a six-hour drive up the coast from the smog of Los Angeles and the demands of Hollywood society. An evening with the Eastwoods is likely to consist of dinner with two or three couples as guests; the only full-scale social event with which they're involved is the annual Clint Eastwood Invitational Celebrity Tennis Tournament at Pebble Beach, the proceeds of which—nearly $50,000 last year—go to local charities.

Another Eastwood quality is intense loyalty to his friends. Before he would sign on for *Fistful*, he insisted that the Italian producer agree to bring over his old army buddy Bill Tompkins (now deceased) to act as stunt coordinator. He promoted Ted Post, a television director who had worked with him on a number of *Rawhide* episodes, to feature films with *Hang 'Em High*—and chose him once more to direct his most recently released starring vehicle, *Magnum Force*, for which Warner Bros. executives are already confidently predicting a $40,000,000 gross. Another close friend is Don Siegel, who directed Eastwood in *Coogan's Bluff*, a contemporary melodrama about an Arizona sheriff sent to New York to extradite a local hood; *Two Mules for Sister Sara*, which featured Eastwood as the protector of a whore in nun's clothing played by Shirley MacLaine; *The Beguiled*, a Gothic horror tale with Eastwood as a wounded soldier who falls into the none-too-gentle hands of the students at a girls' school during the Civil War; and *Dirty Harry*, the saga of a tough San Francisco cop (to which *Magnum Force* is a sequel). Characteristically, when Eastwood set out on his maiden effort as a director, with *Play Misty for Me* (in which he also starred), he cozened Siegel into playing a small role as a bartender.

To learn more about Eastwood, *Playboy* asked longtime contributor, film critic and University of Southern California cinema professor Arthur Knight to interview him. Here's his report:

"Though Eastwood is the world's hottest star, it's hard to believe he believes it. And it's difficult to reconcile the real Clint Eastwood—gentle, soft-spoken, self-effacing—with the violent men he's played onscreen, men who were ready to shoot first and talk later, if at all. There are other contradictions; he's a physical-fitness buff but a chain beer drinker; he enjoys shooting but refuses to hunt; hates giving out autographs, but the fans who besiege him whenever he makes a rare personal appearance are unlikely to discover this unless they become unbearably persistent. You won't find Eastwood in the 'with-it' spots of Hollywood: a big night out, for him, might be spent with a few friends in a bar. One with a good jukebox; he's a former musician who once played piano and jazz trumpet.

"*Playboy's* interview with Eastwood took place in three separate sessions, variously fueled with peach kefir, herb tea, beer, macadamia nuts, sun-dried apricots and saucer-sized oatmeal cookies from the nearest organic-food store. The first session came precariously close to not coming off at all. We had arranged to meet at my hotel in Sausalito at four P.M. (after a day's shooting on *Magnum Force*) to start the interview. But when Eastwood arrived, very much on time, the tape recorder wouldn't work. Eastwood said he thought he could borrow one from a friend, ducked out the back way and returned in about 10 minutes bearing a cassette recorder—but with only one cassette, good for a single hour's worth of conversation. Frantic telephone calls turned up a shop that promised to remain open for us—in a town about 10 miles away. Seeing that I was without wheels, Eastwood drove me over.

"The second session took place in the suite of offices Eastwood maintains over the startlingly named Hog's Breath Inn, a restaurant of which he's part owner in Carmel; and the third—for which I was joined by *Playboy* Associate Editor Gretchen McNeese—in the Malpaso company's offices in a five-room bungalow in Universal City. The walls are decorated with posters; looming in one corner is a life-sized cardboard cutout of Eastwood—which, like his best-known screen characterizations, is curiously one-dimensional and strangely ominous. The most bizarre object in his private office, though, is a three-foot-high, balloon-shaped, shocking-pink, papier-mâché rabbit piggy bank. Definitely not a Playboy Rabbit, the creature wears a sheriff's badge; from his mouth dangles the stub of a cigarette; and protruding from the hat he holds in his hand is the muzzle of a gun. It was, he explained, the gift of a fan—a schoolteacher in New Jersey who described it as her idea of the real Clint Eastwood. It would never have occurred to me to visualize Eastwood as a paunchy pink rabbit. But then, not many people do know the real Clint Eastwood, as I noted when I began this interview."

PLAYBOY: You're the world's number-one box-office star, yet to the public you're almost as much of an enigma as the characters you portrayed in your first screen hits, the laconic loner of the spaghetti Westerns. Why is that?

EASTWOOD: Oh, I guess I'm something of a recluse; when I'm not working, I like to just hide out. And I was never particularly in with the press.

PLAYBOY: You have the reputation of being difficult to interview.

EASTWOOD: Do I? Well, it's not easy for me. I'm not too thrilled with the idea of talking about myself. I have no idea what *Playboy* wants, how I should reply to a *Playboy*-type question.

PLAYBOY: What's a *Playboy*-type question?

EASTWOOD: The kind you answer with something like. "No, I didn't fuck her in 1941." I can't make up anything exciting to jar the readership; it's a talent I distinctly lack.

PLAYBOY: Have you done any interviews you regret?

EASTWOOD: Yes, because of the sheer boredom of it all. I've done talk shows where you get on and it doesn't go right—whether it's because of the mood you're in or the moderator's in, or both, it doesn't jell—and you kind of sit there and think, "Let's cut to the film clip, quick, before you fall asleep. Or the audience falls asleep." But I find myself kind of on the defensive about interviews, because the thing everybody seems to like is shock. I've always admired guys who can do that. Bang-bang. Whoosh. I've read your interviews with people who really work at giving the shock treatment, and they do it well. Like Lee Marvin, Raquel Welch. If I could talk like Lee, my interviews might be more exciting to read. I don't have that capability.

PLAYBOY: Your name doesn't surface often as a participant in those nightclub brawls that are always making the columns. Yet Clint Eastwood onscreen is a guy who's always using his fists. Can you take care of yourself in a real fight?

EASTWOOD: I get by.

PLAYBOY: Do you get in many?

EASTWOOD: No, not too many. I don't provoke a lot of them. You know, there's a lot of actors who claim they're always being harassed. But I'm never harassed. People leave me alone.

PLAYBOY: Maybe that's because you're 6' 4" and weigh 198 pounds.

EASTWOOD: I don't know whether that has anything to do with it. Probably it's because I don't carry a big entourage. When I go someplace, it's usually just for a quiet beer, and then I'm gone before the action starts. I come and go like The Whistler on the old radio program, you know. And I don't do much nightclub crawling. I can't hack that. I don't go to too many functions around here at all. I guess the last big one I attended was the Academy Awards show, and I'm still shaking my head over that one.

PLAYBOY: That was last year, when Charlton Heston got stuck on the freeway ramp and you filled in. Were you nervous?

EASTWOOD: Well, I didn't have time to think about it. Which was probably fortunate. First of all, I thought the guy—Howard Koch, the producer of the show—was joking when he asked me to do it. He came up to me and told me, "Charlton Heston isn't here!" And I said, "So what?" Then he started telling me about filling in for him, and I couldn't believe he was asking me. I said, "Where's Gregory Peck?" You know, some of the more distinguished members of the Academy. "There must be somebody around who could come out here and lend a little class to the thing," I said. But Koch's eyes were kind of twitching; sweat was running down his forehead and the TV guys up there were doing their countdowns: "Ten . . . nine . . . eight . . . seven," and I'm standing there listening to him, and all of a sudden he's whisking me backstage. My wife, Mag, was really kind of responsible for the whole thing. She said, "Go ahead! Help him out!" And then, of course, she was laughing hysterically in the audience. All I could hear out there was her and Burt Reynolds. They both have very distinctive laughs, the kind you can distinguish out of several thousand people, and there they were in the front row, cracking up.

PLAYBOY: What did you say to her afterward?

EASTWOOD: By that time, I didn't care. After I walked off, I went backstage, into a pressroom, and I saw a little ice chest on the floor. I looked in the chest and there was a six-pack of Olympia. It was like, you know, some angel had put it there. So I ripped open about four of them and some page was running back and forth, looking in as I drank them. Finally I went out and sat down in front with Mag, and she said, "A page was just down here asking me how many beers you could drink before you'd get drunk."

PLAYBOY: How many can you?

EASTWOOD: Quite a few, but at that point I needed about 10.

PLAYBOY: Tell us about your wife. How long have you been married?

EASTWOOD: Twenty years last December.

PLAYBOY: With marriages, even those of long standing, breaking up at a rapid rate, why do you think yours has lasted so long?

EASTWOOD: Gee, I don't know. I'd better not say too much; I'm liable to jinx it. I guess people grow away from each other, whether it takes 20 years or one. I don't think that's happened in our case.

PLAYBOY: Why not?

EASTWOOD: I'd say I'd have to give Mag a lot of the credit. She's a bright girl, and she's interested in a lot of the things I'm interested in. You know, we were married very young; I don't really recommend getting married that young. But you can't say exactly; the right age for one person isn't the right age for another. The luck, I guess, is in getting the right partner. There are so many things that can go wrong, it has to be somewhat of a crapshoot. I just think when you're older, sometimes, you know a little more about what you like in a woman.

PLAYBOY: What *do* you like in a woman?

EASTWOOD: Well, many things. What I mean is, when you're older, you appreciate things other than physical attraction, which is the basis of so many young relationships. Though I don't think it was in ours. I mean, we were physically attracted, but we also had everything in common. We both liked the same kind of music—jazz and classical, like Bach—and we'd go to the same kind of places.

PLAYBOY: Your wife's a blonde, but far from a dumb blonde. Have you ever been turned on by that type?

EASTWOOD: For marriage, no.

PLAYBOY: For fooling around, but not for marriage?

EASTWOOD: Sure, fooling around a little, hanky-panky, you know, sitting in the saloon with that old patter: "Do you come here often? Are you new in town?" No, seriously, I'm not turned on by a dumb chick—for anything. What's that old joke: "What do you talk about afterward?" There's an awful lot of afterward, very little during. Before and after, there have to be many other things. And I think friendship is important. Everybody talks about love in marriage, but it's just as important to be friends.

PLAYBOY: How did you meet Mag?

EASTWOOD: On a blind date up at Berkeley. When we got married, I was going to L.A. City College, and she helped support us. She worked for an export firm called Industria Americana—a little company that exported auto parts here in Los Angeles. And she worked for Caltex and Catalina, a couple of those swimsuit manufacturers, as a model. She was a good bathing-suit type.

PLAYBOY: Is she still a good bathing-suit type?

EASTWOOD: Yeah, she is. She worked for a while, and then she got hepatitis very badly—about as badly as you can get it without ceasing to exist. She had to quit, not do anything for a year. By that time, I was steadily employed. Fortunately.

PLAYBOY: Is there any connection between Eastwood the family man and the character you play on the screen—the fanatic cop from *Dirty Harry*, the Man with No Name from *A Fistful of Dollars*, the disc jockey from *Play Misty for Me*, the mysterious avenger from *High Plains Drifter*?

EASTWOOD: Well, I think I'm a little bit of all of those. Everybody has certain elements of himself in every role he plays. Maybe the thing that makes me work in the type of roles I'm more famous for, like the lone Westerner or the rebel police officer, is that I'm an individual in real life.

PLAYBOY: In what way?

EASTWOOD: Well, I've been lucky enough in life to head up my own company at a young age, make my own decisions, shape my own career. With a lot of help, of course. I guess I'm pretty self-sufficient, and I think that's appealing from the audience's point of view, because there are so many things to feel unself-sufficient about in life. Everybody likes to look at a moving picture and say, "That's the way I'd like to be when I grow up," "That's the way I would have handled it if I had lived in 1840" or "If I could just be that self-sufficient, I could dump the shrink and put all the payments in the bank." I think there's a dream in every man's mind of being an individual, but it's harder every year to be one. The tendency is to join something—join the left, join the right, join the Phi Beta this, the Kappa Kappa Gamma that. Everything is joining.

PLAYBOY: Do you join anything?

EASTWOOD: No, it's not my thing. But I've had to join a lot of unions at one time or another, because I had many different jobs before I got into pictures.

PLAYBOY: What kind of jobs?

EASTWOOD: Well, as a kid I had summer jobs all over Northern California—hay baling around Yreka, cutting timber for the Forest Service near Paradise. The forestry job was mostly fire fighting; we'd cut timber when we weren't fighting fires. Then, after I got out of high school, my family moved from Oakland up to Seattle, and I went to Springfield, Oregon, just outside Eugene, to work for the Weyerhaeuser Company.

PLAYBOY: As a lumberjack?

EASTWOOD: Yeah, up in the hills, and in the pulp mill at Springfield.

PLAYBOY: How long were you there?

EASTWOOD: Between the lumberjacking and the millwork, maybe about a year, year and a quarter. The dampness finally got to me and I moved on. Around Eugene, in the Willamette Valley, it's beautiful, but in the winter it socks in. You go six, seven months without seeing blue.

PLAYBOY: What else did you do?

EASTWOOD: I bummed around three, four different jobs around Seattle. I worked for Bethlehem Steel on the graveyard shift, in front of a furnace.

PLAYBOY: Like Peter Boyle in *Joe*?

EASTWOOD: Yeah, I felt like Joe. I wasn't there very long. After that, I went to work for King County as a lifeguard and swimming instructor. That was in Renton, near Seattle.

PLAYBOY: Where the Boeing plant is?

EASTWOOD: I worked there, too, at Boeing, in the parts department. People would call for parts, and you'd get them stuff out of the inventory, fill out the forms. And I drove a truck—short-trip stuff, loaded and unloaded—for the Color Shake organization in Seattle.

PLAYBOY: What's that?

EASTWOOD: It's an outfit that dyes shakes.

PLAYBOY: Shakes?

EASTWOOD: For siding.

PLAYBOY: Not milk shakes.

EASTWOOD: No, no; I would have gotten acne at a very early age. Anyway, just about the time I made up my mind to go back to school—I was going to be a music major—I got this notice from the government: "Greetings from the President."

PLAYBOY: This was during the Korean War?

EASTWOOD: Yeah, but except for the 16 weeks of basic training, I spent all my military career in the swimming pool at Fort Ord.

PLAYBOY: How did you manage that?

EASTWOOD: Well, I'd taught swimming before going into the Army, and they needed a couple of guys to help out at the pool there. So I got up and went into my act as a Johnny Weissmuller type. This was before Mark Spitz and Don Schollander. Anyway, I told them I was absolutely the greatest swimmer going, things like that, and I ended up getting the job. When we started out, there were this buddy of mine and I, and a master sergeant and four sergeants over us, and a lieutenant over them. Everybody got shipped to Korea except me; my name just didn't come up. So I figured I'd make the best of it and went up and talked to the captain. I said, "Look, I'm only a private, but I think I can handle this swimming-pool thing," and he said, "Well, I don't even know how to swim, so go ahead and run it. You're wearing a sweatshirt; nobody will know you're just a private." So I stayed there and hired four other guys to work for me. We had a pretty good swimming-instruction program going, got quite a few excellent ratings—like four-star movie reviews. I even lived down at the pool; it was a terrific deal for being in the service. And then, after I got out, while I was going to school, trying to break into pictures, I worked at a Signal Oil station, right across from the unemployment office on Santa Monica Boulevard in L.A., and for a while I dug swimming pools.

PLAYBOY: Did the physical build-up you got from all these jobs help later in your action-movie roles?

EASTWOOD: Well, they kept me in shape. But I wasn't trying to keep in shape; it was just a matter of survival. Digging swimming pools certainly wasn't mentally stimulating. I'd put down my shovel and sneak off in the middle of the day, get to a public phone and call my agent: "Anything? Anything?" Actually, though, what was important about those jobs was that they provided me with great places to observe the workingman. On those kinds of jobs, you run into some wild characters. I'd like to make a movie about some of them.

PLAYBOY: Do you think your bumming around gave you a greater insight into people and their motivations than you might have gained if you'd gone straight through school as a drama major?

EASTWOOD: Definitely. I think it's helped me judge what audiences like in the way of entertainment: escape from that kind of existence.

I believe that's probably the secret to my whole career. The choice of material—and the judgment of whether an audience will buy the material—is what makes an actor or a director a success.

PLAYBOY: When did you realize you were going to be a success?

EASTWOOD: Not for a long time. The number of people who had faith that I'd make it in show business I could name easily on one hand—and have a few fingers left over.

PLAYBOY: How did you happen to go into showbiz? Had you wanted to be an actor since childhood?

EASTWOOD: No, not really. I remember in junior high school, in Oakland, I had a teacher decide we were going to put on a one-act play, and she made up her mind I was going to be the lead. It was really disastrous. I wanted to go out for athletics; doing plays was not considered the thing to do at that stage in life—especially not presenting them before the entire senior high school, which is what she made us do. We muffed a lot of lines. I swore that was the end of my acting career.

PLAYBOY: What changed your mind?

EASTWOOD: Well, while I was at Fort Ord, I met a lot of actors—Martin Milner, Dave Janssen, Norman Bartold. After discharge, they went back to acting, and I was curious about it, wondered what it would be like. There was also a still photographer named Irving Lasper—he's dead now—who was a friend of mine, and he tried to encourage me to become an actor. So I signed a contract with Universal. They paid me $75 a week, I think; that was an enormous amount, it seemed to me then. I'd been going to school on the GI Bill at $110 a month, plus working in the afternoons at a gas station and nights managing the apartment house I lived in; so $75 a week sounded great.

PLAYBOY: Did you get the contract at Universal through a screen test?

EASTWOOD: In those days, they'd make interview tests, not acting tests. They'd sit you in front of the camera and talk—just as we're talking now. I thought I was an absolute clod. It looked pretty good; it was photographed well, but I thought, "If that's acting, I'm in trouble." But they signed me up as a contract player—which was a little lower than working in the mailroom.

PLAYBOY: What movies did you appear in at Universal?

EASTWOOD: Oh, all the biggies. I think I played in about 13 or 14 films over the year and a half I was there. My parts ranged from one-liners to four-liners—though to look at some of the billings in *TV Guide* these days, you'd think I co-starred in those films.

PLAYBOY: Do you remember your first part?

EASTWOOD: I think it was called *Revenge of the Creature from the Black Lagoon*. No, just *Revenge of the Creature*. Then I was in *Never Say Goodbye*, *Francis in the Navy* and *Tarantula*. None of them were what you'd call top-rank movies. But I learned a lot. There were classes every day, and I went to them, and I'd hang out on sets, behind the scenery somewhere—trying to be very unobtrusive—and watch people operate.

PLAYBOY: What can you learn from watching a second-rate movie being made?

EASTWOOD: I think you learn from seeing a bad movie as much as you do from seeing a good movie. I once went to a film festival where the audience was made up of students—or I gathered they were—and I forget what the film was, but it wasn't very good. And all these kids were yelling, making noises at the film, sort of as if it were a Sunday matinee of five-year-olds. And that seemed kind of stupid to me. I thought to myself, "Don't they realize this piece of crap on the screen can tell them a lot?" It's just like acting in a picture with a bad director; it gives you some point of reference, some comparison, so that when you meet someone who is halfway adequate, you see what makes the difference.

PLAYBOY: Why did you leave Universal at the end of a year and a half?

EASTWOOD: They eighty-sixed me. My salary had gone up to $100 a week after six months, and then it was supposed to go up to $125. They called me in and said they didn't feel I was of any value to them at $125, but I could stay on at $100 if I wanted to. At first I was mad, of course, and I said, "What the hell, if they can't give me a raise, I'll take a hike." Then I decided I'd better hang in there another six months and get a little more experience. So I did, and after *that*, they dropped me. Still wasn't worth $125.

PLAYBOY: Then what did you do?

EASTWOOD: Television was going pretty good then, so I figured there'd be some opportunities for me. I got out and tried the cold world.

PLAYBOY: At that time, wasn't the attitude toward television pretty low among movie people?

EASTWOOD: I guess it was; TV was like a younger brother, or a second-class citizen. But to me, television was a logical place to go to really learn the business. Most of the people in television were doing the newest things, and in TV you had to work twice as fast, twice as hard to get half the credits. I learned a heck of a lot.

PLAYBOY: What shows did you do?

EASTWOOD: Oh, I did the circuit of the series that guys my age did then: *Navy Log, Men of Annapolis, Highway Patrol.* Didn't mean to get you overexcited there. I didn't play any giant parts, but they were improvements over what I'd been doing in those B movies—those three- or four-line bits.

PLAYBOY: On television you got five or six lines?

EASTWOOD: Yeah, well, I'd get a supporting role, or a semilead, because I could ride a motorcycle, jump off a building or some crazy thing. They didn't have to pay for a stunt man.

PLAYBOY: Do you still do your own stunts?

EASTWOOD: Some, but I used to do much more. When you start out, you think, "Aw, I'm gonna do that myself." Just for fun. Authenticity, you know.

PLAYBOY: Were you also trying to prove something?

EASTWOOD: Probably, yeah. But I enjoy doing stuntwork. As you become more important to the film, though, you have problems with the insurance company. In *Magnum Force*, my latest film, we had to use some doubles, because this guy I play drives a motorcycle 60 feet into San Francisco Bay. I wasn't about to do that.

PLAYBOY: Have you ever had any mishaps with a stunt?

EASTWOOD: Oh, I've been punched around a little bit, kicked around, but nothing much. I've done a lot of things—driven over explosions and stuff like that—but I've been pretty lucky.

PLAYBOY: What's it like to drive over an explosion?

EASTWOOD: Well, in *Kelly's Heroes*, which we made on location in Yugoslavia, it was rough, because the special-effects man used dynamite—real explosives—rather than just cork and black powder. He was an excellent special-effects guy—a German, Karli Baumgartner. But those explosions are quite dangerous, if you're ever on top of one.

PLAYBOY: And that's where he put you?

EASTWOOD: Well, he put me close. He's good about setting them off; does it right after you get past. In those situations, they're always careful not to have shrapnel involved.

PLAYBOY: Very considerate.

EASTWOOD: But there's still rocks and things that always get blown loose. Most of the American guys don't use the high explosive that Karli used.

PLAYBOY: Why did *he* use it?

EASTWOOD: Maybe he was getting even for World War II. I don't know; he just liked big explosions. We had one scene in *Kelly's Heroes* where we were supposed to run out and lie down and a barn was supposed to explode behind us. And Telly Savalas, he didn't want to do it. Brian Hutton, the director, said to me, "What do you think?" And I said, "Well, I'll do it, but first we ought to ask Karli what he thinks." So I went to Karli and said, "What's your opinion of this explosion?" He said, "I don't recommend your being in this stunt, because I just don't know." Which I thought was nice. I mean, a lot of guys would have said, "Go ahead, it's not me out there." So a couple of stunt guys did it; Baumgartner set it off and, sure enough, the building disintegrated right behind them. They were walking around talking to themselves, having trouble hearing for a few days. I do my own stunts whenever they're reasonable ones, but, like I said, not as many as in the old days back in television.

PLAYBOY: Were you working pretty regularly when you started out in TV?

EASTWOOD: They'd be two-, three-, four-day jobs, and then I'd be off for a while, collecting unemployment, digging more swimming pools. There were periods when I didn't work for four, five, six months at a time, and I got pretty depressed about it. Along about 1958, I had a sort of supporting role in a small film—it may have been the worst Western ever made—and it didn't do well, and I really thought about giving up.

PLAYBOY: What was the film?

EASTWOOD: *Ambush at Cimarron Pass.* That was sort of the low point of my movie career.

PLAYBOY: What brought you out of that slump?

EASTWOOD: I went down and visited a friend, Sonia Chernus, who was in the story department of CBS-TV. She works for me now, as *my* story editor. Anyway, we were sitting there talking by this coffee wagon in the basement at CBS and this guy came up to me and said, "Are you an actor?" And I said, "Yeah." He said, "What have you done?" So I listed a line of credits, always increasing the importance of the roles by about 50 percent, praying to God the guy would never ask to see *Ambush at Cimarron Pass.* Which, of course, he did. I was taking the whole thing kind of lightly, because, although I knew CBS was casting an hour television show, my agent had told me the lead had to be older than me—about 39 or 40. So the man—I didn't know who the hell he was—called me into an office and another guy came in wearing old clothes. Looked like he'd just been pushing a broom in the back room. I didn't know whether he was going to sweep under the chair or what.

PLAYBOY: Who was he?

EASTWOOD: Charles Marquis Warren, the producer of *Rawhide*. I can hardly wait until he reads his description in this interview. So, anyway, I was being very cool, and I just casually asked him, "What's the lead like?" And he says, "Well, there's two leads, and one is a young guy in his early 20s." My agent wasn't bright enough to find that out. So I started perking up, straightening out the wrinkles in my T-shirt, you know—I was just wearing Levis—and finally the guy said, "Well, we'll get in contact with you." I kind of halfway wrote it off, because I figured once they'd seen *Ambush at Cimarron Pass*, that'd be the end of it.

PLAYBOY: That wasn't one of your better hunches.

EASTWOOD: No; well, they called me about four o'clock that afternoon and said, "Come on down and make a film test," and I did that, and another one the next morning. The big wheels at CBS liked it, and I was picked, and Eric Fleming was picked as the other lead. That was a great day in my life; the money looked to me as if I'd be in a league with Howard Hughes.

PLAYBOY: End of depression?

EASTWOOD: Not yet, because after we made 10 of the 13 episodes we were supposed to do, the network pulled it off and shelved it. Here my career was, lying in the basement of CBS, because the word was that hourlong shows were out. So I decided to go up and visit my parents—they had moved from Seattle back to Oakland by then—and Mag and I got on a train. On the way from Los Angeles to Oakland, I got a telegram saying that the series had sold, after all, and to be ready to work on such and such a day. So Mag and I did a little champagne trick and yelled a lot; I stuck my head out the window and shouted a lot of profane things.

PLAYBOY: Such as?

EASTWOOD: I can't remember. As you get older, you know, you learn other forms of relieving tension. But at a certain age, standing in the middle of Sunset Boulevard and yelling "Shit!" at the top of your lungs does provide a certain release. I can use as big obscenities as the next guy when I'm bugged. I can go on for 15 minutes without a repeat. But don't ask me what they are.

PLAYBOY: Then you *do* get bugged? You're described as being unflappable.

EASTWOOD: Well, I may not be as cool as my exterior. Or maybe I'm the type who doesn't show it. I can't really be objective about it. But sure, some things bug me. Yesterday some guy, making a TV series, called and asked to use my dressing room as a set. So, being an economically minded person, I said, "Fine. Why build a whole set? Just move in and shoot." Then I go back and find the dressing room looks like a public toilet. I mean the place is an absolute shambles. I'm going to tell that producer just what I think of his group, as soon as my secretary nails him down.

PLAYBOY: Let's get back to *Rawhide*. That was one of the longest-running series on television. Didn't there come a time when you got sick of it?

EASTWOOD: Oh, sure, everybody gets sick of it. But I kind of hesitated bitching about it because before you get into a series, you hear actors complaining and you think, "Wow, what's this guy bitching about? He's making $50,000 a year!" So I didn't have any real beefs. Having the security of being in a series week in, week out gives you great flexibility; you can experiment with yourself, try a different scene different ways. If you make a mistake one week, you can look at it and say, "Well, I won't do that again," and you're still on the air next week. It was kind of like being in a stock company on film. You might get three or four scripts in a row that are turkeys, and that can put you in the doldrums if you let it; but you can take those scripts and try to do more with them, rewrite them, upgrade them a little, and if you can take crap and make it adequate, make it palatable to the public, then you feel you've accomplished something. And I learned a lot about crews, too. You do 250 hours of television, you learn what makes one prop man good and another fair and another lousy, and what makes one cameraman better than another one. You learn about leadership, how one week a crew can move very fast and efficiently and the next week drag. About 90 percent of the time, it's the fault of the director. And you just store those things up in your head.

PLAYBOY: But didn't you really want to get back into feature films?

EASTWOOD: Oh, sure; there isn't any television-series performer who would ever say he wouldn't rather be doing a feature film. It's the difference between writing a single story once or twice a year and having to fill a column every day. Some days there's just nothing to put in the damn column and you're having to wring it out, fill the space with something. During the last season of *Rawhide*, I had taken over the sole lead. Eric was having some kind of an argument with CBS over something, so they decided to try it with me alone. But that didn't exactly save the show, and it just kind of quietly died in 1966, as most series do when they go. At their height they give you a vast exposure—immediate recognition of some sort—and then they lose about 30 percent as they go along. So at the end, when it dies quietly, everybody says, "Oh, yeah, him."

PLAYBOY: You made your first Italian Western, *A Fistful of Dollars*, while you were still a regular on *Rawhide*. How did that happen?

EASTWOOD: Well, we had a break in shooting the series, from February or March to late May, early June. And about that time—this was in 1964—my agent called me and asked if I'd be interested in going to Spain to do a very low-budget Western, an Italian/German/Spanish coproduction. I laughed. I told him, "For six years I've been doing a Western every week. Hell, no, I'm not interested in it, especially not a European Western. It would probably be a joke." "Well," he said, "do me a favor. I promised the Rome office that I'd get you to read the script." So I read it, and about the 10th page I recognized it as a Western version of *Yojimbo*, the samurai film by Akira Kurosawa.

PLAYBOY: Had you seen *Yojimbo*?

EASTWOOD: Yeah. The funny thing was that this buddy and I had seen it together, and at the time we were both impressed by what a good Western it would make—the way *The Magnificent Seven* was made from *Seven Samurai*. But we thought it wouldn't sell; it would be too rough. Anyway, I read the script and, although the dialog was atrocious, I could see that it was very intelligently laid out. I said to Mag, who hadn't seen *Yojimbo*, "Read this and tell me what you think of it." And she read it and said, "Wow, it's really interesting. It's wild." So I told the agent. "OK, go ahead. I've really got nothing to lose on this deal, because if the picture turns out to be a bomb, it won't go anywhere." And I had a hunch that if it was handled well, it'd work.

PLAYBOY: Your hunches were improving.

EASTWOOD: Besides, it was a chance to go to Europe. I'd never been to Europe. So I signed on, even though it wasn't as much pay as I had made on TV.

PLAYBOY: What was the fee?

EASTWOOD: It was $15,000 for the total project.

PLAYBOY: No percentages?

EASTWOOD: No percentages, no nothing. The $15,000 was all I ever made from that one.

PLAYBOY: What was it about the *Dollars* character that appealed to you?

EASTWOOD: I was tired of playing the nice clean-cut cowboy in *Rawhide*; I wanted something earthier. Something different from the old-fashioned Western. You know: Hero rides in, very stalwart, with white hat, man's beating a horse, hero jumps off, punches man, schoolmarm walks down the street, sees this situation going on, slight conflict with schoolmarm, but not too much. You know schoolmarm and hero will be together in exactly 10 more reels, if you care to sit around and wait, and you know man who beats horse will eventually get comeuppance from hero when this guy bushwhacks him in reel nine. But this film was different; it definitely had satiric overtones. The hero was an enigmatic figure, and that worked within the context of this picture. In some films, he would be ludicrous. You can't have a cartoon in the middle of a Renoir.

PLAYBOY: Was the character of the Man with No Name defined in the script, or was he somewhat of your devising?

EASTWOOD: I kind of devised it. I even picked out the costumes. I went into Mattsons', a sport shop up on Hollywood Boulevard here, and bought some black Levis and bleached them out, roughed them up. The boots, spurs and gun belts I had from *Rawhide*; the hat I got at a wardrobe place in Santa Monica. The little black cigars I bought in Beverly Hills.

PLAYBOY: You don't smoke, do you?

EASTWOOD: No, I don't. I smoked the cigars only for those films. I didn't really like them, but they kept me in the right kind of humor. Kind of a fog.

PLAYBOY: Did they make you sick?

EASTWOOD: No, they just put you in a sour frame of mind. Those were pretty edgy cigars.

PLAYBOY: What about the poncho?

EASTWOOD: The poncho I got in Spain. Never had any doubles for that. Most of the time, in films you have everything in duplicate or triplicate, just in case you lose things in stunts. But I never had any doubles for the poncho.

PLAYBOY: Didn't it get a little ripe?

EASTWOOD: Well, if you *must* ask! Yeah, the poncho got a little dirty. I never washed it in three films, I'll tell you that.

PLAYBOY: Do you still have it?

EASTWOOD: It's hanging on the wall of a Mexican restaurant that belongs to a friend of mine in Carmel.

PLAYBOY: With a plaque underneath it?

EASTWOOD: Yeah, he's got a plaque with it. He wanted to put it on his wall, so I let him have it.

PLAYBOY: Would you take the poncho off the wall to make another *Dollars* film?

EASTWOOD: You mean if the same director, Sergio Leone, came back and said, "We've got a new place to take you"? I'd make any kind of film if

I liked the script. But I'd have to see the thing. I don't know; I doubt it at the moment.

PLAYBOY: What was working with Leone like?

EASTWOOD: Sergio and I got along fine. Of course, at first we couldn't converse much; he spoke absolutely no English, and my Italian was just *ciao* and *arrivederci*, and that was about it. So I did my own thing and he did his.

PLAYBOY: How long did it take before you could communicate with each other?

EASTWOOD: Well, it took three pictures. *A Fistful of Dollars, For a Few Dollars More* and *The Good, the Bad and the Ugly*. He speaks better English now and I speak a little better Italian. I suppose we met somewhere in the middle.

PLAYBOY: Do you have a faculty for languages?

EASTWOOD: No, I don't. If I majored in language, I wouldn't exactly be at the top of the class. I was speaking Spanish to somebody the other day, though, and I wasn't doing too bad. I wasn't just ripping along; this person, a Mexican, was speaking very fast, and I was doing my usual "*Repite despacio, por favor,*" but we got along. In the present tense. Not conjugating any verbs. But I think Mexican Spanish is easier to understand than what they speak in Spain. Where we were in Spain, making the *Dollars* films, was in Andalusia—Andalu*th*ia. They spoke extremely fast in that Andaluthian dialect. Somebody who doesn't even speak rapid English, like myself, really gets lost.

PLAYBOY: Did you have any misunderstandings with Leone, or with the crew, because of the language problem?

EASTWOOD: Yeah, but I couldn't possibly give you an example. After a while, of course, you do it purposely. Like in Italy, they have *cornettas*—you know what those are? A little sweet roll that you have in the morning with coffee. And I used to go into a store and put on a typical American accent—a kind of Texas-cowboy drawl—and say, "Ah'll have one a them there core-noodos. Raht."

PLAYBOY: Cornutos? You mean cuckolds?

EASTWOOD: Yeah. You can have a lot of fun with that—with the looks on their faces.

PLAYBOY: Did you realize at the time you were making *Fistful* that it would be such a runaway success?

EASTWOOD: I had more faith in it than the producers did. They thought it was going to be an absolute disaster when they saw the dailies. They wanted me to play a more expressive character.

PLAYBOY: Why did you feel the Man with No Name should be played in so deadpan a style?

EASTWOOD: My feeling was that the strength of this character was in his economy of movement and what the audience anticipates he's going to do. This builds up a constant suspense. If you can keep the audience's interest in what he's going to do next, you've really got it. The worst thing you can do is just impress the critics.

PLAYBOY: Is that a dig at critics who have described your performances as deriving from the "Mount Rushmore school of acting"?

EASTWOOD: No, actually, I've been treated well—flatteringly so—by the better, more experienced reviewers, people like Andrew Sarris, Jay Cocks, Vincent Canby and Bosley Crowther. Judith Crist, for some reason, hasn't been knocked out over everything I've done—or *anything* I've done, as a matter of fact. I think she liked *The Devil in Miss Jones*, but she thought *Beguiled* was obscene.

PLAYBOY: How do you feel about negative reviews?

EASTWOOD: I'm not overly affected by them; I figure everybody's entitled to his opinion, and reviewers are employed by publications to express those opinions. I've even seen unfavorable reviews of my pictures that I agreed with. I've always felt, though, that it's easier to write an unfavorable review than a favorable one. Because it takes more knowledge to write a good review. Anybody can do a pan, but to say what really works—that's tough. To take another area, jazz reviewers like Ralph Gleason and Leonard Feather can play musical instruments themselves. They know music. Consequently, if they do or don't like something, they're very specific about it in their reviews. They never make a general statement, like, "This musician is the worst player I've ever heard." Movie criticism is an art, too, but I'm often surprised at how much is left out of reviews. Once in a while, one will mention the music or the photography, but they don't point out the ways in which these blend into the total style of the film, the reasons it does or doesn't work.

PLAYBOY: How much influence have the critics had on your career?

EASTWOOD: Not too much. To me, what's really important is whether the public likes what I do.

PLAYBOY: The public certainly liked *A Fistful of Dollars*. Was the picture an immediate success?

EASTWOOD: Not exactly. What happened was that they had a sneak-preview engagement somewhere outside Naples, and the first night I guess the house was about a quarter full. They had some expert come up from Rome and he said, "It's a well-made film, but it will never make a lira." But the next night the house was full, and the night after that, people were lined up down the street, and pretty soon the major downtown theater men from Naples were asking, "Why can't we have this film? What's it doing out here in the sticks?" So they were forced to release it nationwide and renegotiate all their contracts.

PLAYBOY: Were you back in the States by then?

EASTWOOD: Yeah, making *Rawhide* again, and I kept looking in the trades for news about the movie. One day I saw an item in *Variety*, quoting an Italian from Rome: "Westerns have finally died out here." And I said to myself, "Wouldn't you know it?" But two weeks later, I read another article that said the big deal in Italy was that everybody was enthusiastic about making Westerns after the success of this fantastic new film, *A Fistful of Dollars*. That meant nothing to me, because the title we'd used during the shooting was *Magnificent Stranger*. Then about two days after that, there was another item from Rome, and it said, "*A Fistful of Dollars*, starring Clint Eastwood, is going through the roof here." And I said, "Clint Eastwood? Jesus Christ!" Then, I got a letter from the producer—who hadn't bothered to write me since I left, saying thank you or go screw yourself, or whatever—asking about making another picture.

PLAYBOY: That would be *For a Few Dollars More*, which was followed by *The Good, the Bad and the Ugly*. When did you finally start getting a percentage of the receipts?

EASTWOOD: With the third one. But even then, with three films that were successful overseas, I had a rough time cracking the Hollywood scene. Not only was there a movie prejudice against television actors but there was a feeling that an American actor making an Italian movie was sort of taking a step backward. But the film exchanges in France, Italy, Germany, Spain—all these countries—were asking the Hollywood producers when they were going to make a film starring Clint Eastwood. So finally I was offered a very modest film for United Artists—*Hang 'Em High*. It was a good film, analyzed capital punishment within a good story. I formed my own company, The Malpaso Company, and we got a piece of it and did the film for $1,600,000. It broke even almost immediately, and then went into the black and was a very healthy film. That's kind of when things started picking up.

PLAYBOY: Why did you form your own company?

EASTWOOD: My theory was that I could foul my career up just as well as somebody else could foul it up for me, so why not try it? And I had this great urge to show the industry that it needs to be streamlined so it can make more films with smaller crews. The crews will be employed more, so there'll be just as much work. What's the point of spending so much money producing a movie that you can't break even on it? So at Malpaso, we don't have a staff of 26 and a fancy office. I've got a six-pack of beer under my arm, and a few pieces of paper, and a couple of pencils, and I'm in business. What the hell, I can work in a closet.

PLAYBOY: What does Malpaso mean?

EASTWOOD: In Spanish, it can mean bad pass or bad step. In this case, it means bad pass. I own some property on a creek in the Big Sur country called Malpaso Creek; I guess it runs down a bad pass in the mountains.

PLAYBOY: But you've continued to do films for other companies, as well as for Malpaso.

EASTWOOD: Sure. It depends on the story.

PLAYBOY: What's been your favorite role?

EASTWOOD: It would probably be *Dirty Harry*. That's the type of thing I like to think I can do as well as, or maybe better than, the next guy. He's very good at his job, and his individualism pays off to some degree. What I liked about playing that character was that he becomes obsessed; he's got to take this killer off the street. I think that appealed to the public. They say, "Yeah, this guy has to be put out of circulation, even if some police chief says, 'Lay off.'" The general public isn't worried about the rights of the killer; they're just saying get him off the street, don't let him kidnap my child, don't let him kill my daughter.

PLAYBOY: Aren't you concerned about the rights of the killer—or those accused of killing?

EASTWOOD: There's a reason for the rights of the accused, and I think it's very important and one of the things that make our system great. But there are also the rights of the victim. Most people who talk about the rights of the accused have never been victimized; most of them probably never got accosted in an alley. The symbol of justice is the scale, and yet the scale is never balanced; it falls to the left and then it swings too far back to the right. That's the whole basis of *Magnum Force*, the sequel to *Dirty Harry*. These guys on the police force form their own elite, a tough inner group to combat what they see as opposition to law and order. It's remotely based on a true case, that Brazilian police death squad. It's frightening.

PLAYBOY: When *Dirty Harry* came out, it was accused of being "a fascist masterpiece." Did you expect the same thing to happen with *Magnum Force?*

EASTWOOD: No, I expected some people might call it a left-wing fantasy. Which I don't think it is. I don't think *Dirty Harry* was a fascist picture at all. It's just the story of one frustrated police officer in a frustrating situation on one particular case. I think that's why police officers were attracted to the film. Most of the films that were coming out at that time, in 1972, were extremely anti-cop. They were about the cop on the take, you know. And this was a film that showed the frustrations of the job, but at the same time, it wasn't a glorification of police work. Although some police department in the Philippines, I understand, asked for a 16-millimeter print of *Dirty Harry* to use as a training film.

PLAYBOY: Did you get many letters from policemen after *Harry?*

EASTWOOD: Yeah, I got letters. Still do. I'm asked to speak before police groups, women-police-officers' organizations. But I haven't accepted any of those requests, because I don't claim to be an expert on law enforcement.

PLAYBOY: At the end of the film, when Harry throws away his badge, is that a statement of contempt for his superiors? Something like what happened in *High Noon*, when Gary Cooper tossed his badge into the dust as a symbol of his disgust with the townspeople who didn't support him?

EASTWOOD: Cooper asked for support from the town that he had served so well, and they ended up crapping on him. But Harry wasn't saying the community as a whole had crapped on him, just the political elements of the city. The situation in another of my pictures, *High Plains Drifter*, is more like that in *High Noon*. That community didn't want to get involved, either. They weren't totally evil, they were just complacent, and they just sat back and let their marshal get whipped to death. It's a sort of comment on the thing that's very current today, of not wanting to get involved. Like the Kitty Genovese case a few years back, when something like 38 people witnessed this girl being murdered and not one of them so much as called the police.

PLAYBOY: What would *you* do if you saw a woman being beaten up in the street?

EASTWOOD: I don't know. I would hope that I would, at a minimum, raise the telephone and notify the police. At a maximum, wipe the guy out. I mean, people are capable of heroic action in life, but nobody knows what he'd do before the occasion arises. I'm sure that prior to World War II, Audie Murphy never thought of himself as a war hero.

PLAYBOY: Take another example: What if you were in a liquor store, picking up a six-pack, when a holdup took place. Would you act as Harry would?

EASTWOOD: I probably wouldn't do a thing. I'm sure that if somebody were pointing a gun at me and I were standing there with a six-pack, I'd say, "Care for one?"

PLAYBOY: In other words, you'd be realistic, like the character in the *Dollars* films. Not get mixed up in something you didn't have to. Would you call that character basically an antihero?

EASTWOOD: Yes, he operates on strictly selfish motivations at all times. But he was never the total antagonist of the film; everyone else was so evil that he looked better by comparison.

PLAYBOY: Have you been disappointed in any of the films you've made— not the B-movie bits but the major ones?

EASTWOOD: I was disappointed in *Kelly's Heroes*. That film could have been one of the best war movies ever. And it should have been; it had the best script, a good cast, a subtle antiwar message. But somehow everything got lost, the picture got bogged down shooting in Yugoslavia and it just ended up as the story of a bunch of American screw-offs in World War II. Some of the key scenes got cut out. I even called up Jim Aubrey, who was then the head of MGM, and said, "For God's sake, don't run that picture for the critics until Brian, the director, has had a chance to do some more work on it. You're going to cut off maybe millions of dollars in box-office receipts." Aubrey said he'd think it over, but I'm sure when he hung up the phone, he said to himself, "What does this frigging actor know about millions of dollars? Forget it." It was released without further work, and it did badly.

PLAYBOY: *Beguiled* didn't pack 'em in, either, did it?

EASTWOOD: That probably would have been a more successful film if I hadn't been in it.

PLAYBOY: Why?

EASTWOOD: It was advertised to appeal to the kind of people who were my fans from the action pictures, and they didn't like seeing me play a character who gets his leg cut off, gets emasculated. They wanted a character who could control everything around him. The other people, those who might have liked the film, never came to see it. But it was good for me in a career sense, because it did give the few people who saw it a different look at me as a performer.

PLAYBOY: Since then, do you think you've developed a sense of what's right for you?

EASTWOOD: Yes. You have to cast yourself in things you do well. John Wayne has been the success he has been over the years because he does what he does better than anybody else can. A lot of people have said he doesn't really act. Just let them try to act like he does and they'll find they can't do it. You'll never go to any acting school in the world where people stand around trying to be the lone, enigmatic stranger, either. But at the same time, a lot of actors who play Henry the Fifth can't play my characters. They'd be ludicrous. To me, an actor's success comes not only from the magnetism of his personality but more from his ability to select material that would be commercial with him in it.

PLAYBOY: Which is what you didn't do in *Beguiled*?

EASTWOOD: Yes, although my role in *Beguiled* was easier to play than the lone Westerner was. In those Leone films, I had to establish an image for the audience while saying very little, showing very little. In *Beguiled*, I was dealing with straight, normal emotions.

PLAYBOY: What was so normal about *Beguiled*? It had incest, jealousy, sadism, hints of lesbianism, gore. . . .

EASTWOOD: I was talking about the emotions from my own standpoint, which were simply those of survival.

PLAYBOY: In *Beguiled*, as in several of your movies—most obviously *Play Misty for Me*—it's noteworthy that the moment you appear on the scene, all the girls make a play for you. There seems to be an attitude that women are not only available but eagerly available.

EASTWOOD: Women *are* eagerly available. And so are men. People are eager to be with other people, eager to establish some kind of relationship. Everybody in the world wants to meet somebody. *Play Misty for Me* was strictly a comment on an available guy, a single guy who's somewhat of a celebrity—a disc jockey—in a small town. And this kooky girl becomes intrigued by his show, intrigued by him; she sees herself in a romantic situation and they have an affair. To him, it's just an affair; he's in love with somebody else and he tries to level with her, telling her he's involved elsewhere. *Misty* was a suspense sort of psychodrama, with an added element; it looked at that whole problem of commitment, that misinterpretation of commitment between a man and a woman. The girl who wrote it based it on a real-life story, on a girl she once knew. It appealed to me, too, because I've had this situation happen to me in my own life, this thing of having somebody clinging and clutching at you, not allowing you to breathe.

PLAYBOY: Isn't the Misty type of situation a problem for you today? Don't you have groupies pursuing you?

EASTWOOD: Well, you know, women do make plays sometimes, but I guess I'm at an age where I don't allow myself to be vulnerable. The Misty sort of thing happened to me when I was very young, 21 years old, before I was married. Sick jealousy isn't confined to any particular age, but most people I know, male or female, who have gone through that Misty type of insane jealousy had it happen at a very young age.

PLAYBOY: At what point does jealousy become insane?

EASTWOOD: When people start threatening to kill themselves and do all kinds of silly things. I've never been a real jealous person myself. I don't know why; never even went through it too bad as a kid.

PLAYBOY: Was that something you got from your parents?

EASTWOOD: Maybe, yeah, because of the security of their relationship.

PLAYBOY: Do you have a fairly open relationship yourself, with Mag?

EASTWOOD: Sure. Oh, yeah, we've always had—I'd hate to say I'm a pioneer with women's lib or whatever, but we've always had an agreement that she could enter into any kind of business she wanted to. We never had that thing about staying home and taking care of the house. There's always a certain respect for the individual in our relationship; we're not one person. She's an individual, I'm an individual, and we're friends. We're a lot of things—lovers, friends, the whole conglomerate—but at the same time, I'm not shooting orders to her on where she's supposed to be every five minutes, and I don't expect her to shoot them at me.

PLAYBOY: Does she?

EASTWOOD: No. That's why the relationship has lasted as long as it has.

PLAYBOY: You say you can't claim to be a pioneer in women's lib. But what do you think of the movement?

EASTWOOD: I think it's justifiable; it's probably been too long in coming. So many articles you read on it are absolutely boring and silly, but the basis for it is all there. I think women tend to be smarter than men in a lot of areas, and I don't know what took them so long to get into things like equal pay for equal jobs. There's no reason in the world they shouldn't have it.

PLAYBOY: In what areas do you think women are smarter than men?

EASTWOOD: Well, you see a lot of terribly intelligent men with dumb women, but you never see terribly intelligent women with dumb guys. I can't really articulate it; it's just a feeling I have. I hate to break things down to their smallest parts. I work on more of an animal level, on a feeling level. I don't do a lot of philosophizing and intellectualizing.

PLAYBOY: Yet we've heard you do a great deal of reading.

EASTWOOD: I do a tremendous amount of reading, but a good portion of it, these days especially, is taken up by potential properties—potential films. That's almost 90 percent of my reading. It takes an awful lot of reading to find the right material; you have to wade through miles to get one inch. I've been easing up, though; Sonia and Bob are doing some of the reading and I'm taking their word on more things. I used to have to say, "Well, I'll give it a look myself." Never could take advantage of that old saying, "You don't have to drink the ocean to find out it's salty." I'd read scripts from beginning to end, even if the first 50 pages were just awful.

PLAYBOY: Why?

EASTWOOD: I'd say, "Well, this is so bad, I've got to see how it turns out." And I'd sit up late at night, reading away on these properties. And finally throw them out, saying, "What the hell have I wasted the last two hours on that for?" I could have been sleeping, or walking the dog. Something really creative.

PLAYBOY: When you're selecting scripts, do you play by the conventional Hollywood wisdom—that it's safe to follow trends?

EASTWOOD: No. Why in hell do I have to follow some trend? Like the way I read that Westerns were out just before A *Fistful of Dollars* was released. There's always somebody who's going to say Westerns are out. They said police films were out when we made *Dirty Harry*. All you can do is just do your own thing, follow your instincts. If the project is right, people will go for all kinds of pictures.

PLAYBOY: The trend about which many observers have expressed concern lately is a continuing escalation of violence onscreen. Some critics have traced this to the bloodbaths in your own spaghetti Westerns. When you were making them, were you concerned about their violence?

EASTWOOD: No, I wasn't. I knew they were tough films, but there was a certain satire involved in the violence that I felt was a catharsis. I'm not a person who advocates violence in real life, and if I thought I'd made a film in which the violence inspired people to go out and commit more violence, I wouldn't make those films. But I don't believe that.

PLAYBOY: Why?

EASTWOOD: I believe they're a total-escape type of entertainment. There was an article in the *Los Angeles Times* several years ago; a journalist had been interviewing inmates at San Quentin, and they said their favorite pictures were Clint Eastwood Westerns—their reason being that any pent-up emotions they had were released when they saw those films. After they'd see one, everything would be very calm in the prison for the next few weeks. The basis for drama is conflict, you know, and physical conflict is certainly a very important part of it. You can't have movies and television with people just sitting around having arguments; no physical action, nothing to look at. You might as well tell the story on radio.

PLAYBOY: But is there a point at which the violence becomes excessive?

EASTWOOD: Certainly. Everything can get overdone. I'm sure that since the *Dollars* pictures first came out, the Italians—and the Americans, for that matter—have made 200-and-some-odd Westerns, each of them probably more violent than those were. And with the Kung Fu films, you get one big hit and then the next guy says, "We'll do it twice as bloody." So it gets superviolent. A lot of critics interpreted Sam Peckinpah's *The Wild Bunch* as a statement *against* violence; it was so violent they saw it as antiviolence. I don't think that's true at all. I think Peckinpah just wanted to make a super-violent flick. I don't think he showed how bad violence is; I think he showed how *beautiful* it is, with slow-motion cameras and everything. I liked the picture, but when you have that many shootings, you lose the horror aspect of it and it just becomes comedic.

PLAYBOY: Can't that have a brutalizing effect on an audience?

EASTWOOD: Yeah; after a while, you just sit there and say, "Oh, another guy getting blown to bits in slow motion." But I don't think it has a permanently brutalizing effect. I just think the audience gets tired of it. It's like—you see one person getting stabbed by a guy, and then the killer has to get stabbed by a bigger guy, and then the big guy has to get run over by a steamroller or something. What extremes can you carry this to? It's the same thing with sex in films. You start out with a scene of two people in bed, and then you have a scene intimating sexual relations, and pretty soon you have *Deep Throat* and people doing all kinds of kinky stuff.

PLAYBOY: Have you seen *Deep Throat*?

EASTWOOD: Yes, and I saw that other one, *The Devil in Miss Jones*.

PLAYBOY: What did you think of them?

EASTWOOD: Not much. The old stag films, with the guys in masks and black socks and garters, they were more fun. They were so bad they were good. The plumber with the bony knees looking through the window, watching the girl undress, and all of a sudden he comes in and sets the pipes down—those were the old smoker movies of the 1940s. These new ones aren't any better; they're just done in color.

PLAYBOY: You don't think the new porno films are more artistic?

EASTWOOD: I don't see that ejaculating in a girl's face is more artistic. If that's beautiful sex, if that's socially relevant, you can keep it. What you want to do in your own bedroom is great, but that's not necessarily what I want to look at. I'd like to see a good one, though; I've often wondered what would happen if somebody made a really good porno film.

PLAYBOY: What would make a porno film really good?

EASTWOOD: One that showed tenderness, that had a real, honest love developing, something that was well photographed, well presented, well acted. It would be interesting to see how an audience would respond to explicit sex within a moving story rather than just a gymnastic thing or a gag. You know, I'm surprised some women's group hasn't gone after *Deep Throat*. I mean, it's making a joke out of a woman's anatomy; that's the whole theme of the picture. Personally, I was turned off by sex after watching *Deep Throat*. That kind of stuff—people pouring Cokes into people—turns me off.

PLAYBOY: What turns you on?

EASTWOOD: I'm sure *Playboy* would like to know what turns me on very specifically. But I've never been one to discuss that kind of crap in print. I keep a lot of stuff to myself.

PLAYBOY: We give up. Would you be in favor of censoring hard-core films?

EASTWOOD: No, I'm against censorship. I think it can be dangerous. If the press had been censored, we'd never have found out about Watergate, which needed to be exposed. As far as films are concerned, I think adult human beings ought to be able to see what they want to. I'm too much of an individual to think otherwise.

PLAYBOY: Have you run into censorship problems with your own films?

EASTWOOD: Well, we have a film, *Breezy*, that's R-rated, and I don't think it deserves to be R-rated at all. But it is, because 20-some states in the Union have statutes that say showing the nipple on a woman's breast to children is obscene. That's the first thing we come into contact with when we arrive on this planet: a woman's breast. Why should that be considered obscene? And I understand that someplace in Texas, there was a move to give *Paper Moon* an R instead of a PG, because an underaged girl is swearing and kind of pimping for a hotel clerk in one scene. I don't know. You could argue that the local community has the right to set standards, but if you accept that, you could argue that the community has the right to impose segregation. That's the long-range implication of something like the Supreme Court decisions on obscenity. But I can see how the extremes of a *Deep Throat* have led to the public demand for censorship that put the Court under so much pressure. Sex is a very important topic; it's important to be able to show it artistically. But where do you go from *Deep Throat?* To chickens? It's that old cliché about the pendulum swinging back and forth. You remember, quite a few years ago, there was a period when movies couldn't show a husband and wife in bed together, even if they were just reading magazines. Now you can see that on any TV show. There's a much more honest approach. But what happens—and it's the same thing with politics—is that the pendulum swings too far, the scale tips over and falls back with a crash.

PLAYBOY: How would you characterize yourself politically?

EASTWOOD: I'm a political nothing. I mean, I hate to be categorized. I'm certainly not an extremist; the best thing you can say about extremists, either right or left, is that they're boring people. Not very flexible people. I suppose I'm a moderate, but I could be called a lot of things. On certain things I could be called very liberal; on others, very conservative.

PLAYBOY: Which things?

EASTWOOD: I'm liberal on civil rights, conservative on government spending.

PLAYBOY: What areas of government spending?

EASTWOOD: I think the attitude that Big Daddy's going to take over has become a kind of mental sickness. I don't think government programs should be designed to encourage freeloading. The government has to help people, to some degree, but it should be encouraging people to make something of themselves.

PLAYBOY: You're not against unemployment insurance, are you?

EASTWOOD: No, I've collected it often enough. Though when I see what it is today—something like $85 a week—I wonder what the hell I'm doing working. But I don't know, I suppose with inflation it's not worth much more than the 20-something a week I used to get.

PLAYBOY: You say you're a liberal on civil rights; what about civil liberties? How do you feel about wire tapping, electronic surveillance?

EASTWOOD: Whatever the reasons are, whatever the hell the law finally states, I just don't think it's morally right. Same as I think the morality of President Nixon's making those tapes in the Oval Office was bad. Innocent people were in there talking to him—like the prime minister of some country—very frankly stating their points of view with no idea that their conversations were being taped. President Nixon knew. They didn't. If I knew I was bugging a room and I was going to keep the tapes for history, I sure as hell wouldn't say anything on tape that might convict me. If everything I said in Lew Wasserman's office here at M.C.A., or in the offices of whatever studio I'm dealing with, was taped, I certainly would talk a little more carefully than I usually do. But I don't want to find out all my conversations are going straight to the M.C.A. Tower.

PLAYBOY: Are they?

EASTWOOD: Probably. No, they aren't. I checked it out.

PLAYBOY: Really?

EASTWOOD: No, but that's the way things have gotten these days. Everybody bugging everybody.

PLAYBOY: Or investigating everybody, What's your opinion of the attitude John Ehrlichman expressed during the Watergate hearings—that more character investigations should be conducted to unearth such things as politicians' drinking habits? Would you run such a check on somebody who came to work for you?

EASTWOOD: Every company checks on a person's references. You call his former boss and ask why this guy left, if he was dismissed, and for what reason. If I found out a guy was an absolute lush, I wouldn't hire him. I'm sure that right now a lot of people are asking why President Nixon didn't check further into former Vice President Agnew's background, or why there are so many people around him who seem to be of questionable honor. You'd have to say that he's a very poor judge of character. And, on the other side, a lot of people wondered why Senator McGovern didn't check out Senator Eagleton. But to go back to hiring somebody myself, well, I'm not going to scrutinize the type of women he goes out with and all that, because I don't care. And I wouldn't want him scrutinizing me the same way.

PLAYBOY: How would you react if somebody did run a check like that on you, complete with private detectives?

EASTWOOD: I wouldn't like it, but basically I wouldn't *give* a damn. I'm an actor, and actors are expected to be screwballs. People would say, you know, "What else?" But with politicians, people expect—or at least hope for—the best. They're concerned if their Senator is out getting five-o-twos or out boozing.

PLAYBOY: Five-o-twos?

EASTWOOD: Drunk-driving citations. That kind of thing would probably make *me* vote for the guy, though. When Senator McGovern told that jerk who was harassing him to "Kiss my ass," I started thinking, "This guy is all of a sudden sounding good to me." Not because he used profanity but because he had a human reaction; he was tired of being bugged. When Harry Truman told off that critic who said his daughter couldn't sing, called him a stupid son of a bitch—or whatever the hell he called him—it was the natural reaction of a father expressing resentment at somebody attacking his daughter. I think that appealed to a lot of people. Politics is a tough business and you have to be tough to stay in it. I mean, nobody came over more virtuous than Senator McGovern, but I'm sure that he's a tough guy. I'm sure he isn't quite as Percy Kilbride as his image was presented; to be where he is today, as a Senator of the United States, he must have been in on some good infighting.

PLAYBOY: Whatever your opinion of McGovern, are you suspicious of most politicians?

EASTWOOD: No, I don't think I'm a total negativist on that, but I do think this Watergate thing is making people cynical. I hate to see the public get so callous about it, not care anymore, because they *should* care. So that things like Watergate won't happen again. Same as if maybe the Bobby Baker thing had been pursued as vigorously as the Watergate thing has, to find the connections between Baker and the hierarchy, it might have set an example. If nothing else, Watergate, right through the Ellsberg thing, was the dumbest-handled thing in the world. I'm glad it was exposed, for the sake of turning off what might have been a dangerous trend, but I'd hate to think that our intelligence forces around the world were operating as clumsily as that group. Leaving money in telephone booths. It was like a poor man's James Bond movie.

PLAYBOY: If you were going to do Watergate as an adventure movie—

EASTWOOD: I wouldn't do it. I think Peter Sellers would.

PLAYBOY: Another opinion expressed by Ehrlichman during the Watergate hearings was that virtually any action—such as burglarizing Ellsberg's psychiatrist's office—was justifiable if it was being done in the name of national security, for the President of the United States. How do you feel about that?

EASTWOOD: I don't think that's at all justifiable. I think he was just trying to rationalize his way out of a very difficult situation. Where does this kind of thing end? My latest picture, *Magnum Force*, is all about that:

about what happens when the law decides it's *above* the law. Pretty soon *everybody*'s burglarizing. If breaking and entering are considered legal under *any* circumstances, I think pretty soon we'll all just go breaking into a neighbor's house and lift whatever we happen to want or need. Maybe information, maybe his wallet.

PLAYBOY: What would you do if somebody broke into your house?

EASTWOOD: He'd risk getting shot.

PLAYBOY: Do you keep a loaded gun in your house?

EASTWOOD: Yes, I have guns; but with kids, one has to be very intelligent about where one places them. My kids play with toy guns, or my boy does, but I've taken him out to the range where I fire pistols and I've always instilled in his mind that one kind of gun is a plaything and another is the real thing. There's no use trying to tell him not to have anything to do with guns. You can be an idealist and not buy war toys, but a boy will still pick up a stick and play shoot-'em-up.

PLAYBOY: You had your children rather late in your marriage, in comparison with some couples. How did it feel to become a father after 15 years?

EASTWOOD: I think it felt better for me at this age than it would have when I was 21, trying to start a career. I wasn't broke, like my father was when he had me. I suppose that's the reason we had them late in life. But I think I appreciate kids more now, much more.

PLAYBOY: Your work has required you to be gone from home a great deal, sometimes on long locations—

EASTWOOD: I wasn't even in this country when Kyle was born. I was in Europe on location for *Where Eagles Dare.* I hope that sort of thing won't have to happen again.

PLAYBOY: In any case, your wife has had to be both father and mother to the kids at times. How does she feel about that?

EASTWOOD: Well, she prefers it when I'm around. Naturally. At least I hope so. I *think* she does.

PLAYBOY: Of all the films you've acted in or directed, what was your favorite location?

EASTWOOD: Working in Carmel for *Misty* was great, being near home. I also liked the location for *High Plains Drifter* at June Lake, east of Yosemite. And *Thunderbolt and Lightfoot*—the new film I'm in with Jeff Bridges, George Kennedy and Geoffrey Lewis—was shot near Great Falls, Montana. Beautiful country. I've enjoyed all the locations. What I don't like is *long* locations. I hate long movies.

PLAYBOY: What do you consider a long movie?

EASTWOOD: One that takes more than three months. *Kelly's Heroes*, in Yugoslavia, was about five and a half or six months; *Paint Your Wagon* was five months, in Baker, Oregon. There wasn't anything very exciting there—especially for five months.

PLAYBOY: What did you do for kicks?

EASTWOOD: They had a nine-hole golf course, so I played golf. I rented a farm outside town, about 40 acres, had ducks in a pond. Slopped the hogs for the guy who owned the farm.

PLAYBOY: And in the evening you'd sit around the campfire, singing Lerner and Loewe songs?

EASTWOOD: Right. "Tenting on the Old Campground."

PLAYBOY: Where's your next location?

EASTWOOD: Our next project—we don't even have the title yet, but I'll be directing it, not acting in it—will be on location close by, near Los Angeles. It's a suspense film.

PLAYBOY: Do you plan to go on alternating between acting and directing?

EASTWOOD: Eventually, I would love to give up acting and just direct. I think every actor should direct at least once. It gives you a tolerance, an understanding of the problems involved in making a film. In fact, I also think every director should act.

PLAYBOY: Is that why you cast Don Siegel, your director from *Coogan's Bluff*, *Dirty Harry* and other films, in a role in *Play Misty for Me*?

EASTWOOD: Yeah. On my first day as a director, on the set of *Misty*, the actor in the scene was Don. He kept saying, "You're making a big mistake; you shouldn't be doing this. You should get a good character actor." I said, "Don't worry about it. If I screw up as a director, I've got a good director on the set." And it worked out.

PLAYBOY: Can you distinguish between the qualities that make a good actor and those that make a good director?

EASTWOOD: It's an instinctive thing. Just as acting isn't an intellectual medium, I don't think directing is, either: the instinct to hire the right person—the right cameraman to go with the right director, and the right actors to go with the other actors, and so on, so that the ensemble fits.

PLAYBOY: If you were to win an Academy Award—

EASTWOOD: I don't really expect to. I'm not going to sit here and say I'd hate to win one. But I'm not terribly politically oriented. I don't know if I'd be able to campaign properly, even if I had the vehicle.

PLAYBOY: You mean it's not possible to win one without campaigning?

EASTWOOD: I guess it is, but there's definitely a public-relations aspect to it. You have to keep people aware of whatever it is you're doing.

PLAYBOY: If you did win one, would you rather it be as best actor or as best director?

EASTWOOD: I suppose as director. I don't know. Directing, to me, is somewhat more satisfying.

PLAYBOY: Is that why you said you'd love to give up acting someday?

EASTWOOD: Did I say that? I really wouldn't.

PLAYBOY: You just said it.

EASTWOOD: Well, I was lying. What I meant, I'm sure, is that someday I may just get to the point where I feel I don't come across right on the screen anymore, that I ought to be playing character roles. Then maybe I'd better stick to directing.

PLAYBOY: Have you ever considered investing the money you've made from films in some sort of commercial enterprise?

EASTWOOD: Not really. I do have a few ventures, like the Hog's Breath Inn, a restaurant I own part of in Carmel. It has the atmosphere of an English countryside restaurant and serves some very good organic food.

PLAYBOY: Why that appetizing name?

EASTWOOD: I have to take credit for that. When I was drifting around Great Britain with *Fistful of Dollars*, I went to Wales and Scotland and stopped in all the small towns. Naturally, I stopped at an awful lot of pubs. They all had crazy names, and Hog's Breath Inn was the craziest one I could think up. Somebody raised the objection that that's a bad name for a restaurant, but I said if a customer doesn't have a sense of humor, we don't want him anyway.

PLAYBOY: And why organic food?

EASTWOOD: I like it. Years ago, I walked into a health-food store with a friend; he was looking for some kind of bread. And there was a little old lady in there talking about pesticides and things, in the way that's fashionable today. And I thought, "Gee, what she says makes sense." Although I'm not against all pesticides. But most of the stuff from the health-food stores is quite good. It's also more expensive, but people who like to save money on marketing will turn around and buy four or five bottles of booze and take it home in the same armload. So I just buy two or three bottles of booze and spend the rest on organic food.

PLAYBOY: Do you suppose Olympia, your favorite beer, is made from organically grown hops?

EASTWOOD: I don't know how organically brewed Olympia or any other beer is, but there are certain things you just can't sacrifice.

PLAYBOY: Is the fact that you don't hunt attributable to the same sort of concern for the environment that drew you to natural foods?

EASTWOOD: I guess I have too much of a reverence for living creatures. There's so much beauty in them.

PLAYBOY: There's a story that you once refused to kill a rattlesnake on the set of *Two Mules for Sister Sara*. Is that true?

EASTWOOD: I didn't refuse. I ended up killing the rattlesnake, but I didn't want to. We were in Mexico, and the authorities didn't want a rattlesnake let loose after the filming.

PLAYBOY: How did you kill it?

EASTWOOD: Cut its head off with a knife. It wasn't the happiest thing I ever did. I cut the snake's head off and handed the body to Shirley MacLaine.

PLAYBOY: Of all the actresses you've worked with, who has been your favorite leading lady?

EASTWOOD: Shirley was fun, but in *Beguiled*, I worked with eight leading actresses, and they were all fun, too. Inger Stevens—God rest her soul—was a great gal. In *Rawhide*, we had some sensational people—Julie Harris, Geraldine Page.

PLAYBOY: Who are your close friends? Are they in the movie colony, neighbors in Carmel, business associates?

EASTWOOD: Well, I work with Bob Daley, and we're close friends. We used to live next door to each other when I was a contract player and he was in cost analysis. Bob and Cissy Donner are friends; he's an actor, and I talked him into starting, going into a drama group. Fritz Manes, he's a friend of mine who works for channel two in Oakland. A kid I knew in school, Don Kincade, is still a friend; he's a dentist who lives in Davis. Those are guys I've known for many years. And I've known Don Siegel for about seven years. And I have three or four close friends around Carmel.

PLAYBOY: Are any of them movie people?

EASTWOOD: Not really. But Merv Griffin owns a house there, and Merv I know quite well. He played in the celebrity tennis tournament with me.

PLAYBOY: The Clint Eastwood Invitational Celebrity Tennis Tournament has become quite a bash, hasn't it? How did you get involved?

EASTWOOD: Don Hamilton, who was the pro at the Pebble Beach Beach and Tennis Club, approached me about three years ago. They had had a celebrity tennis tournament, but it was a very small thing, mostly within the Del Monte company. And they wanted to have a big thing for charity. I told him they ought to get a better tennis player, but he talked me into sponsoring it. And it's gone over quite well.

PLAYBOY: How good a player are you?

EASTWOOD: *Cosi, cosi.* Mag is a good tennis player.

PLAYBOY: What are some of your other pastimes?

EASTWOOD: Well, I work out; have a little gym at home with racks of weights around the walls, a punching bag, sandbag. You may not believe it, as I'm sitting here eating macadamia nuts and drinking my 27th beer, but I like to keep in shape. Let's see, what else? I go to an awful lot of movies. I like to see them at regular theaters, along with the general public, and get a feeling of the audience.

PLAYBOY: Aren't you recognized and besieged for autographs?

EASTWOOD: Well, I disguise myself when I go into a theater. I put on a mustache and glasses, and it makes me look quite different. I managed to go to a rodeo at Salinas the other day and not one person recognized me. By the time I get a hat on, and the mustache and glasses, it drops my I.Q. by about 50 points, which makes it about five.

PLAYBOY: Are you a rodeo fan?

EASTWOOD: I used to go to a lot of them. I did weekend stints when I was on *Rawhide*; all the TV guys do, I think. They'd pay you to come out and do an appearance, in Casper, Wyoming, or someplace like that.

PLAYBOY: Have you always done a lot of riding?

EASTWOOD: Most of my life. My cousins had horses, at my grandmother's place, so I rode a lot as a kid.

PLAYBOY: You mentioned wanting to study music when you were younger. Do you play any instruments?

EASTWOOD: No. I used to play the piano. When I was 17, I played in Oakland at the Omar club.

PLAYBOY: For money?

EASTWOOD: I got all the beer I could handle and all my meals. And I used to play the trumpet. I still have it.

PLAYBOY: But you don't play it?

EASTWOOD: No muscles.

PLAYBOY: That's what comes of making those early films in which you barely moved your lips. Recently, though, you've had more varied roles. In the past 12 months, you've acted in *Magnum Force* and *Thunderbolt and Lightfoot* and directed *Breezy*. Besides the new picture you're planning, what's next on the agenda?

EASTWOOD: I'd like to take it easy for about six months, slow down my pace a little, spend some time with my family. I still don't get to do as much of that as I'd like, but I don't think anybody does. It's the nature of the business—this business, anyway.

PLAYBOY: Was your own family closely knit when you were a child?

EASTWOOD: Yes, but not in the conventional sense. That was during the Depression, you know, and my dad traveled around a lot looking for work. Jobs were hard to come by in those days. So there were times when we had to be separated; when times weren't good, I had to live with my grandmother, on her farm up near Sunol, near Livermore. We moved around so much—I must have gone to eight different grammar schools—that the family was about all you had. I didn't have a lot of friends; our family—my parents and my younger sister and I—was a unit. I think my parents and my grandmother—she was quite a person, very self-sufficient, lived by herself on a mountain—probably had more to do with my turning out the way I have than any educational process I may have gone through. They were very young parents—quite the antithesis of my own situation with my children. They were great parents. I was lucky to have them. But I've been lucky with a lot of things: lucky with my acting career, lucky with my directing efforts.

PLAYBOY: You seem to ascribe a great deal to luck. Are you saying that your career has been something of a fluke?

EASTWOOD: Maybe, in the sense that I believe everything in life's kind of a fluke. Luck has played a great part in my whole existence, particularly my existence as an actor. I was lucky to be in the right place at the right time. And for the kind of guy I am, this is the right era to be in the motion-picture business.

PLAYBOY: Why?

EASTWOOD: Today the actor is much more in control of his own fate than he used to be. I'd find it very frustrating to be under one of those old contracts, at the mercy of one of those studio regimes. It's a funny thing; I was never the guy the press agents figured should be on the cover of this or that magazine, never the recipient of the big, glamorous studio push they used to give upcoming actors in the old days. I've never been the darling of any particular group, but somehow—somehow I got there, anyway.

A candid conversation with the tough-guy legend about his life as a Hollywood outsider, his legal battles with Sondra Locke and the secret behind his years as a star.

Clint Eastwood is walking around Mission Ranch, the quiet, secluded property he owns only a few miles from his home in Carmel, California. He purchased the ranch on the Monterey Peninsula in 1986 when businessmen planned to turn the 22-acre site into a condominium development. He enjoys talking about the history of the place—it was one of the first California dairies and, during World War II, an army and navy officers' club with a rollicking reputation.

As soon as Eastwood bought the ranch, he hired craftsmen to turn the series of buildings on the site into a quaint hotel overlooking meadows that join the wetlands and Carmel River Beach. "It would have been wrong to sell this," he says slowly, softly and emphatically, his startlingly blue eyes squinting once more, his craggy face and 6'4" frame somehow giving the words weight, even a touch of menace.

Eastwood's on-screen persona—the flinty, confident, silent loner—mirrors his life in a way that's uncommon among movie stars. Even more uncommon has been his longevity and success. His remarkable 40-year career is unrivaled. He entered the nation's consciousness as a no-talent television heartthrob on *Rawhide*. Even when he switched to motion pictures, critics had no use for him.

"Eastwood doesn't act in motion pictures, he is framed in them," Vincent Canby wrote in *The New York Times* in 1968. In 1971 Pauline Kael said *Dirty Harry* was a film imbued with "fascist medievalism." Eastwood seemed oblivious to the attacks and widened his focus to include directing.

By the mid-1980s many of Eastwood's early critics had reversed themselves. In his review of *Pale Rider*, Canby wrote, "I'm just now beginning to realize that, though Mr. Eastwood may have been improving over the years, it's also taken all these years for most of us to recognize his very consistent grace and wit as a filmmaker." Norman

Mailer wrote, "Eastwood is an artist. You can see the man in his work, just as clearly as you can see Hemingway in A *Farewell to Arms*."

In the youth-dominated entertainment industry, Eastwood continues to confound people. He's 66 years old and still a major box-office draw and sex symbol. As an actor, he remains the longest-running success story in Hollywood. He is such an archetypal movie star it's almost easy to forget that he's one of our most successful directors as well, having presided over more than 20 films.

He stars in his new movie, *Absolute Power*, which opens this month. It is based on a best-selling novel by David Baldacci about a skilled career burglar who inadvertently witnesses a murder in which the president of the U.S. participates. What especially appealed to Eastwood was the troubled relationship in the film between the burglar and his daughter. His next directorial effort is an adaptation of John Berendt's *Midnight in the Garden of Good and Evil*.

Born on May 31, 1930 in San Francisco, the older child of Clinton and Ruth Eastwood, Clinton Eastwood Jr. endured a hardscrabble, Depression-era childhood that profoundly affected him. Because his father had difficulty finding jobs, the family moved from one northern California town to another with a one-wheel trailer in tow. Young Clint attended eight grammar schools and later described himself as having been a lonely, introverted child.

In Oakland, California Eastwood attended Oakland Technical High School, where, aside from swimming and basketball, his major interest was jazz. He played piano for free meals at a club in Oakland and after graduating from high school in 1948 worked as a lumberjack and firefighter in Oregon and a steelworker in Seattle. His motto was "never to be dependent on anyone else."

He was drafted into the army in 1951 and was made a swimming instructor at Fort Ord, California. While there he met several actors, including David Janssen and Martin Milner, who encouraged him to go to Hollywood after his military stint.

Following his discharge in 1953, he enrolled at Los Angeles City College under the GI Bill and started making the rounds as an actor. On the basis of his rugged looks, Universal signed him on as a contract player.

After 18 months of playing bit parts in "Francis the Talking Mule" movies and *Revenge of the Creature* (1955), Eastwood was dropped by Universal. He pumped gas and dug swimming pools in the San

Fernando Valley Hills and thought about returning to college. While he was eating with a friend in the basement of the CBS television studios, a producer asked him to test for the role of good guy Rowdy Yates in *Rawhide*, the TV series about cattle drives on the Great Plains that ran from 1959 to 1966. It was the beginning of Eastwood's lucrative career as a gunslinger.

In 1964, during a four-month break in the *Rawhide* production schedule, Eastwood accepted an offer of $15,000 to fly to Spain and star in *A Fistful of Dollars*, directed by Sergio Leone. As the Man with No Name, Eastwood went out of his way to depart from his clean-cut television cowboy image and play a smoldering, enigmatic, violent loner.

The film was an unexpected hit. Two other successful spaghetti Westerns by Leone followed: *For a Few Dollars More* and *The Good, the Bad and the Ugly*. By the late 1960s, the three films had established Eastwood's reputation as an international superstar, initially more popular abroad than at home.

Returning to Hollywood, Eastwood formed his own production company, Malpaso, and signed on to make *Hang 'Em High* (1968), as a man who survives his own hanging and wreaks revenge on the nine men responsible. Although similar to the spaghetti Westerns, the movie had even darker undertones because it featured a different type of hero—a cowboy who drew his gun first. "I do everything John Wayne would never do," he said at the time. "I play the hero, but I shoot the guy in the back." The movie—for which Eastwood was paid $40,000 plus 25 percent of the profits—was one of his highest-grossing films for that period.

By 1969 Eastwood was one of the world's top box-office draws. He began a partnership with action director Don Siegel, making such successes as *Coogan's Bluff*, *Two Mules for Sister Sara*, *The Beguiled* and *Dirty Harry*. *Dirty Harry*, the 1971 film about Harry Callahan, a San Francisco detective who takes the law into his own hands, not only launched three sequels but, to the amazement of Eastwood and Siegel, also seized the mood of many Americans who were as enraged about urban violence as they were about a legal system that failed to control thugs.

It was Siegel who encouraged Eastwood to direct his first feature film, *Play Misty for Me* (1971), a thriller about a disc jockey (played by Eastwood) who becomes involved with a psychotic fan. There followed a series of films that he directed, many of them dark-edged. Eastwood starred in many of these films, including *The Outlaw Josey Wales* (1976), plus *Bronco Billy* (1980) and *Honkytonk Man* (1982)—which spoofed Eastwood's tough-guy persona—and the mystical Western *Pale Rider* (1985). There were some duds, too, including a James Bond-style mishap, *The Eiger Sanction* (1975).

Eastwood then proceeded to make some even more striking films, including *Bird* (1988), about the destructive life of jazz musician Charlie Parker (played by Forest Whitaker), and *White Hunter, Black Heart* (1990), in which Eastwood gave a broad performance as a macho, self-absorbed director, a character based on John Huston.

Unforgiven (1992) is the most acclaimed film of Eastwood's career, winning an Academy Award as best picture and earning him an Oscar as best director. It was followed by *In the Line of Fire* (directed by Wolfgang Petersen) and two more films, *A Perfect World*, in which he co-starred with Kevin Costner (despite good reviews, the film was a box-office disappointment) and *The Bridges of Madison County*, in which he played a *National Geographic* photographer who has a brief affair with an Iowa housewife played by Meryl Streep.

Over that long career Eastwood had kept his personal life more discreet than most movie stars—until the end of his relationship with Sondra Locke, an actress and director who appeared in six Eastwood films and was his lover and companion for 14 years. In the spring of 1989 Eastwood changed the locks on their Bel-Air home and hired movers to pack and move her clothes while she was on location directing a film.

She retaliated with a palimony suit. In a later, highly public lawsuit she would allege that Eastwood had duped her into dropping the palimony case by dangling a bogus three-year development deal to direct at Warner Bros. Locke said she was undergoing chemotherapy at the time and in a vulnerable state. After the deal, she pitched more than 30 projects; Warner Bros. rejected all of them. Locke said she later learned that her $1.5 million deal was secretly financed by Eastwood. The case was resolved last September when Eastwood gave Locke an undisclosed monetary settlement.

Eastwood has been married twice and seems to have seven children— the number is unconfirmed and Eastwood is reticent about the issue. In 1953 he married Maggie Johnson, a swimsuit model. After a long estrangement, they divorced in the mid-1980s and she reportedly received a $25 million settlement. The couple have two grown children, Kyle, a musician, and Alison, an actress.

The new biography by Richard Schickel mentions the fact, first published in 1989, that Eastwood has another grown daughter, Kimber, born in 1964 to a woman who had an affair with Eastwood and remained somewhat friendly with him. In recent years Kimber has granted press interviews, saying at times that her father is financially and emotionally supportive. He also has a son and daughter born to Jacelyn Reeves, a former flight attendant living in the Carmel area, who, according to Schickel, wanted children but did not want to share Eastwood's public life. He supports the family.

And Eastwood has a three-year-old daughter, Francesca, with Frances Fisher, the stage and film actress who had the top female role in *Unforgiven*.

Last March, after a quiet courtship, Eastwood married then 30-year-old Dina Ruiz, a television reporter in Salinas. The couple had their first child, a daughter, Morgan, on December 12. Eastwood has joked that he married Ruiz "for her money."

We sent writer Bernard Weinraub, whose most recent article in *Playboy* was about the life and death of producer Don Simpson, to get the press-shy actor to open up. Weinraub reports:

"Eastwood has numerous homes—in Bel Air, in Shasta County (the old Bing Crosby estate) and in Sun Valley, Idaho. But the one he favors is in Carmel, a quaint oceanside town that he first visited in his army days. Around Carmel—where he was mayor from 1986 to 1988—Eastwood is treated with a mixture of deference and friendliness. Everyone calls him Clint.

"Friendly but a little moody, Eastwood is an unpredictable interview—terse one moment, talkative the next. He doesn't like to be pressed too hard. There's no nervous chatter. He says exactly what he wants to say, and that's it.

"He's thoroughly unpretentious. What you see onscreen is pretty much what you see offscreen. There's no entourage. He drives himself to the airport. He doesn't mix with the Hollywood crowd. Many of his friends are golf buddies in Carmel—an accountant, a salesman, a schoolteacher. His loyalties seem to run deep. He has used the same talent agent and publicity honchos for decades. He keeps the same film crew.

"As reserved as he is, the one time he became animated was when his wife appeared. Dina Ruiz is outgoing and laughs easily. 'If he doesn't tell you anything, just call me. I'll tell you everything,' she said to me. Eastwood rolled his eyes in mock horror."

PLAYBOY: For years now, you've been considered the archetypal macho guy. How does that feel?

EASTWOOD: It's a burden only when other people impose their thoughts about who I am. Macho was a fashionable word in the 1980s. Everybody was kind of into it, what's macho and what isn't macho. I really don't know what macho is. I never have understood it. Does it mean somebody who swaggers around exuding testosterone? And kicks the gate open and runs sprints up and down the street? Or does handsprings or whatever? Or is macho a quiet thing based on your security? I remember shaking hands with Rocky Marciano. He was gentle, he didn't squeeze your hand. And he had a high voice. But he knew he could knock people around, it was a given. That's macho. Muhammad Ali is the same. If you talked with him in his younger days, he spoke gently. He wasn't kicking over chairs. I think some of the most macho people are the gentlest.

PLAYBOY: Meryl Streep said of you, "I've never encountered anyone who gave less of a damn what any critic, movie wag or trend hound says about him or his work."

EASTWOOD: Well, I don't know. You never purposely make a movie for an empty house. You make it hoping people will see it and enjoy it. But I'm philosophical. At some point you commit yourself to a project and you have to do the project the way you see it. There's a line from the director character in *White Hunter, Black Heart*, patterned after John Huston. He tells a writer, "When you make a film, you must forget that anyone's ever going to see it. Just make the film. And stay true to it." I believe that. You have to tell the story the way you see it and hope people want to come along on the journey. You cannot tell a story and say, "OK, I've got to be careful now because audiences may not like this." Then you become delusional and don't know what you're making anymore. I've always believed that the great thing about a movie theater is the big exit sign that everyone can see. And don't let the door hit you on the rear as you walk out.

PLAYBOY: So you've never cared about what's trendy or fashionable?

EASTWOOD: Oh, absolutely not. I hate trends, I hate fads. And the movie business loves fads, so for 40 years I've been stuck in a business that loves fads. I wasn't a fad. When I came in, it was predicted that I'd go nowhere. And the pictures that were turning points in my career, such as *Fistful of Dollars*, were against the fad. Westerns were out of favor. You just have to go with your instincts. I didn't make *Dirty Harry* because I thought the country needed a detective movie. I just felt it was a good movie. I know that Hollywood is loaded with people who love fads, the studios especially. *Independence Day* was the big picture last year, so I'm sure there are dozens more like it on the drawing board. Would I like to make a movie like that? Not particularly.

PLAYBOY: You once said, "There's a rebel lying deep in my soul. Anybody tells me the trend is such and such, I go in the opposite direction."

EASTWOOD: That just about sums it up.

PLAYBOY: Do you consider yourself an artist?

EASTWOOD: I've never thought about that. If making movies is an art, I guess I'd be considered an artist. But I don't know if it's an art or a craft or whatever anybody wants to call it. A lot of people get pompous and claim a film director has to be an auteur. Or are you really just a craftsman who is in a leadership capacity and who guides people along? Besides, isn't there an art to everything? There's an art to a plumber fixing a sink well. Or a mechanic working on cars. There's an art to it if you know how to do it and you do it well. A good bartender could be an artist. A bad one is not.

PLAYBOY: When you're on a movie set away from home, how inevitable is it that people—the actors, the director, the crew—will have romances?

EASTWOOD: I don't know if it's common. It does happen, though. When you're a young person making movies, it's easy to be exposed to it, to be tempted when you're away from home.

PLAYBOY: Have you been tempted?

EASTWOOD: [*Smiles*] Well, I guess maybe in my youth.

PLAYBOY: Not in your later years?

EASTWOOD: When you get into directing films it becomes a little different because directing is so time-consuming. Once an actor learns his part he has a lot of time on his hands. If you're a young actor and you're playing a romantic scene with somebody, I suppose that temptation would be there. But film directors don't have much time on their hands.

PLAYBOY: Still, don't women throw themselves at you more than they would at an average guy?

EASTWOOD: I can't say. I suppose people fantasize about movie stars. I fantasized about Rita Hayworth and Linda Darnell. But sure, it's something an actor might face regardless of his age. It's the same thing that an older executive feels with a 21-year-old girl chasing him around. He wonders, Does she like me for my personality and looks or is it for something else?

PLAYBOY: And when women throw themselves at you—

EASTWOOD: Today I'm very happy and married to the best woman I have ever known, and that wouldn't cross my mind.

PLAYBOY: But you admit it happens.

EASTWOOD: Oh, yeah. There are a lot of people who throw themselves at you. At a certain time in your life that's flattering, and you're impressed by it. At other times you're realistic about it. You realize it doesn't add up to a whole lot.

PLAYBOY: Are you at least flattered?

EASTWOOD: I think I'm a realist about it. You're a movie actor, people know you. I've been around a long time. Although I appeal to a wide age group, a younger actor would get the younger audience going for him.

PLAYBOY: It must cheer you up that this still goes on when you're 66 years old.

EASTWOOD: [*Laughs*] I don't think about that. Age is biological, but it's also psychological. A lot of people are old before their time because they think old.

PLAYBOY: How do you feel when you see actors who are afraid to play their age?

EASTWOOD: I cringe. Some people can't face it. Like Cary Grant. He just decided one day he didn't want to act anymore because he could no longer play romantic characters. Other people say, "What the hell, I'll just play character parts and play them till I'm 90." And there are other people who insist they can play 45-year-olds for the rest of their life as long as they have a lot of hair dye and stuff like that. But that's not very interesting to me. You've got to be what you are.

PLAYBOY: Do you have much privacy?

EASTWOOD: When you study to be an actor you try to watch people and observe humanity. Then, when you become more well known, you're the one studied and you can't study people anymore. You go places and people interrupt you and say, "Oh God, you're sitting by yourself. I thought maybe I'd give you some company." Which is the last thing you probably want. You're probably sitting by yourself for a reason. It could be that your dog got run over, or you could be in a terrible mood. Everybody deserves to have his moment of privacy. As a well-known person you don't get it, but you deserve it.

PLAYBOY: You have never been part of the Hollywood world—the premieres, parties, restaurants and all of that. Why not?

EASTWOOD: I've gone to a few. I've always maintained a residence here in Monterey County; it's sort of my home base, except when I'm working. I go to restaurants in L.A. once in a while. I don't hold with the fashion that you have to hate L.A. to be happy in the world. I mean, to me, you're happy wherever you are and where things are going well.

PLAYBOY: What do you like about Carmel?

EASTWOOD: It's a smaller town, a smaller community. It's not quite like a small town in mid-America where there may be nothing to do except to hang around the local store and drive the strip with your hair in curlers. There are things to do here—there are rock festivals, jazz festivals, car races, anything a person wants to do. It has exquisite views. You're close to San Francisco, and you're reasonably close to L.A. It's a nice place to be.

PLAYBOY: Your career choices in recent years, as an actor and as a director, don't show much of a pattern. You don't seem to say, I'm doing a comedy this year, I'll do an action film next year.

EASTWOOD: I don't look for anything in particular. What I look for is an interesting story. I'm not sitting there saying, "Well, I'm looking for something to direct." With *Absolute Power*, I liked the gimmick of the book—the guy is outside the law, so he can't go to the police when he sees a situation involving a high-up government official. It's a little different. I haven't done a suspense-oriented film for a while.

PLAYBOY: Your next film is *Midnight in the Garden of Good and Evil*, which you'll direct but not appear in. What appealed to you about that book?

EASTWOOD: I liked the atmosphere of Savannah. The central character, the journalist, goes down there and takes us on a journey. It's a town with a tremendous history and an interesting social structure.

PLAYBOY: When you tackle something that seems so outside your experience, do you get nervous?

EASTWOOD: No. Half the fun of making a movie is doing something that's outside your experience. In fact, if you do something outside your experience, you have a much better chance of bringing a fresh eye to it.

PLAYBOY: If you look at the work of Clint Eastwood, director and actor, do you see many common threads?

EASTWOOD: I sometimes find myself attracted to characters who are searching for some sort of redemption, some sort of reconciliation with their soul. But I don't know if it's a common thread. A lot of the characters I play are outsiders, a lot of them are rebelling against conditions in society. A lot of the people I've played have been lonely for one reason or another, either by their own choice or through fate. Like in *Bridges of Madison County*. He's a loner. I seek out that sort of character. I guess I relate to those kinds of people. In terms of a story, basically, when I look at a character I want him to have something that's bothering him. As in *In the Line of Fire*—a Secret Service guy is guarding the president, who's been threatened. That's a plot. But it isn't half as interesting as a Secret Service guy who's living with guilt because he was guarding another president when that president was killed years ago.

PLAYBOY: And what about your career disappointments?

EASTWOOD: I've had several films that were disappointing. Some were risky to begin with, and I knew the odds were against them. I suppose *Honkytonk Man* and *Bird* would be included in that group. There was *Paint Your Wagon*. I did that in the 1970s. That was just a big waste of money and effort. A blatant waste.

PLAYBOY: Don Siegel, who directed you in *Dirty Harry*, once said, "You can't push Clint. It's very dangerous. For a guy who's as cool as he is, there are times when he has a violent temper."

EASTWOOD: I don't know if I have a violent temper. I don't think I do at this stage in my life. But, yeah, certain things bug me, and I get as bugged as the next person.

PLAYBOY: Give an example.

EASTWOOD: It happens once a picture. If you can go through a movie and lose your temper only once or twice, you're lucky. On the set of *Absolute Power* we were trying to get this particular scene done, and everything was falling apart. People were talking on the radios and everyone looked like they were walking around chasing their tails. I just let go. I didn't say, "Hey, you're all fired." I just let everybody know I was unhappy at that moment.

PLAYBOY: Meryl Streep has echoed what lots of other people have said about you. She said your set is the quietest she's ever worked on and that you work so unnervingly fast that the rehearsal may end up in the film.

EASTWOOD: Yeah, I know. I don't think that's a particularly bad reputation to have in a business that loves excess so much. I do like a quiet set. I think it's better for the actors. I don't depend on nervous energy or insecurity to drive the wagon ahead. I believe there's a comfort zone in which actors work best, and if you keep that atmosphere, actors will sometimes do something brilliant during rehearsal. That doesn't mean I'll use it in a picture, but I might. I remember when Meryl saw *Bridges of Madison County*. She said, "You know what I love? You used all my mistakes, too." And I said, "Yeah, but they were genuine mistakes." They were human mistakes, not an actor's mistakes. They are more like real life.

PLAYBOY: You were married more than 25 years to your first wife. What happened?

EASTWOOD: We just separated. We were separated for 10 years of that marriage.

PLAYBOY: What is your relationship with her like now?

EASTWOOD: We're in business together—we have a partnership in a restaurant and some properties. We get along terrifically. She lives in this area and we talk a lot, and naturally we have certain things in common, because we have two children. We see each other at events and get along much better than when we were married.

PLAYBOY: You received a lot of media attention about the situation with Sondra Locke.

EASTWOOD: I know. I guess maybe I'm the only one who finds it weird that she's still obsessed with our relationship and putting out the same old rhetoric almost 10 years later. But I always think it's best to take the high road and not get involved with that. There are two sides to this whole thing. And I've endured a lot of sensationalist reporting, people making up things out of thin air. She's been married for 29 years, but nobody puts that in their stories. She never wanted children, so she had a tubal ligation, which women opt for mostly after they've had children. I've been accused of forcing that on her—if anybody believes that.

PLAYBOY: She accused you of forcing her to have a tubal ligation?

EASTWOOD: Yeah. It's constantly thrown out there—some tabloid called me about it the other day, or called my agent about it. But it's the same old stuff, and you get on with your life. It's kind of unfortunate. She plays the victim very well. Unfortunately, she had cancer and so she plays that card. But every time these things come up, it makes me knock on wood that I'm here and not there.

PLAYBOY: Do the tabloids drive you crazy?

EASTWOOD: With the tabloids it's a kind of lazy journalism. They don't really want to know your story; they prefer to write about Clint Eastwood and the accusations against him. They regurgitate this stuff. As far as the legal action with Sondra goes, it was my fault. I have to take full responsibility because I thought I was doing her a favor by helping her get a production arrangement with Warner Bros. I prevailed upon Warner Bros. to do it and it didn't work out. So she sued Warner and then she sued me and finally at some point I said, Wait a second, I would have been better off if I hadn't done anything and had let her go ahead and file the palimony suit against me. I tried to help. I thought she would get directing assignments, but it didn't work out that way. So her attorney accused me of going into collusion with Warner Bros. and said that they purposely didn't want her to do anything. I should have known that it would never work out, that it would come back to haunt me. Even if it had worked out, it would have come back to haunt me, because you don't know if somebody is ever going to be satisfied.

PLAYBOY: She said the breakup, after all those years, was sudden.

EASTWOOD: It wasn't sudden. I mean, it was sudden, but it had been coming along for some time. She has a husband. He's gay and was having problems with one of his friends, so she was getting drawn into it all the time. She was constantly on the phone and couldn't go anywhere, and pretty soon we just grew apart. She was busy trying to solve his problems and we didn't spend that much time together. I decided I was tired of it. That's the way things happen sometimes. It was an unhealthy existence, and I didn't want any part of it. My son was living with me in Los Angeles at the time, and I just wanted to be with my family. I didn't want to be with someone who had some strange thing going on. And I don't mind what anybody does, but when it's affecting me and my family relationships, then I have to do something.

PLAYBOY: Her husband is gay?

EASTWOOD: She admitted that during the trial. They were buddies from school days or something. I mean, it's just a different scene. I can't explain it without going into a . . . I mean, your eyes might not stay in their sockets. They're liable to come too far out of your head. They were pals when they were kids, and they both believe in fairy tales and call each other Hobbit and stuff like that. And so they hang out together, and I guess she's supportive of him and he's supportive of her, and somehow they feed each other. She didn't like my son living with me and it just got messy. It just wasn't the kind of existence I wanted.

PLAYBOY: Do you feel burned by the whole thing?

EASTWOOD: Yeah, I guess so. But you go on about your business. I'm going on with my life, and if other people can't get on with theirs, that's their problem.

PLAYBOY: How is your relationship with Frances Fisher? Is it friendly?

EASTWOOD: Good, yeah. It's friendly.

PLAYBOY: You have a child with her?

EASTWOOD: Yes.

PLAYBOY: Was the breakup acrimonious?

EASTWOOD: We were just having a rough time getting along. I love the child, she loves the child. We have that together. Frances is a fine actress. Very successful. Hardworking. I give her a lot of credit. We had a nice relationship, but it was never meant to go to marriage.

PLAYBOY: Is it complicated having a serious relationship with an actress, especially if you're a director?

EASTWOOD: Yes, it is. Very complicated. It's better just to hire people and work with people. But if you're with an actress, especially if you're a director with a certain amount of control, there's sometimes a resentment if you hire somebody else. The attitude is, "Am I not good enough for you to hire me?" Of course it has nothing to do with ability; it has to do with how you see the project.

PLAYBOY: So if you want to cast *The Bridges of Madison County*—

EASTWOOD: Exactly. She would have loved to play the part Meryl played.

PLAYBOY: Was that an issue?

EASTWOOD: Enough said.

PLAYBOY: So is this your final marriage? Is Dina the last Mrs. Eastwood?

EASTWOOD: This is it. Win, lose or draw.

PLAYBOY: Does the age disparity concern you? She's 31, you're 66.

EASTWOOD: Nothing to worry about there. I mean, it's never been an issue. I don't think about that. You're as old as you feel, and I feel great. Certainly if you're a man there are advantages to being older. You're a little more giving and patient. You're not as self-oriented, always out for the brass ring like when you were younger. None of us knows how long fate gives you on the planet. People get so concerned about age, about the future, they don't live out their moment today. Moment to moment. I'm immensely happy with Dina, and I feel I've finally found a person I want to be with. We have a great time.

PLAYBOY: How did you meet?

EASTWOOD: She's an anchorwoman with an NBC affiliate here, and she interviewed me after *Unforgiven*. She seemed very charming and nice and I liked her, but it was a friendly thing and then we just went our separate ways. But I liked her very much. I remembered her. And I think she felt the same way. I went to a function by myself some time later. I walked in and they said, "Oh, why don't you sit with Dina, she's also by herself." So we sat down and talked and laughed and danced and what have you, but we didn't arrange a date or anything. Then I went to another charity function, and again she was there. And we got talking again and by this time I was between relationships, and so we went out and had a beer and talked. The next few times we just went out and grabbed a beer and sat and talked. We started to date occasionally after *Bridges of Madison County*. The one thing we always maintained was a really good level of respect for each other. I've been supportive of her with her job and she's supportive of me with my job. They don't cross or collide. She's a really smart woman.

PLAYBOY: Do you prefer to be with somebody who's not in the movie business?

EASTWOOD: You said it. There's no agenda, no work thing. If I introduce her to friends who are producers, there's no work in that for her. They're just friends. And she's here, she loves it here. I love it here. It's very nice.

PLAYBOY: What kind of women have appealed to you?

EASTWOOD: I've liked women who were smart and OK-looking, and I've liked women who were good-looking and not too smart. I'm no different from any other guy. It's a cliché that an extremely attractive woman has to be a bimbo with a brain the size of a peanut. That's wrong. Just because a woman is attractive doesn't mean she isn't smart. But I think what a man wants from a woman is pretty much what a woman wants from a man. Respect. That's the ultimate to me. Sure there's infatuation. But a person has to respect herself and has to respect you and what you do, and you have to respect each other. If one or the other doesn't, it becomes problematic.

PLAYBOY: What role does your family play in your life?

EASTWOOD: I like them very much. It seems their existence keeps me young. If you have a two-year-old around the house, it keeps you thinking, keeps you young, watching the learning process. My older kids are all off in different directions, but I try to see them as much as I can. I'm seeing my daughter Alison in L.A. tonight. I see the older ones on holidays and on certain occasions when they want something. [*Laughs*]

PLAYBOY: How do you feel about having a three-year-old and a brand-new daughter?

EASTWOOD: It's so much easier when you're in your 60s. When you're young, life is selfish, everything is selfish. You're talking about your next job, what's going to happen to your career and, when you get a break, especially in the acting profession, how long it's going to last. Every actor thinks his last job was his last job. It takes years before that syndrome subsides. And I don't have that. It's a great thing. I'm not compelled to work like I did when I was younger. Check it out with older men who have kids. They have more time, and more patience. Of course, you also get to a certain age and you go, "OK, this is going to be nice." But here's the reality of it: They're going to be here forever, you'll be asked for things forever, you'll feel sometimes like it's a one-way street.

PLAYBOY: Having been mayor of Carmel, have you ever been asked to run for governor or senator?

EASTWOOD: There was a lot of talk like that, but only because Reagan was president at the time and everybody thought, Well, here's another movie actor who is going to try to do something political. But I didn't want to do that. George Murphy and Reagan and all those guys quit acting when they went into politics.

PLAYBOY: Why didn't politics appeal to you as a way of life?

EASTWOOD: It's a lot of work and a lot of frustration, and being a politician is about the last thing I'd want to do. I like independence. I revere independence. And I'm not that good a politician. I get along with people, but to sit there and fudge the truth and promise to do something and know you're not going to do it—that's not what I want to do.

PLAYBOY: Are there issues you feel strongly about?

EASTWOOD: I don't think there should be two four-year terms for the president. I think someone should be president for one six-year term with no chance to run again. I feel that only two years of a four-year term are put to good use. The rest is running for the next four years, and that's very expensive and counterproductive. I think term limitations would be great. I know a lot of congressmen and senators hate to hear that, but I think it's good to have new blood. I quit after one term as mayor because I wanted new blood to come in. When people get in term after term, they forget the meaning of public servant. Then bad things start happening.

PLAYBOY: How would you characterize yourself politically?

EASTWOOD: Libertarian. Everyone leaves everyone else alone. Neither party seems to have the ability to embrace that sort of thing.

PLAYBOY: Are you pro-choice?

EASTWOOD: I've always been pro-choice. It's an individual decision. I don't believe organizations should start taking over the decision-making process for the individual. Absolute power corrupts.

PLAYBOY: Let's talk about another issue. During the 1960s and 1970s, did you see a lot of drugs and craziness in Hollywood?

EASTWOOD: I had friends who died using drugs, and I've had a lot of friends who had problems along the way. I had a particularly close friend who became reclusive and finally gave up. It was very sad.

PLAYBOY: Did you ever take drugs?

EASTWOOD: No, never did. I'm not much of a drinker, either. A glass of wine, a beer, a shot of Patron tequila—that's a treat every now and then. I have a buddy who says, "Anything better than a good glass of beer and a piece of ass would kill me." [*Laughs*] Maybe there's something to that. I mean, how good do you want life to be? I've always liked life, anyway. People who get into drugs are trying to escape themselves. I've never wanted to escape.

PLAYBOY: Let's talk a little bit about your childhood. What was your mother like?

EASTWOOD: I say this without prejudice: She's an extremely giving lady and she was always very flexible, very supportive, when I was growing up. I was always taught to be respectful of her. My father was big on basic courtesies toward women. The one time I ever got snotty with my mother when he was around, he left me a little battered. [*Grins*] Yeah, he taught me little things—like I should leave the toilet seat down out of respect for my mother. I was lucky. I was taught values. I was raised in a good family.

PLAYBOY: You grew up during the Depression. What impact did that have on you?

EASTWOOD: Tremendous impact, tremendous. So many people were unemployed and struggling, and there was no welfare state. People were dying to work, really wanted to work in any kind of job. Nowadays it's different. A friend of mine stopped a guy who was carrying a "need work" sign on the road and asked him if he wanted a job. The guy asked how much he'd be paid, and my friend said $6.80 an hour. The guy said, "Can't do it, not enough." That wouldn't have happened then.

PLAYBOY: Did growing up worrying about money affect you?

EASTWOOD: It made me sort of fiscally conservative. When you have some dough, you should put it away for a rainy day, and you should try to manage your money. The first movie actor I met was Cornel Wilde. We were at a party, and he asked, "What are you doing?" And I said, "Well, I'm trying to be an actor, studying to be an actor." I was a kid at the time, in my early 20s. And he said, "Save your money." I said, "I don't have any." But he said, "If you ever get any money, make sure you save it so you don't have to do all the crap people are going to ask you to do someday." I've always remembered that.

PLAYBOY: You struggled for some time as a bit player at Universal, then got *Rawhide*. Then you went off to Italy to make the spaghetti Westerns. Did it upset you that people years later—maybe even now—still saw you essentially as a Western star?

EASTWOOD: It didn't upset me. I knew that I was different, I knew I wasn't a cowboy. But if you portray a cowboy and people think you're a cowboy, that's fine. That's what every actor strives for. If you're playing a fireman and they believe you're a guy who's with the fire department, that's fantastic. People are always trying to typecast you. I guess I came in in kind of an oddball way too, going off to Italy like that to do those low-budget Westerns. When the movies came out, they were actually more revered—at least for that time—than American-made Westerns. But some people wondered, What the hell kind of crap is this? What are they doing to our Western movie? As for being a Western actor, years ago I was asked if I was afraid of being typed when I started *Rawhide*. I had been unemployed for a long time, I had been struggling as an actor, and I said, "Are you kidding? Just get me the job and I'll worry about getting untyped later." But in reality everyone is typed for something.

PLAYBOY: You're one of only a handful of people who have had extraordinary longevity as stars—for you, 40 years. What's the secret? Good looks?

EASTWOOD: Not at this age.

PLAYBOY: Is it the roles you choose?

EASTWOOD: When I first came on, maybe 30 years ago, I was a sort of an upstart out of television who was doing these Italian-made Westerns. But after the third one, after *The Good, the Bad and the Ugly*, it was time to come back here. And instead of doing a picture more grand in scale, I did a smaller picture, *Hang 'Em High*, which was about capital punishment. Then I did medium-sized pictures throughout the 1960s. And several expensive films, such as *Where Eagles Dare* and *Paint Your Wagon*—with varying success. I started to branch out in the 1970s with *The Beguiled*, trying offbeat things. The next two, *Play Misty* and *Dirty Harry*, were commercial, and then in the 1980s I did *Bronco Billy* and

Honkytonk Man. I was always reaching out for something different. And even *Every Which Way but Loose*, which is a comedy with an orangutan and the sort of stuff people don't necessarily take seriously in cinema, was a reach. I was moving away from gunplay and that kind of stuff, and I think those reaches throughout my career have gotten me some attention. They've kept me interested. I think it's easy for a person to fall into complacency and say, "I could have stayed in Italy and done 25 Westerns instead of three." I could have come back here and done a whole mess of cop dramas, but that would have been boring for the public and boring for me. If you're not going to look interested, there's no reason to expect the audience to be interested.

PLAYBOY: In terms of casting women, you rarely seemed to go after conventional beauties: Geraldine Page in *The Beguiled*, Jessica Walter in *Play Misty for Me*, Kay Lenz in *Breezy*, Bernadette Peters in *Pink Cadillac*.

EASTWOOD: If you get too conventional with glamour girls, all of a sudden it becomes a Hollywood picture rather than a picture that relates to anything realistic. There are beautiful girls who are not models or actresses, but they seem like Barbies. It can kill a movie if you glam things up.

PLAYBOY: You often make the commute from Carmel to Los Angeles by piloting your own helicopter. When did you start flying?

EASTWOOD: I was introduced to helicopters in 1968 or 1969. I was on the set of *Paint Your Wagon*, in Baker, Oregon, and the pilot used to pick me up in the front yard of the home I was renting and we'd fly a half hour to work. He gave me a chance to fly a little. I liked it. Finally about eight years ago I got a license and bought a helicopter at the Paris Air Show.

PLAYBOY: What makes flying a helicopter special?

EASTWOOD: There's great freedom to it. It's sort of the last seat-of-your-pants flying. You can actually go places and land places and not be obliged to have an airport. It's nice to be able to land at a friend's house. And when you're flying you're out on your own, there are no phones, you just kind of relax and think. You're just a number in the sky. It's nice up there.

PLAYBOY: Let's talk about music. We heard you playing piano the other day and you play very well.

EASTWOOD: I used to listen to a lot of rhythm and blues on the radio. When I was growing up in northern California there was a big classic-jazz revival in the Bay Area. I would lie about my age and go to Hambone

Kelly's. I'd stand in the back and listen to Lu Watters and Turk Murphy play New Orleans jazz. I used to think I was really a black guy in a white body.

PLAYBOY: Who were your favorites?

EASTWOOD: I grew up listening to Ella Fitzgerald and Nat King Cole. Big favorites. I still listen. I was raised on Lester Young, Charlie Parker, Dizzy Gillespie, Miles Davis, Clifford Brown, Fats Navarro, all that crowd, and Thelonious Monk, Erroll Garner.

PLAYBOY: *Bird* was an unexpected film for you.

EASTWOOD: It was unexpected because it was out of the genre. People think, If he's not going to be in the picture, he should make a film about something he understands or has done before. But I like music, I love music. Doing a story about a musician was very logical for me. And it came as a shock only to someone who didn't know I was interested. But those are all swings at bat. You don't always get the home run. Sometimes a game can be put together with base hits. That's what happened with *Bird*.

PLAYBOY: Why did you want to make a movie about Charlie Parker?

EASTWOOD: I had seen him when I was a kid. I liked him very much. I thought he was one of the most confident players I'd ever seen. It was a whole new era of music—this is when New York bop was coming out. I saw him in Oakland, California. He was on tour with Lester Young, Coleman Hawkins and Hank Jones. It was an interesting era for me. At that time I was 16 years old in the 1940s and it just kind of knocked me out. And I didn't know about Charlie Parker. I just knew his name. But he came out and started playing. In those days, musicians didn't wear fancy outfits like today. Everybody just wore a suit and tie, everybody. They just played. And you listened. The excitement came out of what they played. Parker got up there and started playing, and I said, "I don't know what this is, but I want to find out about it." He opened up a whole new world. I'd never seen an artist that confident about what he was doing, so completely in control. He was brilliant and innovative. Yet there was great emotion and sensitivity. I bought a lot of his records over the years. When that script became available, I decided it was a story I would like to tell.

PLAYBOY: You've written the main themes for *Bridges of Madison County* and other films. Lennie Niehaus, the composer who scores a lot of your pictures, said you actually think like a jazz musician while directing films, preferring improvisation over constant rehearsal and placing an emphasis on ensemble work over individuality.

EASTWOOD: Jazz has always represented a sort of freedom of expression for me. But a musician has an advantage over an actor. He holds the saxophone or trumpet and channels into it. We just have to stand there and deliver whatever there is. Being behind the camera is certainly a safer feeling than acting in front of it.

PLAYBOY: You still tend to play heroes. Could you play a salesman or a dry cleaner or an average guy?

EASTWOOD: I doubt it. Let's say I wanted to play a remake of Dr. Kildare or someone like that. Old Dr. Kildare, middle-aged doctor, whatever. Eventually, when the last reel comes up, no matter how nice the story is, many people in the audience will expect old Dr. Kildare to shoot somebody. Fortunately, a lot of reviewers have called attention to the fact that I fought my way out of a certain genre, and that's been nice. But still there's a group out there saying: "Eastwood as Dr. Kildare? Let's pass on this one and catch the next one." I entered some projects, such as *White Hunter, Black Heart*, knowing they would probably not be hardcore commercial films. But I had to make them anyway.

PLAYBOY: Any parts you wish you'd had?

EASTWOOD: There are some you turn down because you don't feel instinctively right about the material, or maybe you think you aren't the right guy. One interested me a while back. *The Killing Fields*. You remember the one, where the guy is a New York journalist who goes into Cambodia. I liked the script a lot and thought it would make a good movie. But I thought, If you cast Clint Eastwood in a film called *The Killing Fields*, you know damn well that that's going to send a message to a lot of people who want to see Clint Eastwood gun down 30 people every reel. And they're going to be terribly disappointed. You're going to get that crowd and that crowd only.

PLAYBOY: In the Dirty Harry films you mete out justice to murderers. You take the law in your own hands, mirroring the discontent in a country that was portrayed as being run by bleeding hearts. Pauline Kael said it was fascist.

EASTWOOD: People can call things what they want. In those days everybody wanted to put a label on things. The picture was ahead of its time. This is a guy who's having bureaucratic obstacles thrown up within the police force, judicial system, city politics and all that. Everybody understood that frustration. If there was irresponsibility in *Dirty Harry*, there's irresponsibility in Robin Hood, Tom Mix and the Old Testament. There's violence in them all.

PLAYBOY: Is that why you think that picture struck a nerve?

EASTWOOD: It showed compassion for the victim, which wasn't stylish at the time.

PLAYBOY: What did you think the first time you read "Go ahead, make my day"?

EASTWOOD: I thought, Yeah, this is definitely the key line of the movie.

PLAYBOY: Other stars, including Mel Gibson and Jack Nicholson, have come to you for advice before directing a film. What did you tell them?

EASTWOOD: Get more sleep than your actors.

PLAYBOY: You were once asked if you ever woke up in the morning, looked in the mirror and said, "Can this possibly be me?" Your reply was, "It's like waking up with a hooker—how the hell did I get here?"

EASTWOOD: Actually, it's like waking up with an ugly hooker.

February 1966

FEDERICO FELLINI

A candid conversation with the protean creator of such trailblazing cinematic allegories as La Strada, La Dolce Vita *and* 8 1/2

A few months ago, during the closed-set filming of *Juliet of the Spirits*, Federico Fellini's long-awaited latest film, Roman TV officials congratulated themselves on what promised to be a major video coup when *il grande maestro* unexpectedly rescinded his own ban on press coverage of the production in progress and acquiesced to their repeated requests for a sample snippet from the film. They were understandably baffled and bedazzled by the footage he supplied—an extraordinary comic-opera scene starring the elephantine, wild-haired whore from *8 1/2* outrageously decked out as D'Artagnan in feathers, velvets, boots and blond mustaches, surrounded by a motley chorus of nuns, clowns and gypsies, all cavorting about to the tune of a blaring Neapolitan aria. The viewing public was equally perplexed when the scene was subsequently sneak-previewed on television, but the critics greeted it with learned interpretations of its allegorical significance—or lack of it. Not until the finished film premiered did they discover that they'd been had: Never intended as part of the picture, it was conspicuous by its absence; Fellini had dreamed up the whole thing as a put-on for symbol searchers.

Unamused, some reviewers replied that the joke was on Fellini; though dazzling to behold, the invented scene was no more or less profound, or relevant to the story, they averred, than any given episode in the picture, which one of them contemptuously dismissed as "a fever dream with delusions of grandeur." A kaleidoscopic pasticcio of visions, dreams, memories and hallucinations conjured up by a middle-aged housewife who takes refuge from reality in a private world of fantasy, and finds it peopled with erotic and terrifying specters, *Juliet* has been hailed by other critics as a phantasmagorical master-piece of cinematic psychodrama, and a spectacular affirmation of its creator's status as a protean poet of the cinema. But acclaim or abuse—neither of which is new to Fellini—serves merely to certify his contentious world fame. And the paradoxical appellations he's earned during his 15 years as a director—genius and madman, tragedian and clown, archangel and archdemon, moralist and sensation seeker—testify not only to his defiance of definition ("Tags," he says, "are for suitcases") but also to his prodigious originality as a moviemaker.

Even his detractors acknowledge that whatever else he may be, Fellini is irrepressibly, inimitably, eternally himself. On the visual level, all of his films bear the unmistakable stamp of a flamboyantly inventive directorial technique; and beneath the bravura façade, his protagonists all share a dual quest: for human warmth, usually from the wrong people; and for their own identities, usually in the wrong places. "Sometimes," he told one journalist, "I feel that I am all the time making the same film." By his own admission, this serial screenplay is a chronicle of his own spiritual odyssey, a search for self in a liberation from the past—a past steeped in the guilt-edged moral ideals of stern Church dogma drummed into him as a boy.

Son of a well-to-do wholesaler of wines and groceries in Rimini, a small provincial town on the Adriatic coast of northern Italy, Fellini took to neither the disciplines of parochial schooling nor the sedate comforts of middle-class home life: He quit school at 12 and ran away to join a traveling circus as an apprentice clown. Not quite ready to sever the parental ties, he was back home dead-broke a few months later; and he remained there, restlessly, until a vaudeville troupe hit town soon after his 17th birthday. When it pulled up stakes two days later, so did he—this time for good—following the show from town to town, writing comedy sketches for his keep. Drawn to the bustle and bright lights of the big city, he abandoned the caravan in Florence and decided to seek his fortune as a freelance contributor to local humor magazines. But pickings were slim, and Fellini soon moved on to slightly greener pastures in Milan, where he turned a talent for cartooning into a modest but fairly steady living by pirating American comic strips—banned from Italy by Mussolini—for various city newspapers. Drifting on to Rome a few months later, he spent the war years avoiding the draft and scuffling for bread money as a prolific gagwriter for local humor weeklies.

It was also during this otherwise bleak period that he met and married the struggling young actress who was to become world-famous as his tragicomic star: Giulietta Masina. The war's end, however, found them both pounding the pavement: she in search of movie bit parts, he as a street-corner caricaturist in sidewalk cafés along the Via Veneto—even then a watering place for show-business moguls great and small, hangers-on and has-beens—where he began to mingle and make friends with aspiring moviemakers who were just breaking into the burgeoning postwar film industry. Among them was director Roberto Rossellini, who invited the articulate, energetic young jack-of-all-trades to collaborate with him on the scenario of his first film. They did, and the picture—*Open City*—was hailed as a milestone in the Italian cinema, progenitor of a seminal new movement in moviemaking: neorealism. With *Paisan*, their second joint effort, Rossellini's renown became worldwide, and Fellini was launched on a full-time screenwriting career.

A score of successful film scripts poured from his pen in the next two years, though his income failed to keep pace with his rising reputation. Rankling not at financial frustration but at the creative confinement of the printed word, he leaped in 1950 at the chance to bring a script personally to life as both author and co-director of *Variety Lights*, a poignant portrait of the melancholy faces hidden behind the masks of mirth worn by a troupe of wandering vaudevillians— and, in a larger sense, by most of mankind on an aimless road of life. Though he shared in its creation, even this first directorial effort bears the distinctive imprint of Fellini's potent personality—and of his checkered past, echoing as it does the picaresque period of his own experience as an itinerant entertainer. Then, in 1951, with his debut as a full-fledged director, came the first mature expression of the multileveled, metaphoric vision that has become the trademark of a Fellini film. A seriocomic satire on the *fumetti*—those far-fetched photographic comic strips in which impossibly handsome heroes perform impossibly dashing deeds of derring-do and rescue ladies in impossible extremities of distress—it was called *The White Sheik*, after one of the Valentino-like paladins from this daydream world of Italian pulp-magazine pictorials. On one level, it tells the story of a newlywed fumetti fan so steeped in rosy romantic reveries that she finds it impossible to reconcile herself to the mundane reality of marriage. On a deeper level, the picture warns of the desolation and despair that await those who pursue ideality rather than reality, who hope to hide from the harsh task of finding out who they really are.

Alienation of a more subtle and hopeless kind was the somber theme of I Vitelloni, Fellini's next film. Outwardly, it's the chronicle of a bunch of young loafers—unemployed and unmotivated, believing in and belonging to nothing—who bum around the empty streets and beaches of a seaside resort during the dead winter months in a listless, futile search for nothing more meaningful than something to pass the time. But it can also be seen as an allegory of man's vain quest for a purpose and pattern larger than and beyond his own.

With La Strada, his next picture, Fellini emerged, at 34, into the full flower of his creative powers as a lyrical cinematic poet. Universally applauded not merely as a tragic masterpiece but as one of the screen's authentic classics, it won dozens of distinguished film awards—including an Oscar—and earned its creator his first international recognition. It was also the picture in which Fellini's wife, Giulietta Masina, established her credentials as a Chaplinesque genius of comic pathos with her deeply touching performance as Gelsomina, a simpleminded waif whose childlike love of life is trampled and finally snuffed out by Zampano, a half-human, half-animal circus strong man (played by Anthony Quinn) who buys her, uses her cruelly and finally abandons her, sick and broken, by the roadside. Repenting later, he wants Gelsomina back and goes looking for her—only to learn that she has died. Thunderstruck, he staggers numbly to the beach in the film's final scene and falls weeping to his knees. Shaking his fists in impotent rage and grief at the indifferent stars, he is a mutely eloquent embodiment of man's loneliness, folly and despair.

Equally poetic justice is meted out to the protagonist of Fellini's fifth film, Il Bidone (1955), a merciless indictment of confidence men who prey on other people's illusions—and by extension, of all who knowingly exploit their fellow man. At the end, an aging swindler (Broderick Crawford) is beaten, betrayed and left to die in a ditch by his equally unscrupulous accomplices—after repenting too late, like Zampano, for the error of his ways. Seldom shown in this country, Il Bidone was perhaps Fellini's most humorless and least successful film, both artistically and commercially. Back at the top of his form in 1957, however, with *Nights of Cabiria*, he took home a sizable sum of box-office booty and a mantelpieceful of international prizes, including his second Academy Award. Another tour-de-force vehicle for the talents of Mrs. Fellini, the film starred her as a dumpy, gullible, good-natured prostitute who unknowingly allows herself to be bilked out of her hard-earned little hoard of earnings. But no retribution, in this case, is visited upon the exploiter; the bitter lesson is that wrongdoers, in the real world, don't always pay the piper. The film's last scene, however, as a group of young musicians serenades Cabiria home after learning of her loss, sounds a final note of hope restored and faith instilled—that a crippling loss, even of a limb or a loved one, need not be as tragic as it seems; that a cruel humiliation need not breed disillusionment.

But disillusionment, abject and all-encompassing, provided both theme and variations for Fellini's next creation, in 1960, an epicurean smorgasbord of despair and degeneracy that proferred an eye-filling feast for millions of scandal-hungry moviegoers throughout the world: *La Dolce Vita*, starring Marcello Mastroianni. A brilliantly conceived, graphically etched, bitterly sardonic and morbidly fascinating panorama of Rome's decadent café society, it was seen by Fellini as "an attempt to take the temperature of a sick society." In the opinion of Church spokesmen, censorship groups and even a few reviewers, however, it was little more than a sensational tabloid exposé that exploited as well as indicted the objects of its satire.

Except for his contribution of a brief segment to *Boccaccio '70* in 1961, nothing was heard from Fellini for the next three years; but then came another Oscar winner: *8 1/2*, a creation even more extravagant than the public's expectations, a radical departure from everything he'd ever done before, in a style so unconventional that it can be said to have introduced an entirely new genre of cinematic storytelling. The leading man—again portrayed by Mastroianni—is really a modified mirror image of Fellini: Guido, a self-searching 43-year-old Italian movie director with graying temples. And the story line is a highly impressionistic mosaic of larger-than-life memories, self-indulgent fantasies, bizarre dreams and idealized visions that somehow coalesce into a coherent, deeply insightful and introspective spiritual autobiography. At the end of the film, Guido finally extricates himself from the self-created labyrinth of irrational guilts, fears, hopes and expectations that has immobilized him—and learns to accept himself as he is, not as he might wish he were or hoped he might have been.

The identity crisis, and the epiphany of self-acceptance experienced by the heroine in *Juliet of the Spirits*, Fellini's most recent and precocious brain child, are essentially the same as Guido's. But the dreams, fantasies and memories each summons up perform the opposite functions. In Guido's case, they're actually way stations on his search for self-fulfillment in reality; while for Juliet they're magic carpets of escape from the real world. Setting *Juliet* even farther apart from 8 1/2 is the simple fact that it's in Technicolor, Fellini's first; and the further fact that it was blessed with a multimillion-dollar production budget, a great rarity in European films. Bedaubing and bedizening his cinematic canvas with giddy abandon, Fellini has created for his heroine a dreamworld of eye-drenching and Byzantine extravagance.

To the consternation of his actors, producers, technicians and almost everybody else who works with him, the process of creating these resplendent spectacles of the spirit takes place almost entirely without such traditional prerequisites as finished dialogue and a detailed shooting script; Fellini considers them not only unnecessary but inhibiting to optimum creativity. The outlines of the plot and the drift of the dialogue are jotted down ahead of time, mostly for the record; but all the rest—from the selection of the leading lady's shade of eye shadow to the designation of locations for each scene—is decided on the set, often on the day of the shooting only a moment before the cameras start to roll; and all of it, needless to mention, in every detail, is decreed by Fellini himself and no one else. The complete filmmaker, he feels, must be not only the creator of his own heaven and earth and all the beasts thereof, but also the benevolent despot of all he surveys on set, with final and absolute authority over everything and everyone within his private realm. In the heat of this omnipotent role as god-king, amid the all-consuming throes of filming, Fellini is a man possessed—tireless, foodless, drinkless, oblivious to all else but the birth of the film as a living entity. "Though he's miraculously talented, sensitive and intuitive," says a coworker, "Federico can also be cruel, childish and destructive to those around him at these times." Considering the issue of his prodigious labors, most are willing to forgive such moods.

When he finished filming *Juliet of the Spirits* late last year, we waited a few weeks, on the advice of friends, "for his brain to cool," then telephoned Fellini at his beach house in nearby Fregene, on the Tyrrhenian coast—where he was still recovering from "the exquisite ordeal," as he called it—with our request for an exclusive interview at his leisure. We had heard he'd be wearily reluctant to talk at first, but expansively garrulous once persuaded, which we were told would take no more than a modicum of urging. And so it proved. The following week, at his unpretentious provincial home in Fregene, he received us with warm hospitality for the first of our conversations. Later chats took place on the run, in his black Mercedes sedan en route to the studio from the beach; at his comfortably un-chic apartment in Rome's Parioli district; and at work in the dubbing room, where he supervised the lip-synching of *Juliet* into English. A rumpled, heavy six-footer with a penetrating gaze and a shaggy leonine mane of graying hair, he often wore a heavy black scarf over his shoulders—and a floppy black cloth hat of the Black Bart variety. Punctuating his every sentence with sweepingly expressive gestures and a flashing succession of pantomimic facial expressions to match, he spoke to us (in English and Italian) for a total of 10 hours, his conversation alternately colloquial and poetically baroque, richly metaphorical and metaphysical, laced with a cheerful sense of irony, and marked throughout by an engaging candor about himself. We began the interview with a candid, if less than engaging, personal question.

PLAYBOY: Among your friends, you have a reputation as a teller of tall tales. One of them, in fact, has gone so far as to call you "a colossal, compulsive, consummate liar." What's your reaction?

FELLINI: At least he gives me credit for being consummate. Anyone who lives, as I do, in a world of imagination must make an enormous and unnatural effort to be factual in the ordinary sense. I confess I would be a horrible witness in court because of this—and a terrible journalist. I feel compelled to tell a story the way I *see* it, and this is seldom the way it actually happened, in all its documentary detail.

PLAYBOY: You've been accused of embroidering the truth outrageously even in recounting the story of your own life. One friend says you've told him four completely different versions of your breakup with your first sweetheart. Why?

FELLINI: Why not? She's worth even more versions. *Che bella ragazza!* People are worth much more than truth, even when they don't look as great as she did. If you want to call me a liar in this sense, then I reply that it's indispensable to let a storyteller *color* a story, expand it, deepen it, depending on the way he feels it has to be told. In my films, I do the same with life.

PLAYBOY: Is that how you see yourself—as a storyteller rather than as a "conjurer," "modern moralist," "social satirist" or "ringmaster of a cinematic circus," as you've been variously described?

FELLINI: Those are impressive-sounding occupations, but as far as I'm concerned, I'm just a storyteller, and the cinema happens to be my medium. I like it because it re-creates life in movement, enlarges it, enhances it, distills it. For me, it's far closer to the miraculous creation of life itself than, say, painting or music or even literature. It's not just an art form; it's actually a new form of *life*, with its own rhythms, cadences, perspectives and transparencies. It's my way of telling a story.

PLAYBOY: Most critics agree that your storytelling technique is uniquely compelling; but they disagree, for the most part, on the moral and meaning of your films. Does this concern you?

FELLINI: Do the critics have to understand my films? Isn't it enough that the public enjoys them?

PLAYBOY: Are your films intended primarily as entertainment, then, or is their box-office appeal secondary to philosophic intent?

FELLINI: I'm not concerned with popularity, and it's pointless to speak of philosophic intent. After each picture I often don't recall what my intentions were. Intentions are only instruments to put you into condition to do something, to start you off. Many great works are done well *despite* their original intent. Pascal, for example, wrote the *Pensèes* to demonstrate the nonexistence of God—and ended up doing just the opposite. Take *La Dolce Vita*. What I intended was to show the state of Rome's *soul*, a way of being of a people. What it *became* was a scandalous report, a fresco of a street and a society. But I never go to Via Veneto—it isn't my street. And I never attend *festas* of aristocrats—I don't know any. The left-wing press played it up as headline reportage on Rome, but it didn't have to be Rome; it could have been Bangkok or a thousand other cities. I intended it as a report on Sodom and Gomorrah, a trip into anguish and despair. I intended for it to be a document, not a documentary.

PLAYBOY: Still, if we confine ourselves to the original impulse that inspired them, is there a common theme linking your films?

FELLINI: My work can't be anything other than a testimony of what I am looking for in life. It is a mirror of my searching.

PLAYBOY: Searching for what?

FELLINI: For myself freed. In this respect, I think, there is no cleavage or difference of content or style in all my films. From first to last, I have struggled to free myself—always from the past, from the education laid upon me as a child. That is what I'm seeking, though through different characters and with changing tempo and images.

PLAYBOY: In what sense do you want to escape your past?

FELLINI: I became burdened in childhood with useless baggage that I now want off my back. I want to *uneducate* myself of these worthless concepts, so that I may return to a virginal personality—to a rebirth of real intent and of real self. Then I won't be lost in a collective whole that fits nobody because it's made to fit *everybody.* Wherever I go, from the corner of my eye I see young people moving in groups, like schools of fish. When I was young, we all moved in separate directions. Are we developing a society like ants, in blocs and colonies? This is one of the things I fear more than anything else. I loathe collectivity. Man's greatness and nobility consist in standing *free* of the mass. How he extricates himself from it is his own personal problem and private struggle. This is what my films describe.

PLAYBOY: Can you give us an actual example from one of your films?

FELLINI: In *8 1/2*, society's norms and rules imprisoned Guido in his boyhood with a sense of guilt and frustration. From childhood many of us are conditioned by a similar education. Then, growing up, we find ourselves in profound conflict—a conflict created by having been taught to idealize our lives, to pursue aesthetic and ethical ideals of absolute good or evil. This imposes impossible standards and unattainable aspirations that can only impede the spontaneous growth of a normal human being, and may conceivably destroy him. You must have experienced this yourself. There arrives a moment in life when you discover that what you've been told at home, in school or in church is simply not true. You discover that it binds your authentic self, your instinct, your true growth. And this opens up a schism, creates a conflict that must eventually be resolved—or succumbed to. In all forms of neurosis there is this clash between certain forms of idealization in a moral sense and a contrary aesthetic form. It all started with the Greeks when they enshrined a classical standard of physical beauty. A man who did not correspond to that type of beauty felt himself excluded, inferior, an outsider. Then came Christianity, which established an ethical beauty. This doubled man's problems by creating the dual possibility that he was neither beautiful as a Greek god nor holy as a Catholic one. Inevitably, you were guilty of either nonbeauty or unsaintliness, and probably both. So you lived in disgrace: Man did not love you, nor did God; thus you remained outside of life.

PLAYBOY: And today?

FELLINI: In a modified form, this same ethic-aesthetic still prevails, and there is no escape from it through mere denial, though many have tried. You *can* escape very simply, however: by realizing that if you are not beautiful, it's all right anyway; and if you're not a saint, that's all right, too—because reality is not ideality. But this self-acceptance can occur only when you've grasped one fundamental fact of life: that the only thing which exists is yourself, your true individual self in depth, which wants to grow spontaneously, but which is fettered by inoperative lies, myths and fantasies proposing an unattainable morality or sanctity or perfection—all of it brainwashed into us during our defenseless childhood.

PLAYBOY: Once you've liberated yourself from the past, what then?

FELLINI: Then you are free to live in the present, and not seek cowardly flight toward the past—or toward the future, either.

PLAYBOY: In what way toward the future?

FELLINI: I mean that we must cease projecting ourselves into the future as though it were plannable, foreseeable, tangible, controllable—it's not; or as though it were a dimension existing outside and beyond ourselves. We must learn to deal with matters as they are, not as we hope or fear they may eventuate. We must cope with them as they exist now, today, at this moment. We must awaken to the fact that the future is already *here*, to be lived in the present. In short, wake up and live!

PLAYBOY: Though most of your protagonists, at the end of their spiritual odysseys, do learn to live with themselves as they are and with life as it is, some interpreters have seen their awakening as little more than a fatalistic resignation to the human condition.

FELLINI: No, no! Not a fatalistic resignation, but an *affirmative acceptance* of life, a burgeoning of *love* for life. The return of Guido to life in 8 1/2 is not a defeat. Rather, it is the return of a victor. When he finally realizes that he will never be able to resolve his problems, only to *live* with them—when he realizes that life itself is a continuous refutation of resolution—he experiences an exhilarating resurgence of energy, a return of profound religious sentiment. "I have faith," he says, "that I am inserted into a design of Providence whose end I don't and can't and will never comprehend—and wouldn't want to even if I could. There's nothing for me to do but pass through this panorama of joy and pain—with all my energy, all my enthusiasm, all my love, accepting it for what it is, without expecting an explanation that does not concern me, that does not involve me, that I am not called upon to give." He is at peace with himself at last—free to accept himself as he is, not as he wished he were or might have been. That is the optimistic finale to 8 1/2.

PLAYBOY: Doesn't *Juliet of the Spirits* have essentially the same moral?

FELLINI: Essentially, yes—only carried along another, deeper plane, with more decadent undertones, and told in a less realistic way. *Juliet* touches on myths within human psychology; its images, therefore, are those of a fable. But it treats a profound human reality: the institution of marriage, and the need within it for individual liberation. It's the portrait of an Italian woman, conditioned by our modern society, yet a product of misshapen religious training and ancient dogmas—like the one about getting married and living happily ever after. When she grows up and finds it hasn't come true, she can neither face nor understand it; and so she escapes into a private world of remembered yesterdays and mythical tomorrows. Whatever she does is influenced by her childhood, which she recaptures in otherworldly visions; and by the future, which she brings to life in bizarre and lively fantasies. The present exists for her only in the electronic unreality of television commercials. She is finally awakened from these visions by a grim reality: the desertion of her husband; but this fulfillment of her worst fear becomes the most positive episode of her life, for it forces her to find herself, to seek her free identity as an individual. And this gives her the insight to realize that all the fears—the phantoms that lived around her—were monsters of her own creation, bred of misshapen education and misread religion. She realizes that the spirits have been necessary, even useful, and deserve to be thanked; and the moment she thanks them, she no longer fears and hates them, and they turn into positive, pleasant beings.

PLAYBOY: Is there some specific message in this for all of us?

FELLINI: A lesson—a lesson we must all learn—as *Juliet* finally did: that marriage, if it is to survive, must be treated as the *beginning*, not as the happy ending; that it's something you have to work at; but that it's also not the alpha and omega of human existence; and that it must not be something you accept from the outside, like an inviolate taboo, never to be shattered. Why not admit it? Marriage as an institution needs re-examining. We live with too many nonfunctioning ideologies. Modern man needs richer relationships.

PLAYBOY: What kind?

FELLINI: Extramarital and premarital. Man is not basically a monogamous animal. Marriage is tyranny, a violation and mortification of his natural instincts. A woman, on the other hand, tends to create a world around one man. The tragedy of modern man is that he needs a multiplicity of individual relationships, whereas, at least in the culture in which I live, he is still forced into a single-mated mold. Without it, his life could develop into something interesting, into a higher evolution. Curiously enough, the multiple roles of infidelity seem to bring out the best in some men; were it not for self-negating guilt, it might in *most* men.

PLAYBOY: What you're suggesting, of course, is completely contrary to the teachings of the Catholic Church. Aren't you a Catholic?

FELLINI: It's difficult biologically and geographically *not* to be a Catholic in Italy. It's like a creature born beneath the sea—how can it not be a fish? For one born in Italy, it's difficult not to breathe, from childhood onward, this Catholic atmosphere. One who comes from Italian parents passes a childhood in Italy, enters the Church as a baby, makes his Communion, witnesses Catholic funerals—how can he not be a Catholic? Still, I have a great admiration for those who declare themselves a detached laity—but I don't see how this can happen in Italy. Sooner or later, however—even in Italy—every man must take stock of himself, to determine to what point he is really a Catholic, or perhaps not one at all.

PLAYBOY: Your unsparing caricatures of Catholic clerics, particularly in *8 1/2*, have led some Church theologians to the latter conclusion about *you*. Are they right?

FELLINI: Let them say what they want. In a noncategorized form, I think I'm *deeply* religious, even profoundly so—because I accept life's infinite mysteries without knowing its finite borders, accept them with joy and wonder. Is that being anti-Catholic or anti-religious? When I speak in a polemical manner about deforming our children with Catholic dogma, I'm speaking about an inhuman, inflexible application of Counter Reformation Catholicism. Guido's Catholic teachers in *8 1/2* were monstrous and unfeeling, but they have nothing to do with Pope John XXIII, for example, who sought to wipe away all such ignorance and help us to rediscover the true Christian faith. If a false and misguided type of Catholic education creates guilts, inhibitions and complexes, then I say it's not only right but necessary to identify it—and, if possible, to eradicate it.

PLAYBOY: Would you include the so-called double standard of morality toward women—which divides them into "good" girls and "bad" girls—among the Church-bred afflictions that ought to be eradicated?

FELLINI: Absolutely. Particularly for us Catholics, woman is seen as either the spirit or the flesh, as either the embodiment of virtue, motherhood and saintliness or the incarnation of vice, whoredom and wickedness. Either we dress her up as an ideal, a snow-white inspiration such as Dante's Beatrice, or she becomes the lewd, laboring beast that devours her newborn son. The problem is to find the link between these opposites. But this is difficult, because we don't really know who woman is. She remains in that precise place within man where darkness begins. Talking about women means talking about the darkest part of ourselves, the undeveloped part, the true mystery within. In the beginning, I believe that man was complete and androgynous—both male and female, or neither, like the angels. Then came the division, and Eve was taken from him. So the problem for man is to reunite himself with the other half of his being, to find the woman who is right for him—right because she is simply a projection, a mirror of himself. A man can't become whole or free until he has set woman free—*his* woman. It's his responsibility, not hers. He can't be complete, truly alive, until he makes her his sexual *companion*, and not a slave for libidinous acts or a saint with a halo.

PLAYBOY: Your spectacular exhibition of Anita Ekberg's larger-than-life endowments on a block-long billboard in *Boccaccio '70* has been called a caricature of woman's role, not as man's sexual slave but as a Gargantuan goddess of eroticism. Was that your purpose?

FELLINI: Yes. In the mind of that repressed little man who spies on the billboard every night, of course, she's *anything* but a caricature; she becomes a mountainous creature of flesh and blood, a living embodiment of the grotesquely exaggerated image of female sexuality that stalks his stifled libido—that pressure cooker of puritan sexual inhibitions—and finally escapes to stalk *him.* I wanted to show metaphorically how man's imprisoned appetites can finally burst their bonds and bloat into an erotic fantasy that comes to life, takes possession of its creator and ultimately devours him.

PLAYBOY: Can we conclude, then, that you welcome as a healthy trend the increasing sexual freedom currently enjoyed by movies, magazines and nightclubs—and the nudity on display in them?

FELLINI: It's all to the good, because it lifts the veil of mystery and obscurity, the clandestine aspect of sex which deforms it. Think what a woman must look like to a man in prison, how gross some parts of her body must appear to him. Set free, he hurries home to his girl with deformed visions. Ravenously, he re-explores the forgotten country of the woman's body; but the monstrous desires are soon pacified, and the female myth becomes a normality once again.

PLAYBOY: Do you agree with those who feel that a totally undraped woman loses much of her mystery?

FELLINI: Only her *visual* mystery. Inasmuch as woman represents that hidden half of us, the religious mystery of coupling in birth, the mystical, erotical fusion that integrates the whole man, it's clear she will always possess unfathomable secrets invisible even to the *inner* eye. So I see no reason to keep her covered outwardly, to keep her worldly riches buried like a pirate's treasure in the viscera of the earth.

PLAYBOY: The women in your films—whether prey or predator, saint or sensualist—all seem to be far more vibrantly and affirmatively alive than your self-immobilized male protagonists. Why?

FELLINI: I find my women figures—like Anita Ekberg and Sandra Milo—more exciting to create, perhaps because woman is more intriguing than man, more elusive, more erotic, more stimulating.

PLAYBOY: What inspired you to star Ekberg, whose career was in eclipse, as the voluptuous female in *La Dolce Vita*?

FELLINI: She embodied in every detail my mental image of the role; it's as simple as that. Her previous screenwork was irrelevant.

PLAYBOY: How did you manage to transform her with this one role into the international sex symbol she had failed to become in Hollywood?

FELLINI: I just provided her with the perfect part to elicit, perhaps for the first time, the full impact of her extravagant sensuality. I performed no mysterious alchemy. I did no more to bring out the best in her than I do with all my other actors.

PLAYBOY: And how much is that?

FELLINI: Well, once I find the flesh-and-blood incarnation of my fantasy characters—and it doesn't matter whether they're picked from the street or are professional actors and actresses—the next thing I try to do is to put them at ease, to strip them of their inhibitions, to make them forget technique, to transport them into a climate that allows them to laugh and cry and behave naturally. In other words, I endeavor to coax out the natural talents they already possess. If I have a method, it is to get their most spontaneous reaction. Every human being has his own irrevocable truth, which is authentic and precious and unique; and the truth of Anita Ekberg or Sandra Milo is no different from anyone else's. If the atmosphere is right, *anybody* can be made to express his joys, his sadnesses, his hostilities, everything—entirely of his own accord, honestly and openly. I don't ever want to make the mistake of forcing someone into a given character, or of limiting him in any way. Instead, I try to let him re-create his *own* character for the role. Because of this, I think, my results are richer and more satisfactory; the spectator finds himself in the presence of a creature of unique truth.

PLAYBOY: Most actors are trained to *create* a role, to impersonate someone else, a fictional character. Yet you say you want them to portray themselves. Doesn't this create a conflict of interests?

FELLINI: Not really. Once they get used to the idea of turning inward rather than outward, most find that it comes more naturally, that it enables them to bring far more authenticity to their portrayals. For most roles, of course, only part of the actor's own character will be germane to the character he's playing, so I ask him to be less than completely open and spontaneous, to be only selectively self-revealing. But even where there is a deep personal identification between an actor and his role, he doesn't simply play himself; he doesn't strip himself bare. Complete self-exposure can be both dangerous and irrelevant to the role. I ask him instead to expose himself gradually, layer by layer, until he reaches the level where he merges and meshes completely with the character. Though his subconscious motivations and reactions will now be those of the man he's portraying—and vice versa—the identity of player and part must remain a dramatic illusion, his seeming spontaneity must be studied, his naturalness premeditated. Despite his rapport with the role, all of his acting skills and disciplines will be necessary to bring the character believably to life. Though there may be severe labor pains, the issue of this unlikely union between instinct and technique can be beautiful, indeed. A perfect example is Marcello Mastroianni's wonderfully sensitive performance as Guido in 8 1/2, a part with which he deeply identified.

PLAYBOY: So did you, if one can believe reports that the picture was your own spiritual autobiography.

FELLINI: I did and it was. I wrote a story dealing with myself and my deepest secrets—or at least an idealistic approximation of me. Then I found a man who could become inhabited with all that had been inside me, and I made him the incarnation of an imaginary person closely resembling me. A mysterious air arose on the set: I found myself ordering myself around like a disembodied spirit in limbo.

PLAYBOY: Are you as close to Mastroianni in private life?

FELLINI: Almost symbiotically so. Even though we seldom see each other outside of our work periods, we have such a profound rapport that it is like a mirror before me saying, "It's me. It's not me . . ." and so on. It's uncanny. This is the basic bond of our friendship; but he's also very humanly *simpatico*. I see in him a charge of enthusiasm, innocence and charlatanry—like a smaller brother. And I'm no less an admirer of his professionalism. He's a very gifted actor.

PLAYBOY: Are you as deeply involved with any other actors?

FELLINI: Not so intensely, though I become terribly fond of all my actors, out of all proportion—because they are my puppets, creations of my fantasy. I claim they are the world's greatest actors and become ferociously defensive about them.

PLAYBOY: Your wife, Giulietta Masina, has starred in several of your films. Does your personal relationship make it easy or difficult to direct her?

FELLINI: Both. When I work with her, she seems the ideal actress: patient, docile, obedient, serious. She's not difficult—I am. I'm more impatient with her than with other actors. I get irritated if she doesn't immediately do what I have in mind. It seems incredible to me when she doesn't respond promptly just the way I want. You see, Giulietta is the first character I think about when I do a film with her. The others come slowly to mind, many months afterward, but always around her as the central figure. So when I get impatient and irritated with her, I feel like saying, "Giulietta! You were born first and the others came after you. You've lived in my mind so much longer than the others; why aren't you quicker?" I know that's unjust, but somehow it always goes that way. But I do like to work with her.

PLAYBOY: Is she a good actress, in your opinion?

FELLINI: Excellent. I think that she would have interested me as such even if she hadn't been my wife. Her mimicry, for example, and that little round face which can express happiness or sadness with such poignant simplicity. That little figure, with its tenderness, its delicacy, fascinates me no end. Her type is crystallized, even stylized for me. As an actress, she represents a special type, a very specific humanity.

PLAYBOY: And as a wife?

FELLINI: So many things. I'll try to be objective, but it isn't easy. We've lived together so long. The other day on the set, we celebrated our 21st anniversary. Twenty-one years. It doesn't really seem that long. There are still things to discover. Where were we?

PLAYBOY: Discussing Giulietta as a wife.

FELLINI: And such a wife—tender, affectionate, eternally solicitous. She always wants to know if I feel cold or if I want to eat. When we're shooting outdoors, she asks if my socks are wet. You know how women are. But she is not only my wife; she is also the one who inspires me. Over the years, she has become a stimulant for me, a symbol of certain feelings, certain moods, certain behavior. Our life together has been sprinkled with tragedy and joy, with tears and laughter, and this has given me material, inspiration for my work.

PLAYBOY: Does she make any actual creative contribution?

FELLINI: Only in the sense that she provides the sun and the rain that warms and waters the soil in which the seeds I sow eventually sprout—and occasionally flower into films.

PLAYBOY: To continue your imagery, where do the seeds come from?

FELLINI: I don't always know, but somehow, from somewhere, an idea arrives, and I carry it within me like an embryo for weeks, months, years—until finally it reaches the fetal stage and begins to assume a vague but tangible shape. Then, very tentatively, I begin to work on the first rough pieces of a script.

PLAYBOY: You've said that looking at portrait photos of potential characters is a stimulant to the creative process at this stage. Why?

FELLINI: It's a ritual form with me, a habit, a psychological conditioning to begin work. When I'm planning a picture, I see literally thousands of people in hundreds of mass auditions, and I keep all their photographs. I'm searching for faces to fit the characters I'm creating—or may create.

PLAYBOY: You have a reputation for dragging out this preparatory period for month after month, as though it were a drug, until finally you must be pulled away and forced into actual shooting.

FELLINI: Well, it's not quite that addictive, and it's not always my fault for taking so long at it. Often these protracted preparations are caused by external factors—such as not finding a producer, or a producer who loses faith, or something else beyond my control. But postponements serve the positive purpose of giving me more time to create the right atmosphere for filming—time to create a kind of oxygen tent that will allow my creatures to live. This is made from many things—the script, costumes, photographs, a trip, a meeting with a girl, a fight with a producer, a change of office, an aimless walk around the house. All of this helps create a tent with enough air for the birth of this thing. That, for me, is the real effort: to take these steps that create the condition for the birth of the work. The film I make may not turn out to be the one I had in mind, but the main point is to see if, in the first two or three weeks of shooting, this thing is actually born alive. After that, it becomes self-sustaining—as though I were no longer directing, but rather that the film were directing me, pulling me onward.

PLAYBOY: Is there any truth to the prevalent notion that you begin shooting with little more than the outline of a script; that, in effect, you direct your films off the top of your head, improvising scenes and dialogue as you go along?

FELLINI: If I wanted to commit artistic and economic suicide, that would be a beautiful and spectacular way to go. But since I don't, I arrive on the set with a script in hand—though it doesn't really mean that much, except as a pacifier for actors who fear improvisation, and for producers who crave reassurance that the structure for a film story has been created. What *does* matter is that I have a very precise idea of where I want to go in the film and how I want to get there long before the camera starts to roll. Once it does, of course, I try to remain flexible enough to amend and adorn the action as the need arises—rather than adhere blindly and fanatically to the original scenario as though it were Holy Scripture.

You can't say, "I want a baby with blue eyes, pink ears, blonde hair, that weighs seven pounds, three ounces, and with fingers just so." No, you take a woman, make her pregnant, assist in the childbirth, and the baby is what it is, and you're stuck with it. At the moment of parturition you can't say, "No, no, it doesn't have blue eyes, back it goes!" A film is the same. What does it mean to be faithful to 10 pages of dialogue, written five months previous, without knowing the actors or what language would be used? You don't even know where it will be shot. You might conceive of the scene in a park, but when you get there you realize your actor with his face would not have spoken that way in a park. Or the actress wears a dress that prevents her from saying a certain line.

Also, instead of filming two actors talking, you may discover while you're filming that a close-up of a fountain or a panning shot of the rare furnishings in a drawing room will say more than the entire 10 pages of dialogue. In this sense I make myself available to adaptation; but I do not extemporize.

PLAYBOY: How do you feel after completing a film? Do you ever worry about going stale, or encountering what's called artistic paralysis?

FELLINI: What a strange question. A film never ends abruptly for me. It leaves an echo, a trail, and I live with it. Even after I've finished shooting and cutting, it's still with me, I still hear it, feel it, sense it. When it isn't with me anymore, when I feel it's finally extinguished, then another atmosphere enters, like the arrival of spring. It's the new film—with its new personages, and its undeveloped story. You see, I don't experience blank periods. It seems that ever since I started as a director, it's been the same day—the same long, wonderful day. But am I at all preoccupied with failure or professional impotence? Naturally. As you know, 8 1/2 dealt with this preoccupation. But I don't feel the day is near when I will be empty. When it happens, I hope I'll have the humility and good sense to stop chattering. Meanwhile, I am still filled with enthusiasm and with a consuming urge to do things.

PLAYBOY: Is it true that you go to the movies hardly at all—even to see your own pictures?

FELLINI: Very true. When I finish a film, as I said, I'm possessed by the shaping vision of my next one; and it's always a jealous mistress. Besides, I want to live in the present, not linger in the past. As for other people's films, I go very, very seldom. I'd rather make films than watch them.

PLAYBOY: Surely you've seen a *few* of your contemporaries' pictures.

FELLINI: Enough to form a few impressions.

PLAYBOY: Have you seen any of Kurosawa's films?

FELLINI: Only his *Seven Samurai*, but I think he is the greatest living example of all that an author of the cinema should be. I feel a fraternal affinity with his way of telling a story.

PLAYBOY: How about Ingmar Bergman?

FELLINI: I have a profound admiration for him and for his work, even though I haven't seen all of his films. First of all, he is a master of his métier. Secondly, he is able to make things mysterious, compelling, colorful and, at times, repulsive. Because of that, he has the right to talk about other people and to be listened to by other people. Like a medieval troubadour, he can sit in the middle of the room and hold his audience by telling stories, singing, playing the guitar, reading poetry, doing sleight of hand. He has the seductive quality of mesmerizing your attention. Even if you're not in full agreement with what he says, you enjoy the way he says it, his way of seeing the world with such intensity. He is one of the most complete cinematographic creators I have ever seen.

PLAYBOY: Antonioni?

FELLINI: I have respect for his constancy, his fanatical integrity and his refusal to compromise. Antonioni had a very difficult professional beginning. His films for many years were not accepted, and another man, less honest, less strong, would have made retreats. But Antonioni kept on his solitary road, doing what he believed he should do until he was recognized as a great creator. This has always made an enormous impression on me. He is an artist who knows what he wants to say, and that's a lot.

PLAYBOY: Truffaut?

FELLINI: I'm terribly embarrassed, but I haven't seen anything of his. Sorry.

PLAYBOY: De Sica?

FELLINI: Great power of achievement, and a master of his actors. He stems from our marvelous era of neorealism. He is a very good director, someone almost untouchable, because of the special place he occupied after the war.

PLAYBOY: Some critics have drawn parallels between your work and that of the neorealistic school. Do you think there's any validity to the comparison?

FELLINI: Indeed, yes. But mine is the neorealism of the 1960s—a very different breed of cat from the neorealism of the 1940s, when many of us began with great ideals, but which finally tore itself apart in social polemics and drifted off into nonpolemical comedy. By the time that happened, however, neorealism had lifted filmmaking to the dignified level of an autonomous art, freed the filmmaker from the enslaved conditioning in which cinema was imprisoned—a secondary art subordinate to the mood of the public. The greatness of early neorealism consisted in giving cinema liberty, so that we could finally express ourselves in films as freely as others could with a brush or a pen.

PLAYBOY: Since *La Dolce Vita*, you've been inundated with movie offers from America. Do you think you could express yourself freely as a filmmaker in Hollywood?

FELLINI: Probably not, but I've been sorely tempted to try it anyway. I'd love to do a film there on what caught my imagination during my visits to America. But even if I had a clear idea of what to say, the practical realization of it, the actual translation of this idea into images would embarrass and probably defeat me.

PLAYBOY: Why?

FELLINI: In Italy, I know what I'm doing. I know how to handle my actors, how to dress them, how to make them believable in the surroundings I've created for them. I know what I want them to express because I know what I am talking about myself. Even if I throw in an extra with one line, she has a reason to be there and she'll give truth to that one line and authenticity to those few seconds she's on screen. But how could I do this in a strange country with strange people? How would I know, for example, what a Boston taxi driver would wear at home on Sunday afternoon? How does a cashier from a Bronx drugstore dress, smile or react to a man insulting her? I'd be lost a thousand times a day, and that would be fatal, because cinematography, at least in my opinion, needs an absolute mastery, complete control of everything and everyone—the female star's underwear, the leading man's mustache, the way matches are placed on the left side of the table. This is a true and deep obstacle. It's why an author must stay with the language that has nourished him since childhood, that has left with him a cultural deposit and a bagful of customs and traditions. So you see, the idea of a radical uprooting to work in America—or anywhere else beyond these borders—would be inconceivable to me.

PLAYBOY: Could the right price make you change your mind?

FELLINI: Money doesn't interest me. It's useful and good to have, but it's not an obsession with me, and it wasn't even when I didn't have it. When I first came to Rome at 18, I worked on a newspaper, and at times I didn't have enough money for lunch. But it was *food* I desired—not money. I have no money with me at this very moment; I never have. I even borrow for coffee from friends. Maybe I've been able to make money because of this. Money goes to those who don't court it.

PLAYBOY: And fame, too, in your case. Are you as indifferent to that?

FELLINI: I would be, only it's not as easy to ignore. It keeps impinging on one's time and privacy. Though I've managed to preserve a few small sanctuaries from the unblinking eye of publicity, there are more and more invasions, especially since 8 1/2. When I went to America, I was besieged by women who thought I had the key to happiness, some sort of recipe for joining life. They phoned at all hours and even waited for me in hotel corridors. I told them I had no answers, no amulets, no elixirs, no nothing for them, but they wouldn't believe me. I'm a director, not a seer or a psychiatrist. What I have to say, I say in my work.

PLAYBOY: And your work, as you said earlier, has been an attempt to escape from your past. Do you think you've succeeded?

FELLINI: To some extent. I feel less guilty now about the things my childhood education made me feel guilty about.

PLAYBOY: Such as sex?

FELLINI: Or any intelligent use of the senses that takes you beyond the confines of puritan morality. So I feel more robust, less defenseless. But then, it's high time for maturation, don't you think? At my age a man *should* be somewhat mature. Occasionally, though, I feel that this calm understanding could be destroyed by a single, sudden, violent, unexpected emotional confrontation.

PLAYBOY: With a woman?

FELLINI: I don't know with what or whom. But certainly it's always possible in life, and most possible when you're most sure of yourself.

PLAYBOY: Are you sure of yourself?

FELLINI: Not in an egotistical sense; but I feel less emotional, more collected, more at peace with myself than ever before. Though I've lost some of my power and potential in the process—along with my youthful pugnacity—I feel that a religious sentiment, profound but authentic, has been born within me. But I've had a rather fortunate life, so it's possible that my optimism may stem from not having known much sorrow or pain.

PLAYBOY: Do you fear growing old?

FELLINI: No—probably for the same reason.

PLAYBOY: How about death?

FELLINI: Death is such a strange thought, so contrary to what we think of in our physical life, that it's difficult to speak about it. We don't know what it is, so a vague terror tends to seize us. It's like a legendary continent, a faraway land that you've heard spoken about in contradictory terms. Some say it exists, others that it doesn't. Some say it's most beautiful, others that it's horrible. Some say it's better than this world, while others claim that nothing is as beautiful as life, that death is only silence and a forgetting. But let's face it: There is this country, and sooner or later we're all going there.

PLAYBOY: Do you dread it?

FELLINI: Yes. No. I don't know. One should face death as he embraces life: with a consuming curiosity—but without fear. Nor should he delude himself by approaching either with hope; for hope is a way of idealizing the other side of the coin of fear. *Faith* is what is needed, not hope. You must feel that all is sacred, that all is necessary, that all is useful, that all goes well. I can't understand an artist who seeks to show life as sterile and doomed, that we are alone and abandoned, that there is nothing left. If you deny everything, then you deny art itself, so why create it?

PLAYBOY: Are faith and curiosity, then, your prescriptions to make a happy life?

FELLINI: Let's say a *full* life. Happiness is simply a temporary condition that precedes unhappiness. Fortunately for us, it works the other way around as well. But it's all a part of the carnival, isn't it?

JOHN HUSTON

A candid conversation with the writer-director about real men and real movies—from Bogart in Maltese Falcon *to Nicholson in* Prizzi's Honor.

There's trouble in paradise as John Huston looks up at the sky again and sees no sign of rain. He has been living in Las Caletas, Mexico, which is south of Puerto Vallarta and reachable only by boat, for 10 years, and when the rains don't come, the wells dry up and there's no running water. His hacking, recurring cough expresses his displeasure.

The short-wave connection to his secretary in Puerto Vallarta is not coming through, and when it finally does, he's told that Maricela, the young woman who is both companion and caretaker, missed her flight and won't be back until tomorrow. So even here, where pelicans float on the sea and iguanas rest on boulders, it's beyond SNAFU (situation normal, all fucked up), at TARFU (things are really fucked up) and closing in on FUBAR (fucked up beyond any recognition)—favorite expressions of Huston's—but that's OK with him.

He would probably scoff at being called a national treasure, but if John Huston doesn't fit the cliché, no one in America does. As writer, director and actor, he has been a force in our culture for more than four decades, from his first hyphenated credit as writer-director of the 1941 remake of *The Maltese Falcon* to his recently released and highly charged Mafia black comedy, *Prizzi's Honor,* starring Jack Nicholson, Kathleen Turner and his daughter Anjelica.

Over his long life, Huston has lived in New York, Arizona, California, France, England, Africa, Ireland and now Mexico, which has always fascinated him. In 1948, he wrote and directed *The Treasure of the Sierra Madre* there and received separate Oscars as director and screenwriter. Nearly two decades after that, he decided to film

Tennessee Williams' *The Night of the Iguana* in Puerto Vallarta and helped turn a sleepy village of 2500 into a bustling tourist attraction of 80,000.

Huston is one of the last of a breed of rugged individualists who had enough talent and courage to carve out a life that reads a lot like an overblown Kipling story. Born in Nevada, Missouri, in 1906, Huston has been a semipro boxer, painter, writer of fiction and screenplays, big-game hunter, actor, director, horseman, great drinker, womanizer, husband (five times), father (of five children, one adopted), animal lover, architect, storyteller, narrator and, at appropriate times, the voices of Noah and God.

He has dared to adapt such great works of literature as Melville's *Moby Dick*, Kipling's *The Man Who Would Be King*, Stephen Crane's *The Red Badge of Courage* and Flannery O'Connor's *Wise Blood* and turned B. Traven's *The Treasure of the Sierra Madre*, C. S. Forester's *The African Queen*, Dashiell Hammett's *The Maltese Falcon*, W. R. Burnett's *The Asphalt Jungle*, Arthur Miller's *The Misfits* and Carson McCullers' *Reflections in a Golden Eye* into some of the most memorable stories ever put onto film.

It was his father, actor Walter Huston, who not only encouraged him to direct but showed him the fundamentals of drama when he took his son to the 1923 Dempsey-Firpo heavyweight-championship fight at the Polo Grounds. Dempsey was, to the 17-year-old Huston, a god. "Nobody in my lifetime has ever had such glory about him. He walked in a nimbus." When the fight started, he dropped the much larger Firpo in the first 15 seconds. Firpo got up, went down, got up, went down again—and the crowd went crazy. Then, incredibly, Firpo threw a mighty punch that sent Dempsey through the ropes. Huston thought it was over, but Dempsey got back in and knocked Firpo down at the bell. In the second round, Dempsey won the fight and young John learned a lesson in courage and drama he would always remember.

As a fighter himself, Huston won his 140-pound division at Lincoln Heights High School in Los Angeles and then boxed in clubs for five dollars a fight, winning 23 of 25 bouts, until he discovered painting and enrolled in the Smith School of Art. Painting has remained a passion, but it was the theater that enthralled him. His mother, a journalist, and his father had divorced, but Walter Huston kept in touch with his son—and passed along a love for the theater.

In 1924, John acted for the first time with the Provincetown Players in Greenwich Village. He married his first sweetheart, Dorothy Harvey, and they lived in Malibu, broke but happy; Huston returned to the ring to pick up some cash. His career lasted one bout, in which he was pummeled so hard that he decided to return to the haven of the arts.

His mother had smuggled a copy of James Joyce's *Ulysses* into the country, and it affected Huston in much the same way as Dempsey's flattening Firpo. He tried his hand at writing stories. One, called *Fool*, was accepted by *American Mercury*.

He became a journalist, working for the New York *Daily Graphic*, then wrote a play for marionettes and acted in a short film called *Two Americans* in 1929. When his friend Herman Shulin (who had directed *Grand Hotel*) suggested he go to Hollywood as a contract writer for Sam Goldwyn, Huston gave up journalism and crossed the country once again.

Although he wrote a few scripts (*A House Divided, Law and Order, Murders in the Rue Morgue*), his first experience in Hollywood was disappointing. His marriage dissolved when his wife discovered he was having an affair. He had a car accident in which he ran over and killed a girl crossing the street. Shaken, he took an offer to write scripts in London and moved to England.

The job proved to be a bust, and Huston soon found himself sleeping in London parks and singing cowboy songs in the streets. Twenty-eight and penniless, he returned to the States, where he fell in love with an Irish girl named Lesley Black. They married and went to Hollywood, where Huston was asked by his friend William Wyler to doctor a script he had been writing called *Jezebel*.

Next, Huston wrote *The Amazing Dr. Clitterhouse* for Edward G. Robinson and Humphrey Bogart, collaborated on *Juarez* for Paul Muni and moved to the San Fernando Valley, where he designed his first house. He wrote *Dr. Ehrlich's Magic Bullet* in 1940, and his screenplay was nominated for an Oscar. He then wrote *Sergeant York* for Warner Bros., followed by *High Sierra* and then by his directorial debut, *The Maltese Falcon*.

Before Bogart's death in 1957, Huston directed him in five other films: *Across the Pacific, The Treasure of the Sierra Madre, Key Largo, The African Queen* and *Beat the Devil*.

The outbreak of the Second World War coincided with the break-up of Huston's second marriage, coming soon after he and his wife had lost their daughter, born prematurely. He accepted a commission as a lieutenant in the U.S. Army Signal Corps, and between 1943 and 1946, he made three of the most powerful and controversial war documentaries: *Report from the Aleutians, The Battle of San Pietro* and *Let There Be Light.* The effect of the *San Pietro* documentary was so vivid, its depiction of war so bitter, that it was classified as secret by the War Department; it took a direct order by General George C. Marshall to override the classification. And it wasn't until January 1981 that Walter Mondale, as vice president, got *Let There Be Light* released.

By the war's end, Huston had fallen in love with a married woman, Marietta Fitzgerald. While waiting for her to leave her husband, he met actress Evelyn Keyes, who proposed to him at a restaurant. Ever the gentleman, Huston accepted and they flew to Vegas to marry that night.

During the McCarthy era, Huston helped form a group called the Committee for the First Amendment, which was falsely described as a Communist-front organization. Disgusted with the politics of the time, Huston left the country to make *The African Queen, Moulin Rouge* and *Beat the Devil.* He eventually found a haven in Ireland; he bought an estate in Galway and became a fox-hunting gentleman farmer. By then, he was married to his fourth wife, Enrica "Ricki" Soma. In 1964, he became an Irish citizen. Eleven years after that, ever restless, he moved to Mexico.

To find out more about this legendary man, *Playboy* sent Contributing Editor Lawrence Grobel (who has conducted *Playboy Interviews* with two actors who have worked for Huston, Marlon Brando and George C. Scott) to Las Caletas for a week of intensive conversations. Grobel's report:

"It shouldn't be easy getting to see John Huston and, by God, it isn't. After the flight to Puerto Vallarta, it's a 20-kilometer drive along a narrow road between the mountains and the sea to an unpaved, rocky turnoff at a place called Boca de Tomatlán. José, Huston's boatman, was waiting by his ponga. A washing machine was already in the boat, being transported to Huston's coastal hideaway, and José suggested that I sit behind it as we made our way through choppy seas.

"When I realized that it wasn't secured, the trip became a ride of terror; the machine slid from side to side as we plowed through the waves, and I feared being crushed to death by an errant washing machine.

"The sun was bright, the weather warm, the sky blue and unpolluted. The huge boulders that make up the shore line of the Mexican Pacific are scarred as if sliced by the ax of some angry Mexican god, and the jungle glowers behind the shore.

"The house Huston lives in is a simple one: An arched trellis provides shade over the path to the house, which consists of living room, bedroom and bathroom. A satellite dish and a short-wave radio provide him with all the contact with the outside world he needs. In his bedroom, books and scripts cover his large bed; vials of pills line the top of the bookcase.

"Although racked by emphysema and worn down by heart surgery, he is still a vigorous, unvanquished man whose life force is strong. He takes a daily morning swim in the sea, works a full day and reads long into the night. He was a gracious host, conscientious, thoughtful, insightful. I liked him enormously."

PLAYBOY: Coming to Puerto Vallarta to interview you is an adventure in itself.

HUSTON: Well, this is the most primitive home I have ever had, with the jungle at my back and the ocean a few steps from my house. No running water, either. It hasn't rained in more than three months, so the spring has run dry. You get used to it. It's a hell of a lot better than living in Bel Air, which is the kind of life I can least imagine myself living—where if your neighbor has a Colonial mansion, you have a Swiss chalet and, depending on how rich you are, you live north or south of Sunset Boulevard. [Laughs]

PLAYBOY: At least in Bel Air, you could get help in an emergency. You're 79 years old and an hour's boat ride away from a hospital. Doesn't that concern you?

HUSTON: Not an hour; it's a day from anywhere, because the hospital in Puerto Vallarta is not what I would call space-age outfitted. But what the hell. If you think like that, you can have a heart attack in the Beverly Hills Hotel and be dead before you get to the ambulance—which is how my father died.

PLAYBOY: What kind of shape are you in?

HUSTON: I'm in terrible shape. I've got emphysema as bad as you can have it. A flight of steps is a short climb up Mount Everest for me. I went to Mexico City, where the smog is 10 times as bad as in Los Angeles, and, Christ, I didn't think I could make it to the curb.

PLAYBOY: Do you miss Ireland?

HUSTON: Yes. It was wonderful; I loved it.

PLAYBOY: Why did you leave?

HUSTON: Two reasons. When I went to Ireland, it was one of the cheaper places in Europe to live. But prices kept going up, salaries kept rising, until today it's one of the most expensive countries. The other big consideration was the hunting, which was a strenuous sport. I was joint master of the Galway Blazers for 10 years. But when I couldn't hunt any longer, those two things just decided it for me. But it was one of the best periods of my life.

PLAYBOY: Are you still an Irish citizen?

HUSTON: Yes.

PLAYBOY: Are there any other locations for which you feel nostalgia?

HUSTON: I liked Africa, but a lot of the places that I've been to are quite impossible today. When I was in Africa to shoot *The African Queen*, for instance, there was no conflict, the people were friendly and hospitable, and you felt perfectly safe in places that now no one dares mention, such as the backwaters of Uganda, where you can get killed. It's hard to imagine those gentle, delightful people, who were very well governed, by the way. . . . I was, and theoretically still am, against colonialism, but, my God, they were a lot better off under the English.

PLAYBOY: Wasn't that when your expatriate life began—with *The African Queen*?

HUSTON: Well, I didn't exactly pack my bags and leave America. It's just that I had one son, my wife was going to have another baby, and since I had to cut that movie in England, I took them all over. Then came the idea of doing *Moulin Rouge*, so I went to France, and after that came *Beat the Devil*. During that time, I would go over to Ireland for hunting weekends. It was something I had never experienced before, the best hunting in the world. That led me to rent a house in Ireland.

PLAYBOY: There's lots to talk about—writing, directing, acting, your rich personal life—but since you mentioned it, *The African Queen* seems as good a place as any to begin. What memories do you have of that location—of Katharine Hepburn and your friend Humphrey Bogart?

HUSTON: We had some funny encounters in Africa. To start out with, we had talked with a local king who said that his people would be villagers for us, but when the time came, no one showed up. So we drove a considerable distance to this king's native village. I said, "Why aren't the people coming?" He said, "They are afraid you are going to eat them." I said, "Oh, no, we wouldn't dream of doing anything like that." By that time, there was quite an audience of villagers around us, and he asked for volunteers. Two of the bravest men I have encountered held up their hands. Just two. So we took them back with us, wined and dined them and drove them back to their village. The next morning, they all came. They call it the Third World, but, my God, Africa was the 97th world! It was so far removed from our awareness, there was no basis for comparison.

PLAYBOY: The stories about that film are that Hepburn was very much put off by you and Bogart and the project in general. Just how skeptical was she at first?

HUSTON: Extremely. Katie was born suspicious, and she had great reservations regarding me that she was in no pains to conceal. She knew that both Bogart and I were wastrels, but Katie has a weakness for wastrels. Spencer Tracy was also one. But we put it on for her. We pretended to be even bigger wastrels than we were.

PLAYBOY: How?

HUSTON: By writing dirty things on her mirror in soap—childish things that shocked her. She always rose to the bait. She was suspicious of my advice as a director and wasn't sure how she was going to play her character in the film. I advised her to play her as a lady rather than a shrew. She said, "What lady?" I said, "Eleanor Roosevelt." That made sense to her, and her performance thereafter was everything I had ever hoped for.

PLAYBOY: Did you become close?

HUSTON: I don't think I was ever closer to anybody than I was to Katie out there. Not in a romantic way; there was only one man in her life, and there was no room for anybody but Spence.

PLAYBOY: Wasn't there a story about the two of you getting caught in the middle of a herd of elephants?

HUSTON: Well, that was a bad moment. I used to go out shooting in the morning to get game for the pot. It was always in my mind to get a really impressive trophy, a big tusk. There was a book written about my quest for a big elephant, but I never shot one. I wouldn't commit the sin—not the crime but the sin—of shooting an elephant unless the reward were sufficiently handsome. I wanted nothing less than 100 kilos in the way of a trophy. Anyway, Katie took a very dim view of my shooting. She said, "John, this just doesn't go with the rest of your character. You're not a murderer, and yet you shoot these beautiful animals." I said, "Katie, you can't really understand unless you come with me and experience it." So she did, and from that day on, Katie was a veritable Diana of the hunt. We shot antelope, waterbuck. You couldn't restrain her. She would come into my cabin and wake me before dawn to get in an hour of shooting before we started work on the picture. One of those mornings, there were elephant signs. It was a very heavy forest in Uganda, and we worked very carefully down wind. All of a sudden, there was a very loud growl, which was the elephant's insides digesting, about five feet away. We froze, of course, and the elephant didn't know we were there. But then the breeze changed and our scent drifted and hell broke loose. There were elephants going by like train engines. You must not run under those circumstances, because that only confuses the elephants, which are trying to get away from you. But if they're confused, they're likely to pick you up and throw you away for good. I turned and looked at Katie, who had my light rifle up to her shoulder. She was going to go down like the heroine she is. Fortunately, those locomotives all went by us, and I breathed very deeply and wiped the sweat off my brow. Katie wasn't shaken by the experience. I was profoundly shaken. It was a hell of a note, my taking my star out, submitting her to that sort of thing.

PLAYBOY: You once nearly did away with the picture's other star, too, didn't you?

HUSTON: Yes, in Italy, just before we began shooting *Beat the Devil*. There was an element of absurdity about that whole experience. I found myself in Rome with the company, the crew—everything but a script. It was no spot to be in. I said to Bogey, "Let's forget the whole thing." He surprised me very much, saying, "John, it's only money." Then he and I got a chauffeur-driven car to go to Naples, and at a fork in the road, the driver couldn't make up his mind and went straight ahead through a stone wall. I was sitting in the front seat and braced myself, but Bogey was asleep in the back seat. His teeth had been knocked out; he had bitten through his tongue. We got him to a hospital and had to wait 10 days for his bridge to be duplicated and sent over.

PLAYBOY: You say you were stuck without a script. How did you come up with one?

HUSTON: I met a young man named Truman Capote on the street in Rome and asked him if he could help us out. He said sure. He was an extraordinary little man who had the courage and the determination of a lion. We worked on the script together. We had been writing feverishly for a few days when his face got swollen to half again its size. He had an impacted wisdom tooth. So I called an ambulance and we took him to the hospital; and that night, pages came back to me from the hospital. That was typical of Truman.

PLAYBOY: When you have your writer's hat on, how do you work with a collaborator?

HUSTON: As a rule, I write a scene and the other person writes a scene; then he takes mine and I take his and we rewrite.

PLAYBOY: How good a screenwriter do you think you are?

HUSTON: I think I am one of the best.

PLAYBOY: Are there many others?

HUSTON: There aren't many. Ingmar Bergman. Robert Bolt writes beautifully for the screen. Screenwriting is such a very special branch of literature. In some ways, it's closer to the poetic form than it is to the dramatic. A lot of book writers think that they write down to an audience if they do a motion-picture script.

PLAYBOY: Speaking of writing up or down to your audience, it seems as if some of your latest films, such as *Under the Volcano* and *Wise Blood*, have been smaller, more personal than the adventure films for which you're famous—*The Maltese Falcon, The African Queen, The Treasure of the Sierra Madre, The Man Who Would Be King*. Why have you gone in this direction?

HUSTON: Nothing conscious about it. I don't think of those films as art films, nor do I think of adventure as something that simply implies action or exploit. The consul in *Volcano*, played by Albert Finney, is an adventurer. *Volcano* is an adventure of the mind, of the soul.

PLAYBOY: Nonetheless, these films are different in appeal. Is that what interests you more now?

HUSTON: No, there's no design in any of this. My new movie, *Prizzi's Honor*, is not a small film. But, yes, I am less concerned with having to make a buck.

PLAYBOY: In writing about *Under the Volcano, The New York Times* called you a "bold visionary." Are you?

HUSTON: I'm a bold visionary with other people's work. I haven't originated my films in any true sense. As for the acting, that is largely the work of the artists themselves. Just as I had done with many other actors, I often said to Albert Finney and the others, "Work something out; I'll leave you alone." I'd leave them for an hour or two and they'd come up with something.

PLAYBOY: Isn't that a favorite expression of yours—"Work something out"?

HUSTON: Yes. And if they are the right people playing the part, what they choose to do is right, as a rule, and that's a great help. It's a practice of mine to get as much out of the actor as I can, rather than to impose myself upon his performance.

PLAYBOY: But what happens when you ask your actors to come up with something and they can't—or when a scene isn't working, no matter what you do?

HUSTON: You go back to the sources, to the writing. You may even discover that the scene isn't needed and can be dropped; that's happened a time or two. I'll give you a very good example: I had such a scene in *The Night of the Iguana*. The dialog and the situation were good, but for some reason, the scene wasn't coming off. It was between Richard Burton and the young girl, Sue Lyon. He's in his room at that hotel in Puerto Barrio, and she comes to see him surreptitiously. She wants him to make love to her and he resists. He's shaving, there is a whiskey bottle on a shelf, and they have this dialog that doesn't work.

Well, Tennessee Williams was down there on the set, and I said to him, "I'm having trouble with this; see if you can do anything about it." He had it for me the next morning. What he had done with it made it perhaps the best scene in the picture: When she comes in, instead of dialog, her very appearance startles him and he bumps against the shelf and the whiskey bottle falls off and breaks on the floor. He's barefoot. He begins to tell her why they must not make love and, in talking, he walks up and down, the broken glass cutting his feet. She watches him become a kind of martyr with fascination; then she takes off her shoes and joins him in his martyrdom, cutting her own feet as their dialog is played over that. I think that's a striking example of the answer to your question.

PLAYBOY: Yet Williams wasn't happy with the way you ended *Iguana*, was he?

HUSTON: We talked a lot about the finish of the picture and disagreed on it. The most amusing character in the play was the one played by Ava Gardner, who had the most penetrating remarks. Yet, in the end, he wanted her to be a female spider. But he himself had written her sympathetically, and it seemed to me he was pulling back his sympathy at the end. He resisted the finish as we had written it for the screen but couldn't come up with anything as good. He just wanted to make the Ava Gardner character consuming and destructive. Finally, I said, "Tennessee, I think you've got it in for women; you don't want to see a man and a woman in a love relationship, and that's at the bottom of it." He didn't contest that; he just thought about it and stopped arguing. Yet years later, in London at a luncheon party, the last thing he ever said to me, just before he left, was, "John, I still don't agree with you about the finish. I think that finish was a mistake."

PLAYBOY: Was Williams a genius?

HUSTON: Yes.

PLAYBOY: What *is* a genius?

HUSTON: Someone who see things in a way that illuminates them and enables you to see things in a different way.

PLAYBOY: How many have you known?

HUSTON: Well, one knows men of genius only through their work. I'd say Williams; Eugene O'Neill; Manzù, the sculptor; Henry Moore, the sculptor; Mark Rothko, the painter; Henri Cartier-Bresson; in a funny way, Robert Capa, the photographer; Ernest Hemingway; William Faulkner; Dashiell Hammett; Marlon Brando. I've seen flashes of it in others: Bergman; Vittorio De Sica; Akiro Kurosawa.

PLAYBOY: Brando is the only actor you include. What about some of his peers from the old days, such as Montgomery Clift and James Dean?

HUSTON: Clift and Dean were in the same league, but Brando was something else entirely. Brando had an explosive thing; you felt something smoldering, dangerous, about to ignite at times. Did you see *Julius Caesar?* Christ! I will never forget that; it was like a furnace door opening—the heat came off the screen. I don't know another actor who could do that.

PLAYBOY: You directed him in *Reflections in a Golden Eye.* What comes to mind?

HUSTON: An extraordinary, amazing actor. If you remember the scene where he talks about the Army, standing at the mantelpiece, it's a long speech and he fiddles with a candle. Well, he did it, and after the first time, I could have said, "That's it," as I often do; but knowing Marlon and the way he works, I said, "Let's do it again." We did it three times, and each time was different; any of them could have been used!

In another scene, he gives a lecture on leadership to a class as his wife is in the background, on horseback, with the man she was having an affair with. He did that completely differently two or three times. I've never seen any other actor do that.

PLAYBOY: Do you think Brando's disdain for his profession is real?

HUSTON: Yes, I think it's real, though he takes his acting very seriously. He is not a dilettante in that sense. I'm not sure that he felt about acting the way Laurence Olivier does, or John Gielgud, or those who are dedicated to the art of acting. His doing a season at Stratford is beyond one's imagination. But, God knows, he is a fine actor and a very intelligent man. I don't know whether Brando has done some of the things he has simply because of the money, but I can't imagine him being bad in anything, though I think the worst thing I ever saw Brando do was *Apocalypse Now*, which was just dreadful—the finish of that picture. The model for it, *Heart of Darkness*, has no finish, either, and the moviemakers just didn't find one. It's very good for a picture to have an ending before you start shooting. [*Laughs*]

PLAYBOY: Of your several careers, when did you start thinking of yourself as a writer?

HUSTON: H. L. Mencken, the legendary editor of *American Mercury*, accepted a short story I'd written called *Fool* in 1929. It was the first time anybody had ever published anything of mine. I can't begin to describe the importance Mencken had in my young manhood. He was the most prestigious figure in this country, as far as I was concerned; the arbiter of taste and judgment as the editor of the finest magazine. When his letter came saying he wished to publish my story, why, that was a high moment in my life.

PLAYBOY: Soon after that, you became a reporter for the New York *Daily Graphic*. Did you like being a journalist?

HUSTON: No, I was the world's worst reporter. There was a night city editor who hated my guts. He would fire me and the day city editor would hire me back. I was hired and fired three or four times. All my sympathies, by the way, are with the night city editor. He was quite correct. The thing that finally brought about my separation from the paper forever happened when I was sent to cover a murder in a tobacco factory in New Jersey. One of the workers had killed another one, and I got my notes mixed up and had the owner of the factory down as the murderer. That ended my career as a newspaperman.

PLAYBOY: And when did your career as a director begin?

HUSTON: Let's see: I was a boxer while I was in high school, and I was also going to the Art Students League in California; I had a half notion that I'd be a painter and a half notion I might have the makings of a welterweight champion. Then I went to New York on a visit to my father, whom I wasn't living with. I had only seen him in vaudeville, not in the New York theater. He was in *Desire Under the Elms*. That's when I met O'Neill. I was about 17, and it influenced me enormously, seeing one of the great American plays come together.

Anyway, some years later, when I had had some success as a writer in Hollywood, my father asked me to direct him in a play, *A Passenger to Bali*. I'd never directed, of course. I'm trying to remember whether I had ever expressed the desire to direct. . . . No, it was his idea, as I recall. The play had a modest success, but it confirmed my desire to become a director.

PLAYBOY: So the credit goes to your father?

HUSTON: Yes, yes.

PLAYBOY: But how did you get your chance to direct—getting as your first movie a small property called *The Maltese Falcon*?

HUSTON: It came from my being a writer first. My standing as a writer was quite high at Warner's; and after I had adapted *High Sierra*, my agent had it written into my contract that if they took up my option, they'd let me direct a picture. When it came time, Henry Blanke, who was a producer at Warner Bros. and a man of great taste and discrimination, became something of a champion of mine, and he backed me up. When I said I wanted to direct *The Maltese Falcon*, the studio heads were astonished and delighted, because they owned it. It had been a bad picture twice before, but it makes sense to remake a bad picture.

PLAYBOY: George Raft was Warner's first choice to star, not Bogart. Had he made it, would it have been—

HUSTON: Not nearly as good. I couldn't have been more pleased when Raft turned it down.

PLAYBOY: Did you have any idea that you were making a film classic?

HUSTON: I knew it was a marvelous book. Hammett is one of the great American writers, a great stylist.

PLAYBOY: Did you cast the picture yourself?

HUSTON: Yes. Just think of a completely inexperienced director's bringing Sydney Greenstreet out from New York. They gave me the actors I wanted. Being in charge of my own casting has allowed me not to have to do as much directing through the years. If the actors aren't right, then you have to direct and conceal that fact.

PLAYBOY: Casting your father in another picture, *The Treasure of the Sierra Madre*, was apparently a right decision.

HUSTON: Yes. [*Laughs*] He got the Academy Award for it; I regard that film with great sentiment. And since I learned a lot about direction from seeing my father work, it was very gratifying.

PLAYBOY: Were you close to your father?

HUSTON: I didn't see a great deal of him until I was about 15 years old. I had merely been told by my mother that he was an actor, which meant he was away. Then I remember my mother's saying they were getting a divorce. I stayed with my mother and my grandmother. But every month, he would write a letter and send money. Every year or two, they would send me to see him; and because I saw him so infrequently, he would put himself out, so it was always a very pleasant relationship. And since he had never played a father, he never assumed that role with me. We were more like brothers or good friends. He was a great companion; he loved great humor. I've never laughed with anyone else as much as I did with him.

PLAYBOY: What was your mother like?

HUSTON: Nervous . . . very active . . . smoked. When I say nervous, I mean tending toward the neurotic. She was better with animals than with people. She liked excitement. Still, I was closer to her than to my father, closer to the women in my family.

PLAYBOY: That reminds us of a story we read about your mother's leaving you with your nursemaid when you were a boy. . . .

HUSTON: Oh, yes, I know what you're talking about. I was very young, maybe five or six, and my mother was working and left me alone with this nursemaid. I lay on the bed with her, and somehow her dresses got up and her behind was bare, and I fiddled with her behind and thought it was marvelous. I thoroughly approved of it. I remember my mother coming to the front door, but I didn't tell her what had happened. There was some sense that I should keep this very strictly to myself, looking forward to further exploration.

PLAYBOY: And?

HUSTON: Unfortunately, the nursemaid disappeared from our lives almost immediately. [*Laughs*] But from that time on, I was trying to get little girls to show me their genitals.

PLAYBOY: So you were advanced sexually?

HUSTON: I don't know about that. I was comparatively late in having any coitus. I was about 15 or 16; it was with a girl I met in the park. My mother was away, and I took her to my bedroom and pulled the shade down. My mother later noticed that the shade was down and asked me if I had been home during the afternoon. I confessed ignorance of that mystery.

PLAYBOY: You must have made up for your ignorance by the time you got through school. There's another story we seem to remember involving you, a lady and a commission in the Mexican Army—all before you were 20.

HUSTON: Oh . . . that was when I first came down to Mexico. I loved horses and there was a well-known teacher of dressage in Mexico, and I thought if I could get down here, maybe I could get lessons from him. I had jumped horses, but I had never done dressage. I found the man, who was a colonel in the Mexican army, and he gave me lessons at a stable in Mexico City. We became friends. I didn't have much money, and one day, the colonel said, "Look, you don't have to pay me for the dressage lessons anymore; why don't I just give you an honorary commission so you can ride horses and go to the officers' mess and not have to pay the expenses?" Well, that sounded good, and that's what I did.

The whole scene in Mexico and the army around that time was pretty abandoned. I became a kind of a Mexican-army pet, a mascot. It was a crazy country, much more so than now. I had never seen an outdoor swimming pool owned by an individual, and one night, a powerful bureaucrat named José Avelleneda, who later became secretary of the treasury, invited a group of us to his house in the country, and he had an outdoor swimming pool—and he had it full of whores, without any clothes on. He had brought them out for our visit. We dived right in. Life was a constant revel.

PLAYBOY: And what happened with the woman—and a supposed duel?

HUSTON: That was just an absurd thing. There was a count from South Africa whose main claim to glory was that he had lured Mata Hari, the German spy, over the Spanish border into France to be shot. That was his demonstration of patriotism. He was in hot pursuit of the wife of an American I got to know. She was afraid to tell her husband about the count, but she wanted him warned off. So I undertook to do it. There was a quarrel, we scuffled, were separated and he said, "I will meet you in an hour, where I will kill you."

I hurried downtown, where guns could be bought without a license. I wasn't an expert with handguns at all, so I bought the one with the longest barrel and took up my position, behind a tree, well before the stroke of the hour. I was going to shoot him as he turned the corner, aim the gun like a rifle and just shoot him [laughs]—so there would be no question of the outcome. Well, the count didn't turn the corner; my mother did! She had come down a few weeks earlier, had heard about the duel and had come to disarm me. And that was the end of that.

PLAYBOY: That's not the only time you've been involved with guns and a ladyfriend. We're thinking of the filming of *Moulin Rouge* in Paris, in 1952, and the actress Suzanne Flon.

HUSTON: That happened on Bastille Day. I had been with Aly Khan, Zsa Zsa Gabor, José Ferrer and Suzanne Flon. Afterward, I took Suzanne home in a taxi, and when the taxi door opened, somebody came in and belted me—hit me two or three times before I knew what was happening. I got out of the cab and the man disappeared through an archway. I followed and he came down some steps with a pistol, which he pointed at me. I went toward him and he pulled the trigger, and I heard the pistol click and decided it wasn't loaded. The taxi driver and a bystander got between us, and Suzanne kept begging me to leave, so I did. But he had bruised me around the eyes and I had to put on some dark glasses. He was in love with her; he was jealous and he had been waiting to see who was taking her home.

Well, I found out where he lived, and I had a kind of goon in the company who I asked to come with me, since I knew he had a gun. I knocked on his door and he opened it, and I hit the door hard enough to knock him back, then proceeded to kick the shit out of him. He couldn't fight; he tried to kick me in the balls, so I gave him a little extra punishment for that. [*Laughs*] I was still angry at this son of a bitch. Then he began to beg, saying he had loved her for so many years and so on, and there was a knock at the door—the gendarmes. We answered, said it was just a friendly scuffle—he was bleeding from his nose and mouth. [*Laughs*] I said, "Let me see your gun," and he brought it; it was only a .22, but you can kill somebody with a .22. I took the clip out of the gun and, son of a bitch, the round had misfired.

PLAYBOY: Was Suzanne worth getting killed over?

HUSTON: She was the most extraordinary woman I have ever known.

PLAYBOY: Another, more publicized altercation was an hourlong fistfight you had with Errol Flynn. How serious was that?

HUSTON: He went to one hospital and I went to another. [*Laughs*] To reduce the publicity.

PLAYBOY: You didn't say in your memoirs why you had that fight, but other sources say it was over a remark Errol Flynn had made about Olivia de Havilland.

HUSTON: I've never said that.

PLAYBOY: Still, it seems as if you feel a man needs to test his courage with an occasional fight. True?

HUSTON: It depends on how severe the test. I think it's of primary importance in the make-up of a man, the part that courage plays in his character. It's happened to me frequently. Let's say that I've been able to conceal from others the anxiety that I felt at the time. [*Laughs*]

PLAYBOY: That's straight out of Hemingway—whom you sparred with, correct?

HUSTON: I had been told by someone that Hemingway had his doubts about me as a boxer. I'd been on the boat with Papa in Cuba—I think I began calling him Papa at that time—and instead of swimming directly to shore, he took a long walk instead. That evening, we had some cocktails and we were at his house and I said, "Have you got some gloves here, Papa?" And he said yes, and I said, "Let's put them on; I just want to see what your style is." He said, "You have longer arms and you're supposed to be a good boxer; you wouldn't stay out there and jab my face, jab my nose, would you?" And I said, "No, no, I wouldn't do anything like that." I meant it.

Well, Papa went into the other room with [writer] Peter Viertel, saying, "I'm gonna cool the son of a bitch." But Mary, his wife, said to me, "John, don't box with him, please; he has been having trouble with his heart; that's why he walked in today and didn't swim. No one is supposed to know that, but, please, don't box him." When he came out, I said, "Let's forget it," and that was the end of that.

PLAYBOY: Did you ever consider working with him in any way?

HUSTON: I was going to do a picture of Hemingway's at one time and the idea was for him to do a voice-over, a foreword to it, but it was impossible. His voice had a funny lack of expression in it.

PLAYBOY: Does anyone today remind you of Hemingway?

HUSTON: I'll tell you the actor who looks more like him than anybody else but doesn't resemble him in any other way: Burt Reynolds. He could be his brother.

PLAYBOY: What do you think of Hemingway's choice of death?

HUSTON: I approve completely. He knew he was on the way out; his mind was gone. Papa had been having persecution complexes, phobias, and life was dreadful for him. He had a moment or two of sanity and killed himself in one of those moments.

PLAYBOY: You've been married five times. You're obviously a good judge of actors and actresses; how good a judge of women are you in your personal life?

HUSTON: Quite good. I've delighted in the women I have known, been married to and been in love with. It's really gone to make a very good life. I regret that I wasn't constituted, as some men are, to stay with one woman, though I believed implicitly each time that I would.

PLAYBOY: Do you really regret that? After all, you seem to be in the mold of Hemingway, Norman Mailer, adventurous men who apparently outgrow their women.

HUSTON: No, I think they grew just as fast as I did . . . and for the most part, they were extraordinary women, except the last, who was a crocodile. [*Laughs*] And even she was extraordinary, in a sense. Let me put it this way: I regret that lack within myself that enables a man to pour all his affection into one individual.

PLAYBOY: Why do you call your last wife a crocodile?

HUSTON: It's just the best description I have of her. [*Laughs*] I've been friends with all of my wives except the last. We were never good friends, from the word go.

PLAYBOY: Were you surprised at your lack of perception about her?

HUSTON: I was, indeed. I was shocked by it.

PLAYBOY: Have you ever known a woman who you felt was your equal?

HUSTON: Oh, many. A few, even superior. [*Laughs*] For sheer strength of character, I wouldn't have dared to cross swords with [Maria] Callas. I would rather have gone six rounds with Jack Dempsey! I had an aunt Margaret who was a very strong and intelligent woman. I didn't like her or have great regard for her, though. A woman we've talked about, for whom I have enormous respect and regard for her intelligence and humanity, is Suzanne Flon. Another is Iris Tree.

PLAYBOY: You have five children, including an adopted son. Do you feel differently about each of them?

HUSTON: Yes, I have different emotions toward each.

PLAYBOY: Is it tough for them, being the children of John Huston?

HUSTON: One of my sons has a little difficulty being a son of mine and the other one none at all, and neither of my daughters has any problem. Anjelica has a role in my new movie and is wonderful in it.

PLAYBOY: Anjelica has been living with Jack Nicholson for some time; that makes him a kind of son-in-law. Is he a good one?

HUSTON: As far as I'm concerned, he is.

PLAYBOY: Do rumors linking Nicholson to alleged cocaine use bother you?

HUSTON: I don't think there is any truth to the stories. I have seen a good deal of Jack and never once have I seen him under the influence of drugs.

PLAYBOY: You acted with Nicholson in *Chinatown*; now you've directed him in *Prizzi's Honor*. How do you assess him from both sides of the camera?

HUSTON: Oh, he's a wonderful actor, one of the best. He just illuminates the book. He impressed me in one scene after another; the new movie is composed largely of first takes with him.

PLAYBOY: Let's talk about some of the themes of your movies. There seems to be an element of despair in some of the recent ones. Does that reflect your own philosophy?

HUSTON: I certainly don't know what the point of life is . . . but I don't indulge in depression. I think I see the world very clearly, though.

PLAYBOY: Has life always seemed futile?

HUSTON: Not always. In World War II, I think I had as high hopes as anybody. It looked to me as if we were on our way to some kind of understanding of life.

PLAYBOY: What changed that vision?

HUSTON: The McCarthy era, the whole Red-baiting thing. The idea of America, the America of our founding fathers, was lost. It stopped being that America and became something else. And then one wondered whether it ever had been America except for the founding fathers and a few rare souls. Was it all an illusion? I know that what Roosevelt was doing with the New Deal seemed to hold the promise of a return to those original values. He was the only president in my time I thoroughly approved of. Red baiting did nothing to me and my career, because my nose was completely clean; I had no Communist inclination; but I had a few friends who were Communists, though they never told me they were. The thing is, I saw nothing reprehensible; if they chose to become Communists, that was their business. In America, there is supposed to be political and religious freedom!

PLAYBOY: Your Committee of the First Amendment was described as a Communist front.

HUSTON: Only afterward, you see.

PLAYBOY: Why weren't you subpoenaed by the House Un-American Activities Committee?

HUSTON: Because the members all knew I wasn't a Communist.

PLAYBOY: Still, many Hollywood writers and directors were brought before HUAC.

HUSTON: I think many of them were Communists. I know of one who was not, but he was never called to the stand. That was Howard Koch; he was subpoenaed but not called. HUAC had a pretty good idea of who was a Communist and who wasn't. The people who did get caught up in it were, for the most part, well-intentioned boobs from a poor background. A number of them had come from the Lower East Side of Manhattan, and out in Hollywood, they sort of felt guilty for living the good life. Their social conscience was more acute than the next fellow's.

PLAYBOY: Didn't the head of MGM, Louis B. Mayer, want you to do a documentary tribute to Joe McCarthy?

HUSTON: Yes. I just laughed. L. B. was a great patriot.

PLAYBOY: Did he actually crawl on his knees and kiss your hand, as reported, begging you to make *Quo Vadis* for him?

HUSTON: Yes, he was the kind of man who would do such a thing. [*Laughs*] He wanted that picture to be warm and emotional, and he described to me the way he had once hired Jeanette MacDonald against everyone's advice. Everyone said MacDonald pissed ice water—I'm quoting L. B.—but he knew that she had heart, and he said he sang her a Jewish song and was able to bring tears to her eyes. She went on and did *Ah, Sweet Mystery of Life* in that picture, and it was an experience that no one ever forgot. Now he wanted me to make *Quo Vadis* that kind of picture, and if I were able to, he would get down on his knees and kiss my hand, and then he proceeded to do exactly that. Needless to say, I didn't make the film.

PLAYBOY: Another example of your outlook was *Fat City*, a bleak look at one of your favorite pastimes—boxing—which contrasts, for example, with the upbeat tone of such movies as *Rocky*.

HUSTON: Yes, one asks the question, Why is a prize-fighting film such as *Rocky* a great success and a picture such as *Fat City* not successful at all? *Rocky* isn't the true world of boxing. *Rocky* is a world of boxing that's in people's minds. But the first *Rocky* was very good; there were some extraordinary moments in it—his seduction of the girl, getting her to take off her hat, standing there mute . . . it was memorable.

PLAYBOY: Coming from an old boxer, that's at least some praise. You have a fondness for tough guys, don't you? Robert Mitchum, for instance.

HUSTON: Yes, I like Mitchum enormously.

PLAYBOY: Why?

HUSTON: It's just his viewpoint, his attitude toward life. He doesn't dramatize anything; he's—I don't even like the word, but he's cool, he underplays everything and he has a wonderful humor. He's extremely intelligent, has marvelous powers of observation, can re-create a scene with all the funny aspects that it originally had. Mitchum is, essentially, a gent. I like his easy attitude. God, I've seen some funny things happen with Mitchum.

One night in Tobago, I went into the hotel where we were staying and Mitchum had a sailor over a balcony, holding him by the throat, slapping him around. Dorothy, his wife, was crying and begging him to let go, which Mitchum did. Then he laughed and strolled back to the bar. I said, "What in hell happened?" Turned out these two sailors had bothered him and he put up with them as long as he could and finally they jumped him; he knocked them both down. Mitchum could fight. It ended with them, so one sailor said, trying to be friends, "Give me a free one." Bob said all right, and the sailor hit him once for all he was worth. Bob said, "OK, you've had your free one," and turned away. Then the son of a bitch hit him again! Bob turned loose. That's when I came in, as Bob was throttling the guy, about to throw him over the balcony 80 feet down. [*Laughs*] But there is no element of the bully in Bob, no strutting his stuff. He's quite the opposite.

PLAYBOY: A tough guy for whom you don't have much affection is George C. Scott. You once called him a shitheel in *Rolling Stone*. When you filmed *The Bible*, who was more difficult, the animals or Scott?

HUSTON: Scott was more difficult, because he got drunk.

PLAYBOY: How much abuse did he give Ava Gardner on that film?

HUSTON: Considerable.

PLAYBOY: Did you ever see him slap her?

HUSTON: No. I saw him try to, but I was on his back and stopped him—with six others.

PLAYBOY: Has your opinion of him changed?

HUSTON: No, not in the slightest.

PLAYBOY: Would you ever consider him for another role?

HUSTON: No.

PLAYBOY: Are there any other actors with whom you wouldn't have done a second film?

HUSTON: Paul Muni. He was certainly an amazingly good actor, but he had a huge ego. He ruined a picture that I depended a great deal on—*Juarez*. He really ruined it. I can say this without bragging, because two other men worked with me on the script for almost a year; it was a very fine script and was written so Juarez would just come into the story at vital, special moments and when he spoke, every word counted. This was in contrast to the grace and eloquence of Maximilian. Well, the first thing Muni wanted was more dialog. A humorless man, vastly impressed with himself.

PLAYBOY: Montgomery Clift was supposedly a difficult actor to work with, yet you starred him in two of your pictures—*The Misfits* and *Freud.*

HUSTON: Emotionally, Clift was very fragile. He was a mess; he was gone. I remember that on *The Misfits,* Clark Gable had a bad back, a slipped disk; Monty would slap him on purpose. Gable didn't have much use for him, I must say. But it wasn't Clift who made filming *The Misfits* an ordeal; it was Marilyn Monroe. She was always trying to wake up or go to sleep.

Marilyn and her husband, Arthur Miller, were at odds. I hadn't realized that until we were well into the picture. I was impertinent enough to say to Arthur that to allow her to take drugs of any kind was criminal and utterly irresponsible on the part of anyone who had any feeling for her. It was only shortly after that that I realized that she wouldn't listen to Arthur at all; he had no say over her actions.

PLAYBOY: Do you believe her death was a suicide?

HUSTON: No, no, I think it was an accident. You know, when I cast her in her first big picture [*The Asphalt Jungle*], I didn't have any idea that she was going to become America's sex queen. There was something very touching about her; one felt protective about Marilyn—and this is not simply after the fact, either. You felt that she was vulnerable and might get hurt, and she damn well did. The phrase sex queen may be a misapplication; that was no more than half of her attraction. She moved women as much as she did men.

PLAYBOY: Getting back to Clift, is it true that he would cry when you excluded him from discussions during *Freud?*

HUSTON: Tears came very easily to Monty. I was amazed how good the end result was, because it was really an ordeal.

PLAYBOY: Was your reputation for being cruel to him unjust?

HUSTON: Completely so. I was never kinder to anybody than I was to Clift. Sometimes I spoke harshly to him, but it was an attempt to awaken something in him. The combination of drugs, drink and being homosexual was a soup that was just too much.

PLAYBOY: There was talk of brain damage. Do you think that was true?

HUSTON: Undoubtedly. He was never the same after his automobile accident. He lost the ability to memorize. In *The Misfits,* his lines were easy to learn, short, colloquial. *Freud* called for something entirely different, another language, as it were, the easy deployment of scientific terms—and he couldn't memorize anything.

PLAYBOY: *Freud* didn't get the kind of reception you had hoped it would, did it?

HUSTON: Well, I didn't like the beginning, but I did like the rest of the picture. I was surprised it didn't have an audience—and it certainly didn't. I'd thought that there would be more people curious about Freud's work. At one point, the studio changed the title to get a wider audience—*The Hidden Passion* or some goddamn thing—but that didn't fool anybody.

PLAYBOY: Jean-Paul Sartre wrote the first draft of *Freud*, didn't he?

HUSTON: Yes. I had promised him that we wouldn't be censored, and he understood that to mean we could have an eight-hour picture, so he wrote a script of that length. I then took his material and tried to organize it, and it was a hell of an undertaking. I have never had a worse time writing.

PLAYBOY: What was your impression of Sartre?

HUSTON: I don't think I knew Sartre at his best. He was on drugs—not hard drugs, drugs to stimulate him; he couldn't stop talking. He stayed with me in Ireland for three weeks, during which he talked. He had no English; my French isn't good; there were a couple of interpreters, who just added to the babble. He wore a cheap, ill-fitting three-piece suit with the same necktie, and although his shirts looked laundered, it was always as though he had the same clothes on. He was without egotism and was probably the ugliest man I have ever laid eyes on—one eye going in one direction, and the eye itself wasn't very beautiful, like an omelet. And this pitted face.

PLAYBOY: After *Freud*, you tackled another huge subject. What made you decide to film *Moby Dick*?

HUSTON: I had read *Moby Dick* 20 years before I made it. I hadn't read it as a child. Most people say they read it when they were children—well, they're liars. Nobody in his early teens ever read *Moby Dick*. They've read abridged versions. Ray Bradbury and I wrote the script; we simplified it into picture terms. The fact that multitudes didn't clamor to see *Moby Dick* was a great disappointment. The greatest criticism leveled against the picture was the casting—Gregory Peck as Ahab. Well, I'm a pretty good judge of actors. I saw *Moby Dick* recently on TV, and Peck is good. But the image the audience of that time had of him was different; they wouldn't accept him.

PLAYBOY: That was the only film on which you ever went over budget, wasn't it?

HUSTON: Yes, because we encountered the worst seas in maritime history for that part of the Atlantic. We lost two quite expensive whales, and the picture had to stop while they built a new one. The cable holding it broke three times, and it was a question of rescuing either the men in the boats or the whales. Each time, we allowed sentiment to overcome our better judgment—we saved the men. [*Laughs*] When we were down to our last whale, I knew that if I got inside it, they weren't going to let it go, so I grabbed a bottle of Scotch and got inside the whale.

PLAYBOY: How do you rank *Moby Dick* among your films?

HUSTON: I like particular things about it. I like things about *The Red Badge of Courage* and about *Freud*, too.

PLAYBOY: You're naming three of your least appreciated films. How do you feel about your body of work?

HUSTON: I am delightfully surprised every now and then at something that I see is good. I am not unduly impressed with my *oeuvre*, as some call it, but every now and then I see something of which I approve.

PLAYBOY: Which of your films made you the most money?

HUSTON: For me, *Moulin Rouge*. The producers were unscrupulously honest; instead of trying to conceal profits, they took pleasure in giving me my dues.

PLAYBOY: What about *The African Queen*?

HUSTON: Just a salary. I wanted to get out of my partnership with Sam Spiegel, and giving up my profits got me out of it.

PLAYBOY: What about *The Man Who Would Be King*? Didn't Michael Caine and Sean Connery have to sue to get their money?

HUSTON: Caine and Connery eventually got their money. I never got my full salary.

PLAYBOY: Which of your pictures would you like to either forget or remake?

HUSTON: I'd like to forget *The Barbarian and the Geisha* [with John Wayne], which was a good picture at one point. I went away to Africa for several months, and during that time, they changed it and released it, and it was really a fucked-up proposition, terrible, awful. I would have had my name taken off the picture, but the producer, the head of the studio, was a friend of mine; he was dying of a brain tumor and I didn't want to have a further complication. I would remake *Moulin Rouge* more realistically. At that time, censorship didn't permit the telling of the real Toulouse-Lautrec story.

PLAYBOY: Given your interest in art, do you think there are other painters' lives that might make good pictures?

HUSTON: Yes. I don't think justice was done to either Van Gogh or Michelangelo in *Lust for Life* and *The Agony and the Ecstasy*. Pictures could still be made about them, more serious, deeper pictures. But I've been influenced by painting in my own pictures. One of the things I look for in a color film is the palette: What palette do I use? Just as a painter, when he approaches a subject, decides what colors and tonalities. *Moulin Rouge* was in part an attempt to re-create something of the effect of the Lautrec posters.

PLAYBOY: Which films by other people do you most admire?

HUSTON: I find it easier to talk about the work of the director than about individual films. I like, of course, William Wyler enormously, the whole body of his work. John Ford, George Stevens—not unexpected names. Pictures from my youth—*Covered Wagon*; I was enormously moved by the profundity of *Four Horsemen*. [*Laughs*] Among the French, *Hiroshima, Mon Amour*, Henri-Georges Clouzot's *Wages of Fear*. De Sica's *Bicycle Thief*. The original *Mutiny on the Bounty*.

PLAYBOY: How do you feel about remakes?

HUSTON: Awful. They ought to remake the ones they did badly, but to remake a great picture is the ultimate in absurdity. Even if the remake is good, it can never be as good as the original. By Christ, you would think they would begin to realize that!

PLAYBOY: What contemporary films have impressed you?

HUSTON: The last picture that I saw that I liked without reservation was *Gallipoli*. It was a marvelous picture, unrecognized for how good it was, simply a great picture from every standpoint. Another that impressed me not as a great picture but as interesting was the one about the three old men who robbed a bank, *Going in Style*. *Ordinary People* was well written, not inspired but excellent. That other Australian film, *Breaker Morant*. *Godfather II* was a hell of a picture, beautifully acted. Who played in *Taxi Driver*?

PLAYBOY: Robert De Niro.

HUSTON: Jesus, that was good. I didn't know it was De Niro when I began watching. I just knew it was marvelous. Christ, what a performance! I've seen a few pictures on TV that I would have missed otherwise. One was kind of awful but more interesting than people realized—De Niro in *The King of Comedy*. I found it distasteful and boring at first; then, about the third time I saw it on TV, I was fascinated. It was realism taken to the point of excruciating, sickening truth. It's a rather important document, I think, but mine is the first voice I've heard in praise of it.

PLAYBOY: What about the blockbusters—the *Star Wars* and *Raiders* pictures, *E.T.?*

HUSTON: Yes, fine . . . they've been done now. It's fascinating that such a large segment of mankind fell in love with the E.T. creature. It shows a good impulse.

PLAYBOY: And what do you think of Steven Spielberg as a director?

HUSTON: My God, I think he is as inventive as hell; I take my hat off to him. He's an ordinary man with an extraordinary expression.

PLAYBOY: And George Lucas?

HUSTON: I would lump them together.

PLAYBOY: What do you think of actors, such as Warren Beatty and Barbra Streisand, who turn to directing?

HUSTON: Beatty did an extraordinary job with *Reds*. What I most admired was his taking that subject. He is someone to contend with; his choices of material indicate quite a well-furnished apartment upstairs. I think, by the way, *Bonnie and Clyde* was one of the important pictures of our time.

PLAYBOY: And Streisand?

HUSTON: I'm impressed with her choosing *Yentl*; it was extraordinary. But for some reason, Hollywood turned against her.

PLAYBOY: Why?

HUSTON: I don't know; perhaps because she had some romantic hookup with this guy who was her hairdresser and she was calling the shots and they were out of their depth . . . there was a lack of sympathy toward her, I felt. I always felt Streisand was capable of far more than playing the Pussycat or the little Brooklyn Jewish girl. Christ, she could have played Cleopatra better than Liz Taylor, with her enormous power and the subtlety of her singing. I said to my friend Ray Stark [the producer of *Funny Girl*], "You are not doing the best thing you could with this girl."

PLAYBOY: Would you like to direct her?

HUSTON: I certainly would, because she is one of the great actresses and she hasn't been well used.

PLAYBOY: What do you think of Meryl Streep, Faye Dunaway, Jane Fonda?

HUSTON: Meryl Streep and Faye Dunaway are quite extraordinary. I like Jane Fonda for what she does, but it hasn't that scope to it. I think Jessica Lange has something that's very fine.

PLAYBOY: How about Kathleen Turner, who's in your new film?

HUSTON: Superb. I don't think there's any question she's a major actress. She's got it all. It's the kind of acting that you're born with; it's not learned. It's channeled and, my God, it flows.

PLAYBOY: Does she remind you of anyone?

HUSTON: No, and that's why she's wonderful: The good ones don't remind you of anybody else.

PLAYBOY: How do you feel about your own acting?

HUSTON: I don't put any great store in my acting; I don't take it seriously. I liked myself in *Chinatown*. And when I saw the picture about the Kennedys, *Winter Kills*, I thought that was amusing. But not much else. I just spoke my lines. But do you know who the best reader of lines is—at least on cue cards? The master?

PLAYBOY: Who?

HUSTON: Ronald Reagan. I saw him give a speech when he was in South Korea, and it was a damn good one. He spoke to the audience and he didn't look at the camera, you didn't see him reading his lines. It was the only thing about Ronald Reagan that ever impressed me.

PLAYBOY: You and Reagan go back a long way, don't you?

HUSTON: Yes, I have known him for a long time, since he was working with Warner Bros. I knew his wife, Nancy, who is the daughter of great friends of my father's, Dr. Loyal and Edith Davis. When Nancy went out to Hollywood, she was sort of under my wing for a while, and then she married Ronnie. I'd see them occasionally.

PLAYBOY: Did your opinion of Nancy lower any when she married Reagan?

HUSTON: Oh, no. I love Nancy—and I don't dislike Ronnie, I just disagree with his politics. But I submit one thing: The idea that Nancy is archconservative and reactionary and that she is the influence on Ronnie that has guided his political thinking is absurd, absolute nonsense.

PLAYBOY: Do you miss the old Hollywood?

HUSTON: Yes, I miss the order that the old Hollywood had. It was much easier then to get a picture made than it is today. It's become a cliché that the studio people were picture makers then, but there is a large element of truth in it. They were people who wanted to make pictures, and they knew how to make them. They weren't accountants and bookkeepers, tax consultants and efficiency experts who don't know how to make pictures, or wheeler-dealers; that element just seems to have taken over today—promoters who just want to get a part of the action rather than people who want to make good pictures. They'll get a picture, get an actor, wheel and deal and get a package together and present it to a studio and the studio will then pass on it. It's amazing that pictures ever get made—and a bad picture, a picture with no qualifications whatever, can get made as readily as something like *Terms of Endearment*, which was turned down by every studio in town. As to the Hollywood social scene, I've managed to avoid that for a lifetime, except in very small doses. I like country life—not farming but the sports that attend to country life: huntin', shootin' and fishin', as it were. I like working with and being with animals. I like making a picture if I feel I'm on the way to getting something good. I despair of making a picture if I feel it's going badly, which occasionally happens. Only occasionally, thank God—otherwise, I wouldn't go on making films.

PLAYBOY: After all these years, are you still affected by reviews?

HUSTON: Yes, the bad ones hit me. I read something recently that disturbed me no end. There's a female reviewer for *The New Yorker* who was writing about *The Night of the Iguana*, saying it was a badly made picture. Well, it's not a badly made picture. I know damn well it's not. She is a cunt. I'm prepared to forgive her for a lot of things but not for that. [*Laughs*]

PLAYBOY: With cassettes and cable and satellite dishes, do you think seeing movies in a theater will become a thing of the past?

HUSTON: I should think so. I find it very difficult to go to a theater if I have to line up round the block to see a picture. I'd go to see a fight or a horse race that way, but I would be goddamned if I would go to see a picture under those terms.

PLAYBOY: Did you once tell Bogart that you were forever and eternally bored?

HUSTON: No. Perhaps I was saying I was afraid of being bored, which is true. If I'm threatened with boredom, why, I'll run like a hare.

PLAYBOY: Is there a secret to maintaining your creativity through a long life?

HUSTON: Have I told you the story of a *jai alai* game I attended once? No? Well, there was a point that went on and on, an unbelievable rally that lasted five or more minutes, until one of the players lost. I heard the man behind me say, "He didn't lose it; his grandfather lost it." Well, it's not me; it's my grandparents.

PLAYBOY: It's in the genes?

HUSTON: Yeah, though you have to keep exercising the brain—it's a muscle like any other. I say this as the gates of senility open before me like a Beverly Hills estate.

PLAYBOY: Are you afraid of death? Would you like to be in control of your own death, as Hemingway was?

HUSTON: No, I don't care about that. What I wouldn't want to do is to hang around half out of my mind. I hope death approaches me very quietly, gently, touches me with a sleeve, says, "Lie down," puts its fingers over my eyes.

PLAYBOY: But until then—

HUSTON: There is usually something to do to keep from being bored—read a book, see a painting, ride a horse, skydive. . . .

PLAYBOY: You've left out something.

HUSTON: Oh, yes, make another picture.

STANLEY KUBRICK

A candid conversation with the pioneering creator of 2001: A Space Odyssey, Dr. Strange- love *and* Lolita

Throughout his 17-year career as a moviemaker, Stanley Kubrick has committed himself to pushing the frontiers of film into new and often controversial regions—despite the box-office problems and censorship battles that such a commitment invariably entails. Never a follower of the safe, well-traveled road to Hollywood success, he has consistently struck out on his own, shattering movie conventions and shibboleths along the way. In many respects, his latest film, the epic *2001: A Space Odyssey*, stands as a metaphor for Kubrick himself. A technically flawless production that took three years and $10.5 million to create, 2001 could have been just a superspectacle of exotic gadgetry and lavish special effects; but with the collaboration of Arthur C. Clarke, astrophysicist and doyen of science-fiction writers, Kubrick has elevated a sci-fi adventure to the level of allegory— creating a stunning and disturbing metaphysical speculation on man's destiny that has fomented a good-sized critical controversy and become a cocktail-party topic across the country. An uncompromising film, 2001 places a heavy intellectual burden upon the audience, compelling each viewer to unravel for himself its deeper meaning and significance. Its message is conveyed not through plot or standard expository dialogue but through metaphysical hints and visual symbols that demand confrontation and interpretation.

2001 begins several million years in the past, with a vivid—and, to some, mystifying—sequence on the dawn of man. At first an ape- like vegetarian living peacefully among other animals, he suddenly becomes a carnivorous and warlike protohuman, eager and ready to kill his neighbor in defense of the territorial imperative. The cosmic midwife of this transmogrification is a mysterious black monolith that appears at a crucial point in the ape's evolution and apparently inspires him to employ a bone as both weapon and tool. The monoliths are, in a very real sense, the protagonists of the picture; they appear, Sivalike, to offer man options for both good and evil, as represented by the weapon-tool—which, when flung triumphantly into the air by a jubilant warrior ape, dissolves into a spaceship languidly approaching a satellite space station.

The year is now 2001. Another monolith has been discovered buried beneath the moon's surface—and man is ready for his next evolutionary leap. The monolith broadcasts an earsplitting signal toward the planet Jupiter, and a team of five astronauts (three in hibernation) is sent there to determine the source of the mystery. But in the course of the journey, four of them die at the hands of Hal 9000—the ship's omniscient and omnipresent computer—who is so anthropomorphic that he suffers from the all-too-human sin of hubris. The remaining astronaut (Keir Dullea) performs a mechanical lobotomy on Hal's memory circuits.

Pursuing another monolith, floating among Jupiter's moons, Dullea is suddenly swept into a cosmic maelstrom that hurtles him through inner and outer space into new dimensions of consciousness. Finally, he emerges from his space capsule, death-eyed and white-haired, in an eerie Regency bedroom replete with Watteau paintings, French provincial furniture and a luminously glowing floor. Here he witnesses—and experiences—the successive stages of his life from old age into senescence and death—a death that becomes a mystical rebirth as the astronaut, shrunken and desiccated like the first apes, gazes up at yet another monolith at the foot of his bed and is absorbed into a sunburst of energy. Reborn as the first of a new race, the astronaut in the last scene floats fetally in space within a cosmic placenta—his huge eyes, worldly and otherworldly, turning for a last look at the Earth he has left behind forever.

Critical reaction to 2001 was vehemently divided between those who declared it either an unqualified masterpiece or an absolute disaster. "Technically and imaginatively," wrote Penelope Gilliatt of *The New Yorker*, "it is staggering." *The Washington Evening Star* called it "a gorgeous, exhilarating and mind-stretching spectacle," and *Cue* observed that it "dazzles the eyes and gnaws at the mind." But other reviewers concurred with the film critic for *Women's Wear Daily*, who termed it "not the worst film I've ever seen, simply the dullest," and with John Simon of *The New Leader*, who loftily dismissed the epic as "a kind of space-*Spartacus* and, more pretentious still, a shaggy God story." But Andrew Sarris of *The Village Voice* waxed most passionate of all the critics in his denunciation: "It is anti-human, anti-science and anti-progress . . . completely sexless, soulless: a dirge for the future."

Though Kubrick is by now accustomed to living in the eye of such critical hurricanes, his early background was hardly tempestuous. He was born in the Bronx in 1928, the son of a doctor who still practices there. Kubrick's adolescent ambition to become a jazz drummer was sidetracked at the age of 13, when his father gave him his first camera—a Graflex. Habitually quiet and introspective, young Kubrick made few friends, but his photographic talent blossomed rapidly. In 1945, two months before he graduated from Taft High School in the Bronx (with a lukewarm 67 average), he snapped a picture of a weeping news dealer surrounded by papers announcing FDR's death, submitted the photo to *Look* and received $25 for his first published work. Shortly thereafter, *Look* also gave Kubrick his first job; he became one of the youngest photographers in the magazine's history.

Kubrick stayed with the magazine until 1950, supplementing his modest income by playing chess in Washington Square Park at 25 cents a game (he is still a superior player); but he was becoming increasingly intrigued with cinema. His first film, *Day of the Fight*, was a short documentary about prizefighter Walter Cartier. It cost all of $3900 to make, but Kubrick soon found he couldn't retrieve even this investment. Finally he sold the work to RKO-Pathé at a $100 loss. After one more unheralded documentary, Kubrick decided to try his hand—and his luck—at a feature-length film. He quit his job at *Look*, raised $20,000—mostly from his father and his uncle—and began shooting *Fear and Desire*, the story of four soldiers, isolated behind enemy lines during World War II, who gain insights about themselves in their struggle to rejoin their outfit. Kubrick now regards the film as pretentious and amateurish, but many critics welcomed it as a remarkably sensitive first effort. Though rejected by all major distributors, *Fear and Desire* toured the art-house circuit and eventually broke even.

After a decidedly commercial murder mystery called *Killer's Kiss*, Kubrick went to work on *The Killing*, an intricately contrived melodrama involving a racetrack robbery. The film starred Sterling Hayden and won Kubrick his first widespread recognition. As *Time* breathlessly declared: "At 27, writer-director Stanley Kubrick has shown more audacity with dialogue and camera than Hollywood has seen since the obstreperous Orson Welles." *Time* subsequently called *The Killing* one of the 10 best films of 1956, but the movie proved a box-office dud.

Undismayed, Kubrick again focused his attention on a military subject: the blood-soaked battlefields of the western front in World War I. The result was *Paths of Glory*, the tragic story of three innocent French soldiers who live through a futile engagement with the Germans only to be executed as cowards by their own high command. With Kirk Douglas in the leading role, the film movingly depicted the bleak horror and meaninglessness of war. Though it, too, fared only modestly at the box office, it was universally hailed as a major work of cinematic art, and it made Kubrick a name to be reckoned with. Douglas, impressed with Kubrick's talent, asked him to direct the forthcoming *Spartacus*, in which Douglas was to play the starring role. "It was the only film I didn't have full directorial control over," Kubrick recalls ruefully; but *Spartacus* was viewed by the critics as a cut above the standard Cinemascopic spectacular. It also made money.

Never one to rest on his laurels, Kubrick had already selected his next film: an adaptation of *Lolita*, Vladimir Nabokov's sexy, scintillating bestseller. Undaunted by the looming censorship problems involved in depicting the story of a passionate liaison between a middle-aged man and a sensuous nymphet, Kubrick selected James Mason to play Humbert Humbert and a Hollywood unknown—Sue Lyon—for the lead role. Kubrick then wisely decided to make the film in England, where the chance of censorial intervention was less likely than on home shores. The result was one of the biggest box-office hits in Hollywood history—and a superabundance of rave reviews. Arthur Schlesinger Jr., then moonlighting as a film critic from his presidential advisory post, called *Lolita* "a brilliant and sinister film, wildly funny and wildly poignant."

Well before the returns on *Lolita* were in, Kubrick was characteristically blocking out his next project. He had long been concerned with the prospect of accidental nuclear holocaust; and his fears were reinforced by a novel, *Red Alert*, by Peter George. In collaboration with George—and with an indeterminate amount of assistance from black humorist Terry Southern (Kubrick and Southern still disagree heatedly on the extent of Southern's participation)—Kubrick produced *Dr. Strangelove*, an overwhelming critical and commercial success. The film's darkly satirical antiwar message offended some Cold Warriors and travelers on the ultraright, but critic Stanley Kauffmann described it as "the best American picture that I can remember since Chaplain's *Monsieur Verdoux* and Huston's *Treasure of the Sierra Madre*." And *Time* declared, "It fulfills Stanley Kubrick's promise as one of the most audacious and imaginative directors the U.S. cinema has yet produced."

Kubrick's meteoric career—launched into even higher orbit by his ambitious space odyssey to 2001—has made him a near legend in Hollywood, where he has won the devoted admiration of his co-workers and the respect of fellow directors and actors; no mean feat in Tinseltown. Marlon Brando, who has worked with Kubrick (though not always harmoniously), reports: "Stanley is unusually perceptive and delicately attuned to people. He has an adroit intellect and is a creative thinker, not a repeater, not a fact gatherer. He digests what he learns and brings to a new project an original point of view and a reserved passion." Kirk Douglas is more blunt: "Success can't hurt that kid. Stanley always knew he was good."

To discover what has made Kubrick so respected—and controversial —a director, and to plumb both his own complexities and those of *2001*, *Playboy* interviewed Kubrick at his elegant mansion outside London, a short drive from MGM's studio at Borham Wood, where he is working on his latest film—a biography of Napoleon. Interviewer Eric Norden found Kubrick—"a slim, relaxed man with thinning hair, dark beard and intense eyes"—sprawled in a chair on the spacious expanse of lawn overlooking his elegantly tended gardens. "As Kubrick crossed one scuffed shoe over a wrinkled pants leg," writes Norden, "I began by asking him to decipher the metaphysical message of *2001*. Though his answer was enigmatically evasive, he was far more voluble about his space odyssey, and the destiny it prophesies for the human race, than about himself as man or moviemaker. It may be that he feels his private life is too dull to talk about, or perhaps too interesting, or simply nobody's business but his own. But I think it's more likely that he is one of those rare men whose self-concern is plural and impersonal, to whom the present is less real than the possible, who live less in the world of tangible reality than in the uncharted country of the mind." But not completely uncharted, Norden might have added, since many of Kubrick's imaginative extrapolations are predicated on theories and formulations with which science-fiction fans are fondly familiar. What lifts Kubrick's prognostications beyond the realm of most conventional sci-fi speculation is his preoccupation not with mechanistic externals but with the philosophical implications of man's future.

PLAYBOY: Much of the controversy surrounding 2001 deals with the meaning of the metaphysical symbols that abound in the film—the polished black monoliths, the orbital conjunction of Earth, moon and sun at each stage of the monoliths' intervention in human destiny, the stunning final kaleidoscopic maelstrom of time and space that engulfs the surviving astronaut and sets the stage for his rebirth as a "star child" drifting toward Earth in a translucent placenta. One critic even called 2001 "the first Nietzschean film," contending that its essential theme is Nietzsche's concept of man's evolution from ape to human to superman. What *was* the metaphysical message of 2001?

KUBRICK: It's not a message that I ever intend to convey in words. 2001 is a nonverbal experience; out of two hours and 19 minutes of film, there are only a little less than 40 minutes of dialogue. I tried to create a *visual* experience, one that bypasses verbalized pigeonholing and directly penetrates the subconscious with an emotional and philosophic content. To convolute McLuhan, in 2001, the message is the medium. I intended the film to be an intensely subjective experience that reaches the viewer at an inner level of consciousness, just as music does; to "explain" a Beethoven symphony would be to emasculate it by erecting an artificial barrier between conception and appreciation. You're free to speculate as you wish about the philosophical and allegorical meaning of the film—and such speculation is one indication that it has succeeded in gripping the audience at a deep level—but I don't want to spell out a verbal road map for 2001 that every viewer will feel obligated to pursue or else fear he's missed the point. I think that if 2001 succeeds at all, it is in reaching a wide spectrum of people who would not often give a thought to man's destiny, his role in the cosmos and his relationship to higher forms of life. But even in the case of someone who is highly intelligent, certain ideas found in 2001 would, if presented as abstractions, fall rather lifelessly and be automatically assigned to pat intellectual categories; experienced in a moving visual and emotional context, however, they can resonate within the deepest fibers of one's being.

PLAYBOY: Without laying out a philosophical road map for the viewer, can you tell us your own interpretation of the meaning of the film?

KUBRICK: No, for the reasons I've already given. How much would we appreciate *La Gioconda* today if Leonardo had written at the bottom of the canvas: "This lady is smiling slightly because she has rotten teeth"—or "because she's hiding a secret from her lover"? It would shut off the viewer's appreciation and shackle him to a "reality" other than his own. I don't want that to happen to 2001.

PLAYBOY: Arthur Clarke has said of the film, "If anyone understands it on the first viewing, we've failed in our intention." Why should the viewer have to see a film twice to get its message?

KUBRICK: I don't agree with that statement of Arthur's, and I believe he made it facetiously. The very nature of the visual experience in *2001* is to give the viewer an instantaneous, visceral reaction that does not—and should not—require further amplification. Just speaking generally, however, I would say that there are elements in any good film that would increase the viewer's interest and appreciation on a second viewing; the momentum of a movie often prevents every stimulating detail or nuance from having a full impact the first time it's seen. The whole idea that a movie should be seen only once is an extension of our traditional conception of the film as an ephemeral entertainment rather than as a visual work of art. We don't believe that we should hear a great piece of music only once, or see a great painting once, or even read a great book just once. But the film has until recent years been exempted from the category of art—a situation I'm glad is finally changing.

PLAYBOY: Some prominent critics—including Renata Adler of *The New York Times*, John Simon of the *New Leader*, Judith Crist of *New York* magazine and Andrew Sarris of *The Village Voice*—apparently felt that 2001 should be among those films still exempted from the category of art; all four castigated it as dull, pretentious and overlong. How do you account for their hostility?

KUBRICK: The four critics you mention all work for New York publications. The reviews across America and around the world have been 95 percent enthusiastic. Some were more perceptive than others, of course, but even those who praised the film on relatively superficial grounds were able to get something of its message. New York was the only really hostile city. Perhaps there is a certain element of the lumpen literati that is so dogmatically atheist and materialist and earthbound that it finds the grandeur of space and the myriad mysteries of cosmic intelligence anathema. But film critics, fortunately, rarely have any effect on the general public; houses everywhere are packed and the film is well on its way to becoming the greatest moneymaker in MGM's history. Perhaps this sounds like a crass way to evaluate one's work, but I think that, especially with a film that is so obviously *different*, record audience attendance means people are saying the right things to one another after they see it—and isn't this really what it's all about?

PLAYBOY: Speaking of what it's all about—if you'll allow us to return to the philosophical interpretation of *2001*—would you agree with those critics who call it a profoundly religious film?

KUBRICK: I will say that the God concept is at the heart of *2001*—but not any traditional, anthropomorphic image of God. I don't believe in any of Earth's monotheistic religions, but I do believe that one can construct an intriguing *scientific* definition of God, once you accept the fact that there are approximately 100 billion stars in our galaxy alone, that each star is a life-giving sun and that there are approximately 100 billion galaxies in just the *visible* universe. Given a planet in a stable orbit, not too hot and not too cold, and given a few billion years of chance chemical reactions created by the interaction of a sun's energy on the planet's chemicals, it's fairly certain that life in one form or another will eventually emerge. It's reasonable to assume that there must be, in fact, countless *billions* of such planets where biological life has arisen, and the odds of some proportion of such life developing intelligence are high. Now, the sun is by no means an old star, and its planets are mere children in cosmic age, so it seems likely that there are billions of planets in the universe not only where intelligent life is on a lower scale than man but other billions where it is approximately equal and others still where it is hundreds of thousands of millions of years in advance of us. When you think of the giant technological strides that man has made in a few millennia—less than a microsecond in the chronology of the universe—can you imagine the evolutionary development that much older life-forms have taken? They may have progressed from biological species, which are fragile shells for the mind at best, into immortal machine entities—and then, over innumerable eons, they could emerge from the chrysalis of matter transformed into beings of pure energy and spirit. Their potentialities would be limitless and their intelligence ungraspable by humans.

PLAYBOY: Even assuming the cosmic evolutionary path you suggest, what has this to do with the nature of God?

KUBRICK: Everything—because these beings would *be* gods to the billions of less advanced races in the universe, just as man would appear a god to an ant that somehow comprehended man's existence. They would possess the twin attributes of all deities—omniscience and omnipotence. These entities might be in telepathic communication throughout the cosmos and thus be aware of everything that occurs, tapping every intelligent mind as effortlessly as we switch on the radio; they might not be limited by the speed of light and their presence could penetrate to the farthest corners of the universe; they might possess complete mastery over matter and energy; and in their final evolutionary stage, they might develop into an integrated collective immortal consciousness. They would be incomprehensible to us except as gods; and if the tendrils of their consciousness ever brushed men's minds, it is only the hand of God we could grasp as an explanation.

PLAYBOY: If such creatures do exist, why should they be interested in man?

KUBRICK: They may not be. But why should man be interested in microbes? The motives of such beings would be as alien to us as their intelligence.

PLAYBOY: In *2001*, such incorporeal creatures seem to manipulate our destinies and control our evolution, though whether for good or evil—or both, or neither—remains unclear. Do you really believe it's possible that man is a cosmic plaything of such entities?

KUBRICK: I don't really *believe* anything about them; how can I? Mere speculation on the possibility of their existence is sufficiently overwhelming, without attempting to decipher their motives. The important point is that all the standard attributes assigned to God in our history could equally well be the characteristics of biological entities who billions of years ago were at a stage of development similar to man's own and evolved into something as remote from man as man is remote from the primordial ooze from which he first emerged.

PLAYBOY: In this cosmic phylogeny you've described, isn't it possible that there might be forms of intelligent life on an even higher scale than these entities of pure energy—perhaps as far removed from them as they are from us?

KUBRICK: Of course there could be; in an infinite, eternal universe, the point is that *anything* is possible, and it's unlikely that we can even begin to scratch the surface of the full range of possibilities. But at a time when astronauts are preparing to set foot on the moon, I think it's necessary to open up our earthbound minds to such speculation. No one knows what's waiting for us in the universe. I think it was a prominent astronomer who wrote recently, "Sometimes I think we are alone, and sometimes I think we're not. In either case, the idea is quite staggering."

PLAYBOY: You said there must be billions of planets sustaining life that is considerably more advanced than man but has not yet evolved into non- or suprabiological forms. What do you believe would be the effect on humanity if the Earth were contacted by a race of such ungodlike but technologically superior beings?

KUBRICK: There's a considerable difference of opinion on this subject among scientists and philosophers. Some contend that encountering a highly advanced civilization—even one whose technology is essentially comprehensible to us—would produce a traumatic cultural shock effect on man by divesting him of his smug ethnocentrism and shattering the delusion that he is the center of the universe. Carl Jung summed up this position when he wrote of contact with advanced extraterrestrial life that the "reins would be torn from our hands and we would, as a tearful old medicine man once said to me, find ourselves 'without dreams'. . . we would find our intellectual and spiritual aspirations so outmoded as to leave us completely paralyzed." I personally don't accept this position, but it's one that's widely held and can't be summarily dismissed.

In 1960, for example, the Committee for Long Range Studies of the Brookings Institution prepared a report for the National Aeronautics and Space Administration warning that even indirect contact—i.e., alien artifacts that might possibly be discovered through our space activities on the moon, Mars or Venus or via radio contact with an interstellar civilization—could cause severe psychological dislocations. The study cautioned that "Anthropological files contain many examples of societies, sure of their place in the universe, which have disintegrated when they have had to associate with previously unfamiliar societies espousing different ideas and different life ways; others that survived such an experience usually did so by paying the price of changes in values and attitudes and behavior." It concluded that since intelligent life might be discovered at any time, and that since the consequences of such a discovery are "presently unpredictable," it was advisable that the government initiate continuing studies on the psychological and intellectual impact of confrontation with extraterrestrial life. What action was taken on this report I don't know, but I assume that such studies are now under way. However, while not discounting the possible adverse emotional impact on some people, I would personally tend to view such contact with a tremendous amount of excitement and enthusiasm. Rather than shattering our society, I think it could immeasurably enrich it.

Another positive point is that it's a virtual certainty that all intelligent life at one stage in its technological development must have discovered nuclear energy. This is obviously the watershed of any civilization; does it find a way to use nuclear power without destruction and harness it for peaceful purposes, or does it annihilate itself? I would guess that any civilization that has existed for 1000 years after its discovery of atomic energy has devised a means of accommodating itself to the bomb, and this could prove tremendously reassuring to us—as well as give us specific guidelines for our own survival. In any case, as far as cultural shock is concerned, my impression is that the attention span of most people is quite brief; after a week or two of great excitement and oversaturation in newspapers and on television, the public's interest would drop off and the United Nations, or whatever world body we then had, would settle down to discussions with the aliens.

PLAYBOY: It sounds like you're assuming that extraterrestrials would be benevolent. Why?

KUBRICK: Why should a vastly superior race *bother* to harm or destroy us? If an intelligent ant suddenly traced a message in the sand at my feet reading, "I am sentient; let's talk things over," I doubt very much that I would rush to grind him under my heel. Even if they weren't superintelligent, though, but merely more advanced than mankind, I would tend to lean more toward the benevolence, or at least indifference, theory. Since it's most unlikely that we would be visited from within our own solar system, any society capable of traversing light-years of space would have to have an extremely high degree of control over matter and energy. Therefore, what possible motivation for hostility would they have? To steal our gold or oil or coal? It's hard to think of any nasty intention that would justify the long and arduous journey from another star.

PLAYBOY: You'll admit, though, that extraterrestrials are commonly portrayed in comic strips and cheap science-fiction films as bug-eyed monsters scuttling hungrily after curvaceous Earth maidens.

KUBRICK: This probably dates back to the pulp science-fiction magazines of the 1920s and 1930s and perhaps even to the Orson Welles Martianinvasion broadcast in 1938 and the resultant mass hysteria, which is always advanced in support of the hypothesis that contact would cause severe cultural shock. In a sense, the lines with which Welles opened that broadcast set the tone for public consideration of extraterrestrial life for years to come. I've memorized them: "Across an immense ethereal gulf, minds that are to our minds as ours are to the beasts in the jungle—intellects vast, cool and unsympathetic—regarded this Earth with envious eyes and slowly and surely drew their plans against us. . . ." Anything we can imagine about such other life forms is possible, of course. You could have psychotic civilizations, or decadent civilizations that have elevated pain to an aesthetic and might covet humans as gladiators or torture objects, or civilizations that might want us for zoos, or scientific experimentation, or slaves or even for food. While I am appreciably more optimistic, we just can't be sure *what* their motivations will be.

I'm interested in the argument of Professor Freeman Dyson of Princeton's Institute of Advanced Study, who contends that it would be a mistake to expect that all potential space visitors will be altruistic, or to believe that they would have *any* ethical or moral concepts comparable to mankind's. Dyson writes, if I remember him correctly, that "Intelligence may indeed be a benign influence creating isolated groups of philosopher kings far apart in the heavens," but it's just as likely that "Intelligence may be a cancer of purposeless technological exploitation, sweeping across a galaxy as irresistibly as it has swept across our own planet." Dyson concludes that it's "just as unscientific to impute to remote intelligence wisdom and serenity as it is to impute to them irrational and murderous impulses. We must be prepared for either possibility and conduct our searches accordingly."

This is why some scientists caution, now that we're attempting to intercept radio signals from other solar systems, that if we do receive a message we should wait awhile before answering it. But we've been transmitting radio and television signals for so many years that any advanced civilization could have received the emissions long ago. So in the final analysis, we really don't have much choice in this matter; they're either going to contact us or they're not, and if they do we'll have nothing to say about their benevolence or malevolence.

Even if they prove to be malevolent, their arrival would have at least one useful byproduct in that the nations of the Earth would stop squabbling among themselves and forge a common front to defend the planet. I think it was André Maurois who suggested many years ago that the best way to realize world peace would be to stage a false threat from outer space; it's not a bad idea. But I certainly don't believe we should view contact with extraterrestrial life forms with foreboding, or hesitate to visit other planets for fear of what we may find there. If others don't contact us, we must contact them; it's our destiny.

PLAYBOY: You indicated earlier that intelligent life is extremely unlikely elsewhere within our solar system. Why?

KUBRICK: From what we know of the other planets in this system, it appears improbable that intelligence exists, because of surface temperatures and atmospheres that are inhospitable to higher life forms. Improbable, but not impossible. I will admit that there are certain tantalizing clues pointing in the other direction. For example, while the consensus of scientific opinion dismisses the possibility of intelligent life on Mars—as opposed to plant or low orders of organic life—there are some eminently respectable dissenters. Dr. Frank B. Salisbury, professor of plant physiology at Utah State University, has contended in a study in *Science* magazine that if vegetation exists on a planet, then it is logical that there will be higher orders of life to feed on it. "From there," he writes, "it is but one more step—granted, a big one—to intelligent beings."

Salisbury also points out that a number of astronomers have observed strange flashes of light, possibly explosions of great magnitude, on Mars' surface, some of which emit clouds; and he suggests that these could actually be nuclear explosions. Another intriguing facet of Mars is the peculiar orbits of its twin satellites, Phobos and Deimos, first discovered in 1877—the same year, incidentally, that Schiaparelli discovered his famous but still elusive Martian "canals." One eminent astronomer, Dr. Josif Shklovsky, chairman of the department of radio astronomy at the Shternberg Astronomical Institute in Moscow, has propounded the theory that both moons are artificial space satellites launched by the Martians thousands of years ago in an effort to escape the dying surface of their planet. He bases this theory on the unique orbits of the two moons, which, unlike the 31 other satellites in our solar system, orbit *faster* than the revolution of their host planet. The orbit of Phobos is also deteriorating in an inexplicable manner and dragging the satellite progressively closer to Mars' surface. Both of these circumstances, Shklovsky contends, make sense only if the two moons are *hollow*.

Shklovsky believes that the satellites are the last remnants of an extinct ancient Martian civilization; but Professor Salisbury goes a step further and suggests that they were launched within the past hundred years. Noting that the moons were discovered by a relatively small-power telescope in 1877 and not detected by a much more powerful telescope observing Mars in 1862—when the planet was appreciably nearer Earth—he asks: "Should we attribute the failure of 1862 to imperfections in the existing telescope, or may we imagine that the satellites were launched into orbit between 1862 and 1877?" There are no answers here, of course, only questions, but it is fascinating speculation. On balance, however, I would have to say that the weight of available evidence dictates against intelligent life on Mars.

PLAYBOY: How about possibilities, if not the probabilities, of intelligent life on the other planets?

KUBRICK: Most scientists and astronomers rule out life on the outer planets since their surface temperatures are thousands of degrees either above or below zero and their atmosphere would be poisonous. I suppose it's possible that life could evolve on such planets with, say, a liquid ammonia or methane base, but it doesn't appear too likely. As far as Venus goes, the Mariner probes indicate that the surface temperature of the planet is approximately 800 degrees Fahrenheit, which would deny the chemical basis for molecular development of life. And there could be no indigenous intelligent life on the moon, because of the total lack of atmosphere—no life as we know it, in any case; though I suppose that intelligent rocks or crystals, or statues, with a silicone life base are not really impossible, or even conscious gaseous matter or swarms of sentient electric particles. You'd get no technology from such creatures, but if their intelligence could control matter, why would they need it? There could be nothing about them, however, even remotely humanoid—a form that would appear to be an eminently practicable universal life prototype.

PLAYBOY: What do you think we'll find on the moon?

KUBRICK: I think the most exciting prospect about the moon is that if alien races have ever visited Earth in the remote past and left artifacts for man to discover in the future, they probably chose the arid, airless lunar vacuum, where no deterioration would take place and an object could exist for millennia. It would be inevitable that as man evolved technologically, he would reach his nearest satellite and the aliens would then expect him to find their calling card—perhaps a message of greeting, a cache of knowledge or simply a cosmic burglar alarm signaling that another race had mastered space flight. This, of course, was the central situation of 2001.

But an equally fascinating question is whether there could be another race of intelligent life on Earth. Dr. John Lilly, whose research into dolphins has been funded by the National Aeronautics and Space Administration, has amassed considerable evidence pointing to the possibility that the bottle-nosed dolphin may be as intelligent as or more intelligent than man. He bases this not only on its brain size—which is larger than man's and with a more complex cortex—but on the fact that dolphins have evolved an extensive language. Lilly is currently attempting, with some initial success, to decipher this language and establish communication with the dolphins. NASA's interest in this is obvious, because learning to communicate with dolphins would be a highly instructive precedent for learning to communicate with alien races on other planets. Of course, if the dolphins are really intelligent, theirs is obviously a nontechnological culture, since without an opposable thumb, they could never create artifacts. Their intelligence might also be on a totally different order than man's, which could make communication additionally difficult. Dr. Lilly has written that "It is probable that their intelligence is comparable to ours, though in a very strange fashion . . . they may have a new class of large brain so dissimilar to ours that we cannot within our lifetime possibly understand its mental processes." Their culture may be totally devoted to creating works of poetry or devising abstract mathematical concepts, and they could conceivably share a telepathic communication to supplement their high-frequency underwater language.

What is particularly interesting is that dolphins appear to have developed a concept of altruism; the stories of shipwrecked sailors rescued by dolphins and carried to shore, or protected by them against sharks, are by no means all old wives' tales. But I'm rather disturbed by some recent developments that indicate not only how we may treat dolphins but also how we may treat intelligent races on other planets. The Navy, impressed by the dolphin's apparent intelligence, is reported to have been engaging in underwater-demolition experiments in which a live torpedo is strapped to a dolphin and detonated by radio when it nears a prototype enemy submarine. These experiments have been officially denied; but if they're true, I'm afraid we may learn more about man through dolphins than the other way around. The Russians, paradoxically, seem to be one step ahead of us in this area; they recently banned all catching of dolphins in Russian waters on the grounds that "Comrade Dolphin" is a fellow sentient being and killing him would be morally equivalent to murder.

PLAYBOY: Although flying saucers are frequently an object of public derision, there has been a good deal of serious discussion in the scientific community about the possibility that UFOs could be alien spacecraft. What's your opinion?

KUBRICK: The most significant analysis of UFOs I've seen recently was written by L. M. Chassin, a French air force general who had been a high-ranking NATO officer. He argues that by any legal rules of evidence, there is now sufficient sighting data amassed from reputable sources—astronomers, pilots, radar operators and the like—to initiate a serious and thorough worldwide investigation of UFO phenomena. Actually, if you examine even a fraction of the extant testimony you will find that people have been sent to the gas chamber on far less substantial evidence. Of course, it's possible that all the governments in the world really *do* take UFOs seriously and perhaps are already engaging in secret study projects to determine their origin, nature and intentions. If so, they may not be disclosing their findings for fear that the public would be alarmed—the danger of cultural shock deriving from confrontation with the unknown which we discussed earlier, and which is an element of *2001*, when news of the monolith's discovery on the moon is suppressed. But I think even the 2 percent of sightings that the Air Force's Project Blue Book admits is unexplainable by conventional means should dictate a serious, searching probe. From all indications, the current government-authorized investigation at the University of Colorado is neither serious nor searching.

One hopeful sign that this subject may at last be accorded the serious discussion it deserves, however, is the belated but exemplary conversion of Dr. J. Allen Hynek, since 1948 the Air Force's consultant on UFOs and currently chairman of the astronomy department at Northwestern University. Hynek, who in his official capacity pooh-poohed UFO sightings, now believes that UFOs deserve top-priority attention—as he wrote in *Playboy* [December 1967]—and even concedes that the existing evidence may indicate a possible connection with extraterrestrial life. He predicts: "I will be surprised if an intensive study yields nothing. To the contrary, I think that mankind may be in for the greatest adventure since dawning human intelligence turned outward to contemplate the universe." I agree with him.

PLAYBOY: If flying saucers are real, who or what do you think they might be?

KUBRICK: I don't know. The evidence proves they're up there, but it gives us very little clue as to what they are. Some science-fiction writers theorize half-seriously that they could be time shuttles flicking back and forth between eons to a future age when man has mastered temporal travel; and I understand that biologist Ivan Sanderson has even advanced a theory that they may be some kind of living space animal inhabiting the upper stratosphere—though I can't give much credence to that suggestion. It's also possible that they are perfectly natural phenomena, perhaps chain lightning, as one American science writer has suggested; although this, again, does not explain some of the photographs taken by reputable sources, such as the Argentine navy, which clearly show spherical metallic objects hovering in the sky. As you've probably deduced, I'm really fascinated by UFOs and I only regret that this field of investigation has to a considerable extent been pre-empted by a crackpot fringe that claims to have soared to Mars on flying saucers piloted by three-foot-tall green humanoids with pointy heads. That kind of kook approach makes it very easy to dismiss the whole phenomenon which we do at our own risk.

I think another problem here—and one of the reasons that, despite the overwhelming evidence, there has been remarkably little public interest—is that most people don't really *want* to think about extraterrestrial beings patrolling our skies and perhaps observing us like bugs on a slide. The thought is too disturbing; it upsets our tidy, soothing, sanitized suburban *Weltanschauung*; the cosmos is more than light-years away from Scarsdale. This could be a survival mechanism, but it could also blind us to what may be the most dramatic and important moment in man's history—contact with another civilization.

PLAYBOY: Among the reasons adduced by those who doubt the interstellar origin of UFOs is Einstein's special theory of relativity, which states that the speed of light is absolute and that nothing can exceed it. A journey from even the nearest star to Earth would consequently take thousands of years. They claim this virtually rules out interstellar travel—at least for sentient beings with life spans as short as the longest known to man. Do you find this argument valid?

KUBRICK: I find it difficult to believe that we have penetrated to the ultimate depths of knowledge about the physical laws of the universe. It seems rather presumptuous to believe that in the space of a few hundred years, we've figured out most of what there is to know. So I don't think it's right to declaim with unshakable certitude that light is the absolute speed limit of the universe. I'm suspicious of dogmatic scientific rules; they tend to have a rather short life span. The most eminent European scientists of the early 19th century scoffed at meteorites, on the grounds that "stones can't fall from the sky"; and just a year before *Sputnik*, one of the world's leading astrophysicists stated flatly that "space flight is bunk." Actually, there are already some extremely interesting theoretical studies under way—one by Dr. Gerald Feinberg at Columbia University—which indicate that shortcuts could be found that would enable some things under certain conditions to exceed the speed of light.

In addition, there's always the possibility that the speed-of-light limitation, even if it's rigid, could be circumvented via a space-time warp, as Arthur Clarke has proposed. But let's take another, slightly more conservative, means of evading the speed of light's restrictions: If radio contact is developed between ourselves and another civilization, within 200 years we will have reached a stage in genetic engineering where the other race could transmit its genetic code to us by radio and we could then re-create their DNA pattern and artificially duplicate one of their species in our laboratories—and vice versa. This sounds fantastic only to those who haven't followed the tremendous breakthroughs being made in genetic engineering.

But actual interstellar travel wouldn't be impossible even if light speed *can't* be achieved. Whenever we dismiss space flight beyond our solar system on the grounds that it would take thousands of years, we are thinking of beings with life spans similar to ours. Fruit flies, I understand, live out their entire existence—birth, reproduction and death—within 24 hours; well, man may be to other creatures in the universe as the fruit fly is to man. There may be countless races in the universe with life spans of hundreds of thousands or even millions of years, to whom a 10,000-year journey to Earth would be about as intimidating as an afternoon outing in the park. But even in terms of our own time scale, within a few years it should be possible to freeze astronauts or induce a hibernatory suspension of life functions for the duration of an interstellar journey. They could spend 300 or 1000 years in space and be awakened automatically, feeling no different than if they had had a hearty eight hours' sleep.

The speed-of-light theory, too, could work in favor of long journeys; the peculiar "time dilation" factor in Einstein's relativity theory means that as an object accelerates toward the speed of light, time slows down. Everything would appear normal to those on board; but if they had been away from Earth for, say, 56 years, upon their return they would be merely 20 years older than when they departed. So, taking all these factors into consideration, I'm not unduly impressed by the claims of some scientists that the speed-of-light limitation renders interstellar travel impossible.

PLAYBOY: You mentioned freezing astronauts for lengthy space journeys, as in the "hibernacula" of *2001*. As you know, physicist Robert Ettinger and others have proposed freezing *dead* bodies in liquid nitrogen until a future time when they can be revived. What do you think of this proposal?

KUBRICK: I've been interested in it for many years, and I consider it eminently feasible. Within 10 years, in fact, I believe that freezing of the dead will be a major industry in the United States and throughout the world; I would recommend it as a field of investment for imaginative speculators. Dr. Ettinger's thesis is quite simple: If a body is frozen cryogenically in liquid nitrogen at a temperature near absolute zero—minus 459.6 degrees Fahrenheit—and stored in adequate facilities, it may very well be possible at some as-yet-indeterminate date in the future to thaw and revive the corpse and then cure the disease or repair the physical damage that was the original cause of death. This would, of course, entail a considerable gamble; we have no way of knowing that future science will be sufficiently advanced to cure, say, terminal cancer, or even successfully revive a frozen body. In addition, the dead body undergoes damage in the course of the freezing process itself; ice crystallizes within the bloodstream. And unless a body is frozen at the precise moment of death, progressive brain-cell deterioration also occurs. But what do we have to lose? Nothing—and we have immortality to gain. Let me read you what Dr. Ettinger has written: "It used to be thought that the distinction between life and death was simple and obvious. A living man breathes, sweats and makes stupid remarks; a dead one just lies there, pays no attention, and after a while gets putrid. But nowadays nothing is that simple."

Actually, when you really examine the concept of freezing the dead, it's nowhere nearly as fantastic—though every bit as revolutionary—as it appears at first. After all, countless thousands of patients "die" on the operating table and are revived by artificial stimulation of the heart after a few seconds or even a few minutes—and there is really little substantive difference between bringing a patient back to life after three minutes of clinical death or after an "intermezzo" stage of 300 years. Fortunately, the freezing concept is now gaining an increasing amount of attention within the scientific community. France's Dr. Jean Rostand, an internationally respected biologist, has proposed that every nation begin a freezer program immediately, funded by government money and utilizing the top scientific minds in each country. "For every day that we delay," he says, "untold thousands are going to an unnecessary grave."

PLAYBOY: Are you interested in being frozen yourself?

KUBRICK: I would be if there were adequate facilities available at the present time—which, unfortunately, there are not. A number of organizations are attempting to disseminate information and raise funds to implement an effective freezing program—the Life Extension Society of Washington, the Cryonics Society of New York, etc.—but we are still in the infancy of cryobiology. Right now, all existing freezer facilities—and there are only a handful—aren't sufficiently sophisticated to offer any realistic hope. But that could and probably will change far more rapidly than we imagine.

A key point to remember, particularly by those ready to dismiss this whole concept as preposterous, is that science has made fantastic strides in just the past 40 years; within this brief period of time, a wide range of killer diseases that once were the scourge of mankind, from smallpox to diphtheria, have been virtually eliminated through vaccines and antibiotics; while others, such as diabetes, have been brought under control—though not yet completely eliminated—by drugs such as insulin. Already, heart transplants are almost a viable proposition, and organ banks are being prepared to stock supplies of spleens, kidneys, lungs and hearts for future transplant surgery.

Dr. Ettinger predicts that a "freezee" who died after a severe accident or massive internal damage would emerge resuscitated from a hospital of the future a "crazy quilt of patchwork." His internal organs—heart, lungs, liver, kidneys, stomach and the rest—may be grafts, implanted after being grown in the laboratory from someone's donor cells. His arms and legs may be "bloodless artifacts of fabric, metal and plastic, directed by tiny motors." His brain cells, writes Ettinger, "may be mostly new, regenerated from the few which would be saved, and some of his memories and personality traits may have had to be imprinted onto the new cells by microtechniques of chemistry and physics." The main challenge to the scientist of the future will not be revival but eliminating the original cause of death; and in this area, we have every reason for optimism as a result of recent experience. So before anyone dismisses the idea of freezing, he should take a searching look at what we have accomplished in a few decades—and ponder what we're capable of accomplishing over the next few centuries.

PLAYBOY: If such a program does succeed, the person who is frozen will have no way of knowing, of course, if he will ever be successfully revived. Do you think future scientists will be willing, even if they're able, to bring their ancestors back to life?

KUBRICK: Well, 20th century man may not be quite the cup of tea for a more advanced civilization of even 100 years in the future; but unless the future culture has achieved immortality—which is scientifically quite possible—they themselves would be frozen at death, and every generation would have a vested interest in the preservation of the preceding frozen generation in order to be, in turn, preserved by its own descendants. Of course, it would be something of a letdown if, 300 years from now, somebody just pulled the plug on us all, wouldn't it?

Another problem here, quite obviously, is the population explosion; what will be the demographic effect on the Earth of billions of frozen bodies suddenly revived and taking their places in society? But by the time future scientists have mastered the techniques to revive their frozen ancestors, space flight will doubtless be a reality and other planets will be open for colonization. In addition, vast freezer facilities could possibly be constructed on the dark side of the moon to store millions of bodies. The problems are legion, of course, but so are the potentialities.

PLAYBOY: Opponents of cryogenic freezing argue that death is the natural and inevitable culmination of life and that we shouldn't tamper with it—even if we're able to do so. How would you answer them?

KUBRICK: Death is no more natural or inevitable than smallpox or diphtheria. Death is a disease and as susceptible to cure as any other disease. Over the eons, man's powerlessness to prevent death has led him to force it from the forefront of his mind, for his own psychological health, and to accept it unquestioningly as the unavoidable termination. But with the advance of science, this is no longer necessary—or desirable. Freezing is only one possible means of conquering death, and it certainly would not be binding on everyone; those who desire a "natural" death can go ahead and die, just as those in the 19th century who desired "God-ordained" suffering resisted anesthesia. As Dr. Ettinger has written, "To each his own, and to those who choose not to be frozen, all I can say is—rot in good health."

PLAYBOY: Freezing and resuscitation of the dead is just one revolutionary scientific technique that could transform our society. Looking ahead to the year of your film, 2001, what major social and scientific changes do you foresee?

KUBRICK: Perhaps the greatest breakthrough we may have made by 2001 is the possibility that man may be able to eliminate old age. We've just discussed the steady scientific conquest of disease; even when this is accomplished, however, the scourge of old age will remain. But too many people view senile decay, like death itself, as inevitable. It's nothing of the sort. The highly respected Russian scientist V. F. Kuprevich has written, "I am sure we can find means for switching off the mechanisms which make cells age." Dr. Bernard Strehler, an eminent gerontology expert, contends that there is no inherent contradiction, no inherent property of cells or of Metazoa that precludes their organization into perpetually functioning and self-replenishing individuals.

One encouraging indication that we may already be on this road is the work of Dr. Hans Selye, who in his book *Calciphylaxis* presents an intriguing and well-buttressed argument that old age is caused by the transfer of calcium within the body—a transfer that can be arrested by circulating throughout the system specific iron compounds that flush out the calcium, absorb it and prevent it from permeating the tissue. Dr. Selye predicts that we may soon be able to prevent the man of 60 from progressing to the condition of the man of 90. This is something of an understatement; Selye could have added that the man of 60 could *stay* 60 for hundreds or even thousands of years if all other diseases have been eradicated. Even accidents would not necessarily impair his relative immortality; even if a man is run over by a steamroller, his mind and body will be completely re-creatable from the tiniest fragment of his tissue, if genetic engineering continues its rapid progress.

PLAYBOY: What impact do you think such dramatic scientific breakthroughs will have on the lifestyle of society at the turn of the century?

KUBRICK: That's almost impossible to say. Who could have predicted in 1900 what life in 1968 would be like? Technology is, in many ways, more predictable than human behavior. Politics and world affairs change so quickly that it's difficult to predict the future of social institutions for even 10 years with a modicum of accuracy. By 2001, we could be living in a Gandhiesque paradise where all men are brothers, or in a neofascist dictatorship, or just be muddling along about the way we are today. As technology evolves, however, there's little doubt that the whole concept of leisure will be both quantitatively and qualitatively improved.

PLAYBOY: What about the field of entertainment?

KUBRICK: I'm sure we'll have sophisticated 3D holographic television and films, and it's possible that completely new forms of entertainment and education will be devised. You might have a machine that taps the brain and ushers you into a vivid dream experience in which you are the protagonist in a romance or an adventure. On a more serious level, a similar machine could directly program you with knowledge; in this way, you might, for example, easily be able to learn fluent German in 20 minutes. Currently, the learning processes are so laborious and time-consuming that a breakthrough is really needed.

On the other hand, there are some risks in this kind of thing; I understand that at Yale they've been engaging in experiments in which the pleasure center of a mouse's brain has been localized and stimulated by electrodes; the result is that the mouse undergoes an eight-hour orgasm. If pleasure that intense were readily available to all of us, we might well become a race of sensually stultified zombies plugged into pleasure stimulators while machines do our work and our bodies and minds atrophy. We could also have this same problem with psychedelic drugs; they offer great promise of unleashing perceptions, but they also hold commensurate dangers of causing withdrawal and disengagement from life into a totally inner-directed kind of Soma world. At the present time, there are no ideal drugs; but I believe by 2001 we will have devised chemicals with no adverse physical, mental or genetic results that can give wings to the mind and enlarge perception beyond its present evolutionary capacities.

Actually, up to now, perception on the deepest level has really, from an evolutionary point of view, been detrimental to survival; if primitive man had been content to sit on a ledge by his cave absorbed in a beautiful sunset or a complex cloud configuration, he might never have exterminated his rival species—but neither would he have achieved mastery of the planet. Now, however, man is faced with the unprecedented situation of potentially unlimited material and technological resources at his disposal and a tremendous amount of leisure time. At last, he has the opportunity to look both within and beyond himself with a new perspective—without endangering or impeding the progress of the species. Drugs, intelligently used, can be a valuable guide to this new expansion of our consciousness. But if employed just for kicks, or to dull rather than to expand perception, they can be a highly negative influence. There should be fascinating drugs available by 2001; what use we make of them will be the crucial question.

PLAYBOY: Have you ever used LSD or other so-called consciousness-expanding drugs?

KUBRICK: No. I believe that drugs are basically of more use to the audience than to the artist. I think that the illusion of oneness with the universe, and absorption with the significance of every object in your environment, and the pervasive aura of peace and contentment is not the ideal state for an artist. It tranquilizes the creative personality, which thrives on conflict and on the clash and ferment of ideas. The artist's transcendence must be within his own work; he should not impose any artificial barriers between himself and the mainspring of his subconscious. One of the things that's turned me against LSD is that all the people I know who use it have a peculiar inability to distinguish between things that are really interesting and stimulating and things that *appear* so in the state of universal bliss the drug induces on a "good" trip. They seem to completely lose their critical faculties and disengage themselves from some of the most stimulating areas of life. Perhaps when *everything* is beautiful, nothing is beautiful.

PLAYBOY: What stage do you believe today's sexual revolution will have reached by 2001?

KUBRICK: Here again, it's pure speculation. Perhaps there will have been a reaction against present trends, and the pendulum will swing back to a kind of neo-puritanism. But it's more likely that the so-called sexual revolution, midwifed by the pill, will be extended. Through drugs, or perhaps via the sharpening or even mechanical amplification of latent ESP functions, it may be possible for each partner to simultaneously experience the sensations of the other; or we may eventually emerge into polymorphous sexual beings, with the male and female components blurring, merging and interchanging. The potentialities for exploring new areas of sexual experience are virtually boundless.

PLAYBOY: In view of these trends, do you think romantic love may have become unfashionable by 2001?

KUBRICK: Obviously, people are finding it increasingly easy to have intimate and fulfilling relationships outside the concept of romantic love—which, in its present form, is a relatively recent acquisition, developed at the court of Eleanor of Aquitaine in the 12th century—but the basic love relationship, even at its most obsessional, is too deeply ingrained in man's psyche not to endure in one form or another. It's not going to be easy to circumvent our primitive emotional programming. Man still has essentially the same set of pair-bonding instincts—love, jealousy, possessiveness—imprinted for individual and tribal survival millions of years ago, and these still lie quite close to the surface, even in these allegedly enlightened and liberated times.

PLAYBOY: Do you think that by 2001 the institution of the family, which some social scientists have characterized as moribund, may have evolved into something quite different from what it is today?

KUBRICK: One can offer all kinds of impressive intellectual arguments against the family as an institution—its inherent authoritarianism, etc.; but when you get right down to it, the family is the most primitive and visceral and vital unit in society. You may stand outside your wife's hospital room during childbirth muttering, "My God, what a responsibility! Is it right to take on this terrible obligation? What am I really doing here?"; and then you go in and look down at the face of your child and—zap!—that ancient programming takes over and your response is one of wonder and joy and pride. It's a classic case of genetically imprinted social patterns. There are very few things in this world that have an unquestionable importance in and of themselves and are not susceptible to debate or rational argument, but the family is one of them. Perhaps man has been too "liberated" by science and evolutionary social trends. He has been turned loose from religion and has hailed the death of his gods; the imperative loyalties of the old nation-state are dissolving and all the old social and ethical values, however reactionary and narrow they often were, are disappearing. Man in the 20th century has been cut adrift in a rudderless boat on an uncharted sea; if he is going to stay sane throughout the voyage, he must have someone to care about, something that is more important than himself.

PLAYBOY: Some critics have detected not only a deep pessimism but also a kind of misanthropy in much of your work. In *Dr. Strangelove*, for example, one reviewer commented that your directorial attitude, despite the film's antiwar message, seemed curiously aloof and detached and unmoved by the annihilation of mankind, almost as if the Earth were being cleansed of an infection. Is there any truth to that?

KUBRICK: Good God, no. You don't stop being concerned with man because you recognize his essential absurdities and frailties and pretensions. To me, the only real immorality is that which endangers the species; and the only absolute evil, that which threatens its annihilation. In the deepest sense, I believe in man's potential and in his capacity for progress. In *Strangelove*, I was dealing with the inherent irrationality in man that threatens to destroy him; that irrationality is with us as strongly today, and must be conquered. But a recognition of insanity doesn't imply a celebration of it—nor a sense of despair and futility about the possibility of curing it.

PLAYBOY: In the five years since *Dr. Strangelove* was released, the two major nuclear powers, the U.S. and the U.S.S.R., have reached substantial accommodation with each other. Do you think this has reduced the danger of nuclear war?

KUBRICK: No. If anything, the overconfident Soviet-American détente *increases* the threat of accidental war through carelessness; this has always been the greatest menace and the one most difficult to cope with. The danger that nuclear weapons may be used—perhaps by a secondary power—is as great if not greater than it has ever been, and it is really quite amazing that the world has been able to adjust to it psychologically with so little apparent dislocation.

Particularly acute is the possibility of war breaking out as the result of a sudden unanticipated flare-up in some part of the world, triggering a panic reaction and catapulting confused and frightened men into decisions they are incapable of making rationally. In addition, the serious threat remains that a psychotic figure somewhere in the modern command structure could start a war, or at the very least a limited exchange of nuclear weapons that could devastate wide areas and cause innumerable casualties. This, of course, was the theme of *Dr. Strangelove*; and I'm not entirely assured that somewhere in the Pentagon or the Red army upper echelons there does not exist the real-life prototype of General Jack D. Ripper.

PLAYBOY: Fail-safe strategists have suggested that one way to obviate the danger that a screwball might spark a war would be to administer psychological-fitness tests to all key personnel in the nuclear command structure. Would that be an effective safeguard?

KUBRICK: No, because any seriously disturbed individual who rose high within the system would have to possess considerable self-discipline and be able to effectively mask his fixations. Such tests already do exist to a limited degree, but you'd really have to be pretty far gone to betray yourself in them, and the type of individual we're discussing would have to be a highly controlled psychopathic personality not to have given himself away long ago. But beyond those tests, how are you going to objectively assess the sanity of the president, in whom, as commander in chief, the ultimate responsibility for the use of nuclear weapons resides? It's improbable but not impossible that we could someday have a psychopathic president, or a president who suffers a nervous breakdown, or an alcoholic president who, in the course of some stupefying binge, starts a war. You could say that such a man would be detected and restrained by his aides—but with the powers of the presidency what they are today, who really knows? Less farfetched and even more terrifying is the possibility that a psychopathic individual could work his way into the lower echelons of the White House staff. Can you imagine what might have happened at the height of the Cuban Missile Crisis if some deranged waiter had slipped LSD into Kennedy's coffee—or, on the other side of the fence, into Khrushchev's vodka? The possibilities are chilling.

PLAYBOY: Do you share the belief of some psychiatrists that our continued reliance on the balance of nuclear power, with all its attendant risks of global catastrophe, could reflect a kind of collective death wish?

KUBRICK: No, but I think the *fear* of death helps explain why people accept this Damoclean sword over their heads with such bland equanimity. Man is the only creature aware of his own mortality and is at the same time generally incapable of coming to grips with this awareness and all its implications. Millions of people thus, to a greater or lesser degree, experience emotional anxieties, tensions and unresolved conflicts that frequently express themselves in the form of neuroses and a general joylessness that permeates their lives with frustration and bitterness and increases as they grow older and see the grave yawning before them. As fewer and fewer people find solace in religion as a buffer between themselves and the terminal moment, I actually believe that they unconsciously derive a kind of perverse solace from the idea that in the event of nuclear war, the world dies with them. God is dead, but the bomb endures; thus, they are no longer alone in the terrible vulnerability of their mortality. Sartre once wrote that if there was one thing you could tell a man about to be executed that would make him happy, it was that a comet would strike the Earth the next day and destroy every living human being. This is not so much a collective death wish or self-destructive urge as a reflection of the awesome and agonizing loneliness of death. This is extremely pernicious, of course, because it aborts the kind of fury and indignation that should galvanize the world into defusing a situation where a few political leaders on both sides are seriously prepared to incinerate millions of people out of some misguided sense of national interest.

PLAYBOY: Are you a pacifist?

KUBRICK: I'm not sure what pacifism really means. Would it have been an act of superior morality to have submitted to Hitler in order to avoid war? I don't think so. But there have also been tragically senseless wars such as World War I and the current mess in Vietnam and the plethora of religious wars that pockmark history. What makes today's situation so radically different from anything that has gone before, however, is that, for the first time in history, man has the means to destroy the entire species—and possibly the planet as well. The problem of dramatizing this to the public is that it all seems so abstract and unreal; it's rather like saying, "The sun is going to die in a billion years." What is required as a minimal first corrective step is a concrete alternative to the present balance of terror—one that people can understand and support.

PLAYBOY: Do you believe that some form of all-powerful world government, or some radically new social, political and economic system, could deal intelligently and farsightedly with such problems as nuclear war?

KUBRICK: Well, none of the present systems has worked very well, but I don't know what we'd replace them with. The idea of a group of philosopher kings running everything with benign and omniscient paternalism is always attractive, but where do we find the philosopher kings? And if we do find them, how do we provide for their successors? No, it has to be conceded that democratic society, with all its inherent strains and contradictions, is unquestionably the best system anyone ever worked out. I believe it was Churchill who once remarked that democracy is the worst social system in the world, except for all the others.

PLAYBOY: You've been accused of revealing in your films, a strong hostility to the modern industrialized society of the democratic West, and a particular antagonism—ambivalently laced with a kind of morbid fascination—toward automation. Your critics claim this was especially evident in *2001*, where the archvillain of the film, the computer Hal 9000, was in a sense the only human being. Do you believe that machines are becoming more like men and men more like machines—and do you detect an eventual struggle for dominance between the two?

KUBRICK: First of all, I'm not hostile toward machines at all; just the opposite, in fact. There's no doubt that we're entering a mechanarchy, however, and that our already complex relationship with our machinery will become even more complex as the machines become more and more intelligent. Eventually, we will have to share this planet with machines whose intelligence and abilities far surpass our own. But the interrelationship—if intelligently managed by man—could have an immeasurably enriching effect on society.

Looking into the distant future, I suppose it's not inconceivable that a semisentient robot-computer subculture could evolve that might one day decide it no longer needed man. You've probably heard the story about the ultimate computer of the future: For months scientists think of the first question to pose to it, and finally they hit on the right one: "Is there a God?" After a moment of whirring and flashing lights, a card comes out, punched with the words: There is now. But this problem is a distant one and I'm not staying up nights worrying about it: I'm convinced that our toasters and TVs are fully domesticated, though I'm not so sure about integrated telephone circuits, which sometimes strike me as possessing a malevolent life all their own.

PLAYBOY: Speaking of futuristic electronics and mechanics, *2001*'s incredibly elaborate gadgetry and scenes of space flight have been hailed—even by hostile critics—as a major cinematic breakthrough. How were you able to achieve such remarkable special effects?

KUBRICK: I can't answer that question technically in the time we have available, but I can say that it was necessary to conceive, design and engineer completely new techniques in order to produce the special effects. This took 18 months and $6.5 million out of a $10.5 million budget. I think an extraordinary amount of credit must go to Robert H. O'Brien, the president of MGM, who had sufficient faith to allow me to persevere at what must have at times appeared to be a task without end. But I felt it was necessary to make this film in such a way that every special-effects shot in it would be completely convincing—something that had never before been accomplished in a motion picture.

PLAYBOY: Thanks to those special effects, *2001* is undoubtedly the most graphic depiction of space flight in the history of films—and yet you have admitted that you yourself refuse to fly, even in a commercial jet liner. Why?

KUBRICK: I suppose it comes down to a rather awesome awareness of mortality. Our ability, unlike the other animals, to conceptualize our own end creates tremendous psychic strains within us; whether we like to admit it or not, in each man's chest a tiny ferret of fear at this ultimate knowledge gnaws away at his ego and his sense of purpose. We're fortunate, in a way, that our body, and the fulfillment of its needs and functions, plays such an imperative role in our lives; this physical shell creates a buffer between us and the mind-paralyzing realization that only a few years of existence separate birth from death. If man really sat back and thought about his impending termination, and his terrifying insignificance and aloneness in the cosmos, he would surely go mad, or succumb to a numbing sense of futility. Why, he might ask himself, should be bother to write a great symphony, or strive to make a living, or even to love another, when he is no more than a momentary microbe on a dust mote whirling through the unimaginable immensity of space?

Those of us who are forced by their own sensibilities to view their lives in this perspective—who recognize that there is no purpose they can comprehend and that amidst a countless myriad of stars their existence goes unknown and unchronicled—can fall prey all too easily to the ultimate anomie. I can well understand how life became for Matthew Arnold "a darkling plain . . . where ignorant armies clash by night . . . and there is neither love nor hope nor certitude nor faith nor surcease from pain." But even for those who lack the sensitivity to more than vaguely comprehend their transience and their triviality, this inchoate awareness robs life of meaning and purpose; it's why "the mass of men lead lives of quiet desperation," why so many of us find our lives as absent of meaning as our deaths.

The world's religions, for all their parochialism, did supply a kind of consolation for this great ache; but as clergymen now pronounce the death of God and, to quote Arnold again, "the sea of faith" recedes around the world with a "melancholy, long, withdrawing roar," man has no crutch left on which to lean—and no hope, however irrational, to give purpose to his existence. This shattering recognition of our mortality is at the root of far more mental illness than I suspect even psychiatrists are aware.

PLAYBOY: If life is so purposeless, do you feel that it's worth living?

KUBRICK: Yes, for those of us who manage somehow to cope with our mortality. The very meaninglessness of life forces man to create his own meaning. Children, of course, begin life with an untarnished sense of wonder, a capacity to experience total joy at something as simple as the greenness of a leaf; but as they grow older, the awareness of death and decay begins to impinge on their consciousness and subtly erode their joie de vivre, their idealism—and their assumption of immortality. As a child matures, he sees death and pain everywhere about him, and begins to lose faith in faith and in the ultimate goodness of man. But if he's reasonably strong—and lucky—he can emerge from this twilight of the soul into a rebirth of life's élan. Both because of and in spite of his awareness of the meaninglessness of life, he can forge a fresh sense of purpose and affirmation. He may not recapture the same pure sense of wonder he was born with, but he can shape something far more enduring and sustaining. The most terrifying fact about the universe is not that it is hostile but that it is indifferent; but if we can come to terms with this indifference and accept the challenges of life within the boundaries of death—however mutable man may be able to make them—our existence as a species can have genuine meaning and fulfillment. However vast the darkness, we must supply our own light.

PLAYBOY: Will we be able to find any deep meaning or fulfillment, either as individuals or as a species, as long as we continue to live with the knowledge that all human life could be snuffed out at any moment in a nuclear catastrophe?

KUBRICK: We *must*, for in the final analysis, there may be no sound way to eliminate the threat of self-extinction without changing human nature; even if you managed to get every country disarmed down to the bow and arrow, you would still be unable to lobotomize either the knowledge of how to build nuclear warheads or the perversity that allows us to rationalize their use. Given these two categorical imperatives in a disarmed world, the first country to amass even a few weapons would have a great incentive to use them quickly. So an argument might be made that there is a greater chance for *some* use of nuclear weapons in a totally disarmed world, though less chance of global extinction; while in a world armed to the teeth, you have less chance for *some* use—but a great chance of extinction if they're used.

If you try to remove yourself from an earthly perspective and look at this tragic paradox with the detachment of an extraterrestrial, the whole thing is totally irrational. Man now has the power in one mad, incandescent moment, as you point out, to exterminate the entire species; our own generation could be the last on Earth. One miscalculation and all the achievements of history could vanish in a mushroom cloud; one misstep and all of man's aspirations and strivings over the millennia could be terminated. One short circuit in a computer, one lunatic in a command structure and we could negate the heritage of the billions who have died since the dawn of man and abort the promise of the billions yet unborn—the ultimate genocide. What an irony that the discovery of nuclear power, with its potential for annihilation, also constitutes the first tottering step into the universe that must be taken by all intelligent worlds. Unhappily, the infant-mortality rate among emerging civilizations in the cosmos may be very high. Not that it will matter except to us; the destruction of this planet would have no significance on a cosmic scale; to an observer in the Andromeda nebulae, the sign of our extinction would be no more than a match flaring for a second in the heavens; and if that match does blaze in the darkness, there will be none to mourn a race that used a power that could have lit a beacon in the stars to light its funeral pyre. The choice is ours.

July 1991

SPIKE LEE

A candid conversation with the outspoken actor-director about being black in America, sounding white on the streets and causing trouble everywhere else

There are many logical places you might find a famous director, writer, producer or actor—in a bungalow office on the studio back lot, poolside in Bel Air or maybe at a prominent table at Le Dome. But if you're looking for the most successful hyphenate in movies—a man who is the writer, producer, director *and* star of a series of commercially and critically successful films—forget Hollywood and head for a renovated three-story firehouse in the Fort Greene section of Brooklyn.

The fact that Spike Lee has chosen to oversee his burgeoning show-business empire from Fort Greene, his childhood home, is simply one example of his fierce independence. He demands complete control over his often controversial movies, such as *Do the Right Thing, School Daze, She's Gotta Have It, Mo' Better Blues* and the upcoming *Jungle Fever.* He directs and stars in a string of Nike commercials with Michael Jordan. He directs music videos. He oversees books and documentaries about himself and his films. He's starting a record company. He owns a store—Spike's Joint—that merchandises every conceivable type of paraphernalia based on his movies.

"Spike is first and foremost a damn good businessman," says actor-director Ossie Davis, who played Da Mayor in *Do the Right Thing* and Coach Odom in *School Daze.* But Lee is much more than that. With his movies, he has clearly raised the consciousness of Hollywood toward black filmmakers and, more importantly, he has shown that black-themed films can be both commercially and critically viable. But Lee is not satisfied with putting blacks *on* the screen; he is a vocal advocate for getting blacks jobs behind the scenes as well. He stipulates in his contracts—whether for movies or commercials—that blacks be hired, often in capacities that have not been available to them previously. He insists, for instance, that black artists do the posters for his movies and he has built a loyal repertory company of actors and crew, some of whom have been with him since his days as a student filmmaker.

Probably no movie director since Hitchcock has become so immediately identifiable to the public. Part of that fame stems from Lee's acting, both in his films and in commercials. But Lee, 34, has also positioned himself as a spokesman on a variety of racial issues. *Vogue* dubbed him a "provoc-auteur," and he seems dedicated to living up to that image.

Shelton Jackson Lee—who was nicknamed Spike by his mother— is the eldest child of a middle-class Brooklyn family. His mother, who died in 1977, was a teacher who demanded educational excellence from all five Lee children; his father is a musician who has written the scores for most of his son's films. Lee was the third generation of his family to attend Morehouse College, the so-called black Harvard, and later went to New York University when he decided to pursue filmmaking. His *Joe's Bed-Stuy Barbershop: We Cut Heads* won a student Academy Award and became the first student film ever shown at Lincoln Center's "New Directors, New Films" series.

Despite that success, he was unable to land serious filmwork. Since Hollywood wasn't helping him, Lee decided to help himself. Armed with spit, prayers and a budget of $175,000, he made *She's Gotta Have It*, a dizzying, up-to-the-minute look at a relationship through the eyes of an independent and charismatic young black woman and her three suitors. Lee himself played one of those suitors—Mars Blackmon, the fly-mouthed messenger who does everything, including make love, in a pair of Air Jordans that seem to be as large as he is. (Mars lives on in Lee's Nike commercials.) The movie made $8,000,000 and turned Lee into an overnight sensation.

Had Spike's first film been a fluke? Was it a lucky break or was he really a filmmaker?

Lee answered that with *School Daze*, an ambitious, multilayered tale about life at a black college. Not only did he attempt to examine such sensitive issues as the stratification of light- and dark-skinned blacks and the cliquish assimilation into the middle class that takes place at black colleges, he did it as a musical comedy. *School Daze* was one of Columbia Pictures' biggest-grossing films of 1988.

It was in 1989 that Lee tackled his most heated subject: race relations on the hottest day of the year on a tense Bedford-Stuyvesant block in *Do the Right Thing*. From the flamboyant opening to the tragic climax that ends in one character's death at the hands of the police to the double-barreled closing quotes from Martin Luther King Jr., and Malcolm X, *Do the Right Thing* was proudly combative. When it failed to earn a chance at an Oscar for Best Picture, Lee was publicly outraged, claiming the snub was racially motivated.

Lee changed pace with *Mo' Better Blues*, a movie about a single-minded jazz musician, but he continued to be a controversy magnet, he was branded as anti-Semitic because of the movie's portrayal of two avaricious, small-minded Jewish club owners. Since his newest movie, *Jungle Fever*, a story about interracial love, promises to be one of his most controversial, we decided the time was right to send Elvis Mitchell, a freelancer and National Public Radio's "Weekend Edition" entertainment critic, to check in with Lee. Mitchell reports:

"Lee has made my life miserable for the past couple of months. The line 'Elvis was a hero to most, but he never meant shit to me' comes from 'Fight the Power,' the bracing and hard-charging theme of *Do the Right Thing*, and invariably, in phone-tag intramurals preceding our meetings, every message Lee left on my answering machine began with those deathless words, followed by his trademark cackle.

"I first met with him in his office in Fort Greene, where he was putting together an assemblage of *Jungle Fever* to show the studio before leaping into his next picture, an epic on the life and times of Malcolm X. The place is cluttered with boxes and people and Lee was extremely busy. We did manage to talk briefly and schedule our first session, which was to take place on a flight from New York to Los Angeles. He was good-humored and prickly; he loves to catch people off-guard and make incendiary comments. For instance, he demanded the right to approve this interview before it was published, but when I told him no, he simply cackled.

"Our first lengthy session, squeezed in between drops during a bumpy flight and a showing of *Dick Tracy*, demonstrated that Lee was a man of many moods. He preferred judging questions to answering them and seemed more combative than comfortable. But our second session, which took place at his New York apartment a few blocks from his office, was far more relaxed and productive. He responded to the questions with candor and enthusiasm and even posed some of his own. He asserted his shyness and spoke about his difficulty with interviews, even as he talked at length.

"We started with the obvious question."

PLAYBOY: You like to cause trouble, don't you?

LEE: Sure. I was an instigator as a kid. I just like to make people think, stir 'em up. What's wrong with that?

PLAYBOY: *Jungle Fever* certainly seems likely to stir things up.

LEE: [*Laughs*] You think that one's gonna cause some trouble?

PLAYBOY: When you write lines such as "You never see black men with fine white women"? What was the word in the script—mugly? Wasn't that the way you described the white women black men go out with?

LEE: [*Laughs*] But that's true. I've never seen black men with fine white women. They be ugly. Mugly, dogs. And you always see white men with good-looking black women. But, hey, every time you see an interracial couple somewhere, people stare at 'em.

PLAYBOY: Come on, Spike. That's a big generalization. We've seen good-looking interracial couples.

LEE: I said what I meant to. Never see it.

PLAYBOY: We know you've said in the past that you won't get involved with white women.

LEE: I don't need the trouble. Like I don't have enough as it is. Black women don't go for that, don't like that shit. I just don't find white women attractive, that's all. And it's way too many fine black women out there.

PLAYBOY: Isn't there an interracial marriage in your family?

LEE: Yes. My father. My father remarried. He married a white woman.

PLAYBOY: Did that have any effect on your making *Jungle Fever*?

LEE: Why? Why would it? I didn't talk to my father about it. I talk to my father only when it comes to scoring my movies. This isn't about him.

PLAYBOY: There's another potential controversy in *Jungle Fever*. In the opening, you address the audience directly, not as a character, and tell them that if they think you're a racist, they can kiss your "black ass." You say it twice. Why?

LEE: I felt it was justified. I wanted to hit all that, about race, before anybody else.

PLAYBOY: How did test audiences respond to it?

LEE: The test audiences liked it. I don't think Universal is crazy about that shit.

PLAYBOY: Will it stay in the movie?

LEE: I guess it will. I do have final cut.

PLAYBOY: Why does so much of *Jungle Fever* emphasize racial anger?

LEE: Why shouldn't it? It's out there.

PLAYBOY: You've said that black people are incapable of racism. Do you really believe that?

LEE: Yeah, I do. Let me clear that up, 'cause people are always taking stuff out of context. Black people can't be racist. Racism is an institution. Black people don't have the power to keep hundreds of people from getting jobs or the vote. Black people didn't bring nobody else over in boats. They had to add shit to the Constitution so we could get the vote. Affirmative action is about finished in this country now. It's through. And black people had nothing to do with that, those kinds of decisions. So how can black people be racist when that's the standard? Now, black people can be prejudiced. Shit, everybody's prejudiced about something. I don't think there will ever be an end to prejudice. But racism, that's a different thing entirely.

PLAYBOY: You've been quoted as saying that no white man could properly do the Malcolm X story, which you're preparing to direct.

LEE: That's right.

PLAYBOY: You don't think Norman Jewison, who was originally scheduled to direct, could pull it off?

LEE: No, I don't. Why do people pull that shit with black people? Don't you think Francis Coppola brought something special to *The Godfather* because he was an Italian? Don't you think that Martin Scorsese brought something special to *GoodFellas* because he was Italian?

PLAYBOY: Marlon Brando's not Italian and he was in *The Godfather*. Isn't the point that there simply aren't enough minorities to be considered?

LEE: Yeah. Now, when that shit changes, then we can talk. Until there are enough black directors, minorities working in movies so it's not an issue, we have to address it different.

PLAYBOY: But what about one director having skills another director doesn't?

LEE: I like Norman Jewison's movies. I respect what he does. I saw *In the Heat of the Night, A Soldier's Story*. I respect his work. But I think a black man is more qualified, especially in this case. Now, I do think black people are qualified to direct movies about white people.

PLAYBOY: How does that work?

LEE: Because we grow up with white images all the time, in TV, in movies, in books. It's everywhere; you can't get around it. The white world surrounds us. What do white people see of black people? Look at the shit they have us do in movies: "Right on, jive turkey!" [*Laughs*]

PLAYBOY: There's a line in *Jungle Fever* that says a black man won't rise past a certain level in white corporate America.

LEE: It's true. How many black men do you see running Xerox? How many black men you see running IBM? Shit, we need to be black entrepreneurs, run our own shit. That's what it's about.

PLAYBOY: Is that what's behind your store, Spike's Joint?

LEE: It started off as this mom-and-pop operation. We sold T-shirts for the movies and stuff, but we just had too much stuff going on. So, yeah, I wanted to get it going the way I wanted. I want to control the business, and it's easier to do it from the store. Black people just have to understand we need to become owners. Ownership is important. I don't mean to get down on Eddie Murphy, but he only owns 50 percent of Eddie Murphy Productions. His two white managers each own 25 percent of Eddie Murphy Productions. He don't even own a 100 percent of himself.

PLAYBOY: You have some other complaints about Murphy, don't you?

LEE: My problem with Eddie has to do with the hiring of black people. He will maintain he can't do nothin' about getting black people hired at Paramount. That's bullshit. A man who makes them a billion dollars can't do nothing about getting black people hired at Paramount? I can't believe that. In my contract, I demand a black man does the design and artwork for my poster. Eddie built Paramount. He built their house, he can bring some people in there if he wants to.

PLAYBOY: Overall, you seem to have become less critical about other black performers. Have you mellowed?

LEE: Look, I was never that critical. When I said that shit about Whoopi Goldberg, I was talking about the contact lenses, she was wearing blue contact lenses. She don't wear them blue contact lenses no more, do she?

PLAYBOY: What's the deal between you and Arsenio Hall?

LEE: [*Smiles*] Deal? What deal? I been on his show twice. You have to be specific.

PLAYBOY: Wasn't there a quarrel between the two of you?

LEE: I criticized him once. I never criticized him as a talk-show host.

PLAYBOY: Our understanding is that you appeared on his show last summer and were supposed to go back about a month later and were disinvited.

LEE: Yeah. They canceled on me at the last minute. Didn't even hear from him. Some assistant said they didn't want me on the show. It's in the past. Nothing to say about it. It's all been worked out. I was on his show for *Mo' Better*.

PLAYBOY: *Jungle Fever* and *Do the Right Thing* both deal with the relationships between blacks and Italians in the outer boroughs of New York. Why did you choose to deal with that twice?

LEE: Well, history has proven that in New York City, those are the two most violent, volatile combinations of ethnic groups. Black people and Jewish people have static, but it rarely ever elevates to a physical thing. Little Italy, Bensonhurst, Bay Ridge, Canarsie—black people know that these are neighborhoods that you don't fuck around in.

PLAYBOY: What do you remember as a kid about that kind of thing—that feeling of fear you talk about?

LEE: Well, I grew up in sort of an Italian neighborhood. I lived in Cobble Hill before I moved here to Fort Greene. A lot of Italian people there. And we were really the first black family to move into Cobble Hill. For the first couple of days, we got called "nigger," but we were basically left alone. We weren't perceived as a threat, because there was only one of us. In fact, some of my best friends who lived down the block were the Tuccis. Louis Tucci, Joe Tucci. Annabella's [Sciorra] family [in *Jungle Fever*], they're the Tuccis.

PLAYBOY: While growing up in that kind of neighborhood, what was your feeling about Italians?

LEE: I think Cobble Hill is a lot different than Bensonhurst. You had a lot of Jewish people in Cobble Hill, too, so it just seemed to be more—I don't want to use the word intelligent, but—

PLAYBOY: Tolerant?

LEE: Yeah, that would be a good word.

PLAYBOY: It just seems odd that the kind of neighborhood you depict in your pictures is so different from the kind you grew up in. Did you ever have an encounter in one of those places like Bensonhurst?

LEE: No. See, I went to John Dewey High School on Coney Island. But some of my friends went to other high schools, like FDR, Fort Hamilton, schools like that. They used to chase the black kids from the school to the subway station. A lot of my friends got chased.

PLAYBOY: Do you ever go to Bensonhurst just to see what it's like over there?

LEE: A couple of days after Yusef Hawkins got murdered, this reporter from *Newsday* invited me to walk around Bensonhurst with him. Other than that, I never went to it until we shot *Jungle Fever* over there.

PLAYBOY: What was that walk like?

LEE: Well, I was a celebrity, so it was "Spike, sign an autograph." "Spike, you bringing Michael Jordan around here?" "Spike, you bringing Flavor Flav?" It was exactly like the scene in *Do the Right Thing* between me and Pino over the cigarette machine, with an allowance. Pino says Magic Johnson, Eddie Murphy and Prince aren't black, they're more than black. That's the way I thought I was being viewed. I was "Spike Lee," I wasn't a black person, so they asked me for my autograph. If I was anybody else, I could have gotten a bat over the head.

PLAYBOY: How does it make you feel to be a celebrity in the neighborhood where you more or less grew up?

LEE: Well, I think that people don't necessarily look at me as a celebrity, because they know I grew up here. It's no big thing; they see me every day, buying the paper or walking to work and stuff like that. People say hello, but it's not like [*a throaty scream*] "Spike Lee!" It's not no Beatles shit or anything like that.

PLAYBOY: What do people on the street say? Do they tell you what they like or dislike about your movies?

LEE: They come up and tell me how much they like Mars Blackmon, or they tell me what they think I should do for my next movie. I'm always getting these comments from people who know exactly what my next movie should be. It's funny—I guess everybody's a director. Or a critic.

PLAYBOY: When you were a kid, did you know you wanted to make movies?

LEE: I didn't grow up thinking I wanted to make movies, be a director. Everybody in my neighborhood saw a lot of movies. There was nothing special about going to the movies. I didn't know what I wanted to do. At Morehouse College, I had a combined major, communications: radio-television, journalism, film—not film right away.

PLAYBOY: Do you remember the first film you saw that made you want to make movies?

LEE: Wait a minute. I never had a moment like that. It was never, "I saw *Lawrence of Arabia* when I was two and suddenly I was hit by the magic power of film." That's bullshit. Like I told you, I just went to the movies. Nobody thought about being a director, not me or anybody else. I read that all the time—"After I saw that picture, I knew there was nothing else for me to do"—that's a lie. It's just bullshit when people say that.

PLAYBOY: Maybe it's a lie sometimes, but certainly, some directors see movies as kids and want to make films.

LEE: I think it's bullshit. It's just something almost every director says. I have never believed it. I tell you this: It wasn't that way for me. "That's what makes movies seem like this magical thing" or somethin'. That's just Hollywood bullshit, people saying that shit because it makes makin' movies special, and the people who make movies special. The first time I went on a movie set, it didn't look like nothin' magical to me. [*Laughs*] It was the exact same thing I was doing on my student movies, only it was bigger and they were spendin' more money. That's what keeps black people out of movies—the idea that makin' movies is some special thing, some calling or something. That's what I'm about—demystifying movies. I want to do away with that bullshit.

PLAYBOY: Do you remember the first Sidney Poitier film you saw?

LEE: It had to be *Lilies of the Field*. I hated that movie. I must have been six, seven years old, but even at that age, I felt like putting a rock through the screen. Later with these nuns! You better get outa here before one of 'em says that you raped 'em! But we owe a lot to Sidney Poitier, because in order for us to get to where we are today, those films had to be made. And Sidney had to do what he had to do. He was the perfect Negro.

PLAYBOY: What did you think when you saw *Guess Who's Coming to Dinner*—especially now that you're doing a movie about interracial romance?

LEE: It was white liberal BS. You have to look at it in the context of when this film came out. This film came out in the 1960s, during the whole civil rights movement. At that time, it was a great advance for black people in the cinema.

PLAYBOY: That aside, what were you thinking as you were sitting there watching it? Were you bored? Angry?

LEE: I wasn't angry. It was just that the only way they would accept this guy was because he was a perfect human being: a doctor, from Harvard or whatever it was. Making a long-distance call and leaving the money out. That's the only way the audience would accept him, because he was such a fine, upstanding citizen.

Sidney had a great burden. He was carrying the whole weight of the hopes and aspirations of the African Americans on his shoulders. I think that had a lot to do with the roles that he chose. I think he felt he could not do a "negative" character. That's something I have tried to do, not get into that whole positive-negative image thing.

PLAYBOY: You must hear that sometimes.

LEE: *Sometimes?* All the time. Black folks tell me all the time that my image is not a positive portrayal of black people.

PLAYBOY: Did that start with *She's Gotta Have It?*

LEE: *She's Gotta Have It* has Nola Darling. She's a negative portrayal of black women and just reinforces what white people think about black women being loose, anyway. And *School Daze*—again, it was negative images of black people, showing fighting all the time. I was airing dirty laundry with our differences, which I feel are petty and superficial.

Do the Right Thing, I've got more negative images. None of the black people in *Do the Right Thing* have a job. It shows we're all lazy or whatever. It shows Sweet Dick Willie pissing against the wall, and that's a negative image of black people.

PLAYBOY: But obviously, you understand the complaints.

LEE: I understand what that means, positive black role models, because of the way black people have been shown in movies and on TV. But it's unrealistic to make every character I come up with a doctor or a lawyer or something that's just a flat character. Like, in *Jungle Fever,* I bring in drugs because it's time. One of the characters is a basehead, because it's appropriate.

PLAYBOY: What about a movie such as *School Daze,* in which you're showing the environment at a black college? Did that get a negative reaction?

LEE: Yeah. The schools themselves were saying it would be a negative portrayal of black higher education. That's one of the reasons why, three weeks into shooting, we got kicked off Morehouse's campus. Spelman refused to let us shoot there at all.

PLAYBOY: In *School Daze,* you showed a part of the black culture—the black middle class—that's not usually shown. Didn't they want that to be shown?

LEE: Yeah, but a lot of the administration and faculty in these schools, these are *old* schools. To me, they're very backward.

PLAYBOY: Did many of your fellow students rebel at middle-class traditions at Morehouse?

LEE: Yeah. We never got a really big thing, but there were students who were not going along with the program. They didn't want to be that "Morehouse Man."

PLAYBOY: How many films did you shoot when you were in school?

LEE: At Morehouse? I might have done one or two. It was there that I had my appetite whetted. That's where I became interested in film and that's where I decided I wanted to become a filmmaker. That's why I went to NYU. At NYU, I started making films.

PLAYBOY: It took you three years to get any work after you graduated from NYU. Did that bother you?

LEE: I have no bitterness. The way it happens is the way it should happen. We had to struggle for three years, but I was a better filmmaker. I don't think I could have made *She's Gotta Have It* straight out of film school.

PLAYBOY: What did it take for you to be ready to make it?

LEE: More maturity. And to be hungrier.

PLAYBOY: Where did the money come from?

LEE: Everywhere. Even though the budget for the film was $175,000, we never had that money all at one time. When we began the shoot that July, we only had $13,000 in the bank.

Man, that movie was so hard to make. We were cashin' in bottles for change, because we had so little money. I remember, we were shootin' in Nola's loft in the middle of the summer—it musta been a hundred and four degrees up there. When it's so hot, people drink a lot and I remember sayin', "Don't throw away the bottles." That's one of my movies that I can't watch again, *She's Gotta Have It*.

PLAYBOY: Was it so painful to make?

LEE: Yeah, it was hard. We only shot for 12 days, but every night, after we finished the day's work, I had to think about tryin' to go out and raise money for the very next day. Things have changed so much now, you know. We have money for contingencies, reshoots or whatever. Each picture is a little easier. But also, with *She's Gotta Have It*, the acting was bad.

PLAYBOY: So you don't like the performances?

LEE: No, not at all. They just weren't very good. I didn't really know how to direct. I wasn't good with the actors, in telling 'em what I wanted from 'em. I was just out of film school, and that was my only experience. In film school, you don't really get to work with actors, you never really have much contact with the actors, and so you're kinda intimidated by 'em. You don't deal with 'em much at all.

PLAYBOY: What was your personal life like at the time?

LEE: Everything was wrapped up in getting this film made. We invited the American independent distributors to come to the San Francisco Film Festival, because that's where the world premiere was going to happen. In the middle of the film, there was a blackout in San Francisco. Not the whole city but that particular neighborhood. So for half an hour—the theater was packed, too—people just sat there. I was sitting there in a chair in the dark, on the stage. There was a question-and-answer period while we waited for the lights to come back on. So I answered questions in the dark, and nobody left.

PLAYBOY: Did you start laughing at that point? You had been through so much.

LEE: No. I said it was an act of God. What is happening? At the beginning of the movie, a blackout. But that's where the bidding war started. We sold it to Island Pictures for $475,000 and went on to make eight million.

PLAYBOY: How long before you made your next picture?

LEE: That has been the biggest gap of all my films, between *She's Gotta Have It* and *School Daze*. I had to stay with that film a long time. Promote it, get it out there. It came out in 1986, and *School Daze* didn't come out until 1988. But since then, we've made a film every year.

PLAYBOY: *School Daze* sounds like it was overly ambitious, going from a four-character piece essentially in one room to a big musical with lots of production numbers and lots of characters.

LEE: I didn't think that was overly ambitious. I know that has been reflected in some people's reviews of the film. What I wanted to do in *School Daze* was, in that two-hour movie, compress my four years of Morehouse.

PLAYBOY: Were you surprised by the response that your next film, *Do the Right Thing*, got at the Cannes Film Festival?

LEE: That was a big response. You don't know. Sometimes, what might play in the States might not go in Europe, and vice versa. But I knew they would like *She's Gotta Have It*. It had a very European feel to it, the way it was cut and shot and that kind of stuff.

PLAYBOY: What about what German director Wim Wenders said?

LEE: Oh, yeah, he said that *Do the Right Thing* was "not heroic"? Yeah, very. I was disappointed. I hold no grudges against Wim Wenders now. I never had anything against Steven Soderbergh [*who won the Golden*

Palm that year], because it was not his doing. He made a very good film with *sex, lies, and videotape*. It was not his fault that he got the award. I know he's happy he got it, but I had no ill feelings toward Steven, and we're still friends today. [*sex, lies, and videotape*] was *very, very* heroic. Especially this James Spader character, this guy jerking off all the time to the TV. Taping sexual confessions of women. *Very* heroic.

PLAYBOY: You said that *Mo' Better Blues*, your fourth film, was consciously noncontroversial. Not only are you dealing with interracial romance in *Jungle Fever* but you're also dealing with drugs. Why add two controversial elements?

LEE: I don't know. I might have given it the interracial thing, but how is drugs controversial?

PLAYBOY: Because you purposefully avoided, you said, drugs as a subplot previously in *Do the Right Thing*.

LEE: Yeah, but I don't think the word is controversy. I'm not gonna let any critic determine my agenda. I find it preposterous that critics would attack me for not having drugs in *Do the Right Thing*, as if drugs were the complete domain of black people. How could you do a film set in Bed-Stuy without any drugs? Easy. We black people aren't the only people on drugs. The reason you've got drugs on the so-called agenda is because you've got young white kids in middle-class America and white suburbia who are doing crack and whatever. *Then* it becomes a national problem. As long as it was contained within the black ghettos, you would never see that problem being dealt with on the covers of *Time* or *Newsweek*. And if that is the case, which it is, then why have I never read of any white filmmakers being chastised for not having drugs in their films?

PLAYBOY: Obviously, the critics thought the criticism was valid because of that particular neighborhood.

LEE: Hey, there's as much drugs in Bed-Stuy as there is on Wall Street or the Upper East Side.

PLAYBOY: How did you get hooked up with the Fruit of Islam? Some people criticize that group's militancy and its association with Louis Farrakhan.

LEE: When we did location scouting for *Do the Right Thing*, we needed a block in Bed-Stuy that had two empty lots on the corner that faced each other. We had to build a pizzeria, and build a Korean fruit and vegetable stand. It turned out there were two or three crack houses on the block, or in the vicinity, so knowing the Fruit—they don't play that—we brought them in. They closed down the crack houses and they stayed on for security for the rest of the film.

PLAYBOY: It seems ironic that the movie doesn't deal with drugs and you had to run the crack dealers off the block.

LEE: I don't find it ironic. Drugs is a part of our society, but I felt they should not be a part of this story. This film was really about 24 hours in the life of this block on the hottest day of the summer. It was really about race relations. I didn't want to put drugs in this.

PLAYBOY: You seem very sure of yourself, and yet you've consistently portrayed the characters you play in your films as powerless and ineffectual.

LEE: Yeah, well, I don't see the need to make myself the hero in my movies. What's the point in that?

PLAYBOY: Why do you keep playing the same kind of character?

LEE: I'm not that impressed with myself as an actor. I don't think much of myself that way. I don't have a lot of range as far as acting. Mars Blackmon, that was all right. I didn't expect people to like him, the way they did.

PLAYBOY: What makes you continue to act in your pictures?

LEE: It really has to do with box office, with having somewhat of a little appeal with the audience. People will be more apt to come to one of my films if I'm in it.

PLAYBOY: Will you be in *Malcolm X*?

LEE: Probably. [*Laughs*] I still need to be in my films.

PLAYBOY: *Mo' Better Blues* was criticized for its portrayal of Jews. There's even a story about your father having gone down to apologize to the owner of a Village jazz club because of your portrayal of Jews in that film.

LEE: Huh? I can't respond to that, because I never heard it before. Look, Siskel and Ebert—I shouldn't say this, 'cause they're fans of mine. Soon as *Mo' Better Blues* comes out, they [start talking about] stereotypes. Then came [*New York Times* critic] Caryn James with her stupid-ass article. Nobody was supposed to take those guys as representin' all Jews. Besides, where was everybody when that what's-his-name movie with Steven Seagal came out?

PLAYBOY: *Marked for Death*?

LEE: What about that racist piece of shit? That's a number-one hit for a couple of weeks, and where was everybody when that came out? They had nothin' to say about it.

PLAYBOY: What did you think when you saw it?

LEE: I didn't see it.

PLAYBOY: One of the best things about your films tends to be their improvisational quality, the way you handle the interplay between people.

LEE: Yeah, it helps to have actors who know how to improvise. Not everybody's good at it.

PLAYBOY: Like who?

LEE: I don't wanna say.

PLAYBOY: Wait a second. You're worried about hurting somebody's feelings? When the Oscars came around in 1990, you didn't seem so worried about hurting people's feelings.

LEE: That didn't have nothin' to do with hurting people's feelings. It was that Fred Schelp—Sheep—What's that guy's name? That Australian guy?

PLAYBOY: Fred Schepisi? What about him?

LEE: You know, the one who did *Driving Miss Daisy?*

PLAYBOY: You mean Bruce Beresford.

LEE: Him. Yeah, him. Bruce Beresford. When he was complaining about not getting a nomination for Best Director, nobody made anything of that. Or when [Richard] Zanuck, he started complaining, you know, about *Driving Miss Daisy,* how could it get a Best Picture nomination and not get a Best Director nomination? It was as soon as *I* started sayin' we got robbed on *Do the Right Thing,* suddenly, I'm the one. I'm the problem.

PLAYBOY: People think you're an artist and they have higher expectations of you. When you complain about being shut out, people are let down by it.

LEE: I don't buy that. I don't believe that. I was complaining about the Oscars because we should've got a Best Picture nomination.

PLAYBOY: A lot of movies that stand the test of time never get nominated for Oscars or they never win Oscars.

LEE: Oscars, they can mean money. You know, you get a Best Picture nomination and the studios, they can promote a picture, advertise. They can get more people to come out and see it. People were afraid to come see *Do the Right Thing* as it was, afraid there would be riots and shit.

PLAYBOY: Some people claim that you use racism as a tool to strike out at others, such as in your attack of *New York Times* critic Janet Maslin's review of *School Daze,* when you said, "I bet she can't even dance. Does she have rhythm?"

LEE: She didn't get the point of *School Daze,* and the way she dissed it, talking about "my little musical." Race is an issue, and I don't always use it. You'd think I don't like critics. I don't like *The New York Times.* Well, I read Vincent Canby.

PLAYBOY: You've always had a dicey relationship with the press. Stanley Crouch, in his essay "Do the Race Thing," discusses how you tried to have it both ways with *Do the Right Thing*, by quoting Martin Luther King *and* Malcolm X.

LEE: That ignorant motherfucker. He has no idea what he's talking about. Shit, what about all those motherfuckers like Joe Klein at *New York* sayin' *Do the Right Thing* would cause a riot, because it was released during the summer? Or David Denby callin' it irresponsible? That's irresponsible. And it's lazy. When the riots didn't happen, when Dinkins got elected, neither one of them, none of the people who said that shit, said they were wrong in print or apologized.

PLAYBOY: What about the Nike Air Jordan controversy? *New York Post* columnist Phil Mushnick wrote that you and Michael Jordan glamorize expensive shoes and sometimes kids are killed in robberies over them.

LEE: Shit. What about it? It's my fault, it's Michael Jordan's fault, that kids are buying those shoes? That's just the trigger. There's more to it than that. Something is wrong where these young black kids have to put so much weight, where their whole life is tied up—their life is so hopeless—that their life is defined by a pair of sneakers. Or a sheepskin coat. The problem is not the coat or the sneakers. I mean, we tried to explore that with *Do the Right Thing* with the radio. These young black kids who are lost. Radio Raheem [*the character who's killed by the police*]—his life was that radio. That really defined his existence. I mean, without that radio, he's invisible; people don't notice him. But with that radio blasting Public Enemy and "Fight the Power," you had to deal with him. It made people notice him. It gave him self-worth. And when Sal killed his radio, he might as well have killed his mother or his father, or himself. That's why he tried to choke the shit out of Sal.

PLAYBOY: What about that *Sports Illustrated* article where Jordan was almost reduced to tears? He's publicly remorseful, disturbed by what his endorsement may have caused.

LEE: What the fuck? You think I'm happy black men are dying over shoes? Hell, no! Hell, no! I'm upset about it, too. Is every black man who wears those shoes a drug dealer? Hell, no! You know how that is. Look at you. You're wearing Pumps. Are you a drug dealer? Hell, no! They're oversimplifying the issue.

PLAYBOY: OK, let's ask an easy question. From your experience, what is Michael Jordan really like?

LEE: Mike's a down brother. Mike just had a lot of confidence in me. He was a young brother. He liked *She's Gotta Have It*. He felt like I did, that it was important that we hook up. Mike pulled me to the side and said,

"Look, there's been some grumbling where Nike is trying to ease you out. But as long as I'm around, you're around." I said, "I hear you, Mike. Thank you for getting my back." That's why I did those commercials. I thought it was important that me and Mike do something together. Young black people in different fields, hooking up.

PLAYBOY: Did your parents encourage you to go into the arts?

LEE: Not really. Whatever you wanted to do was fine with them. They encouraged us, but they never pushed me in any direction. I will say that we had great exposure to the arts at a young age. We had to. My mother taught art; she liked the theater and liked music. My father is a jazz musician—he played with folk singers, too, like Theodore Bikel and Josh White—so music was always being played in the house. I remember my mother dragging me to *The King and I* with Yul Brynner when I was little. I started crying; I was scared to death. She had to take me home.

PLAYBOY: What was the first thing you remember sitting through and really enjoying as a kid, even if it didn't make you want to be a filmmaker?

LEE: When I was real little, I saw *Hatari*. Remember that? John Wayne in a safari film, with the rhinoceros. And *Bye Bye Birdie*. My mother would take me to see James Bond films, *Goldfinger* and *Dr. No.* I remember her taking me to see *A Hard Day's Night.*

PLAYBOY: Did you like that?

LEE: Yeah. I liked the Beatles when I was little. My father would turn down the radio when he came in the house.

PLAYBOY: He didn't like the Beatles?

LEE: He didn't like *no* music besides jazz. [*Shouts*] "Turn that bad music off!"

PLAYBOY: Did you always know you were going to college?

LEE: Yeah. I mean, what else was I gonna do? My father and my grandfather, they went to college, so it was there for me, too. What else would I do, work at a McDonald's? Go work for somebody else? I never thought about rebellin', not goin' to college. It was what I was gonna do.

PLAYBOY: You sound like you were a practical kid, not a troublemaker.

LEE: I grew up as the oldest, so I had to be practical. The oldest child has to take care of the younger kids. They're always the most practical.

PLAYBOY: What was your relationship with the kids in the neighborhood?

LEE: I was always a leader. I was the one organizing stuff.

PLAYBOY: Did you like school as a kid?

LEE: Not really.

PLAYBOY: Did you do well?

LEE: Just good enough to get by.

PLAYBOY: Which must not have made your mother too happy, since she was a teacher.

LEE: She was always on me. I'd get an 80 and I'd be happy, but she'd be like, "Well, you shouldn't be content with an 80. Them Jewish kids are getting 95." [*Laughs*] But she was right.

PLAYBOY: Do you wonder what it would be like if you were growing up now?

LEE: It would be frightening, with the violence and the access to weapons and guns, and the drugs. Before, we used to be terrified if we even saw somebody taking a puff on a joint. But now, if you're a parent, you pray to God that's all your child is doing is smoking marijuana.

PLAYBOY: Do you think there's a lack of emphasis on education now?

LEE: Right. Half of the young black males here in New York City don't even finish high school. But this is not to say that I'm blaming them. I'm not trying to point a finger at the victim. I think that the educational system has failed. At the same time, I've never been one just to blame white people for everything, for all of our ills. We have to take some responsibility. If stuff's going to be corrected, it's up to us. It's up to the parents. What are these kids doing outside late at night? Eight years old and hanging out later than I am. Running in the streets at two, three, four in the morning. Where are their parents?

When we were growing up, people looked out after one another. Other parents could tell you something. If somebody else's mother saw you doing something wrong, that mother would treat you as if you were her child.

PLAYBOY: But you also got straightened out in school, right?

LEE: Yeah. I think that discipline, that's what's really lacking. I'm not saying let's go back to the Dark Ages when they were hitting kids in school with rulers, but discipline is really lacking.

PLAYBOY: Does it make you leery of having a family?

LEE: No, not really at all. When I do have a family, I don't want to send them to private school, because I feel that's too sheltered.

PLAYBOY: Even given the problems with the educational system?

LEE: I will be able to get my kids in the best public schools here. I mean, there are good public schools here, but there aren't that many. I went to public school, my brother Chris went to public school. But David, Joie and Cinque went to private school. I always could tell a difference in them because they went to private school. Their negritude got honed or harnessed going into these predominantly white private schools. That's where my mother was teaching.

PLAYBOY: Do you talk about this?

LEE: They know it. Most of their friends were white. Not that I have anything against that, it's just that there is definitely an argument for being around your own people.

PLAYBOY: A lot of the parents who send their kids to private schools today went to public schools themselves. They fear their children won't get a good education or be safe at a public school.

LEE: They're justified in thinking that. People are getting shot and stabbed in school. That's not supposed to happen in a school.

PLAYBOY: Did your mother try to keep you away from the bad kids in the neighborhood?

LEE: No. There were never any gangs. I don't remember ever seeing any. There were people who would steal your lunch money, but that wasn't no gang thing. I mean, now they'll shoot you. When I was growing up, they might take a quarter from you. You give it up.

PLAYBOY: Or fight.

LEE: Yeah, but it's not like "Give us your leather coat or I'll shoot you."

PLAYBOY: Since the educational system is so bad, why should kids be unemployed college grads when they could sell crack and make a lot of money?

LEE: That is something that is going to have to be dealt with, the economics. Forget about the moral issue, even though it should play into it. It's not going to weigh when these kids are faced with the fact of making minimum wage at McDonald's or making three and four thousand a week selling crack. Not everybody, but a lot of them are going to sell that crack and make that money. You're not thinking about how you might end up dead, eventually, or end up in jail. That's not the point. Now you can buy that BMW or whatever. Gold chains and gold teeth. Kangols [*hats*] and Kazals [*glasses*].

PLAYBOY: Where do you think that materialism comes from?

LEE: Well, when people don't have anything, they have to try to show they do have something. And you show that by what you wear or the car you drive. "I'm not like all the rest of these poor niggers. I got something."

PLAYBOY: Don't some black kids view education itself as white?

LEE: There's something very sick where if you speak well and you speak articulately, that's looked at as being negative and speaking white. I remember when I was growing up, people used to tell me, "You sound white." I've been reading of various cases where kids flunk on purpose so they'll be considered "down" with the homeboys and stuff. That's crazy when intelligence is thought of as being white and all the other stuff is being black and being down. I think that one has to be able to navigate both worlds. You ought to be able to speak with your brothers on the street but at the same time be able to go to a job interview, fill out the application and speak proper English. You've got to have both. I don't think it makes you any less black by being articulate.

PLAYBOY: Where do you think that attitude comes from?

LEE: I think all this stuff you could really trace to our hatred of ourselves. Everything we do, eventually, if you keep going back far enough, you'll see that we've been taught to hate ourselves. And until we stop that, all this other shit we're doing is just going to continue to happen.

PLAYBOY: Comedian Franklyn Ajaye said that one of the things he didn't like about In Living Color when he was a writer there was that everybody talked like they were down. He didn't see any kind of reflection of articulate black life in the show, and that bothered him.

LEE: Me and Keenen [Ivory Wayans] talked about it. He was on the cover of New York magazine, and in the article, they said they had thirteen writers and only three or four were black. The rest were all these Jewish kids that went to Harvard. So I just asked Keenen what's up. He explained to me all he's done for black people, as far as the show is concerned. I'm not going to dispute that. I'm not saying it's because they did the skit on me, but if you have some white kid from Harvard joking about Malcolm X-Lax—I don't think that shit is funny. I don't think they'd allow a black person to make a joke about Golda Meir.

PLAYBOY: Do you think being educated means that you're not black?

LEE: In a perverse kind of way. Everything has been kind of turned upside down. I think we've just got a lot of things turned around.

PLAYBOY: When did that happen?

LEE: A lot of things happened after the civil rights movement, where we thought we were making strides and progress. Somewhere from the end of the 1960s up to now, we got off the path. Or we were led off the path. I think that we really haven't advanced a lot. For me, the biggest problem is that people get tricked. Because of the visibility of a couple of African Americans who are able to split through, mostly in entertainment or the sports industry, it gives off the perception that black people have made great strides and that everything is all right. But the reality is, we're not all right. You look at all the black people who are dying of cancer, hypertension, AIDS. The permanently unemployed. The black underclass now is larger than it's ever been. But people are tricked into not really taking that stuff into account. I'm not blaming these people. They're tricked because they see Oprah Winfrey, they see Bill Cosby, they see Spike Lee, they see Eddie Murphy, they see Michael Jordan, they see Bo Jackson, Paula Abdul, M. C. Hammer, Janet Jackson, Arsenio Hall. But we're just a couple of people. We were the exception, not the rule. We were able to slide through that microscopic crack that was open for a second.

PLAYBOY: Is that your opinion because you think there are so many visible black people that—

LEE: Wait. If you look at the context of all the shows that are on TV and all the movies that are made, and then look at the percent, it's not that many. It's just the *perception* that there's a lot of us.

PLAYBOY: Based on that perception and the fact that you can say there may be more successful, visible black people than ever, the perception is that—

LEE: We've arrived. And that's not the case at all. I mean, there's not one person outside of Eddie Murphy, really, not *one* African American in Hollywood who can green-light a picture. Who can say, "I want this picture made," and that's it.

PLAYBOY: You can't get that done?

LEE: No matter what? For me to get a film made, I have to present a script, and they either do it or they don't. But every studio has people who are the guardians of the gate. They're the ones who say this picture gets made and this picture doesn't. And there are no black people in that position in Hollywood. I mean, we're getting ready to have a big fight with the Teamsters here in New York because they don't have *no* black people. We used the Teamsters on *Do the Right Thing, Mo' Better* and *Jungle Fever,* and the amount that we paid for the Teamsters for all three films is like three quarters of a million dollars. And there are only three or four black Teamsters in the whole union here in New York. I refuse to give money to organizations that are openly into hiring practices that may exclude blacks. So we're about to go toe to toe with them on *Malcolm X.*

PLAYBOY: You're not going to use them?

LEE: If they don't get some more black people in it, they can kiss our ass. We told them that. They even refused to sit down with us and meet. They said, "We will let no one dictate to us who to hire."

PLAYBOY: So they deny any discriminatory practices?

LEE: The Teamsters, man, it's predominantly Irish. This particular branch I'm talking about here in New York. The Teamsters who work on movies.

PLAYBOY: How long have you been talking to them about this? Since you started to use them?

LEE: Yeah. They've been appeasing us. They might give us one or two, but we told them we wanted a black Teamster captain and we wanted five black people to get their books. They trick you sometimes. Let me not use the word trick, but they might put black people on your film, but they don't have their books. Meaning they're not full-fledged members of the union and don't receive the full benefits of the union. If you're a Teamster here in New York, they have the best benefits of any union in the country. Any of their children, they can go to college—free. Whatever college you choose. The union will pay for it.

PLAYBOY: And there are just a handful of black people in the union?

LEE: A handful. I mean, they just admitted one who got his book recently. But the last time one got admitted before that was 1962. There's too much money being made. I refuse to give money to an organization like that that's just so overtly racist in their hiring practices.

PLAYBOY: There is obviously now a big trend toward trying to increase the African-American inclusion in the movie mainstream. We've heard that people are already expecting a backlash. Remember when *The Wiz* and *Ragtime* failed—

LEE: That was it. They said, "Black people don't support these films. Let's stop making black films." The blame was never put on Sidney Lumet, or the score, or the casting of Diana Ross. That is not to disrespect any of them, but the blame was put solely on "black people who failed to support this film." Whereas, if a white film doesn't work, it would be the director or whoever.

PLAYBOY: In some ways, there seems to be a renaissance of black participation in popular culture. There's you and Robert Townsend, *In Living Color* and the enormous effect of rap.

LEE: Yeah, that's true. They've finally realized black people contribute, and black audiences are a power in the entertainment market. Studios know there's just too much money to be made now from black audiences. And that people wanna see us, too.

PLAYBOY: Do you worry that history will repeat itself?

LEE: I think that this is a very crucial time. Every film studio, if you're black and even look like you're a director, they're signing you. And it's very important that all these people who are getting opportunities really be serious. I'm not trying to speak like I'm the grandfather of black cinema. But I think that there are a lot of people who are getting deals now—and more power to them—but I don't know if they're going to last. They just think that you can just walk off the street and direct a movie—and it is not true. This ain't just no bullshit; "Well, I'm just directing a film. I don't need to know nothing about film grammar or film history," or any other thing that one needs to know to become a film director.

PLAYBOY: You talked about being attacked for the Nola Darling character in *She's Gotta Have It*. Do you think you're becoming more enlightened about your portrayals of women?

LEE: This is something I've known all along. Every filmmaker has a weakness, just like athletes.

PLAYBOY: But we're not talking about every filmmaker.

LEE: No, I'm saying every filmmaker, every athlete, has weaknesses. If you come into the league hitting 50 percent at the free-throw line, you've got to do something about your foul-shooting if you want to be a complete ballplayer. My female characters were something I needed to work on. It was lacking. It's something I've tried to concentrate on.

PLAYBOY: We always thought one of the interesting things about Nola was that she lived her life the way she wanted to.

LEE: Yeah, but that wasn't the only film where they talked about the female characters. *School Daze*—they weren't as multidimensional as the male characters. There weren't enough of them in *Do the Right Thing*. And in *Mo' Better*, all they wanted was the man; they didn't have a life of their own—which I don't agree with for that particular film.

PLAYBOY: How does this affect your personal relationships? Do women have preconceived notions about you?

LEE: I don't really think you can break that question down to a sex thing, as far as male-female. I think that's just in general. Any time you're out in the public eye, people, when they meet you in person, they expect you to live up to that expectation of what that persona is. A lot of people expect me to be more animated, and they're kind of disappointed. "I didn't know you were quiet." So that really has nothing to do with male-female.

PLAYBOY: What about your relationships with white people? It's clear that a lot of white people are afraid of you.

LEE: I guess you fear stuff you don't understand. I don't think any white folks have anything to fear from me.

PLAYBOY: Still, almost all of the movie industry is white. All they ever see are other white people.

LEE: With a small smattering of Jewish people. [*Laughs*] I don't know why some Jewish people get upset when you say that there are a lot of Jewish people in the movie industry. That's the truth. That's like saying there are blacks in the NBA. That's not making a judgment, that's just a fact.

PLAYBOY: Do they really get sensitive when you say there are lots of Jews in the industry?

LEE: Yeah. *The New York Times*, there was this whole black-Jewish Hollywood thing. It was sparked by the convention the NAACP had in Hollywood where they said that Hollywood is racist and so on and that it was run predominantly by Jewish people.

PLAYBOY: You must get a lot of calls whenever something like that happens.

LEE: Hooo, from around the world! The phone rings off the hook at our office. I think that this is what happens when the media appoints their so-called spokesperson for black people. This is something I have never wanted to achieve. It's not something I've chased after. And, for the most part, I don't say anything. But there are instances where stuff has to be spoken on. But, for the most part, I only answer about 5 percent of their questions.

PLAYBOY: What do you think about the future for African Americans?

LEE: If you look at the eight years of Reagan and maybe another eight of Bush, and the way they're dismantling affirmative action and all that stuff we fought for and died for, or the Supreme Court that's being appointed—Bush tried to pull this thing where it's discriminatory for schools to have scholarships for black students, and then they get this Uncle Tom handkerchief-head Negro to announce it as assistant secretary [of the Education Department]. Nobody even heard of this motherfucker, but the moment that this program has to be implemented and an announcement has to be made, they pull this Negro off the shelf. How are we supposed to go to school? It's a shame that we've still got Uncle Toms like this around. That guy should be beat with a Louisville Slugger in an alley. He got used. That's the only reason they hired him, for something specific like that that was going to affect black people. So by the Bush Administration's having this black person make this announcement, it can't be racist—we got a black person saying it.

PLAYBOY: Do you wonder if there has been some complacency since the civil rights movement?

LEE: I think America just really arrived at the point where it said, Look—and I think the mandate was handed down by Reagan—where it said, Look, we are tired of you niggers. You've got about as much as you're gonna get from us, and that's it. Period.

PLAYBOY: Some black people say they don't want special consideration.

LEE: Special? I don't think it's special, the fact that we were brought here as slaves and we've been robbed of our heritage and everything else. I mean, I don't consider that special.

PLAYBOY: So we take it that you don't have much truck with black conservatives.

LEE: They'll sell you out in a minute. They sold us out. I mean, they're trying to make a big deal out of this what's-his-name, Colin Powell.

PLAYBOY: You don't think that he's a formidable figure? He's the Chairman of the joint Chiefs of Staff—that shows black progress, doesn't it?

LEE: So what? So we've got a black general that's going to be head of the army that kills black people in Panama? Kills black people in Nicaragua? People of color in the Middle East? How come every war now is against people of color in Third World countries? They talk about fighting for democracy: Is South Africa democratic? I know it would be too far-fetched to ask Bush to send troops into South Africa to fight for black people, so let's not talk about that. But how about sanctions? He's trying to lift the motherfucking sanctions! Saddam does not compare to what De Klerk and all them crooks down there in South Africa are doing and have been doing. But they're white, so it's not perceived as that.

PLAYBOY: So you think it's another instance of racism?

LEE: Yes. I'm not going to say that Saddam might not be a maniac, but if you just study the way the press portrays Noriega, Ortega, Hussein, the ayatollah and the way they portray people like Botha, De Klerk, Cecil Rhodes—I mean, it's the difference between night and day. I have to give in, they have a point on Hitler and Mussolini, but since World War II, there is a difference in the way they portray dictators.

PLAYBOY: But look at the way the Soviets were portrayed.

LEE: That was really during the Cold War. They didn't send no troops into Lithuania and shit. They bogarted that country the same way that Hussein bogarted Kuwait. For me, the United States is not on the moral ground to judge anybody, because it's the most hypocritical country in the world. So, to me, they really can't say shit about nobody, because they got a lot of shit with themselves.

PLAYBOY: Do you think that after the civil rights movement lost its figureheads—Martin Luther King and Malcolm X—it lost momentum?

LEE: It did, but that's a mistake of putting emphasis on personality and people instead of the movement. As long as we continue to do that and make cults around our leaders, all they have to do to stop it any time we're making ground is just kill us off, kill off that leader.

PLAYBOY: What have you learned in your research for the Malcolm X movie?

LEE: That Malcolm was a very complex person. There were three or four different Malcolms. He was constantly evolving, his outlook and his ideology, and always trying to seek the truth. If he found it, he was not scared of being called a hypocrite. If he found a higher truth, he would say, "I was wrong. All that stuff I said before is wrong, and this is what I believe." That's something that very few people do.

PLAYBOY: Have your feelings about him changed since you started doing the research?

LEE: I think that I've really grown to love Malcolm more. What he stood for and what he died for.

PLAYBOY: What did you think when you first read his autobiography?

LEE: It was just a revelation. I have deep respect for Dr. King, but I've always been drawn more to Malcolm. I just cannot get with Dr. King's complete nonviolence philosophy.

PLAYBOY: Malcolm was moving in that direction himself, wasn't he?

LEE: No. Malcolm never moved away from defending oneself, the right to protect the self. He never moved away from that. Malcolm would never say, "Go to a march, get hit upside the head, and hopefully, after you get enough knocked upside the head, the white man will see how evil he is and will stop." He never said that and he was never moving toward that. He's always been about the right to protect oneself.

Malcolm never advocated violence. He said one should reserve the right to protect oneself.

PLAYBOY: Doesn't it seem interesting that there has finally come a time when a major studio will give you—

LEE: Yeah, 20 years and more since he's been dead and buried. He no longer seems such a threat. This film would not have been done in 1966, the year after he got assassinated. No way.

PLAYBOY: But look at what you get a chance to do now.

LEE: It's a great opportunity.

PLAYBOY: Are you up for it?

LEE: Yeah. Everything I've done has really prepared me for this film. It's led me in this direction. I've got no intention of dropping the ball.

.

April 1995

DAVID MAMET

*A candid conversation with
America's foremost dramatist
about tough talk, TV violence,
women and why government
shouldn't fund the arts*

In a joke that made the rounds not long ago, a beggar in New York City's theater district approaches a well-dressed man for a handout. "'Neither a beggar nor a borrower be,'" the man says sanctimoniously. "William Shakespeare."

"Yeah?" the beggar fires back. "Well, 'fuck you.' David Mamet."

It is a measure of Mamet's influence that he could claim title to that line.

But even if somebody else (Shakespeare, maybe) said it first, nobody has said it better, or put it in a more secure context, than David Mamet—playwright, essayist, novelist, scriptwriter and director. If Arthur Miller is to be remembered for his plays about the sorrows of capitalism—*Death of a Salesman*—and the witch-hunting side of the American character—*The Crucible*—then Mamet has been bold enough to take on those same themes in a raw, bare-knuckled fashion in two of his best-known plays—*Glengarry Glen Ross* and *Oleanna*. The latter play touched a hot wire to the already nervous issue of sexual harassment in America. The public responded viscerally, even physically. Shouting matches and fistfights broke out in some audiences. To anyone who has followed Mamet's career, this was both surprising and predictable. It is never certain where Mamet will go next, only that the next move will be ambitious and that it will strike at the heart.

Mamet was born in 1947 to Jewish parents who divorced when he was young, and he was raised in Chicago. Mamet's father was a labor lawyer. His stepfather was—according to Mamet's own writings—a heartless and sometimes violent man. As a young boy, Mamet was exposed to the sort of cruelties that are prevalent in his work. Asked once where he picked up his ear for abusive, obscene talk, Mamet answered, "In my family, in the days prior to television, we liked to while away the evenings by making ourselves miserable, based solely on our ability to speak the language viciously. That's probably where my ability was honed."

He was also exposed to the theater at a young age as a child actor (he once danced onstage with Maurice Chevalier). Although he was, by his own estimation, "the worst actor in the history of theater," he spent most of his college years at Goddard (which he dismisses as "intellectual summer camp"), hanging around the campus theater. That was the advent of Mamet the playwright.

First, however, there were jobs that exposed him to life as it is lived away from the suburbs. He cooked on a merchant ship in the Great Lakes, drove a cab, sold rugs and real estate and even did a short stint as an editor, writing copy for the pictorial features in *Playboy*'s sister publication, *Oui*. During these years, however, his focus remained on the theater. In 1975, when Mamet was 27, he announced his arrival, emphatically, with *American Buffalo*.

That play, like all of Mamet's work, was full of the kind of rough talk that people were unaccustomed to hearing onstage. Brutal, elliptical and obscene, it sounded like the streets (or the pawnshop, which was its setting)—only different. "Eloquent stammering" was the way Mamet's dialogue was described by one of the many critics who have tried to parse his language. That David Mamet was a unique and disturbing new voice seemed undeniable.

And if anyone wanted to deny it, they were quickly disabused by the body of work that piled up: *Glengarry Glen Ross* (for which he won both a Pulitzer Prize and the New York Drama Critics' Circle Award), *Speed-the-Plow* and *Oleanna*, among others.

In the late 1970s, after his play *Lone Canoe* was less than generously reviewed, he wrote the screenplays for *The Postman Always Rings Twice* and *The Verdict*. This initial exposure to film led Mamet to direct his own projects—*Homicide* and *House of Games*, starring Lindsay Crouse, whom he had married in 1977. They were divorced in 1990. Mamet also wrote the screenplays for *Hoffa* and *The Untouchables* as well as an episode of *Hill Street Blues*.

In addition, Mamet has written a book of poems (*The Hero Pony*), three collections of essays (*Writing in Restaurants, Some Freaks* and

The Cabin), a children's book, *Warm and Cold*, with illustrations by Donald Sultan, and a novel (*The Village*). Mamet's private life is of a distinctively masculine nature. Though his plays are set in the rough, crowded, contemporary urban world, Mamet lives in rural Vermont in an old farmhouse with his wife, actress and singer Rebecca Pidgeon. He is known to collect guns and knives, to hunt and to play serious poker. Facile comparisons to Hemingway follow Mamet, who does not bother to refute them. He has, in mid-career, stopped giving interviews. (He used to send out a form letter to people who wrote objecting to the language or violence in his plays. The letter read: "Too bad, you big crybaby.")

Mamet did agree, however, to a *Playboy Interview* late last summer in Massachusetts. He was editing the final cut of the film *Oleanna*. Geoffrey Norman and *Playboy* Assistant Managing Editor John Rezek conducted the interview. Their report:

"Mamet met us punctually at nine A.M. on the third floor of a walk-up where he works, a block or two from the Harvard campus. He looked fit and alert but more the scholar than the macho man of reputation. The office was a working space with theater posters on the walls and books on the shelves. Before we started, Mamet, who had just started drinking it again, sent out for what he said was the 'best coffee in Cambridge.' While we waited for it to arrive, we made small talk and were struck that this man who is known for the rawness of his dialogue would speak so softly, and so deferentially. What surprises you is that Mamet is flawlessly polite, bordering on the courtly. He reminisced affectionately about Chicago and then described his labors on the film version of *Oleanna*, his controversial play (he has been called a 'vicious misogynist' and 'politically irresponsible' for writing it). When the coffee arrived (it was as good as advertised), it seemed like a good time to switch on the tape recorder. In three days of discursive conversation, Mamet spoke at times with the crude wit of his best characters and at others with an informed, recondite precision. He quotes a wide range of writers; some, such as Kipling and Veblen, are long out of fashion. His answers were sometimes enigmatic, occasionally evasive, often elaborate, frequently funny. David Mamet, people might be surprised to learn, is a very funny man. He likes jokes and he loves show-business stories, which he tells with relish.

"But he is also deeply serious about his work. We began our talk by asking about *Oleanna* and the storms it generated."

PLAYBOY: Your film *Oleanna*—and the play—pushed the culture's hot buttons, with a man and woman winding up, literally, each at the other's throat. Why is there such tension between the sexes?

MAMET: This has always been a puritan country and we've always been terrified of sex. That terror takes different forms. Sometimes it is overindulgence and, of course, at other times it's the opposite.

PLAYBOY: Why should this be a time of repression?

MAMET: For one thing, there is economic scarcity. People tend to get cranky when there aren't so many jobs to go around. Also, I think our expectations are scrambled. Sexual drive is designed to make sure the species will survive, as much as we fight the fact. But for young people today, it is very difficult to say, "Fine, either with you this year or with someone else next year, I'm going to get married, buy a house, get a job, settle down and raise kids." It's terrifying for them to say that. They can't get married. There aren't any jobs. They can't buy the house and have the dog named Randy. Our expectations have become greater than our ability to meet them.

PLAYBOY: So the alternative is the kind of antagonism we see between the sexes?

MAMET: Alternatives are going to emerge. In the 1970s and 1980s, there was the notion of continual romantic involvement. You said, "I don't want to get married; I just want to go out there and have a good time." That worked for a while and then, suddenly, it didn't seem like such a good idea anymore. Back in the 1960s or 1970s, *National Lampoon* published a story of a rumor about a new strain of the clap that guys brought back from Vietnam. If you got it, you died. Very funny.

So now you can't become committed to somebody because you can't support a family, and recreational sex is out because AIDS might kill you. As a result, society is going to bring us to some sort of intermediary mechanism, something to keep people wary about getting involved with each other. Here it comes—sexual harassment. The culture has to supersede. Alternatives will emerge to take the problem off our shoulders.

"Gee, what does she want of me?" It's a rhetorical question. It means, "I don't understand, better back off." On the other hand, "I need him to be more sensitive to me." That's poetry. It doesn't mean anything. It means, "I'd better back off because of my fear."

PLAYBOY: Your timing with *Oleanna* was perfect. When the play was first performed, sexual harassment was probably the most incendiary issue around. Were you influenced by the Clarence Thomas hearings?

MAMET: No. I didn't follow those hearings, actually. It was weird. I wrote the play before the hearings and I stuck it in a drawer.

PLAYBOY: Why?

MAMET: Two reasons. First, I didn't have a last act. Second, when I wrote the play, it seemed a little far-fetched to me. And then the Thomas hearings began and I took the play out of the drawer and started working on it again. One of the first people to see the play was a headmaster at a very good school here in Cambridge. He said to me, "Eighteen months ago, I would have said this play was fantasy. But now, when all the headmasters get together at conferences, we whisper to one another, 'You know, all of us are only one dime away from the end of a career.'"

PLAYBOY: Was that a typical response?

MAMET: There was a great deal of controversy at a level I've never encountered in the theater. In the audience, people got into shouting matches and fistfights. People stood up and screamed "Oh bullshit" at the stage before they realized they'd done it. A couple of people got a little crazy and lost their composure.

PLAYBOY: So it isn't a good date play?

MAMET: It is a terrible date play. But I never really saw it as a play about sexual harassment. I think the issue was, to a large extent, a flag of convenience for a play that's structured as a tragedy. Just like the issues of race relations and xenophobia are flags of convenience for *Othello*. It doesn't have anything to do with race. This play—and the film—is a tragedy about power. These are two people with a lot to say to each other, with legitimate affection for each other. But protecting their positions becomes more important than pursuing their own best interests. And that leads them down the slippery slope to a point where, at the end of the play, they tear each other's throat out. My plays are not political. They're dramatic. I don't believe that the theater is a good venue for political argument. Not because it is wrong, but because it doesn't work very well.

PLAYBOY: Do you think you can understand and empathize with the female point of view in this hostile climate? Your critics would say your point of view is almost exclusively male. Cheap shot?

MAMET: Not cheap, but inaccurate. Take Oleanna, for instance, the points she makes about power and privilege—I believe them all. If I didn't believe them, the play wouldn't work as well. It is a play about two people, and each person's point of view is correct. Yet they end up destroying each other.

PLAYBOY: So it is possible, then, that Anita Hill and Clarence Thomas were both telling the truth?

MAMET: Yeah, sure. You know, the whole notion of American jurisprudence is that you can't determine who is telling the truth. That's not the job of the jury. The jury is supposed to decide which side has made the best case. Polls—which are replacing the judicial system as the way we settle disputes—are no better.

PLAYBOY: But they do provide clarity, which some critics find lacking in your work. They find your dialogue almost intentionally obscure. What do you say to them?

MAMET: First of all, I'd like to thank them for their interest in my work.

PLAYBOY: Then?

MAMET: Then, I suppose, I'd like them to think about *Oleanna*. They say the play is "unclear," and it occurs to me that what they mean is "provocative." That rather than sending the audience out whistling over the tidy moral of the play, it leaves them unsettled. I've noticed over the past 30 years that a lot of what passes in the theater is not drama but rather a morality tale. "Go thou now and do likewise." That's very comforting to someone who is concerned or upset. When you leave the theater and you say, "Oh, now I get it. Women are people, too." Or, "Now I get it, handicapped people have rights," then you feel very soothed for the amount of time it takes you to get to your car. Then you forget about the play. If, on the other hand, you leave the theater upset, you might have seen a rotten play. Or, you might be provoked because something was suggested that you could not have known when you came into the theater. Aristotle said we should see something at the end of tragedy that is surprising and inevitable.

PLAYBOY: But while your structure is classical, the speech is entirely modern and urban, and, some critics have said, free of content. How do you get your characters to convey anything?

MAMET: There is always content in what's being said. That content is not necessarily carried by the context of the words. There has never been a conversation without content. If you're in a room where a lot of people are talking with one another and you can't hear a word of what's being said, you can still tell what the people are saying because their intent communicates itself.

One of the things I learned when I studied acting is that the content of what is being said is rarely carried by the connotation of the words. It is carried by the rhythm of the speech and the posture of the speaker and a lot of other things. All conversations have meaning.

PLAYBOY: Do men and women use speech differently?

MAMET: Probably. But men talk differently to other men under different circumstances. Conversations with their peers in a bar vary from conversations with strangers in a bar. No one ever talks except to accomplish an objective. This objective changes according to the sex of the person, the age of the person, the time of day. Everybody uses language for his or her own purpose to get what he or she wants. I think the notion that everyone can be everything to everybody at all times is a big fat bore. Men have always talked with one another. I find it interesting that in the past five or six years, women have started talking with one another. It's called "consciousness-raising," whereas men talking with one another is called "bonding."

PLAYBOY: Is the rough, profane talk characteristic of your plays an exclusively male language?

MAMET: Anyone who would think that apparently hasn't met my sister [screenwriter Lynn Mamet Weisberg]. I have never found the issue of profanity to be very important. In the plays I was writing, that's how the people actually spoke. It would have been different if I had been writing bedroom farce. But I wasn't. I was writing about different kinds of people, people whom I knew something about.

PLAYBOY: Including con men.

MAMET: Absolutely.

PLAYBOY: The con game is one of the fixtures in your work. What's behind your fascination with the con?

MAMET: Well, I have spent some time around con men, and they are fascinating people. I've always been interested in the continuum that starts with charm and ends with psychopathy. Con artists deal in human nature, and what they do is all in the realm of suggestion. It is like hypnosis or, to a certain extent, like playwriting.

PLAYBOY: How?

MAMET: Part of the art of the play is to introduce information in such a way, and at such a time, that the people in the audience don't realize they have been given information. They accept it as a matter of course, but they aren't really aware of it so that later on, the information pays off. It has been consciously planted by the author.

PLAYBOY: And he is working a con?

MAMET: Right. Now, in a bad play, the author will introduce the information frontally. You actually tell the audience that you are about to give them some information and that it is important to what happens later in the play. In a good play, the information is delivered almost as an aside. The same mechanism holds true in the con game. If you're giving the mark information that he—or she, in the case of a film of mine called *House of Games*—is going to need in order to be taken advantage of, and you don't want him to know that he has been given the information, then you would bring it in through the back door. Let's say my partner and I are taking you to the cleaners. The three of us are talking and my partner and I get into an argument. We start saying things that you aren't supposed to hear. I say to you, "Excuse me for a second, I'm sorry about this, and blah, blah, blah." Then I take my partner aside and we start screaming at each other, really out of control. You have not only been given information, you've been told to please look the other way. Well, that is going to put your mind on afterburner. Later you use that information, which you think you got accidentally, to put together what you think are the pieces.

PLAYBOY: A useful skill, then?

MAMET: Sure. The con game is what people do, most of the time, with few exceptions. After we reach a certain economic level, we try to say that we're no longer trying to talk you out of your money. We're doing "investment banking" or we've got a film "in development."

PLAYBOY: Films in development is a world you know something about. You've written scripts and directed films.

MAMET: Yes.

PLAYBOY: And used Hollywood as material in your play *Speed-the-Plow*, which painted a pretty bleak picture of a world where the con is everything.

MAMET: Well, any business will eventually degenerate into a con game. The cause of the process is any kind of boom. If you get a boom, certain myths will crystallize around that success and cause eventual failure. If you get a boom in American virtue, like you did in World War II when the citizen-soldiers of this country flat-out saved the world from Nazism, it is inevitable that you are going to have a military-industrial complex and wind up fighting a whole bunch of wars because you want to find a place to be virtuous again. Vietnam was the inevitable outcome of D-day. We had the golden age of cinema and the consequences of it.

PLAYBOY: This sense of corruption was almost overwhelming in *Speed-the-Plow*. Because this is a world you know, was there some personal malice reflected in the play?

MAMET: Not nearly enough.

PLAYBOY: Is your work in movies a way to make money or a way to do interesting things?

MAMET: Well, both. I love making movies. I love writing them and I love directing them.

PLAYBOY: At the end of the day, do you ever get a sense that you should go back to your room and to your real work, which is writing plays; that maybe moviemaking is a lesser form?

MAMET: I don't think it is a lesser form. I do, however, feel absolutely that the theater is my real work, and when I'm making movies I sometimes feel like I'm playing hooky. I'm like the pilot flying multimillion-dollar airplanes, landing them on aircraft carriers, and when he gets out of the cockpit he says, "And they pay me to do this, the fools."

PLAYBOY: Do you feel like you have to cultivate that part of your career fairly assiduously? Or can you stay in Vermont and write plays and go back to films when the spirit moves you?

MAMET: I think I am hanging on by my fingernails. But I also think most people feel the same way out there and don't show it. And I do spend a lot of time in Vermont.

PLAYBOY: In the theater—as a writer and a director—you worked with the same tight core group of actors. Has it been tougher in movies, with the kind of egos you find there?

MAMET: I've heard all the stories about big egos, but I have never encountered them myself. Maybe if I stay in the business long enough, I will. But I think it might be a bum rap. I've found on movie sets the most hardworking people I've ever seen. There is an ethic of help out, pitch in, get the job done, keep quiet about how hard it is to do. It is kind of the modern equivalent of a cattle drive. I'm sure there are bad apples. You'll find that in any business.

PLAYBOY: You like actors, then?

MAMET: They are absolutely the most interesting people I know. I loved hanging around them when I was young and I still love having them for friends. I'm especially lucky that way.

PLAYBOY: You've written scripts that were altered and, when the movies were finally made, had other people's names on them. Do you resent that your own work wasn't accepted?

MAMET: Sure, of course. Like everybody else in the world, I would like everything to be exactly my way all the time. You know that old line about the scriptwriter who gives something to somebody to read. It's a first draft, and he's looking for a reaction. "Tell me," he says, "how much do you love it?"

PLAYBOY: Is there any story you especially want to do?

MAMET: Oh yeah. There's one project I want to do. A Hemingway novel—*Across the River and Into the Trees*. I was talking with some of the people who have the rights and I finally figured out a way to do the movie. It isn't one of Hemingway's better novels, but that could work in its favor. Somebody once told me that the better a play is, the worse the movie version will be. I think the same may be true of the novel.

PLAYBOY: Like a lot of other American writers, you have been compared to Hemingway.

MAMET: A heavy, impossible burden. You know, you can't play Stanley Kowalski without being compared to Marlon Brando—even by people who never saw Marlon Brando in the movie, let alone onstage. He revolutionized that role and the American notion of what it meant to act. The same is true of Hemingway and writing.

PLAYBOY: Any validity to the Hemingway comparisons?

MAMET: No, I don't think so.

PLAYBOY: The way you live? Your interest in hunting and guns?

MAMET: I have always felt that my private life is nobody's business except my own and, of course, that of the readers of this magazine.

PLAYBOY: What is the most curious description of yourself that you've read?

MAMET: I read only the good stuff. But seriously, there is a kind of flawed thinking in the world today that has to do with celebrity, with the idea that there are special people who are somehow different from the rest of us, who lack the usual human weaknesses. So inevitably we revere them and then, when we get closer, we are disappointed by them and turn on them. We're all the same. That's why I stopped doing the press. Until this interview.

In one of my last interviews I explained that I didn't like talking to the press because it made me feel stupid.

The interviewer said to me, "That is ridiculous."

I said, "See."

I stopped talking to the press because I just didn't know how to answer most of the questions. And my inability was seen as reluctance or coyness. I thought, Why should I subject myself to that? And so I quit.

PLAYBOY: Perhaps celebrities are no different from the rest of us. But don't people develop unique skills? Doesn't your gift for dialogue give you a better-than-average ability to size up people from what they say? To tell, for instance, when they are lying?

MAMET: I have a good sense of what people are like and when they are lying. Except when I'm emotionally involved. Then, like everyone else, I am hopeless.

PLAYBOY: How do you see through a lie—or a con?

MAMET: There are clues—they are called "tells," because they tell you something.

PLAYBOY: What are some examples between men and women?

MAMET: We see them all the time but sometimes we choose not to be-cause we're emotionally involved. It is in our interest to disregard the fact that someone was late, forgot a telephone number, got the wrong size or forgot a birthday.

But these are things most of us know. Or, if we don't, you can't learn them from me. I think it's natural that when someone has a little noto-riety, we start to assign certain magical attributes to him that just aren't true. People say to me, "Can you tell us about the art of playwriting?" I say it isn't an art, it is a trick. There are no magic properties that go with a little publicity.

PLAYBOY: People nevertheless find fame to be irresistible.

MAMET: Absolutely. Let me tell you my favorite story about that. Gregory Mosher is flying from Chicago to New York because he's casting a play and he wants to see Rex Harrison. The plane is late and he gets in the cab and says, "47th and Broadway, I'm going to the theater."

So the cabdriver says, "What are you going to see?"

And Mosher tells him.

"Who's in it?" the cabdriver asks.

"Rex Harrison and Claudette Colbert." The driver stands on the brakes, pulls over to the side, turns around in the seat and says, "Claudette Colbert? Claudette Colbert? I fucked her maid."

That is absolutely my favorite theatrical story.

PLAYBOY: If celebrity is a current American obsession, then violence is another. Do you think that we live in more violent times?

MAMET: More violent than what? The world is a very violent place. It always has been. Why is it a violent place? Because human beings are wired with a touchy survival mechanism that goes off very easily.

PLAYBOY: What is your personal response to actual flesh-and-blood violence? To a fistfight on the street, perhaps.

MAMET: Well, it's pretty shocking, isn't it? Not at all what we've been led to expect.

PLAYBOY: Are you attracted to violence? In prizefights, say? Or bullfighting?

MAMET: No. I've never been.

PLAYBOY: Do you consider your work to be violent?

MAMET: Violent? No.

PLAYBOY: As an artist, do you find it more challenging to deal with the evil and violent side of human nature? In your script for *The Untouchables*, the Al Capone character—played by Robert De Niro—stole the movie from Kevin Costner's Eliot Ness.

MAMET: Drama can't be about nice things happening to nice people. Anyone who has ever been around gangsters knows that they are extremely charming. They speak colorfully, they're sentimental. Generous. They are interesting to write about, interesting to create.

PLAYBOY: In your work, women are frequently the victims of violence, beginning with the violent seduction in *The Postman Always Rings Twice*—

MAMET: I should point out here that what I wrote for that scene was, "They kiss."

PLAYBOY: The tabletop scene—you didn't write that?

MAMET: "They kiss."

PLAYBOY: OK. But there is a pattern in your work. Paul Newman decks Charlotte Rampling in *The Verdict* and now, in *Oleanna*—

MAMET: Look, you mention *Oleanna*. People might want to know why these two characters are at each other's throat. Well, you have a two-character drama. One person is a man and one person is a woman. Two people in opposition. That's what drama means. I sincerely believe that my job as a dramatist is to explicate human interactions in such a way that an artistic—not mechanical but artistic—synthesis can happen.

It is just dead wrong to suggest that my work incites—or supports—violence. My job is exactly to the contrary. My job is to show human interactions in such a way that the synthesis an audience takes away will perhaps lead to a greater humanity, a greater understanding of human motives. I don't know how successful I am at it, but that absolutely is my job. If the net effect is otherwise, which I don't think that it is, then they should throw me in jail.

PLAYBOY: Are the best American characters people who get things done by violent means? Capone and the gangsters. Hoffa. Gunfighters in a Western.

MAMET: Well, that's the American myth. See it and take it.

PLAYBOY: Going all the way back to *The Deerslayer* and other Cooper novels?

MAMET: It goes back as far as America. See it and take it. There's nobody there, boys, jump in and take what you want. Manifest Destiny. I mean, Lord have mercy, if it's Manifest Destiny to take over the country from the Atlantic to the Pacific, what is that except pillage, plunder and steal?

PLAYBOY: Is there excessive violence in films and on television?

MAMET: Sure.

PLAYBOY: There are serious suggestions—from the attorney general, among others—that society needs to control the depiction of violence. Could you live with that?

MAMET: The question, of course, becomes, What is violence and who gets to say so? It is a serious question when the community standard gets so broad. Any law is going to be interpreted by community standards, because people aren't machines. Laws probably work as long as we have a community that understands them in more or less the same way, or is willing to trust one another to interpret them ad hoc. When you don't have that community, it's like the blind men trying to describe an elephant.

PLAYBOY: What if the attorney general and her team could identify exceedingly and unacceptably violent content? Would it be helpful for them to eliminate it?

MAMET: Once you set up a czarship of any kind, rest assured that however brilliant the original people are, those who come after will be swine. That's the way it works.

The problem is, who's going to decide and what are his or her qualifications? There was a story in the papers recently about a fellow who calls himself a performance artist, and he very well may be. If I knew what performance art was, I'd be better qualified to say. Anyway, he is HIV-positive, and in his act he has an associate score his back with a scalpel and then press paper towels against the cuts to take blood impressions, which he hangs on a clothesline to dry. His performance is funded in small part by government money, and that has caused some controversy. Is it art? Hell, I don't know. And if I don't know, then Janet Reno sure doesn't know.

PLAYBOY: OK. Then if the government shouldn't be in the business of censoring expression, should it be in the business of supporting it? There is a lot of discussion about cutting off federal funding of the National Endowment for the Arts and the Public Broadcasting System. Do you think that this would be a disaster for the arts?

MAMET: Right. I'm going to say something heretical. My experience has been that literal, actual art flourishes better without government support. On the other hand, having come up the hard way as everybody does in show business, it would be nice if some people could be helped. I'm torn between wanting to see them helped and wondering if the government is the best way to do it. I mean, people object to the government's subsidizing—even a little—this fellow's performance art. Well, I object to a lot of the pablum that gets grant money. I think people who get that money would be better left to their own devices and eventually to lapse back into the real estate business.

PLAYBOY: Without public television, won't children be deprived of an alternative to repetitive violence, which some people say is the real threat? Doesn't the sheer number of killings they see on the screen eventually desensitize them?

MAMET: I don't buy it. The violence you see on television and the violence you see in real life have nothing to do with each other. Even kids know it. The reports of violence in the news, on the other hand, may desensitize them. Too much exposure to the O.J. Simpson case may desensitize them. The answer is, one does not have to watch television.

PLAYBOY: You're a father. Is it part of your role as a parent to censor what your kids watch on television?

MAMET: I don't think kids should watch television. Period.

PLAYBOY: Not even *Sesame Street?*

MAMET: Not even *Sesame Street.* And I love *Sesame Street.*

PLAYBOY: Then what's the problem with kids watching it?

MAMET: The problem isn't with *Sesame Street.* The problem is with television. If you aren't watching television, then you could be learning some other skill like carving wood, or even reading. I was talking with a friend of mine, a guy who is something of a scholar of show business, and I said, "I don't get television. I believe I understand certain things about the essential nature of live performance and the central nature of radio and movies. But I don't understand television." He said, "Television is essentially a medicine show." And he was right. For X minutes of supposed entertainment, television is going to have your attention for 30 seconds so it can sell you a bottle of snake oil. That is its essential nature. It's a sales tool.

PLAYBOY: Can't technology change that? With some cable channels, for instance, you have no ads.

MAMET: No. Not at all. It's possible to have television without ads, but that doesn't alter its essential nature. You can describe a painting—a Renaissance masterpiece—on the radio and it might have a certain amount of value. But it is not the best way to do painting.

PLAYBOY: You've done some work for television. Didn't it change your opinion of the medium?

MAMET: What is television's agenda? It is a tool to sell you products. What are the tools it uses? Guilt. Shame. Envy. It tells you to be like Ozzie and Harriet. I grew up in the first television generation and I spent a lot of time wondering why my life was so inferior to—and unlike—the lives I saw depicted on television.

PLAYBOY: Which brings to mind the British reviewer who called you "one of our chief critics of capitalism."

MAMET: I don't think I was ever a critic of capitalism. I'm a dramatist. The drama is not a prescriptive medium. Part of what the drama can offer—because it should work on the subconscious level—is the relief that comes with addressing a subject previously thought unaddressable. I'll give you an example.

On the day John F. Kennedy was shot, Lenny Bruce was performing in San Francisco. Everybody was waiting to hear what Lenny Bruce would say. He came out onstage, shook his head and said nothing for five full minutes. Then he looked up at the audience and said, "Vaughn Meader." That was the comedian who'd made his career out of imitating one character—John Kennedy. Saying that—making that joke—was an incredible relief. Does that mean Lenny Bruce was insensitive to the terror and horror and tragedy inflicted on the country, on the Kennedy family? No. He was doing his job as a humorist and he was doing it bravely.

Anything I might know about American capitalism is not going to be found in a play.

PLAYBOY: Just the same, your play—and film—*Glengarry Glen Ross* could be called an indictment of the kill-or-be-killed nature of business.

MAMET: Yeah. Well, Robert Service said it best. He said there isn't a law of God or man that goes north of 10,000 bucks. You know, money makes people cruel. Or has the capacity to do so. Human interactions—that's what I hope my plays are about. The rest of it is just a way to get somewhere.

PLAYBOY: How do you feel about money? Is it better to have money than not to have money?

MAMET: I'd say so. But you can get carried away. There's a story about Herb Gardner, who wrote A *Thousand Clowns*. First a play, then a movie.

He's hot and his agent comes to him with a deal for a television show. Gardner thinks it's a dumb idea and says, "I don't want to do the show." The agent says, "Herb, listen, do this show and you'll never have to write another word."

PLAYBOY: And?

MAMET: Well, you have to ask yourself if that's why you became a writer. So you'd never have to write another word?

There is another story. I was talking to a guy who'd been in the CIA and had an idea for a script. He said, "You know, you could probably make 50 million off this deal. For a half hour's work."

I said, "Fifty million for half an hour's work, huh? That works out to four billion a week, if you don't put in any overtime. That comes to 200 billion a year, if you take two weeks off for vacation."

"Listen," this guy said, "when you're making that kind of money, you can't afford to take a vacation."

PLAYBOY: All right. Getting back to earth here, you mentioned Lenny Bruce, who made his reputation by saying what couldn't be said. Is there anything left that you can't say?

MAMET: You can't say Wayne Newton's head is too small. Or that Richard Simmons is too pudgy. Other than that, you can say anything. Or you can say anything you want so long as you don't mean it. If you mean it, you're in a lot of trouble.

PLAYBOY: Aren't we actually moving back, in a way, to a climate like the one that existed during Lenny Bruce's time? Isn't that what some aspects of the political correctness on American college campuses is all about, that there are some things you can't be allowed to say?

MAMET: Well, sure, but I think centralization will do away with free speech before PC does.

PLAYBOY: Centralization?

MAMET: Sure. One day, three corporations will own all the means of disseminating public information. We'll have to get through their censors, who will make the PC kids look like mice.

There was a Russian dramatist who described working during the Stalin era. He had to sit down with this guy whose job was to censor plays for the Party. The guy would say, "You can't put this and that onstage," and the playwright would say, "Sit down, for Christ's sake. Have a cigar, have a drink, let me tell you what this play is about. Blah, blah, blah."

So the censor listens and says, "Well, OK, but I got to check it out with my boss. Tell you what, when the guy says so and so, in act three, take that out so I can tell my boss."

And the playwright says, "Fine, I can live with that."

And the censor says, "Good, can I have two tickets for Wednesday?" And he goes back to the building where he works.

I would much rather deal with that guy than with some idiot who just got out of the Yale drama school and works as a script reader at the XYZ studio in Hollywood. Those are the people who will eventually control publishing and movies.

PLAYBOY: You don't see a danger in fundamentalist groups that want to get J. D. Salinger out of the library? Or black groups that try to do the same with *Huckleberry Finn*?

MAMET: Of course. There is a vast danger. But, again, I say that's a minor threat. I noticed some black group wants to get *Uncle Tom's Cabin* out of the library somewhere. I wonder if they've even read the book. If there were ever a more beautifully written novel that was an indictment of slavery. . . .

PLAYBOY: Well, it is no secret that people are sensitive about these questions. You wrote an article in *The Guardian* calling *Schindler's List* "emotional pornography" and "*Mandingo* for Jews." Can you elaborate on that?

MAMET: I don't think you can get more elaborate than "*Mandingo* for Jews."

PLAYBOY: Is anti-Semitism something you are especially worried about?

MAMET: As a Jew I'm very concerned that we are falling back on the traditional answer of the Jewish intellectuals in the 1920s, which was to assimilate. To try to hide. You say, "I am an Austrian or a German or a German Jew, and I am such a part of the culture that I don't have this other identity." I was talking to a survivor of the Holocaust, who had lost all his family. He said the worst fear of intellectuals was not in seeing their families killed and their possessions confiscated and their race destroyed. Their worst nightmare was in winding up naked in the field with a bunch of Jews.

But there is no ticket of admission. During the Holocaust, all they cared about was if you were a Jew. They didn't care how much money you had or if you'd won the Iron Cross in World War I. To be Jewish meant to be dead.

PLAYBOY: Do you think this desire to assimilate is still a problem?

MAMET: Before I went to Israel, I talked to my rabbi and he said, "You are in for a shock." And I said, "Why? It is a Jewish country." He said, "No, that's easy. You are going to be in for a shock because what you will find is that there are rapists, murderers, litterbugs and grumpy people in Israel, just like in any place in the world." He said that the lesson in Israel is that Jews are just like anybody else. That's what we've been fighting for 3,000 years—to have a country just like anyone else.

But if you look at the depictions of Jews in the movies, it's the kindly little old lady, Molly Goldberg, or it's the Nobel physicist. People are bending over backward to say, "See, we're treating Jews with kid gloves."

I wrote another essay in which I said that you find few Jewish heroes in the movies. The Jewish answer has always been, "Well, that's OK. It's not important." Earlier you asked about things you cannot say—well, here are two: You cannot say you are a Jew first and then an American. And you cannot say that the movie business is a Jewish business. If there is anything wrong with that, I don't know what it is. Except that the Jewish moguls kept the Jews out of the movies. Where are the Jewish characters? When you find a Jew in the movies, it is probably something like the character in Spike Lee's *Mo' Better Blues*, which was a straight-up anti-Semitic portrait. It's not right. The end of it is murder.

PLAYBOY: Should Spike Lee have his wrist slapped?

MAMET: By whom? I sent him a letter.

PLAYBOY: Did he respond?

MAMET: No. It's not his job to respond. But it is my job to write a letter.

PLAYBOY: In those situations, how do you respond when people challenge your characterizations?

MAMET: The first time we did *Oleanna*, we had about 15 young people from universities who came to see the play. Afterward I asked them, "Well, what do you think?" One young woman said, "Don't you think this is politically irresponsible?" I didn't know what it meant and I still don't know.

PLAYBOY: Is this sort of thinking going to be with us for a while?

MAMET: I hope not, but I think so. Like I said earlier, young people are frightened. They wonder why they're in college, what they are going to do when they get out, what has happened to society. Nobody's looking out for them and there's nothing for them to go into. It's no wonder they're trying to take things into their own hands.

PLAYBOY: Were your college years fearful or did you find your vocation during college?

MAMET: There was a light verse I heard once about Hamlet. It goes like this:

Young Hamlet was prince of Denmark,
A country disrupted and sad,
His mother had married his uncle,
His uncle had murdered his dad.
But Hamlet could not make his mind up,
Whether to dance or to sing.
He got all frenetic
And walked round pathetic,
And did not do one fucking thing.

The last three lines sum up my college career. I spent a lot of time in the theater in college.

PLAYBOY: Was that the genesis of your interest in the theater?

MAMET: Actually, I grew up as something of a child actor in Chicago. My uncle was the head of broadcasting for the Chicago Board of Rabbis and I used to do a radio show for Jewish children Sunday mornings. I was an amateur actor as a kid, then I got involved at Hull House in Chicago in the early 1960s.

PLAYBOY: And playwriting? Did you suddenly find your calling when you read *Death of a Salesman* at 16, or something like that?

MAMET: None of it ever made any sense to me until I started reading Beckett and Pinter. That was my wake-up call.

PLAYBOY: When would that have been? College?

MAMET: I was 14.

PLAYBOY: That must have made you some kind of nerd.

MAMET: Not really. I hated school. But I was on the wrestling team and I played football. I was sports editor for the school paper. And I read a lot. I used to hang out at the Oak Street Book Shop in Chicago. It was a magic place for me. In back they had a room full of books by playwrights, and I used to dream about what it would be like to have a book I had written on one of those shelves.

PLAYBOY: Did your feeling for drama sustain you through college?

MAMET: Yeah. That's all I did. Hung out at the theater.

PLAYBOY: When you were starting out professionally, back in Chicago, were you able to support yourself with your work in the theater?

MAMET: Lord, no. I had jobs. I worked as a real estate salesman and as a cabdriver.

PLAYBOY: How did you do as a real estate salesman?

MAMET: I never got out of the office. I was in charge of the leads, like the character in *Glengarry Glen Ross*.

PLAYBOY: Was that as unpleasant an experience as the play depicts?

MAMET: It was harsh. I also sold carpet over the phone. Cold calling. Anybody who has ever done it knows what I'm talking about.

PLAYBOY: How did you describe color over the phone?

MAMET: They had all these names that sounded like they could have been ice cream. Or horses.

PLAYBOY: If you learned business from handling real estate leads, what about cabdriving? Did you get any material from conversations you overheard?

MAMET: No. But I always enjoyed driving a cab. For two reasons. You could start in the morning with no money, even to eat, and after a couple of fares, you would have enough to buy breakfast. The other reason was those Checker cabs, which we all drove in those days. They had the best heaters in the world. It could be 30 below in Chicago and you could drive all day in a T-shirt. It was so wonderfully warm. It was great.

PLAYBOY: Since *American Buffalo*, your breakthrough work that had you on Broadway when you were 27, you have been a prolific playwright. Do you have dry spells?

MAMET: Sure. You always have dry spells as a writer. What I usually do when I'm in a dry spell is write something else. I just like to write. And I reap all sorts of rewards from it. It supports me and I've made a lot of friends doing it and it gives me a feeling of accomplishment. If I can't do it one way, I'll do it another.

PLAYBOY: Do you pay much attention to the mechanics? Are you fussy about whether or not you are writing with number two pencils, that kind of thing?

MAMET: Oh, sure. If I've got nothing else to do, I'll bitch about that. For years I worked with the same manual typewriter. And I drank coffee. I'd sit down to write, take a sip of coffee, put the cup down on the right side of the typewriter, light a cigarette and type the first line. Then I'd hit the carriage return and it would hit the cup and the coffee would go everywhere. I did that every day for 20 years. Then I quit drinking coffee.

PLAYBOY: And smoking cigarettes.

MAMET: That came first.

PLAYBOY: It has been reported that you like cigars.

MAMET: I gave them up, too.

PLAYBOY: Are you one of those writers who need a routine?

MAMET: Sure. I have all kinds of routines. But I like to describe myself as a free spirit will-o'-the-wisp. So I keep myself blissfully ignorant of my routines.

PLAYBOY: Do you write every day?

MAMET: Sometimes.

PLAYBOY: What's the source of your feeling for speech?

MAMET: My family, I suppose. I had a grandfather who was a great talker and storyteller. His name was Naphtali. I was reading in the Bible the story of when Jacob is about to die and he is giving his sons his blessings. One of the sons, whose people became the tribe Naphtali, was given the blessing of speech, of being able to talk the birds out of the trees.

PLAYBOY: For all your success, there have been some setbacks, such as *Lone Canoe* onstage and *We're No Angels* on film. How do you bounce back?

MAMET: Rudyard Kipling said, "If you can meet with triumph and disaster and treat those two impostors just the same." I'm getting to be middle-aged enough to see that there is more than superficial truth in his assertion that they are both impostors. It's nice to have people like your work. I also hope as a writer that I am my own best judge and worst critic.

When you're young, everything seems like it's the end of the world. Bad review? OK, that's it. Oh my God, what's happened? You've just been excoriated in every newspaper in the country. How can you ever go on? Goddamn them all. I hope they all get the mumps.

Having spent too many years in show business, the one thing I see that succeeds is persistence. It's the person who just ain't gonna go home. I decided early on that I wasn't going to go home. This is what I'll be doing until they put me in jail or put me in a coffin.

Kids today say they are going to go to graduate school so they'll have something to fall back on. If you have something to fall back on, you're going to fall back on it. You learn how to take the criticism. You have to, or you get out. I was talking with a friend the other day about something I was working on that wasn't going right. I said, "I don't like it. It's a piece of shit."

He said, "Dave, never berate yourself. There are people who are paid to do that for you."

PLAYBOY: Any other advice for the young playwright?

MAMET: My best friend, Jonathan Katz, was for a number of years the kid ping-pong champion of New York State. And when he was 12 or 13, he wandered into Marty Reisman's ping-pong parlor in New York City. Reisman was then the U.S. champion in table tennis and a genius, an absolute genius. Jonathan asked him, "What do I have to do to play table tennis like you?"

Reisman said, "First, drop out of school."

That would be my advice to aspiring playwrights.

PLAYBOY: And how did you break into movies?

MAMET: I got my first job in pictures through my ex-wife. She was going to audition for a part in *Postman* and I told her to tell Bob Rafelson, who was directing, that he was a fool if he didn't hire me to write the screenplay. I was kidding, but she did it. And when it turned out he needed a writer, he called. When he asked why he should hire me, I told him, "Because I'll give you either a really good screenplay or a sincere apology."

PLAYBOY: One last question. Where do you get your titles?

MAMET: I don't know. But I thought of a good one the other day: *In These Our Clothes*. I think of titles and I write to fit.

ROMAN POLANSKI

A candid conversation with the brash, brilliant director of Knife in the Water, Rosemary's Baby *and* Macbeth

There was virtually no action, and the plot was starkly simple: A successful middle-aged Polish journalist, his restless wife and a young hitchhiker they have picked up spend a weekend on a yacht, with subtle, potentially murderous psychosexual tensions developing among them. But *Knife in the Water*, Roman Polanski's first feature film (which he co-authored), won an Academy Award nomination for best foreign film of 1963 and made its director internationally famous at the age of 30.

All the violence in *Knife* was in the characters' minds, but Polanski's next two films (which he also co-authored) revealed what some began to consider a morbid fascination with scenes of gruesome death. In *Repulsion*, the frenzied insanity of a beautiful young Belgian girl (Catherine Deneuve) drives her to murder her suitor, and *Cul-de-Sac* told a black-humor tale of two criminals who take refuge in the isolated island home of a weak transvestite and his tarty bride. Polanski kept some of his allies among the critics who had heaped praise on *Knife*, but others couldn't stomach his taste for the macabre. *Time* saw *Cul-de-Sac* as "a jittery, tittery comedy of terrors . . . In frame after frame, the danger lurks just out of sight until the onlooker feels like a man cooped up with a cobra he can't really see." But Judith Crist complained that the film was entertaining only "for those who can laugh while fighting off nausea."

After a mildly amusing side step in *The Fearless Vampire Killers*, a harmless parody of old horror movies, Polanski pushed on to somewhere near the outer limits of suspense with *Rosemary's Baby*, his adaptation of Ira Levin's best-selling novel about a modern-day witchcraft cult in Manhattan. Starring Mia Farrow and John Cassavetes, the film was a spectacular success both with the critics and at the box office.

Polanski's personal brushes with suspense and brutality in life began at an early age. When he was eight, his mother died in a Nazi concentration camp and not long after, he escaped from the infamous Jewish ghetto in Kraków and survived the war by shunting among various families willing to take him in. One day, he had to dash for cover as a German soldier decided on some casual target practice and whizzed a bullet over Polanski's head. Then, when he was 16, a thug nearly beat him to death.

After he was graduated from Poland's superlative State School of Filming in Lodz, Polanski scrabbled to make a living in Paris for a couple of years before the Polish government finally gave him a budget for his screenplay of *Knife in the Water* and sent him on his way up in the world. He quickly established a reputation as one of the celebrity circuit's most successful bachelors; and in 1968 he married Sharon Tate, a beautiful young American actress. Moving at a fast pace between film sets and their homes in London and Los Angeles, they were known as a jet-set couple until the night of August 9, 1969 when Sharon and three friends—Voyteck Frykowski, men's hair stylist Jay Sebring and coffee heiress Abigail Folger—plus an 18-year-old boy who was visiting the caretaker, were sadistically murdered at Polanski's rented house in Los Angeles. The press gave the case saturation publicity and made it one of the most sensational mass murders in the country's history.

For months, the popular theory was that the murders were committed by someone from the "rich hippie" crowd in which Miss Tate and Polanski were such popular figures. Eventually, the theory proved false, when police apprehended Charles Manson and his bizarre "family" of young men and runaway girls who were living at an abandoned ranch a few miles outside L.A. After a long and widely reported trial, Manson and two of his followers were sentenced to death for the murders and Polanski's name dropped out of the news and the gossip columns. Now, three years after *Rosemary's Baby* and two years after the murders, he has completed the filming of Shakespeare's *Macbeth*, adapted for the screen by Polanski and British author-critic (and Contributing Editor) Kenneth Tynan and produced by Playboy Productions. To explore Polanski's vision of himself, his films and his life today, *Playboy* sent freelance writer Larry DuBois to London for the first interview he's granted in more than two years. DuBois writes of his experiences:

"Roman Polanski inspires strong, and often conflicting, feelings in people; and after you've been around his pals, women and professional associates for a while, you get used to a frustrating ambivalence about him that is most often expressed in remarks that go something like: 'God, how I like that little bastard.' I couldn't say it any better myself. During the extended course of this interview, there were moments when I'd have fought for Polanski, moments when I only wanted to fight with him—or with the editor responsible for the assignment—and moments when I passionately wished I'd never met either one of them. After most of two and a half months chasing Polanski to wrench from him the 20-odd hours of taped conversation I finally acquired, I see that my own ambivalence fits neatly into four stages, which assumed an almost perfect symmetry as my affection and my irritation deepened simultaneously.

"Stage one: You enjoy him as a gloriously colorful figure, with a keen sense of humor, who takes great pleasure in entertaining whoever happens to be around him with anecdotes—vigorously re-enacted—or a showman's monolog that can go on for an hour or more. But his ego is as unbending as a natural law, and he has a fierce suspicion of anyone, especially a journalist, whose goal is to penetrate the wall of emotional invulnerability he has constructed around himself. So you soon begin to feel this interview is going to be difficult.

"Stage two: Endlessly following him around as he works, you begin to perceive his large talent and his tenacious determination to have any project he is concerned with done his way. I felt quite a sympathy for the technicians at Shepperton Studios who had to cope with Polanski's relentless drive to get every frame of *Macbeth* absolutely perfect for maximum dramatic effect. I also felt quite a sympathy for myself when Polanski either ended one of our sessions abruptly because he didn't feel in top form or ordered me to 'turn that fucking recorder off' while he paced, pulled at his hair, yelled, told jokes or whatever else he felt like doing while he searched for exactly the word or thought to express what he meant. His Polish accent is thick and his grammar isn't perfect, but his vocabulary and his feel for the nuances of English are simply astonishing for someone who learned it only a few years ago. This talent, and his striving for perfection, makes him an artist to admire. But, as I now realized with a sinking heart, they make an interview even more difficult than I had feared.

"Stage three: Traveling with him, and staying for a week at the lovely 19th century farmhouse he rents in the countryside a few kilometers from St.-Tropez, you discover that he is a superb companion. He likes to go there to relax in privacy, but he also zooms through the resort's cafés, yachts, discothèques, penny arcades and dinner parties, and gradually a body of empirical evidence accumulates to indicate that he is more than just a talented eccentric. Behind the charm is a remarkable grace, and he turns out to be a generous, considerate, even sentimental man, with real warmth for his friends and even many of his casual acquaintances. By now, however, it is apparent that he is not difficult at all but nearly impossible to interview, being beyond reason about such niceties as schedules, deadlines and questions he can't get excited about.

"Stage four: Unbelievably, you finish. And the sense of accomplishment and relief can only be described as pure joy, because almost without realizing it, you've come to agree with Polanski's friends, who have the same high opinion of his worth that he does; but, as you explain to your editor, you would rather spend the next several months interviewing, say, an insurance salesman about actuarial charts for men over 50 than ask Polanski one more question. Ever.

"My memory barely extends as far back as the beginning of this assignment, but I recall that from his films and the press after the murders of his wife and friends, I had the image of Polanski as a flaky, perhaps even macabre character. On the contrary. He is as cavalier about his work as an ambitious executive and about as macabre as a California beach boy. His disposition is cheery and optimistic. He is straightforward to the point of discomfiting bluntness. He tends to surround himself with intelligent, serious people and gets bored quickly with what he calls 'the aimless, futile individuals' he sometimes encounters in St.-Tropez.

"His only genuine indulgence is women, which is what he does with most of whatever free time he has in St.-Tropez and elsewhere; and in that, he lives up to his image. At least superficially, his seductive style is roughly that of a wily street urchin (he's 5'5") faced with rich tourists, disarming them with a kind of youthful enthusiasm and naïveté. It works. In his other personal habits, he is almost depressingly disciplined. He exercises diligently. His diet includes wheat germ, yogurt and other health foods. He rarely drinks more than a glass of wine or beer and he is not above lecturing his friends about the evils of cigarette smoking.

"Now that the interview is over, only one of our many differences still bothers me: He is a most terrifying driver of automobiles. I find nothing endearing about having rocketed with him in an XK-E through the French holiday traffic around St.-Tropez at 110-120 miles per hour. When I tried to explain my own concept of personal safety, he just said, 'You must understand: What seems like a risk to you may not seem like a risk to me.' The uninitiated might read all sorts of meanings into that about his background, and some hidden fatalism. But I dropped the subject, because I knew that, as usual, he meant exactly what he said and no more. He is, quite simply, so goddamn arrogant about his abilities that it's never occurred to him that such speeds might confront him with a situation he can't handle. And as for those who may be unhappy with his pace, well, they're completely free to take a taxi.

"Finally, I should note that there is one section of this interview that didn't require a struggle to extract. One Sunday evening, we sat on the porch of his farmhouse with nothing around for miles but the silent French countryside, and I hesitantly brought up the subject of Sharon and the murders. For two straight hours, without any further coaxing, he told his story, simply and with none of his usual interruptions. He obviously wanted to go through it all once, let it all out; and when he was finished, I think he felt better. For myself, I was unspeakably depressed. It was a couple of days before either of us mentioned the interview again. The transition from that subject to another was a difficult one then, as it is now. So just one last thing: All along, Polanski kept telling me, when the tape recorder was off, that it would be impossible to translate his personality onto paper, since he expresses so much of his irresistibly high-spirited and playful nature through antics rather than words. He's like a movie, he said; he has to be seen to be appreciated. I think he was wrong. I think readers will be able to develop their own affectionate ambivalence about him."

PLAYBOY: Your films have earned you a reputation as a master of the macabre. How do you explain your fascination with it?

POLANSKI: I don't know why I like it. Why do some people like boxing, or writing? I'm a filmmaker; I make pictures. I don't like to talk about them and I don't think about why I make them. You're asking me to psychoanalyze myself and this is not something that interests me at all.

PLAYBOY: We're not really asking you to psychoanalyze yourself—just to tell us about the personal vision you convey in your films.

POLANSKI: All right. I'm not preoccupied with the macabre—I'm rather more interested in the behavior of people under stress, when they are no longer in comfortable, everyday situations where they can afford to respect the conventional rules and morals of society. You can really learn something about a person when he's put into circumstances in which civilized values place his own identity, even his very being, in jeopardy. In a way, *Knife in the Water* was my minute example of this. I took three people and put them in a situation that subjected them to stress, due to their confinement on the yacht and the competition between the two males. In a way, *Cul-de-Sac* was the same situation, where the people could not react the way they were accustomed to. Before the death of my wife, I was working on a film about the Donner Pass group, which got stranded in the Sierra Nevada Mountains in 1847. It's an extremely interesting story, because besides being symptomatic of the problems the pioneers faced in the beginning of that country, it shows civilized people reduced to circumstances where they have to decide on the most drastic moral issues, like eating each other, in order to survive. I don't know what I would do in that situation. But I don't think I would eat your flesh. I think I would rather die. Not because I would think there was something morally wrong with eating you after you were dead. I simply don't think I would be willing to swallow your flesh. Would you swallow mine?

PLAYBOY: Who knows? Our cultural aversion to the idea would probably make us throw up, anyway.

POLANSKI: Only in the beginning, my friend.

PLAYBOY: Do you film characters under stress in order to find answers you're seeking for yourself or to force the audience to confront problems you think you already understand?

POLANSKI: Neither. It simply fascinates me. When something fascinates you, you talk about it, and making films is my way of talking about it.

PLAYBOY: Why are you more fascinated by characters under stress than by those who aren't?

POLANSKI: I sometimes surprise myself that I don't ask myself these questions, but I don't. Perhaps if I did, I would know the answers, but I don't feel any need for that. That's the way I am. Perhaps it's because as a child I had plenty of opportunities to see how people behave under stress. I often think: How would a friend with whom you've drunk a lot of vodka and had a lot of fun respond when one morning you plant yourself on his doorstep and say, "Hide me. I'm being chased by the Nazis." And now he has to decide whether or not to risk his life for your friendship. But it's difficult for me to judge how much part the war plays in what I create. I don't think I'm obsessed by what I lived through. I was a child during the war, and children are resilient. Whatever you create, it's an accumulation of millions of things in you, of what you go through as a boy, as a young man, of what you read, of what you see in the cinema, of the people you know. All these have affected my emotional life. I remember, for instance, that one of the profound experiences of my youth was seeing *Of Mice and Men*. That has stayed with me. I couldn't stop thinking about this big, lovely man and his friend, and their friendship, and I thought that if I were ever a filmmaker, I would certainly try to do something along those lines, something against injustice and intolerance and prejudice and superstition. And I have. These elements are weaved through my films.

PLAYBOY: Why, then, did you decide to make *Rosemary's Baby*, which could be said to have celebrated, or at least popularized, superstition?

POLANSKI: You don't have to be superstitious to enjoy a fantasy. If you are around me for long, you will see that I have no belief at all in the supernatural of any kind. It's just a fashionable distraction for people seeking easy explanations to certain phenomena they are otherwise incapable of understanding. Myself, I am down to earth in my philosophy of life, very rationally and materialistically oriented, with no interest in the occult. The only obsession that compelled me to make that film was my liking for good cinema. When Bob Evans, the head of production for Paramount, called me and asked me to read the galleys of the book before it was published, I found it fascinating material for a film, with a terrifically suspenseful plot.

PLAYBOY: Suspense is another of the hallmarks of your films. What makes it so important to you?

POLANSKI: I'm in the drama business, and suspense is the essence of drama. In my films, I'm concerned with the unexpected and with making what is unbelievable believable. *Life* is like that to me. We can never control what will happen out there. I don't live my life suspensefully, but in cinema I like the constant unexpected because that's what makes a story interesting. The essential is not to allow the audience to be able to anticipate what is going to happen next.

I remember when I was six, some friends and I made this skull out of clay and put these pieces of glass in it for eyes and hung it on the wall, thinking that anyone who walked by would be scared of it. I also remember making a mask of the devil with a red tongue made out of a candy wrapper, then putting a flashlight behind it. These are the things that intrigued me—but not for any supernatural or bizarre reasons, only because I already liked the show business aspect of this mask making. My fondness for the dramatic and the unexpected has always been so obvious to me that I never stopped to ask why. I must have been born with it.

PLAYBOY: Your past films have been contemporary suspense stories. Now you've chosen to direct a medieval Shakespearean tragedy? Why?

POLANSKI: After the murders, everything I was considering seemed futile to me. I couldn't think of a subject that seemed worthwhile or dignified enough to spend a year or more on it, in view of what happened to me. That may sound extremely pompous, but I couldn't make another suspense story. And I certainly couldn't make a comedy; I couldn't make a casual film. In the state of mind I found myself, this type of project seemed most acceptable. As a kid, I loved Shakespeare, and when I was a teenager I saw Laurence Olivier's *Hamlet* 20 times. I always had this great desire to make a Shakespearean movie someday, and when I finally decided I must go back to work, I thought to myself: "That's something I could do, that's something I could give myself to. That's worth the effort."

PLAYBOY: From all of Shakespeare's plays, what made you choose *Macbeth*?

POLANSKI: *Macbeth* was the most seductive because there are a lot of lines and descriptions that are verbal but can be easily translated into great action scenes, and because there is a great character in Macbeth, who can be developed and shown a new way on the screen.

PLAYBOY: *Macbeth* is also a tragedy full of violence and murder. In view of your personal memories, wasn't it difficult for you to film those scenes?

POLANSKI: No. When you're actually staging such scenes, it's amusing. It has nothing to do with reality. You never even associate it with reality. It's all artifice, special effects. A knife is not a knife and blood is not blood. You can play with it, and we all laughed and behaved like children doing those scenes. It's only when you put it together later and show it to an audience that you realize there's something horrific in it. But certainly not during the actual filming.

PLAYBOY: Some critics and moviegoers may feel that you chose *Macbeth* as a kind of catharsis, to purge yourself of the kind of violence you had so recently experienced in your own life. What would you say to them?

POLANSKI: I would say they are full of shit, because it's not so. I've told you why I decided to make this film, and once I decided to do it, I had to do it according to my own standards. If you make a film about a murder, you have to *show* the murder, or do a film about something else. If you use the screen as a medium, then what you tell has to be told by visual means. Of course, you could put a guy in front of a camera and have him read the play and the same story would be told to your audience in a different, perhaps more gentle way. I happen to think it would also be a very boring way. When you're telling a story about a man who kills a head of state to take his place, you are absolutely obligated to show the act that is the culmination of the whole play.

PLAYBOY: There's still the question of taste and finesse. Some critics have said that you've indulged in excessive violence on the screen.

POLANSKI: The way I've done it is with finesse. Others do it euphemistically. They are afraid to show what is essential to the story. I will never forget a growing tension in the churchyard scene of *Zorba the Greek*, which culminates with a throat cutting that unfortunately happens just below the bottom edge of the screen. That was the end of the movie for me, because the director had copped out. He showed his cowardice. If you tell a joke that requires the use of four-letter words, then you have to say them. It's not good to say, "He grabbed her and . . . dot, dot, dot, dot." It's better to tell another story. Showing the violence is an analogous situation, isn't it?

PLAYBOY: But critics might argue that the graphic portrayal of violence is analogous to pornography, not only with no redeeming social value but with harmful effects on those who see it.

POLANSKI: These people delude themselves that violence can be caused by what is on the screen. They should ask little children on the street what causes violence and they would become more enlightened. For me, when I see something violent happening on the screen, I react *against* it; I think this is most people's reaction. If there is violence on the screen that *can* make people act violently in their lives, it's the sterilized Hollywood conception of violence. It's the Western where the bad guy aggravates you so much for 90 minutes that finally, when the good guy gets rid of him in a tidy way, you feel relieved and happy. So what develops in young minds is that when somebody is bad enough, you can get rid of him—and without a mess. This is murder committed the "clean" way, murder that can be endorsed by movie-rating authorities who miss its real meaning. To me, *this* is immorality.

But if you show killing in an agonizing, realistic way, with the spurting of blood and people dying slowly and horribly, that is reality, because very rarely does a man die instantly, and to witness that on the screen can do nothing but repel you from engaging in it in real life. Look at literature. The Bible is enough to make you faint. And when Sholokhov tells you about the atrocities in Russia in *And Quiet Flows the Don*, he describes them with utmost detail and nobody would ever think of criticizing it, because that's how literature evolved, whereas cinema is something young, something much more commercial, and boundaries were forced upon it, at least in the Anglo-Saxon countries, so it couldn't evolve in the proper way. Instead, the cinema has tended to draw hypocritical, gilded pictures of life and death.

But even if *Macbeth* weren't a play about murder, the critics would be asking why I chose to make it after Sharon's death. What if I had made a scene with Macbeth, dagger in hand, going to the king's chambers, and then . . . dot, dot, dot, dot? They would say, "After what happened to him, he lost his balls." Or what if I had decided to make a comedy? They would say, "After the murders, he has the bad taste to do a comedy."

PLAYBOY: For the past two years, you've remained silent about the murder of your wife and friends, despite the enormous and lurid exposure it has received in the press. Are you willing to tell your side of the story now?

POLANSKI: It's not something I talk about with friends, but I would like to go through it once from beginning to end. I have terrific difficulty in trying to reconstruct that period, but I have some definite things to say about it. I lost something most precious to me, and I'm sure that the people who were close to us feel the same way. But when it happened, the press said in unison, "Yes, of course, that's the way he lived, that's what he created in his films, and here is the result." That was the first outburst. *Time* magazine said, "It was a scene as grisly as anything in Polanski's film explorations of the dark and melancholy side of the human character." I was baffled, to say the least, by the cheapness and platitude of such writing. I remember their headline: "Nothing But Bodies." It was sickening, the way the press sensationalized something that was already sensational.

This was a subject I knew more about than anybody else, a subject very near to my heart. I had long known that it was impossible for a journalist to convey 100 percent of the truth, but I didn't realize to what extent the truth is distorted, both by the intentions of the journalist and by neglect. I don't mean just the interpretations of what happened; I also mean the facts. The reporting about Sharon and the murders was virtually criminal. Reading the papers, I could not believe my eyes. *I could not believe my eyes!* They blamed the victims for their own murders. I really despise the press. I didn't always. The press made me despise it.

Some of those articles! From *Pageant:* "Those Sharon Tate Orgies: Sex, Sadism, Celebrities." Incredible! Particularly in view of the fact that a woman eight and a half months pregnant has limited desires for orgies. It was like the press suddenly had a new dictionary, with words like masochism, sadism, sodomy, suicide, witchcraft, rituals, drug abuse and necrophilia. They put in everything they could imagine. One magazine ran a photograph of Sharon with the four other victims floating around behind her like champagne bubbles while she is dancing. God*damn* them! The victims were assassinated two times: once by the murderers, the second time by the press.

PLAYBOY: Why, do you think?

POLANSKI: I don't know. I really don't know. I think because of some resentment, some bitterness, some jealousy; and let me tell you, a lot of journalists and nonjournalists who wrote "personal" accounts of what they claimed to know made a lot of money off the case. I wonder to myself: Were the people who wrote those slanderous articles any better than the murderers? I don't think so. They just use different forms of expression. Tell me, what makes the press so fucking vituperative?

PLAYBOY: There's no question that certain elements of the press had a field day exploiting the murders, but the legitimate press made a more serious and responsible effort to find out if there was some connection between the victims and the murderers. Wasn't that both logical and understandable?

POLANSKI: Yes. I suppose. But they all groped for the "irony" in the murders, which was nonsense, and then turned my films into a metaphor for the murders. And they all believed there had to be a logical motive, so they slandered us with articles about "the wild parties that led to the massacre"—which is an exact title of one newspaper story—and the connections of Jay Sebring and Voyteck with certain anonymous drug dealers. These articles remind me of the story about the guy who says to his friend, "Imagine. *Pâté de foie gras*, two-inch steak, with spinach and French fries, chocolate pudding and coffee, all for 25 cents," and his friend says, "That's impossible. Where?" And he answers, "I didn't say where. I said, 'Imagine.'"

There is a couple who live in Hollywood, Joe Hyams and Elke Sommer. He's supposed to be a writer and she's supposed to be an actress, yet they were both out there peddling articles saying that they knew the way we lived and the people we hung around with, and so they knew that tragedy would happen to us sooner or later. Astonishing! I met them once in my life. Once! But there is something magical about the printed word, so the average reader says, "Well, if they print it, it must be true," and the press was booming about this sort of thing so often and with such assurance that even some of our friends were affected by it. They would read something and say, "We didn't know about that." And I would say, "I didn't either."

What people read about us after the murders would make them ask one question: When did they have the time to work, between their orgies and rituals and drug taking? How did I have time to make four films in three and a half years? How did Sharon have the time to make even more? How did Jay Sebring run a business? Abigail Folger was a social worker who got up at six in the morning to go to Watts to work, then to a speed-reading class after work, and she would come back at 11 at night, utterly exhausted and hardly able to perform rituals and orgies before getting up at six again the next morning. And Voyteck was desperately trying to get something together in films. I had promised him a job on a film about dolphins I was preparing, and he was very excited about that and doing his own research on the subject. *Time* magazine said he had "sinister connections to which even the tolerant Polanski objected." Where do they get this stuff? I ask you. Where do they get it?

PLAYBOY: Perhaps from the reputation you and many of your friends had around Los Angeles for being sort of "rich hippies" whose lifestyle revolved around parties, drugs, casual sex and the like.

POLANSKI: All us sinful hedonists, eh? Should that have made the tragedy seem understandable to people? How could the press accept that as the explanation? These were all very good people, and this was a happy, blameless period of my life. There were lots of parties at people's houses, on the beach or in the mountains, and often Sharon would make dinner, and there was this magnificent group of friends who would come to our house, and we would sit outside where it was warm, with the sky full of stars, and listen to music or talk for hours—films, sex, politics or whatever. We all tried to help each other, we were all happy at each other's successes, and it was beautiful, and so new to me. I never knew life could be a luxury. It had always been hotel rooms and struggle, and now I loved this life, I loved the place, I loved the people, I loved my work. I was paying my maid over $200 a week, which is probably what a Polish worker earns in six months. I could not believe such affluence and comfort. Sharon and I had great prospects. We wanted to settle for good in Los Angeles. We had big plans. It seemed to be a kind of peculiar, happy dream. But there was nothing freaked out, sinister or immoral about it.

PLAYBOY: There were stories that Sebring and Frykowski were into a drug-dealing scene.

POLANSKI: Those stories were nonsense. The most they would ever do was buy pot from someone for their own use.

PLAYBOY: At the time, the press stressed that Frykowski and Abigail Folger had been living in your house for several months, even while you were away, and that Sebring always seemed to be around. The implication was that this was evidence of bizarre goings-on.

POLANSKI: Jay was a frequent visitor, but he *never* stayed at the house. It seemed reasonable to have Voyteck and Gibby stay there to watch the house while we were gone, and when Sharon returned from London to Los Angeles before I did, we both felt better that she would have someone there with her. So it could hardly be considered some bizarre scene. You've seen how people come and go from my house in St.-Tropez. You've also seen that it's pretty innocent, in a college fraternity sort of way.

PLAYBOY: What about the occult rituals that stories said were taking place—stories that gained momentum from the fact that you had directed *Rosemary's Baby?*

POLANSKI: Do you want me to be rude with you? As I said before, not only do I not endorse the occult but it is something so foreign to my rational, materialistic philosophy of life that I protest against those implications. And Sharon—it was *fantastic* what they were attributing to her. In death, they made a monster out of her. A monster out of the sweetest, most innocent, lovable human being. She was kindness itself to everybody and everything around her—people, animals, everything. She just didn't have a bad bone in her body. She was a unique person. It's difficult to describe her character. She was just utterly good, the kindest human being I've ever met, with an extreme patience. To live with me was proof of her patience, because to be near me must be an ordeal. She never had a bad temper, she was never moody. She enjoyed being a wife. The press and the public knew of her physical beauty, but she also had a beautiful soul, and this is something that only her friends knew about. Before I met Sharon in 1966, my love life, as opposed to my sex life, had been unsuccessful and painful, and I guarded my freedom. My first marriage had been a very traumatic experience.

PLAYBOY: In what way?

POLANSKI: After I left Poland and was wandering around Paris in circles, young and full of enthusiasm, I was married briefly to a Polish actress—but I really hate talking about it for some reason. Not because it's painful to talk about but because it's so futile. So let's not talk about it. OK?

PLAYBOY: OK. You were saying you met Sharon in 1966.

POLANSKI: While filming *The Fearless Vampire Killers*, in which she had a role. I was living what you would call the life of a playboy, and marriage was the last thing in my mind. Except for the few months of my first marriage, I had lived all my life like a nomad. I grew up sitting on suitcases in the midst of war. My mother was taken to the concentration camp when I was eight and my father was taken a few months later. I felt that any type of family tie, anything that means nest, ends in tragedy. But seeing Sharon more and more often, I knew a sentimental relationship was developing. At the beginning, I was afraid of this. But she was so extremely understanding, tactful and clever. Being around me, she still made me feel absolutely free, and she made it clear that she was not going to engulf me. I remember once her words, "I am not one of those ladies who swallow a man." And it was true. Finally, she moved to my house in London and we began to live together, and a new emotional adventure started. After two years, I realized that she would like to get married. She never asked me, never said a word about it. So finally I said, "I'm sure you would like to get married," and she said she would. So I said, "We'll get married, then," and we did. By that time, I wasn't nervous about it at all.

Sharon was the first woman in my life who really made me feel happy. I mean literally aware of being happy. That's a very rare state. Strangely enough, about a week or two before her death, I remember an instant when I was thinking of it, and I was actually thinking: "I am a happy man!" And it was a sentiment that I hadn't known before, because there had always been something missing from my happiness, some little thing that always needed adjusting. I also remember thinking—and here is my middle-European background, probably—I remember thinking: "This cannot possibly last. It's impossible to last." And I suddenly got scared. I was thinking that you can't maintain such a status quo. I didn't have anything tragic in mind, but I was afraid, being quite a realist, that such a state cannot last indefinitely.

PLAYBOY: How did the news of the murders come to you?

POLANSKI: I was in our house in London, working on a script for *The Day of the Dolphin*, with my friends Andy Braunsberg and Michael Brown. I was walking around the room talking about one scene and the phone rang. It was my agent in Los Angeles. He said, "Roman, there was a disaster in a house." I said, "Which house?" "Your house," and then quickly, in one go, he said, "Sharon is dead, and Voyteck and Jay and Abigail."

PLAYBOY: What then?

POLANSKI: I just kept saying, "No, no, no, no." My first reaction was that there must have been a hill slide, with the mountains sliding down or something. I said, "How?" He said, "I don't know, I don't know." He was crying on the other end of the line, and I was crying, and I just kept saying it was insane, and finally he told me they had been murdered. A little while later, another friend came to our house and we went out and walked the streets for a while. When we came back, they called a doctor, who gave me a shot, and I slept.

PLAYBOY: How did you happen to be in London just then, when Sharon was eight and a half months pregnant, rather than with her?

POLANSKI: I had been working on that script for several months, while Sharon was doing a film in London. She was quite pregnant but working until the last possible moment. We were planning that I could finish the script and we would return to Los Angeles together, but the script kept dragging on. By this time, Sharon couldn't fly anymore, because the airlines don't allow you to after a certain period of pregnancy, so she decided to take the boat home. I couldn't take the boat, because it took so long, so I was supposed to take a plane as soon as I finished the script, and this was to be just days after she arrived in Los Angeles.

When she left London, I took Sharon to the boat, the *Queen Elizabeth II*, and we had lunch. When they asked visitors to leave the boat came the moment when we had to say goodbye to each other—the saddest moment of my life, because we were seeing each other for the last time and didn't know it. I remember I called her on the ship later that afternoon. She was telling me the news about our new dog, named Prudence. She told me the dog was very happy on the boat because her rubber ball never stopped rolling around the cabin. After that, we talked daily on the phone. The bill was astronomical. On the last call, just 10 hours before it happened—it was a Friday—she told me that they had found a wild kitten and they were trying to feed it with an eyedropper, and they were keeping him in the bathtub because he was absolutely wild, jumping on people, etc. Funny how life is weaved out of these little banal moments that make it worthwhile. At the end of that call, I said, "I'm coming Monday." I was annoyed that I had to say Monday, because she couldn't wait for me to come, and I couldn't wait to leave, but the goddamn script kept dragging on. So I told her, "I'm coming Monday, whether I'm through or not." That was our last conversation.

PLAYBOY: How long did it take you to accept the fact of her death?

POLANSKI: A long time. At first the reaction is panic. Completely disjointed, you can't concentrate, you can't put things together to realize what has actually happened. You can't believe. You can't conceive of the fact that she and the others are no longer alive. I could not grasp this very thin moment that separated their existence from nothingness. After that came a period of utter grief that lasted as long as the investigation. Somehow, those two things were parallel. For months, I thought of nothing else and then, all at once, when the crime was solved, my obsession stopped. Then came the period of dismissal, of withdrawal. I moved to Switzerland and started skiing myself silly with a bunch of friends, hedonists you would call them. They were wonderful to me. Kind and gentle and tactful, but I was able to do it all only for the dismissal.

And after the period of extensive skiing and social life, I decided to go back to work. Right after the murders, everyone kept patting me on the shoulder and saying I must go back to work, and work would make me forget, make my life worthwhile. But I couldn't even have tried to pull myself together at that point, and I remember talking to Stanley Kubrick and he said, "I'm sure that everybody tells you to work. You can't work in this state of mind, but there will come a moment when you feel suddenly, 'I have to go out and work.'" And that is exactly what happened after the period in Switzerland. I have worked for over a year on *Macbeth* and now, two years after it happened, you talk to me, ask me questions, and it seems as though it all happened two weeks ago. So it's a kind of trial for me.

PLAYBOY: Do you want to go through with it?

POLANSKI: Absolutely.

PLAYBOY: When your period of grief set in, how did you feel about not having been there that night?

POLANSKI: I had, and still have, a tremendous feeling of guilt, a feeling that if I had been there, it wouldn't have happened, contrary to what our friends thought. They thought if I had been there, I wouldn't be here now.

PLAYBOY: Do you think you could have defended Sharon and the others from the murderers?

POLANSKI: I think I would have been able to prevent it. I don't think I would let myself be intimidated or overcome by anybody. I think I could have prevented it.

PLAYBOY: During the investigation of the murders, were you questioned by the police?

POLANSKI: Extensively. I stayed in Los Angeles because I thought my presence could be useful to them. As a matter of fact, along with our friends, the cops were the best people of all in this situation. Unlike the press, the police were realistic, but human and with genuine feeling. They were devoted to their job and I had occasion to see all sides of their personalities and their own personal problems. They were great people. I think of them with a lot of sentiment.

PLAYBOY: How did you think you might be useful to them?

POLANSKI: I thought maybe there would be some minute clue they had overlooked. And I thought I could think of people, people who had come to our house, for instance, who wouldn't occur to the police. The press was writing so much about Jay and Voyteck being the probable motives, or essential persons, that I finally started to believe there could be someone I didn't know about. So I tried to establish step by step what everybody who knew us was doing at the time. It was quite difficult without seeming too obvious, and I didn't want anyone to know I was in constant touch with the police. I never believed it was some drug supplier of Jay's. I thought it was the work of some insane person, terribly jealous of one of us for some reason, but I couldn't give myself any plausible answer. I just kept listening and looking.

It's very difficult for me to talk about it. There are things I'm not sure we should even talk about. I was under this tremendous illusion that by solving the crime, it would be easier on me, somehow. Only after months did I understand that I was just chasing rabbits, running around in circles, that finding the murderers wouldn't bring her back. And I had to explain this to Sharon's parents, who I felt were under the same illusion. Colonel Tate, Sharon's father, was also seeing the police every day, for the same reasons I was. Thank God, Sharon's parents never allowed themselves to believe the trash the press was printing about us.

PLAYBOY: You never felt the Tates somehow blamed you?

POLANSKI: No. They were with me all the time. They knew the people who were our friends and they knew the press was lying about the way we lived.

PLAYBOY: As it turned out, did you do anything during the investigation that now seems to have been helpful?

POLANSKI: How could I? No one I knew had anything to do with it. I remember, at the very beginning, Lieutenant Bob Helder told me about this group of hippies living at that ranch with this guy they called Jesus Christ. Bob said they were suspected of being involved in the killing of some musician and writing a note on his body, and there was a possibility that these people had something to do with it. I said, "Come on, Bob, you're prejudiced against hippies." And I remember his words: "You should suspect everyone. Don't dismiss it so easily." But I didn't think much about it, because I could see *no* connection and I had nothing instinctively against them as hippies. The hippies, with their "Make love, not war" philosophy, were sympathetic figures to me.

PLAYBOY: Before you knew who was guilty for the murder, didn't you fear for your own life?

POLANSKI: In such a state, you don't give a damn for your own life. I was *hoping* that he, or they, would show up. I was living on the beach with a dear friend of mine, Dick Sylbert, the art director of *Rosemary's Baby*. He was mother and father and brother—I won't say wife—to me for three months, with me being constantly preoccupied. Poor guy. The neighbors were all up in arms about me being there. They believed what they read in the papers and thought they might have a scandal, or a murder, in their neighborhood. But I was prepared to defend myself if anything happened.

PLAYBOY: Were you carrying a gun?

POLANSKI: I asked the police and they said I shouldn't, because if something happened and I used a weapon, there would be all sorts of trouble. I didn't really want a gun anyway. I felt I could take care of myself; and anyway, it didn't matter, because I was obsessed with finding who was responsible. Then suddenly, when the police announced to the press that they had the murderers, the press had to somehow pretend they had known it was something like this all along, something totally unconnected with us and with my films, and I remembered the policemen laughing sarcastically about how the press had now decided that the victims were not actually the guilty ones after all. Suddenly, it was obvious to them that it had been a bunch of crazy hippies, and people like Mr. Elke Sommer promptly forgot that he "saw the murder coming." The victims were now dismissed within 24 hours and new things started appearing—phony interviews with me and quotes that I was "overjoyed" at the news. That word hardly describes my emotions. But at that moment, a strange thing happened to me: I was relieved. I lost all interest in what was going to happen.

PLAYBOY: Why?

POLANSKI: I finally realized that the only way to get over it was to dismiss it completely, and also I knew I couldn't change anything. It's like the only way to cope with the stress was to dismiss everything, to erase that part of the tape from my memory bank. It just disappeared in my head. I had no reason to follow what the press said about Manson, because I had no reason to believe they would be any more accurate about him than they were about Sharon and me, so I didn't read at all about him. All that I do know about Manson I knew from the police in those days before they broke the news to the press. For my own good, I completely ignored him and that trial, particularly because the press made a real circus out of it. The way they handled it was as deplorable as the way they handled the reporting of the murders. Before you ask how I know if I didn't read about it, I'll tell you: There are headlines you can't avoid, and the radio. You can't *escape* knowing certain things. I can't reconstruct the trial period for you at all, but I suspect that the ritualistic element of the crazy sect was grossly exaggerated by the press and that the assassins willingly capitalized on that, being aware that this aura would give him more chance of publicity, which would render the trial more complicated.

PLAYBOY: What makes you suspect that?

POLANSKI: One of the policemen told me about one of Manson's friends being in jail—this was before the murders—and Manson was trying to get the money somewhere to bail him out, and they went to Terry Melcher, who had been renting the house before we moved in. I don't know the details and I don't even know if this was ever brought up at the trial, but in any case, I think they were after money that night, and Manson was clever enough to know that if money came to be viewed as the motive, he wouldn't seem such a mystifying figure, because materialistic motives are always regarded as more easily understandable, and therefore dismissed, than any kind of ideological motives. Even if the ideological motives are pure evil, people will pay much more attention to them than to robbery by an ordinary criminal, because then they have to contest the *ideology*. Manson knew if he was seen as a false god, not only would he get more attention but he would even force the middle-class hypocrites he hated so much to look at him more closely and compare his values with theirs. But his ideological, ritualistic motives for the murders were tremendously exaggerated.

PLAYBOY: From what you know of him, how would you analyze a man like Charles Manson?

POLANSKI: In any hippie area, you see sometimes an older guy, maybe even middle-aged, maybe with a fat stomach, who without the cover of hippiedom would only be a fat, perhaps pathetic man. But here he is with the long hair and wearing flowery shirts, and he seems to be an entirely different individual, and he enjoys the promiscuity of this type of life, and he becomes an attractive person to the hippies, who may be very naive and ignorant. Now, this guy is basically the same as he was in straight society, with all the same impulses and motivations he had developed there, whatever those may be, but he becomes a part of the hippies and masquerades as one of them. Christ, it's so difficult to explain what I mean. I'm not a verbalist. I express myself every way better than with words. I want to tell you a story that will perhaps explain what I mean.

PLAYBOY: Go ahead.

POLANSKI: When I was 16 in Poland, and tremendously interested in bicycle racing, I met a guy in his 20s, and I hung around with him a little bit and kind of liked him. He was what you would call now a groovy guy. He offered to sell me a racing bicycle for a very cheap price and I got greedy. I had this appointment to meet him in an old German bunker near the park, and I went down to meet him and he got me alone and hit me on the head with a stone five times. I still have the scars on my scalp. I lost consciousness for a few seconds, and then I saw him standing above me asking where the money was. He took it and my watch and ran away. I couldn't understand why he had done that. A few minutes later, he was caught by some truck drivers, and a week later, the detectives came to the hospital to ask me for details. I said, "Will he get a long sentence?" They laughed at me. "He's going to be hanged," one of them said. "He killed three people before this."

It was the first time I was acquainted with this type of individual. People seem to dismiss the fact that Manson had a criminal track record, too. He spent a great deal of his life in prison. He had a record long before he tried to be a hippie. This man who hit me with the stone was another Manson, only Manson was lucky to live in a period when certain attributes are considered virtues: He could wear long hair and a beard for his hippie masquerade, while preaching a philosophy that was basically criminal. This other guy, who was trying to murder me, he was just a murderer, and no one would view him as anything but a criminal. No one would have mistaken *him* for a Jesus.

PLAYBOY: You mentioned earlier that the hippies were sympathetic figures for you. Are they still?

POLANSKI: Remember the first be-ins in Central Park, when they would throw flowers at the policemen? How blameless. I think these people were sincere at that time. But the hippies don't really exist anymore. The hippie movement has degenerated, but the degeneration came from the top, not from the bottom. When the kids began preaching new values, the government tried to beat their ideas out of them. The reaction, from Berkeley on, was only what you could expect: violence.

PLAYBOY: Critics feel that drugs were an integral part of the hippie philosophy and a principal reason for the psychological degeneration of some of them, including the girls who carried out Manson's orders.

POLANSKI: I don't have a professional knowledge about drugs to say anything really sound about it, but I do know that marijuana and the other hallucinogenic drugs are rather a source of indolence. They are dropout drugs. They make people passive. In this respect, you could say that these drugs make people more easily influenced; but, on the other hand, they would not incite you to take any action, any active enterprise, and they are certainly not murderous drugs. You know what marijuana does to people: They want to lay about and do nothing, smile and listen to music. So you have to decide which way you want it. You can't blame these drugs for making people indolent and also for inciting them to violent crime.

PLAYBOY: But weren't hallucinogenic drugs a part of the whole pathology that turned Manson from a common criminal into a Jesus Christ figure in the eyes of his followers—a pathology that would require a certain passivity on the part of those being manipulated?

POLANSKI: I think definitely that the people who are submitted to this kind of life are more vulnerable than regular members of society; but whatever the drugs do, they don't make you lose the ability to distinguish between right and wrong. Do you think you could commit a murder under the influence of drugs?

PLAYBOY: No. But we're talking now about those emotionally crippled young girls who, without exposure to a cult of mind-bending drugs, slavelike promiscuity and the rituals of a would-be Jesus Christ, would almost certainly never have been galvanized into committing murder.

POLANSKI: Don't forget that certain individuals have a talent to draw masses behind them. Hitler did the same thing with normal, straight, square German society.

PLAYBOY: Even given the historical fact of Hitler, aren't you willing to admit that drugs, which you accept or at least defend, played some role in what happened?

POLANSKI: No. Which drugs? I think there is nothing wrong with marijuana. There are millions of people smoking pot, but there is no parallel of Manson's story within any other group of people that I could speak of. I can think of more similarities between Manson and *In Cold Blood* than with the pot smokers of this world. People are just looking for an easy excuse, an easy explanation for the murders. Personally, I don't think it had anything to do with smoking marijuana.

PLAYBOY: What about LSD?

POLANSKI: I have never endorsed LSD. I took about three trips on acid several years ago, and they were all bad and I swore off. But that's still an answer that's too easy. How about those people in West Pakistan, who maybe in their ordinary lives were just quiet peasants or office clerks before they were sent off with the army on its binges of murder? How about the German soldier committing atrocities during the war, who might have been an ordinary man with a family and children? Were these people under the influence of LSD? How about Charles Whitman and Richard Speck? How about Lieutenant Calley? He seems to me a very straight person by conventional standards. I just think that certain people need very little excuse to commit criminal acts, and maybe the drugs were an excuse for Manson and these girls to vent their murderous instincts.

PLAYBOY: How did you react to the death sentences they received?

POLANSKI: In principle, I'm against capital punishment. I think the world would be a better place if it were abolished. I don't think capital punishment is moral, because we should not presume to terminate somebody's life.

PLAYBOY: Then you oppose the sentences?

POLANSKI: You're asking a very difficult question. A very difficult question. Because I really don't know. I feel very often a need for revenge. I suspect revenge may be one of the most important motives in human progress and in seeking justice. But it remains to be determined how the revenge should be performed. If the criminal kills eight people and is captured and tried, is it moral or immoral to take his life? I think it's immoral. Capital punishment is just another brutalizing aspect of modern life.

I don't know if I'm being clear. If you ask me should there be capital punishment, I say no. But if you ask me about a particular case of someone who engineered a murder—and remember, my emotional state is involved—in a jurisdiction where capital punishment exists within the system in which he was judged, then I would say to give him anything less than the maximum that exists is immoral. Who should be given more? I think Manson did the utmost, and within the set of rules that exists, he should be given the utmost sentence. He committed his crime while capital punishment was still the maximum sentence that could be handed out in California. At one point, I was asked to make the gesture of asking for clemency for him and I said I wouldn't do that. I think that would be an act of hypocrisy on my part; but I do ask for abolition of capital punishment for everyone, not just for Manson.

PLAYBOY: Was it an act of hypocrisy for Ted Kennedy to ask clemency for Sirhan Sirhan?

POLANSKI: Yes, I think so. That's precisely what I was thinking of when I said I wouldn't be willing to do that. I wouldn't be against siding with Ted Kennedy, saying that we are against capital punishment as part of the system of law. But I think it's phony nobility to go to bat, as it were, for your "pet" murderer, the one who caused *you* so much suffering.

PLAYBOY: You said earlier that your experiences during the war had taught you that family ties end in tragedy. After a little more than two years since the murders, do you feel they were yet another lesson that one's happiness will always be snatched away?

POLANSKI: You mention the word lesson. Unfortunately, there is no lesson to be taken. There is just nothing. It's absolutely senseless, stupid, cruel and insane. I'm not sure it's even worth talking about. Sharon and the others are dead. I can't restore what was.

PLAYBOY: But has the experience changed your vision of life?

POLANSKI: I don't know. I wouldn't call myself a fatalist, because those are people who just sit and wait for whatever will happen to them, and I'm not like that. I have always been sentimental and not a cynic, and that hasn't changed, but these are wounds that don't leave you without scars. I think I was probably a better human being before. It's difficult to define, but I think I was more gentle with people before. I don't think my emotional state now would permit me to develop serious new emotional ties with anybody.

PLAYBOY: Understandable, yet you appear to have feeling for, and ties with, those around you.

POLANSKI: You don't change your character drastically. It's only a note that changes. There was more youth in my feeling for people, more naïveté. I don't even know if the change is visible to my friends. I think it is.

PLAYBOY: Yet you give the impression of having adjusted. You seem a happy enough man.

POLANSKI: How could you even suspect me of such a thing? How could I be happy? There must be something that *makes* you happy.

PLAYBOY: You seem to enjoy your friends, and your women, and your work.

POLANSKI: These are things that give me pleasure, even make me content. But there's nothing that really makes me *happy*. Not anymore.

PLAYBOY: Then what keeps you going?

POLANSKI: I'm asking myself that question. What is it in the human being that makes him overcome practically everything and keep going? I don't know. There are endless people with tragedies more atrocious than mine, and they keep plowing away, too. After a period of mourning, they somehow restore their way of life. But I tell you, I know myself and I feel there's something gone. I don't have the same desires, the same dreams I used to have. I don't know why. It's something that's troubled me for quite some time now. It must be connected somehow with the death of Sharon, but also I think it's partly the fact that I have already achieved what I always dreamed of.

PLAYBOY: You mean that having achieved major success as a filmmaker, you're not as driven as you once were?

POLANSKI: Precisely. Throughout the years, my basic engine was the desire to make films. I dreamed of doing films, and somehow I don't feel this overpowering urge anymore. I first noticed the symptoms of my loss of enthusiasm when I went to Hollywood to make *Rosemary's Baby*. The first day I went onstage with 70 people waiting for me, I remembered the day I had first gone on location to shoot *Knife in the Water*. Then, I'd had butterflies in my stomach and that incredible feeling of anticipation that prevents you from going to sleep the whole night before. Now, here I was in Hollywood, in the place that belonged more to my dreams than to my reality, at the threshold of where everything would be handed to me, and I felt absolutely no thrill. I felt I was just going to work for the day—work I loved doing, but there was no *thrill* in it. Do you understand?

PLAYBOY: Yes. But how, then, did you turn in your best work? Or did you?

POLANSKI: I did a good job, but not my best work. Maybe it's just pride in craft. Maybe that is the way to achieve the maximum in what you do. I care about what I make. It's a dear thing to me and I think it remains so because it's a part of human nature to want to do something durable. Who was the Pharaoh who built the biggest of the pyramids? He must have been quite persistent, making these people put one stone on top of another for years in order to create something that would last. I'm quite persistent myself, only lately I am asking myself sometimes: "Why bother?" Maybe it's just that I am more sure of myself and my abilities. Maybe that's it. Or maybe I'm just more relaxed. But, on the other hand, a cow is relaxed. Maybe I should ask some maharishi. Maybe he would tell me that I have become wiser. I would have to become wiser, but I think that, in a way, that's what has happened.

PLAYBOY: Why do you resist wisdom?

POLANSKI: Because wise people are boring and they usually lack the enthusiasm and spontaneity to make things come together. I'm afraid it's inevitable that the more experience you acquire, the more you lose your desires, your dreams, your fantasies. It's the same thing in sex. I just don't enjoy it as much as I used to. It's getting a bit repetitious. It's very much like making films; your wisdom and security and experience bring your craft up to a high standard, but you get less thrill out of it as an individual.

PLAYBOY: Maybe your ordained role is to serve as a craftsman, bringing pleasure to moviegoers and women.

POLANSKI: I like that idea. I wish it were true. They say that happiness is seeking the fulfillment of our desires, and usually people spend their lives seeking that fulfillment. But I am at a stage where I'm seeking the *desires*. Have you got any ideas? Help me. Tell me what is the problem here. If not for the sake of the interview, then at least maybe I'll get something out of it.

PLAYBOY: Perhaps you're just suffering from the onset of middle age.

POLANSKI: I do start feeling that now, and I'm very surprised, because I thought it would never happen. Being a born optimist, who never thinks he's going to fail in anything he undertakes, I'm caught off guard by it. But I don't think it's going to last long. It's just a passing stage that will go away as I grow younger.

PLAYBOY: In the meantime, you seem to be doing a successful, if not inspired, job of living the life of what you would call a hedonist.

POLANSKI: I don't know whether I'm a hedonist. It's just my reputation. If I am, I work harder than any other hedonist I've ever met. I'm quite spartan in some ways. I get up early, I exercise to keep myself in shape; I rather like the Boy Scout, sportive way of life. Yet I do love everything life has to offer; so I don't reject luxury if I can afford it, and I don't reject any source of joy that you can acquaint yourself with in your lifetime—particularly sex.

PLAYBOY: Would one be correct to attribute your refusal to deny yourself any of life's luxuries or pleasures to your childhood during the war, when you were deprived of them?

POLANSKI: No. What if I had had a marvelous childhood with rows of lackeys and nannies bringing me hot chocolate and chauffeurs driving me to the cinema? Then you would say I am this way because I *had* such a luxurious childhood. The truth is I am just this way. Period. But I will tell you, I did have sexual problems as a youth.

PLAYBOY: What kind?

POLANSKI: I had an absolute patent on masturbation when I was 12. I thought I invented it. But it made me feel terrifically guilty, and each time I was doing it, I was promising myself it was the last time, definitely the last time I was touching it. Until the next morning. I didn't make it with a chick until I was 17 and a half, which I think is very late.

PLAYBOY: According to the press, you've certainly made up for lost time ever since.

POLANSKI: I found out I like sex. How about that? I like fucking. You remember Kafka's story about the man who fasts professionally in a circus? He was breaking his own records, fasting longer and longer, and finally he fasts so long that everybody forgets all about him. They even forget to mark on his little blackboard the number of days of his fast, which already was incredible. Finally, a cleaning man comes and finds him agonizing under a pile of straw, and he leans down and asks, "Why did you do it? Why?" And with his dry lips and his fading voice, the faster says, "I hated food!" It's beautiful. There was no other reason for fasting. I'm the opposite. I screw because I like screwing. That's all there is to it.

PLAYBOY: Do you concern yourself with the moral issues involved with sex?

POLANSKI: Of course. I don't want to sound pompous, but in a way, I'm actually a moralist. I cherish certain qualities of a civilized mind, qualities that are very difficult to measure or describe, because they have quite flimsy names like nobility, loyalty, etc. This applies, for instance, to my friends. Friendship to me is a very Sicilian thing. It's a matter of life and death. I would do absolutely anything for my friends, and I demand the same in return. Because friendship is a form of love. I separate love from sex. For many people, fornication is immoral. Strangely enough, it seems supremely moral to me to have sex with a girl I've met in the harbor at St.-Tropez. Sex is beautiful. No one gets hurt. Just the opposite. It's simple, isn't it? So if it's true that I'm a playboy, it's only in this respect. The rest of being a playboy doesn't have much attraction for me.

PLAYBOY: Does it ever bother you that some people are more interested in your image as a playboy than in your films?

POLANSKI: I think it's great.

PLAYBOY: Wouldn't you rather be known as a film director whose personal life is of little curiosity?

POLANSKI: Do you mean like Walt Disney? My only disappointment is that people created this conception of me as a decadent man of excess without my active participation. In the beginning, I resented it, but finally I thought, so what? People never know the truth about an individual, anyway. Among all the movies I've seen, I like *Citizen Kane* the most, not only for the way it's done but for what it says. It says that you never know the real truth about anyone. So who cares? This image of a hard worker laboring all day doesn't go well with me. It doesn't help me in my social life. People would get bored with me if I told them. "Hey, listen, guys, I really work very hard. I get up at seven in the morning and I rush from one place to another on business and I don't have a spare minute to take a holiday." I only tell people I'm a busy man when I want to get rid of them. Like a *Playboy* interviewer, you understand? Otherwise, I prefer to seem frivolous, a guy who socializes all the time. For one thing, I realized that this reputation helps me in my relations with women. I've noticed that as my reputation grows worse, my success with women increases.

PLAYBOY: How do you account for this?

POLANSKI: When I meet a new girl, she's already prejudiced against me. She's put off by my image and she thinks, "I'll never make it with *him*!" She wants to prove something to herself. She doesn't want to lower herself to the level of, let's say, her predecessors. But she's intrigued and she wants to know me as an individual, and underneath there is something difficult to describe—a kind of curiosity about me. People are intrigued by the devil and attracted when they discover that on top of having horns and a tail, he's also charming. So you see, she meets me and she's tremendously surprised that I'm not at all the way she thought I was, and already she begins to switch her attitude. She's thrown off guard. I know all this talk about women sounds pretentious and arrogant and megalomaniac. Jesus, it begins to sound that way even to *me*.

PLAYBOY: *Are* you a megalomaniac?

POLANSKI: Of course. Haven't you noticed? But I do have some good qualities.

PLAYBOY: Such as?

POLANSKI: I don't smoke tobacco. In fact, I am more admirable than our friend Doug Rader, the Houston Astros' third baseman, who says he is better at smoking than anything else. "I smoke good and I smoke consistent," he says.

PLAYBOY: What have you got against smokers?

POLANSKI: They don't bother me if they want to ruin their own health. It's their problem, and I'm not one to force the issue, but what bothers me is that they stick their cigarette butts *everywhere*. You find them in the washbasin, in the toilet, all over the house, in the backyard, burns in the curtains, the smell of smoke in your own hair. They take some perverted pleasure in uglifying their own closest surroundings by sticking these butts even into their food—into eggshells, in the cucumbers, in the mashed potatoes, in the half-empty bottle of beer, everywhere. Sometimes I'm afraid to screw.

PLAYBOY: Sorry we asked. So much for smokers. Let's get back to women. Kenneth Tynan, your friend and co-writer of the screenplay for *Macbeth*, implied in a recent article that your attitude toward women approaches the feudalistic.

POLANSKI: Ken, who is a good friend, knows absolutely nothing about my emotional-sexual relationships with women. He is a left-wing intellectual who feels he must support liberation movements, including the one by women, so I very often tease him by saying something about how reactionary I am on the subject. This causes complete outrage on his part, so you shouldn't treat seriously what Ken says about my feelings toward women.

PLAYBOY: In what way are you reactionary about them?

POLANSKI: Well, you must admit that most women one meets do not have the brain of Einstein. I have a very firm theory about male and female intelligence. It causes an absolute outrage if you say that women on the average are less intelligent than men, but it happens to be true.

Since society is becoming more and more democratic about these things, though, we'd better not mention that.

PLAYBOY: That's a highly debatable allegation, but in any case, Tynan wrote that you also dislike *bright* women. His exact words, as we recall, were that Polanski feels the only two acceptable positions for a woman are sitting down and lying down.

POLANSKI: That's a marvelous line, but it's complete crap. First of all, my wife, although people may not know it, was an extremely bright person. But she would never be pushy about her intelligence in order to show people how clever she was. She knew it's feminine to not try to *compete* with men and seem dominating. But I must admit that I rarely find an intelligent female companion with whom I can get along, for the reason that most women who are smart try to compete with the man, and I can't stand the competition of a female.

PLAYBOY: Why?

POLANSKI: Because that brings our relationship onto the wrong level. It becomes like between a man and a man, a masculine relationship. I'm too sensitive about a woman's behavior, and there are too many things that can put me off. Sometimes the most beautiful woman can put me off completely by doing something ungraceful. I'm certain, by the way, that a sensitive woman feels the same toward men. I think even more so. Sometimes I'm charmed by the fact that there are women with whom you can discuss the molecular theory of light all evening and at the end, they will ask you what is your birth sign. But there is nothing more enjoyable than a genuinely brilliant female companion who doesn't turn the relationship into a contest of ego.

PLAYBOY: In short, you simply prefer to dominate them.

POLANSKI: I *do* dominate them. And they like it! I know, I know, this is regarded today as a Neanderthal attitude. But I know one women's lib leader who, friends tell me, is a great cocksucker. By the way, what exactly is the women's lib position on fellatio? That it's OK, but only on an equal-time basis? And why do women sometimes use words like, "He's a *real* man"? It doesn't mean that he knits well or that he looks after the kids well. It has always meant a man who is more creative, more aggressive than a woman, because these are the qualities that have always been essential for the survival of our kind.

PLAYBOY: Is there anything about women's lib with which you would agree?

POLANSKI: Anyone with a civilized mind endorsed the concept of equal pay for equal results long before women's lib, and I endorse that concept.

The problem is that women's lib wants equal pay for equal *work*. What if the results are not the same? What if the man is better at the job? He should be paid more. And vice versa. On abortion, however, I agree absolutely with women's lib. They *should* have control of their own bodies. That's obvious. But I have noticed that many of these women who want to control their own bodies don't even *like* their bodies. They are women who don't like being women. Or at least they don't like being feminine.

The basic premise of women's liberation is that they are in some kind of slavery or subservient position. Even the name of the movement implies they are enslaved. Well, this premise sounds quite absurd to me, because sex isn't a social class; it divides humanity horizontally, not vertically. A woman proletarian can become a woman capitalist, but a proletarian woman cannot become a proletarian man. The women's libbers argue that they weren't given equal opportunities, but what I want to know is what were they doing when the opportunities were given? Were they just passed out one fine day? Or did it happen that men have dominated women for centuries because they were superior in the areas necessary to dominate the other sex? It isn't by accident that we are called Homo sapiens. If you look at the history of our species through science, you realize that in order to survive, we had to divide into two parts, one that brings the offspring, the other that brings the means of survival. And once the functions were divided, it was inevitable that the abilities would come to be divided, and I see this as the source of the differences.

PLAYBOY: Women's lib theorists would maintain that the social structure of prehistoric man is hardly relevant anymore, since times and sex roles have changed along with the nature of society.

POLANSKI: I think men and women are still and will always be fundamentally different, even though they belong to the same species. Just *look* at men and women: They are physically different, their organs are different, their muscles are different, their behavior—even as infants—is different. How can their brains also not be different? If you saw another species in which the female role was one of strong dependence, you wouldn't say that something was wrong with the species, would you? If you observed the female spider eat the male after copulation, you wouldn't say there was something fundamentally unjust about that species. That's the nature of some spiders. You wouldn't try to "improve" their relationship. Somewhere along the line, it became necessary for their survival to evolve this way. It is a built-in characteristic.

PLAYBOY: Some readers may be concluding that Tynan was right about your feudalism on the subject.

POLANSKI: Listen, in many ways, I'm more progressive than a lot of liberal intellectuals. I give women complete freedom to come and go as they please, and I don't make them do anything they don't want to do. I want it to be clear that even though I don't say all the things I know I'm supposed to about this subject, I'm in some ways a greater admirer of women than those who do. I love women! I really *love* them. As people, I hasten to add, not as playthings.

PLAYBOY: Does it frustrate you, or offend your male ego, when you meet a woman you want who seems to take no interest in you? Or has that ever happened?

POLANSKI: Once, I think, it happened, many years ago. No, it doesn't bother me at all, as long as she doesn't try to play games with me.

PLAYBOY: For example.

POLANSKI: To give examples, for me, is more or less like the effort of writing a screenplay. I have to sit and think, but if I were doing a screenplay, people would pay me for it.

PLAYBOY: No deal. You were talking about games people play.

POLANSKI: Let's say I meet a girl and she tries to give me the impression that she desires to go to bed with me that same evening, although I can sense immediately that it's not her intention. That's what I call games, and it lasts about 10 minutes. Then I simply lose interest. I don't mind if she doesn't want to have sexual relations with me. Here you must believe me, because most males say that. But I really *don't* mind as long as she states it clearly by her behavior.

PLAYBOY: Why do you see yourself as different from most males in that regard?

POLANSKI: Because I can't demand every female to want me. I'm just being realistic about it. Or maybe it's because enough of them *do* want me that I don't feel rejected in general.

PLAYBOY: When you tell people things like that, do they consider it arrogant?

POLANSKI: Certainly. But it's really just a kind of optimism, a belief in yourself, which in itself seems an arrogance to many people because of this code of behavior in our society that demands you to be humble. Boasting about your abilities makes you regarded as an arrogant individual, like Cassius Clay, when he was running and screaming, "Float like a butterfly, sting like a bee," and saying that he was the greatest, the fastest, etc. But this is essential to success, at least in certain endeavors, like filmmaking or seduction. It's like a war. It's necessary when you attack to be convinced that you're going to take the town, to be convinced that you're superior to the foe and that food and drink and women are in the town. It's inconceivable to take the town when your commanding officer tells you that you *may* take it, but then again, you may not, and even if you do, you may have to go on to the next town before you find something to eat. So, especially when I'm making a film, I have to prepare myself for victory.

PLAYBOY: How do you do that?

POLANSKI: I run around shouting, "Float like a butterfly, sting like a bee." Unfortunately, I end up different not only to the people I work with but to my friends as well. I don't think I could do it any other way. I go through a complete state of mental preparation. It's not a deliberate thing, as though I said, "OK, now I change myself." It's automatic, and the moment I start a film, I develop this certainty in myself. I boost my ego. I warm myself up by telling myself that I'm the best, the most talented, the genius of filmmaking. I believe the film is going to be a success, and this changes my attitude toward people. I ask of them things I would never ask otherwise. It projects to all areas of my life—"Do this, give me that." And I've learned that it must be said without the slightest hesitation in your attitude, or they won't put up with it. They'll tell you, "Go fuck yourself."

The problem with this is that it's impossible to shift gears twice a day, at eight-thirty A.M. and at seven-thirty in the evening, when you leave the set, so it's an attitude I must live with for a year or more at a time, and when I finish a film and I have to become normal again, the withdrawal symptoms are painful, and I'm undergoing them right now. People are starting to hate me by this time. Toward the end of the film, I have so many enemies that I consider whether I should flee the country. But this ballsiness that everybody is accusing you of is necessary to deflect all the vicious attacks that people will make on your film, from its start to its finish. If you're in a normal state of mind, you may find yourself yielding, so you have to make yourself psychologically invulnerable. If I've learned one thing about filmmaking, it's that it requires not only talent but the stamina to resist all these attackers.

PLAYBOY: Who are all these attackers?

POLANSKI: Everybody. The actors have their own ideas of what their parts are about, the prop man has his own problems, the producers have their financial statements to worry about. Then comes the interviewer, who wants you to sit around and answer questions like this, and you're in the middle of these vicious, inhuman attacks, sometimes for a year. They all say that you're a stubborn, narrow-minded bastard who doesn't accept any criticism. They're right. I already told you I'm a megalomaniac. You have to be one to make a good film, because you have to believe that whatever decision you make, you're right. Even if I'm wrong, I'm right! Because it's my film. And the decision has to be mine. When a painter is painting a picture, whatever he does, it's *his* picture. You can like it or not, but you can't stand behind him saying, "No, you shouldn't make this stroke like that. Make it a little more to the left and put some red in it."

You must understand: You have a certain goal when you make a movie. The goal is to materialize your idea of the film, which is somewhere visualized in your mind. At that moment, it's the cinema of one person, and I'm the only one who knows how to bring this vision into reality. If you allow yourself to be vulnerable to what these people suggest, the movie will end up as a mongrel, or you'll simply abandon it and drop out with an ulcer. Both these solutions are not in my character. I'm afraid I have rather a shark's character in that sense. When it grabs something, there ain't no going back. Incidentally, the shark is one of the oldest species on earth and most perfectly suited to survival: all teeth and no brains. That's why, when all of these people transform themselves into obstacles, I don't let them interfere with the route I'm taking. I can't.

PLAYBOY: But surely some of these people have good ideas, perhaps worth listening to and incorporating into the film.

POLANSKI: It's very difficult to be so narrow-minded as to stick to your own ideas and at the same time to be an objective critic of your own work. This doesn't mean that I don't accept criticism. Often I listen to somebody and it occurs to me that he's right, and I accept the criticism, but I accept it because I think it's right, because his criticism improves the film by *my* standards, not by anybody else's.

I really think that people seriously suspect there is an element of malice in the way I insist on everything being done exactly the way I want it; but if there were malice, I can assure you, it would be an acute case of masochism, because nobody suffers more than the director in his struggle to get what he wants. Often you know that something is not as it should be. You can't put your finger on it; you just know there is something missing in a scene, often a tiny detail, but you know it's wrong and won't fit with the entirety of the movie. Yet the people around you can't understand why you keep repeating a scene, making more and more takes. Sometimes, at the 15th take, they start getting a bit irritated and nervous. I don't want to tell you what happens when you get to 55 takes.

PLAYBOY: When did that happen?

POLANSKI: It's happened to me on, well, I think several occasions. It's not that I'm cavalier at other people's expense. The reason for it is that some scenes turn out with better potential than I had anticipated, and that causes them to be more expensive. Say you need to film a brief insert of a cigarette held between a man's fingers. Some directors would stick a cigarette between a man's fingers and film it, and that would be that, and this would take a few minutes. But maybe the shot could be made more interesting if the cigarette had a long piece of ash that fell at the right moment, and you could see the smoke better if you lit the scene differently, and maybe there is a table in the background, and maybe you could get something to happen at that table—a woman's hand toying with a glass—and maybe there is a piece of floor visible behind that hand, with maybe a dog playing on it. Both these things, the woman's hand and the dog, the goddamn dog, may be connected with the rest of the action and make it more interesting. You can increase the tension by having all these things happen within the one second, or one and a half feet of film, of that insert. But the odds are that these will not all coincide on the first 50 takes, so the scene is much more involved and time-consuming. And who foots the tab? Hefner! Everyone says what a perfectionist I am, but I'm not a perfectionist. I just demand the minimum. You know what I mean?

PLAYBOY: This minimalism of yours always seems to take you unnervingly over budget.

POLANSKI: Billy Wilder once said, "Did you ever hear of someone saying, 'Let's go to the Roxy. They're playing a movie that was made within its schedule.'?" The Polish proverb is: "The better you make your bed, the longer you sleep." There's something in my character that appears to all my financiers as something bad—which is that I care. Whereas some other directors, the ones who give up and yield to these attacks, do not care. The other guys who make good films, as God is my witness, go over budget as much as I do. Only they don't feel bad about it. With me, it's a trauma. I don't sleep, I'm sick, I'm tired, I'm a nervous wreck. You should ask my friends, because what I'm saying is maybe not plausible, as I have a reputation as a nut case, anyway, but ask people who work with me. I wish I could say I *don't* give a damn, but I can't. I just refuse to maim my films. The pressure I had on *Rosemary's Baby* was so tremendous that I had my usual dilemma about whether to get it over with and produce something mediocre or to withstand the pressure and produce something very good.

PLAYBOY: Tell us about it.

POLANSKI: Bob Evans, the creative head of Paramount, and Bernie Donnenfeld, who ran the business end of their productions, were receiving unbelievable heat from New York, where they were all panicky. In corporate headquarters, they didn't know what was going on and they couldn't understand what the film was all about, anyway. Already, they were up to their tonsils in bills, and then suddenly they realized it was getting up to their eyeballs, so they had Bob and Bernie meet with me. Bernie said, "Listen, Roman, we can't take it any longer. The rushes are terrific, we couldn't be more pleased, Mia is doing a fantastic job, it's going to be a great film—but what can we do to go faster?" And I said, "You think *you* can't take it? I can't either. Let's not talk about it anymore. You want me to go faster? OK, I go faster. I know how to finish the last fourth of the script in about three days. If you go onto the back lot, they're shooting a television series, and if you watch for just 15 minutes, you'll realize how easy it is to go fast. I know how they do it. They say, 'OK, guys. Set it up. Lights. Act fast. One take. In the can.' We can do a whole bunch of scenes every day that way. Then what do you do with it when it's finished?" At that point, Bob turned to Bernie and said. "We're masturbating." He said, "Roman, why don't you go back onstage and do what you've been doing? Just make a good movie." And that was the last time we talked about it. He stuck his neck out for me and showed himself to have quite a courage. You know, when they all scream "Faster, faster," it reminds me of the story about the guy who comes to a resort for a weekend and wants to seduce this girl he's dancing with. He says, "Miss, I don't have much time. I only came for the weekend." And she says, "Well, I'm dancing as fast as I can."

PLAYBOY: As Tynan tells the story, you brazened out an episode during the filming of *Macbeth* when the English insurance company was ready to jerk you for being so slow. What would you have done if they had shut you down?

POLANSKI: I would go home. I thought you were going to ask me what if the picture had not been good as a result.

PLAYBOY: OK, what if it hadn't been good, as a result?

POLANSKI: It's as if you were asking Christopher Columbus what if there hadn't been land after flogging and starving all those seamen who were afraid of falling off the end of the world. What kind of question is this?

PLAYBOY: You make up your own question, put it in our mouth and then complain because we ask it.

POLANSKI: You know how to do an interview. I don't. To express my ideas about life is not my profession. I'm a dilettante at it, so it's not easy for me. I've never given a good interview in my life, although I did literally hundreds of them before I learned how simple it is to say no to most of them. As I told you before—but you won't listen—I'm not a verbalist. I never was and never will be. I never tried to develop my speech, and the way I communicate is rather by suggesting something, some atmosphere, some feeling. I've always had rather visual and graphic talents, and it was these that I developed. I don't speak well, although when I'm with friends and there is an animated conversation, I have no difficulty in conveying my argument, you know, by gestures and mimicry.

But you asked what would I do if they had thrown me off *Macbeth*. I would have made another movie. There are people who know how to run corporations and others who know how to make films. I am one of the latter. If they took a film away from me, I wouldn't be crushed, because I believe I could do dozens of others just as well or better, because when I do something good, it isn't a fluke. I don't think most people have any idea how much work and effort are being put into a film. You go to the cinema and see a film like *Macbeth* set in medieval times and you just assume that certain things were there all along. You're not aware that every single thing you see on that screen has been devised, starting with the actions of the characters, going through the costumes they wear, the set where they move about, the lights with which they're lit, the sound they produce, the music, the wind that whispers in the trees. Even the titles. And it's not just one long scene but hundreds of pieces stuck together and then printed in color.

Some directors, people with rather documentary or *Nouvelle Vague* or underground backgrounds, resent all these crews and equipment. I don't. I know how to deal with it. It's like one of those big yellow machines larger than bulldozers that look like gigantic insects and have this sort of claw that can fumble through tons of earth and pick up two little stones. When you watch one of those, you understand about filmmaking. I wouldn't know where is the end and the beginning of such a piece of machinery, but when you watch the operator who sits behind all those levers and with the utmost virtuosity and speed picks up these two little stones from tons of earth, you know how I feel running a movie machine. I know how to use this machinery to transform a vision of my own into a film. I know how to deal with the technical problems.

PLAYBOY: Tell us about them.

POLANSKI: More examples? All right: One of my favorite ones was that I always had great difficulties getting onto film exactly what I had seen through my view finder before the camera has been set up. I always had these problems with my camera operators. All directors who have firm visual, graphic views have these problems, but I had it especially bad. Besides explaining exactly what I had in mind and trying to convey it to the operator and get our ideas conformed, there was always something missing, and I couldn't find out what it was. Finally, on *Rosemary's Baby*, it was working very well and I realized this important detail: Besides this cameraman's willingness to understand me and follow my ideas, he was hardly any taller than I am. And then I understood: He was on the same altitude above sea level as I am. It's important that his camera sees exactly what I see. On *Macbeth*, you can know that I have a camera operator exactly my size, and that works wonders, because it means he sees the world the way I see the world.

PLAYBOY: Is there any larger, metaphorical point to that?

POLANSKI: I don't think of any, but you're a journalist, so I'm sure you would be able to make one.

PLAYBOY: Now why do you have to say that?

POLANSKI: Just a wisecrack, because people who write are usually inspired to think to metaphors on their own terms, not on the terms of the person telling the story. The fact that you asked if there is a metaphor implies that there is a strong possibility you will be inspired to find one.

PLAYBOY: All right, let's ask the question a different way. Is there anything of the Napoleonic about you—of the short man proving himself?

POLANSKI: My height must have some effect on me, but again, I don't psychoanalyze myself to discover it. I actually look smaller than I am. How tall do you think I am?

PLAYBOY: 5' 6"?

POLANSKI: Incredible! You are the first *ever* to give me extra height. I am 5' 5", which is a good size for a female. Maybe I should have been born a girl. Newsmen usually describe me as even shorter than I am. I barely reach four feet in these articles they write. Little do they know that from my point of view, it doesn't seem that I'm small. In fact, it seems to me as if I'm a giant. The terrible thing is that if people didn't tell me I was short, I would never notice. I once had this Yorkshire terrier, a wonderful little dog, and an Irish wolfhound—the largest dog in captivity—and the Yorkshire absolutely terrorized the wolfhound. I'm quite sure the terrier didn't realize he was smaller.

PLAYBOY: You're also something of a physical-fitness nut, with your exercises and karate kicks, and wheat germ and yogurt. How did that begin?

POLANSKI: One day when I was 14, I looked at myself in the mirror and I said to myself, "Jesus, what is this?" So I took a pillowcase and went down to where they were building a road and filled it up with cobblestones and started exercising. I wanted to make something of myself, so I wanted to be strong. At the same time, I started bicycle racing and skiing. Any kind of individual competition. I was totally uninterested in any kind of team effort like football. I like the drama and the glory of racers. They are individuals, and dreamers. To me, an appealing character is Jackie Stewart, because he has a lust for glory and he fulfills it.

You see sometimes men in their 20s who have let their bodies deteriorate, and they look like they're 40, and they look extremely tired and bored. These are the people who probably never had dreams they believed could be fulfilled. As a representative of a capitalist society, you must forgive me for quoting Lenin, but he said that the essential quality of a revolutionary is to be able to fantasize. To create revolution, you must be able to imagine its success. The same is true of films, and I was always dreaming of making great films.

PLAYBOY: When you were a boy, you mean?

POLANSKI: Yes. Even as a child, I always loved cinema and was thrilled when my parents would take me before the war. Then we were put into the ghetto in Kraków and there was no cinema, but the Germans often showed newsreels to the people outside the ghetto, on a screen in the marketplace. And there was one particular corner where you could see the screen through the barbed wire. I remember watching with fascination, although all they were showing was the German army and German tanks, with occasional anti-Jewish slogans inserted on cards. When I escaped from the ghetto, the first thing I looked forward to was the cinema. It was very cheap, since the Germans wanted people to go see German films, and I made the ticket money selling newspapers. It was regarded as something very low to go to the cinema, and the audience was mostly youngsters who weren't aware of their patriotic duty not to go. You could read slogans on the wall—Only Pigs Go To Movies, etc. But I didn't really care too much about being called a pig as long as I could go.

PLAYBOY: How do you explain this fascination?

POLANSKI: I don't know why, but I just loved it. Maybe the liking for cinema is no more mysterious than my liking for suspense; the show business and drama of cinema thrilled me as much as the purely technical aspect of *lanterna magica*—being able to project a picture on the wall and make it move.

PLAYBOY: How did you set about getting started in films?

POLANSKI: Right after the war, I got a job broadcasting on the radio as a child actor and, through that, I got a lead in a successful play in the theater. It was kind of a big splash for a kid. Later, I tried to get into acting school, but I didn't make it. Some of the professors were actors who knew me, and they thought I was too cocky. Already I was quite different from a majority of the applicants, who were scared and running around the corridors of the drama school with diarrhea and showing all the symptoms of submission and humility. I didn't have any of those symptoms, so they thought I wouldn't be good material to mold, and, thank God, I wasn't, because I would have ended up in some provincial theater in Poland making 2000 zlotys a month. At the time, I wasn't seeing much future in films, because my father ran a small plastics company, which the government considered "private initiative." That meant my political background was not the best, so the State School of Filming in Lodz seemed an impossible dream, because there was a tremendous number of applicants, and your political background was terribly important.

PLAYBOY: But you did get into Lodz, which had the reputation at that time of being probably the finest film school in the world. How did Poland, with a drab political regime and a poor economy, come to have such a school?

POLANSKI: I suspect that the school has lost its quality, but from a few years before I went until two or three years after I left, it was definitely the best film school in the world. I think it was just a happy conjunction of certain elements. There was a group of progressive, extremely talented filmmakers in Poland who were in terrible difficulties before the war, when Polish cinema was one of the lowest, producing only cheap exploitation films that took about four days to make. Some of these filmmakers went to the Soviet Union during the war to work on the propaganda films, which had a high priority, and when they came back they were asked by the government to start a center, because this was an industry that was needed by the government. Luckily, there is another line in Lenin saying that among all the arts, cinema is the most important for the Communist state. And since the Communist system clings to dogma, they gave big resources to these men to create an institute.

PLAYBOY: The curriculum at Lodz required five years for a diploma. Was it worthwhile to spend that much time studying instead of getting on-the-job training?

POLANSKI: When you analyze it, you see how advantageous it is to study cinema for five years. Besides all the practical training, like editing, camera operating, etc., you had courses in the history of art, literature, history of music, optics, theory of film directing—if such a thing exists—and so forth. The first year was very general and theoretical, and you got to know intimately the techniques of still photography, which is essential, I think, for anyone who later wants to be an expert in cinematography. The second year, the students made two one-minute films of their own. The third year, a documentary of eight to 15 minutes. The fourth year, a short fictional film of the same length; and then in the fifth year, you made your diploma film, which could go up to 20 minutes. Mine ran 25 minutes and was over budget; already they were screaming at me to dance faster. It was called *When Angels Fall*, a kind of fantasy about an old lady who is a public-toilet attendant. And on top of everything else at the school, we also saw an incredible number of films—and not only each other's.

PLAYBOY: Including films from the West?

POLANSKI: Almost anything. The school was tightly connected with the Polish film archives and we could see anything we wanted. An important part of our education was a baroque wooden stairway where we would sit for hours arguing about films, which sometimes we were screening all day and all night. Occasionally, the discussions became rather heated. In fact, I have a scar under my eye from one of them. There were schools of cinema within the school. My school was *Citizen Kane*, and the school of the older students, the ones who were about to graduate when I was a cocky beginner, was *The Bicycle Thief*, and the postgraduates who were still hanging around were the Soviet Socialist Realism school—films like *Potemkin*. It was a fantastic place and I left it with very firm aesthetic ideals about films.

PLAYBOY: Can you express them in words?

POLANSKI: I'll try. For me, a film has to have a definite dramatic and visual shape, as opposed to a rather flimsy shape that a lot of films were being given by the *Nouvelle Vague*, for example, which happened in more or less the same period. It has to be something finished, like a sculpture, almost something you can touch, that you can roll on the floor. It has to be rigorous and disciplined—that's *Citizen Kane* vs. *The Bicycle Thief*.

PLAYBOY: When did you make *Knife in the Water*?

POLANSKI: In 1960. But it took a long time. After we wrote the screenplay, it was rejected by the government film bureau, so I went to France, and when I came back two years later, it was a better period politically, so I submitted it again and they accepted it and gave me a very limited budget—which I went over, of course.

PLAYBOY: *Knife in the Water* was an original, and unusual, screenplay. Where did you get the idea for it?

POLANSKI: It was the sum of several desires in me. I loved the lake area of Poland and I thought it would make a great setting for a film. I was thinking of a film with a limited number of people in it as a form of challenge. I hadn't ever seen a film with only three characters, where no one else even appeared in the background. The challenge was to make it in a way that the audience wouldn't be aware of the fact that no one else had appeared even in the background. As for the idea, all I had in mind when I began the script was a scene where two men were on a sailboat and one fell overboard. But that was a starting point, wouldn't you agree?

PLAYBOY: Certainly, but a strange one. Why were you thinking about a man falling out of a sailboat?

POLANSKI: There you go, asking me to shrink my head again. I don't know why. I was interested in creating a mood, an atmosphere, and after the film came out, a lot of critics found all sorts of symbols and hidden meanings in it that I hadn't even thought of. It made me sick.

PLAYBOY: You went back to Paris and stayed on there for a couple of years—even after *Knife* had its big success in America. Why?

POLANSKI: The fact that the film was a success didn't make me in such great demand by American producers. But it did make me think that I should seek the Anglo-Saxon world rather than remain forever in France, where the film was a total flop. But those were good years in Paris. I was writing with my friend Gerard Brach, and we wrote *Repulsion* and *Cul-de-Sac* during this period, though we couldn't find anyone to produce them. In France, they aren't looking so much for new talent as for established figures. So Gerard and I were living in miserable conditions. I didn't make any money on *Knife in the Water* and we were penniless and living in little hotels and places like that. Once we were stuffed together in a broom-closet sort of room where in the 18th century, I think, they used to stash one domestic—because two wouldn't have fit. It was virtually a cupboard. But I think of those years with tremendous nostalgia. Whenever we got together 100 francs, we were as happy as kings. The first thing was to run to the cinema to see a movie. The second thing was to have dinner in one of the little restaurants of St. Germain des Prés. And the third thing was to try to pull some girls. Whenever I return to those cafés and see the same characters sitting at the same tables in the identical positions—only much older—I have a very mixed sensation, and these are moments of fear, because I think, "Christ, *I* could have been sitting here still."

PLAYBOY: Was it more difficult for you to "pull" the girls then, before you had celebrity as well as notoriety, not to mention money?

POLANSKI: It was much harder, not only because of the lack of notoriety but also because I didn't have the necessary experience. I wasn't so cool. I was too eager, and I think that's the case with every young man.

PLAYBOY: What made you decide to leave Paris and go to the U.S.?

POLANSKI: Events precipitated themselves suddenly. In late 1963, I was invited to the New York Film Festival, where *Knife in the Water* was being shown. The United States used to be a very popular country in Europe, so it was in my dreams to go there.

PLAYBOY: What was your first impression of New York?

POLANSKI: I had somehow imagined the streets of New York to be very wide, very clean, with a very even surface, and surrounded by bright, shiny buildings. I found it dense and dirty and not smooth at all. At the time, that felt familiar and stimulating. The theaters, the restaurants all seemed exciting, and a lot of the New York intellectuals, who didn't seem so left-wing and tiresome at the time, I found very exciting—maybe because I didn't speak a word of English. As you may have noticed, I still don't. I also found the constant competition—the rat race, you call it—very exciting. But now it's to an extreme that is unbearable. In those days, the rats were still eating each other; now they're eating themselves. That makes it less exciting. Anyway, not long after that trip, I was called by Gene Gutowski, later my business partner, and he suggested that I go to England to try something there. So I made *Repulsion* in London. It was quickly a financial and critical success. You know the rest.

PLAYBOY: After *Repulsion* and *Cul-de-Sac*, you drew extraordinarily strong comment from the reviewers, who either loved you or hated you. Do you pay much attention to them?

POLANSKI: In all honesty, I must say they were helpful to me in the beginning because of their sympathetic treatment of *Knife in the Water*. But a common thing among critics, many of whom are frustrated filmmakers, is that they like to discover young people, and then when the young person becomes popular, the critic feels betrayed and puts him down. So now, when someone I regard as good writes a favorable review, I read it. Otherwise, no, because hardly ever do I read a critic on somebody else's film when I agree with what he says. I read it and I think the man is obviously an imbecile who didn't understand the film, and how could he not like it? Or vice versa. Then later, if I read a review of my own film by the same man, there are only two alternatives. Either he gives me a good review, which means I'm really in trouble and I wonder where I've gone wrong, or he gives me a bad review, which is a good sign, but it's not pleasant reading. So I don't bother. The breaking point for me was *Cul-de-Sac*, which in my opinion is the best thing I've ever done. If I'm remembered for something I've done in the cinema, it will be for this film. But it got terrible reviews.

PLAYBOY: How do you explain that?

POLANSKI: First, because it was ahead of its time in a way, like *Dr. Strangelove*, which is one of the cinema's classics but came out two or three years too soon. And second, because critics are in general dumb and didn't understand the film. And third, because the more a reviewer can get stuck on his own piece and admire it, the happier he is. He's more interested in showing his own brilliance than in seriously assessing a film for the reader.

PLAYBOY: You said *Cul-de-Sac* is your best work. Why do you think so?

POLANSKI: I think it is the most cinematic of all my films, and remember that in a way, I see myself as a technician, so that's very important to me. It's the most cinematic because it's a piece that's virtually untranslatable into any other medium. Popularity and reviews mean nothing in this judgment. The films that are considered masterpieces, like *Citizen Kane* or *L'Avventura* or *A Space Odyssey*, when you look back and start going through the reviews to find out how they were received at the time, you're often surprised to find that it was not that well. Somehow certain films make their reputation throughout the history of cinema *despite* the critics and often despite the public, and sometimes despite both. I think *Cul-de-Sac* is already on the way, from what I hear about it whenever I talk to young people or cinema buffs. *Cul-de-Sac* is going to be a very durable movie.

PLAYBOY: For all those who've panned you, there are some writers in the film journals, especially in Europe, who rank you among the handful of the world's great directors. Would you agree with them?

POLANSKI: Guess! There aren't very many great directors. I think about five or six, like Fellini, Kubrick. . . . No, wait a minute. I can either say that I'm one of the five or six best directors without naming the rest or I can name my five or six favorites without telling you that I think I'm a part of this group, because to do that would seem too presumptuous. Which do you prefer?

PLAYBOY: Both. Before we finish this interview, there's one subject we haven't even touched on: politics. Though you crossed the Iron Curtain to live and work in the capitalist West, nothing you've said has indicated even a passing interest in affairs of state.

POLANSKI: I vaguely follow politics, but I don't think a knowledge of it is essential to lead an intellectually satisfying life. You can be involved with society without being at all interested in politics. I used to be quite political, but I quit when I understood that I couldn't do much about the situation. I'll tell you exactly my motivations, because this one I know the answer to. You know already my character. You know that I'm determined when I set out to do something, and when I'm determined, I do it. I set a goal and I desperately try to achieve it. When I'm not able to achieve what I want to, I become desperately angry and frustrated, and that's the feeling I have for politics. When I was in my 20s and living in Poland, I was concerned, and gradually I understood that all my efforts were so futile that I was reduced to some kind of mental masturbation. So I just stopped trying. I think that if I had chosen politics for a full-time career, I would certainly not only talk about it but I would do a lot about it. In general, though, I think that people who go into politics are a pretty stupid, uninspired race. I suspect that politics is quite easy, and the fact that the results are so poor everywhere is primarily because mostly second-rate people go into it. Really talented and ambitious people are usually interested in other fields of life.

My perceptions of this occurred about the same time I understood one other thing that I think also kept me away from politics, and that is the essential problem of human character, as explained so well by

Oscar Hammerstein—that too many people are too early in their lives too certain of too many things. So they are ready to die or kill for these things. You gradually come to understand that whichever side they're on, it's only by accident. The same baby who grew up as a Protestant in Ireland could just as easily have grown up as a Catholic in Ireland, so this man is fighting against someone he could have very easily been himself. My point is that what fucks up the world is idealism. Idealism is usually associated with the good guys, but I'll tell you, whoever is the Imperial Wizard of the Ku Klux Klan is as much an idealist in his mind as anyone else who believes deeply in his convictions and is willing to die for them or have others killed for them. These people don't expose their prejudices to a healthy doubt.

PLAYBOY: You hardly seem one to criticize others for lack of self-doubt.

POLANSKI: My self-confidence has to do with creative activity, not political activity. These political idealists I'm talking about are the do-gooders who want to do their number for the best interests of other people, not themselves. I do it for myself, not for some ideal of what I think is best for other people and for future generations. There is a whole world of difference.

PLAYBOY: Before we leave the subject, can we persuade you to give us some general idea, using at least broad conventional labels, about whether you consider yourself on the left or the right?

POLANSKI: I definitely don't identify with the right wing in America, but that doesn't mean I have any nostalgia for communism. Come to think of it, I do know one certainty about politics: Communism is a system that doesn't work. Terrible things happen when you start going against human nature, and having lived under communism, I can say that this is exactly what it does. It's basically structured on the assumption that everybody will be performing according to good will, according to the needs of the society, which is absolutely divorced from any conception of human nature. The result is expressed in another contemporary Polish proverb: "*Czy sie stoi czy sie lezy 2000 sie nalezy*"—which I'll bet is the first Polish sentence that *Playboy* has ever published [It is. —*Ed.*]—so don't misspell it. It means: "Whether you're standing up or lying down, they still pay you your 2000 zlotys." Most people are lying down.

I'm more sympathetic to capitalism, because it's not an artificial system that was invented by a group of brilliant people. It's a stage to which people naturally evolved. It's not the ideal system. Far from it. Anyone with any feeling has to be outraged by things like Vietnam, but

I don't think there is anything about it that's peculiar to capitalism. I always hear that this war made America lose her virginity, but the truth is that this war buggered America. If the Soviet Union found herself in a similar situation, I can assure you she would deal with the problem the same way—only faster, as it happened in Hungary, Poland and Czechoslovakia. God, politics is so vague. I don't want to talk politics. I really only do it when it's thrust upon me, mostly by intellectual friends, and I end up spending my energy in unnecessary arguments. So let's talk about something else—or nothing else.

PLAYBOY: One more question: What are your plans, now that you've finished *Macbeth*?

POLANSKI: I don't like to make plans, I don't know what I'll be doing. I'll make another film, but I don't know what. There's only one thing for sure: There will be no castles, no crowd scenes, no special effects, no horses, no costumes—preferably no clothes at all. Just two people on the beach! And perhaps not so much dialogue as in this interview. As I told you, I'm not a man of words, and I've run completely out of them. I'm drained. Enough said, *Playboy*. OK?

PLAYBOY: OK.

April 1991

MARTIN SCORSESE

A candid conversation with the director of Raging Bull and GoodFellas about violence in films, working with Robert De Niro and the Oscar he's yet to win

As unlikely as it seems, Martin Scorsese has never made a picture that was a mega box-office hit. Of course, that's easy enough to understand: Scorsese's films don't take place in outer space or in Beverly Hills. They never feature precocious kids, ambitious secretaries, ghost chasers, fraternity high-jinks, the undead in hockey masks nor any kind of military equipment. Even when his subject matter parallels the stuff hits are made from, Scorsese's vision is unique: His Mafia lives, and works in the streets, not in a posh family compound; when Scorsese went to the boxing ring, his pugilist was a self-destructive putz, not a come-from-behind hero. As if that were not enough to court box-office disaster, Scorsese avoids two subjects that most moviegoers crave: sex and romance.

While the result will never be *Batman*, *Rocky* nor even *Home Alone*, Scorsese occupies a singular place in American cinema. "[He's] one of a handful of American movie directors whose movies really matter," says critic David Ansen. He has won the Golden Palm at Cannes and numerous film-critics' awards (the New York, the Los Angeles and the National Society associations named *GoodFellas* best picture of the year and Scorsese best director). He has been nominated for an Academy Award two times as Best Director but has yet to win. Some of his associates have been luckier: Paul (*The Color of Money*) Newman, Robert (*Raging Bull*) De Niro and Ellen (*Alice Doesn't Live Here Anymore*) Burstyn all won Oscars under his direction.

After making some student films, Scorsese worked as a teacher in New York University's cinema department from 1968 to 1971. Since then, he has made 13 major motion pictures, four documentaries (including *The Last Waltz*), two Giorgio Armani commercials, an episode of *Amazing Stories* and a music video, Michael Jackson's "Bad." He has also done film editing (notably, *Woodstock*), producing (Stephen Frears's *The Grifters*) and acting (he has made 14 brief appearances in movies ranging from his own to Akira Kurosawa's *Dreams* and the upcoming *Guilty by Suspicion*). And then there are the hundreds of hours spent passionately hounding anyone who will listen about the necessity of film preservation and the evils of colorization.

His 20 year career has been both illustrious and rocky. His first three major films—*Mean Streets, Alice Doesn't Live Here Anymore* and *Taxi Driver*—instantly catapulted him into the top rank of directors. But he followed that trio with a well-intentioned but costly failure, *New York, New York,* and found himself a Hollywood outcast. Both his private life and his films have been dogged by controversy. When an obsessed *Taxi Driver* fan shot Ronald Reagan, the film was blamed. *The Last Temptation of Christ* was picketed, vilified and boycotted—even Scorsese's parents were castigated. On the personal front, he nearly died from a bout with drugs. He has been married four times, divorced three, including once from actress Isabella Rossellini.

Whether he was in favor or out, Scorsese still managed to make memorable films. *Raging Bull* is widely considered to be one of the best movies—if not the best movie—of the 1980s. Few directors have even attempted to plumb the depth of urban despair evoked in movies such as *Mean Streets, Taxi Driver* and *GoodFellas.* His artistry has yielded dozens of classic scenes: De Niro shadowboxing under the opening credits of *Raging Bull;* De Niro asking his mirror image, "You talkin' to me?" in *Taxi Driver;* Willem Dafoe as Christ pulling his heart from his chest; De Niro, Joe Pesci and Ray Liotta segmenting a dead gangster's body for a hurried burial in *GoodFellas.* Scorsese's camera slips, slides and pries into his characters' public and private lives—lives often without redeeming qualities.

Even when working closer to the mainstream (*The Color of Money, After Hours, Alice Doesn't Live Here Anymore,* the eerie *The King of Comedy* or the upcoming genre thriller *Cape Fear*), Scorsese routinely eschews the commercial approach in favor of personal subtext. When he directed *New York, New York,* with De Niro and Liza Minnelli, he couldn't resist using the film as a dark mirror. Years later, *Life Lessons,* Scorsese's segment of the *New York Stories* trilogy, was a discourse on an artist's dependence on borrowing creative inspiration from the pain of his deteriorating romantic relationships. His films resonate with echoes of his childhood in New York's Little Italy on the Lower East Side, where he grew up with the violence, the wise guys and the Italian-Catholic mystique that shape and color so much of his work. Currently separated from his fourth wife, producer Barbara De Fina (despite their marital difficulties, they still work together), and living in New York, Scorsese is certainly no pariah in Hollywood. Now rehabilitated and redeemed, he has become an éminence grise in the entertainment industry, having demonstrated his ability to direct more traditional movies, such as *The Color of Money*, as well as produce on-budget films for other directors. "The establishment joined Marty, not vice versa," maintains his friend Steven Spielberg, who is the executive producer of Scorsese's remake of *Cape Fear*. With the success of *GoodFellas*, the possibility of an Oscar for the maverick director seems less elusive.

Playboy sent Contributing Editor David Rensin to meet with Scorsese in Fort Lauderdale, Florida, just four days before *Cape Fear* started filming. Rensin reports:

"The interview took place in Scorsese's rented home. For each session, he appeared at the appointed hour wearing a pressed shirt, olive slacks and a wide belt with a formidable buckle—though for our final meeting, on the morning of his 48th birthday, he was shoeless, unshaven, wearing jeans and a blue T-shirt. I'm still unsure if he was finally relaxing or just happy the interview would soon be over, allowing him to turn to the more pressing business of beginning a motion picture.

"Scorsese's wiry intensity offsets his obvious fragility. He speaks in brisk cadences, punctuated by deep breaths and routine use of his handy asthma inhaler and nose drops. In fact, he prefaced our opening talk with a history of his lifelong asthma problem and its various medications; and it was as detailed and impassioned as a later explanation of why he has become bored with questions about violence in his films.

"His focus and range required uncommon energy. To ask a question meant being prepared for a one-sentence answer, followed by a five-minute detour into film history or philosophic speculation.

"For a guy saddled with such a serious reputation, Scorsese laughed often and maniacally loud, his lips stretching into a wild, teeth-baring smile. Although we ended up meeting four times—twice as many as planned—and then talked more on the phone, that first morning, Scorsese seemed unsure of what to expect. He appeared agitated and somewhat preoccupied but nonetheless attacked the job at hand with ferocity. We made some initial chat about a possible forthcoming Oscar nomination for *GoodFellas,* but the subject quickly turned to anxiety.

PLAYBOY: All three major film-critics' organizations have named *Good-Fellas* as best picture and you as best director. Now it's Academy Award time. Do you want to go out on a limb and predict if this is finally your year for an Oscar?

SCORSESE: What does "This is your year" mean, ultimately? When you're an asthmatic kid from the Lower East Side and you're watching television and you're movie-obsessed because the movies and church are all your parents will let you go to, then I suppose it means a great deal. [*Pauses*] I get chills now thinking about the Academy Awards televised in black and white in the early 1950s. But as I grew up, I understood that when they give you an Oscar, it doesn't mean it's always for your best picture. Howard Hawks never got one. Alfred Hitchcock never got one. Orson Welles never got one. Cary Grant, Marilyn Monroe. Everything has to be kept in perspective. If I win, it doesn't mean that *GoodFellas* is better directed than *Raging Bull* or *Alice Doesn't Live Here Anymore.* I think a great deal of the Academy, but much of it has to do with timing. The only thing you can do is to make more pictures. In other words, it's the old story: You keep proving yourself time after time after time. [*Smiles*] It's like this *Playboy Interview:* Where were *you* 10 years ago?

PLAYBOY: Well, you've reached a certain level, and—

SCORSESE: Reached a certain level? I didn't reach that level with *Raging Bull* 10 years ago? I certainly did; it's the same picture I've been making for 15 years. I think people just began to understand and realize that. And maybe you've interviewed everyone else so there's *only* me around. And while you were doing all the other people, Scorsese's still chopping away and making these pictures.

PLAYBOY: Back to the Oscars. You *do* want one don't you?

SCORSESE: I'd love to have a bunch of Oscars. It would be fun. But I'm at a point in my life where I'm just happy enough to make the pictures.

But I feel good about any awards. I love the film-critics' awards from different cities; I'd love the grand prize again in Cannes if I could get it. *GoodFellas* got the Golden Pit Award [for insensitivity], along with the soap opera *Santa Barbara*. That was good, because I don't want *GoodFellas* to be *too* respectable.

PLAYBOY: Let's talk about the work. Why do you direct?

SCORSESE: I don't think I can do anything else.

PLAYBOY: You can give us a better answer than that.

SCORSESE: Well, despite all the pain of it, all the difficulty, a lot of times, I've made things happen that I really enjoy. Actors do something that I don't expect, or they interpret what's there perfectly. You hear me laugh on the tracks a great deal. The beauty of it is when I get into the editing room and combine what they did on the set with my pre-thought-up cuts and camera moves. I'm fascinated by the moving image. It's like a miracle to me. I'm obsessed with those sprocket holes. Sometimes, in editing, we stop on the little frame and go, "Look!" Perhaps it's half-flash-framed because it's the end of the tape. Or the expression on the actor's face is so beautiful we have the frame printed up and we put it on the wall. And *then* putting music on: the music in *GoodFellas* or *Taxi Driver*. I just want to listen to it over and over. Those are the joys, the rewards. That's it. That's a lot.

PLAYBOY: What are the problems?

SCORSESE: On certain films, every day was anxiety-producing, just wondering if I was going to get enough done for the day—let alone if it was going to be the shots that I had planned, the performances I had worked on. Let alone if it was going to be *any good*. Another problem, of course, is not having enough money to make the picture.

PLAYBOY: It's never enough, is it?

SCORSESE: Well, when you *really* know it's enough, *that* can be a problem, too.

PLAYBOY: In four days, you'll start shooting a new film, *Cape Fear*, with Robert De Niro, Nick Nolte, Jessica Lange and other surprise stars. Are you excited?

SCORSESE: I'm nervous.

PLAYBOY: But you've made 13 films.

SCORSESE: Yeah, but it's a matter of being afraid of becoming complacent about the ability to make films. If I'm not nervous, then there's something to be nervous about.

PLAYBOY: But you seem to be on something of a hot streak lately. *Good-Fellas* is widely respected: *Life Lessons*, your section of *New York Stories*, was the best reviewed; and just last year, *Raging Bull* was selected as the best film of the 1980s by a consortium of "film-world notables" in *Premiere* magazine. Doesn't that inspire a certain amount of self-confidence?

SCORSESE: The award made me feel really good, especially after five or six years in the 1980s when I had trouble with *The Last Temptation of Christ* and made *After Hours* and *The Color of Money*. Even the British, in *Time Out* magazine, had the hundred best films of all time, and *Raging Bull* was number eight. That was great. I had a dinner for my birthday last year at The Russian Tea Room. I remember we had a lot of champagne because *Raging Bull* had been called the best picture of the past 10 years. So it was more than a birthday celebration, it was like having been vindicated. Remembered. That was nice.

PLAYBOY: So even though you told Paul Schrader in 1982 that you'd rather be fulfilled than remembered, you *do* like being remembered.

SCORSESE: Oh, don't believe anything I said back then. [*Laughs*] Being remembered is what it's all about. It's all a way of getting past the notion of death. Woody Allen always talks about it. Maybe at the time I felt that way. I thought the only thing going for me then was being fulfilled by knowing my work *had* been good.

PLAYBOY: Meaning?

SCORSESE: I felt good about *Raging Bull*, but I thought while making it that people would be repulsed. Some were, and I don't blame them. It's not everybody's cup of tea. It was a very strong picture. But most of the pictures I make are not made with "the audience" in mind. I don't mean that badly; I mean that *I'm* the audience. *Raging Bull* is a special movie for me. It was made on a purely personal level and I knew a lot of people wouldn't go for it. It was kamikaze filmmaking. I just poured everything I knew into the film—threw it all in without caring what anyone thought. It was done with such passion that I figured, If they don't like this, then I'll have no choice. I'll have to go away, do documentaries about saints in Rome. I suspected my career would be over.

Instead, we got some wonderful feedback right away. And all those Academy nominations. [De Niro won the Best Actor Oscar; Thelma Schoonmaker won for Best Editing.] I'm not complaining. And remember, nobody had a print of the film until three or four days before it opened. It wasn't like *GoodFellas*, where we had three months to work on publicizing it.

PLAYBOY: Isn't it true that at one time, you *didn't* want to make the picture?

SCORSESE: Right. I didn't really want to do *Raging Bull*; Bob [De Niro] wanted to. And I didn't really understand it until a period of excess I was going through, which landed me in the hospital, was over. I didn't understand what the film was going to be about from my side. From Bob's point of view, it was something else. But then I found my hook. When I made it through and I was all right, and I survived, I understood what the movie was about.

PLAYBOY: Which was?

SCORSESE: Self-destruction. I understood the character I wanted Jake to be. That's why I made the ending as I did. Jake is able to reach some sort of peace with himself, and then subsequently with the people around him. He's able to look at himself in the mirror and talk to himself, reciting lines from *On the Waterfront*, flat. You want to put meanings into the lines? Fine. Those aren't the meanings that we're talking about. It's just flat. He takes it easy on himself and the people around him. That was a goal that *I* wanted to get to.

PLAYBOY: How did De Niro act as a catalyst?

SCORSESE: He kept pushing until finally I saw what I needed to see. I got out of the hospital and went to Italy for a week or two. When I came back, Bob and I went to an island and spent three weeks rewriting the script. That was the epitome of the collaboration.

PLAYBOY: Maybe De Niro pushed you to do that because he wanted you to see what *you*, personally, needed to see.

SCORSESE: No, I don't think so at all. [*Pauses*] Well, when he came to talk to me in the hospital, yes, to a certain extent. I think he really loved the project and wanted to get it made.

PLAYBOY: You mention a period of excess. That was when you were roommates with the Band's Robbie Robertson in the Hollywood Hills. What happened?

SCORSESE: It was pretty self-destructive. Lucky to get out of it alive. I nearly died. But I did it; it's over.

PLAYBOY: Did what?

SCORSESE: [*Uncomfortable*] Knock around, party after party.

PLAYBOY: Drugs?

SCORSESE: Whatever. Everything you could get your hands on. We had some good times, but eventually, I began to ask myself, What was this life ultimately going to be like? Were we going to hit *the ultimate party*? Meet *the ultimate young woman*? *The ultimate drug*? What? No!

PLAYBOY: When did you realize that?

SCORSESE: Toward the end. Of course, Robbie and I had extremely creative, interesting discussions. We'd have little soirees in our house on Mulholland, and we'd screen movies—Jean Cocteau, Sam Fuller, Luchino Visconti—all night. We'd close off all the windows so we didn't see any light coming up in the morning. We didn't want *any* light coming in. It really got to the point where I got so bewildered by it all that I couldn't function creatively. I realized that something had to be done about my having "checked out" this way of life.

PLAYBOY: Checked out? Come on. This wasn't case of mere curiosity.

SCORSESE: Whatever you want to call it. It's a symptom of my having developed later in life than other people. You go out and say, Well, I'm going to have some fun. It's like watching some old cartoon where people do stupid things. It gets very boring after a while. I was just acting out like a child would.

All that stuff eventually found its way into *Raging Bull.* I also put some of it into *The Last Waltz.* In fact, when I finished *The Last Waltz,* I thought that it was the best work that I had done. That's what I felt. And I *still* wasn't happy. Even the *good* work wasn't making me happy. That's when I had to really start to find out what was going on.

PLAYBOY: We've heard a rumor that you had to alter the final print of *The Last Waltz* in order to excise some cocaine visible on Neil Young's nose. Is that true?

SCORSESE: We had to fix it because the song is so beautiful. The audience's eyes would have gone right to that in the middle of "Helpless." Plus, it's such a beautiful, moving shot—simple and emotional. It cost $10,000 or something. I think Neil has the contract framed.

PLAYBOY: How did those years end?

SCORSESE: I started to physically fall apart. Toward the end of the summer of '78, during the week, I'd spent maybe three days in bed, because I couldn't function. Maybe, *maybe* two and a half days of work. It got to the point where I couldn't work anymore, and then around Labor Day of 1978, I had to be hospitalized. I was bleeding internally. I realized, What am I doing? Well, I guess I did it all, so I'd better move on.

PLAYBOY: Is there a reason you haven't used the word cocaine in reference to your excesses, considering what we've just discussed?

SCORSESE: Using it reminds me of people telling all. I just don't like it. I *do* think it's important for people to understand that if you go through excess, whether you're using cocaine, speed, liquor or whatever you can get your hands on, you're going to reach the point of what excess is all about.

That is, you realize that you have a choice: You can either go under—die in your sleep like Fassbinder—or stop it. That's *all* it's about, if there's any message for people reading this. [*Pauses*] I'm just embarrassed about too much breast-baring. Look at my movies, instead. The emotion: the violence, the anger, the rage, the childishness. It's all there.

PLAYBOY: You've said before that you use your films as personal therapy.

SCORSESE: Yeah, that was another stupid thing I've said—as if there's an inner rage in you when you make, say, *Taxi Driver*, and at the end of it, you think the rage has been expelled. It hasn't. No movie is going to do that for you.

PLAYBOY: Bearing in mind the very personal nature of the experiences that fed *Raging Bull*, how did you feel in 1981, at the Academy Awards, when *Ordinary People*, a film that is not on anybody's 10-best-of-the-decade list, won Best Picture and Robert Redford got the Oscar for Best Director?

SCORSESE: That's a good picture. I thought I had a good chance. But I realized I wasn't going to get it when the Directors Guild didn't give me its Best Director of the Year. Usually, Oscar-winning films are certain kinds of pictures. The year *Citizen Kane* was nominated, John Ford's *How Green Was My Valley* won. A wonderful picture. It's about family. It's a good, wholesome film, more in the mainstream and easier to take. So it's more understandable that a *Driving Miss Daisy* rather than a *Born on the Fourth of July* or an *Ordinary People* rather than a *Raging Bull* would win.

PLAYBOY: When did you realize you weren't mainstream?

SCORSESE: Actually, I thought I was until *New York, New York*. I thought it was going to be a blockbuster. The idea is an homage to the style of the musicals of the late 1940s and early 1950s, with characters grafted onto it who are more out of *Scenes from a Marriage* or a John Cassavetes picture. It was a naturalistic documentary approach.

But the more we shot, the more money it cost and the more I got involved with the reality of the characters. I knew they weren't going to wind up together at the end, and I knew that the picture wasn't going to do anything at the box office. I had changed whatever was commercial about it to something more experimental and, again, personal.

PLAYBOY: How shocking was the reaction to *New York, New York*, considering your earlier successes?

SCORSESE: Three films people loved—or at least they got a strong reception: *Mean Streets*, *Alice Doesn't Live Here Anymore* and *Taxi Driver*. The minute *New York, New York* came out, there was such ridicule. It made me think, What the hell am I doing here? Up to that point, I thought I'd belonged within the industry and the Hollywood tradition of classic directors. A real director is someone who can do a swashbuckler, then a *film noir*, then a gangster picture, then a love story. They had a great deal of range; they were pros who could probably have done anything. I always wanted to be that kind of director. But after *New York, New York*, I realized the studio system was over. There was no way I could get that back or re-create it. I didn't know what I was going to do with my life.

PLAYBOY: Why, when it's clear that you're so respected for your originality, did you even *want* to be mainstream?

SCORSESE: Well, I don't want to be considered an adjunct to the business, or some sort of strange punctuation that's on the margins. All my life, I've been on the outside. A good example: I lived in California more than 10 years, but at every party I went to—and I went to *every* party—there was one person who would say, "Well, how long you out here for?" I'd say, "No, no, I *live* here." Or they'd come into my house and say, "You just renting this?" "No, I bought it." It's that kind of thing.

PLAYBOY: And you were an outsider as a kid, too?

SCORSESE: Right from the beginning, because of my asthma. I couldn't join in and play stickball. In the summertime, they'd open the fire hydrants. Water would go all over the street, and I was never allowed to go into that. That sounds like some poor little kid behind a window staring at kids playing, but that's *really* what it was. So my parents would take me to the movies a lot.

PLAYBOY: Was it fear of being an outsider that eventually made you direct more mainstream films, such as *After Hours* and *The Color of Money*?

SCORSESE: No. It was just a good way of getting back into shape after *The Last Temptation* fell through. I got a big dose of humility. I didn't bang any walls, though. I decided to get stronger and rehabilitate myself. I realized I just couldn't walk into a film anymore and say, "OK, it's going to take as long as it takes."

PLAYBOY: Or cost as much as it costs.

SCORSESE: There were three pictures where I didn't really worry about the money: *New York, New York, Raging Bull* and *The King of Comedy*. Those films *were* made in a period when it was a little easier. *King of Comedy* was maybe three hours a day shooting—but I was tired, had just had pneumonia and had to start the picture before I was ready because of an imminent directors' strike. Now I shoot 10 hours. By the end of that film, I realized I wouldn't be able to sustain a career that way any longer. Also, a few days after *Raging Bull* came out, *Heaven's Gate* was released by the same studio. That was the end of complete autonomy budgetwise for most directors. And I realized that with less money, in most cases, you have more freedom to make the picture, and more of a chance of surviving in the theater.

PLAYBOY: Is that why *The Color of Money*, with Tom Cruise and Paul Newman, seems so traditional? It's not exactly a Scorsese picture.

SCORSESE: Funny. Spielberg also said he felt that *The Color of Money* wasn't a Scorsese picture. And he's right, in the traditional sense. It *became* a mainstream film. I couldn't believe it. I didn't do it intentionally. We applied the same principles of production, which was very low budget, that we used on *After Hours* to a picture with a big star like Paul Newman. Those standards seemed to work very much in our favor. We came in a million and a half under budget.

PLAYBOY: Was working with Newman intimidating?

SCORSESE: Yes. In the beginning, my talks with him were a little difficult for me. It was the "under 21 syndrome" that Woody Allen spoke about in trying to direct Van Johnson in *The Purple Rose of Cairo*. When he was under 21, Woody had seen Johnson in so many movies that he was like an idol. Newman was an idol to me and it was tough to be fully myself until I understood what he needed.

PLAYBOY: What did he need?

SCORSESE: A reason for making the film.

PLAYBOY: For *that* film, of all films?

SCORSESE: He never felt that there should have been a sequel to *The Hustler*.

PLAYBOY: But he came to you, didn't he?

SCORSESE: Yeah. In this business, you say, "Well, let's see if so-and-so can do something with it. Maybe if this guy comes up with something, I might really think about it seriously." He didn't believe at the time in the continuation of characters in different movies. So I told him, "I just don't believe that 'Fast Eddie' Felson would give up. He'd become something else. He'd become everything he hated. He'd become the character George C. Scott was." Newman was skeptical. Or cautious. But he thought what I'd said was interesting. I came up with the idea of doing sort of a road movie: take a young boy under his wing and teach the kid all these terrible things. Corrupt the kid and then be bitter with his own corruption, until he does what he was supposed to do all his life, anyway: play the game. Maybe not win but play the game.

PLAYBOY: Can you describe the ideal film you'd like to make?

SCORSESE: Pictures that interest me as much as possible *personally*, are experimental and stay within the system somehow so that they can be shown in theaters. I've *always* tried to blend "personal" movies with being inside the industry. A lot of my success has to do with sacrifice: being paid very little for certain types of pictures and learning to work on a very, very small budget.

PLAYBOY: Isn't that increasingly difficult in the era of the megahit?

SCORSESE: Yeah. I've got to be lucky just to make 50 or 60 million dollars on a picture. I have a great love for organized studios in Hollywood and the way the system works. I'll argue, I'll discuss. I'll complain and I'll say, "Yeah, but if you're making too many films that you expect to make 200 million dollars on, where are the new people going to come from?" And, sure enough, there's a wonderful sturdiness about independent filmmaking in America. For example where was Tim Burton a few years ago? Doing smaller pictures. It isn't as if we got some guy who had worked 10, 15 years in the business to direct *Batman* and that's why it became the $400 million epic.

PLAYBOY: You once said that a crucial aspect of *Mean Streets* was that Charlie and Johnny Boy don't die, they go on. You've had some hard personal times. Have you ever not wanted to keep living?

SCORSESE: Only when I was a kid. I read the book *The Heart of the Matter*, by Graham Greene. Scobie is the character's name. As I remember, his wife had been hurt in an accident, so they couldn't make love anymore. There's an airplane crash and he nurses one of the victims back to health. She's a young woman, and he falls in love with her. He can't leave his wife and he can't stop the adultery. By the end, he decides to commit suicide, because he can't go on offending God.

I had those thoughts when I was 15 or 16, as I was encountering natural sexuality: impure thoughts, masturbation, the whole thing. I thought that if these impurities continued, then maybe I should do what Scobie did. But then I said it in confession to my parish priest, who's now dead, and he said, "No, no, no. You mustn't think *those* thoughts." [*Laughs*] I guess I took it *too* seriously.

PLAYBOY: When did you make your last confession?

SCORSESE: Oh, 1965, I think. I've been confessing most of the time since then on film, so it doesn't matter. My old friends who are priests, they look at my films and they *know*. Still, I can't help being religious. I'm looking for the connection between God and man, like everybody else.

Some say there is no God, and that's the end of the connection. We exist and then we don't exist.

PLAYBOY: Do you believe that?

SCORSESE: I believe the more you know, the less you know.

PLAYBOY: When do you feel the most Catholic?

SCORSESE: When I'm making pictures like *Cape Fear*. Bob De Niro's character, Max, is the avenging angel, in a way. Nick Nolte and Jessica Lange's characters, Sam and Leigh, are representative, for me, of humanity. They're basically good people who have had some hard times and are trying to go through them and piece their lives together. Now they're being tested, like Job, by Max.

PLAYBOY: Can't you help yourself from Catholicizing everything?

SCORSESE: [*Laughs*] No. It's an embarrassment. It just seems to fall into place that way. I have to ground everything in a bedrock of spiritual motivation.

PLAYBOY: Do you think you'll ever go back to the Church?

SCORSESE: A couple of friends of mine think I will. I don't think I've ever left, really.

PLAYBOY: At one time, you wanted to be a priest. What happened?

SCORSESE: I couldn't become a priest because I couldn't resolve how one could take the concepts of Christianity and make them apply to daily life. You hear how life's supposed to work from priests, then you watch how it really works on the streets. That shows in *Mean Streets*, where Charlie is trying to lead a life philosophically tied in with Roman Catholic teaching: offering up penances, suffering for atonement of his own sins, dealing with the sins of pride and selfishness *and* trying to take the concept of loving your enemy and fellow man and reconcile it with rules of living in a total jungle. I couldn't resolve that for myself, because the microcosm of Little Italy is just that: It's a microcosm of us today. It's a microcosm of troops in Saudi Arabia, it's a microcosm of everything. The same concepts apply in every form of society throughout the world, in different degrees of intensity.

Another reason, of course, was that I'd become aware of girls. There was no way to resolve the sexuality that I felt. I was very, very shy that way because of wanting to be a priest, and even more introverted because I had asthma. I was a late bloomer. I'd discovered girls but didn't act on it like some of the other guys who had healthier attitudes. And that, too, figured into *Mean Streets*. During the pool-playing scene, Charlie talks about his priest, who had told him a story about a young boy and girl who were nice kids but who went out and had sex—and paid for it. The kids have never made love. One night they decide to go all the way. They park the car, they're making love and a truck comes by and smashes into the car and they burn up in flames. And the priest said he knew these two kids. Charlie believed it.

I'd heard the same story on retreat and years later, a girl I knew told it to me, too. She said the priest she'd heard it from also *knew the kids personally*. Well, it couldn't have been the same priest. So I talked to a friend who had been on that retreat with me and he said, "Of course it was not true."

PLAYBOY: *You* believed it?

SCORSESE: Totally. I saw those bodies writhing in flames because they had dared to have sexual thoughts and act on them. Priests are great actors. [*Smiles*] I was a fool. I was very gullible and naive. I felt that the priest had lied to me personally.

You've got to understand: I was still a baby in that way. I was living with my parents. A lot of these other guys around me, they were more on their own. I stayed very much a family boy until after I shot *Taxi Driver*.

PLAYBOY: But by the time you heard the story about the car's going up in flames, you'd already had sex?

SCORSESE: No.

PLAYBOY: When was the first time?

SCORSESE: Oh, very late. Very late.

PLAYBOY: In college?

SCORSESE: No, I was married. The idea was one person, and *that* was the one person.

PLAYBOY: Would you have had sex earlier if your religion had allowed it?

SCORSESE: No, absolutely not. I was going to be a priest—and I harbored a desire to go back to the seminary right up until I made my first short film in 1963.

PLAYBOY: Should priests get married?

SCORSESE: Oh, I go the party line on that. Maybe that's one reason I never became a priest. There's supposed to be a devotion, a selflessness; they cannot share their life with anybody else. There has to be a sense of sacrifice, discipline and asceticism. If somebody gets run over by a train, the priest is called in and he has to perform the last rites on what's left of the body. Then he goes back to his rectory. If he were married, what would his wife say? "What was it like today, dear?"

PLAYBOY: You got married at 20 and had a daughter, but the marriage didn't last very long.

SCORSESE: Right. My upbringing was so parochial. Kids from other cultures might have lived together first to try to see if their lifestyles meshed. If I'd had any inkling what this film business was like, I would have wanted to, as well. I was 20 or 21, I was doing films at New York University. I had one foot in one world and one foot in the other. In order to continue the films, I think, I had to really concentrate on that and let the personal life slide. I was late in everything in my life, because I came from a very closed, parochial environment. I didn't let my hair grow until 1969. I went to Woodstock—to work, mind you—in a shirt with cuff links and didn't buy my first pair of jeans or start wearing cowboy shirts until afterward.

PLAYBOY: So you do think business and artistic pressures tend to make successful relationships between two creative people difficult, as in *New York, New York*?

SCORSESE: Actually, it took Jean-Luc Godard to tell me, when I finally met him, what that movie was about: the impossibility of two creative people sustaining a marriage. There *are* great married teams: Nicolas Roeg and Theresa Russell, Blake Edwards and Julie Andrews. They seem to be doing fine. You should ask them. I don't think I've ever really tried it that way. Over the years, you get involved with people and many of them are also creative, and you usually find that the drive for fulfillment of their own work starts to clash.

PLAYBOY: And once again, you put it on the screen?

SCORSESE: No matter what I do, [my personal experiences] seem to get up there. *Not* to betray the people who are with me; not to betray my wife or my close friends. It's not as if I think, I'm going to take that and put it up on the screen. I'm just trying to find a truthfulness, and I look into myself first.

It isn't easy to do, by the way. I don't know if you ever get into an argument with somebody you love and think, Oh, that would be *incredible* on film. Your emotions are in the way; you can't do that. And once you calm down, you forget every word. Later, maybe things come to you, so you try to put them into different characters.

PLAYBOY: Do you think that if you and your second wife, writer Julia Cameron, had stayed together, the *New York, New York* characters might have stayed together?

SCORSESE: [*Very uncomfortable*] I don't know. When you mention her name . . . I can't talk about it that way. It would have been kind of schizophrenic if we hadn't stayed together to put them in the movie that way. In that particular instance, it seemed to be the most honorable way of ending the movie. Everything else would have been a lie if they had walked off together. But the movie is not just about my marriage at the time. It drew from all kinds of relationships.

PLAYBOY: Does that mean if you had focused more off screen on your relationships with women, your movies might have been different?

SCORSESE: [*Bristles*] I'm *always* focused on my relationships. It's just that at a certain point in my life, I realized I could focus only *up to a certain point*, and then you need glasses. The moment you realize you need glasses, and what kind of prescription it is, you tend to take it a little easier on yourself. You think, I can stay in for the long haul *if* I can. But you know that it will probably end.

PLAYBOY: At some point, you couldn't give as much as they demanded?

SCORSESE: Not necessarily what the *people* demanded but what the relationship needed. Up to a certain point, I probably give as much as possible. And I have reacted differently over the years, with depression or rage, at the realization that I couldn't continue.

PLAYBOY: You once told Roger Ebert that you couldn't look at ads or movies with Isabella Rossellini—or even Nastassja Kinski, who looks like her—after your marriage dissolved.

SCORSESE: Well, that was *right after* the breakup of our marriage. There was a great longing. But that was 1982, 1983, an interesting time. That was when *King of Comedy* finished. And within a week or two, I started preproduction on *The Last Temptation of Christ* and I was completely happy again. I was able to put our marriage into some sort of perspective, and now we're pretty good friends.

PLAYBOY: Did you like her in *Blue Velvet*?

SCORSESE: She's quite good, but that's a weird role for an ex-husband to look at. I cannot be totally objective. All I know is that it was a believable performance.

PLAYBOY: Did you get angry at Dennis Hopper when he was hitting her?

SCORSESE: No. [*Laughs*]

PLAYBOY: Are you, like Nick Nolte's character, Lionel Dobie, in *Life Lessons*, someone who needs emotional pain to create?

SCORSESE: Not anymore. [*Laughs*] But remember, you're talking to an Italian. I had to have drama off screen as well as on screen. Now the drama on screen is pretty much enough.

PLAYBOY: Let's talk about another of your important relationships: Robert De Niro.

SCORSESE: Let's not. [*Laughs*] Just kidding.

PLAYBOY: Well, it's true you rarely discuss your relationship. Yet you've done six pictures together and other actors and directors regard your working relationship as a model. Now, after nearly 10 years of not working together, he has been part of the ensemble in *GoodFellas* and plays the lead in *Cape Fear*. Why the long break?

SCORSESE: It was important, after *King of Comedy*, that I did less with Bob and concentrated on my own work again. We had explored so much together. We needed time to learn more about ourselves. I realized that a man lives his life alone. I don't believe in teams, ultimately. Eventually, it's you and the material. But now, after a whole series of pictures on my own, it will be interesting to see if Bob and I can do something that will further our experience in filmmaking.

PLAYBOY: When you watch De Niro's work with other directors, do you ever get jealous? Feel proprietary?

SCORSESE: In the early days, when I was making films with him all the time, yes. When I saw him in *The Deer Hunter*, for example, I felt a bit nervous watching. It was like somebody who was extremely close to me having an affair with someone else. But I admired his work in that film and others.

PLAYBOY: Why does it work so well between you?

SCORSESE: Trust, creatively. He has instincts that just turn out right for me. And also personally. He and I can say the stupidest things to each other about anything, and it's not going to find its way past us. We identify with each other somewhat through the characters he acts out and I direct. We also seem to be growing older in the same way.

PLAYBOY: Is it true you wanted De Niro to play Christ originally?

SCORSESE: No. I flew to Paris for one night to talk to him about it. He felt he didn't know enough about religion to understand what was needed. I knew that before I asked him. It was more a discussion. At one point, he said, "Listen, if there's any problem, if you can't get the picture made without me, I'll do it." For a guy to hang on a cross for three days, you've really got to want to do that. But he meant it wholeheartedly, and I appreciated that.

PLAYBOY: Just before your deal was made for a second try at *The Last Temptation of Christ*, you both visited Marlon Brando on Tetiaroa. Why?

SCORSESE: Brando had an idea for a comedy he wanted me to do. He said he was a fan of *King of Comedy*. He said, "Would you like to come down? Tahiti's beautiful." Bob just happened to be around and said,

"Why don't I come down, too?" I don't think he'd met Brando. Plus, he likes islands. I live in buildings; I don't understand islands. I see a palm tree, I get nervous. We went for seven days and spent about three and a half weeks.

PLAYBOY: Why the change in plans?

SCORSESE: Brando said, "I'll come around, just enjoy yourself." He put me in a small house. The island is very small; you can walk around it in less than 40 minutes. There's nothing to do there. Then he waited until I got into the rhythm of Tahiti, and that took three or four days. He'd come by and say, "Did you walk around the island yet this morning?" I'd say, "Yeah." He'd say, "What are you going to do this afternoon, go the other way?" I'd say, "Yeah." Then I'd be reading a book. "Still reading that book?" Soon I began to understand that you don't do *anything*. You don't know what time it is, you don't know what day it is. You get up, you walk around, you go into the water.

It was the first and only time in my life when I was very sad to leave a place—despite having a hard time because I was being eaten by the mosquitoes.

PLAYBOY: What did you talk about?

SCORSESE: Brando is a raconteur and he has wonderful stories. You get a sense of what's important to him in his life. He would read poetry to me. I liked him. I really wish we could have worked together. But it's hard for me to do other people's dreams, other people's projects that *they*'re burning to do. Over the years, with so many people I admire, we'd get together, we'd like to work together, but it was usually something that I had to do for *them*. Or something that came out of their soul. It's very, very hard, at this stage of the game, for me to become as excited as they are over that particular project. I've got only so much time left. I'm 48 years old. Each film has got to mean something to me. I don't care who it is—if it were my brother's project, I couldn't do it. I've got to do what is important to me.

PLAYBOY: Let us read you something.

SCORSESE: Are these my bad reviews? I don't read the bad reviews. [*Laughs*]

PLAYBOY: It's a letter to the editor from the *Los Angeles Times Magazine*, in response to an article about you when *GoodFellas* was released. It reads, in part, "Like other hack directors, Scorsese uses mayhem to excite audiences, not reveal meaning."

SCORSESE: Oh, the violence question. It comes up.

PLAYBOY: Obviously, this is a criticism you're familiar with. Does it upset you?

SCORSESE: Only because, as I've said many times, the violence comes out of the things that I really know about. It would be very difficult for me to do a war picture. Take Oliver Stone and *Platoon*. He saw war, you get that sense of absolute horror and panic. Maybe it's no justification that these things come from *my* experience. But that's why I make personal movies. I make them about what I think I understand.

I grew up in the tenements. I lived only half a block away from the Bowery. I saw the dregs, the poor vagrants and the alcoholics. I saw everything. Most mornings on the way to grammar school, I'd see two bums fighting each other with broken bottles. Blood all over the ground. I had to step around the blood and the bottles—and I'm just eight years old. Or I'd be sitting in the derelicts' bar across the way. We'd go in—we were only kids, nine years old—and sit there. We'd watch guys get up and struggle over to another table and start hallucinating and beating up someone.

The first sexual thing I ever saw was at night: two derelicts performing fellatio on each other and then vomiting it up. I was about 13 then. But I'll never forget the images. Never forget them. The first aspect of life I remember seeing was the death of it. You don't even have to go to the Bowery now to see it. In Manhattan, it's all over the streets.

PLAYBOY: Sounds like a disturbing childhood.

SCORSESE: It wasn't. This was just the environment I was in. It was like the wild West, the frontier. When it came to your apartment in the tenement where you lived, you were protected, usually. Though at night, coming back late, you found derelicts in the halls, or people robbing each other in the halls. After a while, in the early 1960s, they put locks on the street doors and two lights on each doorway.

PLAYBOY: And these are the experiences you've embraced on film. Why?

SCORSESE: Violence is just a form of how you express your feelings to someone. Take this situation: Let's say you're growing up in this area you want to be a gangster. Well, you can get into somebody's crew, and you start working, but you've got to prove yourself. And what you have to do, you know, is very clear. For instance, an old friend who got into that lifestyle for a while told me this incredible story.

He had to go collect money—because it's always about money. He's told by the man running his crew, "You go to the guy in the store, take this bat and break it over his head. Get the money." The guy says, "Why?" And he says, "Well, because he's been late a few weeks and he owes me the vig. He should be hit. Get the money if you can." So he gets there. He also takes a younger guy with him. They get in the store and he sees there are a lot of people waiting to buy things. So he takes the owner in the back and threatens the guy for money.

The guy says, "Oh, I have it. I have it here. Glad you came. Here's the money." So he takes it and leaves. On the way out, the young guy who was learning from him says, "You were supposed to hit him." "No, he had the money. We don't have to hit him; he gave us the money." So he went back to his boss and said, "Here's the money." The boss said, "Did you hit him? Did you break his head?" "No." "Why not?" "He *had* the money. And there were people there." "That's the point. He's late, isn't he? Take the bat and break his head. Even when he *gives* you the money, *especially* if there's people there. That's how you do it."

And not only do you have to do it, you have to learn to *enjoy* it. And that's what I think people started to get upset about again lately, with *GoodFellas*.

PLAYBOY: In stories about you, there's always the suggestion that although you were too sickly to join in, you *wanted* to be a wise guy—much like Henry Hill in *GoodFellas*.

SCORSESE: I *couldn't* do it personally, but as a boy of 13 or 14, I had to harden my heart against the suffering. I had to take it. My friends go to beat up somebody, I went with them. I didn't jump in, but I watched or set it up.

PLAYBOY: Really?

SCORSESE: Oh, of course. Sure, you do all that. It's part of growing up there. So it's *my* experience. I don't expect this person who wrote the letter you read to have the same experience. Maybe he had experience with violence in another way. I don't know, but that's for him to make a film or write about; I have no argument.

PLAYBOY: As an adult, what were your violent experiences about?

SCORSESE: Years ago, oh, God, the tension of shooting, the frustration of trying to get everything. I had this constant thing of having incredible energy and then suddenly, if things weren't going right, I'd punch a wall. I would traumatize the knuckles on this right hand. When we had only 20 days to shoot and something went wrong, I'd go into the trailer, pound the wall and come out smiling as if nothing was wrong. Now I know what's going to happen if something goes wrong on the set, and I'll either try to make it right or move on. All the screaming and the yelling is not going to help. That doesn't mean I don't still have insecurities. And the anger is there; it simmers. I just don't necessarily act out violent rages anymore.

PLAYBOY: Perhaps the violence in your films *is* some wishful extension of your inability to participate earlier.

SCORSESE: No. It's so destructive, the violence. Look at Jake in *Raging Bull*.

PLAYBOY: When do you find violence in film exultant?

SCORSESE: *The Wild Bunch* has a choreographed excitement. Meaning like ballet. Plus, you also like the characters for some reason.

Bonnie and Clyde is another example of a very important film where you really like the people. The violence is overblown. The violence is just amazing. [*New York Times* critic Vincent] Canby said that it really was a watershed film. It opened the door to a new understanding of violence on screen during the time we were in Vietnam. It was a way to keep abreast of how things were changing.

PLAYBOY: Does violence in films cause violence in the streets?

SCORSESE: It depends on the person. I don't believe any one movie or any one book makes people *in their right mind*, whatever that is, go out and act some way because they saw it in a movie. [But I can't satisfy] America's need for quick, one-statement answers here. American readers seem to want to read a clear statement and say, "You know, they're right." As simple as that, like taking polls on CNN. It's crazy. That's not a one-statement answer, it's a very complicated question.

PLAYBOY: Roger Ebert said he didn't think you could make *Taxi Driver* today, because it had the wrong kind of violence. He said it was meaningful, well-thought-out violence, as opposed to random violence.

SCORSESE: I suppose the kind of random violence he's talking about is in films like *Total Recall*—which I haven't seen—which are really the action-adventure B films from the 1930s and 1940s taken to another level. That violence confuses me and perplexes me. I really don't understand it. Violence in films today is so abstract. Horror films and the disemboweling of people. Maybe that satisfies a need in human beings that was satisfied by real blood lust 2,000 years ago. I don't know what's happened to our society. I don't know why we have to see our entrails being dragged out. I don't get it.

PLAYBOY: What about *Taxi Driver*? The film is perhaps the pre-eminent example of how the public associates you with violence.

SCORSESE: Well, I didn't do the violence scenes in *Taxi Driver* for titillation, for instance, or for an audience to have *fun* with. It was just a natural progression of the character in the story. And the total tragedy of it.

PLAYBOY: Can you defend Travis Bickle?

SCORSESE: Travis Bickle, the character that Paul Schrader wrote, is the avenging angel. He comes in and he wants to clean up the streets. He wants to clean everybody out. He really means well. The problem is the old story of what constitutes madness. We have this fantasy sometimes, in the city, where you look at it and you say, "God, how could this exist? Look at the poor people in the streets. What's going on? What's happened in the past 15 years to America? I wish I could do this; I wish I could do that." You even get a sense of violence walking in the streets.

PLAYBOY: Many of us don't walk in those places because—

SCORSESE: Exactly. You don't have to finish your sentence, because I know what you're saying. A lot of people may read this and they may not understand that, because they may live somewhere else. But in most urban centers, you get that sense of incredible violence.

The point is that Travis sees this, and although *we* have *fantasies* about it in our weakest moments, Travis acts out the fantasy.

PLAYBOY: You said you understood Travis having gone about it the wrong way. Are you saying you tried to get the message across incorrectly about how horrible all this violence is?

SCORSESE: I don't know. There are lots of mistakes you make. What's the old cliché—The road to hell is paved with good intentions? Or the line that always brings tears to my eyes in *The Last Temptation:* "I'm so ashamed of all the wrong ways I looked for God." I did take that rather personally.

PLAYBOY: One person who got it wrong was John Hinckley. He used having seen *Taxi Driver,* and having become obsessed with Jodie Foster, as part of his defense.

SCORSESE: To use the film as a defense is such an oversimplification. A horror. But attempted assassinations are so horrible, and the country is so frightened by this phenomenon, that using the film as a defense kind of sedates the public. It makes them feel, "It's OK, we've got everything under control. It was the fault of these guys who made this picture, and it was the fault of *Catcher in the Rye.*" Does this then mean it has really nothing to do with his *family,* it has nothing to do with *maybe* there's something wrong physically with his brain?

PLAYBOY: When did you hear the news linking the film and the assassination attempt?

SCORSESE: We were in Los Angeles for the Academy Awards. Afterward— Bob won the Academy Award for *Raging Bull*—at a party at Ma Maison, someone said, "Didn't you hear the news?"

PLAYBOY: How did you feel at that moment?

SCORSESE: I said it was absurd. Then they explained the details about Hinckley. Oddly enough, and I've never told this story before, when I was attending the Academy Awards years before, when *Taxi Driver* was nominated for Best Picture, I'd gotten a threatening letter from somebody. Jodie Foster had been nominated, and the letter read, "If Jodie Foster receives an Academy Award for what you made little Jodie do, you'll pay for it with your life. This is no joke."

I remember showing it to Marcia Lucas, George Lucas' wife at the time, who was my film editor. There were so many things going on. We were trying to finish *New York, New York* and we said, "That's all we need." So the FBI came by, I gave them the letter, they looked into it, and a few nights later, I had to go to the Academy Awards. Billy Friedkin was the producer of the show and he let me in first. It was great. They pointed out the FBI agents who were there at the door, some of them women in gowns, and said if anything happens. . . . They thought Jodie might win that night and—who knows?—maybe the person was in the audience. Of course, she didn't win and it was forgotten.

PLAYBOY: OK. Given the violent moments in your movies, how have you resisted what so many other filmmakers haven't—violence against women, especially the connection between violence and sex?

SCORSESE: There isn't that much sex in the films I make. Seriously, in *Taxi Driver*, the sex is all repressed. If you had any real sex in it, it would blow the entire picture.

You have to remember that most of the pictures I make deal with worlds in which the men predominate, and I've gotta be true to those particular worlds. All the Italian women are very strong. Don't believe that nonsense that the man runs the house. No way. Ultimately, it's the matriarch. So when I saw certain scripts in which the woman was just an appendage, I didn't do them. That's why, especially in *GoodFellas*, I chose to make sure that the woman's role was as strong as possible. But it still says good *Fellas*, and the men chopped up the bodies, not the women.

PLAYBOY: And the women in your other films are also allowed to be strong. *Taxi Driver*, for instance.

SCORSESE: You're the first person in 15 years to say that.

PLAYBOY: Do you agree?

SCORSESE: Oh, totally. Others have missed it, though I've really tried to make it clear. Even in *Alice Doesn't Live Here Anymore*, I was trying to do something radical in terms of women. But ultimately, we all came to the conclusion that it was *OK* if she wanted to live with somebody. I felt bad about it and thought maybe it wasn't a radical enough statement for that time of feminism.

But I like women. A lot of the people who've worked with me for years are women: my editor, my producers, my production managers. I find that they have a whole other point of view. It's fascinating to me. I was the first instructor at New York University to allow women to direct. They didn't have any women directors.

PLAYBOY: The question, of course, is how women react to your films.

SCORSESE: I'll tell you one interesting anecdote about this. After the [American Film Institute] tribute to David Lean, there were some cocktails. I'd been working with a number of the archivists and one of them introduced me to another archivist, a young woman. We talked awhile, then she said, "I must say that I'm an admirer of your films. After all, I am a woman." I don't get it.

PLAYBOY: Could you make a movie from a woman's point of view?

SCORSESE: I think so. I could *try*.

PLAYBOY: What about one that deals more directly with sex?

SCORSESE: That's a very good question. I guess when I find the right angle for the interest I have in it. The subject matter that I seem to be attracted to—for example, Edith Wharton's *Age of Innocence*; Jay Cocks and I are doing a script—has the *yearning* for sex, which I believe at times can be more satisfying than the actual consummation. I'm exploring those areas—material that has to do more with the repression of sexuality than the actual sex itself. *Raging Bull* has tons of repressed sexuality. The love scene where she gets him to a point of desire, and then he pours ice water on himself. That's interesting sexually to me.

PLAYBOY: What do you think about onscreen nudity? Again, there's not much in your films.

SCORSESE: I like it. [*Laughs*] I don't have time to go to many movies, so I see most of it on cable or videotape. I'll always look, and then maybe change the channel anyway. Sometimes in a theater, I feel a little uncomfortable with it.

PLAYBOY: Sexuality, or the mere suggestion of it, seemed to play a significant role in your troubles making *The Last Temptation of Christ*. Paramount was going to make the picture in 1983 but pulled the plug in fear of potential protests. Then, four years later, Universal Studios became interested. What appealed to you so much about the Kazantzakis book that you never gave up?

SCORSESE: There are many reasons. Because it's about humanity. It deals with everybody's struggle. You don't have to be Catholic. I had hoped it would be the kind of film that would engender very healthy discussions on the nature of God and how the Church should change to meet today's needs.

PLAYBOY: The Catholic Church wasn't nearly as vocal about the film as the fundamentalist groups. Their outrage focused not on the issues you'd hoped but on whether or not the film should even be shown. When you saw footage of the protesters on *Nightline*, you said, "The film was gone." What did you mean?

SCORSESE: Well, I meant that selfishly. I knew there would be problems. I knew that the fundamentalist movement was difficult in 1983, and that's why the film was canceled, but I didn't think they would be as vociferous the second time around. There were a number of people from Protestant groups who were *for* the film. *They* kept pointing out on television that the fundamentalists—that Reverend Donald Wildmon and the other man, Reverend Hymers, who was doing all the demonstrations in Los Angeles—were only a very small minority. But the fundamentalists got the coverage. So, after *Nightline*, I figured, Well, that's enough; I guess they don't have to release the film if they don't want to. The hell with it; just let it go.

PLAYBOY: That was it? That easily?

SCORSESE: Of course not. But, as I said, I was being selfish. My thought was of the film; I should have been thinking about the *people* for whom the film was made—people like me who are not necessarily involved with the daily ritual of the Church but still believe to a certain extent, who have questions they want to discuss and who want to feel that there is a Jesus for *them*. Remember, Jesus was on Eighth Avenue with the prostitutes. He wasn't uptown or in Washington, D.C.

PLAYBOY: Did your parents suffer in any way from this?

SCORSESE: I think so, yes. They weren't harassed, but I think they were very hurt by the circus on TV. My mother was very upset about it. One religious leader said that she was a whore. I said, "He was using it to make a point, Mom. He's saying that people are hurt that I may be saying things about Jesus that are the equivalent of my saying their mother is a whore. That's what the priest was saying."

PLAYBOY: What was Christ's last temptation?

SCORSESE: In the film, the last temptation was to live the life of an ordinary man and die in old age.

PLAYBOY: Since you identify with your characters, can we assume you harbor the desire to live an ordinary life at some point, to get off the directional cross?

SCORSESE: No, no. I accept who I am. In the film, giving in to the last temptation was kind of like a copping out, even though life as an ordinary man looked very attractive. Eventually, Christ rejected the last temptation. [*Smiles*] So what else am I going to do but direct? And whatever happens, I'll always have something to do with film.

PLAYBOY: Let's start wrapping this up, with one of your favorite subjects. Why did you once say you hated the phrase Italian-American sensibility?

SCORSESE: Did I say that? [*Laughs*] I get upset about the happy, dancing, singing peasants, organ-grinder's monkey, everybody eating pasta cliché of the Italian-American. Any ethnic group would be a little annoyed by the stereotypes.

PLAYBOY: Italian-Americans seem to be annoyed at you for stereotyping them as wise guys and mobsters.

SCORSESE: OK. But I want to be clear about this: It's not the experience for *all* Italian-Americans. Not everybody in my neighborhood was a wise guy. This is a very annoying area to talk about without the Italian-Americans' getting upset. I point out, and Nick Pileggi [author of the book *Wiseguy* and co-author of the screenplay *GoodFellas*] points out, that out of 20 million Italian-Americans, there are only four thousand known organized-crime members. Yet there is a reality to how those organized-crime figures are interlaced into the Italian-American lifestyle. To best understand the importance and the unimportance of it is to come from that lifestyle. It's very difficult to describe.

PLAYBOY: Why does Hollywood love mob movies?

SCORSESE: Actually, what's more interesting is that it was easier for me to make *Mean Streets* because of *The Godfather*. I had tried to get *Mean Streets* made earlier, and I couldn't get any money. My film school professor Haig Manoogian said, "Nobody cares about these people." At the time, he was right. It was the late 1960s, you know, free love.

PLAYBOY: Did you know Francis Ford Coppola at the time?

SCORSESE: We met at the Sorrento Film Encounter in Italy. I was there with *Who's That Knocking?*, working every angle, working every room, getting to every cocktail party I could get to, to get money to make another picture. We had a great time. We ate lots of pasta, told stories. Francis was working on the script for *The Godfather* right there in Sorrento. I said, "When you come back to New York, eat at my parents' house."

PLAYBOY: Did he?

SCORSESE: Yeah. My parents would tell him stories. My father's voice was recorded to listen to the accent. My mother was constantly giving him casting suggestions.

PLAYBOY: Did he take any?

SCORSESE: Yeah, sure. One night at dinner, she told him she wanted Richard Conte in the picture and he put him in. Another time, she asked him how many days he had to shoot and he said, "A hundred days." She said, "That's not enough." This is 1970. I said, "Mom, don't get him terrified!" As it was, he went over budget somewhat. He was fighting every day. I remember one story where he had one day to shoot the funeral of the Godfather. And he just sat down on one of the tombstones in the graveyard and started crying. But out of that torture came a wonderful film.

PLAYBOY: Did you contribute?

SCORSESE: I took [set designer] Dean Tavoularis around for set ideas. I remember finding the olive-oil factory. He also used the interior of my church, St. Patrick's Cathedral, the old cathedral. They shot the baptism scene there.

PLAYBOY: So you were more involved than is generally known.

SCORSESE: Yeah, for a lot of the locations, and my parents helped out a lot. We got a lot of people they knew to be in it, too.

PLAYBOY: Are you and Coppola still close?

SCORSESE: It has always been kind of a constant thing with us. We don't see each other that much anymore. He was like a big brother who helped me a lot.

PLAYBOY: How would you compare your Italian-American films with *The Godfather, Married to the Mob, Prizzi's Honor?*

SCORSESE: Demme was using stereotype for *Married to the Mob,* but for a farce, you can get away with it. *Prizzi's Honor?* Forget it; it's a whole different thing. Jack Nicholson and Anjelica Huston went right over the top with those accents. It was a wonderful self-parody in a way, and it's very difficult to do.

PLAYBOY: Are you at all offended or cynical about those films?

SCORSESE: Yeah. Certain films about Italian-Americans are exaggerations. They're not made by Italian-Americans. *Moonstruck,* for example, is an enjoyable picture, but it's a little exaggerated in terms of the ethnicity of it. It sometimes is disturbing. When the titles come up and you hear "That's Amore" by Dean Martin, as an Italian-American, you cringe a little bit. Or "Mambo Italiano" in the titles of *Married to the Mob*. I told Demme, "You can't do that, you're not Italian. Only Italians can play that music. Only Italians can say the bad things about ourselves."

PLAYBOY: Have you ever gotten compliments on these kind of films from, say, Mafia types?

SCORSESE: Nick Pileggi told me that Henry Hill told him that [Mafia kingpin] Paulie Vario never went to the movies. One night, they said, "Paulie, we're going to take you to see this picture." They took him to see a movie, and it was *Mean Streets*. And he loved it. It was his favorite picture. And I got the same response from Ed McDonald, who was head of the Brooklyn organized-crime strike task force.

PLAYBOY: Why was it so appealing?

SCORSESE: Because it had a truth to it. And that was the highest compliment.

PLAYBOY: Have you ever packed any heat yourself?

SCORSESE: No. I'd shoot myself by accident. People would knock on the door and they'd be killed. I'd be so nervous, I'd be like Barney Fife.

PLAYBOY: This has been a whirlwind—and not only because you speak so fast between breaths and shots from your inhaler. When do you slow down?

SCORSESE: When I'm sleeping. Sometimes. Playing with my dog. When Jay Cocks and I are together, looking at old 16 millimeter films.

PLAYBOY: Don't you go out?

SCORSESE: I don't really see many people anymore.

PLAYBOY: When are you most alone?

SCORSESE: A few minutes before falling asleep. That's when I have a sense of mortality.

PLAYBOY: When you're alone in your New York apartment then, 75 stories above the city, looking out the picture window, surveying New York, what goes through your mind?

SCORSESE: The city looks like a painting that keeps changing. I keep thinking that I don't know how much longer I'll be there—I'm renting— that eventually I want to get my own place. But I realize I don't belong back on the Lower East Side. I don't belong in Rome, I don't belong in London. Where do I belong? Maybe just above New York—and me, afraid of flying. But I don't have to think about where I belong when I'm up there. I can just enjoy it, look over it and think about where I came from and what I'm doing now.

PLAYBOY: If you had to do it over again, would you do it the same?

SCORSESE: Oh, there's no doubt. I would have to, because the mistakes are even more important than the successes.

PLAYBOY: Any other wisdom to share?

SCORSESE: I'm reminded of a sequence I always loved from *Diary of a Country Priest*. The priest is listening to a woman's problems. She's had a very hard time. He tells her something I've always felt deep down: "God is not a torturer. He just wants us to be merciful with ourselves."

PLAYBOY: Is that the kind of advice you'd give to Martin Scorsese?

SCORSESE: It's good advice. I'm just trying to get through every minute of the day. It's the continuing struggle. It sounds pretentious, but I mean it in a good way. I don't mean being an achiever. I mean accomplishing whatever there is to accomplish between friends and in relationships. I was pretty strongly single-minded when I was young. I knew that I wanted to be a director, and I got that. And when you get it, when you get your dream, what do you do with it?

PLAYBOY: Good question.

SCORSESE: You go minute by minute.

OLIVER STONE

A candid conversation with the award-winning director of Platoon *about his odyssey through the jungles of Vietnam, Hollywood and Wall Street*

Two Olivers made news last year: One, a gap-toothed lieutenant colonel in the U.S. Marines, became a temporary TV folk hero as he explained how he had tried to vindicate the "noble cause," by implication, of American intervention in Vietnam by promoting a winnable war against the Communists of Nicaragua. The other Oliver, a gap-toothed screenwriter and movie director, walked away with the year's best-picture Oscar for a landmark movie that preached the opposite point of view: that Vietnam was a tragic folly and that Central America could become the next generation's debacle.

It's a good bet that the second Oliver, the showbiz Oliver, will end up winning more hearts and minds than the military Oliver. For Oliver Stone, 41-year-old Yale dropout, former GI, doper, angry rebel and scourge of Hollywood, is now one of the true powers that be, with a body of work that has reflected—and perhaps affected—his generation's obsessions: war, politics, drugs, money.

Indeed, the fact that Stone went directly from his cathartic vision of the Vietnam war in *Platoon* to an up-to-the-minute drama on greed in America, *Wall Street*, says something about his sense of symbolism and timing. Or about his luck.

It was only after 10 years of excuses, postponements, delays and rejections from every major studio in Hollywood that Stone, a journeyman screenwriter, finally got his independently produced, low-budget, no-stars Vietnam movie on the screen. The result was a film that has grossed $138,000,000 and garnered four Oscars—including best picture and best director. For a time, *Platoon* became a kind of movable Vietnam memorial as men wearing fatigues wept in movie theaters over the film's closing credits. Not a small part of its appeal was the fact that it was embraced both by veterans who felt that their agony had gone unappreciated and by war resisters who felt that the film captured, definitively, the waste that was Vietnam.

The portrayal of U.S. soldiers in Stone's script as emotionally volatile youngsters who drank, smoked dope and occasionally fragged their officers so unnerved the Pentagon that it refused to offer any technical assistance in the shooting of *Platoon*. From his right flank, Stone was barraged by columnists such as John Podhoretz, who damned the film for being "one of the most repellent movies ever made in this country." But after a decade of pious, ineffective lip service from both left and right about the need to heal the wounds of Vietnam, *Platoon* emerged as a hardy curative. *Platoon*, the picture, became, in the words of *Time*, "*Platoon* the Phenomenon."

Back in Hollywood, the topic of Vietnam—a long-standing taboo in studio corridors—suddenly became chic. *Platoon* was followed by a parade of Vietnam-genre movies: *Full Metal Jacket, Gardens of Stone, The Hanoi Hilton* and *Hamburger Hill*. Studio executives and producers who for the past five years had wanted to talk only about teen comedies and middle-of-the-road spoofs now wanted projects with "social significance."

However belated his world-wide fame, Stone has been known to Hollywood insiders for a long time. The movies he has written or on which he has collaborated have nearly all been visceral, noisy, controversial. In 1978, his screenplay *Midnight Express*, about an American in the hellish world of a Turkish prison, won a screenwriting Oscar and launched his career—which nose-dived three years later with the flop of his second directorial effort, a gimmicky movie about a monster hand called, well, *The Hand*. Stone rehabilitated his career slowly, painfully, by writing and collaborating with a group of Hollywood's quirkier, more demanding directors: John Milius, of *Conan the Barbarian*; Brian De Palma, of *Scarface* (a cult film today); Michael Cimino, of *Year of the Dragon*; and Hal Ashby, of *Eight Million Ways to Die*.

Although it kept him busy, Stone's screenplay work drew mixed reviews, and he built up a reputation as a violence-obsessed xenophobe. Stories about his days as a druggie and carouser circulated freely. Although respected, he was considered a wild card, and it

wasn't until he managed to turn *Salvador*, his stinging film indictment of U.S. policy in Central America, into a small hit that Stone
finally got financing for *Platoon* from a small independent company,
Hemdale Film Corporation.

Stone went off to the Philippines with a relatively modest
$5,000,000, shot the film with the Aquino revolution raging around
his location, then came home with a classic. It was also on time and
within budget.

His early personal history does not hint at the discipline or the
toughness that were to become Stone's trademarks: The privileged
son of a New York Jewish stockbroker and a French Catholic mother,
Oliver had a comfortable, conservative childhood. He attended
prep schools and entered Yale with the class of 1969; there, he was
suddenly afflicted with the fear that he was on a "conveyer belt to
business." Influenced by his reading—mainly Joseph Conrad—and
the changing times, he quit Yale, bummed around the world and
wound up teaching Catholic school in Saigon in 1965. More exotic
travels followed, then more romantic reading, and in a desperate,
suicidal state, he returned to Vietnam in 1967 and enlisted in the
U.S. Infantry.

Stone began his combat tour a gung-ho patriot. "I believed in the
John Wayne image of America," he says. He earned a Bronze Star and
a Purple Heart with oak-leaf cluster. But he returned from Vietnam
an embittered anarchist, landing in a San Diego jail on dope charges
just 10 days after his discharge. A failed marriage, stints as a cabdriver
and training at the NYU film school matured him personally; the
collapse of the Vietnam war and Watergate matured him politically.
Ending his carousing, drug-taking, "sexually wild" days, Stone has
settled into a posh Santa Monica home, a new marriage and domestic
concerns with a three-year-old son, Sean.

To find out about the twists and turns in Stone's life, *Playboy*
sent freelance writer Marc Cooper (who co-conducted the *Playboy Interview* with Salvadoran president José Napoleón Duarte in
November 1984) to talk with him during the filming of *Wall Street*.
Cooper's report:

"My first meeting with Stone was at his Santa Monica home—just
hours before last spring's Academy Awards ceremony. 'I better win,'
he said, grinning, 'or you guys won't publish this interview.' I assured
him we were interested, win or lose. He immediately asked how I

felt he had done on ABC's *20/20*, on which he had described the Pentagon's refusal to help in the filming of *Platoon*.

"'I mean, the Army *did* come off as assholes, didn't they?' he asked.

"I didn't think he cared in the personal sense; it was a political question. Throughout our interview sessions, he would speak intensely, but he was monitoring each word, each turn of phrase as he spoke, always watching my face for hints of reaction. There was nothing personal or insecure about it—he had points to make and was looking for the best openings. His manner—broad, outward, forceful—is as potent as his films. But it seemed to me the way of a writer rather than a director. A writer with a mission. A writer with battles yet to win.

"We spoke through some of the location shooting of *Wall Street*, in the summer, between setups that included actor Michael Douglas and Stone's own toddler, Sean. The atmosphere was frantic, but Stone seemed totally focused and inexhaustible. Snatching time in Southampton as the production hurtled on, he pushed the two of us as hard as he pushed his crew, making sure we covered all the ground we had agreed upon. There was no room for distraction, for ambiguity, for drift. He was *directed*.

"Finally, as the interview concluded, Stone's inborn skepticism surfaced. Perhaps it was the cynicism he had acquired after 10 years of betrayal and rejection in Hollywood.

"He pulled off the lapel microphone and said gruffly, 'Hell, you guys'll probably concentrate on all the stuff that's not important. Then you'll cut out the politics.'"

PLAYBOY: Not a bad year for Oliver Stone—from your four Oscars for *Platoon* to the release of *Wall Street*. For a guy who couldn't get a directing job for 10 years, life has certainly changed.

STONE: I feel like the beggar who gets invited to the party but who always keeps a wary eye on the back door. [*Laughs*] I'm a bit like the Nick Nolte character in *Down and Out in Beverly Hills*. Kind of like I'm not quite sure I'm supposed to be at this party. From ugly duckling to Cinderella.

PLAYBOY: And do you feel a sense of getting even, considering all those people who turned down *Platoon*?

STONE: No, the turnaround was so enormous it forgives all the no's and the rejections. That's the way the game goes in Los Angeles. What are you going to do? An asshole who hated you and blackballed you at some studio two years ago comes up to you and says you're a genius all of a sudden—you've got to laugh.

But, sure, there *are* a number of phone calls I haven't been returning lately. There is a certain satisfaction there. As an old English proverb says, "Vengeance is a dish that should be eaten cold."

PLAYBOY: We'll get back to *Platoon* and the hungry days of *Midnight Express*, *Scarface* and *Salvador*; but first, what about your newest film, *Wall Street*? The word is that it's another war movie—jungle warfare in Manhattan.

STONE: It's not that black and white. It's a tough story, but it simply has business as a background. It's about greed and corruption amid these takeover wars we've all read about.

PLAYBOY: Your timing is certainly interesting—the stock-market crash, the wild trading since then.

STONE: Yeah, I'm not amazed or surprised. Our movie doesn't deal directly with the prospects of a crash, but it reflects the hyperinflation of the times—not just of the market but also of personal values and individual egos.

PLAYBOY: And, as usual, the movie is controversial. Didn't *The Wall Street Journal* take off after it?

STONE: *The Wall Street Journal* has had a strange attitude toward the movie. We asked to use the paper as a prop, but they turned us down. We also asked about shooting in their offices and they turned us down for that. But I'm not surprised. They are very conservative, and they're nervous. There's a scene in the movie where a journalist gets an inside tip and uses that information to get what he needs for his story.

PLAYBOY: So, *Platoon* was denied technical assistance by the Pentagon; *Salvador* was denied assistance by the Salvadoran army; now *The Wall Street Journal* has turned you down—you're going to offend everyone, aren't you?

STONE: Yeah. [*Laughs*] We even had *Forbes* complaining about our using *Fortune* in some scene—but that was over *wanting* to be included in the movie. We used both magazines as props.

PLAYBOY: How much of *Wall Street* is a personal story? Weren't you originally groomed for a business career?

STONE: Well, my father was a stockbroker, and there's a character in the movie, played by Hal Holbrook, who is the voice of an older Wall Street.

The Wall Street that my father worked in, the one I grew up around, is wholly different from that of today. There were no computers; they didn't trade in such volume; there were fixed commissions.

My father did very well in the 1950s and the 1960s. Then he had a reversal of fortune and had very bad luck in the late 1960s, into the 1970s. He never recovered. It sort of belongs in a Theodore Dreiser novel. But he was a man who supported the ranks of the rich—until the end, when he began to question the whole economic fabric.

Anyway, I always wanted to do a business movie. Always. My father used to take me to movies and would often say, "Why do they make the businessman such a caricature?" Then he'd explain to me what business *is*. The business of America, as Calvin Coolidge said, is business. He made me aware of what serious business is.

My father believed America's business brought peace to the world and built industry through science and research, and that capital is needed for that. But this idea seems to have been perverted to a large degree. I don't think my father would recognize America today. Personally, I think most corporate raids are good. Not always, but most times.

PLAYBOY: That may surprise people who think your politics are liberal to radical.

STONE: Well, it's what I think about American business. Management's become so weak in this country, so flaccid. These guys are into their salaries, their golf trips, their fishing trips; there's so much fat and waste in these companies. A lot of these corporate raiders are guys who want to make the money, but in doing so, they clean up these companies. So corporate raiding is a reformation of the system. It's a natural correction.

PLAYBOY: Do you take a similarly benign view of insider trading?

STONE: I think insider trading goes on and has been going on for centuries, in all businesses. It goes on in movies; it goes on in taxicabs; everybody is always looking for an inside thing. It's the natural human impulse. How do you legislate against that? The Street has been doing a fairly strong job of policing itself. My father would say there was more inside tipping in the old days than there is now. Apparently, in this new paranoid environment in Wall Street, brokers don't even talk with one another about what they know, they're so scared.

PLAYBOY: Then all the busts have been healthy?

STONE: Probably, yes. I think the past two years have shaken it out a lot. My movie is based on 1985. It's important to note that. It could not have taken place in 1987.

PLAYBOY: You know, it sounds a little as though rebel Stone is defending Wall Street interests.

STONE: God. Here I go. This is a tough one. Look, you know something of what I've fought against in the U.S. establishment, but—McDonald's is *good* for the world, that's my opinion. Because I think war is the most dangerous thing. Nationalism and patriotism are the two most evil forces that I know of in this century or in any century and cause more wars and more death and more destruction to the soul and to human life than anything else—and can still do it with nuclear war. The prime objective we have in this era is to prevent war, to live in peace. The best way you can do that is to bring prosperity to as many people across the world as you can. And when you spread McDonald's all over the world, food becomes cheaper and more available to more people. Won't it be great when they can have McDonald's throughout Africa?

The *Pax Americana*, to me, is the dollar sign. It works. It may not be attractive. It's not pretty to see American businessmen running all around the world in plaid trousers, drinking whisky. But what they're doing makes sense. Now it's been picked up more intelligently by the Japanese, the British and the Germans. But it brings education, health and welfare to the rest of the world.

PLAYBOY: That may be, as we've suggested, the last thing people expected to hear from the maker of *Platoon*. That movie was a landmark for the Vietnam generation, but don't most people assume that you were strongly against the American war effort, against the establishment?

STONE: No, I got as much mail from people who thought I was supportive of that war as from people who thought I was against it. That's part of the appeal of *Platoon*—and the controversy.

PLAYBOY: But the criticism from the right was that you undermined the military, wasn't it?

STONE: From right *and* left. Some right-wing veterans—many officers, many Marines—said they never shot villagers in Vietnam, never took drugs, never killed other servicemen, so the movie was unfair and unbalanced. But I don't agree. I think the movie portrays a wide range of behavior in Vietnam. I think it treats people as human beings. Some are weaker than others, some are stronger morally.

PLAYBOY: What was the left's criticism?

STONE: That *Platoon* doesn't show the causes of Vietnam, of "American imperialism." That it glorifies America's action in Vietnam instead of denouncing it.

PLAYBOY: In fact, *Platoon* doesn't deal with the causes of Vietnam. Was it a conscious decision on your part to omit the war's political origins?

STONE: I dealt with that in another screenplay that didn't get made—*Born on the Fourth of July* [Vietnam veteran Ron Kovic's memoir, excerpted in *Playboy* in July 1976]. That really broke me up, and at that point, in 1978, I felt that nothing serious would come out of Hollywood. I had written *Platoon* prior to that, in 1976, and it always dealt solely, relentlessly, with the jungle. I wrote it as a specific document of a time and a place.

In the real Vietnam, there was no political discussion, as far as I remember. And people had not really seen the true Vietnam combat-grunt story. That bothered me. I hadn't seen it in history books. Certainly not in the army official history books, which all glossed over Vietnam. It was going to be flushed down the toilet, and I was afraid I would end up being an old man like Sam Fuller, who did a World War II movie, *The Big Red One*, that I don't think was effective because of the lapse in years.

PLAYBOY: You've said *Platoon* was meant not to put down the U.S. military but to oppose a certain mythology. Which myths?

STONE: It's a huge question. You have to start with the way we fought the war. There was no moral purpose for the war. There was no geographic objective, no defined goal. There was not even a declaration of war. There was no moral integrity in the way it was fought. It started with President Johnson's defrauding the Congress with the Gulf of Tonkin incidents. Then it deteriorated noticeably when Johnson refused to send anyone except the poor and the uneducated off to fight the war. Anybody in the middle or upper class was able to avoid the war by going to college or getting a psychiatric discharge or numerous other things. This split the country from the git-go, because there's no question that had the middle class and the upper class gone to that war, their parents—the politicians and the businessmen—would have stopped it by 1966 or 1967, as soon as their little kids were getting killed.

PLAYBOY: You weren't poor or uneducated when you went to Vietnam.

STONE: I was the exception. They sent in these poor draftees, not in units but as single replacement troops, where there's no geographic objective and an attitude—which I found in '67—that everybody wanted only to survive. Everybody was counting days. I remember arriving—and I had exactly 360 days to go. I was the last guy on the totem pole. Survival, period. Forget about military heroism and all of that stuff you saw in the movies.

PLAYBOY: Surely, the military establishment was aware of the attitude it had created among the draftees.

STONE: I'm not so sure. The U.S. military had one of the sickest infrastructures, I've ever seen in my lifetime, outside of Miami Beach and Las Vegas. What the United States did, in fact, was bring Miami Beach and Las Vegas to Vietnam! There were seven to eight noncombatants per combatant. They fought a different war from the rest of us. They ate steaks and lobsters every night and watched the bombs and mortars falling from a safe distance.

And it went beyond that. It went to a huge rip-off of American supplies and money. Many of the South Vietnamese we worked with were corrupt and saw in this a possibility to make a lot of money. And when we brought in our PXs, we brought our refrigerators, our cars, our televisions.

PLAYBOY: And the black market.

STONE: This was the basis of the black market. And people made a fortune. There was a huge scandal during the war in which the sergeant major of the army was busted, along with about four other sergeants, for illegal kickbacks. And if you worked in the rear, it *became* Las Vegas. You went back to China Beach; you had the hookers; you had the bars; you had the slot machines. You had the good food. It wasn't a war, it was a scam.

PLAYBOY: As a Yale dropout with well-off parents, you were the exception among the grunts. But campuses were hotbeds of protest and dissent. How could you not have known what you were getting into when you enlisted for combat?

STONE: The fact was that in '65 at Yale, there was no political discussion about the war. That didn't come till a couple of years later. When I was there, I was faced with an overriding conformity of outlook in the Yale ambience. I felt as if I were on an assembly line turning out a mass product: highly educated technocrats who could make money in Wall Street or banking, or run corporate America.

PLAYBOY: What were your politics when you were young?

STONE: I was born a Cold War baby. When *Sputnik* was launched, I was shocked. It was like the end of the American dream for me. I supported Goldwater in 1964 while at the Hill School. I think I might have even joined the Young Republicans. [*Laughs*] I hated liberals.

PLAYBOY: And your father was a rich Republican.

STONE: One out of two. Staunch Republican, yes. But after a lifetime of devotion to his Republican masters, you'd think he'd have walked away a rich man. He walked away poor at the end, and when he died, he was still working.

PLAYBOY: So after dropping out of Yale, you went straight to Vietnam—but not in the military, right?

STONE: Yes. I felt a yearning for something exotic. To break the gray wall of the Hill School, of Yale, of my family. It was an urge that came from novels and movies. From *Zorba the Greek*. Wow! From George Harrison's Indian sitar music. Conrad's book *Lord Jim* really shook me up. I saw the world of Conrad out there: jungle steamers, Malaysia, dealing with the Asiatics. And Lord Jim's redemption. I knew there was another reality out there that I was not experiencing, and if I didn't do something about it, it would be too late.

PLAYBOY: How far out did that romantic pull take you?

STONE: Far enough that I investigated the possibility of going to the Belgian Congo as a mercenary. Check that out! I was so far into it, I was skydiving. In those days, I really needed to find something. I think it was really the equivalent of a nervous breakdown—an intellectual breakdown.

PLAYBOY: How close did you come to becoming a mercenary?

STONE: Very close. I made the contacts. It was adventure. It was Hemingway. It was Conrad. It was Audie Murphy and John Wayne. It was going to be *my* war, as World War II had been my father's war.

PLAYBOY: But, instead, you ended up in 1965 in Saigon for about a year and a half as a teacher. What were your first impressions of Vietnam?

STONE: At that point, it was still a great adventure. I remember seeing Teddy Kennedy on the streets of Thu-dau-mo. Hey, we were going to win. We were the good guys. To see the First Infantry in all its full flash arriving in Saigon was a tremendous thrill. The Marines were already there. Guys were walking around with guns. There were shoot-outs in the street. It was like Dodge City. There was no curfew in those days. Hookers were everywhere. Bars were everywhere. I was 19 years old.

PLAYBOY: The romantic paradise you dreamed about at Yale?

STONE: Oh, yeah! It seemed as if I had finally found the war of my generation. In fact, I was terribly concerned that year, as a teacher, that the war was going to be over too quickly, that I would miss it.

PLAYBOY: You went back to Yale, though, tried to write a novel and dropped out again. But then you went back to Vietnam, after you enlisted.

STONE: Right. I was disgusted with myself. I believed my father's warnings that I was turning my back on humanity by leaving Yale. I was convinced I couldn't write. I gave up and just basically said, "I'm going back to

Vietnam, and either I'm going to kill myself or I'm gonna experience life at the lowest possible level. If I survive, I'm going to be another person." So I joined the army.

PLAYBOY: In a suicidal frame of mind?

STONE: Partly, yes. The failure of the book was really eating at me. I wanted anonymity. And the army offered that.

PLAYBOY: Did the army live up to your expectations?

STONE: I made sure it did. I was offered Officer Candidate School. I turned it down.

PLAYBOY: Not many people do that.

STONE: I did. I was really in a rush; I was afraid I would miss the war. All these generals were saying, "It's almost over" and all that shit. So I went the fastest way. I insisted on Infantry and I insisted they send me to Vietnam. Not Korea or Germany, but Vietnam. April '67, I got inducted at Fort Jackson; and, oddly enough, on September 14, 1967, the night before my 21st birthday, I got on the plane to Vietnam. I started smoking cigarettes on that fucking plane. [*Laughs*] To celebrate my manhood.

PLAYBOY: Given your father's politics, was he happy you went into the military?

STONE: My dad was an *intelligent* right winger. His feeling at that time was that it was a ridiculous waste.

PLAYBOY: It was a waste for you or the entire war was a waste?

STONE: He believed in the domino theory. And he felt that the war was fine as long as other boys less economically sufficient would fight it.

PLAYBOY: How long did it take you after you got off the plane to change your mind about the romance of your decision?

STONE: I'd say one day in the bush. It was like the scene in *Platoon*, the kid on the point. I was put on point my first fucking day in the field. It was just so hard, so grimy, so tough. I thought I couldn't take it. I was about to pass out with 50 pounds of equipment. Then, about seven or eight days in, we had that night-ambush scene—

PLAYBOY: Real life or movie?

STONE: It happened to me, and the scene was pretty closely depicted in the movie: I saw these three NVA [North Vietnamese Army] soldiers. They were huge. Tough! And they walked right up on me. I just fucking forgot everything I had learned. I knew the rules. I knew what you were supposed to do in an ambush. You blow your Claymore. You throw your grenades. Then you use your '16, because you don't want them to spot your fire pattern.

PLAYBOY: And what did Private Stone do?

STONE: None of the above! [*Laughs*] I just stood there. Wow!

PLAYBOY: You laugh now; were you scared?

STONE: I was. I remember my logical, worldly brain, of course, trying to rationalize this whole thing. I said about the North Vietnamese, "These must be lost GIs." Because they had helmets on, I thought they were coming back into the perimeter.

PLAYBOY: But it wasn't just fear that changed you so quickly. Or talk—you said there was no discussion of ideology there.

STONE: No, never. But all of a sudden, I was with black guys, poor white guys for the first time. And these poor people see through that upper-class bullshit. They don't buy into the rich guy's game. They don't buy into the Pentagon bullshit. They know the score. That score is, "We've been fucked [*laughs*], and we are over here in Vietnam." [*Laughs*]

PLAYBOY: Did knowing the score mean you dropped your Cold War view of the world?

STONE: Well, let's say it went into abeyance during the war. I mean, over there, we were still feeling a certain hostility toward the antiwar protesters. Like, you know, "Well, fuck them. Let *them* come over here and fight. Let *them* experience it."

PLAYBOY: Was that a generalized sentiment among the grunts?

STONE: Not among everybody, but among a lot of people. No, I'd say a lot of black guys—especially black guys—and people like the Elias character in *Platoon* were more hippie-ish in their attitude. Like Muhammad Ali said, I had no beef with the VC You know? Or like, just, "I'm here, man; I'm gonna smoke dope and I'm gonna make it and I'm gonna survive and I'm gonna make a lot of money." And the dope was great!

PLAYBOY: We take it from *Platoon* that you hung out with the dope smokers.

STONE: Yes. It was the first time in my life. With black guys. I had never had any black friends before. They also introduced me to black music. I had never known about Motown. I had never heard Smokey Robinson and Sam Cooke. I remember the first time we heard *Light My Fire*. It was a fucking revolution! Grace Slick's *White Rabbit*. I loved her. Jimi Hendrix. Janis Joplin was very important.

PLAYBOY: How long had you been in Vietnam when you started smoking marijuana?

STONE: I actually did not smoke any dope until I'd been wounded twice.

PLAYBOY: Did you begin as a model soldier?

STONE: Not exactly. I was in the 25th Infantry first, which was where I saw most of my combat. Then, when I got wounded the second time, they shipped me to another unit, because if you had two wounds, you could get out. I went to a rear-echelon unit in Saigon. Auxiliary military police. But I was gonna get an Article 15, insubordination, because I had a fight with a sergeant. So I made a deal, essentially. I said, "Send me back to the field and drop the charges." I couldn't stand this rear-echelon bullshit. They put me in this long-range recon patrol, and that's where I met the basis for the Elias character in *Platoon*.

PLAYBOY: What was Elias' real name?

STONE: Elias. I don't know if it was his last name or his first name, but it was always Elias. A sergeant. Apache. A black-haired kid, very handsome. He looked like Jimmy Morrison; he truly was a Jimmy Morrison of the soldiers. Very charismatic. The leader of the group. He was killed.

PLAYBOY: What happened to you there?

STONE: I got this horrible grease-bag lifer sergeant, one of these guys who were raking off the beer concession. He had a waxed mustache; I'll never forget that. He didn't like my attitude, and I told him to go fuck himself. [*Laughs*]

So they sent me across the road to a regular combat unit, which was the First or the Ninth Armored Cav, or whatever the fuck they called it. Basically, it was infantry. And there was the Sergeant Barnes character. My squad sergeant.

There, among the First Cav with the black guys, is where I started smoking dope. There were a lot of guys over the edge in that unit. We had a bunker where we used to smoke a lot of dope. I was wearing beads, started to talk black dialect. "Hey, what you doin', man?" All that shit. "What's happenin'?" I'd do all the raps, and when I came home from the war, my father was freaked out. He hated me. He said, "You turned into a black man!"

PLAYBOY: Did you ever smoke dope in combat?

STONE: Yeah.

PLAYBOY: Even on the day you earned your Bronze Star?

STONE: Yeah. I had been stoned that morning and the fire fight was that afternoon. But it wasn't really a big deal. There were so many other acts of valor from other guys; it was just that in my case, somebody saw me doing it.

PLAYBOY: How did you feel about the Vietnamese enemy?

STONE: I never thought about them. My tour included the Tet offensive of January '68. So from September '67 to January we were running into crack troops that were coming from Cambodia down to Saigon, moving equipment. We thought they were pretty tough and skilled and mean. We didn't like 'em. We wanted to kill 'em, because they wanted to kill us. There was no thinking about it.

PLAYBOY: That's true in all wars. But in Vietnam, there was the added factor of the civilians you couldn't trust, wasn't there?

STONE: Civilians were another matter. A lot of the guys, as I showed in the movie, had racist feelings about the Vietnamese. Their attitude was, "All gooks are the same. The only good gook is a dead gook," and that meant women and kids. "They're all the same rotten bunch." A lot of that—I'd say that was a *very* strong feeling in many of the platoons.

PLAYBOY: Isn't that the mentality that leads to massacres?

STONE: There were random killings. Nothing ever preordained, nothing ordered. It would be like we'd go to a village; Bunny, for example—the Kevin Dillon character—he really killed that woman. He battered her. He smashed her head with the stock of a '16, burned her hooch down, but it was in an isolated part of the village. Nobody saw it. It was just like a really quiet thing.

PLAYBOY: How did that happen?

STONE: We'd be pissed off on certain days. We'd walk up to a village, you'd see an old lady, an old gook lady going down the trail, right? The guy would be pissed off. He'd say, "Hey, gook, come here." She wouldn't hear or she wouldn't want to turn around; she'd be scared. She'd just keep walking a few more steps. The guy wouldn't ask her a second time. He'd raise the fuckin' '16—boom, boom, boom—dead. No questions asked. She hadn't come when he told her to.

PLAYBOY: In *Platoon*, your character—played by Charlie Sheen—has a scene in which he comes very close to shooting an old man. Did that happen to you?

STONE: Yes. The time I almost blew the gook away, when I made him dance . . . I mean, I could have gotten away with it. I could have fuckin' killed him, and nobody would have busted me.

PLAYBOY: In the movie, Sheen seems as terrified as his victim.

STONE: The holes, the pits, used to make us all nervous, because you never knew what the fuck was down there. You'd yell, "Get the fuck *out*! Get *out*!" And you'd find weapons and arms and rice stores in these villages, so you hated the civilians. A lot of guys hated them.

I felt sorry for them, because I could see that they were getting pressure from the other side. I mean, I don't know where their actual political sympathies lay. I have no idea to this day. They probably were into survival, just like we were.

PLAYBOY: Did you take part in any of those random killings?

STONE: No, I *saved* a girl from getting killed. I put that in the movie, too, the rape. They would have killed that girl.

PLAYBOY: The murder of Sergeant Barnes in *Platoon* seems to suggest that fragging of officers and noncoms was fairly common.

STONE: It happened a lot. We knew that there was no moral objective from day to day—that there was no victory in sight. And you're out on the front lines. What are you going to do? Risk your life and get killed for this? So that was the source of the tension leading to the murders and the fraggings. The officer corps—not just the officers but especially the top sergeants—were pretty much hated, most of them.

PLAYBOY: Did you hate them?

STONE: I came to hate them, yes. Because they were guys who for the most part were fat cats, sitting there getting rich off the PX deals or making assignments but very rarely risking their lives.

PLAYBOY: How widespread was fragging?

STONE: It's hard to say.

PLAYBOY: You saw some, though?

STONE: I heard about it. But some people have suggested that if I really participated in some of the scenes in *Platoon*, I should be tried for war crimes—a pamphlet was sent around UCLA saying that I'm a war criminal. So I'm not going to be any more specific. You kill somebody during a battle, you put your M-16 on somebody and you just do him. Nobody's going to see it. Types like General Westmoreland don't want to admit how widespread it was. Maybe six, 10 times more than the official count.

I think one of the other figures that are very interesting that I came across is that about 20 percent of our total casualties in Vietnam were accidents or people killed by our own side. I showed it in *Platoon*, in the scenes of artillery landing on our own troops. I think my first wound in my neck was caused by an American sergeant who threw a grenade. It's just—so confusing.

PLAYBOY: The U.S. lost more than 50,000 men in Vietnam. The Vietnamese lost perhaps 2,000,000 of their people, but they are barely mentioned in *Platoon*. Do you think this sort of self-absorption may be what gets us into places like Vietnam?

STONE: I know what you're saying. But it's not just self-absorption that leads us into Vietnams. Ideology is what leads us into Vietnams. Fear of communism is what leads us into Vietnams. What you're asking for would be a different kind of movie. I did *Platoon* the way *I* lived it. I did a white infantry boy's view of the war.

Platoon is not a definitive film. It's simply a look at the war, a slice of the war. A great film would be the story of a North Vietnamese army guy who lives in a tunnel for six years, and you only see the American soldiers like blurs occasionally. And he blows them away. Because they were as scared of us as we were of them.

PLAYBOY: Would Hollywood ever make that film, with the Vietnamese as heroes?

STONE: No, I don't think so. But I agree totally with what you're suggesting. I think that the biggest, most recent example of that—what do you call it?—blindness to foreign concern is the situation in El Salvador. Because very few Americans have been killed—maybe fewer than a dozen in Salvador—America is not interested in the fact that it aided and abetted a death-squad regime that killed more than 50,000 Salvadorans between 1980 and 1986: as many citizens as the U.S. lost in 10 years in Vietnam. We don't seem to care because no Americans were killed. We cared only briefly when four nuns got killed, because they were American nuns. But nobody said anything when the archbishop of the country got greased.

PLAYBOY: Staying with *Platoon* a bit longer, what did the studios tell you during those years they refused to make the movie?

STONE: Basically, that it was too grim. It was too depressing. It wouldn't make a buck. Too real. Who cares?

PLAYBOY: Do you think that *Platoon* would not have been as well received eight years ago as it has been now?

STONE: I think it would have done OK. But in a way, it's better that it came out now. It became an antidote to *Top Gun* and *Rambo*. It's an antidote to Reagan's wars against Libya, Grenada and Nicaragua. It makes people remember what war is really like. It makes them think twice before they go marching off to another one. Maybe now *is* a better time for it than '76, because in '76 we didn't have this rebirth of American militarism that we're seeing now. I think *Platoon* makes kids think twice. Because fuckin' *Top Gun*, man—it was essentially a fascist movie. It sold the idea that war is clean, war can be won, war is a function of hand-eye coordination. You push your computer button; you blow up a Mig on a screen. A Pac-Man game. Get the girl at the end if you blow up the Mig. The music comes up. And nobody in the fuckin' movie ever mentions that he just started World War III!

PLAYBOY: Until *Platoon* came along, *Top Gun* was the biggest military-theme movie of the decade.

STONE: Yeah, it certainly sobered me and made me realize that the American audience is very divided. I think there are a lot of people who learned nothing from Vietnam. Nothing! Because of them, all the men who died in Vietnam have died for nothing—that is, if we haven't learned anything from that war. If we commit troops to Nicaragua, then all those men died in Vietnam for nothing.

I'm sick of these revisionists who want to refight that war. Why don't they just understand that we *never* could have won it? Never! The only way we could have won it was to nuke Hanoi, and even then I'm not sure we could have won. These people are bad losers. That's what it comes down to.

PLAYBOY: What about Stanley Kubrick's *Full Metal Jacket*, which was released a few months after *Platoon*?

STONE: Oh, God. I don't want to get into that. . . . Look, I don't think Stanley—I don't think Kubrick was as concerned in *Full Metal Jacket* with Vietnam as with making a generic war picture. It wasn't specific to Vietnam. It was more like his *Paths of Glory*. It could easily have been about World War II or Korea. It felt a lot like it, what with the rubble and the metallic look it had. There were some very powerful scenes in it: That last sniper scene was very strongly done. He's a master filmmaker. [*Pauses*] Master angle shots. That's about all I can say.

PLAYBOY: *Full Metal Jacket* was made before *Platoon* but was released later, right?

STONE: Right.

PLAYBOY: Since you were aware that *Full Metal Jacket* was already in production, were you concerned that *Platoon* might come in second best?

STONE: Oh, yes. But back in '84, when I had just about given up on the idea of making *Platoon*, Michael Cimino, with whom I had written the script for *Year of the Dragon*, convinced me that we could take the project off the shelf. He said that Vietnam was coming around and that Kubrick would bring a lot of attention to the issue. But our big concern was that, because he is the master filmmaker that he is, our film would be unfavorably compared with *Full Metal Jacket* if it came out afterward. You don't want your movie to be compared, if you can possibly help it, with a Kubrick movie!

PLAYBOY: When you were shooting *Platoon*, were you aware of the plot line of *Full Metal Jacket*?

STONE: I had read Gustav Hasford's book [*The Short-Timers*], which the film was based on, after *Platoon* was written.

PLAYBOY: Well, since you're being diplomatic about Kubrick's movie, what did you think of Hasford's book?

STONE: I didn't much care for it. I thought it was pumped-up, *macho-man*, true-life man's-adventure-story stuff. It could easily have been in the old *Argosy* magazine. I didn't think it was real.

PLAYBOY: Summing up your Vietnam experience, you ended up agreeing with the antiwar protesters you so distrusted when you were in Vietnam, didn't you?

STONE: There's just no question that, ultimately, they were right. The protesters were a force for social change. They brought about the end of the war. They forced Johnson to resign and they boxed Nixon in. They were a movement that hadn't been seen in America since the 1930s, when people had gotten together in groups and united. But it all bypassed me. I didn't realize its import until later.

PLAYBOY: Do you think the Vietnam vets are still not understood by the rest of us?

STONE: Oh, no, I think there's been a tremendous reintegration. I think many vets are doing very well. There's obviously a very large minority of vets who have had severe problems. But you have to keep a balanced view about this. The Korean vets have had enormous problems, too. Nobody has really examined the Korean War as a fraud or a deceit, and it, too, has become a sacred cow.

Yes, Korean vets were as much victims of the Cold War ideology as Vietnam vets. So I don't want to make a special thing about being a Vietnam vet. We are all victims of this ridiculous Cold War ideology.

PLAYBOY: Now to Central America. Some consider *Salvador* a better movie than *Platoon*. But you had plenty of trouble getting anyone to make *that*, didn't you?

STONE: I sent the script around and got extremely negative reactions. Anti-American, they said.

PLAYBOY: Well, *isn't* your portrayal of the U.S. as the mastermind behind the terror in Salvador fairly anti-American?

STONE: No. It's anti-American foreign policy. It's anti-American government—which is truly one of the worst governments in the world.

Because we're always on the side of repression. We're always on the side of the dictators.

PLAYBOY: Didn't you try to hoodwink the Salvadoran government into providing you assistance with the film?

STONE: Yeah. We went down there and we met with the military bigwigs, and [co-writer] Richard Boyle had concocted this scheme, because they have tons of American equipment. He said if we could only get them on our side, we could ride anywhere in the country and film anything. We could follow the army. We could do the helicopter assaults in the north. He said we could do *Apocalypse Now*—for about $5000 or $10,000. [*Laughs*]

PLAYBOY: How did you try to persuade the Salvadoran army to help?

STONE: We showed them a different script, which reversed everything and made *them* look good!

PLAYBOY: And did they go for it?

STONE: Oh, yes! They bought it. They liked the script. It was all set to go. What scotched it was a combination of events that culminated in our Salvadoran military advisor, who was our liaison with them, being shot and killed on a tennis court by the guerrillas. So we basically dropped the plans to shoot there, and we moved the production to Mexico.

PLAYBOY: As brutally explicit as *Salvador* is, you cut out a lot of scenes before releasing it, didn't you?

STONE: Oh, yes. The film was about two hours, 40 minutes, and we had many discussions with the producers. The film was difficult enough to distribute at two hours. We took out a lot. The original concept was that it would go from light to dark a lot. We wanted to use that Latin sort of blending that you find in a García Márquez novel—jumping from high seriousness to absurdity.

PLAYBOY: Weren't there also some explicit sex scenes that you cut?

STONE: Sure. We had this party scene where James Belushi gets a blow job under a table and Jimmy Woods is trying to get information from the colonel while he's screwing this hooker and the colonel is drunk and throwing ears—human ears—into a champagne glass. His line was, "Left-wing ears, right-wing ears; who gives a fuck? Here's to Salvador," and he makes a toast. Belushi throws up.

We showed a version of the film with that scene in it to preview audiences here in the U.S., and the comment cards that came back didn't like it. The feeling was that people in America didn't know how they were supposed to react to the movie, which I found kind of sad. *Dr. Strangelove* was a perfect amalgam of humor and seriousness about a subject that is extremely dark. There's no reason the subject of Salvadoran death squads has to be solemn. You can have fun with these guys, 'cause they're assholes. It's too bad. I think Latin American audiences would have gotten the blend much easier; but apparently, when the North American audience wants to see a political film, it wants to see a political film, period.

PLAYBOY: Did El Salvador remind you of Vietnam in the early days?

STONE: It was Honduras that reminded me of Vietnam, because of the volume and presence of the American military there. You see a lot of young American guys in Honduras, technicians, too, that sense of Saigon in '65, that same sense of "We're doin' the right thing. We're beatin' the Commies in Nicaragua." I talked with these kids. I said, "Do you remember Vietnam?" And they kind of looked at me with a disturbed look. They don't remember. They don't fuckin' remember!

PLAYBOY: Did that attitude affect you?

STONE: Yeah, it's why I made *Platoon*. To yell out, "This happened, kids! People got killed here. This is what war is really like. This is it! This is what your kid is going to go through if it happens again. This is what it means. Think twice before you buy another used war from these fuckin' politicians with their 'Communism is everywhere' routine."

PLAYBOY: Let's move on to your personal life. Drugs seem to be a theme in every one of your movies. Were they a central part of your life?

STONE: I think drugs are very much a part of my generation's experience. We were not only the Cold War generation, we were the drug generation. And marijuana, with its origins in the 1960s, was good. It was a force for good. As was acid. It transformed consciousness. And in Vietnam, it certainly kept us sane.

PLAYBOY: What was *your* drug use like?

STONE: After the war, I took it to excess. I was using as much LSD as anybody. Even slipped it into my dad's drink once. What I did turned bad in the sense that it got heavier. My usage became heavier, but not for a purpose. It became an indulgence.

PLAYBOY: How much and what were you using?

STONE: Well, I started more acid, and grass, I suppose, in the beginning. And then I touched on some other things here and there.

PLAYBOY: Heroin? Cocaine?

STONE: Cocaine, certainly. But that was in the late 1970s. Cocaine is what took me to the edge. I finally realized that coke had beaten me and I hadn't beaten it. So in 1981, I went cold turkey on everything. Except an occasional drink here or there, or an occasional, you know, thing, but basically cold turkey. I moved to Paris that year and wrote *Scarface*, which was a farewell to cocaine.

PLAYBOY: *Scarface* became a cult hit. Had you quit using cocaine before or after you wrote it?

STONE: I wrote it totally straight. But I researched it stoned, because I had to research it in South America, in various spots where I had to do it in order to talk with these people.

PLAYBOY: Before you quit, how deeply were you into it?

STONE: I would say it was an everyday thing. Hollywood in the late 1970s was—there was a kind of cocaine craze. And it lasted until later in the 1980s.

PLAYBOY: And now? Are you supporting Nancy Reagan's "just say no" compaign?

STONE: No. I don't agree with her phony policies. I think she's a hypocrite— no, her *policies* are hypocritical. The government, with its left hand, is basically importing drugs, and with its right hand, it's trying to stop it. It's wasting a lot of money.

PLAYBOY: What do you mean, the government is importing drugs?

STONE: I think we barely scratched the surface in the Iran/Contra affair of what this government has been up to. It's a filthy story, and I know that the Cuban right wing is heavily involved with drugs. Our government is really very bad, acting basically like gangsters. I mean, all the tie-ups through the years with the Mafia, the tie-ups with the dictators, the re-pressions are totally against the spirit of what Jefferson and Washington and Lincoln wanted for this country.

PLAYBOY: Back to your own experience: Don't you think the Hollywood community is now more inclined to go with Mrs. Reagan's view of things than with yours?

STONE: Oh, sure! Yes. Throw another two billion dollars at the problem and *fight drugs!* Any jerk-off Congressman is going to vote so the apple-pie moms will say, "Hey, we're fighting drugs." It's all horseshit! That money just goes down the tubes. The DEA does nothing. In fact, there are quite a few DEA agents who are suspects themselves. [*Laughs*]

This whole thing is sick. I mean, the way to beat it is to legalize drugs, out and out. Legalize heroin, cocaine, marijuana. Yeah. Let kids try it. Let them get it out of their system. Take out the allure. Take out the glamor. Make it cheap. Make it available. People kill to get it. The gangsters will scurry like rats to find another enterprising activity. It'll take the fuckin' mystique off it and the price tag off it. But no! We won't cut the price of drugs, because organized crime makes too much money. And the bankers make too much money. And the attorneys make too much money. It's a *100-billion-dollar-a-year business!* Too many people are making too much money, including establishment people in south Florida and Houston and all over the country.

PLAYBOY: What were the circumstances of your drug arrest in 1969?

STONE: I had been out of the Army 10 days. I had gone to Mexico. I got busted at the border carrying two ounces of my own weed. They threw me in county jail, facing federal smuggling charges—five to 20 years.

PLAYBOY: Were you formally charged?

STONE: Oh, yes. Everything. The papers were there.

PLAYBOY: How long were you held?

STONE: A couple of weeks. There were about 15,000 of us kids jammed into a place built to hold 3,000. No lawyer showed up, and these kids were telling me they had been in there for six months and they hadn't seen a lawyer, either.

PLAYBOY: Did you panic?

STONE: Almost. The kids said to me, "Hey! Wake up! This is what America's really like, man!" There were two fucking judges. One judge was a little lenient guy. He sat on Tuesday and Thursday. If you came up on Monday or Wednesday or Friday, you hit the hard-balls guy. He would have hit me for five years; I might have gotten out after three.

PLAYBOY: You got the lenient judge?

STONE: What happened is interesting. I finally called my father. I had a hard time doing that, because he thought I was still in Vietnam.

PLAYBOY: He didn't know you'd gotten out of the army?

STONE: Well, he knew that I was due out but not exactly when. So I called him and I said, "Dad, the good news is I'm out of Vietnam. Do you want to hear the bad news?" [*Laughs*] He said, "Oh, shit. What is it?" I said, "I'm in jail in San Diego." He said, "Oh, shit." He knew the score and he knew what it was about. So I could have sat in that prison for six months. My court-appointed lawyer might never have showed up. My father called him. The moment the guy knew he was going to get paid, he showed up beaming.

PLAYBOY: Exactly like the lawyer in your script for *Midnight Express*.

STONE: Same idea. I think we paid him $2,500. He got my case dismissed "in the interest of justice." I guess they had 20,000 other kids to prosecute [*laughs*], so they let it go. What happened beyond his receiving the money, I don't know.

PLAYBOY: Getting busted 10 days after your tour of Vietnam must have made you quite an angry young man.

STONE: Yes. I suppose if I went over to Vietnam right wing, I came back an anarchist. Radical. Very much like Travis Bickle in *Taxi Driver*. Alienated. A walking time bomb. Hateful and suspicious.

PLAYBOY: What did you believe in?

STONE: Direct action. When Nixon invaded Cambodia, I was at the NYU film school, and everyone went nuts. I thought they were a bunch of jerks just running around shooting film. I thought, Why don't we get a gun and just do Nixon, you know? *I'll do him.* [*Laughs*] You know, "Let's go kill, man." I thought, If you want to shake up the system, if you want a revolution, let's fuckin' have one. Let's kill cops. Back then, I was feeling pure anger. Hatred. Well, actually, I'm right. [*Laughs*] That's the only way revolution is ever going to occur.

PLAYBOY: Do you still consider yourself to be outside the system? A revolutionary?

STONE: No. That anarchy gave way finally to some kind of reintegration into American society, I suppose. [*Laughs*] The Pentagon papers, Watergate, a lot of reading gave seed to what has become a sort of mature liberalism. I think I've been on that track since around 1975. And although some critics have said otherwise, I think my films have all been on that track.

PLAYBOY: With a little help from a healthy bank account.

STONE: I understand money. I know what it's like to move overnight from golden boy to ugly duckling. Success and disaster seem to be two sides of the same coin. I've seen disaster, because I saw it after my first Academy Award, in 1978, for writing *Midnight Express*. And before that, for 10 years, when I was a starving writer.

PLAYBOY: How did you manage to turn that initial success into prolonged failure?

STONE: I buried myself with my own hand, so to speak. Whatever possessed me to spend half my time on the set of the second movie I directed—*The Hand*, in 1981—fighting Michael Caine, I'll never know.

PLAYBOY: After that movie was panned, you suffered another setback when you couldn't get *Born on the Fourth of July* produced, right?

STONE: Actually, I wrote it before *The Hand*. I spent a year on it. It was a very defeating experience. I worked with a series of directors on it, and Al Pacino was committed. I came up with a really good script. We rehearsed it; Al played it. I saw all the roles played. It was really happening. And then the money fell out at the last possible second and the film collapsed and Pacino went on to work on another film. It sort of soured me on the possibility of doing something serious in Hollywood.

PLAYBOY: So you gave up for a while?

STONE: In a way, yes. Part of the reason I did *The Hand* was that it was obvious that studios weren't going to do the more dramatic material. So I thought, At least they'll do a horror movie for money. That's why I compromised, and I made a serious mistake. I wanted to work as a director. So I really should have been directing *Platoon* or *Born on the Fourth of July*. But there was no way they were even going to make those movies, let alone let me direct them. So I went into a phase of cynicism from around 1980 to 1985, which was a period in which nobody was making any serious movies.

PLAYBOY: Why?

STONE: The execs were very much into high-concept, kid-gloss movies— *War Games* rip-offs, *Star Wars* rip-offs. It was a depressing time. I worked on *Scarface* during that period only because Al Pacino wanted me. And I worked on *Dragon* because Cimino wanted me. I didn't work for a studio; I never had an office in a studio. I had a miserable four or five years writing other people's movies, but I did learn from them.

PLAYBOY: What got your enthusiasm for *Platoon* going again?

STONE: Seeing Warren Beatty's *Reds* in 1981. I loved it. The fact that Beatty had spent so much time doing a film that was so unconventional really reminded me that, hey, you can make good movies if you stick it out. So at that point in time, I said, "I'm going to do it." And I wrote my Russian thing—

PLAYBOY: What Russian thing? Is this another unproduced script?

STONE: Yeah. I wrote a great script about dissidents in Russia. Universal Studios sent me to Russia to research it, but nobody wanted to make it. Frank Price was in charge of the studio. He's a right winger and was too busy doing movies like *Fletch* and *Breakfast Club*.

PLAYBOY: A movie about Soviet dissidents wouldn't offend the right wing.

STONE: That's true. But Price was probably offended just because it was a serious film. He was not doing dramas. Go check the books. Universal did one drama in that year [1985], probably, and it was *Out of Africa*. You know why they did it? Because it had Meryl Streep, Robert Redford and Sydney Pollack. An unknown filmmaker comes in and wants to do something serious, they're not going to make that.

PLAYBOY: Hasn't it always been hard to make political films in Hollywood?

STONE: No, in the 1930s and the 1940s, studios did them. Darryl F. Zanuck [former head of 20th Century Fox] did them; they did a lot of stuff like that. Now they're just afraid of anything that's controversial, that stirs up emotions. Most of them want a very bland Chevy Chase comedy that gets a lot of people in to buy popcorn. I'm convinced that there's a conspiracy to make blander films.

PLAYBOY: Does this mean that the distributors are dictating taste?

STONE: No. Taste is dictated by a mass consensus of distributors, exhibitors—a floating circle of players. A guy in Cleveland saying, "You gave me six dogs last year," puts pressure on the distributors. It all gets passed along. A consensus emerges.

Comedies, the least offensive category, are still "in." Comedies are the least offensive medium. They shouldn't be, but they are—though Eddie Murphy is getting to be offensive. But Chevy Chase—a very safe man. And he's one of the hottest movie stars today, as the American middle-class boob, you know, in plaid trousers, walking around with a happy face and a pretty wife, and I guess America wants to see itself that way. Put Chevy Chase up against the Libyans, I don't think he'd last two seconds.

PLAYBOY: What was it like to go in and pitch ideas after having written two big-time scripts?

STONE: From '80 to '85, miserable. Often I'd go in and have a meeting with some real smartass baby exec, maybe 24, who'd just gotten out of film school. He or she was supposed to have his or her finger on the pulse of what the new kids wanted, and I'd sit there, discussing a serious story and being patronized. You know the crap: "Well, we know from *Midnight Express* that you like those dark films, but you're not really getting the point of where America is at. America wants Steve Martin, Eddie Murphy, Dan Aykroyd."

After '85, I vowed never to go to a development meeting again, and I never did. Since *Salvador*, I've never had a script conference. On *Wall Street*, I never even saw a development person. The so-called development process is just a series of 25 meetings to make the script as obsolete and harmless and banal and inoffensive as possible. When 25 people agree that it's all of the above, then they make the movie. If the star agrees to come along! [*Laughs*]

PLAYBOY: And yet some very good movies do get made.

STONE: I think it's a random thing. It depends on the persistent vision of two or three people, and they push it through a system that's geared to compromise and obstacles. Nobody deliberately sets out to do a bad movie, but people have different tastes. There are just so many collaborative elements. You have so many actors; you have to depend on locations; you have to depend on money; you depend on whether you woke up that day with a headache. It all comes down to thousands of little choices. And if you miss one of them, the movie is not going to be good.

Sometimes a political movie gets made that people don't know is political—George Lucas' *Star Wars*, for instance, which teaches us that the forces of authoritarianism and fascism can be defeated by a good conscience. By listening to your inner voice—which is, I think, a great liberal message. Steven Spielberg has never professed political interest in his films, yet he seems to be moving toward a greater awareness of it, which I think is good. *The Color Purple*, I think, is an excellent movie, and it was an attempt to deal with an issue that had been overlooked, and it wouldn't have been done if it hadn't been Spielberg. And it's not like everyone says, that he ruined the book. That's horseshit. Nobody was going to *do* the book.

PLAYBOY: Let's talk about some of the criticism of your films. You say they are in the liberal tradition, but critics slammed you for racism in your characterization of the Turks in *Midnight Express*.

STONE: I think that there was a lack of proportion in the picture regarding the Turks. I was younger. I was more rabid. But I think we shouldn't lose sight of what the movie was about. It was about the miscarriage of justice, and I think it still comes through. In the original script, there was more humor. There were some very funny things that the Turks did, where they were portrayed as rather human, too. But [director] Alan Parker does not really have a great sense of humor, and I think he moved it in a direction where the humorous scenes were cut out so that the Turks came out looking tougher, meaner.

PLAYBOY: Next case, *Scarface*. The charge: racist portrayal of the Cubans.

STONE: In *Scarface*, I don't back down for one second. I think it's clear that not all Cubans are drug dealers. The guy is, and his mother even says he is, no good. It's classic gangster stuff. But people get oversensitive, like when the Italians objected to Francis Coppola's doing *The Godfather*. It's like "We're not gangsters." I mean, every nationality wants to believe there are no gangsters. And *Scarface* is a political movie, but the Cuban right wing is a very scary group. Honestly, even to talk about them is dangerous; they may be the single most dangerous group of guys I've ever met.

PLAYBOY: Aren't you exaggerating the politics of the movie?

STONE: The politics in it are buried by a lot of superficial trivia. To some, it's a movie about cars, palaces, money and coke. It's not just about that. It's about what those things do to you and how they corrupt you. That theme got lost. I think Tony Montana—Al Pacino—has a Frank Sinatra dream of the United States, OK? So he becomes a right-winger in this sense: "I hate Communists, and this is the good life with the big steaks and the cigars in fancy restaurants and the blonde and the limousines and the whole bit."

It's the whole group from the Bay of Pigs. A few of them are drug dealers and use drug money to keep their political work going. A lot of these guys have disguised drug dealing as legitimate anti-Castro political activities, and that is mentioned in the movie. Tony's mother tells him, Don't give me this bullshit that you're working against Castro, you know. I know you. You've always been a gangster and you're going to die one.

PLAYBOY: What about the Chinese, who organized protests and boycotts against another movie you co-wrote, *Year of the Dragon*?

STONE: The Chinese want to believe that there are no gangsters among them. That's all horseshit! The Chinese are the greatest importers of heroin in this country. We knew this five years ago! As for the lead character, played by Mickey Rourke, he is a racist and we *wrote* him that way.

PLAYBOY: But didn't you write the character to make people cheer him on?

STONE: Yes. But I think people cheered him for other reasons, not for his racism. At least I hope not. But there might be an element of it. The guy, no matter how prejudiced, is still trying to get something done—as an underdog. That's why I'm rooting for him. But I should say that I think it was the least successful of my scripts.

PLAYBOY: Next charge: All your movies have a locker-room feeling to them. No strong women.

STONE: OK. I think this is true. I have not done movies about women. I have always picked areas that involve extremist ideas that to date have involved men, mostly. The Vietnam war, the drug trade at the highest levels, the heroin trade in Chinatown, men's prisons in Turkey, Wall Street; all—at the top, anyway—were and are run by men. Though I do have women in my films and I happen to like the portrayals—Cindy Gibb as the nun in *Salvador*; Michelle Pfeiffer as the basic bimbo hanging around this Cuban gangster in *Scarface*. I know they're smaller roles, but I don't think any of them are inauthentic.

PLAYBOY: Is there going to be a sequel to *Platoon*?

STONE: I had contracted before *Platoon* was ever released to write a film called *Second Life*, to be based on my own experiences in coming back to the States. I wanted to do that whole period of the late 1960s and early 1970s in America, a period of extreme ideological conflict between the left and the right. The age of *Easy Rider*—the landmark film of that era. I'd like to go back to that. But it wasn't meant as a sequel. Now, with *Platoon*, if Charlie Sheen does it, it will be deemed a sequel. After *Wall Street* comes out.

PLAYBOY: Can we assume that the studios had a friendlier attitude toward *Wall Street* after the runaway success of *Platoon*?

STONE: *Wall Street* was like a Porsche to *Salvador*'s broken-down jeep—a smooth, cushioned ride. And I must tell you that I enjoy working this way, because there's so much tension in making any movie. When you have money worries, it makes things impossible. I'm now a believer in Flaubert's advice to live a bourgeois life but to have an exciting mind.

PLAYBOY: After the boom of *Platoon*, do you expect critics to be gunning for you?

STONE: It would be nearly impossible ever to follow *Platoon* with something that could be as big at the box office, or as critically well received. That I know. There is the king-must-die theory. I think that you have to keep your head down. You somehow have to ignore the critical storms that come and go. And you've got to continue to do good work for your life, like Ford did, like Stevens, like Hawks and Huston and Renoir. That's the only way to get through this madness: Wear blinders and keep to the work.

 **November 2004**

A candid conversation with the controversial director about enemies, drugs, conspiracies, bisexuality and why Alexander the Great was a rock star.

Oliver Stone's movies have been in the news as often as they have been about the news. *JFK*, Stone's divisive drama about a conspiracy to murder President John F. Kennedy, is still hotly debated. Only last year, on a television special commemorating the 40th anniversary of the Kennedy assassination, ABC *News*'s Peter Jennings noted that a significant number of Americans remain convinced of a conspiracy based entirely on Stone's movie. Stone has created indelible stories about Richard Nixon (in *Nixon*) and Jim Morrison (in *The Doors*) and tackled the American culture of violence in *Natural Born Killers*. His films about the Vietnam war—*Heaven & Earth, Platoon* and *Born on the Fourth of July*—are inextricably tied to the nation's collective memory of the conflict and the 1960s antiwar movement.

Recently, Stone turned his attention to Cuba, in a pair of documentaries about Fidel Castro. "Newspapers can have trouble keeping up with him," wrote Gary Wills in the *Atlantic Monthly*. And Stone not only helps shape—or distort, according to some—history, he predicts it. With uncanny prescience, he depicted corporate insider-trading scandals in *Wall Street* (1987) and the rise of the right-wing media in *Talk Radio* (1988) years before they happened.

For Stone's newest, and most ambitious, movie, the director retreats from modern-day controversies, venturing back in time to 356 to 323 B.C. Stone spent more than a decade writing *Alexander*—the story of Alexander the Great—which he filmed at the end of 2003 in Thailand, Morocco and England. In Stone's hands, even Alexander the Great is somehow tied to the current political debate. "There are similarities between the ambitions of ancient Macedonia under Alexander and the United States under George Bush," Stone claims. "They made similar journeys into Iraq and Afghanistan. And both men, though of entirely different character, want to conquer the world."

Almost no one is indifferent to Stone. He has die-hard fans, and film critics have praised many of his movies. Leonard Maltin called *JFK* "a masterful cinematic achievement." Norman Mailer called *Nixon* "a major work by a major artist." And Stone's detractors are equally impassioned. Some dismiss him as a paranoid nutcase: *Time* magazine dubbed him Mr. Conspiracy. After Stone described the September 11 terrorist attack on America as "a rebellion against globalization, against the American way," journalist Christopher Hitchens called Stone "a moral and intellectual idiot."

Stone is the only child of a wealthy stockbroker father and a French-born mother who divorced when he was 15. He attended private boys' schools in New York City and in 1965 enrolled at Yale, where he was a classmate of George W. Bush's and John Kerry was a few years ahead of him. Stone dropped out, joined the military and was sent to Vietnam in 1967. Twice wounded, he was awarded a Bronze Star and a Purple Heart. He returned to the U.S. embittered and began writing *Platoon,* an indictment of the war.

He enrolled at New York University to study filmmaking and wrote and directed his first movie, *Seizure,* in 1974. He won his first Oscar, in 1979, for his screenplay for *Midnight Express.* A decade after writing *Platoon,* he finally made the film, which was released in 1986. It won the Academy Award for best picture, and Stone won the best director award. He was also nominated that year for a best screenwriting Oscar for *Salvador.* Screenwriting nominations for *JFK* and *Nixon* followed, and he won another best director statue for *Born on the Fourth of July.*

At times Stone's personal life has been as controversial as his movies. In 1999 he was arrested in Los Angeles for driving while under the influence and for possession of hashish and other drugs. (He had also been arrested in 1968 in Mexico for possession of marijuana.) Stone entered a drug-treatment program in 2000.

Playboy Contributing Editor David Sheff, who last interviewed Google founders Larry Page and Sergey Brin for *Playboy,* met Stone in Santa Monica, California, where he was editing *Alexander.* Reports Sheff: "When I arrived at Stone's office for the interview, his gorgeous British assistant explained that Stone would be late. In the meantime, she said, 'Oliver says you should lie on the floor and I should give you a massage.' Once we began the interview, it was a challenge to keep Stone, who sucked on a Cuban cigar and drank coffee, focused on any given subject. Many conversations returned to his obvious concern about American politics. Still, it was clear he was enjoying his immersion in the pre-Christian time of Alexander the Great. 'Maybe I'll stay here,' he said, sounding serious. 'I may have found a time where I fit in much better.'"

PLAYBOY: You're associated with so many topical contemporary dramas. What inspired you to tackle Alexander the Great?

STONE: I've been interested in him since I was in college. I'd always wondered why his story had never been dramatized. It's one of the most extraordinary stories in history. Why hadn't Shakespeare tried? Why hadn't other great playwrights or screenwriters?

PLAYBOY: And what was your conclusion?

STONE: I think he scares people off because he was so fucking successful. There's an inherent dislike or fear or distrust of somebody who is that much bigger than life. It seemed too much for a story—the decadent politics, the outrageous ambition, the decadent lifestyle. So I struggled with how to make the movie that has eluded everyone. I loved the character, but I never thought I would get to do him.

PLAYBOY: You weren't the only director to decide to tackle Alexander's story. Mel Gibson was planning a miniseries for HBO, and producer Dino De Laurentiis and director Baz Luhrmann signed Leonardo DiCaprio and Nicole Kidman for a version.

STONE: As far as I know, they've all given up, but not before they damaged us.

PLAYBOY: How did they damage you?

STONE: We did not get financed in Hollywood. We were rejected there. We got financed in Europe only, and it didn't help to have Dino De Laurentiis telling his friends in various countries, "Don't buy that movie." Without foreign sales you're dead in the water. There were a lot of shenanigans, and there was a lot of ugliness. I was called names. I tried to stay out of it. I'm not going to be left with bad karma on my set. I just stuck to the work, and we eventually pulled people together and got the movie made.

PLAYBOY: Could you have made the movie without the success of *Troy* and *Gladiator*?

STONE: No. Without them the movie never would have been made. There was new interest in big epics. When Warner Bros. finally signed up in the U.S., I could go to them and say, "Gentlemen, you've got to sign on to our movie. We're making a movie about the son of Achilles." They were high on *Troy*, of course, and they went for it.

PLAYBOY: How did you decide to cast Colin Farrell as Alexander the Great?

STONE: I liked Brad Pitt very much in *Troy*, but like Achilles, his character in the movie, he is as mythic as Steve McQueen is in *The Magnificent Seven*. Unreal. From the myth, I wanted to find the man. Colin was right. He is equally handsome and of a younger generation. It's thrilling to watch him as Alexander, who lived up to and went beyond the Achilles myth. Achilles conquered Troy; Alexander went after the world. Colin may well be a modern-day Alexander, and Angelina Jolie, who is Olympias, is a modern-day queen. If we had them, she would be queen. She's as strong and determined.

PLAYBOY: You once said that Alexander was a rock star of his time. Were you thinking of Jim Morrison of the Doors?

STONE: Him or others. Like Morrison, Alexander ran up against the forces of life and surmounted them.

PLAYBOY: Morrison didn't surmount them. He succumbed to them and died young.

STONE: But he accomplished an enormous amount. Every man reaches and falls. Some attain greatness along the way. Alexander did, of course. Morrison did. I'm fascinated by all who achieve greatness.

PLAYBOY: You produced a movie about the attempted assassination of Ronald Reagan. When the former president died, were you surprised by the intensity of the tributes?

STONE: It was theater. It was television. Parades with people in baseball caps and shorts and ugly T-shirts. A hollowness. It's what Reagan was all about. He was a scary man. I used to have nightmares about him, literally. Smile, head of hair. He was a stage prop, an actor. That's what Americans want. They want the shell. Look at Arnold.

PLAYBOY: You've known Schwarzenegger since you wrote the script for *Conan*. Do you keep in touch with him?

STONE: I see him here and there. I like him.

PLAYBOY: Even as governor?

STONE: I'm not sure, but he's what America wants. I'm not surprised he's governor. He's got an amazing face. He's got a great smile. He has great willpower. The guy pulls off amazing things with his charisma. Unless he really fucks up, he can go right to the White House.

PLAYBOY: How will he overcome the requirement that a president be born in this country?

STONE: They'll change it for him. He's a hell of a lot more attractive and sexy than Bush. He would be a far better president, too.

PLAYBOY: Now that you've directed movies about presidents Kennedy and Nixon and produced a movie about Reagan, have you considered taking on President Bush?

STONE: It's too soon. You need some historical perspective. We had to wait 20 years to do *Nixon*. As a dramatist, you have to wait. Right now Bush is in full play. It's not time for a biography.

PLAYBOY: Would Bush be a good subject for a drama?

STONE: A scary one. He looks like a tiny little chamber of commerce guy. In the 1950s he would have been considered distasteful. He's worse than Nixon in his vulgarity. He looks like he shops at Wal-Mart.

That's not what a president is supposed to be. He has no intellectual curiosity and is proud of it. He says his wife does the book thing. He's a liar, hiding behind a shallow and dangerous patriotism: "We're number one." "The American way." It's a Superman comic-book idea of the world. It covers up the complicated realities, and it's very dangerous.

PLAYBOY: After September 11, 2001 you spoke out against the president. After your statement that America may have brought on the type of hatred that led to the terrorist attack, journalist Christopher Hitchens called you an idiot.

STONE: A moral and intellectual idiot, to be exact. In the 1980s I admired Hitchens. He was strongly pro-Nicaragua and right about it. He seemed very intelligent. Since then he has gotten into an extremist groove. He has become an ideologue. I thought it behooved us to understand how America's unilateralism, arrogance and history of pushing around the rest of the world enrages people. Since Iraq, the outrage is worse than ever. It's why this election is so damn important.

PLAYBOY: Did you know Bush when you were at Yale together?

STONE: No, but I met him before he was president. He wanted to meet me.

PLAYBOY: But as a well-known leftist, you seem like the last person he would want to meet.

STONE: I don't know why, but he did. When we met, he reminded me that we'd been in the same class at Yale. I said, "But you know, Governor, I didn't make it all the way through. I went off to Vietnam." He said, "I had a friend who went over there and didn't come back." He looked at me, and it was a moment. I don't think he had much interest in me beyond that. He knows how to talk to you, though. He's good for a few seconds. I don't know, maybe this is Oliver Stone paranoia, but I felt like he was looking through me, like he wished his friend had come back instead of me. I felt a whiff of discontent.

PLAYBOY: John Kerry was at Yale too. Did you run into him?

STONE: When I was a freshman, he was a senior. He was a big shot. I saw him debate, and he was powerful—he looked like Lincoln. People said he was pompous—that was the rap. He had a funereal groove about him, like some Dickensian character. He was always too old for his years. I remember him in the post-Vietnam era, too, and he was very somber. I've met him a few times since.

PLAYBOY: What's your opinion of him?

STONE: There's a fundamental decency about him. I think he'd make a good president. He's a public servant in the Brahmin sense of the word. The guy knows his A's, B's and C's.

PLAYBOY: What's your take on the polls? In the end, who will win?

STONE: I worry that the Republicans will do anything to win. For a long time I've worried that Bush will start another war before the election to get people fearful. Voters are nervous about changing leadership in the middle of a war. He bills himself as Mr. Security, which of course he's not. He's Mr. Insecurity. Every decision he has made has led to a worse military conclusion and a less secure nation. He has generated enormous hatred, and hatred begets violence. He shovels up the worst kind of patriotic crap. Thirty or 40 years ago, even in the 1920s, they would have run him out of town. Patriotic stuff works occasionally, as it did during Joe McCarthy's time, but Bush is overdoing it.

PLAYBOY: Some critics of *Fahrenheit 9/11* lump Michael Moore and you together, charging that you're left-wing loonies and conspiracy-theory nuts.

STONE: That's typical. Rather than look at what we say, they try to discredit us. I'm glad to be lumped in with such great company. We fucking need him. He's becoming a folkloric Mark Twain figure. The movie is very powerful.

PLAYBOY: How much of a difference will his movie make in the election?

STONE: It's hard to know, but I think a movie can make a huge difference. *JFK* helped Clinton win. It came out right before the election. *Salvador* and *Platoon* may have had an impact on Reagan's downturn in popularity. *Salvador* took shots at Reagan and led to an early sense that the Reagan thing was going to end. A month before *Platoon*, Ollie North got booby-trapped. The whole thing turned.

PLAYBOY: Yet Reagan remained popular.

STONE: At the time, though, he lost a lot of power. He couldn't do as much evil. The movies were part of a change in sensibility. Movies can help evolve consciousness, as Michael Moore's movies have. You risk a lot when you speak out, though. That's always been true, but more so since September 11. After September 11 no one would speak out.

PLAYBOY: You did.

STONE: And I was pilloried. Most were quiet. We all felt the chill. We became so cautious that we self-censored. For a while it killed the impulse we have for greatness and creativity.

PLAYBOY: Did you self-censor because of fear of reprisals?

STONE: The fear of rocking the boat, yes. We all have it. In school you don't want to rock the boat, but at times you have to. I had movies shut down, sometimes for mysterious reasons. I was never in the middle of a storm like Moore is, but there were controversies even before September 11. Since then, however, they can call you unpatriotic if you don't go along. If you came out against Vietnam they pulled the unpatriotic thing too. It's a warped definition of patriotism. A patriot cares deeply about this country, enough to want it to do right. Michael Moore is a great patriot.

PLAYBOY: If you were to make a new version of *Platoon*, focusing on Iraq rather than Vietnam, how would it be similar?

STONE: I haven't been to Iraq, but from the letters home and glimpses of the soldiers, I think it's pretty much the same for a young man in Iraq as it was in Vietnam. There's the dilemma about how you behave, morally or immorally. Most people just follow orders, but some step up. The fighting is about the same, though the military has gotten better at making people more like robots. They're able to control firefights better; they move clumps of men more easily. But basically it's the same strategy as in Vietnam. They bring in maximum firepower, wipe out what they can and then send in the soldiers to mop up. You blow the shit out of everybody and then move forward, minimizing your own casualties. As a result they've maximized civilian casualties. Whatever they say about precision bombing, it's not that precise. The news triumphs when we take out some terrorist, but what about the 3,000 civilians? What difference does it make? Why is a baby in a well in Pennsylvania more important than 3,000 civilians in Iraq? Because it's an American baby?

War was and is a bureaucratic fuckup. Nothing goes right, and everything costs twice as much as they say it will. For the most part it's a nightmare and inefficient. They said that My Lai was just a few bad apples. It wasn't. The system allows it to happen, just as it did in the prison camps in Iraq. One of the great things about writing *Platoon* was that I looked deeply into the different reactions of ordinary boys from every state. The boy you thought would be a weasel wasn't, and the boy who was a weasel was a hero. Then the soldiers came home. I fought in Vietnam in 1967 and 1968. When we came back here, we were nobodies. Vets live with what the public never sees. Here I am again, raving, the conspiracy nut.

PLAYBOY: You're joking, but how do you feel about those stereotypes?

STONE: Conspiracy nut, leftist, madman. These are terms of dismissal so you don't have to listen to the argument. It's an ugly way of doing business and not logical, either. It would be healthier and, frankly, more fun to hear what someone has to say. I'm just looking at the facts and asking questions. Meanwhile, the press, which is supposed to ask the questions, usually just smiles and nods. Donald Rumsfeld said the abuses in Iraq are un-American. What the fuck does that mean? Does he mean that the rest of the world does it and we don't? Yet no one challenges him. Another thing that bothers me is that we've created a ball game in which unless you're a winner, you're seen as a loser. It's a zero-sum game that Michael Douglas talked about as Gordon Gekko in *Wall Street*. Why? Why do you have to see life that way? It goes to the fundamental mindset of what schoolchildren are taught. When I made *Born on the Fourth of July*, I got to know Ron Kovic well. He said he grew up on John Wayne in *Sands of Iwo Jima*, and everything was black and white, good and evil, winners and losers. Trying to emulate John Wayne is how he wound up in Vietnam, but of course he came to see that things are not black and white at all. Not in war, not ever. America should be about many definitions of being a winner. America's greatness—what's left of it—comes from the fact that we're a melting pot. We're Portuguese, Latin, French, Chinese, African. We're all mutts. It should make us more forgiving and tolerant, but instead it has made us fearful and arrogant, two sides of the same coin. At 18 you are allowed to go to Iraq and get killed, but you can't get a drink in California. Why can you die and not fuck? Why can't there be legal whorehouses? Why can't there be places where kids can have sex safely? Why can't we be more honest about sexuality?

PLAYBOY: Not sure how we got from conspiracies to legal whorehouses, but are you advocating them?

STONE: I'm talking about hypocrisy. Our puritanism allows boys to kill and be killed but not have sex. It's ludicrous. Once again we pretend things are one way. Alexander lived in a more honest time. We go into his bisexuality. It may offend some people, but sexuality in those days was a different thing. Pre-Christian morality. Young boys were with boys when they wanted to be. Sometimes it was physical and sometimes platonic. Nonetheless, a man was expected to marry. They didn't know how heirs were made. At the time, many thought sperm itself contained the whole thing and that the vagina was merely the receptacle. It led them to view women as second-class citizens, as baggage carriers. Sexuality wasn't necessarily tied to procreation and morality, and men were allowed to have a homosexual side as well as a heterosexual side.

PLAYBOY: A lot of American men would deny that they have a homosexual side.

STONE: I think if we were allowed the freedoms we were promised, we might find out more about ourselves than we know. Perhaps people would be happier, too. Instead of having 14 shotguns, they might have an erection. But children are taught to be fearful of AIDS, to shy from the other sex unless you marry them, to repress any natural sexual feelings, not to drink, not to fuck, not to dance, not to take ecstasy, but to fight in Iraq. They're scaring kids to death. Heterosexual and homosexual sex can be fun. You don't have to live an antisex, antidope, antibooze, anti-everything life. Let people do whatever the fuck they want and stay the fuck out and don't ask them about it.

PLAYBOY: Have you felt a puritanical reaction to your movies?

STONE: I've been shot down for most of them. I've taken a lot of shots in my life.

PLAYBOY: Undeserved?

STONE: Maybe they were deserved and I just never understood. Or maybe if you start messing around with Richard Nixon or JFK, you have to expect people to attack you. Not only that, if you move from *Heaven & Earth* to *JFK* to *Natural Born Killers* to an interview with Castro, people can't get a take on you. *Heaven & Earth* and *Natural Born Killers* were played at the Paris Film Festival back-to-back. What a 180 degree fucking turn! One was a Buddhist film about pacifism, according to some people, and the other is supposedly a violent, insane, lurid piece of trash. They can't figure you out, and that bothers them. From that point on it's opinions and gossip.

PLAYBOY: Why have you swung from genre to genre?

STONE: I follow whatever motivates me, whatever puts the wind in my sails at the moment. I have to be zealous about a project, because it requires years. You have to be consumed by it. Whether it's *Alexander* or *U Turn*, you give it your all. I've always changed genres. I'll do a film noir and then a sports drama like *Any Given Sunday*. This is the first time I've done a historical epic. Ideas come to me, some people say too fast. Perhaps they're right and I have to learn to slow down, but age takes care of that anyway. I just have to keep going. When I have been shut down, I've found a new way. I'm misunderstood and I keep going. I was accused of promoting violence. Anyone who knows me understands that I promote peace.

PLAYBOY: The accusation that you promote violence comes from *Natural*

Born Killers. One teenage couple, after watching the movie, went on a killing spree.

STONE: *Natural Born Killers* was an experiment. I wanted to make an action film. I'd never done a summer movie and wanted to. Once I started, I explored the idea, and it became about cartoon violence. *Natural Born Killers* is a breakthrough in experimentation. I tried to explore the flexibility and elasticity of film. I don't think film had ever been used like that. The people in the movie were cartoon characters. We scraped the edges off the behavior perimeters to see how far we could go. Correct me if I'm wrong, but isn't the definition of satire overexaggeration? You can't expect everyone to get satire.

PLAYBOY: Did you feel any guilt over the copycat murders?

STONE: You can't account for every person in the world. The kid who killed John Lennon was reading *Catcher in the Rye*. Is Salinger responsible? Give me a break. Anybody who'd kill is psychotic in a deeper way and was psychotic before they saw a movie.

PLAYBOY: Writer John Grisham said you were responsible in the same way that Ford Motor Co. was responsible for the deaths caused by its Pintos.

STONE: He got involved because a personal friend of his was killed. He became one of those outsize caricatures—in this case, American novelist turned vigilante. I don't know the guy at all, but he's still gloating. He recently said how glad he is that he put a spike into Hollywood. I don't know if the films you've seen in the past seven or eight years are far better than *Natural Born Killers*, but they certainly are violent, some far more violent and far more realistically violent. Look at *Black Hawk Down*. I think that movie has done far more disservice to this country than *Natural Born Killers*.

PLAYBOY: What disservice?

STONE: *Natural Born Killers* is satire, whereas movies like *Black Hawk Down* and *Saving Private Ryan* contribute to an aura of patriotic inevitability and an awe of the military.

PLAYBOY: Did the *Natural Born Killers* controversy weigh heavily on you?

STONE: It was an ugly time. I'd just finished *JFK* and was editing *Heaven & Earth* and shooting *Natural Born Killers*. I was going through a divorce. Can you imagine what that was like? At the time I had two kids. I had an amazingly complicated life. Yeah, the controversy was difficult. I get people so mad.

PLAYBOY: Even cartoon violence can be upsetting. So can conspiracy theories.

STONE: Let's look at *JFK*. *JFK* doesn't say the things some people say it does. It's very much a hypothesis. It's a philosophical inquiry into what is truth, what is reality. If you look closely at the film, it's written precisely with conditional tenses, what-ifs. It's a timeworn method of drama. And we put out an entire book with footnotes to explain our sources. We made every effort to be honest, and we were raked over the coals. I was in Europe, thank God, but Peter Jennings took me apart on ABC on the 40th anniversary of the Kennedy assassination.

PLAYBOY: Do you admit that you are conspiracy-minded?

STONE: In Europe everyone is conspiracy-minded. They assume that things happen behind the scenes in government and business. They aren't naive enough to believe the evening news and the soundbites from politicians. Americans want to believe the evening news. They want to believe the press conference. Don't people realize that they've been lying to us for years? So they attack Michael Moore. They attack me.

PLAYBOY: Are you immune to the attacks?

STONE: Sometimes. The reaction to *Natural Born Killers* wounded me.

PLAYBOY: You were also attacked for that movie by the author of the original script, Quentin Tarantino.

STONE: I bought the script from Quentin for a lot of money. He accepted the money. Nobody forced it down his throat. Contrary to what my critics say—that I took it away from him and ruined it and blah-blah-blah—it had been at the bottom of a pile of rejected scripts. I happened to see it and liked the title. I read it and thought it was a great idea. But I never could have made that movie as it was written. Quentin was pissed that I changed it, but since then I've spoken to him, and we get along fine. I respect him, and I think he respects me. But there's no question he hurt the movie quite a bit.

PLAYBOY: How did he hurt the movie?

STONE: He went around the world saying it was a bad movie.

PLAYBOY: He apparently retaliated in his script for *True Romance* with the character of a filmmaker who made a movie called *Coming Home in a Body Bag*. It was a none too subtle attack on you.

STONE: I guess that's what he saw me as. It's an ugly character. God, a horror show. But if that's the way he saw me, that's the way he saw me. Since then, he's gotten to know me better, I hope. At the time, for whatever reason, I was politically incorrect. I couldn't figure out why *Pulp Fiction* was politically correct but *Natural Born Killers* was white trash. I still can't. The movie was meant to be over-the-top. *The Doors* was another. Maybe that's partly why I still get dragged down by the political jackals who run alongside the pack. My movies excite the audience. To tell a story like the Kennedy assassination in an exciting way is a dramatist's delight. If I pull off *Alexander*, it'll be the greatest coup of my life. But yes, I got whipped a lot. Fine. I got some bad press, some awful reviews. I got good reviews, too. It's a steady kind of whiplash. I'm fine with it both ways, and I think I understand it, but for a while I lost confidence.

PLAYBOY: When did you lose confidence?

STONE: I just had a period of adversity. I got worn down by 10 years of attacks. I did 10 films from 1985 to 1995. I wrote a book. I did three documentaries and three commercials. Every time I made a movie I was perhaps overachieving in that I was working fast. I was always fearful that I wouldn't be able to make another movie, so I would start the next movie before I'd finished the first. I had a group of people to support, too, a team I work with. I tried to run a production company and produced 12 movies. I started to have my fill of this business. There were the attacks against *Natural Born Killers*, the attack by John Grisham, the attacks against *JFK*, bad reviews, *Nixon* was ignored. Yeah, it eventually got to me. I took a break at that point, which is exactly what I needed. I had a beautiful daughter then. I was devoted to my wife. I felt comfortable not working. I lost my team and lived more and more like a pariah, but I saw my daughter grow up, unlike my sons.

PLAYBOY: How were you a different father to her than to your sons?

STONE: It's not that I became a model father, but I enjoyed witnessing it. I'm still not the guy who likes taking his daughter to volleyball practice, but yes, I spend quality time with her. I have no patience to read to her, though. I can't stand reading to a child at bedtime.

PLAYBOY: Do you feel you treated your children from your first marriage any differently?

STONE: I love them all. I'm so proud of them. But with the older kids I was away a lot more. I just wasn't around. I wasn't taking the kids to the movies, but how many of these stupid fucking kids' movies can you see anyway? Now I go to the movies with my older son, Sean, who is 18, and it's different. He's a great movie companion.

PLAYBOY: Are you substantially different from your parents?

STONE: I'm sometimes different, sometimes the same. We all wrestle with that one. We don't want to make the same mistakes, but sometimes we do.

PLAYBOY: Was your childhood happy?

STONE: Not particularly. I grew up in Manhattan. There was no nature anywhere. I wore ties and suits every day. I was an outsider, I think. I tried to stay anonymous. I wanted to be Willie Stone, which was the name I used then. I used Willie because of Willie Mays. Willie had a crewcut. He attended all-boys boarding schools and all-boys summer camps. I was never around women.

PLAYBOY: Is it true that your father brought you to a prostitute so you could lose your virginity?

STONE: Yes, because I guess I needed his help. There were no women around at school. My father was a generous man, and I love him to this day for it.

PLAYBOY: Some people might find it inappropriate for a father to bring his son to a prostitute.

STONE: There's a great tradition of that, I believe. For me it was great. There were no scars. I can see that bad habits could develop, but they didn't for me. I've had healthy relationships since then. I think more, not less, fucking is good—1960s love is not a bad thing.

PLAYBOY: When did you first use drugs?

STONE: I lived an isolated life before I went to Vietnam. I didn't know who Elvis Presley was. I didn't know rock and roll. I didn't know grass. I didn't know what a black man was. I didn't know any of that until I went to Vietnam. It all hit there. It's all in *Platoon*.

PLAYBOY: After Vietnam you were arrested for possession of drugs.

STONE: And the charges were dismissed in the interest of justice. [*Laughs*] Basically I was doing light drugs like grass and psychotropics. I never heard of harder drugs until much later, when I got to Hollywood.

PLAYBOY: Did you become addicted to those drugs?

STONE: No, but I had a troubled period with them.

PLAYBOY: Did you go into rehab?

STONE: No, I quit cold turkey and went to Paris. I never did those fucking drugs again. It beat the shit out of me. I thought I was becoming a worse writer. It was dangerous. I thought I was blowing my life. I cut my ties and moved to Paris with my then wife.

PLAYBOY: Do you still use drugs?

STONE: Maybe. It's not smart to talk too much about it. I believe in natural things, but I also take care of myself.

PLAYBOY: Do you exercise?

STONE: I do. I go to the gym. I have exercised for most of my life.

PLAYBOY: How is your current relationship different from your marriages?

STONE: I found a South Korean woman who is terrific. She's amazing, supportive. I'm so lucky to have found this love in my life. She was there when I'd retreated and my daughter was born. Finally I found the time to write *Alexander*. It could have happened only when I was demoralized and withdrawn, so ultimately it was a good thing. Going into *Alexander* was symbolic as much as anything else. I had to persevere, and I did. The movies tend to reflect where I am emotionally. I'd been deluding myself, and so I was drawn to a movie about self-delusion, which was *Nixon*. The football movie, *Any Given Sunday*, came from anticorporate fires that were brewing in me. It was a protest against those forces. On and on.

PLAYBOY: If your movies are emotional barometers, what does *Alexander* say about you now?

STONE: The process helped raise me out of the morass of the present world. It took me back in time to an ancient place where men had higher ideals and strived to execute them. When I decided to make the movie, I thought, What harm can come to me by being associated with that kind of energy for three years? It helped me enormously. It made me more positive, stronger. It may sound ridiculous, but I feel Alexander's spirit helped me surmount huge obstacles.

PLAYBOY: In the meantime you made two television documentaries about Fidel Castro. What prompted them?

STONE: I'd met him in 1987 when I showed *Salvador* at the Havana Film Festival. I didn't return there until 2002, when a Spanish producer set up an interview. It wasn't going to be a big documentary, just an interview for Spanish television. We talked a lot about Brigitte Bardot.

PLAYBOY: For which you were accused of pandering to him.

STONE: Unfairly. I saw great value in a deep look into a man who has had an enormous impact on history. I was never a journalist, grilling him on his human rights record. That wasn't my purpose. I wanted to get inside his head. I did, too. I was accused of humanizing him, but what does that mean? I suggest that it's useful to understand world leaders on the deepest possible level. Once again, though, people want a black-and-white story—Castro, Cuba, communist. What more is there to be said?

PLAYBOY: Didn't you have the opposite agenda, to deify Castro? You have described him as moral, selfless and wise.

STONE: I didn't go in with much of an impression at all. I admired him because he'd done something extraordinary with his life. Through the interviews, I came to respect him. What other world leader would talk so straight to you, with the camera rolling and without a PR assistant? Let him be heard, for Christ's sake. The American people have a right to hear the guy who lives 90 miles away on a hostile little island. I was criticized for humanizing him, but if I had demonized him, they would have loved it.

PLAYBOY: Did you hear from him again?

STONE: Yeah, he likes *Comandante* [a film with a Q&A format that ran on Spanish television] very much. It was shown in Havana, and it's a huge success. I returned to do the HBO documentary *Looking for Fidel.* I'm not sure he liked me after that, because I interviewed dissidents in Cuba, and he didn't want me to do that.

PLAYBOY: For the HBO movie, you held a bizarre discussion with men who tried to flee Cuba. They were being tried. Castro was present. They were contrite, but it seemed phony. They would have been punished had they spoken to you freely. Did you feel that Castro orchestrated the conversation?

STONE: No, because he had no idea what they would say.

PLAYBOY: Yet he held all the power. Had they criticized him or his government, he could and probably would have punished them.

STONE: It was still an amazing opportunity to show them and their plight. The sentences they received were horribly severe. I hope he reconsiders. It seems to me he could have taken a more reformist line after the fall of the Soviet Union, but he would argue that the anti-Castro forces in the United States are very dangerous for him.

PLAYBOY: Are you bitter and pessimistic?

STONE: I hope not.

PLAYBOY: How do you retain a sense of optimism when things are as corrupt and bleak as you depict them?

STONE: You find other kinds of beauty. Moments can be deadly, so moments can be beautiful. You must find the beauty. So get on with it. If one door is blocked, move to another door. Adapt. If they try to stop you, find a way to persevere. Yes, if you call attention to yourself, you'll get nailed. I try to shake it up, and sometimes I suffer for it. But I won't stop. It's my duty.

QUENTIN TARANTINO

A candid conversation with Hollywood's punk auteur about doing drugs, getting laid, the secrets of Pulp Fiction *and how* Kill Bill *ended up as a two-parter*

At first Quentin Tarantino wanted *Kill Bill* to be a small homage to samurai films, a modest vehicle for his *Pulp Fiction* star Uma Thurman. She would play the Bride, a sword-wielding assassin who rises from her deathbed to carve up hundreds of villains standing between her and the mysterious Bill.

Just as in a Tarantino movie, though, strange twists were in store. Somewhere between original concept and final production, *Kill Bill*, Tarantino's first feature in more than five years, became an epic. After nine months of shooting, a budget that surpassed $50 million (compared with the $8 million he spent on *Pulp Fiction*) and three hours of final footage, the decision was made to slice Bill into two freestanding movies that will hit theaters in quick succession. It's a risky, groundbreaking, in-your-face move, and that's exactly how the boy wonder of arthouse violence likes it.

Tarantino forever will be known for *Pulp Fiction*. That gloriously bloody follow-up to *Reservoir Dogs* had far-reaching impact, way beyond winning Tarantino the Palme d'Or at Cannes and an Oscar for best screenplay and beyond making Tarantino the indie-film equivalent of a rock star who spawns a legion of imitators.

Pulp Fiction instantly turned John Travolta from a has-been into a $20 million-a-picture superstar. More significantly, it transformed Miramax from an art-house haven into a major studio. Tarantino's impact on Miramax has been so profound that studio chief Harvey Weinstein has likened it to Mickey Mouse's on Disney. Weinstein gives Tarantino more artistic freedom than just about any other

Hollywood director. Who else but Tarantino could have gotten the notoriously tough Weinstein to say yes to casting the long-forgotten David Carradine as Bill in *Kill Bill*?

Born in Tennessee and raised in Torrance, California, Tarantino dropped out of school in the ninth grade. After jobs that included working as an usher in a porn theater, he got the equivalent of a film degree working behind the counter of a video-rental store in Manhattan Beach, California. He watched thousands of movies belonging to every imaginable genre before finding his own voice writing the films *True Romance*, *From Dusk Till Dawn* and *Natural Born Killers* and directing *Reservoir Dogs* and *Pulp Fiction*.

Still, it has been six years since Tarantino followed *Pulp Fiction* with his critically and commercially disappointing Elmore Leonard novel adaptation, *Jackie Brown*. In the interim he's annoyed critics by starring in numerous films and a Broadway play, and he has become renowned for a series of high-profile celebrity brawls. It was clearly time to get back to work.

Kill Bill is based on Tarantino's first original screenplay since *Pulp Fiction*. He met with *Variety* columnist Michael Fleming on several nights in Hollywood, once coming from a screening of his favorite film, *The Good, the Bad and the Ugly*, another time from the editing room where he was putting the finishing touches on a *Kill Bill* fight scene so huge it cost nearly as much as the entire budget for *Pulp Fiction*. Despite a bad-boy image, Tarantino was charming and disarming, no matter who interrupted him. He was even polite to a woman who tried to engage him in a long-winded discussion of numerology.

PLAYBOY: It has been six years since *Jackie Brown*. Why so long? The rumors were that you had writer's block and anxiety because you were doing your first original work since *Pulp Fiction*.

TARANTINO: I didn't have writer's block at all. I did so much writing in those six years, I'm hooked up for a while now. I wrote a big war film, and it was like a gigantic novel. I ended up writing about three war films in the course of writing one, *Inglorious Bastards*. I had no anxiety about writing *Kill Bill*, but I was precious about it. It wasn't like I was afraid to let the world see it. I just wanted it to be really good. It took me a year to write one big fight sequence in *Kill Bill.*

PLAYBOY: Orson Welles and Peter Bogdanovich also made groundbreaking films early on. They failed to measure up afterward and seemed shackled by people's expectations. Is that perilous?

TARANTINO: I love being shackled with expectations. I've never had a problem with that. I'm not trying to re-create the phenomenon of *Pulp Fiction,* but I intend to keep breaking ground. There is nothing about the success and recognition *Pulp Fiction* got that is bad or negative in any way. *Blade Runner* didn't get appreciated until 10 years later. That's how I thought my life was going to go. I didn't think I'd get such cause and effect—bam!—during the theatrical release of the movie.

PLAYBOY: What ground are you breaking with *Kill Bill?*

TARANTINO: I don't think that way. People will view it and filter it back to me. I've been having this conversation for some time, because as far as some people were concerned, *Reservoir Dogs* was as good as it was going to get. This poor, silly boy is trying to follow up *Reservoir Dogs?* If somebody had asked what ground was being broken in *Pulp Fiction,* I'd have said none. It's just what I wanted to see in a movie, what I thought would be cool. I'm not surprised when people are surprised. They haven't seen all the movies I have, and they're not prepared for all the jerking around of the senses. They're not as bored with movies as I am. I need to do those things to make the experience worthwhile.

PLAYBOY: This film was supposed to be a small movie before your big World War II film. Now *Kill Bill* is so big it has been split into two movies that cost six times what *Pulp Fiction* did. How did that happen?

TARANTINO: When Uma's husband, Ethan Hawke, read it the first time, he said, "Quentin, if this is the epic you're doing before you do your epic, I'm afraid to see your epic." It's become a full-on epic exploitation movie. Hopefully, it's the movie that every exploitation-movie lover has always wished for. It doesn't have the pretentiousness of a big movie epic. This is made for black theaters, for exploitation cinema that covers the entire globe.

PLAYBOY: Isn't it awkward, splitting a single movie into two parts?

TARANTINO: There were no obstacles. I've always designed movies to be malleable. For instance, I've always designed different versions for Asia and for America and Europe. I don't make movies for America; I make movies for the world. In the last month of shooting, when Harvey Weinstein came to the set and brought up the idea of splitting the movie into two parts, within an hour I had figured out how it would work. We shot two opening sequences, all kinds of stuff. This is my tribute to grind-house cinema, and something was bothering me about releasing a three-hour grind-house movie. It seemed pretentious, like an art film meditation on a grind-house movie. Two 90-minute movies coming out fairly rapidly, one after another—that's not pretentious, that's ambitious.

PLAYBOY: Will the abundance of blood in *Kill Bill* limit your audience?

TARANTINO: I like that it's violent as hell, but it's also fun as hell. It doesn't take place in this universe but in the movie universe these movies take place in. This is a movie that knows it's a movie. You may like the movie, you may not like the movie. But if you're a movie lover and have good knowledge, you can't help but smile at this thing, because it's just so movie-mad obsessed. It makes its own universe out of all these different genres. Harvey Weinstein was worried at one point that women would be turned off by the violence. I said, "Don't worry. They're going to love the movie. They'll be very empowered by it." I think 13-year-old girls will love *Kill Bill*. I want young girls to be able to see it. They're going to love Uma's character, the Bride. They have my permission to buy a ticket for another movie and sneak into *Kill Bill*. That's money I'm okay not making. When I was a kid, I used to go into theaters when they didn't have the name of the movies on the ticket. I'm a theater-sneaker-inner from way back.

PLAYBOY: You conceived *Kill Bill* with Uma Thurman on the set of *Pulp Fiction*. Then she and Ethan Hawke conceived a child. You had to decide whether to wait or to replace her. Your long layoff must have left you tempted to find someone else.

TARANTINO: I definitely thought about it for two to three weeks. It was a decision I had to make.

PLAYBOY: Did she talk you out of it? This is her meatiest role since *Pulp Fiction*.

TARANTINO: Uma was so invested, so in love with this movie, it would have broken her heart if I'd gone with anybody else. At the same time, she didn't want to ruin my life. She was having her baby, and this was mine. She was going to let me decide. And I decided. It needed to be her. If you're Sergio Leone and you've got Eastwood in *A Fistful of Dollars* and he gets sick, you wait for him. If you're Josef von Sternberg doing *Morocco* and Marlene Dietrich breaks her leg, you wait.

PLAYBOY: Warren Beatty signed on to play Bill. He was replaced by David Carradine, which keeps alive your tradition of recycling forgotten actors such as John Travolta, Pam Grier and Robert Forster. Why didn't Warren make the film?

TARANTINO: He wanted to. Then, as it got a little closer, things changed. He thought it was a bit more of a commitment than I'd let on. Bill doesn't show up until almost the end, but Warren would have had to go through the three months of kung fu training that everyone else went through. He wasn't prepared for two months in L.A. and a month in China.

PLAYBOY: So he would have had to leave his family.

TARANTINO: Just like everybody else. Vivica Fox left her family, and she worked only a week and a half. She spent three months in training, including a month in Beijing, and her scene was shot here six months later. She didn't like it, but when that week and a half came, she kicked ass like you wouldn't believe. I needed that commitment.

PLAYBOY: Who thought of Carradine?

TARANTINO: Warren did. I'd thought of Carradine after reading his autobiography but never told anybody. Warren suggested him out of the blue, and I laughed. The minute he said that, that kind of became the deal.

PLAYBOY: David Carradine has a reputation for being somewhat eccentric.

TARANTINO: I'm a huge fan of his. Along with a few actors such as Jack Nicholson and Christopher Walken, David is one of the great mad geniuses of the acting community. There is also the aspect of having Gordon Liu, representing Hong Kong, Sonny Chiba, representing Japan, and David Carradine, star of *Kung Fu*, representing America—a literal roundup of the three countries that made martial arts the genre that it is.

PLAYBOY: What is it like for a young guy to be transformed overnight from a film geek into a rock star, as you were when *Pulp Fiction* came out?

TARANTINO: Let's make it clear that we're using the rock-star thing because you brought it up.

PLAYBOY: Did your sudden fame change the way women regard you? Do rock star directors have groupies?

TARANTINO: Even before *Pulp Fiction* I started discovering how cool it is to be a director. When I started going on the film festival circuit, I was getting laid all the time. I'd never been out of the country before, and not only was I getting laid, I was getting laid by foreign chicks. When I wasn't getting laid I'd find myself making out with some Italian girl who was the spitting image of Michelle Pfeiffer.

PLAYBOY: Were these women you would dream about when you were a minimum-wage guy?

TARANTINO: No, it wasn't quite *Revenge of the Nerds*. I always really liked beautiful women and interesting women. I never walked around thinking I was this geek who could never get anybody. I never felt any girl was unattainable, as long as she got to know me. But when you spend most of your time renting videos at the Video Archives, it's hard to meet girls unless you're in a situation where they're around. The entire time I was at the video store, my only dates were with customers. Other than that, I'd hang out with my dateless friends and go to movies. The minute I started working at places where I had more natural contact with women, it became a whole different story. I felt like Elvis when I was meeting girls on the festival circuit. I went crazy for a little bit—a lot of making out. I love kissing. I'm a good kisser.

PLAYBOY: What about foot massages, the kind you popularized in *Pulp Fiction?*

TARANTINO: I've been known to give a good foot massage. But with *Reservoir Dogs* and *Pulp Fiction* it just went off the hook. There was a lot of making up for lost time. What handsome guys did in their 20s, I did in my 30s. When you become famous, it's cool. I can go by myself into a bar I've never been in before, and in no time I'll have a couple girls around me, if not more. I usually go home with a couple phone numbers, and I'm not asking for them. If I go into a strip club now and play my cards right, I can take one of the strippers home. If I go to get a lap dance when it's close to the end of the night, when they're getting ready to close up, and the girl knows who I am, she'll probably ask if I want to go out for coffee.

PLAYBOY: What was the biggest surprise about the women?

TARANTINO: One thing I wasn't expecting—I really got a kick out of it—was getting really sexy fan mail.

PLAYBOY: Do you mean nude pictures?

TARANTINO: I never really got nude pictures. I would get girls who have really big crushes on me writing about that, whether they're 12 or 13 or 25. I also got sex letters, and those were pretty cool. The girls had done some thinking about my sexuality. Some of the pictures and letters were brilliant.

PLAYBOY: Highlights, please.

TARANTINO: One girl sent me a can of tennis balls, with a picture and a note that said, "Now you've got the balls, give me a call."

PLAYBOY: Did you call?

TARANTINO: I did, but she was in St. Louis, and I wasn't going to travel.

I followed up on a few of the letters. One girl, I'll never forget her. I don't think I called her; I was afraid she was a little too young. In her picture, she could have been 20, or she could have been 15. She was a young black girl. I was doing *From Dusk Till Dawn* with George Clooney. After I read the letter, I went banging on his trailer. I went in and read it to him, and he was like, "Whoa!"

PLAYBOY: He gets good letters too.

TARANTINO: We had a good time reading each other our sex mail. This one was so imaginative. First she's telling me what movies she'd like to watch with me, talking like a cool film-geek kind of girl, and then she starts getting into dirty stuff. She mentions kissing for hours. Then she writes, "I want to dress you in a French maid outfit, and while I sit in a chair in a garter belt and panties, smoking a cigarette, I'll make you pick up every piece of lint off the carpet. And I'm not going to be easy about it! You're going to have to get right down on your hands and knees, and I want that carpet completely clean as I smoke cigarettes."

PLAYBOY: You spent four months in China shooting *Kill Bill*. How does a guy entertain himself in a communist country?

TARANTINO: The nightlife in China is off the hook. If you've ever seen Sixth Street in Austin, Texas, that street with all the bars, well, they've got five streets like that in Beijing, and the bars are open all night. We worked six-day weeks in China and did a lot of partying on our day off. When we finished shooting, we would go out. We were up all night on Saturdays, and we would sleep all day on Sunday. China is the ecstasy capital of the world right now. They have E there that's beyond acid. It's wild. We had a good goddamn time in China.

PLAYBOY: You did ecstasy?

TARANTINO: Yes. The first time I went to the Great Wall of China it was like an all-night rave. They had rock bands, fireworks. We were smoking pot and doing E. It was great. Me and a bunch of the crew partied like rock stars all night. It's a great way to see the wall the first time.

PLAYBOY: You write about bad guys who navigate through the worst trouble imaginable. What's the worst situation you've had to get out of? Was it the time you spent in jail?

TARANTINO: I went to the county jail three different times, all for traffic stuff. I was in my 20s and broke, barely making $8,000 a year. If I got caught for traffic stuff, I had to do the days because I couldn't pay. When your car's outlawed and you have no insurance, if you get a ticket you can't fix it. You just do the days and try not to get caught again for a while.

PLAYBOY: You pummeled a producer of *Natural Born Killers* at a Hollywood restaurant and scrapped in a New York City bar with a guy who objected to the way you refer to blacks in your movies. Do you have too quick a temper?

TARANTINO: I don't think I have a quick temper. I can get into a discussion, and that argument can get heated. I'm not going to take it to a violent place, because I know there is no limit to where I could go with that. Depending on how thick the shit gets, I'll go all the way if I need to. I don't want to. Life will be a lot easier if I don't. I can get really mad at somebody, but I'm never afraid that I'll hit them or step over that line. But the minute they do, I'm all there.

PLAYBOY: When was the last time you got into a physical altercation?

TARANTINO: Well, for a while it was happening a lot. There was a third incident that nobody knew about, with a cabdriver. I was with a girl, and he was really rude. I got into an argument with him. We were yelling at each other, and he said something about her. I went around the side of the cab and beat him up. Bouncers from a club pulled me off him, and he drove away. Those two other things had just happened, and I remember thinking, Is this worth $30,000, the amount I'll have to pay when this guy figures out who I am? How much do I want to whip this guy's ass? He was a big black guy, and they're used to white guys backing down. I don't back down, especially to big black guys. That gives me a psychological advantage. When I don't back down, they have to stop and think, Why didn't he back down? He came out of the car and said, "Come on, motherfucker!" Right then the $30,000 went out of my head, and all I was thinking was, I'm going to get my money's worth.

PLAYBOY: Did you?

TARANTINO: I did. *Boom!* I punched him. The bouncers grabbed me, and then the guy tried to bite me in my breast. He took a big bite out of me, right by my nipple. What a fucking asshole!

PLAYBOY: Talk about a plot twist. You probably never expected to get milked.

TARANTINO: The only reason he didn't really fuck me up was he was too greedy. He took too big a bite. Had he taken a small bite, I might not have a nipple now. He barely broke the skin because he had too much flesh in his mouth.

PLAYBOY: Did it cost you $30,000?

TARANTINO: No, I did something smart. I said to myself, I'm not going to call my publicist; I'm not telling anybody. I didn't want to release it into the atmosphere, figuring I had about five days before he figured out who I was. It wasn't till two months later that I told friends I'd gotten into this fight.

PLAYBOY: Fighting lends to your mystique. Why are people so intrigued by you?

TARANTINO: Two things. They are digging on my movies. Maybe I turned them on to movies they'd never seen before. Then there's my personal American-dream story that maybe they saw me tell on *The Tonight Show* or read in interviews. I'm open, and what you see is what you get. That is something that made me sick of the media for a bit, because it seemed like they were making fun of me for being me. That sounds like some poor-baby thing, but once you're an adult, people don't make fun of you anymore—not to your face.

PLAYBOY: You become a caricature.

TARANTINO: You'll read about someone taking a swipe, making fun of your looks—my hair, my jaw or the way I talk. I've gotten over it, but it hurt my feelings. I wasn't expecting that. Who needs that shit? I didn't want to go through that shit in high school; that's why I dropped out. You think, They're always complaining about everybody being so guarded. I'm not guarded, and I'm paying for it. I'm over it now, though.

PLAYBOY: For both *Reservoir Dogs* and *Pulp Fiction* you were accused of borrowing elements from obscure Hong Kong films. Tell us the influences that went into *Pulp Fiction*. The scene in which Bruce Willis and Ving Rhames are brawling, fall into a pawnshop and end up captured by redneck homosexual rapists, where did that come from?

TARANTINO: I don't know exactly how those things happen. I'm about not getting too analytical beforehand and just letting stories take the turns they take.

PLAYBOY: You could compare that pawnshop scene to John Boorman's *Deliverance*, if only for the homosexual rape.

TARANTINO: Roger Avary came up with the idea. He'd written a whole script for a movie. I didn't want to do the whole thing, only one section that fit into *Pulp Fiction*. I bought that script the way you'd buy a book to make into a movie, just to adapt the part that I liked. That was the scene when the boxer throws the fight and gets chased down by the other guy and they end up in a pawnshop with two guys who are serial killers.

PLAYBOY: Did the "Wake the gimp" sequence come from Avary?

TARANTINO: The gimp and the whole anal-rape torture sequence were his ideas. I wanted to do it because it was a flip reworking of something that was a big deal in *Deliverance*. This crazy, anal-sex rape was so out of nowhere that I thought it was funny. I thought, Wow, he's made anal rape really funny.

PLAYBOY: Finally.

TARANTINO: We were worried about getting an X rating. Right around that time, *American Me* came out, and it had three anal rapes. It helped our cause.

PLAYBOY: Ned Beatty has been permanently linked with being raped in *Deliverance*. Was it tough to get Rhames to play the mob boss who gets sodomized by rednecks?

TARANTINO: It was a stumbling point for almost all the black male actors I talked to. It's very hard to talk a black man into doing anything where he's being raped. It wasn't even a matter of how much to show but rather, if the audience sees that, will they ever not see that? But I'd written it with Ving in mind. I'd always heard his voice saying that dialogue. The words trickle off Ving's tongue because I wrote it for his cadence. He came in, did his audition, and he was just magnificent. Then came the time to have the conversation. I was thinking, Please, let him not have as much of a problem as everybody else, because he's just so good. Ving sensed this and said, "Let me ask you, how explicit is this shit gonna get?" I said, "It's not going to be that bad, but you're going to know what's going on. Do you have a problem with that?" He says, "Not only do I not have a problem, you have to understand that because of the way I am, I don't get offered many vulnerable characters. This man might end up being the most vulnerable motherfucker I will ever play."

PLAYBOY: So he was game.

TARANTINO: Ving was a man of his word, but there was one sequence with Duane Whitaker, who plays Maynard, one of the guys who's fucking him in the movie. I wanted this wild, "yee haw!" kind of anal-rape thing. Ving says, "Okay, so we're going to see his butt, right? Well, what's going to be down there to protect that?" I say, "You won't see anything." And he says, "I'm not talking about what you're going to show. I don't care if it's on camera, in focus or not. I don't want dick touching anus. What are you going to put down there?" It's Duane, Ving and me, and this prop guy brings in this turquoise velvet bag that you put diamonds in. We burst out laughing, and Ving says, "Duane, you just put your dick in this little bag and I'll be okay."

PLAYBOY: You've said of *Jackie Brown* that you most identified with Sam

Jackson's badass gun-runner character, Ordell Robbie. Is there a bit of badass in you?

TARANTINO: People misunderstood what I said about Ordell. I'm a method writer. I become one or two characters when I'm writing. When I was doing *Kill Bill*, I was the Bride. People noticed that when I was writing, I was getting much more feminine in my outlook. All of a sudden I was buying things for my apartment or house. I'd see something cool in a shop in Greenwich Village, and I'd buy it. An item could jump off a shelf at me, through a window. I'd have to buy it, take it home and try it out. I'd buy flowers for the house and start arranging them. I don't normally wear jewelry, and suddenly I'm wearing jewelry. My friends said, "You're getting in touch with your feminine side. You're nesting, adorning yourself." In the case of *Jackie Brown*, the character I assimilated was Ordell. I walked around like Ordell that whole year. I'd leave the house as Ordell. When I stopped writing, I had to let go and let Sam Jackson take over.

PLAYBOY: You clashed with Oliver Stone at his peak when he vastly changed your script for *Natural Born Killers*. Why did you hate the film so much?

TARANTINO: I'd never really seen the movie from beginning to end. I watched it only in bits and pieces, out of defiance at first. Then I actually went to the movies to see it.

PLAYBOY: And you walked out?

TARANTINO: Yes. I just hated that whole Rodney Dangerfield sequence so much. It was so unfunny, so disgusting. It did the number one thing I would never do: It came up with a little peanut psychological origin for why these people were the way they were. I rejected that in every way, and then that awful scene gives you a little pop psychology analysis.

PLAYBOY: It was modeled like a sitcom, with a laugh track, and it made clear that Dangerfield's character had molested his daughter.

TARANTINO: I had my name taken off the script just so people wouldn't think I had written that.

PLAYBOY: You sparred with Spike Lee over your liberal use of the word nigger in your films. Did that feud also go by the wayside?

TARANTINO: It didn't go by the wayside per se. Spike and I bumped into each other once after all that crap was over, and I was all set to kick his ass.

PLAYBOY: Why?

TARANTINO: Because he'd been talking all this shit instead of talking to me about it. My biggest problem with Spike was the completely self-serving aspect of his argument. He attacked me to keep his "Jesse Jackson of cinema" status. Basically, for a little bit of time before I came along, you had to get Spike Lee's benediction and approval if you were white and dealing with black stuff in a movie. Fuck that. This destroyed that, and he's never had that position again. I wasn't looking for his approval, and so he was taking me on to keep his status. I hated it, because a celebrity feud is one of the most tasteless, trite, trivial things somebody in my position can engage in, to be drawn into something so beneath you.

PLAYBOY: Do you think some of his arguments had merit?

TARANTINO: It's funny, because he talks in these grandiose terms, but as much of a loudmouth as he can be, the press doesn't really listen to what he says. They print his tone. If you boiled down what he was saying, it wasn't that I didn't have the right to say "nigger" as many times as I did. It was why do I have the right to say "nigger" 37 times, but he doesn't have the right to say "kike" 37 times? That is really what he was saying.

PLAYBOY: He did get flack for using two stereotypical Jewish characters in *Mo' Better Blues*.

TARANTINO: The words nigger and kike are not the same word. Kike is not common parlance among Jews. The other word has maybe 12 different meanings, depending on the context it's spoken in, who is saying it and the way he's saying it. So to equate nigger with kike does not take into account the way the English language works today. And I am working with the English language. I am not just a film director who shoots movies. I'm an artist, and good, bad or indifferent, I'm coming from that place. All my choices, the way I live my life, are about that. He came back with, "Quentin isn't any more of an artist than Michael Jackson is, and when Michael said 'Jew me' in a song, they made him change it." It was almost worth the whole damn thing to hear him say that.

PLAYBOY: Rate yourself from one to 10 on your level of skill as a writer, as a director and as an actor.

TARANTINO: Wow, you're nailing me down here. Look, I don't want to rate myself with numbers. If I say 10, I'm being a jerk, and if I don't say 10, I'm being a liar. [*Laughs*] I'll answer the question, just not by your scale. As far as acting is concerned, I think I could be a great actor. If I got a chance to do more characters and get more time into it, I could be a really good character actor. People have been really tough on me.

PLAYBOY: Why?

TARANTINO: Probably because they didn't realize how serious I was about it, and film critics didn't want it. One critic told me exactly as much. I was this great white hope, a young auteur, and they didn't want me to divide my focus. They wanted me sitting in a room, coming up with the next thing they can watch. "Why aren't you saving cinema from itself?"

PLAYBOY: George Clooney and your *Reservoir Dogs* cast mates Tim Roth and Steve Buscemi directed films and were roundly applauded for stretching. Double standard?

TARANTINO: Thank you for noticing, because it hasn't been lost on me. I actually confronted Roger Ebert after he named this movie I did years ago, *Somebody to Love*, as some kind of booby prize on his show. It was released way after the fact, and I'm in it for two seconds. Buscemi directs *Trees Lounge* and gets the door prize for directing and stretching his talents. The booby prize went to me for daring to act in a movie. Why is it okay for him to stretch his talent and not me?

PLAYBOY: You started acting as an Elvis impersonator on *The Golden Girls*. What was it like, being near Bea Arthur with stars in your eyes?

TARANTINO: The job lasted two days, and what was fantastic was how much money I made. That was when I had no money whatsoever. All of a sudden I made $700 in a lump sum. You get it again when it's repeated. They liked that bit so much they put it in a "Best of *The Golden Girls*" episode. I got paid $700 for that. And then the show was in tremendous repeat mode, on NBC and in syndication. I had two episodes in repeat rotation and ended up making $2,500. Just when I was flat broke, a check would come in for $150, then $75, then $95. I got a check the other day for 85 cents.

PLAYBOY: How was your Elvis?

TARANTINO: I was the best of the bunch. The others were all the Vegas Elvis. I was the Sun Records Elvis, the hillbilly cat.

PLAYBOY: This was your first big acting job after quitting school. How did you negotiate that exit?

TARANTINO: My mom and I have different recollections. I had ditched school for about three weeks, so I was in this weird phase when I couldn't go back because I'd get busted. I went back, and I got busted. Me and my mom were arguing, and in the heat of it I said, "Well, I want to quit anyway." She said, "You're not going to quit." I thought that was that. A week later, she was putting on makeup in the bathroom, getting ready for work. She said, "About your quitting school, I've thought about it, and I'm going to let you quit. But you have to go out and get a job." I was gob-smacked. I thought, Doesn't she realize I was bluffing? So I quit.

PLAYBOY: You dated Mira Sorvino, a Harvard grad, and you didn't go near college. Do you ever regret dropping out?

TARANTINO: No, there's a slight pride in quitting junior high and achieving what I have. It makes me look a little bit smarter. When I tell somebody that, they're genuinely impressed. I'm not very enamored with the American public school system. I hated school so much, I dropped out in ninth grade. I never went to high school. There's a cool cachet about it now. My only regret—and it's not even a big regret—is that I hated school so much I thought that's what it was going to be like forever. I didn't realize college would be different. So if I had to do it all over I probably would stay in school so I could have my college experience. I'm sure I would have had a ball.

PLAYBOY: Your mom raised you without your biological father. *Premiere* magazine trotted him out after you became famous. Was that unfair?

TARANTINO: That really bothered me for a long time. It was one of those crappy byproducts of fame. I've never met him and don't have any desire to. He's not my father. Just because you fucked my mom doesn't make you my father. The only thing I've got to say to him is "Thanks for the fucking sperm." He had 30 years to look me up, and he tries after I'm famous? It was sad. For a while, when I was going by that name and he didn't look me up, I thought, Well, that's cool of him. He's showing some class. Stay the fuck out of the picture. But that limelight is a little hard for people to turn down.

PLAYBOY: We can't leave without asking the one question you always refuse to answer. What's glowing inside that briefcase in *Pulp Fiction?* And for that matter, what happens when Mr. Pink runs off after the shootout in *Reservoir Dogs?*

TARANTINO: I'll never explain what was in that briefcase—not to be a prick but because people come up with their own explanations, and that is the explanation. Same with Mr. Pink. I once said this as a dig to Oliver Stone, but I don't really mean it as a dig anymore. When Oliver Stone does his movies, he has a big idea he wants to get across, and he wants everyone to leave the theater with that idea. They can reject the idea, but they'd better get it or he'll think he didn't do his job. I want to do a whole lot of work for you, but I want to leave 10, maybe even 20 percent for you to imagine so the movie is really yours. You have a version. Stuff that's open for interpretation, I want your interpretation. The minute

I tell you what I think, you'll throw away whatever you've come up with in your head. You can't help it. I would too. You'd feel like a fool. So you tell me what's in the briefcase. If you think it's Marsellus' soul and he's bought it back from the devil, which is one guess I've heard, well, you are right: It's his soul. That I actually did a movie that can inspire such wildly imaginative readings makes me proud. It's funny where a throwaway line can lead you. You know what my favorite line is in the pawnshop scene in *Pulp Fiction*? Holly Hunter noticed it. It comes when they're deciding who they're going to fuck first. They choose Marsellus, and it's "You want to do it here?" The other guy says, "No, let's take him into Russell's old room." You're left thinking, Who the fuck is Russell and how did it become his old room? I'll leave you guessing on that one, too.

ORSON WELLES

A candid conversation with the protean actor-writer-producer-director and Falstaffian bon vivant

Our interviewer is England's eminent drama critic Kenneth Tynan, whom readers will remember as the author of previous *Playboy Interviews* with Richard Burton and Peter O'Toole, as well as several trenchant *Playboy* articles. Of this month's larger-than-life subject, Tynan writes:

"The performing arts have now enjoyed the professional services of George Orson Welles for 35 years—ever since 1931, when he arrived at the Gate Theater in Dublin, passed himself off as a well-known actor from the New York Theater Guild and began playing leads at the age of 16. The previous year, just before graduating from a progressive boys' school in Woodstock, Illinois, he had put an ad in an American trade paper. It read, in part: 'Orson Welles—Stock, Characters, Heavies, Juveniles or as cast . . . Lots of pep, experience and ability.' Already George Welles had begun to behave as if he were Orson Welles.

"He was born in Kenosha, Wisconsin, in 1915. Both his parents were then approaching middle age. Through his mother—an aesthete, a beauty and a talented musician—he met Ravel and Stravinsky. Through his father—a globe-trotting gambler who loved star quality—he met numerous actors, magicians and circus performers. The milestones of Welles's career are dotted all over the landscape of show business in the middle decades of the 20th century.

"He had only to train his sights on an art for it to capitulate. Theater fell first. Just 30 years ago, he directed a famous all-Negro *Macbeth* in Harlem. Moving downtown, he launched the Mercury

Theater with his modern-dress production of *Julius Caesar*, in which Caesar was a bald-pated replica of Mussolini. Almost in passing, he conquered radio: Blood froze all over America when he celebrated Halloween in 1938 with a broadcast version of H. G. Wells's *War of the Worlds*. The movie industry was the next to surrender. A quarter of a century has passed since the premiere of *Citizen Kane*, Welles's first film; but Hollywood seismographs still record the tremors left by its impact. It gave the American cinema an adult vocabulary, and in a recent poll of international critics, it was voted the finest film ever made. *The Magnificent Ambersons*, which followed in 1942, confirmed the arrival of a revolutionary virtuoso. In every art he touched, Welles started at the top. That was his triumph, and also his problem. Whenever his name appeared on anything less than a masterpiece, people instantly said he was slipping.

"During the past 20 years, living mainly in Europe, Welles has been a rogue elephant at large in most of the performing media. He may turn up in Morocco, filming *Othello* on a frayed shoestring; in London, directing his own brilliant stage adaptation of *Moby Dick*; in Paris, shooting Kafka's *The Trial* in a derelict railway station; in Spain, making a still-unfinished movie of *Don Quixote*; in Yugoslavia or Italy, hamming away for money in other people's bad epics; and even in Hollywood, where in 1958 he made a startling and underrated thriller called *Touch of Evil*. You can never tell how or where he will manifest himself next. In the course of his career—apart from writing and directing films and plays, and acting in both—he has been a novelist, a painter, a ballet scenarist, a conjurer, a columnist, a television pundit and an amateur bullfighter. There's symbolic if not literal truth in the story about how he once addressed a thinly attended meeting of admirers with the words: 'Isn't it a shame that there are so many of me and so few of you?'

"He has grown fat spreading himself thin. A passive figure sculpted in foam rubber, he is preceded wherever he goes by his belly and an oversized cigar; and his presence is immediately signaled, even to the blind, by the Bacchic earthquake of his laughter. His first European base was a villa near Rome, but nowadays he lives with his Italian wife and their daughter Beatrice in an expensive suburb of Madrid. 'I used to be an American émigré in Italy,' he says. 'Now I'm an Italian émigré in Spain.' At 51, he has long since joined the select group of international celebrities whose fame is self-sustaining, no matter how widely opinions of their work may vary, and no matter how much the work itself may fluctuate in quality. (Other members of the club in recent times have been Chaplin, Ellington, Cocteau, Picasso and Hemingway.)

"My interview with him took place last spring in London. Welles was appearing with Peter Sellers and David Niven in *Casino Royale*, the James Bond film that has everything but Sean Connery. Characteristically, Welles had insisted on living in a furnished apartment directly over the Mirabelle, one of the most expensive and arguably the best restaurant in London. Thus, he could be sure of gourmet room service. Empty caviar pots adorned every table. Imposingly swathed in the robes of a Buddhist priest, he sipped Dom Pérignon champagne and talked far into the night.

"Shortly afterward, Welles took his Falstaff film, *Chimes at Midnight* [released in the U.S. as *Falstaff*], to the Cannes Festival. Not all the critics were ecstatic; one said that Welles was the only actor who ever had to slim down to play Falstaff. But the jury reacted warmly; and so did the audience at the prize-giving ceremony, which began with the announcement of a special award to 'M. Orson Welles, for his contribution to world cinema.' Jeers and whistles greeted many of the other prizes; but for this one, everybody rose—avant-garde critics and commercial producers alike—and clapped with their hands held over their heads. The ovation lasted for minutes. Welles beamed and sweated on the stage of the Festival Palace, looking like a melting iceberg and occasionally tilting forward in something that approximated a bow.

"Later, at his hotel, he talked with me about his next production— *Treasure Island*, in which he would play Long John Silver. Then he would complete *Don Quixote* and make a film of *King Lear*. After that, there were plenty of other projects in hand. 'The bee,' he said happily, 'is always making honey.'"

PLAYBOY: You've been a celebrity now for 30 years. In all that time, what's the most accurate description anyone has given of you?

WELLES: I don't want *any* description of me to be accurate; I want it to be flattering. I don't think people who have to sing for their supper ever like to be described truthfully—not in print, anyway. We need to sell tickets, so we need good reviews.

PLAYBOY: In private conversation, what's the pleasantest thing you ever heard about yourself?

WELLES: Roosevelt saying that I would have been a great politician. Barrymore saying that Chaplin and myself were the two finest living actors. I don't mean that I *believe* those things, but you used the word "pleasant." What I really enjoy is flattery in the suburbs of my work—about things I'm not mainly or even professionally occupied with. When an old bullfighter tells me I'm one of the few people who understand the bulls, or when a magician says I'm a good magician, that tickles the ego without having anything to do with the box office.

PLAYBOY: Of all the comments, written or spoken, that have been made about you, which has displeased you the most?

WELLES: Nothing spoken. It's only written things I mind—for example, everything Walter Kerr ever wrote about me. It takes a big effort for me to persuade myself that anything bad I read about myself isn't true. I have a primitive respect for the printed word as it applies to me, especially if it's negative. I can remember being described in Denver, when I was playing Marchbanks in *Candida* at the age of 18, as "a sea cow whining in a basso profundo." That was more than 30 years ago, and I can still quote the review verbatim. I can never remember the good ones. Probably the bad ones hurt so much and so morbidly because I've run the store so long. I've been an actor-manager in radio, films and the theater; and in a very immediate way, I've been economically dependent on what's written about me, so that I worry about how much it's going to affect the gross. Or maybe that's just a justification for hypersensitivity.

PLAYBOY: Talking about critics, you once complained: "They don't review my work, they review *me*." Do you feel that's still true?

WELLES: Yes—but I suppose I shouldn't kick about it. I earn a good living and get a lot of work because of this ridiculous myth about me. But the price of it is that when I try to do something serious, something I care about, a great many critics don't review that particular work, but me in general. They write their standard Welles piece. It's either the good piece or the bad piece, but they're both fairly standard.

PLAYBOY: In an era of increasing specialization, you've expressed yourself in almost every artistic medium. Have you never wanted to specialize?

WELLES: No, I can't imagine limiting myself. It's a great shame that we live in an age of specialists, and I think we give them too much respect.

I've known four or five great doctors in my life, and they have always told me that medicine is still in a primitive state and that they know hardly anything about it. I've known only one great cameraman—Gregg Toland, who photographed *Citizen Kane*. He said he could teach me everything about the camera in four hours—and he did. I don't believe the specialist is all that our epoch cracks him up to be.

PLAYBOY: Is it possible nowadays to be a Renaissance man—someone who's equally at home in the arts and the sciences?

WELLES: It's possible and it's also necessary, because the big problem ahead of us today is synthesis. We have to get all these scattered things together and make sense of them. The wildest kind of lunacy is to go wandering up some single street. It's better not only for the individual but for society that our personal horizons should be as wide as possible. What a normally intelligent person can't learn—if he's genuinely alive and honestly curious—isn't really worth learning. For instance, besides knowing something about Elizabethan drama, I think I could also make a stab at explaining the basic principles of nuclear fission—a fair enough stab to be living in the world today. I don't just say: "That's a mystery that ought to be left to the scientists." Of course, I don't mean that I'm ready to accept a key post in national defense.

PLAYBOY: Since World War II, you've lived and worked mostly outside the United States. Would you call yourself an expatriate?

WELLES: I don't like that word. Since childhood, I've always regarded myself as an American who happens to live all over the place. "Expatriate" is a dated word that relates to a particular 1920ish generation and to a romantic attitude about living abroad. I'm prejudiced against the word rather than the fact. I might very well cease to be an American citizen someday, but simply because, if you're forming a production company in Europe, it's economically helpful to be a European. I'm not young enough to bear arms for my country, so why shouldn't I live where I like and where I get the most work? After all, London is full of Hungarians and Germans and Frenchmen, and America is full of *everybody*—and *they* aren't called expatriates.

PLAYBOY: Isn't it true that you chose to live in Europe because the U.S. government refused to allow you tax deductions on the losses you suffered in your 1946 Broadway production of *Around the World in Eighty Days*?

WELLES: My tax problems began at that time, but that wasn't why I went to Europe. I spent many of these years in Europe paying the government back all that money I lost, which they wouldn't let me write off as a loss because of some bad bookkeeping. I like living in Europe; I'm not a refugee.

PLAYBOY: You aren't a Catholic, yet you decided to live in two intensely Catholic countries—first Italy and now Spain. Why?

WELLES: This has nothing to do with religion. The Mediterranean culture is more generous, less guilt-ridden. Any society that exists without natural gaiety, without some sense of ease in the presence of death, is one in which I am not immensely comfortable. I don't condemn that very northern, very Protestant world of artists like Ingmar Bergman; it's just not where I live. The Sweden I like to visit is a lot of fun. But Bergman's Sweden always reminds me of something Henry James said about Ibsen's Norway—that it was full of "the odor of spiritual paraffin." How I sympathize with that!

PLAYBOY: If you could have picked any country and period in which to be born, would you have chosen America in 1915?

WELLES: It wouldn't have been all that low on my list, but anyone in their senses would have wanted to live in the golden age of Greece, in 15th century Italy or Elizabethan England. And there were other golden ages. Persia had one and China had four or five. Ours is an extraordinary age, but it doesn't even look very silver to me. I think I might have been happier and more fulfilled in other periods and places—including America at about the time when we started putting up roofs instead of tents.

PLAYBOY: Are there any figures in American history you identify with?

WELLES: Like most Americans, I wish I had some Lincoln in me: But I don't. I can't imagine myself being capable of any such goodness or compassion. I guess the only great American whose role I might conceivably have occupied is Tom Paine. He was a radical, a true independent—not in the comfortable, present-day liberal sense, but in the good, tough sense that he was prepared to go to jail for it. It's been my luck, good or bad, not to have been faced with that choice.

PLAYBOY: Your parents separated when you were six, but you traveled widely with your mother, who died two years later. You then went around the world with your father, who died when you were 15. What places do you remember most vividly from this early globetrotting period?

WELLES: Berlin had about three good years, from 1926 onward, and so did Chicago about the same time. But the best cities were certainly Budapest and Peking. They had the best talk and the most action right up to the end. But I can't forget a party I attended somewhere in the Tyrol sometime in the mid-1920s. I was on a walking tour with several other little boys, and our tutor took us to eat at a big open-air beer garden. We sat at a long table with a lot of Nazis, who were then a little-known bunch of cranks, and I was placed next to a small man with a very dim personality. He made no impression on me at the time, but later, when I saw his pictures, I realized that I had lunched with Adolf Hitler.

PLAYBOY: In many of the films you've written and directed, the hero has no father. We know nothing about Citizen Kane's father: and George, in *The Magnificent Ambersons*, ruins the life of his widowed mother by forbidding her to remarry. In your latest film, *Falstaff*, the hero is Prince Hal, whose legitimate father, Henry IV of England, is a murderous usurper; but his spiritual father, whom you play yourself—

WELLES: Is Falstaff.

PLAYBOY: Right. Does this attitude toward fathers reflect anything in your own life?

WELLES: I don't think so. I had a father whom I remember as enormously likable and attractive. He was a gambler, and a playboy who may have been getting a bit old for it when I knew him, but he was a marvelous fellow, and it was a great sorrow to me when he died. No, a story interests me on its own merits, not because it's autobiographical. The Falstaff story is the best in Shakespeare—not the best play, but the best story. The richness of the triangle between the father and Falstaff and the son is without parallel; it's a complete Shakespearean creation. The other plays are good stories borrowed from other sources and made great because of what Shakespeare breathed into them. But there's nothing in the medieval chronicles that even hints at the Falstaff-Hal-King story. That's Shakespeare's story, and Falstaff is entirely his creation. He's the only great character in dramatic literature who is also good.

PLAYBOY: Do you agree with W. H. Auden, who once likened him to a Christ figure?

WELLES: I won't argue with that, although my flesh always creeps when people use the word "Christ." I think Falstaff is like a Christmas tree decorated with vices. The tree itself is total innocence and love. By contrast, the king is decorated only with kingliness. He's a pure Machiavellian. And there's something beady-eyed and self-regarding about his son—even when he reaches his apotheosis as Henry V.

PLAYBOY: Do you think *Falstaff* is likely to outrage Shakespeare lovers?

WELLES: Well, I've always edited Shakespeare, and my other Shakespearean films have suffered critically for just that reason. God knows what will happen with this one. In the case of *Macbeth* or *Othello*, I tried to make a single play into a film script. In *Falstaff*, I've taken five plays—*Richard II*, the two parts of *Henry IV*, *Henry V* and *The Merry Wives of Windsor*—and turned them into an entertainment lasting less than two hours. Naturally, I'm going to offend the kind of Shakespeare lover whose main concern is the sacredness of the text. But with people who are willing to concede that movies are a separate art form, I have some hopes of success. After all, when Verdi wrote *Falstaff* and *Otello*, nobody criticized *him* for radically changing Shakespeare. Larry Olivier has made fine Shakespearean movies that are essentially filmed Shakespearean plays; I use Shakespeare's words and characters to make motion pictures. They are variations on his themes. In *Falstaff*, I've gone much further than ever before, but not willfully, not for the fun of chopping and dabbling. If you see the history plays night after night in the theater, you discover a continuing story about a delinquent prince who turns into a great military captain, a usurping king, and Falstaff, the prince's spiritual father, who is a kind of secular saint. It finally culminates in the rejection of Falstaff by the prince. My film is entirely true to that story, although it sacrifices great parts of the plays from which the story is mined.

PLAYBOY: Does the film have a "message"?

WELLES: It laments the death of chivalry and the rejection of merry England. Even in Shakespeare's day, the old England of the greenwood and Maytime was already a myth, but a very real one. The rejection of Falstaff by the prince means the rejection of that England by a new kind of England that Shakespeare deplored—an England that ended up as the British Empire. The main change is no excuse for the betrayal of a friendship. It's the liberation of that story that justifies my surgical approach to the text.

PLAYBOY: May we check on a few of the popular rumors about you? It's been said that your pictures always go over the budget. True or false?

WELLES: False. I'm not an overspender, though I've sometimes been a delayed earner. *Citizen Kane*, for instance, cost about $850,000. I've no idea how much profit it's made by now, but it must be plenty. That profit took time, and it didn't go to me. All the pictures I've directed have been made within their budgets. The only exception was a documentary about South America that I started in 1942, just after I finished shooting *The Magnificent Ambersons*. I was asked to do it by the government for no salary but with $1 million to spend. But it was the studio's money, not the government's, and the studio fired me when I'd spent $600,000, on the basis that I was throwing money away. This is when the legend started. The studio spent a lot of dough and a lot of manpower putting it into circulation.

PLAYBOY: Another prevalent rumor is that you have the power of clairvoyance. Is that true?

WELLES: Well, if it exists, I sure as hell have it; if it doesn't exist, I have the thing that's mistaken for it. I've told people their futures in a terrifying way sometimes—and please understand that I hate fortunetelling. It's meddlesome, dangerous and a mockery of free will—the most important doctrine man has invented. But I was a fortuneteller once in Kansas City, when I was playing a week's stand there in the theater. As a part-time magician, I'd met a lot of semi-magician racketeers and learned the tricks of the professional seers. I took an apartment in a cheap district and put up a sign—$2 Readings—and every day I went there, put on a turban and told fortunes. At first I used what are called "cold readings"; that's a technical term for things you say to people that are bound to impress them and put them off their guard, so that they start telling you things about themselves. A typical cold reading is to say that you have a scar on your knee. Everybody has a scar on their knee, because everybody fell down as a child. Another one is to say that a big change took place in your attitude toward life between the ages of 12 and 14. But in the last two or three days, I stopped doing the tricks and just talked. A woman came in wearing a bright dress. As soon as she sat down, I said, "You've just lost your husband"; and she burst into tears. I believe that I saw and deduced things that my conscious mind did not record. But consciously, I just said the first thing that came into my head, and it was true. So I was well on the way to contracting the fortuneteller's occupational disease, which is to start believing in yourself; to become what they call a "shuteye." And that's dangerous.

PLAYBOY: A third charge often leveled against you is that you dissipate too much energy in talk. The English critic Cyril Connolly once said that conversation, for an artist, was "a ceremony of self-wastage." Does that phrase give you a pang?

WELLES: No, but it reminds me of Thornton Wilder and his theory of "capsule conversations." He used to say to me: "You must stop wasting your energy, Orson. You must do what I do—have capsule conversations." Just as a comic can do three minutes of his mother-in-law, Thornton could do three minutes on Gertrude Stein or Lope de Vega. That's how he saved his energy. But I don't believe that you have more energy if you save it. It isn't a priceless juice that has to be kept in a secret bottle. We're social animals, and good conversation—not just parroting slogans and vogue words—is an essential part of good living. It doesn't behoove any artist to regard what he has to offer as something so valuable that not a second of it should be frittered away in talking to his chums.

PLAYBOY: It's also been said that you spend too much time in the company of ski bums and pretenders to Middle European thrones. Do you agree?

WELLES: I don't know many people in either of those categories. Those that I do know are all right, but they're certainly not my constant companions. However, I have nothing against being known as a friend of *any* sort of person.

PLAYBOY: A good deal of space and veneration is lavished on you in such avant-garde movie magazines as *Cahiers du Cinéma*. What do you think of the New Wave French directors so admired by these journals?

WELLES: I'm longing to see their work! I've missed most of it because I'm afraid it might inhibit my own. When I make a picture, I don't like it to refer to other pictures; I like to think I'm inventing everything for the first time. I talk to *Cahiers du Cinéma* about movies in general because I'm so pleased that they like mine. When they want long highbrow interviews, I haven't the heart to refuse them. But it's a complete act. I'm a fraud; I even talk about "the art of the cinema." I wouldn't talk to my friends about the art of the cinema—I'd rather be caught without my pants in the middle of Times Square.

PLAYBOY: How do you feel about the films of Antonioni?

WELLES: According to a young American critic, one of the great discoveries of our age is the value of boredom as an artistic subject. If that is so, Antonioni deserves to be counted as a pioneer and founding father. His movies are perfect backgrounds for fashion models. Maybe there aren't backgrounds that good in *Vogue*, but there ought to be. They ought to get Antonioni to design them.

PLAYBOY: And what about Fellini?

WELLES: He's as gifted as anyone making pictures today. His limitation— which is also the source of his charm—is that he's fundamentally very provincial. His films are a small-town boy's dream of the big city. His sophistication works because it's the creation of someone who doesn't have it. But he shows dangerous signs of being a superlative artist with little to say.

PLAYBOY: Ingmar Bergman?

WELLES: As I suggested a while ago, I share neither his interests nor his obsessions. He's far more foreign to me than the Japanese.

PLAYBOY: How about contemporary American directors?

WELLES: Stanley Kubrick and Richard Lester are the only ones that appeal to me—except for the old masters. By which I mean John Ford, John Ford and John Ford. I don't regard Alfred Hitchcock as an American director, though he's worked in Hollywood for all these years. He seems to me tremendously English in the best Edgar Wallace tradition, and no more. There's always something anecdotal about his work; his contrivances remain contrivances, no matter how marvelously they're conceived and executed. I don't honestly believe that Hitchcock is a director whose pictures will be of any interest a hundred years from now. With Ford at his best, you feel that the movie has lived and breathed in a real world, even though it may have been written by Mother Machree. With Hitchcock, it's a world of spooks.

PLAYBOY: When you first went to Hollywood in 1940, the big studios were still omnipotent. Do you think you'd have fared better if you'd arrived 20 years later, in the era of independent productions?

WELLES: The very opposite. Hollywood died on me as soon as I got there. I wish to God I'd gone there sooner. It was the rise of the independents that was my ruin as a director. The old studio bosses—Jack Warner, Sam Goldwyn, Darryl Zanuck, Harry Cohn—were all friends, or friendly enemies I knew how to deal with. They all offered me work. Louis B. Mayer even wanted me to be the production chief of his studio—the job Dore Schary took. I was in great shape with those boys. The minute the independents got in, I never directed another American picture except by accident. If I'd gone to Hollywood in the last five years, virgin and unknown, I could have written my own ticket. But I'm not a virgin; I drag my myth around with me, and I've had much more trouble with the independents than I ever had with the big studios. I was a maverick, but the studios understood what that meant, and if there was a fight, we both enjoyed it. With an annual output of 40 pictures per studio, there would probably be room for one Orson Welles picture. But an independent is a fellow whose work is centered around his own particular gifts. In that setup, there's no place for me.

PLAYBOY: Is it possible to learn how to direct movies?

WELLES: Oh, the various technical jobs can be taught, just as you can teach the principles of grammar and rhetoric. But you can't teach writing, and directing a picture is very much like writing, except that it involves

300 people and a great many more skills. A director has to function like a commander in the field in time of battle. You need the same ability to inspire, terrify, encourage, reinforce and generally dominate. So it's partly a question of personality, which isn't so easy to acquire as a skill.

PLAYBOY: Do you think it would help if there were a federally subsidized film school in the United States?

WELLES: If they *made* movies instead of *talking* about making movies, and if all classes on theory were rigorously forbidden, I could imagine a film school being very valuable, indeed.

PLAYBOY: Do you think movie production ought to be aided by public money, as it is in many European countries?

WELLES: If it is true—and I believe it is—that the theater and opera and music should be subsidized by the state, then it's equally true of the cinema, only more so. Films are more potent socially and have more to do with this particular moment in world history. The biggest money should go to the cinema. It needs more and has more to say.

PLAYBOY: What do you see as the next development in the cinema?

WELLES: I hope it *does* develop, that's all. There hasn't been any major revolution in films in more than 20 years, and without a revolution, stagnation sets in and decay is just around the corner. I hope some brand-new kind of moviemaking will arise. But before that happens, some form of making films more cheaply and showing them more cheaply will have to be evolved. Otherwise, the big revolution won't take place and the film artist will never be free.

PLAYBOY: Given worldwide distribution, do you think any film could change the course of history?

WELLES: Yes. And it might be a very bad film.

PLAYBOY: Let's turn to the theater. Five years ago you said, "London is the actor's city, Paris is the playwright's city and New York is the director's city." Do you still agree with that judgment?

WELLES: Today, I'd say that New York is David Merrick's city. Paris has ceased to be interesting at all as far as theater is concerned. London is still the great place for actors—but not for actresses. The English theater is a man's world. "London is a man's town, there's power in the air: And Paris is a woman's town, with flowers in her hair." I don't know who wrote that terrible old poem, but it continues to be true. Nobody in England writes great parts for women.

PLAYBOY: Have you any unfulfilled theatrical ambitions?

WELLES: I'd like to run a theater school, but not—and it makes me very sad to say this—not in America. Especially not in New York. Two generations of American actors have been so besotted by the Method that they have a built-in resistance to any other approach to theater. I don't want to drive the Method out of New York, but I wish it would move over and leave room for a few other ideas about acting. The last time I tried to work in New York, I found no one who wasn't touched by it.

PLAYBOY: Do you think American actors are equipped to play the classics?

WELLES: They should be, but they're less able to than they were when we were running the Mercury Theater around a quarter of a century ago. Part of the reason is that New York was a much more cosmopolitan city in those days. We were still within speaking distance of the age when it was called the melting pot. People were still first- and second-generation Europeans, and there was a genuine internationalism that did not come from the mass media. It just came from Uncle Joe having been born in a Warsaw suburb, and there were foreign-language theaters and I don't know how many foreign-language newspapers. All this gave a fertilizing richness to the earth that has now gone. New York has become much more standardized. Nowadays it's a sort of premixed Manhattan cocktail, with a jigger of Irishness, Jewishness, WASP, and so forth. And that's your modern New Yorker, no matter where his grandfather came from. He may be just as nice a guy, but he isn't as various.

PLAYBOY: Have you any predictions about the future of the theater in general?

WELLES: I believe that the theater, like ballet and grand opera, is already an anachronism. It still gives us joy and stimulation: It still offers the artist a chance to do important work—qualitatively, perhaps, work as good as has ever been done. But it isn't an institution that belongs to our times, and it cannot expect a long future. It's not true that we've always had the theater. That's a dream. We've had it for only a few periods of history, no matter what its partisans say to the contrary. And the theater as we know it is now in its last stages.

PLAYBOY: Looking back on your career in the performing arts, do you ever regret that you didn't go into politics?

WELLES: Sometimes very bitterly. There was a time when I considered running as a junior senator from Wisconsin; my opponent would have been a fellow called Joe McCarthy. If you feel that you might have been useful and effective in public office, you can't help being disappointed in yourself for never having tried it. And I flatter myself that I might have been. I think I am—at least potentially—a better public speaker than an actor, and I might have been able to reach people, to move and convince them. Oratory today is an almost nonexistent art, but if we lived in a society where rhetoric was seriously considered as an art—as it has been at many periods in world history—then I would have been an orator.

PLAYBOY: What are your politics—and have they changed in the last 25 years?

WELLES: Everyone's politics have changed in the last 25 years. You can't have a political opinion in a vacuum; it has to be a reaction to a situation. I've always been an independent radical, but with wide streaks of emotional and cultural old-fashionedness. I have enormous respect for many human institutions that are now in serious decay and likely never to be revived. Although I'm what is called a progressive, it isn't out of dislike for the past. I don't reject our yesterdays. I wish that parts of our dead past were more alive. If I'm capable of originality, it's not because I want to knock down idols or be ahead of the times. If there's anything rigid about me, it's a distaste for being in vogue. I would much rather be thought old-fashioned than "with it." But in general, I still belong to the liberal leftist world as it exists in the West. I vote that way and stand with those people. We may disagree on one issue or another, but that is where I belong.

PLAYBOY: Where do you stand on the Vietnam war?

WELLES: There's a newspaper in front of me right now that says that, according to a poll, popular support for Johnson's Vietnam program is going down. By the time this appears in print, anything I say will probably be shared by many more people. America doesn't have a history of losing wars and it has only a few bad wars on its conscience; this is one of them.

PLAYBOY: You've met many of the great men and women of your time. Is there any living person you'd still like to meet?

WELLES: Mrs. Sukarno, for obvious reasons, and Chou En-lai, mostly out of curiosity—I don't know if he'd be as interesting now as I always heard he used to be. He might be old and stiff and sad. I wish I'd known George Marshall, Winston Churchill and Wilson Mizner [an early-20th century American playwright] better than I did. I never knew Pope John and that's a real regret. And although it may sound a little demagogic, I'd love to talk to an old lady named Elizabeth Allen: She's English, she's been living in a tin hut in a forest for about 80 years and she makes the most beautiful pictures you ever saw out of rags. She's just had her first exhibition in London and she is superlative. But above everybody else, I'd like to meet Robert Graves. Not only because I think he's the greatest living poet, but because he has given me through the years the kind of pleasure that you get from close friends. I'd like to have some more of that stuff, only firsthand.

PLAYBOY: Is there anyone, living or dead, with whom you'd like to change places?

WELLES: If you've had as much luck as I have, it would be a sort of treachery to want to be anyone but yourself.

PLAYBOY: What is your major vice?

WELLES: *Accidia*—the medieval Latin word for melancholy, and sloth. I don't give way to it for long, but it still comes lurching at me out of the shadows. I have most of the accepted sins—envy, perhaps, the least of all. And pride. I'm not sure that is a sin; it's the only place where I quarrel with the Christian list. If it's a virtue, I don't recognize much of it in myself; the same is true if it's a vice.

PLAYBOY: Do you consider gluttony a bad vice?

WELLES: All vice is bad. A lot of vices are secret, but not gluttony—it shows. It certainly shows on me. But I feel that gluttony must be a good deal less deadly than some of the other sins. Because it's affirmative, isn't it? At least it celebrates some of the good things of life. Gluttony may be a sin, but an awful lot of fun goes into committing it. On the other hand, it's wrong for a man to make a mess of himself. I'm fat, and people shouldn't be fat.

PLAYBOY: What is your attitude toward pornography and the literary use of four-letter words?

WELLES: Four-letter words are useful tools, but when they cease to be more or less forbidden, they lose their cutting edge. When we wish to shock, we must have something left in our verbal quiver that will actually do the job. As for pornography, I don't agree with the present permissiveness in publishing it. By this I don't mean *Lady Chatterley's Lover*—the sort of book about physical love that used to be banned. I mean hard-core pornography—the blue novel and the blue movie. The difference is quite clear; it becomes blurred only when you have to testify in a court. We all know perfectly well what we mean by what the French call *cochon*. It's not only piggish but lonely. Hard-core pornography may begin as a fairly benign sexual stimulant, but it ends up pretty vicious and sick. Then it isn't a harmless release for that which is sick in us; it excites and encourages the sickness, particularly in young people who have yet to learn about sex in terms of love and shared joy. The sexual habits of consenting adults are their own business. It's the secondhandedness of the printed thing that I don't like; not the fact that people *do* it, but that other people sit alone and read about it.

PLAYBOY: If the decision were yours, would you censor anything in films or the theater?

WELLES: I am so opposed to censorship that I must answer no—nothing. But if there were no censorship, I have a little list of the things I would prefer not to have shown. Not too often, anyway. Heavy spice isn't good for the palate; and in the theater and films, when there's too much license, what is merely raw tends to crowd out almost everything else, and our dramatic vocabulary is impoverished. If you show the act of copulation every time you do a love scene, both the producers and the public get to feel that no other kind of love scene is worth doing, and that the only variations on the theme are variations of physical position. No, artists should not be censored, but I do think they should restrain themselves, in order not to weaken the language of their art. Take the old Roman comedies: Once you bring out those great leather phalluses, you get so there isn't any other sort of joke you can do. It's the same with violence, or any theatrical extreme. If it's pushed too far, it tends to erode the middle register of human feeling. However, propaganda against any kind of loving human relationship is despicable and probably ought to be censored.

PLAYBOY: But how do you reconcile that with—

WELLES: For 30 years people have been asking me how I reconcile X with Y! The truthful answer is that I don't. Everything about me is a contradiction, and so is everything about everybody I know. We are made out of oppositions; we live between two poles. There's a Philistine and an aesthete in all of us, and a murderer and a saint. You don't reconcile the poles. You just recognize them.

PLAYBOY: Did you have a religious upbringing?

WELLES: Quite the contrary. My mother was born a Catholic but then became a student of Oriental religions, in which she later lost interest. She taught me to read the Bible as a wonderful piece of literature. My father was a total agnostic, and Dr. Bernstein—the guardian who looked after me when my parents died—always made fun of the Bible stories. That shocked me as a child. I have a natural sense of veneration for what man has aspired to beyond himself, in East or West. It comes easily and instinctively to me to feel reverence rather than a gleeful skepticism. I read the mystics, though I'm not a mystic myself.

PLAYBOY: Do you believe in God?

WELLES: My feelings on that subject are a constant interior dialogue that I haven't sufficiently resolved to be sure that I have anything worth communicating to people I don't know. I may not be a believer, but I'm certainly religious. In a strange way, I even accept the divinity of Christ. The accumulation of faith creates its own veracity. It does this in a sort of Jungian sense, because it's been made true in a way that's almost as real as life. If you ask me whether the rabbi who was crucified was God, the answer is no. But the great, irresistible thing about the Judeo-Christian idea is that man—no matter what his ancestry, no matter how close he is to any murderous ape—really is unique. If we are capable of unselfishly loving one another, we are absolutely alone, as a species, on this planet. There isn't another animal that remotely resembles us. The notion of Christ's divinity is a way of saying that. That's why the myth is true. In the highest tragic sense, it dramatizes the idea that man is divine.

PLAYBOY: Does your idealization of man apply equally to woman? Are there any limitations on what a woman can achieve?

WELLES: No. There's a limitation on what she is *likely* to do, but not on what she *can* do. Women have managed to do everything; but the likelihood that they're going to do it often is statistically small. It's improbable that they will ever be as numerous as men in the arts. I believe that if there had never been men, there would never have been art—but if there had never been women, men would never have made art.

PLAYBOY: Whom would you choose as a model of the way men ought to behave toward women?

WELLES: Robert Graves. In other words, total adoration. Mine is less total than it ought to be. I'm crazy about the girls, but I do like to sit around the port with the boys. I recognize in myself that old-fashioned Edwardian tendency—shared by many other societies in other epochs—to let the ladies leave us for a while after dinner, so the men can talk. We'll join them later. I've talked endlessly to women for sexual purposes—years of my life have been given up to it. But women usually depress or dominate a conversation to its detriment—though, of course, there are brilliant and unnerving exceptions. In a sense, every woman is an exception. It's the generality that makes a male chauvinist like me.

PLAYBOY: In the opinion of some, the frontiers of art—and reality—may soon be pushed back by the use of hallucinogenic drugs. What do you think about these so-called aids to perception?

WELLES: The use of drugs is a perverse expression of individualism, antisocial and life-denying. It's all part of a great reaction—especially in the West—against the inevitably collective nature of society in the future. Let me put it discursively. European women are painting their eyelids to look Chinese. Japanese women are having operations to look American; white people are getting suntanned and Negroes are having their hair dekinked. We are trying to become as much like one another as possible. And with this great mass movement—which is both good and bad, both a denial of cultural heritage and an affirmation of human solidarity—there goes a retreat from the crowd into one's lonely self. And that's what this drug business is all about. It isn't an assertion of individuality; it's a substitute for it. It's not an attempt to be different when everyone else is becoming more alike; it's a way of copping out. And that's the worst thing you can do. I much prefer people who rock the boat to people who jump out.

PLAYBOY: If art is an expression of protest, as some philosophers have felt, do you think it's possible that in an automated world of abundance, devoid of frustrations and pressures, nobody would feel compelled to create art?

WELLES: I don't believe that, even in a perfect oyster shell, there will never be another grain of sand, and therefore never another pearl. And I don't accept that art is necessarily based on unhappiness. It's often serene and joyous and a kind of celebration. That isn't to deny the vast body of work that has been created in conditions of spiritual and economic wretchedness and even torment, but I see no reason to think that culture will be poorer because people are happier.

PLAYBOY: Some critics assert that modern art can be produced by accident—as in action painting, aleatory music and theatrical Happenings. Do you think it's possible to create a work of art without intending to?

WELLES: Categorically no. You may create something that will give some of the pleasures and emotions that a work of art may give, just as a microscopic study of a snowflake or a tapeworm or a cancer cell may be a beautiful object. But a work of art is a conscious human effort that has to do with communication. It is that or it is nothing. When an accident is applauded as a work of art, when a cult grows up around the deliciousness of inadvertent beauty, we are in the presence of the greatest decadence the West has known in its history.

PLAYBOY: Do you agree with those modern artists who say: "I don't care what happens to my work tomorrow—it's only meant for today"?

WELLES: No, because an artist shouldn't care what happens today, either. To care about today to the exclusion of any other time, to be self-consciously contemporary, is to be absurdly parochial. That's what is wrong about the artist's association with the huckster. Today has been canonized, beatified. But today is just one day in the history of our planet. It's the be-all and the end-all only for somebody who is selling something.

PLAYBOY: What effect do you feel the advertising industry is having on artists—on writers as well as painters and designers?

WELLES: The advertisers are having a disastrous effect on every art they touch. They are not only seducing the artist, they are drafting him. They are not only drawing on him, they are sucking the soul out of him. And the artist has gone over to the advertiser far more than he ever did to the merchant. The classic enemy of art has always been the marketplace. There you find the merchant and the charlatan—the man with goods to sell and the man with the snake oil. In the old days you had merchant princes, ex-pushcart peddlers turned into Hollywood moguls, but by and large honest salesmen, trying to give the public what they believed was good—even if it wasn't—and not seriously invading the artist's life unless the artist was willing to make that concession. But now we're in the hands of the snake-oil boys. Among the advertisers, you find artists who have betrayed their kind and are busy getting their brethren hooked on the same drug. The advertising profession is largely made up of unfrocked poets, disappointed novelists, frustrated actors and unsuccessful producers with split-level homes. They've somehow managed to pervade the whole universe of art, so that the artist himself now thinks and functions as an advertising man. He makes expendable objects, deals in the immediate gut kick, revels in the lack of true content. He paints a soup can and calls it art. A can of soup, well enough designed, could be a work of art; but a painting of it, never.

PLAYBOY: Have you any theories about what will happen to you after death?

WELLES: I don't know about my soul, but my body will be sent to the White House. American passports ask you to state the name and address of the person to whom your remains should be delivered in the event of your death. I discovered many years ago that there is no law against putting down the name and address of the president. This has a powerful effect on the borders of many countries and acts as a sort of diplomatic visa. During the long Eisenhower years, I would almost have been willing to die, in order to have my coffin turn up some evening in front of his television set.

PLAYBOY: How would you like the world to remember you?

WELLES: I've set myself against being concerned with any more worldly success than I need to function with. That's an honest statement and not a piece of attitudinizing. Up to a point, I have to be successful in order to operate. But I think it's corrupting to care about success; and nothing could be more vulgar than to worry about posterity.

June 1963

BILLY WILDER

*A candid conversation with the
master of filmic seriocomedy*

For solo and collaborative efforts as director and scenarist, Billy
Wilder has been nominated 24 times for Academy Awards, amassing
nine Oscars during 28 years in the movie capital. Recently *Playboy*
interviewed him in his suite of offices on the Goldwyn lot in downtown
Hollywood, where he and co-writer I. A. L. Diamond—having just
completed *Irma La Douce*—were brainstorming over the script for his
next picture. They would be working and reworking it right up to the
final day of shooting, for Wilder has conceded that although he always
knows where he's going with his plots, he's never quite sure how he's
going to get there. Between intermittent sips of a vodka martini, he
answered our questions with a rapid-fire delivery reminiscent of the
brisk dialogue from one of his own films. He strode restlessly up and
down as he spoke, slapping his thigh occasionally with an ornately
carved walking stick, his colloquial English enunciated in the guttural
accents which still bespeak his beginnings as a struggling screenwriter
in Berlin between the wars. Much of Wilder's work—from such
eminently unfunny films as *The Lost Weekend, Double Indemnity* and
Sunset Boulevard to such comedic tours de force as *Some Like It Hot,
The Apartment* and *One, Two, Three*—has been touched by a cynicism which reflects the mood of that worldly city during the 1920s.
We began with an exploration of these early years and influences.

PLAYBOY: Are you conscious of any kinship in your films or your philosophy, as several critics have suggested, with the savage satire of Bertolt Brecht, or with the intellectual cynicism he articulated for his generation?

WILDER: I knew him in Germany, and I knew him when he lived for a time here in Hollywood, and I regard him with Mr. Shaw—George Bernard, not Irwin—as one of the monumental dramatists of this first half-century, but I was never aware that he influenced me. Brecht was dealing with enormous subjects of the hungry, exploited masses which neither my brain nor my attention span can cope with. His was a much vaster canvas than mine. After all, was Mickey Spillane influenced by Tolstoy? That's Leo Nikolaevich, not Irwin. If there was any influence on me in those days, it must have come more from American books and plays I read. One of the most popular writers was Upton Sinclair. I read him, and Sinclair Lewis, Bret Harte, Mark Twain. I was also influenced by Erich von Stroheim and by Ernst Lubitsch, with whom I first worked on *Bluebeard's Eighth Wife*. But I don't believe I have been influenced by the cynicism of the times or even shown any of it on the screen. When they say that I have, they could be referring to, say, *Double Indemnity*, but this was done from a short story by James M. Cain, an American. It is not sugar-coated, my work, but I certainly don't sit down and say, "Now I am going to make a vicious, unsentimental picture."

PLAYBOY: As a native-born Viennese, you were already living in one of Europe's principal artistic and cultural capitals. What made you leave it to go to Berlin?

WILDER: Simple. After one year at the University in Vienna, I became a space-rates reporter. Paul Whiteman played a concert in town, liked my review, and took me along to Berlin with him. There I danced as a gigolo for a while in the Eden Hotel, and at the Adlon I served as a teatime partner for lonely old ladies.

PLAYBOY: How did you make the transition from dance floor to sound stage?

WILDER: Well, before long I got another reporting job. I was already trying to break into film writing, but having as much luck as the New York Mets. During this time I was living in a rooming house where there was a daughter who was engaged but also playing around a little on the side. One night her fiancé came pounding at the front door. I was in bed—my own bed—asleep, and before I knew what was going on, she had pushed this scared old man with his shoes in his hand into my room while she went to answer the front door and admit Helmut or Irwin or whatever his name was. I recognized the old man immediately as the head of the company called Maxim Films. He looked at me sheepishly and said, "Have you got a shoehorn?" I said, "I have a shoehorn, but I also have this script I would like you to read." "Yes, yes, send it along to the office," he said. "No. *Now*," I said, so he sat down and read it, and he gave me 500 marks for it on the spot, and I gave him my shoehorn. After a while Helmut went away and he was able to sneak out, and that was how my film career began. Soon I was up to my ears in movies. I must have written 50 silent pictures: Sometimes I did two a month. One, *People on Sunday*, directed by Robert Siodmak, is still shown in places where they call movies "the cinema."

PLAYBOY: This was about the time when Hitler began his rise to power. Did political events have any effect on your career?

WILDER: They ended it. I was having my dinner in the Kempinski Hotel the day after the Reichstag fire. I knew I had to get out. The Nazis were getting too warm. I rolled up the paintings I was collecting, packed a small bag and got on the train to Paris. A year later I came to the United States. I've been here ever since and eventually found my way to Hollywood.

PLAYBOY: Your long-time collaborator, Charles Brackett, once said your work was characterized by "an exuberant vulgarity." What is your own appraisal?

WILDER: Did you read that piece by somebody called Simon—or Irwin—who really crapped all over me in *Theatre Arts*? It boiled down to this: What he objected to was not the vulgarity in my art but the lack of art in my vulgarity. I have been pursued for years by that nasty word there. The bad taste thing. They sit there in the theater and laugh their heads off, and then they go out and say, "Cheap! Vulgar!" Then they go and see *Pillow Talk* and pronounce it urbane humor. Maybe my work is a little robust, but one has to work with what one has. It would be disaster if I used the sugar tongs and tried to regiment myself into something unnatural for me.

PLAYBOY: Less critically, Brackett has also said that you have a "sure sense of audience reaction." Do you feel that's true?

WILDER: When you start a movie script, it's like entering a dark room: You may find your way around all right, but you also may fall over a piece of furniture and break your neck. Some of us can see a little better than others in the dark, but there is no guaranteeing audience's reaction. I've been lucky; I've taken a lot of chances in treading on new ground which could have slipped out from under me. Though I've got away with it about 90 percent of the time, I don't flatter myself that I can hit all the time. But I have to live in the hope—or perhaps under the delusion—that if I like it, a great many other people will like it, too.

PLAYBOY: Your films in this country have been written in collaboration. Why have you chosen to do it that way?

WILDER: Here I have the handicap of working in a new language—even after 28 years. Then there is the question of time. A movie is not like a novel. Sometimes the publisher may want to bring a novel out by Christmas; but in films we *always* have time limitations. Certain stars are available at a certain time, so you have, say, six months to write a screenplay. If they're compatible, two people can stimulate each other and get it done a little faster and, most of the time, better.

PLAYBOY: A friend of yours once said "Billy's collaborators are $50,000 secretaries." Is your creative hand really that authoritative in writing a scenario?

WILDER: First of all, whoever said that is no friend of mine. If that were the case I would hire my relatives and make the money I give them tax-deductible, at least. But my collaborator, Iz Diamond, and I work together from the word go, and after it's done it cannot be said that this was his idea, this was mine, this was my joke, this was his. It all occurs together, like playing a piano piece four-handed.

PLAYBOY: Since your native language is not English, how have you managed to become so adept at mastering the nuances of the American comic idiom?

WILDER: If you think I have an accent—which unquestionably I do—you should have heard Ernst Lubitsch. But he had a wonderful ear for American idiom and dialogue. You either have an ear or you don't, as Van Gogh said—that's Irwin, not Vincent. I suppose I have it. Many foreigners do. When I arrived in the U.S., I couldn't speak a word of English. Well, let's say I knew a dozen the Johnson Office wouldn't tolerate. I learned by not associating myself with the European refugee colony, by going around with new American friends, by listening to the radio. Perhaps it helps you to learn the language if you go into it cold. It pours into you and it stays.

PLAYBOY: Bucking the trend toward overseas location pictures, you've said you prefer to make movies right here in Hollywood. Why? Wouldn't you save thousands on budgets by filming abroad?

WILDER: To make pictures in Europe would be like going to a cathouse not as a lover but to fix the plumbing. I go to Europe for fun, not to work. But seriously, it's much easier technically to shoot a picture in Hollywood. If you're going to perform a delicate operation, why not do it in the best hospital?

PLAYBOY: Many moviemakers claim to have found an intellectual stimulation and creative freedom in Europe that's unattainable in Hollywood. Have you?

WILDER: Remember, the movie scripts that Hollywood people go to Europe to shoot are still written in Hollywood, don't forget. So they make *La Dolce Vita* in Rome; but they also make *Hercules and the Seven Dwarfs*. As for freedom, all the Mirisch Company asks me is the name of my picture, a vague outline of the story, and who's going to be in it. The rest is up to me; can you get more freedom than that? And as for there being more intellectual stimulation in Europe, some of my best friends have gone to Europe and then to seed intellectually. I don't believe any of that "intellectual stimulus" crap. Take Confucius—he said some pretty stimulating things, but he never got to Paris in his life.

PLAYBOY: Hollywoodians often speak enviously of you as a man of uncompromising standards. How is it that you and a few other filmmakers have managed to resist the pressures of compromise?

WILDER: To me, it is a matter of dollars and cents. It doesn't have only to do with Hollywood, it has to do with a man's approach to the problem of making those dollars and cents. Some compromise, some do not. Look at Fellini. He cleaned up with *La Dolce Vita*. When I saw it I couldn't decide if it was the greatest or dreariest picture I'd ever seen, and finally I decided it was both. A remarkable film, excellent because he had stuck to his own principles. But the worst thing that can happen to us in this business is if a dog picture makes a hit, then we all have to make dog pictures because the people with the money trust dogs. But if one like Fellini's makes a hit, it is the greatest thing—as long as it is not loaded with the stars who are always advertising themselves in the trades. It's a question of money, and yet it is not a question of money anymore in Hollywood. The beauty of our capitalist system is that you can't keep what you make even if you make a lousy picture that's a hit; so why not try to make something good? Today's capitalist system is for those who already have the money, not for those who are making it. There is really very little use in my working, since I can't keep the money. I can never get richer than I am. So why am I beating my brains out? I go to the studio because I can't stand listening to my wife's vacuum cleaner at home, and also because I can't find three bridge partners or somebody to go to the ball game with. Also I work to waylay some of the phonies from getting Academy Awards.

PLAYBOY: How do you view the decline of Hollywood as the world movie capital?

WILDER: The future of major studios as we have known them, I view with tremendous pessimism. They are all but dead. But that makes me *optimistic*. The breakup of the major studios, the advent of the independent producers, and the growing influence of really good foreign films—all these developments are very much for the best.

PLAYBOY: Analytically inclined reviewers are fond of "discovering" secondary levels of social and satirical comment in your films, even in the comedies. Do you consciously inject such messages?

WILDER: I am not really a message man. Pictures like *Love in the Afternoon* and *Sabrina* are not in any way a comment on the world. Maybe *The Apartment* had a few things to say about our society, but it was not meant to be a deep-searching exploration of how we are. On certain levels, once in a while, maybe we smuggle in a little contraband message, but we try never to jump in their faces with our naked pretensions showing, because they'll recoil. In certain pictures I do hope they'll leave the theater a little enriched, but I never make them pay a buck-and-a-half and then ram a lecture down their throats. In Munich not long ago I saw Chaplin's *Limelight* for the first time; it was never shown on the West Coast, and I was anxious to see it. A girl in our party said she had seen it eight times, and later I told her I knew how she felt, because I saw it once and it *seemed* like eight times. I found it completely shallow and commonplace. If only he had stuck to comedy. In the silents he never philosophized. In sound he never *stopped* philosophizing; when he finally found a voice to say what was on his mind, it was like a child writing lyrics to Beethoven's *Ninth*. I found it shocking to think that he was attacked for his political convictions and forced to leave the U.S. when everything he was saying was on a grammar school level. Mind you, I still think he was an authentic genius, and I would do a picture with him today for free—if he would only shut up.

PLAYBOY: Some critics have asserted that you do have a message: that man is essentially mean. Playwright George Axelrod has said flatly that you yourself are mean, that "he sees the worst in everybody, and he sees it funny." True?

WILDER: I cop the Fifth. There are certain traits in certain characters that make them interesting to me, but I don't think I go too far from reality in emphasizing their meanness. I stylize, maybe, but not too much. And if I'm so mean personally, how come I've managed to go through life with a good number of very close friends?

PLAYBOY: Though it certainly didn't dwell on the subject of human meanness, *One, Two, Three* was an incisive satire of both sides involved in the Cold War. Were you concerned, while filming in Berlin, that the authorities on one side or the other might cause trouble?

WILDER: We got to Berlin the day they sealed off the Eastern sector and wouldn't let people come across the border. It was like making a picture in Pompeii with all the lava coming down. Khrushchev was even faster than me and Diamond. We had to make continuous revisions to keep up with the headlines. It seemed to me that the whole thing could have been straightened out if Oleg Cassini had sent Mrs. Khrushchev a new dress. But we weren't afraid of creating an incident like Mr. Paar. We minded our manners and were good boys. When they told us we couldn't use the Brandenburg Gate in Berlin, we went to Munich and built our own.

PLAYBOY: Was there any negative reaction to the picture as a flip treatment of a serious subject?

WILDER: Of course. There is a little group of people who always say I'm not Spinoza. The thinner the magazine, the fatter the heads of the reviewers. They were shocked because we made fun of the Cold War. Others objected because it was very quick-paced and they could not catch everything. People either loved it or hated it.

PLAYBOY: Why did you switch to comedy after establishing yourself as a director of such grimly ironic dramas as *Double Indemnity* and *Sunset Boulevard*?

WILDER: It wasn't done deliberately. What I make depends on what tickles me at the moment—and what I hope will show a profit. But I *will* be making serious pictures again; this is a warning.

PLAYBOY: You seem to enjoy taking heavy subjects—the Cold War, transvestitism, adultery, prison camps—and turning them into funny pictures. What is your attraction to such themes, and how do you manage to make them funny?

WILDER: It's not the subject as such, it's the treatment. Those thin-magazine people I mentioned before said *Some Like It Hot* had homosexual overtones as well as transvestite undertones. Well, I know that transvestites are cases for Krafft-Ebing, but to me they are terribly funny. Wasn't

Charlie's Aunt one of the most successful comedies ever written? The stronger the basic story, the better the jokes play against it. I think the funniest picture the Marx Brothers ever made was A *Night at the Opera*, because opera is such a deadly serious background. I saw a picture about sex the other day. It was a crashing bore. Unless treated with humor, wit and gaiety, even sex is unbelievably dull. I can't take it seriously. I'm not talking about love, mind you, but about sex.

PLAYBOY: You have been accused of playing down to your audiences, via the use of puns and slapstick. Do you?

WILDER: You run into people who shudder when you make a pun, but it's only because they can't make one themselves. I don't make pictures for the so-called intelligentsia; they bore the ass off me. I think they're all phonies, and it delights me to be unpopular with them. They are pretentious mezzo-brows. My pictures seem to appeal more to the true highbrows and lowbrows. I happen to think that puns and slapstick are funny. Those who look down on it and on me, they are overestimating me, they are overestimating my ambition in life. I have at no time regarded myself as one of the artistic immortals. I am just making movies to entertain people and I try to do it as honestly as I can. I don't want anything more rewarding than to travel halfway around the world, as I did, and hear them roaring at *Hot*. That was good enough for me.

PLAYBOY: Your films have been criticized for being overloaded with visual bits of business and breakneck action. True?

WILDER: I am not James McNeill Whistler. Nor am I O'Neill—Irwin, not Eugene. I hate to have people face each other and talk-talk-talk-talk-talk, even if they are in a moving taxicab. I make *moving pictures*. On the other hand, you will not find in my pictures any phony camera moves or fancy setups to prove that I am a moving-picture director. My characters don't rush around for the sake of being busy. I like to believe that movement can be achieved eloquently, elegantly, economically and logically without shooting from a hole in the ground, without hanging the camera from the chandelier and without the camera dolly dancing a polka.

PLAYBOY: The fast plot pace and dialogue which have characterized your last three pictures have become for the public the expected ingredients of a Wilder movie. Are you concerned about being typecast, or about the possibility of falling back on tried-and-true comic situations for the sake of a sure laugh?

WILDER: If you develop a certain style you inevitably repeat yourself to some extent—but never consciously. Every writer-director with his own distinctive signature will do things reminiscent of pictures he has done before. But I would never do it intentionally. Iz and I always try to be original, though sometimes we do say, "Remember when we did *this?*"—and then do a switch on it. But I would never do a remake of one of my own pictures. I never even look at my pictures after they're finished—not on 35 millimeter, not on 16 millimeter, not on eight millimeter. All I have are a few bound scripts at home which are gathering dust there. *Witness for the Prosecution* was on television a few Sundays ago and I would have dreaded to look at it again. It would have made me sick.

PLAYBOY: Are there any of your own pictures to which you're still partial?

WILDER: As soon as I'm done, I go on to something else. But there are certain parts in a few of them which I remember with fondness: maybe parts of *Sunset Boulevard* and *Double Indemnity*; some of *Lost Weekend* and *Hot.* I also like the runt of my litter, *Ace in the Hole.* It didn't make a nickel here even after we changed the title to *The Big Carnival,* but it cleaned up in Europe and won at the Venice Festival. But believe me, most of the time I remember only the booboos I've committed.

PLAYBOY: Many of the stars you've worked with have vowed they would "work for Billy for nothing." Which of them have you most enjoyed working with?

WILDER: Promises, promises. If they would work for me for nothing, I wish they would tell that to their agents. But I have enjoyed working with nearly all of them, with just a few exceptions. There have even been some pleasant surprises. Outstanding among them was Gloria Swanson. You must remember that this was a star who at one time was carried in a sedan chair from her dressing room to the sound stage. When she married the Marquis de la Falaise and came by boat from Europe to New York and by train from there to Hollywood, people were strewing rose petals on the railroad tracks in her direction. She'd been one of the all-time stars, but when she returned to the screen in *Sunset,* she worked like a dog. Or take Shirley MacLaine; she was infected with that one-take Rat Pack all-play-and-no-work nonsense, but when she came to work for Iz and me in *The Apartment,* she got serious and worked as hard as anybody. Now she's playing drama. And of course Lemmon I could work with forever. Some stars I have trouble with, of course, but it can't be avoided because, after all, they *are* actors. In *Sabrina,* Bogart gave me some bad times, but he was a needler anyway and he somehow got the idea that Bill Holden, Audrey Hepburn and I were in cahoots against him. Bill at one point was ready to kill him. Eventually we smoothed it out and everything worked out well. But in most cases there haven't been any problems. In fact, one of the things I am proud of is that tension is totally absent from my sets. People extend themselves to do their best when they're happy, and I feel it's my job to make them feel that way.

PLAYBOY: Are there any stars you haven't worked with yet whom you'd like to direct in a movie?

WILDER: Sure. Grant—Cary, not Irwin. I thought I had him for *Sabrina*, but at the last minute he changed his mind and told me he wouldn't do it, although I never found out why; so the part had to be rewritten for Bogart. And I'd like to work with Brando. If he wanted me, and we could have a meeting of the minds, it would be worthwhile to take a little beating just to have him in a picture. Jackie Gleason—one of the great, great talents. Dean Martin is a doll. Chaplin of course. And Guinness—an aristocrat; I would like to work with him. And Peter Sellers . . . but I think I *am* going to be working with him; Iz and I are planning our picture after *Irma La Douce* with Sellers.

PLAYBOY: What are your movie plans after *Irma* and the Peter Sellers picture?

WILDER: Iz and I bought an Italian play, *L'Hora della Fantasia*; it takes place in the 18th Century, but we are going to do it in the present. After that, who knows? Maybe I'll rest a while, then it will be a year before I'm ready to do the next one, or at least six to nine months.

PLAYBOY: What will you do with yourself during the interim? Isn't it true that when you're between pictures you've been known to volunteer your services to other producers and directors?

WILDER: Only when asked. I enjoy making movies, I enjoy the problems. If I'm not working on something of my own and someone calls me up and says, "Look here, Billy, I have a problem," I will try to do what I can to help out. I'm restless. My stomach hurts when I'm working, but it also hurts when I'm not. It's exasperating—I should get into something else. But that's the way it is, and I'm stuck with it. After 30 years of making films I'm used to trouble and well-acquainted with grief.

Do you remember my telling you earlier about that rooming house I lived in when I first was trying to get into the movies in Berlin? Well, next to my room was the can, and in it was a toilet that was on the blink. The water kept running all night long. I would lie there and listen to it, and since I was young and romantic, I'd imagine it was a beautiful waterfall—just to get my mind off the monotony of it and the thought of its being a can. Now we dissolve to 25 years later and I am finally rich enough to take a cure at Badgastein, the Austrian spa, where there is the most beautiful waterfall in the whole world. There I am in bed, listening to the waterfall. And after all I have been through, all the trouble and all the money I've made, all the awards and everything else, there I am in that resort, and all I can think of is that goddamned toilet. That, like the man says, is the story of my life.

INDEX

ABC, 376, 400, 411

A Fistful of Dollars, 103, 104, 109, 118, 120-122, 128, 142, 420. *See also* Eastwood, Clint

A Hard Day's Night, 263

A Night at Camp David, 25

A Night at the Opera, 460. *See also* Marx Brothers

A Soldier's Story, 251

A Star is Born, 29

A Streetcar Named Desire, 428. *See also* Brando, Marlon

A Summer Place, 67

Agnew, Spiro, 132

Ajaye, Franklyn, 266

Albee, Edward, 40

Ali, Muhammad. *See* Clay, Cassius

All Hands on Deck, 67

All the President's Men, 24

Allen, Elizabeth, 446

Allen, Woody, 51, 52, 57, 348, 353

Almodóvar, Pedro, 64

Altman, Michael, 31-32, 35-36

Altman, Robert, 11-37:
 Academy Awards, 12, 15, 19, 20, 27, 28
 alcohol, 18
 American culture, 17
 artistic duty, 36-37
 biographies, 35-36
 Breakfast of Champions, 14, 24, 30, 36.
  See also Vonnegut, Kurt Jr.
 Brewster McCloud, 13, 36
 Buffalo Bill and the Indians, 11, 14, 15, 16, 26
 California Split, 13, 26
 Cannes Film Festival, 13, 14, 27
 Catherine Hearst, 23
 childhood, 12, 35
 colonialism, 16-17
 commercial success, 21
 critics, 22, 26-28
 feminism, 25
 filmmaking, 25-26, 29-30
 gambling, 12, 35
 Golden Globes, 20
 Hollywood, 19, 21, 26
 Images, 12, 25
 Jeff Alexander, 19

Jerry Bick, 20

Johnny Green, 19

Keith Carradine, 19, 33

Lily Tomlin, 20, 31

Lion's Gate Films, 13, 14, 18, 34

Louise Fletcher, 20

marriage, 36

*M*A*S*H*, 11, 13, 16, 25, 30, 31

McCabe & Mrs. Miller, 13, 15, 16

Nashville, 12, 14, 15, 17, 19, 20, 21, 22, 24-30, 33, 34

New York Film Critics' Award, 12, 23

Patricia Hearst, 22-23

politics, 22, 25

Ragtime, 23, 30. *See also* Doctorow, E. L.

ratings board, 26

rehearsals, 29-30

Richard Nixon, 23, 24

screenings, 29

spending habits, 35

tattooing dogs, 34

That Cold Day in the Park, 12

The Book of Daniel, 23

The Extra, 31

The Late Show, 31

The World of Robert Altman, 35

They Shoot Horses, Don't They?, 19

Thieves Like Us, 13, 20, 26

Welcome to L.A., 31

Whirlybirds, 12

work ethic, 18

Yig Epoxy, 31

American Civil Liberties Union, 23

American Humane Society, 62

Amores Perros, 64

And Quiet Flows the Don, 306

Ansen, David, 52, 343. *See also Newsweek*

Apocalypse Now, 93, 196, 391

Archer, Lew, 15

Arnold, Matthew, 244

Ashby, Hal, 374

Atlantic Monthly, 401

Aubrey, Jim, 125. *See also* MGM Studios

Axelrod, George, 458

Aykroyd, Dan, 397

Baker, Bobby, 133
Baskin, Richard, 22
Batchelor, Ruth, 27
Beatty, Ned, 426
Beatty, Warren, 13, 30, 32, 83, 210, 396, 420:
    McCabe & Mrs. Miller, 13, 30, 32
    Reds, 396
Beery, Wallace, 35
Beethoven, Ludwig van, 220, 458
Bergan, Ronald, 54, 64
Bergman, Ingmar, 11, 32, 39-50, 179, 193, 195,
    438, 442-443:
    All the Women, 50
    artistic control, 42
    Brink of Life, 40
    censorship, 46-47
    childhood, 39-40
    critics, 39, 44
    dislike of the press, 40, 43
    eroticism, 39, 46
    gender representation, 49
    love, 46, 48
    Lutheranism, 39
    obscenity, 39
    Smiles of a Summer Night, 40
    Sweden, 39, 40, 42, 44
    temper, 43
    The Seventh Seal, 40
    The Silence, 39, 46-49
    The Virgin Spring, 40
    Through a Glass Darkly, 39, 48
    Wild Strawberries, 40, 49
    Winter Light, 39, 48, 49
Berkeley, Busby, 65
Bernstein, Carl, 24-25
Bertolucci, Bernardo, 32
Bickle, Travis, 363, 364, 395. See also Scorsese,
    Martin
Bikel, Theodore, 263
Bite the Bullet, 33. See also Brooks, Richard
Black Hawk Down, 410
Blakley, Ronee, 30
Bogart, Humphrey, 185, 187, 190, 191, 197,
    212, 461-462
Bogdanovich, Peter, 33
Bonnie and Clyde, 210
Born on the Fourth of July, 395, 396, 402, 408.
    See also Stone, Oliver
Brackett, Charles, 455
Bradbury, Ray, 207
Brando, Marlon, 15, 16, 60, 79-83, 86, 188,
    195, 196, 219, 251, 284, 359-360, 462:

A Streetcar Named Desire, 284
The Godfather, 79-83, 86, 251
Braunsberg, Andy, 311
Breaker Morant, 209
Brecht, Bertolt, 40, 454
Breakfast of Champions, 14, 24, 30, 36. See also
    Altman, Robert
Breezy, 130
Bridges, Jeff, 53, 60, 61
Brin, Sergey, 402
Bronson, Charles, 15
Brooks, Richard, 33, 79
Brown, Clifford, 158
Brown, Jerry, 17, 25
Brown, Michael, 311
Bruce, Lenny, 289, 290
Brynner, Yul, 263
Burstyn, Ellen, 343
Burton, Richard, 61, 194, 433
Burton, Tim, 55
Buscemi, Steve, 52, 53, 59, 60, 66, 429
Bush, George W., 270, 271, 401, 404, 405, 406
Bye Bye Birdie, 263
Byrne, Gabriel, 61

CBS, 115, 116, 117, 142
Caan, James, 12, 80, 82, 83, 87
Cain, James M., 52, 65, 67, 454
Caine, Michael, 208, 395
California Split, 13, 26
Callas, Maria, 202
Cameron, Julia, 357
Canby, Vincent, 121, 140, 261, 363. See also
    The New York Times
Cannes Film Festival, 13, 14, 27, 53, 56, 258,
    343, 347, 417, 435
Capote, Truman, 193
Capra, Frank, 53
Carnegie, Andrew, 96
Carney, Art, 31
Carradine, David, 418, 420, 421
Cartier-Bresson, Henri, 195
Cassavetes, John, 33, 298, 351
Castro, Fidel, 399, 401, 409, 414, 415
Catcher in the Rye, 364, 410. See also Salinger,
    J. D.
Champlin, Charles, 26-27. See also The New
    York Times
Chaplin, Charlie, 164, 435, 436, 458, 462
Charlie's Aunt, 460
Chase, Chevy, 397
Chicken Run, 64

Chinatown, 77
Christie, Julie, 13, 25
Churchill, Winston, 242, 446
Cimino, Michael, 374, 389, 396
Citizen Kane, 323, 336, 337, 339, 351, 434, 437, 439, 440. *See also* Welles, Orson
City of Nets, 67. *See also* Friedrich, Otto
Clan of the Cave Bear, 71
Clarke, Arthur C., 215, 221, 232
Clay, Cassius, 145, 327, 384
Clinton, Bill, 406
Clooney, George, 53, 59, 65, 423, 429
Clouzot, Henri-Georges, 209. *See also Wages of Fear*
Cobb, Tex, 61
Cocks, Jay, 28, 90, 121, 366, 370. *See also Time*
Cody, Buffalo Bill, 15-16
Coen, Joel & Ethan, 51-71:
    Academy Awards, 53
    artistic freedom, 56-57
    Barton Fink, 52, 56, 64, 65, 66, 67
    Blood Simple, 52, 54, 58, 63, 65, 66, 69
    budgets, 56-57
    casting, 60
    childhood, 53-54, 68
    collaboration, 55, 69-70
    exploding animals, 62-63
    fame, 59
    film noir, 52, 66
    filmmaking, 56-58, 69
    Judaism, 68
    marriage, 54
    Miller's Crossing, 52, 54, 59, 61, 66
    New York City, 68
    O Brother, Where Art Thou?, 52, 53, 56, 57, 62-65
    originality, 66
    Princeton University, 54
    pseudonyms, 54, 69
    Raising Arizona, 52, 56, 61-63
    recognition, 56
    selling out, 57
    sentimentality, 71
    62 Skidoo, 61
    storytelling, 68
    The Big Lebowski, 53, 56, 60, 64
    The Hudsucker Proxy, 53
    The Man Who Wasn't There, 52, 53, 55, 56, 64, 65
    violence, 70-71
Cohn, Harry, 94, 443
Cole, Nat King, 158, 403

Columbia Pictures, 249
Columbia University, 232
Conan, 374, 404. *See also* Milius, John
Connery, Sean, 208
Conrad, Joseph, 375, 382
Cooke, Sam, 384
Cooper, Alice, 30
Cooper, Gary, 124. *See also High Noon*
Coppola, Francis Ford, 25, 33, 73-101, 368-369, 391, 398:
    Academy Awards, 73, 74, 75, 77, 100
    American Graffiti, 75
    American Zoetrope, 75
    August Coppola, 74
    Marlon Brando, 79-83
    childhood, 74, 100
    critics, 89
    ego, 91-92
    Eleanor Coppola, 75, 76, 98
    family, 75, 93, 96, 100
    female characters, 90
    Finian's Rainbow, 74, 94
    happiness, 98
    Hollywood, 94-96
    Mario Puzo, 74, 78, 79, 80, 87-89
    organized crime, 85-87
    politics, 97
    power, 92
    Patton, 74
    success, 91-92
    THX 1138, 75
    Talia Coppola, 74
    The Conversation, 75, 77, 79, 80, 90, 426
    The Godfather, 73-93, 100
    The Godfather: Part II, 73-93, 100
    The Godfather: Part III, 101
    The Rain People
    violence, 92
    wealth, 97-98
    women, 99
Corman, Roger, 58, 74
Costa-Gravas, Constantin, 79
Costner, Kevin, 286
Crouch, Stanley, 261

DaVinci, Leonardo, 221
De Laurentiis, Dino, 403
De Niro, Robert, 209, 210, 286, 343, 347, 348-349, 352, 355, 358, 359:
    Cape Fear, 347, 355,
    Raging Bull, 343, 344, 348-349
    Taxi Driver, 209

The King of Comedy, 210, 352
The Untouchables, 286
De Palma, Brian, 374
De Sica, Vittoria, 80, 195, 209
Darnell, Linda, 147
David Copperfield, 67
Davis, Edith, 211
Davis, Miles, 158
Day, Doris, 53
Dean, James, 12, 195
Death of a Salesman, 275, 293. See also Miller,
    Arthur
Deep Throat, 129, 130, 131
Del Monte Company, 138
Delon, Alain, 15
Denby, David, 262
Deneuve, Catherine, 297
Dennis, Sandy, 12
DiCaprio, Leonardo, 403
Diamond, I. A. L. (Iz), 453, 456
Dickey, James, 53, 70
Directors' Guild of America
Disney Pictures, 64, 417
Disney, Walt, 73, 323
Doctorow, E. L. 23, 24
Dog Day Afternoon, 19
Donnenfeld, Bernie, 331. See also Paramount
    Pictures
Donner, Bob, 137
Donner, Cissy, 137
Douglas, Kirk, 66, 218, 219
Douglas, Michael, 20, 376, 408
Dr. No, 263
Dr. Strangelove, 31, 219, 239, 240, 391. See also
    Kubrick, Stanley
Dreiser, Theodore, 378
Driving Miss Daisy, 261, 351
Dunaway, Faye, 210-211
Duvall, Robert, 20, 80, 82
Duvall, Shelley, 13, 30
Dylan, Bob, 36

Eagleton, Thomas, 132
Eastwood, Clint, 74, 103-160, 420:
    A Fistful of Dollars, 103, 104, 118, 120-122,
        128, 142
    Absolute Power, 141, 148, 155
    Academy Awards, 107, 135-136
    acting, 111-113, 126, 139
    age, 147, 152
    alcohol, 155
    Ambush at Cimarron Pass, 115, 116

Bird, 143, 149, 158
Brian Hutton, 115
Bridges of Madison County, 149, 152, 153, 158
Bronco Billy, 143, 156
Charles Marquis Warren, 116
childhood, 112, 134, 139, 141, 155, 157
community, 124-125
critics, 121, 140, 159
Dina Ruiz, 144, 145, 152
directing, 135, 141
Dirty Harry, 104, 109, 123, 124, 128, 135,
    140, 142, 146, 149, 159
Don Siegel, 104, 135, 137, 142, 149
drugs, 155
Every Which Way but Loose, 157
family, 134, 139, 153, 154
firearms, 134
For a Few Dollars More, 103, 120, 122, 142
Frances Fisher, 144, 152
Francis in the Navy, 113
Hang 'Em High, 103, 104, 122, 142, 156
High Plains Drifter, 109, 124, 134
Highway Patrol, 114
hobbies, 137, 138, 156
Hog's Breath Inn, 135
Hollywood, 148
Honkytonk Man, 149
In the Line of Fire, 143, 149
interviews, 106
Karli Baumgartner, 114, 115
Kelly's Heroes, 103, 114-115
machismo, 145
Magnum Force, 104, 105, 114, 123, 124,
    133, 138
Margaret Johnson, 104, 107, 108
marriage, 108, 127, 143, 150-152
Midnight in the Garden of Good and Evil, 141,
    148
military service, 111, 141
music, 138, 157, 158-159
Navy Log, 114
Never Say Goodbye, 113
odd jobs, 110-111, 115, 141-142
Olympia Beer, 108, 136, 137
organic food, 136
Paint Your Wagon, 103, 135, 149, 156, 157
Pale Rider, 140, 143
Play Misty for Me, 104, 109, 126, 135, 142, 156
politics, 129-130, 131, 133, 147-148, 154-155
Rawhide, 103, 104, 116-119, 122, 137, 138,
    140, 142, 156
Revenge of the Creature, 113

Robert Daley, 104, 137
screenplay selection, 128
sex, 129-130
Sondra Locke, 140, 143, 150-152
Sonia Chernus, 104, 115
stardom, 138
stunts, 114
Tarantula, 113
Telly Savalas, 115
television, 113-117
temper, 149
The Beguiled, 104, 142, 156, 157
The Clint Eastwood Invitational Celebrity
    Tournament, 104, 137-138
The Good, the Bad and the Ugly, 103, 120,
    122, 156
The Malpaso Company, 103, 104, 122-123
The Man with No Name, 119, 121
Thunderbolt and Lightfoot, 134, 138
trends, 109, 145-146
Two Mules for Sister Sara, 104, 137, 142
typecasting, 156
unemployment, 131
violence, 128-129
Westerns, 118, 156
Where Eagles Dare, 103, 134, 156
women, 108, 126-127, 146-147, 153
work ethic, 149-150
Easy and Hard Ways Out, 31. See also
    Grossbach, Robert
Easy Rider, 400
Edison, Thomas, 96
Ehrlichman, John, 132, 133
8 1/2, 161, 165-166, 169, 170-171, 172, 175-
    176, 179, 181
Eight Million Ways to Die, 374. See also Ashby, Hal
Einstein, Albert, 231, 232, 324
Ellsberg, Daniel, 133
Evans, Robert, 80-82, 303, 331. See also
    Paramount Pictures

Faces of Death, 71
Fahrenheit 9/11, 406. See also Moore, Michael
Falk, Peter, 30, 31
Farber, Stephen, 28
Farrell, Colin, 403
Farrow, Mia, 298
Faulkner, William, 65, 195
Feather, Leonard, 121
Felker, Clay, 28
Fellini, Federico, 11, 45, 340, 442, 457:
    Academy Awards, 164, 165

Anita Ekberg, 173, 174, 175
Anthony Quinn, 164
Boccaccio '70, 165, 173
Catholicism, 172
cartooning, 162
childhood, 162, 169, 182
circus experience, 162
critics, 168, 172, 180
death, 182-183
8 1/2, 161, 165-166, 169, 170-171, 172,
    175-176, 179, 181
embellishing, 167
eroticism, 173-174
fame, 181
film themes, 169
François Truffaut, 180
Giulietta Masina, 163, 164, 165, 176-177
Hollywood, 180-181
I Vitelloni, 164
Il Bidone, 164
instructing actors, 175
interview details, 167
intentions, 168
Juliet of the Spirits, 161-162, 166, 167, 171
La Dolce Vita, 161, 165, 168, 174, 180
La Strada, 161, 164
marriage, 171-172, 176-177
Marcello Mastroianni, 165, 175, 176
money, 181
Nights of Cabiria, 165
Open City, 163
Paisan, 163
Pope John XXIII, 172-173
reputation, 161
Sandra Milo, 174, 175
screenwriting, 163, 177
storytelling, 168
The White Sheik, 163
Variety Lights, 163
vaudeville troupe experience, 162
women, 173-174, 181-182
work ethic, 166, 178-179
Firpo, Luis, 186, 187
Fitzgerald, Ella, 158
Fleming, Eric, 116
Fletch, 396
Flynn, Errol, 200
Fonda, Jane, 210-211
Ford, Gerald, 21, 23
Forester, C. S., 186
Forman, Milos, 19
400 Blows, 53. See also Truffaut, François

Friedkin, Billy, 21, 33, 365. *See also Wages of Fear*
Friedrich, Otto, 67
Fuller, Sam, 380
Full Metal Jacket, 374, 389-390. *See also* Kubrick, Stanley

Gable, Clark, 206
Gabor, Zsa Zsa, 200
Gandolfini, James, 52, 63
Gardner, Ava, 194, 195, 205
Gardner, Herb, 289
Garner, Erroll, 158
Genovese, Kitty, 124
Genovese, Vito, 86, 88
Gibson, Mel, 160, 403
Gillespie, Dizzy, 158
Gladiator, 403
Gleason, Jackie, 462
Gleason, Ralph, 121
Goldberg, Whoopi, 252
Goldfinger, 263
Goldwyn, Samuel, 74, 187, 443, 453
Goodfellas, 251, 343-348, 359, 360, 362, 365, 368. *See also* Scorsese, Martin
Goodman, John, 52
Gordon, Ruth, 30
Gould, Elliott, 13
Grand Hotel, 12, 187
Grant, Cary, 462
Griffin, Merv, 137
Grisham, John, 410, 412
Grobel, Lawrence, 188
Grossbach, Robert, 31
Gutowski, Gene, 338

Hackman, Gene, 15
Hamburger Hill, 374
Hamilton, Don, 137
Hammett, Dashiell, 186, 195, 197
Harris, Julie, 137
Harrison, George, 382
Hatari, 67, 263
Hawks, Howard, 32, 346
Hayden, Sterling, 30, 31, 218
Hayworth, Rita, 147
HBO, 403, 415
Hearst, Patricia, 22, 23. *See also* Altman, Robert
Hearts and Minds, 77. *See also* Schneider, Bert
Hemingway, Ernest, 141, 195, 201, 202, 213, 277, 284, 382, 435

Hendrix, Jimi, 384
Hepburn, Audrey, 462
Hepburn, Katharine, 190-191
Hercules and the Seven Dwarfs, 457
Heston, Charlton, 107
High Noon, 124
Hill, Anita, 280
Hitchcock, Alfred, 12, 52, 57, 64, 248, 346, 443: *Shadow of Doubt*, 64
Hitchens, Christopher, 401
Hitler, Adolf, 87, 241, 272, 318, 439, 455
Hoberman, J., 66
Holbrook, Hal, 377
Holden, Bill, 462
Hope, Bob, 78
Hughes, Howard, 116
Hunter, Holly, 52, 53, 61, 431
Huston, John, 66, 143, 145, 185-213, 219, 400:
A House Divided, 187
Academy Awards, 185, 187, 198
Africa, 186, 190-192, 199
Ah, Sweet Mystery of Life, 204
Albert Finney, 193, 194
American Mercury, 187, 196
Anjelica Huston, 185, 202
Beat the Devil, 187, 188, 190, 192-193
boxing, 186, 187, 201, 204
childhood, 186, 196
Chinatown, 203, 211
Committee for the First Amendment, 188, 203
Covered Wagon, 209
critics, 193, 212
Daily Graphic, 187, 196
death, 201, 213
Dr. Ehrlich's Magic Bullet, 187
Enrica "Ricki" Soma, 188
E.T., 210
Evelyn Keyes, 188
family, 186, 187, 198, 202
Fat City, 204
Four Horsemen, 209
Freud, 206, 207, 208
Gallipoli, 209
George C. Scott, 188, 205
Heart of Darkness, 196
Henry Blanke, 197
High Sierra, 187, 197
Hiroshima Mon Amour, 209
Hollywood, 211-212
House Un-American Activities Committee, 203

hunting, 190, 191, 192
Ireland, 188, 190, 207
Jack Dempsey, 186, 187, 202
Jeanette MacDonald, 204
Jessica Lange, 211
John Gielgud, 196
José Avelleneda, 199
José Ferrer, 200
journalism, 187, 196
Juarez, 187, 205-206
Julius Caesar, 195
Lesley Black, 187
Loyal Davis, 211
Luis Firpo, 186, 187
Marietta Fitzgerald, 188
Mata Hari, 199
Mexico, 185, 186, 188, 189, 199
Montgomery Clift, 195, 205-206
Moulin Rouge, 190, 200, 208-209
Olivia de Havilland, 200
painting, 186
Paul Muni, 187, 205-206
Peter Viertel, 201
Prizzi's Honor, 185, 193, 203
Quo Vadis, 204
Raiders of the Lost Ark, 210
Ray Stark, 210
Reflections in a Golden Eye, 186, 195
residences, 185
Robert Bolt, 193
Robert Capa, 195
Robert Mitchum, 204-205
Sam Spiegel, 208
sexual exploration, 198-199
Suzanne Flon, 200, 202
Sydney Greenstreet, 197
Terms of Endearment, 212
The African Queen, 186, 187, 188, 190-191,
     193, 208
The Agony and the Ecstasy, 209
The Asphalt Jungle, 186, 206
The Barbarian and the Geisha, 208
The Bible, 205
The Hidden Passion, 207
The Maltese Falcon, 185, 186, 187, 193, 197
The Man Who Would Be King, 186, 193,
     208
The Misfits, 186, 206-207
The Night of the Iguana, 186, 194, 212
The Red Badge of Courage, 186, 208
The Treasure of the Sierra Madre, 185, 186,
     187, 193, 197-198

Under the Volcano, 193
William Wyler, 187, 209
Winter Kills, 210
Wise Blood, 186, 193
women, 187, 188, 198-200, 201-202

I Wanna Hold Your Hand, 67.
In the Heat of the Night, 251
Independence Day, 146
Intimate Lighting, 33

Jaffe, Stanley, 80-82
Jaws, 21, 33. See also Spielberg, Steven
Jennings, Peter, 400, 411. See also ABC
     Network
Johnson, Magic, 254
Jolie, Angelina, 403
Jones, Dean, 53
Joplin, Janis, 384
Joyce, James, 187
Jung, Carl, 224

Kael, Pauline, 28, 140, 78, 90, 140, 159. See also
     The New York Times
Kennedy, Edward, 17, 319, 386
Kennedy, John F., 241, 289, 400, 404, 411, 412
Kerry, John, 401, 405
Kidman, Nicole, 403
Kilbride, Percy, 133
Kill Bill, 417, 418- 420, 423, 427. See also
     Tarantino, Quentin
King Kong, 12, 21
King of Comedy, 352, 358, 359. See also De
     Niro, Robert; Scorsese, Martin
Kipling, Rudyard, 186
Kissinger, Henry, 23
Klein, Joe, 262
Knight, Arthur, 105
Koch, Howard, 107, 204
Kovic, Ron, 380, 408
Kubrick, Stanley, 11, 25, 32, 33, 94, 215-245,
     340, 389
  aliens, 223-228, 231
  André Maurios, 226-227
  Andrew Sarris, 217, 221
  Bernard Strehler, 236
  Calciphylaxis, 236
  computers, 242-243
  critics, 216-217, 221-222, 242
  cryobiology, 232-235
  Day of the Fight, 217
  death, 235

dolphins, 229
Dr. Strangelove, 219, 239-240
drugs, 237-238
Eleanor of Aquitaine, 238
family, 217, 239
Frank B. Salisbury, 227
Freeman Dyson, 226
Gerald Feinberg, 232
interstellar travel, 231-233
Ivan Sanderson, 231
J. Allen Hynek, 230
Jean Rostand, 233
John Lilly, 229
Josif Shklovsky, 227
John Simon, 217, 221
Judith Crist, 221
L. M. Chassin, 230
Lolita, 215, 218
love, 238
LSD, 237-238, 241
Mars, 224, 227-228, 231
metaphysical symbols, 220
monoliths, 216, 220
moon, 228
mortality, 244-245
NASA, 224, 229
nuclear holocaust, 218, 240, 242, 245
nuclear power, 224, 241
old age, 236
pacifism, 241-242
Phobos, 227
religion, 222-223, 244
Renata Alder, 221
Robert Ettinger, 233
Robert H. O'Brien, 243
satellites, 227
Shternberg Astronomical Institute, 227
special effects, 243
Stanley Kauffmann, 21
theory of relativity, 231, 232
2001: A Space Odyssey, 215-217, 220-223,
    228, 230, 233, 242, 243
UFOs, 230-231
V. F. Kuprevich, 236
Venus, 224
war, 218, 240-241
Kurosawa, Akira, 32, 118, 179, 195, 344

La Dolce Vita, 32, 45, 161, 165, 174, 180, 457.
    See also Fellini, Federico
L'Avventura, 339
La Terra Trema, 45. See also Visconti, Luchino

Lassie Come Home, 53
Last Tango in Paris, 32. See also Bertolucci,
    Bernardo
Lawrence of Arabia, 254-255
Lean, David, 50, 366
Lee, Shelton Jackson. See Lee, Spike
Lee, Spike, 247-273, 292, 427-428:
    acting roles, 256
    Arsenio Hall, 252-253, 267
    Bensonhurst, 253, 254
    black conservatives, 271
    black filmmakers, 247, 251-252, 269
    black ownership, 252
    Bruce Beresford, 261
    childhood, 248, 253-254, 263-264, 265
    Civil Rights movement, 266-267
    Cobble Hill, 253
    contract stipulations, 248
    controversy, 250, 261, 262
    critics, 260, 261, 262, 269
    directing aspirations, 254-255
    Do the Right Thing, 247, 249, 254, 256, 258,
        259, 261-262, 267, 269
    drugs, 259-260
    Eddie Murphy, 252, 254, 267
    education, 264-266
    family, 248, 250, 263-265
    Fort Green 247, 249, 253
    Fruit of Islam, 259
    Hollywood, 247, 267, 268, 270
    Guess Who's Coming to Dinner, 255
    In Living Color, 266, 268-269
    improvisation, 260-261
    interracial couples, 250, 259
    Italians, 251, 253
    Jewish Religion, 260, 270
    Joe's Bed-Stuy Barbershop: We Cut Heads, 248
    Jungle Fever, 247, 249, 250-251, 252, 254,
        256, 259, 267
    Keenen Ivory Wayans, 266
    Louis Farrakhan, 259
    Malcolm X, 249, 251, 262, 272-273
    Malcolm X, 260, 267, 273
    Marked for Death, 260
    Mars Blackmon, 248, 260
    Martin Luther King Jr., 249, 262, 272
    Michael Jordan, 247, 254, 262-263, 267
    Mo' Better Blues, 247, 249, 259, 250, 267, 269
    Morehouse College, 248, 254, 256-257
    Nike campaign, 247, 248, 262-263
    Norman Jewison, 251
    race relations, 249, 253

racism, 250-251, 270, 271
Saddam Hussein, 271, 272
School Daze, 247, 248-249, 256, 258, 261, 269
She's Gotta Have It, 247, 248, 256, 257-258,
    262, 269
siblings, 264-265
Sidney Poitier, 255-256
Spelman College, 256
Teamsters, 267-268
Uncle Tom, 270-271
white women, 250
Wim Wenders, 258-259
Lemmon, Jack, 461
Lennon, John, 410
Leonard, John, 12. *See also The New York Times*
Leone, Sergio, 119-120. *See also* Eastwood, Clint
Levin, Ira, 298
Lilies of the Field, 255
Limelight, 458. *See also* Chaplin, Charlie
Lion's Gate Films, 13, 14, 18, 34. *See also*
    Altman, Robert
Little, Cleavon, 14, 30
Locke, Sondra, 140, 143, 150
Lord Jim, 384. *See also* Conrad, Joseph
Los Angeles Times, 21, 120, 360
Lubitsch, Ernst, 456
Lucas, George, 75, 92, 210, 365, 398
Lyon, Sue, 194, 218

MacLaine, Shirley, 104, 137, 461
MacMurray, Fred, 61
Macbeth, 40, 297-299, 304-306, 312, 324, 331-
    333, 342, 433, 440
Mahoney, John, 65
Mailer, Norman, 141, 202, 401
Maltin, Leonard, 401
Mamet, David, 275-296:
    American Buffalo, 276, 294
    Anita Hill, 280
    AIDS, 278
    antisemitism, 292
    artist funding, 288
    childhood, 275-276, 293
    college, 292-293
    con artists, 281-282, 285
    critics, 276, 295
    dialogue, 280-281, 295
    Glengarry Glen Ross, 275, 276, 289, 293
    Hill Street Blues, 276
    Hollywood, 282
    Homicide, 276
    House of Games, 276, 282

interviews, 284
Jonathan Katz, 295
Judaism, 291-292
Lenny Bruce, 289, 290
Lindsay Crouse, 276
Lone Canoe, 276, 295
Lynn Mamet Weisberg, 281
Oleanna, 275, 276, 277-280, 286
Othello, 279
playwriting, 281-285
political correctness, 290-291
politics in theater, 278
profanity, 280-281
Rebecca Pidgeon, 277
sex, 278-279
Speed-the-Plow, 276, 282
television, 288-289
The Postman Always Rings Twice, 276, 286, 296
The Untouchables, 276, 286
The Verdict, 276, 286
violence, 286-287
We're No Angels, 295
writing, 294
Manes, Fritz, 137
Manzù, Giacomo, 195
Marciano, Rocky, 145
Martin, Dean, 462
Martin, Steve, 397
Marx Brothers, 460
Maslin, Janet, 261
Mayer, Louis B., 94, 204, 443
Mays, Willie, 413
Mazursky, Paul, 33
McCarthy, Gene, 25
McCarthy, Joseph, 23, 188, 203, 204, 406, 445
McCullers, Carson, 186
McDormand, Frances, 52, 53, 54, 56, 59, 60, 69.
    See also Coen, Joel & Ethan
McGovern, George, 25, 132, 133
McKenna, Kristine, 55
McQueen, Steve, 14, 403
McNeese, Gretchen, 105
Melville, Herman, 186
Mencken, H. L., 196
MGM Studios, 18, 103, 125, 204, 219, 222, 243
Mildred Pierce, 67. *See also* Cain, James M.
Miller, Arthur, 186, 206, 275
Milius, John, 374
Miramax Pictures, 417. *See also* Weinstein, Harvey
Mitchell, Elvis, 249
Monk, Thelonius, 158
Monroe, Marilyn, 206

Montana, Lenny, 83
Montana, Tony, 399. *See also* Stone, Oliver
Moore, Michael, 406, 407, 411
Morrison, Jim, 385, 401, 404. *See also* Stone, Oliver
Mr. Hulot's Holiday, 45
Murphy, Eddie, 252, 254, 267, 397
Murphy, Michael, 13
Murphy, Turk, 159
Murray, William, 75
Mussolini, Benito, 162, 272, 434

NBC, 74, 100, 152, 429
Nabokov, Vladimir, 218
Naked Prey, 53
National Endowment of the Arts, 287
Natural Born Killers, 418, 424, 427. *See also* Stone, Oliver
Navarro, Fats, 158
Nelson, Tim, 65
New Leader, 217, 221
New Wave, 39, 44-45, 332, 337, 442
New West, 28
New York Film Festival, 23, 338
New York Magazine, 28
New York Post, 262
New York University, 54, 248, 257, 343, 357, 366, 375, 395, 402
Newsday, 254
Newman, Paul, 11, 14, 15, 16, 29, 53, 59, 60, 286, 343, 353
Newsweek, 18, 52, 259
Nicholson, Jack, 15, 16, 83, 160, 185, 202, 203, 369, 421
Nixon, Richard, 23, 24, 132
Nolte, Nick, 376
Norden, Eric, 219-220
Noriega, Manuel, 271
North, Oliver, 373, 406
Northwestern University, 230
Nouvelle Vague. See New Wave

O'Connor, Flannery, 186
Of Mice and Men, 303
Olivier, Laurence, 80, 196, 304, 440
O'Neal, Ryan, 83
One Flew Over the Cuckoo's Nest, 19, 20
O'Neill, Eugene, 195, 197
Out of Africa, 396
Out of the Past, 66

Pacino, Al, 80, 82-87, 396

Page, Geraldine, 137
Paper Moon, 130
Papillon, 26
Paramount Pictures, 19, 26, 73, 80, 81, 85, 100, 103, 252, 303, 331, 366
Parker, Alan, 398
Parker, Charlie, 158
Pascal, Réné, 168
Passer, Ivan, 33
Paths of Glory, 218, 389. *See also* Kubrick, Stanley
Pearl Harbor, 56
Peck, Gregory, 107, 207
Peckinpah, Sam, 11, 129
Peter, Jon, 29
Pillow Talk, 455
Pitt, Brad, 53, 59, 63, 70, 71, 403
Platoon, 361, 373-385, 387-390, 392, 396, 399-402, 406, 407, 413. *See also* Stone, Oliver
Polanski, Roman, 297-342:
    Billy Wilder, 330
    capital punishment, 319
    Charles Manson, 298, 314-319
    childhood, 303, 304, 316, 322, 334
    communism, 341-342
    critics, 339
    Cul-de-Sac, 297, 302, 337, 339, 340
    death, 312-313
    drugs, 309, 313, 317-318
    film school, 335-336
    filmmaking, 302, 320-321, 328-330, 332, 333, 335
    Gerard Brach, 337
    hedonism, 321-322
    height, 333-334
    idealism, 341
    interviews, 329-330, 332
    Knife in the Water, 297, 298, 302, 320, 337, 339
    lifestyle, 299, 324, 334
    macabre, 302-303
    Macbeth, 297-299, 304-306, 312, 324, 331-333, 342
    marriage, 310-311
    masturbation, 322
    murder investigation, 313-316
    Paris, 337-338
    politics, 340-342
    press, 306-310, 313
    Repulsion, 297, 337, 339
    revenge, 318-319
    Rosemary's Baby, 297-298, 303, 314, 320, 331, 333

sex, 321, 325, 322-323, 342
Sharon Tate, 298, 299, 306-311, 313, 315,
 319, 320
Stanley Kubrick, 340
suspense, 303-304
The Day of the Dolphin, 311
The Fearless Vampire Killers, 297, 310
violence, 297, 304-306
When Angels Fall, 336
William Shakespeare, 304
women, 298, 323-327, 338
Pollack, Sydney, 396
Ponti, Carlo, 80
Potemkin, 336
Powell, Colin, 271
Preminger, Ingo, 31-32
Princeton University, 54, 226
Profaci, Joseph, 86
Pull My Daisy, 45
Pulp Fiction, 411, 417-419, 421, 422, 425, 430-
 431. *See also* Tarantino, Quentin
Puzo, Mario. *See* Coppola, Francis Ford

Rader, Doug, 324
Raging Bull, 343, 344, 346, 348, 349, 350-353,
 363, 364, 366. *See also* Scorsese, Martin
Ragtime, 23, 30, 268
Rambo, 388
Rashomon, 45
Reagan, Nancy, 211, 393
Reagan, Ronald, 154, 211, 270, 271, 344, 388,
 393, 404, 406
Redford, Robert, 15, 83, 351, 396
Reds, 210, 396. *See also* Beatty, Warren
Reed, Rex, 27-29
Reeves, Jacelyn, 144
Remsen, Bert, 13
Reynolds, Burt, 107
Rhames, Ving, 425-426
Rickard, Jim, 34
Robbins, Tim, 53
Robertson, Robbie 349-350
Robinson, Smokey, 384
Rocky, 204, 343
Rolling Stone, 205
Roosevelt, Eleanor, 191
Roosevelt, Franklin Delano, 203, 436
Roseanne, 60
Rosenberg, Ethel, 22-23
Rosenberg, Julius, 22-23
Ross, Diana, 268
Rossellini, Isabella, 344

Rossellini, Roberto, 163
Rota, Nina, 100
Rothko, Mark, 195
Rourke, Mickey, 399
Ruddy, Al, 79, 80, 88, 91
Rudolph, Alan, 31
Ruiz, Dina, 144
Rumsfeld, Donald, 409

Sabrina, 458, 461, 462. *See also* Bogart,
 Humphrey; Wilder, Billy
St. Cloud State, 53
Salinger, J. D., 291, 410
Sands of Iwo Jima, 408. *See also* Kovic, Ron
Sarris, Andrew, 217, 221
Sartre, Jean-Paul, 207
Saving Private Ryan, 410
Scarface, 374, 377, 393, 396, 398, 399. *See also*
 De Palma, Brian; Stone, Oliver
Scorsese, Martin, 33, 68, 251, 343-371, 395:
 After Hours, 348, 352, 353, 358
 Alice Doesn't Live Here Anymore, 343, 344,
 346, 351, 365
 Allen, Woody, 51, 52, 57, 348, 353
 asthma, 345, 346, 352, 355, 370
 awards, 343, 346-347, 348, 351, 364-365
 Cape Fear, 344, 345, 347, 355, 359
 Catholicism, 354-356
 childhood, 352, 361
 critics, 360, 363
 directing, 347
 drugs and partying, 349-351
 Ellen Burstyn, 343
 Francis Ford Coppola, 368-369
 Goodfellas, 344, 348
 independent filmmaking, 354
 Hollywood, 352, 354
 Italian-Americans, 368-371
 Julia Cameron, 357
 King of Comedy, 352, 358, 359
 Marlon Brando, 359-360
 Mean Streets, 344, 351, 354, 355, 368, 370
 mobsters, 369-370
 New York City, 370
 New York, New York, 344, 351, 352, 357, 365
 New York Stories, 344, 347-348
 New York University, 343, 357
 Paul Newman, 353
 relationships, 358
 success, 348
 Robertson, Robbie, 349-350
 Rossellini, Isabella, 344, 358

Raging Bull, 343, 344, 346, 348-353, 363, 364, 366
    Robert De Niro, 343, 347, 348-349, 355, 358, 359
    sex, 355, 365
    Taxi Driver, 344, 347, 351, 356, 363-364, 395
    The Color of Money, 343, 344, 345, 348, 352, 353. *See also* Newman, Paul
    The King of Comedy, 344, 352
    The Last Temptation of Christ, 344, 348
    The Last Waltz, 344, 350
    violence, 361-364
Schickel, Richard, 144
Schlesinger Jr., Arthur, 218. *See also The New York Times*
Schneider, Bert, 77-78
Schwarzenegger, Arnold, 404
Screen Extras Guild, 31
Seagal, Steven, 260
Seconds, 61
Segal, George, 13
Sellers, Peter, 92, 133, 435, 462
Seven Samurai, 118, 179
sex, lies, and videotape, 259
Sexy Beast, 64
Shadows, 44
Shakespeare, William, 275, 304, 402, 439, 440
Shaw, George Bernard, 454
Sheen, Charlie, 386
Sheff, David, 402
Shrek, 64
Siegel, Don, 104, 135, 137, 142, 149
Silver, Joel, 58
Simon & Schuster, 36
Sinatra, Frank, 78, 88, 89, 399
Sinclair, Upton, 454
Siodmak, Robert, 455
Slick, Grace, 384
Sling Blade, 51. *See also* Thornton, Billy Bob
Simon, John, 28, 32, 217, 221
Sommer, Elke, 315
Sonnenfeld, Barry, 54
Spader, James, 259
Spielberg, Steven, 21, 33, 210, 345, 353, 398:
    Cape Fear, 345
    Jaws, 21, 33
    Schindler's List, 291
    The Color Purple, 398
Splendor in the Grass, 67
Sports Illustrated, 262
Star Wars, 210, 396, 398. *See also* Lucas, George
Stevens, Inger, 137

Stewart, Jackie, 334
Stone, Oliver, 361, 373-416, 427, 430:
    AIDS, 409
    Alexander the Great, 400-404, 408, 409, 412, 414
    Academy Awards, 373, 375, 395, 402
    American business, 378-379
    Any Given Sunday, 415
    bisexuality, 408-409
    Born on the Fourth of July, 380, 395-396, 401, 402
    casting, 403
    childhood, 375, 378, 412-413
    Christopher Hitchens, 401, 405
    comedy, 397
    Commandante, 415
    conspiracies, 397, 400, 401, 406, 407, 410, 411
    critics, 374, 398, 400, 411
    drugs, 384-385, 392-395, 399, 413
    El Salvador, 388
    epics, 403
    fatherhood, 412
    Heaven & Earth, 401, 409, 410
    Hollywood, 396-397
    homosexuality, 408-409
    jail, 394-395
    JFK, 400, 402
    Joseph Conrad, 382
    Looking for Fidel, 415
    Midnight Express, 374, 377, 394, 395, 397, 398, 402
    Nixon, 390, 395, 401, 402, 404, 409, 412
    Pentagon, 374, 376, 377, 384
    pessimism, 415
    Platoon, 361, 373, 374-377, 379-390, 392, 396, 399, 400, 401, 402, 406, 407, 413
    politics, 376, 381-383, 393-395, 398, 403-408
    Puritanism, 409
    Quentin Tarantino, 411-412
    racism, 398-399
    Salvador, 375, 377, 388, 390-393, 397, 399, 400, 402, 406, 414
    satire, 410
    Scarface, 374, 377, 393, 396, 398-399
    Seizure, 402
    September 11, 401, 405, 406
    sex, 409
    Stanley Kubrick, 11, 389-390
    Talk Radio, 401
    The Doors, 401, 404, 411

The Hand, 374, 395-396
The Wall Street Journal, 377
Vietnam war, 379-387, 405, 407
violence, 409
Wal-Mart, 404
Wall Street, 373, 375-379, 397, 400, 401, 408
Yale University, 373, 375, 381, 382, 401
Year of the Dragon, 374, 389, 399
Streep, Meryl, 143, 145, 149, 210-211, 396
Streisand, Barbra, 39, 210
Sturges, Preston, 53, 67
Suicide is Painless, 31. See also Altman, Michael
Sundance Film Festival, 58
Susskind, David, 16
Sutherland, Donald, 30
Swanson, Gloria, 461
Sylbert, Dick, 314

Tarantino, Quentin, 411-412, 417-431:
    acting, 428-429
    China, 423
    David Carradine, 418, 420, 421
    dropping out, 425, 429-430
    drugs, 423
    father, 430
    femininity, 427
    fighting, 424-425
    From Dusk Till Dawn, 418, 423
    Harvey Weinstein, 420
    Jackie Brown, 418, 426, 427
    John Travolta, 417, 421
    Kill Bill, 417-420, 423, 427
    kissing, 422
    Natural Born Killers, 418, 424, 427. See also
        Stone, Oliver
    Oliver Stone, 427, 430
    Pulp Fiction, 417-419, 421, 422, 425-426,
        430-431
    Reservoir Dogs, 417-419, 422, 425, 429, 430
    sex, 422
    Spike Lee, 427-428
    success, 419, 421
    Uma Thurman, 417, 420
    Ving Rhames, 425-426
Taxi Driver, 209, 344, 347, 351, 356, 363-364,
    395. See also Scorsese, Martin
Ten Days That Shook the World, 74
The Beatles, 254, 263
The Bicycle Thief, 336, 337
The Big Red One, 380. See also Fuller, Sam
The Birth of a Nation, 73
The Book of Daniel, 23. See also Altman, Robert

The Breakfast Club, 396
The Coen Brothers. See Coen, Joel & Ethan
The Color of Money, 343, 344, 345, 348, 352, 353
The Connection, 45
The Devil in Miss Jones, 129
The Drowning Pool, 15
The Exorcist, 21
The Final Days, 24
The French Connection, 82
The Godfather, 73-93, 100, 209, 251, 368, 369,
    398. See also Coppola, Francis Ford
The Good, the Bad and the Ugly, 103, 120, 122,
    156, 418
The Grand Ole Opry, 22
The Hanoi Hilton, 374
The Incredible Hulk, 57
The King and I, 263
The Lady with the Dog, 45
The Long Goodbye, 13, 16
The Magnificent Seven, 118, 403. See also
    McQueen, Steve
The Maltese Falcon, 66
The Manchurian Candidate, 61
The Miracle of Morgan's Creek, 67
The New York Times, 28, 79, 140, 193, 261, 270
The New Yorker, 28, 78, 90, 212
The Postman Always Rings Twice, 276, 286, 296
The Sopranos, 52, 63
The Village Voice, 217, 221
The Washington Evening Star, 216
The Wild Bunch, 129, 363. See also Peckinpah,
    Sam
The Wild Palms, 65. See also Faulkner, William
The Wiz, 268
The Wizard of Oz, 64-65
Thornton, Billy Bob, 51
Time, 42, 306, 308
To the White Sea, 70. See also Dickey, James
Top Gun, 388
Toscanini, Arturo, 74
Toulouse-Lautrec, Henri de, 209
Townsend, Robert, 268
Tracy, Spencer, 191
Travolta, John, 417, 421
Treasure of the Sierra Madre, 185, 186, 187, 193,
    197-198, 219. See also Huston, John
Troy, 403
True Romance, 411. See also Tarantino, Quentin
Truffaut, Francois, 53
Truman, Harry, 133
Tucci, Joe, 253
Tucci, Louis, 253

Tucker, Preston, 96
Turner, Kathleen, 185, 211
Turturro, John, 53, 59, 64, 65, 70
Twain, Mark, 406, 454
2001: A Space Odyssey, 215-217, 219, 220-223,
    228, 230, 233, 242, 243, 339
Tynan, Kenneth, 298, 324, 325, 327, 331, 433

Udall, Morris, 25
Umberto D., 45
    Universal Studios, 113
University of Minnesota, 53
University of California, 74:
    Los Angeles, 74, 387
    Berkeley, 109, 317
University of Colorado, 230
Used Cars, 67. See also Sturges, Preston
Utah State University, 227
Van Gogh, Vincent, 209, 456
Visconti, Luchino, 45, 350
Viva Villa!, 35. See also Beery, Wallace
Vonnegut, Kurt Jr., 14, 24

Wages of Fear, 21, 209
Warner Bros., 104, 403
Wasserman, Lew, 132
Watergate, 132-133, 375, 395
Watters, Lu, 158
Wayne, John, 126, 142, 208, 263, 375, 382, 408
Welles, Orson, 433-452:
    advertising industry, 451
    Antonioni, Michelangelo, 44, 45, 180, 442
    Around the World in Eighty Days, 437
    artistic intention, 450
    Candida, 436
    censorship, 448
    childhood, 433, 438-439, 440
    Citizen Kane, 434, 437, 439, 440
    clairvoyance, 441
    conversation, 441-442
    critics, 436
    death, 451-452
    directing, 443-444
    Don Quixote, 434, 435
    drugs, 449-450
    expatriation, 434, 437, 438
    Falstaff, 435, 439
    Federico Fellini, 442
    gluttony, 447
    Hollywood, 443
    idols, 438
    John Ford, 443

    Macbeth, 433, 440
    Method acting, 445
    New Wave, 442
    politics, 445
    pornography, 447
    religion, 448-449
    taxes, 437-438
    The Magnificent Ambersons, 434, 439
    theater, 444-445
    Thornton Wilder, 441-442
    William Shakespeare, 440
    women, 449
Weinraub, Bernard, 144
Weinstein, Harvey, 417, 419, 420. See also
    Miramax Pictures
Wertmuller, Lina, 32
White Hunter, Black Heart, 145
White Rabbit, 384. See also Slick, Grace
Wilder, Billy, 330, 453-463:
    Ace in the Hole, 461
    awards, 453, 458, 461
    beginnings, 454-455, 462-463
    Bertolt Brecht, 454
    Bluebeard's Eighth Wife, 454
    Humphrey Bogart, 461-462
    Charles Brackett, 455
    Charlie, Chaplin 458, 462
    collaboration, 456
    comedy, 459
    Double Indemnity, 453, 454, 459, 461
    English, 456
    Europe, 457-458
    George Axelrod, 458
    George Bernard Shaw, 454
    Gloria Swanson, 461
    Hollywood, 456-458
    I. A. L. (Iz) Diamond, 453, 456
    influences, 454
    Irma La Douce, 462
    Jack Lemmon, 461
    James M. Cain, 65, 67, 454
    L'Hora della Fantasia, 462
    Love in the Afternoon, 458
    Nazism, 455
    Nikita Khrushchev, 459
    Paul Whiteman, 454
    One, Two, Three, 453, 459
    originality, 461
    personality, 458-459
    Robert Siodmak, 455
    Sabrina, 458, 461-462
    Shirley MacLaine, 461

slapstick, 460
Some Like It Hot, 453, 459-460, 461
Sunset Boulevard, 453, 459, 461
The Apartment, 453, 458, 461
The Big Carnival, 461
The Lost Weekend, 453
Upton Sinclair, 454
vulgarity, 455
Witness for the Prosecution, 461
Wilder, Thornton, 441-442
Williams, Tennessee, 186, 194-195
Williamson, Bruce, 14
Woodward, Bob, 24-25
Wynn, Keenan, 13

Yale University, 373, 375, 381, 382, 401
Year of the Dragon, 374, 389, 399. *See also*
    Cimino, Michael; Stone, Oliver
Yojimbo, 118
York, Susannah, 13, 25
Young, Lester, 158

Zanuck, Daryl, 94, 397, 443
Zanuck, Richard, 94
Zorba the Greek, 382